The Gentleman
from Indianapolis

The Gentleman
from Indianapolis

A TREASURY OF BOOTH TARKINGTON

EDITED BY

John Beecroft

ILLUSTRATED BY JOHN ALAN MAXWELL
DOUBLEDAY & COMPANY, INC., GARDEN CITY, N. Y.
1957

BOOKS BY JOHN BEECROFT

Stories to Remember (with Thomas B. Costain)
A Treasury of Great Mysteries (with Howard Haycraft)
The Best Stories of W. Somerset Maugham
Kipling: A *Selection of His Stories and Poems*
Mr. Maugham Himself
The Modern Reader

Contents

COMPLETE NOVEL

ALICE ADAMS   7

SHORT STORIES

The One-Hundred-Dollar Bill—from *The Fascinating Stranger*   191
Mary Smith—from *The Fascinating Stranger*   207
"Dolling"—from *Women*   221
Mrs. Protheroe—from *In The Arena*   241
Mrs. Dodge, Mrs. Cromwell and Mrs. Roderick Brooks Battle—
    from *Women*   259
Great Men's Sons—from *In The Arena*   279
Stella Crozier   285

COMPLETE NOVEL

PENROD   305

FROM OTHER NOVELS

Little Florence—from *Gentle Julia*   441
Love at Seventeen—from *Seventeen*   491
Little Marie From Kansas City—from *Little Orvie*   509

COMPLETE NOVEL

THE MAGNIFICENT AMBERSONS   523

A Brief Introduction

Booth Tarkington was born in Indianapolis on July 29, 1869, and died there on May 19, 1946. His literary career was one of the most productive and successful in the history of American writing. He is one of the few authors who have become wealthy solely from their literary work. Most of his plays were Broadway hits; magazine editors eagerly bought his short stories; he had a large number of best sellers, and two of his novels—*Alice Adams* and *The Magnificent Ambersons*—won the Pulitzer Prize. He created characters that have become a part of the American literary tradition.

Tarkington loved his home country, and when writing about his Indiana town and the people who lived there, Tarkington did his best work. His town was "made of friendly neighborhoods," he says in his autobiographical book, *The World Does Move*. The principal residential street was "amply broad for family carriages, bicycles, phaetons, buggies, and light delivery wagons; and was shaded by maples, by sycamores and old elms, hickory and black walnut trees, relics of the original forest. Most of the houses were solidly built of brick and trimmed with white stone; the windows were all plate glass; the ceilings high; the staircases were walnut and the verandas were of stone or painted wood. The lawns were broad, often generously without fences to mark dividing lines; there were shade and orchard trees in every yard; some yards had fountains and one or two cast-iron deer were left. . . . In the milder seasons the verandas were the foregathering place of youth and courtship. . . . Pleasures were simpler then; but that never meant less pleasure. Life was slower; but that means there was time to enjoy it a little copiously. There was a tremendous universal respect for respectability. Beauty was there, outdoors, and in the tranquil, friendly life of the people." This sort of living and this sort of town, so close to Tarkington's heart and so deeply a part of our American tradition, are reflected in the writings of Booth Tarkington that I have chosen for this volume.

In Tarkington were mingled the North and the South. His paternal grandfather was a Methodist minister from North Carolina; his mother's family prided themselves on their New England ancestry. Newton Booth, his mother's brother (after whom he was named), became governor of California and later senator; and it was his financial help that eased the way for Tarkington to start his career. Two years in the Indianapolis high school, two years at Phillips Exeter, two years at Purdue, and two years at Princeton gave Tarkington his education. The years at Princeton were among the happiest in his life. He was so active in writing and staging plays and working for the literary yearbooks that he neglected to fulfill Princeton's requirements for a degree. He was well liked by everyone and was loyal to Princeton and his classmates throughout his life. After college Tarkington tried to earn his living by drawing and by writing. Lean years, full of rejection slips and of little encouragement, except from his family, came after his happy time at Princeton.

But the publication of *The Gentleman from Indiana* catapulted Tarkington into fame. *Monsieur Beaucaire* had been serialized and was then published in book form to ride on the success of the novel. *Cherry*, which had been accepted, but which the publisher had hesitated to produce, was also published.

From that time on, Tarkington found no lack of market for his manuscripts. He stepped directly from a struggling and discouraged young writer into the position he held throughout his lifetime as an important figure in American letters.

During his long career as a writer Tarkington won a secure place in the hearts and minds of his readers. He wrote about people he understood. He was sincere and he was honest, and it is his integrity as a writer that has made him one of America's greatest authors.

Alice Adams, Penrod, The Magnificent Ambersons are works that grace our literature and will endure as important and beloved books, increasingly cherished as the years go on.

John Beecroft

Conway, Massachusetts
June 22, 1957.

The Gentleman
from Indianapolis

Alice Adams

CHAPTER I

The patient, an old-fashioned man, thought the nurse made a mistake in keeping both of the windows open, and her sprightly disregard of his protests added something to his hatred of her. Every evening he told her that anybody with ordinary gumption ought to realize that night air was bad for the human frame. "The human frame won't stand everything, Miss Perry," he warned her, resentfully. "Even a child, if it had just ordinary gumption, ought to know enough not to let the night air blow on sick people—yes, nor well people, either! 'Keep out of the night air, no matter how well you feel.' That's what my mother used to tell me when I was a boy. 'Keep out of the night air, Virgil,' she'd say. 'Keep out of the night air.'"

"I expect probably her mother told her the same thing," the nurse suggested.

"Of course she did. My grandmother——"

"Oh, I guess your *grand*mother thought so, Mr. Adams! That was when all this flat central country was swampish and hadn't been drained off yet. I guess the truth must been the swamp mosquitoes bit people and gave 'em malaria, especially before they began to put screens in their windows. Well, we got screens in these windows, and no mosquitoes are goin' to bite us; so just you be a good boy and rest your mind and go to sleep like you need to."

"Sleep?" he said. "Likely!"

He thought the night air worst of all in April; he hadn't a doubt it would kill him, he declared. "It's miraculous what the human frame *will* survive," he admitted on the last evening of that month. "But you and the doctor ought to both be taught it won't stand too dang much! You poison a man and poison and poison him with this April night air——"

"Can't poison you with much more of it," Miss Perry interrupted him, indulgently. "To-morrow it'll be May night air, and I expect that'll be a lot

7

better for you, don't you? Now let's just sober down and be a good boy and
get some nice sound sleep."

She gave him his medicine, and, having set the glass upon the center table,
returned to her cot, where, after a still interval, she snored faintly. Upon this,
his expression became that of a man goaded out of overpowering weariness
into irony.

"Sleep? Oh, *certainly*, thank you!"

However, he did sleep intermittently, drowsed between times, and even
dreamed; but, forgetting his dreams before he opened his eyes, and having
some part of him all the while aware of his discomfort, he believed, as usual,
that he lay awake the whole night long. He was conscious of the city as of
some single great creature resting fitfully in the dark outside his windows. It
lay all round about, in the damp cover of its night cloud of smoke, and tried
to keep quiet for a few hours after midnight, but was too powerful a growing
thing ever to lie altogether still. Even while it strove to sleep it muttered
with digestions of the day before, and these already merged with rumblings
of the morrow. "Owl" cars, bringing in last passengers over distant trolley-
lines, now and then howled on a curve; far-away metallic stirrings could be
heard from factories in the sooty suburbs on the plain outside the city; east,
west, and south, switch-engines chugged and snorted on sidings; and everywhere in the air there seemed to be a faint, voluminous hum as of innumer-
able wires trembling overhead to vibration of machinery underground.

In his youth Adams might have been less resentful of sounds such as these
when they interfered with his night's sleep: even during an illness he might
have taken some pride in them as proof of his citizenship in a "live town";
but at fifty-five he merely hated them because they kept him awake. They
"pressed on his nerves," as he put it; and so did almost everything else, for
that matter.

He heard the milk-wagon drive into the cross-street beneath his windows
and stop at each house. The milkman carried his jars round to the "back
porch," while the horse moved slowly ahead to the gate of the next customer
and waited there. "He's gone into Pollocks'," Adams thought, following this
progress. "I hope it'll sour on 'em before breakfast. Delivered the Andersons'.
Now he's getting out ours. Listen to the darn brute! What's *he* care who
wants to sleep!" His complaint was of the horse, who casually shifted weight
with a clink of steel shoes on the worn brick pavement of the street, and
then heartily shook himself in his harness, perhaps to dislodge a fly far
ahead of its season. Light had just filmed the windows; and with that the
first sparrow woke, chirped instantly, and roused neighbours in the trees of
the small yard, including a loud-voiced robin. Vociferations began irregularly,
but were soon unanimous.

"Sleep? Dang likely now, ain't it!"

Night sounds were becoming day sounds; the far-away hooting of freight-
engines seemed brisker than an hour ago in the dark. A cheerful whistler
passed the house, even more careless of sleepers than the milkman's horse

had been; then a group of coloured workmen came by, and although it was impossible to be sure whether they were homeward bound from night-work or on their way to day-work, at least it was certain that they were jocose. Loose, aboriginal laughter preceded them afar, and beat on the air long after they had gone by.

The sick-room night-light, shielded from his eyes by a newspaper propped against a water-pitcher, still showed a thin glimmering that had grown offensive to Adams. In his wandering and enfeebled thoughts, which were much more often imaginings than reasonings, the attempt of the night-light to resist the dawn reminded him of something unpleasant, though he could not discover just what the unpleasant thing was. Here was a puzzle that irritated him the more because he could not solve it, yet always seemed just on the point of a solution. However, he may have lost nothing cheerful by remaining in the dark upon the matter; for if he had been a little sharper in this introspection he might have concluded that the squalor of the night-light, in its seeming effort to show against the forerunning of the sun itself, had stimulated some half-buried perception within him to sketch the painful little synopsis of an autobiography.

In spite of noises without, he drowsed again, not knowing that he did; and when he opened his eyes the nurse was just rising from her cot. He took no pleasure in the sight, it may be said. She exhibited to him a face mismodelled by sleep, and set like a clay face left on its cheek in a hot and dry studio. She was still only in part awake, however, and by the time she had extinguished the night-light and given her patient his tonic, she had recovered enough plasticity. "Well, isn't that grand! We've had another good night," she said as she departed to dress in the bathroom.

"Yes, you had another!" he retorted, though not until after she had closed the door.

Presently he heard his daughter moving about in her room across the narrow hall, and so knew that she had risen. He hoped she would come in to see him soon, for she was the one thing that didn't press on his nerves, he felt; though the thought of her hurt him, as, indeed, every thought hurt him. But it was his wife who came first.

She wore a lank cotton wrapper, and a crescent of gray hair escaped to one temple from beneath the handkerchief she had worn upon her head for the night and still retained; but she did everything possible to make her expression cheering.

"Oh, you're better again! I can see that, as soon as I look at you," she said. "Miss Perry tells me you've had another splendid night."

He made a sound of irony, which seemed to dispose unfavourably of Miss Perry, and then, in order to be more certainly intelligible, he added, "She slept well, as usual!"

But his wife's smile persisted. "It's a good sign to be cross; it means you're practically convalescent right now."

"Oh, I am, am I?"

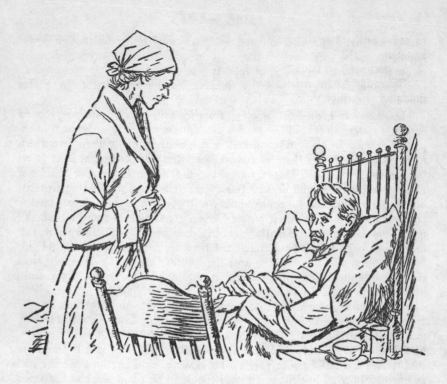

"No doubt in the world!" she exclaimed. "Why, you're practically a well man, Virgil—all except getting your strength back, of course, and that isn't going to take long. You'll be right on your feet in a couple of weeks from now."

"Oh, I will?"

"Of course you will!" She laughed briskly, and, going to the table in the center of the room, moved his glass of medicine an inch or two, turned a book over so that it lay upon its other side, and for a few moments occupied herself with similar futilities, having taken on the air of a person who makes things neat, though she produced no such actual effect upon them. "Of course you will," she repeated, absently. "You'll be as strong as you ever were; maybe stronger." She paused for a moment, not looking at him, then added, cheerfully, "So that you can fly around and find something really good to get into."

Something important between them came near the surface here, for though she spoke with what seemed but a casual cheerfulness, there was a little betraying break in her voice, a trembling just perceptible in the utterance of the final word. And she still kept up the affectation of being helpfully preoccupied with the table, and did not look at her husband—perhaps because they had been married so many years that without looking she knew just what his expression would be, and preferred to avoid the actual sight of it as long as possible. Meanwhile, he stared hard at her, his lips beginning to move with little distortions not lacking in the pathos of a sick man's agitation.

"So that's it," he said. "That's what you're hinting at."

"'Hinting?'" Mrs. Adams looked surprised and indulgent. "Why, I'm not doing any hinting, Virgil."

"What did you say about my finding 'something good to get into?'" he asked, sharply. "Don't you call that hinting?"

Mrs. Adams turned toward him now; she came to the bedside and would have taken his hand, but he quickly moved it away from her.

"You mustn't let yourself get nervous," she said. "But of course when you get well there's only one thing to do. You mustn't go back to that old hole again."

"'Old hole?' That's what you call it, is it?" In spite of his weakness, anger made his voice strident, and upon this stimulation she spoke more urgently.

"You just mustn't go back to it, Virgil. It's not fair to any of us, and you know it isn't."

"Don't tell me what I know, please!"

She clasped her hands, suddenly carrying her urgency to plaintive entreaty. "Virgil, you *won't* go back to that hole?"

"That's a nice word to use to me!" he said. "Call a man's business a hole!"

"Virgil, if you don't owe it to me to look for something different, don't you owe it to your children? Don't tell me you won't do what we all want you to, and what you know in your heart you ought to! And if you *have* got into one of your stubborn fits and are bound to go back there for no other reason except to have your own way, don't tell me so, for I can't bear it!"

He looked up at her fiercely. "You've got a fine way to cure a sick man!" he said; but she had concluded her appeal—for that time—and instead of making any more words in the matter, let him see that there were tears in her eyes, shook her head, and left the room.

Alone, he lay breathing rapidly, his emaciated chest proving itself equal to the demands his emotion put upon it. "Fine!" he repeated, with husky indignation. "Fine way to cure a sick man! Fine!" Then, after a silence, he gave forth whispering sounds as of laughter, his expression the while remaining sore and far from humour.

"And give us our daily bread!" he added, meaning that his wife's little performance was no novelty.

CHAPTER II

In fact, the agitation of Mrs. Adams was genuine, but so well under her control that its traces vanished during the three short steps she took to cross the narrow hall between her husband's door and the one opposite. Her expression was matter-of-course, rather than pathetic, as she entered the pretty room where her daughter, half dressed, sat before a dressing-table and played with the reflections of a three-leafed mirror framed in blue enamel. That is, just before the moment of her mother's entrance, Alice had been playing with the mirror's reflections—posturing her arms and her expressions, clasping her hands behind her neck, and tilting back her head to foreshorten the face in a tableau conceived to represent sauciness, then one of smiling weariness, then one of scornful toleration, and all very piquant; but as the door opened she hurriedly resumed the practical, and occupied her hands in the arrangement of her plentiful brownish hair.

They were pretty hands, of a shapeliness delicate and fine. "The best things she's got!" a cold-blooded girl friend said of them, and meant to include Alice's mind and character in the implied list of possessions surpassed by the notable hands. However that may have been, the rest of her was well enough. She was often called "a right pretty girl"—temperate praise meaning a girl rather pretty than otherwise, and this she deserved, to say the least. Even in repose she deserved it, though repose was anything but her habit, being seldom seen upon her except at home. On exhibition she led a life of gestures, the unkind said to make her lovely hands more memorable; but all of her usually accompanied the gestures of the hands, the shoulders ever giving them their impulses first, and even her feet being called upon, at the same time, for eloquence.

So much liveliness took proper place as only accessory to that of the face, where her vivacity reached its climax; and it was unfortunate that an un-gifted young man, new in the town, should have attempted to define the effect upon him of all this generosity of emphasis. He said that "the way she used her cute hazel eyes and the wonderful glow of her facial expression gave her a mighty spiritual quality." His actual rendition of the word was "spirichul"; but it was not his pronunciation that embalmed this outburst in the perennial laughter of Alice's girl friends; they made the misfortune far less his than hers.

Her mother comforted her too heartily, insisting that Alice had "plenty enough spiritual qualities," certainly more than possessed by the other girls who flung the phrase at her, wooden things, jealous of everything they were incapable of themselves; and then Alice, getting more championship than she sought, grew uneasy lest Mrs. Adams should repeat such defenses "outside the family"; and Mrs. Adams ended by weeping because the daughter so distrusted her intelligence. Alice frequently thought it necessary to instruct her mother.

Her morning greeting was an instruction to-day; or, rather, it was an admonition in the style of an entreaty, the more petulant as Alice thought that Mrs. Adams might have had a glimpse of the posturings to the mirror. This was a needless worry; the mother had caught a thousand such glimpses, with Alice unaware, and she thought nothing of the one just flitted.

"For heaven's sake, mama, come clear inside the room and shut the door! *Please* don't leave it open for everybody to look at me!"

"There isn't anybody to see you," Mrs. Adams explained, obeying. "Miss Perry's gone downstairs, and——"

"Mama, I heard you in papa's room," Alice said, not dropping the note of complaint. "I could hear both of you, and I don't think you ought to get poor old papa so upset—not in his present condition, anyhow."

Mrs. Adams seated herself on the edge of the bed. "He's better all the time," she said, not disturbed. "He's almost well. The doctor says so and Miss Perry says so; and if we don't get him into the right frame of mind now we never will. The first day he's outdoors he'll go back to that old hole— you'll see! And if he once does that, he'll settle down there and it'll be too late and we'll never get him out."

"Well, anyhow, I think you could use a little more tact with him."

"I do try to," the mother sighed. "It never was much use with him. I don't think you understand him as well as I do, Alice."

"There's one thing I don't understand about either of you," Alice returned, crisply. "Before people get married they can do anything they want to with each other. Why can't they do the same thing after they're married? When you and papa were young people and engaged, he'd have done anything you wanted him to. That must have been because you knew how to manage him then. Why can't you go at him the same way now?"

Mrs. Adams sighed again, and laughed a little, making no other response; but Alice persisted. "Well, *why* can't you? Why can't you ask him to do things the way you used to ask him when you were just in love with each other? Why don't you anyhow try it, mama, instead of ding-donging at him?"

"'Ding-donging at him,' Alice?" Mrs. Adams said, with a pathos somewhat emphasized. "Is that how my trying to do what I can for you strikes you?"

"Never mind that; it's nothing to hurt your feelings." Alice disposed of the pathos briskly. "Why don't you answer my question? What's the matter with using a little more tact on papa? Why can't you treat him the way you probably did when you were young people, before you were married? I never have understood why people can't do that."

"Perhaps you *will* understand some day," her mother said, gently. "Maybe you will when you've been married twenty-five years."

"You keep evading. Why don't you answer my question right straight out?"

"There are questions you can't answer to young people, Alice."

"You mean because we're too young to understand the answer? I don't see that at all. At twenty-two a girl's supposed to have some intelligence, isn't she? And intelligence is the ability to understand, isn't it? Why do I have to wait till I've lived with a man twenty-five years to understand why you can't be tactful with papa?"

"You may understand some things before that," Mrs. Adams said, tremulously. "You may understand how you hurt me sometimes. Youth can't know everything by being intelligent, and by the time you could understand the answer you're asking for you'd know it, and wouldn't need to ask. You don't understand your father, Alice; you don't know what it takes to change him when he's made up his mind to be stubborn."

Alice rose and began to get herself into a skirt. "Well, I don't think making scenes ever changes anybody," she grumbled. "I think a little jolly persuasion goes twice as far, myself."

"'A little jolly persuasion!'" Her mother turned the echo of this phrase into an ironic lament. "Yes, there was a time when I thought that, too! It didn't work; that's all."

"Perhaps you left the 'jolly' part of it out, mama."

For the second time that morning—it was now a little after seven o'clock —tears seemed about to offer their solace to Mrs. Adams. "I might have expected you to say that, Alice; you never do miss a chance," she said, gently. "It seems queer you don't some time miss just *one* chance!"

But Alice, progressing with her toilet, appeared to be little concerned. "Oh, well, I think there are better ways of managing a man than just hammering at him."

Mrs. Adams uttered a little cry of pain. "'Hammering,' Alice?"

"If you'd left it entirely to me," her daughter went on, briskly, "I believe papa'd already be willing to do anything we want him to."

"That's it; tell me I spoil everything. Well, I won't interfere from now on, you can be sure of it."

"Please don't talk like that," Alice said, quickly. "I'm old enough to realize that papa may need pressure of all sorts; I only think it makes him more obstinate to get him cross. You probably do understand him better, but that's one thing I've found out and you haven't. There!" She gave her mother a friendly tap on the shoulder and went to the door. "I'll hop in and say hello to him now."

As she went, she continued the fastening of her blouse, and appeared in her father's room with one hand still thus engaged, but she patted his forehead with the other.

"Poor old papa-daddy!" she said, gaily. "Every time he's better somebody talks him into getting so mad he has a relapse. It's a shame!"

Her father's eyes, beneath their melancholy brows, looked up at her wistfully. "I suppose you heard your mother going for me," he said.

"I heard you going for her, too!" Alice laughed. "What was it all about?"

"Oh, the same danged old story!"

"You mean she wants you to try something new when you get well?" Alice asked, with cheerful innocence. "So we could all have a lot more money?"

At this his sorrowful forehead was more sorrowful than ever. The deep horizontal lines moved upward to a pattern of suffering so familiar to his daughter that it meant nothing to her; but he spoke quietly. "Yes; so we wouldn't have any money at all, most likely."

"Oh, no!" she laughed, and, finishing with her blouse, patted his cheeks with both hands. "Just think how many grand openings there must be for a man that knows as much as you do! I always did believe you could get rich if you only cared to, papa."

But upon his forehead the painful pattern still deepened. "Don't you think we've always had enough, the way things are, Alice?"

"Not the way things *are!*" She patted his cheeks again; laughed again. "It used to be enough, maybe—anyway we did skimp along on it—but the way things are now I expect mama's really pretty practical in her ideas, though, I think it's a shame for her to bother you about it while you're so weak. Don't you worry about it, though; just think about other things till you get strong."

"You know," he said; "you know it isn't exactly the easiest thing in the world for a man of my age to find these grand openings you speak of. And when you've passed half-way from fifty to sixty you're apt to see some risk in giving up what you know how to do and trying something new."

"My, what a frown!" she cried, blithely. "Didn't I tell you to stop thinking about it till you get *all* well?" She bent over him, giving him a gay little kiss on the bridge of his nose. "There! I must run to breakfast. Cheer up now! *Au 'voir!*" And with her pretty hand she waved further encouragement from the closing door as she departed.

Lightsomely descending the narrow stairway, she whistled as she went, her fingers drumming time on the rail; and, still whistling, she came into the dining-room, where her mother and her brother were already at the table. The brother, a thin and sallow boy of twenty, greeted her without much approval as she took her place.

"Nothing seems to trouble you!" he said.

"No; nothing much," she made airy response. "What's troubling yourself, Walter?"

"Don't let that worry you!" he returned, seeming to consider this to be repartee of an effective sort; for he furnished a short laugh to go with it, and turned to his coffee with the manner of one who has satisfactorily closed an episode.

"Walter always seems to have so many secrets!" Alice said, studying him shrewdly, but with a friendly enough amusement in her scrutiny. "Everything he does or says seems to be acted for the benefit of some mysterious audience inside himself, and he always gets its applause. Take what he said just now: he seems to think it means something, but if it does, why, that's just another secret between him and the secret audience inside of him! We don't really know anything about Walter at all, do we, mama?"

Walter laughed again, in a manner that sustained her theory well enough; then after finishing his coffee, he took from his pocket a flattened packet in glazed blue paper; extracted with stained fingers a bent and wrinkled little cigarette, lighted it, hitched up his belted trousers with the air of a person who turns from trifles to things better worth his attention, and left the room.

Alice laughed as the door closed. "He's *all* secrets," she said. "Don't you think you really ought to know more about him, mama?"

"I'm sure he's a good boy," Mrs. Adams returned, thoughtfully. "He's been very brave about not being able to have the advantages that are enjoyed by the boys he's grown up with. I've never heard a word of complaint from him."

"About his not being sent to college?" Alice cried. "I should think you wouldn't! He didn't even have enough ambition to finish high school!"

Mrs. Adams sighed. "It seemed to me Walter lost his ambition when nearly all the boys he'd grown up with went to Eastern schools to prepare for college, and we couldn't afford to send him. If only your father would have listened——"

Alice interrupted: "What nonsense! Walter hated books and studying, and athletics, too, for that matter. He doesn't care for anything nice that I ever heard of. What do you suppose he does like, mama? He must like something or other somewhere, but what do you suppose it is? What does he do with his time?"

"Why, the poor boy's at Lamb and Company's all day. He doesn't get through until five in the afternoon; he doesn't *have* much time."

"Well, we never have dinner until about seven, and he's always late for dinner, and goes out, heaven knows where, right afterward!" Alice shook her head. "He used to go with our friends' boys, but I don't think he does now."

"Why, how could he?" Mrs. Adams protested. "That isn't *his* fault, poor child! The boys he knew when he was younger are nearly all away at college."

"Yes, but he doesn't see anything of 'em when they're here at holiday-time or vacation. None of 'em come to the house any more."

"I suppose he's made other friends. It's natural for him to want companions, at his age."

"Yes," Alice said, with disapproving emphasis. "But who are they? I've got an idea he plays pool at some rough place down-town."

"Oh, no; I'm sure he's a steady boy," Mrs. Adams protested, but her tone was not that of thorough-going conviction, and she added, "Life might be a very different thing for him if only your father can be brought to see——"

"Never mind, mama! It isn't me that has to be convinced, you know; and we can do a lot more with papa if we just let him alone about it for a day or two. Promise me you won't say any more to him until—well, until he's able to come downstairs to table. Will you?"

Mrs. Adams bit her lip, which had begun to tremble. "I think you can trust me to know a *few* things, Alice," she said. "I'm a little older than you, you know."

"That's a good girl!" Alice jumped up, laughing. "Don't forget it's the same as a promise, and do just cheer him up a little. I'll say good-bye to him before I go out."

"Where are you going?"

"Oh, I've got lots to do. I thought I'd run out to Mildred's to see what she's going to wear to-night, and then I want to go down and buy a yard of chiffon and some narrow ribbon to make new bows for my slippers—you'll have to give me some money——"

"If he'll give it to me!" her mother lamented, as they went toward the front stairs together; but an hour later she came into Alice's room with a bill in her hand.

"He has some money in his bureau drawer," she said. "He finally told me where it was."

There were traces of emotion in her voice, and Alice, looking shrewdly at her, saw moisture in her eyes.

"Mama!" she cried. "You didn't do what you promised me you wouldn't, did you—*not* before Miss Perry!"

"Miss Perry's getting him some broth," Mrs. Adams returned, calmly. "Besides, you're mistaken in saying I promised you anything; I said I thought you could trust me to know what is right."

"So you did bring it up again!" And Alice swung away from her, strode to her father's door, flung it open, went to him, and put a light hand soothingly over his unrelaxed forehead.

"Poor old papa!" she said. "It's a shame how everybody wants to trouble him. He shan't be bothered any more at all! He doesn't need to have everybody telling him how to get away from that old hole he's worked in so long and begin to make us all nice and rich. *He* knows how!"

Thereupon she kissed him a consoling good-bye, and made another gay departure, the charming hand again fluttering like a white butterfly in the shadow of the closing door.

CHAPTER III

Mrs. Adams had remained in Alice's room, but her mood seemed to have changed, during her daughter's little more than momentary absence.

"What did he *say?*" she asked, quickly, and her tone was hopeful.

" 'Say?' " Alice repeated, impatiently. "Why, nothing. I didn't let him. Really, mama, I think the best thing for you to do would be to just keep out of his room, because I don't believe you can go in there and not talk to him about it, and if you do talk we'll never get him to do the right thing. Never!"

The mother's response was a grieving silence; she turned from her daughter and walked to the door.

"Now, for goodness' sake!" Alice cried. "Don't go making tragedy out of my offering you a little practical advice!"

"I'm not," Mrs. Adams gulped, halting. "I'm just—just going to dust the downstairs, Alice." And with her face still averted, she went out into the little hallway, closing the door behind her. A moment later she could be heard descending the stairs, the sound of her footsteps carrying somehow an effect of resignation.

Alice listened, sighed, and, breathing the words, "Oh, murder!" turned to cheerier matters. She put on a little apple-green turban with a dim gold band round it, and then, having shrouded the turban in a white veil, which she kept pushed up above her forehead, she got herself into a tan coat of soft cloth fashioned with rakish severity. After that, having studied herself gravely in a long glass, she took from one of the drawers of her dressing-table a black leather card-case cornered in silver filigree, but found it empty.

She opened another drawer wherein were two white pasteboard boxes of cards, the one set showing simply "Miss Adams," the other engraved in Gothic characters, "Miss Alys Tuttle Adams." The latter belonged to Alice's "Alys" period—most girls go through it; and Alice must have felt that she had graduated, for, after frowning thoughtfully at the exhibit this morning, she took the box with its contents, and let the white shower fall from her fingers into the waste-basket beside her small desk. She replenished the card-case from the "Miss Adams" box; then, having found a pair of fresh white gloves, she tucked an ivory-topped Malacca walking-stick under her arm and set forth.

She went down the stairs, buttoning her gloves and still wearing the frown with which she had put "Alys" finally out of her life. She descended slowly, and paused on the lowest step, looking about her with an expression that needed but a slight deepening to betoken bitterness. Its connection with her dropping "Alys" forever was slight, however.

The small frame house, about fifteen years old, was already inclining to become a new Colonial relic. The Adamses had built it, moving into it from the "Queen Anne" house they had rented until they took this step in fashion. But fifteen years is a long time to stand still in the midland country, even for a house, and this one was lightly made, though the Adamses had not realized how flimsily until they had lived in it for some time. "Solid, compact, and convenient" were the instructions to the architect; and he had made it compact successfully. Alice, pausing at the foot of the stairway, was at the same time fairly in the "living-room," for the only separation between the "living-room" and the hall was a demarcation suggested to willing imaginations by a pair of wooden columns painted white. These columns, pine under the paint, were bruised and chipped at the base; one of them showed a crack that threatened to become a split; the "hard-wood" floor had become uneven; and in a corner the walls apparently failed of solidity, where the wall-paper had declined to accompany some staggerings of the plaster beneath it.

The furniture was in great part an accumulation begun with the wedding gifts; though some of it was older, two large patent rocking-chairs and a footstool having belonged to Mrs. Adams's mother in the days of hard brown plush and veneer. For decoration there were pictures and vases. Mrs. Adams had always been fond of vases, she said, and every year her husband's Christmas present to her was a vase of one sort or another—whatever the clerk showed him, marked at about twelve or fourteen dollars. The pictures were some of them etchings framed in gilt: Rheims, Canterbury, schooners grouped against a wharf; and Alice could remember how, in her childhood, her father sometimes pointed out the watery reflections in this last as very

fine. But it was a long time since he had shown interest in such things—"or in anything much," as she thought.

Other pictures were two water-colours in baroque frames; one being the Amalfi monk on a pergola wall, while the second was a yard-wide display of iris blossoms, painted by Alice herself at fourteen, as a birthday gift to her mother. Alice's glance paused upon it now with no great pride, but showed more approval of an enormous photograph of the Colosseum. This she thought of as "the only good thing in the room"; it possessed and bestowed distinction, she felt; and she did not regret having won her struggle to get it hung in its conspicuous place of honour over the mantelpiece. Formerly that place had been held for years by a steel-engraving, an accurate representation of the Suspension Bridge at Niagara Falls. It was almost as large as its successor, the "Colosseum," and it had been presented to Mr. Adams by colleagues in his department at Lamb and Company's. Adams had shown some feeling when Alice began to urge its removal to obscurity in the "upstairs hall"; he even resisted for several days after she had the "Colosseum" charged to him, framed in oak, and sent to the house. She cheered him up, of course, when he gave way; and her heart never misgave her that there might be a doubt which of the two pictures was the more dismaying.

Over the pictures, the vases, the old brown plush rocking-chairs and the stool, over the three gilt chairs, over the new chintz-covered easy chair and the gray velure sofa—over everything everywhere, was the familiar coating of smoke grime. It had worked into every fibre of the lace curtains, dingying them to an unpleasant gray; it lay on the window-sills and it dimmed the glass panes; it covered the walls, covered the ceiling, and was smeared darker and thicker in all corners. Yet here was no fault of housewifery; the curse could not be lifted, as the ingrained smudges permanent on the once white woodwork proved. The grime was perpetually renewed; scrubbing only ground it in.

This particular ugliness was small part of Alice's discontent, for though the coating grew a little deeper each year she was used to it. Moreover, she knew that she was not likely to find anything better in a thousand miles, so long as she kept to cities, and that none of her friends, however opulent, had any advantage of her here. Indeed, throughout all the great soft-coal country, people who consider themselves comparatively poor may find this consolation: cleanliness has been added to the virtues and beatitudes that money can not buy.

Alice brightened a little as she went forward to the front door, and she brightened more when the spring breeze met her there. Then all depression left her as she walked down the short brick path to the sidewalk, looked up and down the street, and saw how bravely the maple shade-trees, in spite of the black powder they breathed, were flinging out their thousands of young green particles overhead.

She turned north, treading the new little shadows on the pavement briskly, and, having finished buttoning her gloves, swung down her Malacca stick from under her arm to let it tap a more leisurely accompaniment to her quick, short step. She had to step quickly if she was to get anywhere; for the closeness of her skirt, in spite of its little length, permitted no natural stride; but she was pleased to be impeded, these brevities forming part of her show of fashion.

Other pedestrians found them not without charm, though approval may have been lacking here and there; and at the first crossing Alice suffered what she might have accounted an actual injury, had she allowed herself to be so sensitive. An elderly woman in fussy black silk stood there, waiting for a streetcar; she was all of a globular modelling, with a face patterned like a frost-bitten peach; and that the approaching gracefulness was uncongenial she naïvely made too evident. Her round, wan eyes seemed roused to bitter life as they rose from the curved high heels of the buckled slippers to the tight little skirt, and thence with startled ferocity to the Malacca cane, which plainly appeared to her as a decoration not more astounding than it was insulting.

Perceiving that the girl was bowing to her, the globular lady hurriedly made shift to alter her injurious expression. "Good morning, Mrs. Dowling," Alice said, gravely. Mrs. Dowling returned the salutation with a smile as convincingly benevolent as the ghastly smile upon a Santa Claus face; and then, while Alice passed on, exploded toward her a single compacted breath through tightened lips.

The sound was eloquently audible, though Mrs. Dowling remained unaware that in this or any manner whatever she had shed a light upon her thoughts; for it was her lifelong innocent conviction that other people saw her only as she wished to be seen, and heard from her only what she intended to be heard. At home it was always her husband who pulled down the shades of their bedroom window.

Alice looked serious for a few moments after the little encounter, then found some consolation in the behaviour of a gentleman of forty or so who was coming toward her. Like Mrs. Dowling, he had begun to show consciousness of Alice's approach while she was yet afar off; but his tokens were of a kind pleasanter to her. He was like Mrs. Dowling again, however, in his conception that Alice would not realize the significance of what he did. He passed his hand over his neck-scarf to see that it lay neatly to his collar, smoothed a lapel of his coat, and adjusted his hat, seeming to be preoccupied the while with problems that kept his eyes to the pavement; then, as he came within a few feet of her, he looked up, as in a surprised recognition almost dramatic, smiled winningly, lifted his hat decisively, and carried it to the full arm's length.

Alice's response was all he could have asked. The cane in her right hand stopped short in its swing, while her left hand moved in a pretty gesture as if an impulse carried it toward the heart; and she smiled, with her under lip caught suddenly between her teeth. Months ago she had seen an actress use this smile in a play, and it came perfectly to Alice now, without conscious direction, it had been so well acquired; but the pretty hand's little impulse toward the heart was an original bit all her own, on the spur of the moment.

The gentleman went on, passing from her forward vision as he replaced his hat. Of himself he was nothing to Alice, except for the gracious circumstance that he had shown strong consciousness of a pretty girl. He was middle-aged, substantial, a family man, securely married; and Alice had with him one of those long acquaintances that never become emphasized by so much as five minutes of talk; yet for this inconsequent meeting she had enacted a little part like a fragment in a pantomime of Spanish wooing.

It was not for him—not even to impress him, except as a messenger. Alice was herself almost unaware of her thought, which was one of the running thousands of her thoughts that took no deliberate form in words. Nevertheless, she had it, and it was the impulse of all her pretty bits of pantomime when she met other acquaintances who made their appreciation visible, as this substantial gentleman did. In Alice's unworded thought, he was to be thus encouraged as in some measure a champion to speak well of her to the world; but more than this: he was to tell some magnificent unknown bachelor how wonderful, how mysterious, she was.

She hastened on gravely, a little stirred reciprocally with the supposed stirrings in the breast of that shadowy ducal mate, who must be somewhere "waiting," or perhaps already seeking her; for she more often thought of herself as "waiting" while he sought her; and sometimes this view of things became so definite that it shaped into a murmur on her lips. "Waiting. Just waiting." And she might add, "For him!" Then, being twenty-two, she was apt to conclude the mystic interview by laughing at herself, though not without a continued wistfulness.

She came to a group of small coloured children playing waywardly in a puddle at the mouth of a muddy alley; and at sight of her they gave over their pastime in order to stare. She smiled brilliantly upon them, but they were too struck with wonder to comprehend that the manifestation was friendly; and as Alice picked her way in a little detour to keep from the mud, she heard one of them say, "Lady got cane! Jeez'l!"

She knew that many coloured children use impieties familiarly, and she was not startled. She was disturbed, however, by an unfavourable hint in the speaker's tone. He was six, probably, but the sting of a criticism is not necessarily allayed by knowledge of its ignoble source, and Alice had already begun to feel a slight uneasiness about her cane. Mrs. Dowling's stare had been strikingly projected at it; other women more than merely glanced, their brows and lips contracting impulsively; and Alice was aware that one or two of them frankly halted as soon as she had passed.

She had seen in several magazines pictures of ladies with canes, and on that account she had bought this one, never questioning that fashion is recognized, even in the provinces, as soon as beheld. On the contrary, these staring women obviously failed to realize that what they were being shown

was not an eccentric outburst, but the bright harbinger of an illustrious mode. Alice had applied a bit of artificial pigment to her lips and cheeks before she set forth this morning; she did not need it, having a ready colour of her own, which now mounted high with annoyance.

Then a splendidly shining closed black automobile, with windows of polished glass, came silently down the street toward her. Within it, as in a luxurious little apartment, three comely ladies in mourning sat and gossiped; but when they saw Alice they clutched one another. They instantly recovered, bowing to her solemnly as they were borne by, yet were not gone from her sight so swiftly but the edge of her side glance caught a flash of teeth in mouths suddenly opened, and the dark glisten of black gloves again clutching to share mirth.

The colour that outdid the rouge on Alice's cheek extended its area and grew warmer as she realized how all too cordial had been her nod and smile to these humorous ladies. But in their identity lay a significance causing her a sharper smart, for they were of the family of that Lamb, chief of Lamb and Company, who had employed her father since before she was born.

"And know his salary! They'd be *sure* to find out about that!" was her thought, coupled with another bitter one to the effect that they had probably made instantaneous financial estimates of what she wore—though certainly her walking-stick had most fed their hilarity.

She tucked it under her arm, not swinging it again; and her breath became quick and irregular as emotion beset her. She had been enjoying her walk, but within the space of the few blocks she had gone since she met the substantial gentleman, she found that more than the walk was spoiled: suddenly her life seemed to be spoiled, too; though she did not view the ruin with complaisance. These Lamb women thought her and her cane ridiculous, did they? she said to herself. That was their parvenu blood: to think because a girl's father worked for their grandfather she had no right to be rather striking in style, especially when the striking *was* her style. Probably all the other girls and women would agree with them and would laugh at her when they got together, and, what might be fatal, would try to make all the men think her a silly pretender. Men were just like sheep, and nothing was easier than for women to set up as shepherds and pen them in a fold. "To keep out outsiders," Alice thought. "And make 'em believe I *am* an outsider. What's the use of living?"

All seemed lost when a trim young man appeared, striding out of a cross-street not far before her, and, turning at the corner, came toward her. Visibly, he slackened his gait to lengthen the time of his approach, and, as he was a stranger to her, no motive could be ascribed to him other than a wish to have a longer time to look at her.

She lifted a pretty hand to a pin at her throat, bit her lip—not with the smile, but mysteriously—and at the last instant before her shadow touched the stranger, let her eyes gravely meet his. A moment later, having arrived before the house which was her destination, she halted at the entrance to a driveway leading through fine lawns to the intentionally important mansion. It was a pleasant and impressive place to be seen entering, but Alice did not enter at once. She paused, examining a tiny bit of mortar which the masons had forgotten to scrape from a brick in one of the massive gate-posts. She frowned at this tiny defaccment, and with an air of annoyance scraped it away, using the ferrule of her cane—an act of fastidious proprietorship. If any one had looked back over his shoulder he would not have doubted that she lived there.

Alice did not turn to see whether anything of the sort happened or not, but she may have surmised that it did. At all events, it was with an invigorated step that she left the gateway behind her and went cheerfully up the drive to the house of her friend Mildred.

CHAPTER IV

Adams had a restless morning, and toward noon he asked Miss Perry to call his daughter; he wished to say something to her.

"I thought I heard her leaving the house a couple of hours ago—maybe longer," the nurse told him. "I'll go see." And she returned from the brief errand, her impression confirmed by information from Mrs. Adams. "Yes. She went up to Miss Mildred Palmer's to see what she's going to wear to-night."

Adams looked at Miss Perry wearily, but remained passive, making no inquiries; for he was long accustomed to what seemed to him a kind of jargon among ladies, which became the more incomprehensible when they tried to explain it. A man's best course, he had found, was just to let it go as so much sound. His sorrowful eyes followed the nurse as she went back to her rocking-chair by the window; and her placidity showed him that there was no mystery for her in the fact that Alice walked two miles to ask so simple a question when there was a telephone in the house. Obviously Miss Perry also comprehended why Alice thought it important to know what Mildred meant to wear. Adams understood why Alice should be concerned with what she herself wore—"to look neat and tidy and at her best, why, of course she'd want to," he thought—but he realized that it was forever beyond him to understand why the clothing of other people had long since become an absorbing part of her life.

Her excursion this morning was no novelty; she was continually going to see what Mildred meant to wear, or what some other girl meant to wear; and when Alice came home from wherever other girls or women had been gathered, she always hurried to her mother with earnest descriptions of the clothing she had seen. At such times, if Adams was present, he might recognize "organdie," or "taffeta," or "chiffon," as words defining certain textiles, but the rest was too technical for him, and he was like a dismal boy at a sermon, just waiting for it to get itself finished. Not the least of the mystery was his wife's interest: she was almost indifferent about her own clothes, and when she consulted Alice about them spoke hurriedly and with an air of apology; but when Alice described other people's clothes, Mrs. Adams listened as eagerly as the daughter talked.

"There they go!" he muttered to-day, a moment after he heard the front door closing, a sound recognizable throughout most of the thinly built house. Alice had just returned, and Mrs. Adams called to her from the upper hallway, not far from Adams's door.

"What did she *say?*"

"She was sort of snippy about it," Alice returned, ascending the stairs. "She gets that way sometimes, and pretended she hadn't made up her mind, but I'm pretty sure it'll be the maize Georgette with Malines flounces."

"Didn't you say she wore that at the Pattersons'?" Mrs. Adams inquired, as Alice arrived at the top of the stairs. "And didn't you tell me she wore it again at the——"

"Certainly not," Alice interrupted, rather petulantly. "She's never worn it but once, and of course she wouldn't want to wear anything to-night that people have seen her in a lot."

Miss Perry opened the door of Adams's room and stepped out. "Your father wants to know if you'll come and see him a minute, Miss Adams."

"Poor old thing! Of course!" Alice exclaimed, and went quickly into the room, Miss Perry remaining outside. "What's the matter, papa? Getting awful sick of lying on his tired old back, I expect."

"I've had kind of a poor morning," Adams said, as she patted his hand comfortingly. "I been thinking——"

"Didn't I tell you not to?" she cried, gaily. "Of course you'll have poor times when you go and do just exactly what I say you mustn't. You stop thinking this very minute!"

He smiled ruefully, closing his eyes; was silent for a moment, then asked her to sit beside the bed. "I been thinking of something I wanted to say," he added.

"What like, papa?"

"Well, it's nothing—much," he said, with something deprecatory in his tone, as if he felt vague impulses toward both humour and apology. "I just thought maybe I ought to've said more to you some time or other about—well, about the way things *are*, down at Lamb and Company's, for instance."

"Now, papa!" She leaned forward in the chair she had taken, and pretended to slap his hand crossly. "Isn't that exactly what I said you couldn't think one single think about till you get *all* well?"

"Well——" he said, and went on slowly, not looking at her, but at the ceiling. "I just thought maybe it wouldn't been any harm if some time or other I told you something about the way they sort of depend on me down there."

"Why don't they show it, then?" she asked, quickly. "That's just what mama and I have been feeling so much; they don't appreciate you."

"Why, yes, they do," he said. "Yes, they do. They began h'isting my salary the second year I went in there, and they've h'isted it a little every two years all the time I've worked for 'em. I've been head of the sundries department for seven years now, and I could hardly have more authority in that department unless I was a member of the firm itself."

"Well, why don't they make you a member of the firm? That's what they ought to've done! Yes, and long ago!"

Adams laughed, but sighed with more heartiness than he had laughed. "They call me their 'oldest stand-by' down there." He laughed again, apologetically, as if to excuse himself for taking a little pride in this title. "Yes, sir; they say I'm their 'oldest stand-by'; and I guess they know they can count on my department's turning in as good a report as they look for, at the end of every month; but they don't have to take a man into the firm to get him to do my work, dearie."

"But you said they depended on you, papa."

"So they do; but of course not so's they couldn't get along without me." He paused, reflecting. "I don't just seem to know how to put it—I mean how to put what I started out to say. I kind of wanted to tell you—well, it seems funny to me, these last few years, the way your mother's taken to feeling about it. I'd like to see a better established wholesale drug business than Lamb and Company this side the Alleghanies—I don't say bigger, I say better established—and it's kind of funny for a man that's been with a business like that as long as I have to hear it called a 'hole.'. It's kind of funny when you think, yourself, you've done pretty fairly well in a business like that, and the men at the head of it seem to think so, too, and put your salary just about as high as anybody could consider customary—well, what I mean, Alice, it's kind of funny to have your mother think it's mostly just—mostly just a failure, so to speak."

His voice had become tremulous in spite of him; and this sign of weakness and emotion had sufficient effect upon Alice. She bent over him suddenly, with her arm about him and her cheek against his. "Poor papa!" she murmured. "Poor papa!"

"No, no," he said. "I didn't mean anything to trouble you. I just thought——" He hesitated. "I just wondered—I thought maybe it wouldn't be any harm if I said something about how things are down there. I got to thinking maybe you didn't understand it's a pretty good place. They're fine people to work for; and they've always seemed to think something of me; —the way they took Walter on, for instance, soon as I asked 'em, last year. Don't you think that looked a good deal as if they thought something of me, Alice?"

"Yes, papa," she said, not moving.

"And the work's right pleasant," he went on. "Mighty nice boys in our department, Alice. Well, they are in all the departments, for that matter. We have a good deal of fun down there some days."

She lifted her head. "More than you do at home 'some days,' I expect, papa!" she said.

He protested feebly. "Now, I didn't mean that—I didn't want to trouble you——"

She looked at him through winking eyelashes. "I'm sorry I called it a 'hole,' papa."

"No, no," he protested, gently. "It was your mother said that."

"No. I did, too."

"Well, if you did, it was only because you'd heard her."

She shook her head, then kissed him. "I'm going to talk to her," she said, and rose decisively.

But at this, her father's troubled voice became quickly louder: "You better let her alone. I just wanted to have a little talk with you. I didn't mean to start any—your mother won't——"

"Now, papa!" Alice spoke cheerfully again, and smiled upon him. "I want you to quit worrying! Everything's going to be all right and nobody's going to bother you any more about anything. You'll see!"

She carried her smile out into the hall, but after she had closed the door her face was all pity; and her mother, waiting for her in the opposite room, spoke sympathetically.

"What's the matter, Alice? What did he say that's upset you?"

"Wait a minute, mama." Alice found a handkerchief, used it for eyes and suffused nose, gulped, then suddenly and desolately sat upon the bed. "Poor, poor, *poor* papa!" she whispered.

"Why?" Mrs. Adams inquired, mildly. "What's the matter with him? Sometimes you act as if he weren't getting well. What's he been talking about?"

"Mama—well, I think I'm pretty selfish. Oh, I do!"

"Did he say you were?"

"Papa? No, indeed! What I mean is, maybe we're both a little selfish to try to make him go out and hunt around for something new."

Mrs. Adams looked thoughtful. "Oh, that's what he was up to!"

"Mama, I think we ought to give it up. I didn't dream it had really hurt him."

"Well, doesn't he hurt us?"

"Never that I know of, mama."

"I don't mean by *saying* things," Mrs. Adams explained, impatiently. "There are more ways than that of hurting people. When a man sticks to a salary that doesn't provide for his family, isn't that hurting them?"

"Oh, it 'provides' for us well enough, mama. We have what we need—if I weren't so extravagant. Oh, I know I am!"

But at this admission her mother cried out sharply. " 'Extravagant!' You haven't one tenth of what the other girls you go with have. And you *can't* have what you ought to as long as he doesn't get out of that horrible place. It provides bare food and shelter for us, but what's that?"

"I don't think we ought to try any more to change him."

"You don't?" Mrs. Adams came and stood before her. "Listen, Alice: your father's asleep; that's his trouble, and he's got to be waked up. He doesn't know that things have changed. When you and Walter were little children we did have enough—at least it seemed to be about as much as most of the people we knew. But the town isn't what it was in those days, and times aren't what they were then, and these fearful *prices* aren't the old prices. Everything else but your father has changed, and all the time he's stood still. He doesn't know it; he thinks because they've given him a hundred dollars more every two years he's quite a prosperous man! And he thinks that because his children cost him more than he and I cost our parents he gives them—enough!"

"But Walter——" Alice faltered. "Walter doesn't cost him anything at all any more." And she concluded, in a stricken voice, "It's all—me!"

"Why shouldn't it be?" her mother cried. "You're young—you're just at the time when your life should be fullest of good things and happiness. Yet what do you get?"

Alice's lip quivered; she was not unsusceptible to such an appeal, but she contrived the semblance of a protest. "I don't have such a bad time—not a good *deal* of the time, anyhow. I've got a good *many* of the things other girls have——"

"You have?" Mrs. Adams was piteously satirical. "I suppose you've got a limousine to go to that dance to-night? I suppose you've only got to call a florist and tell him to send you some orchids? I suppose you've——"

But Alice interrupted this list. Apparently in a single instant all emotion left her, and she became business-like, as one in the midst of trifles reminded of really serious matters. She got up from the bed and went to the door of the closet where she kept her dresses. "Oh, see here," she said, briskly. "I've decided to wear my white organdie if you could put in a new lining for me. I'm afraid it'll take you nearly all afternoon."

She brought forth the dress, displayed it upon the bed, and Mrs. Adams examined it attentively.

"Do you think you could get it done, mama?"

"I don't see why not," Mrs. Adams answered, passing a thoughtful hand over the fabric. "It oughtn't to take more than four or five hours."

"It's a shame to have you sit at the machine that long," Alice said, absently, adding, "And I'm sure we ought to let papa alone. Let's just give it up, mama."

Mrs. Adams continued her thoughtful examination of the dress. "Did you buy the chiffon and ribbon, Alice?"

"Yes. I'm sure we oughtn't to talk to him about it any more, mama."

"Well, we'll see."

"Let's both agree that we'll *never* say another single word to him about it," said Alice. "It'll be a great deal better if we just let him make up his mind for himself."

CHAPTER V

With this, having more immediately practical questions before them, they dropped the subject, to bend their entire attention upon the dress; and when the lunch-gong sounded downstairs Alice was still sketching repairs and alterations. She continued to sketch them, not heeding the summons.

"I suppose we'd better go down to lunch," Mrs. Adams said, absently. "She's at the gong again."

"In a minute, mama. Now about the sleeves——" And she went on with her planning. Unfortunately the gong was inexpressive of the mood of the person who beat upon it. It consisted of three little metal bowls upon a string; they were unequal in size, and, upon being tapped with a padded stick, gave forth vibrations almost musically pleasant. It was Alice who had substituted this contrivance for the brass "dinner-bell" in use throughout her childhood; and neither she nor the others of her family realized that the substitution of sweeter sounds had made the life of that household more difficult. In spite of dismaying increases in wages, the Adamses still strove to keep a cook; and, as they were unable to pay the higher rates demanded by a good one, what they usually had was a whimsical coloured woman of nomadic impulses. In the hands of such a person the old-fashioned "dinner-bell" was satisfying; life could instantly be made intolerable for any one dawdling on his way to a meal; the bell was capable of every desirable profanity and left nothing bottled up in the breast of the ringer. But the chamois-covered stick might whack upon Alice's little Chinese bowls for a considerable length of time and produce no great effect of urgency upon a hearer, nor any other effect, except fury in the cook. The ironical impossibility of expressing indignation otherwise than by sounds of gentle harmony proved exasperating; the cook was apt to become surcharged, so that explosive resignations, never rare, were somewhat more frequent after the introduction of the gong.

Mrs. Adams took this increased frequency to be only another manifestation of the inexplicable new difficulties that beset all housekeeping. You paid a cook double what you had paid one a few years before; and the cook knew half as much of cookery, and had no gratitude. The more you gave these people, it seemed, the worse they behaved—a condition not to be remedied by simply giving them less, because you couldn't even get the worst unless you paid her what she demanded. Nevertheless, Mrs. Adams remained fitfully an optimist in the matter. Brought up by her mother to speak of a female cook as "the girl," she had been instructed by Alice to drop that definition

in favour of one not an improvement in accuracy: "the maid." Almost always, during the first day or so after every cook came, Mrs. Adams would
say, at intervals, with an air of triumph: "I believe—of course it's a little
soon to be sure—but I do really believe this new maid is the treasure we've
been looking for so long!" Much in the same way that Alice dreamed of a
mysterious perfect mate for whom she "waited," her mother had a fairy theory
that hidden somewhere in the universe there was the treasure, the perfect
"maid," who would come and cook in the Adamses' kitchen, not four days
or four weeks, but forever.

The present incumbent was not she. Alice, profoundly interested herself,
kept her mother likewise so preoccupied with the dress that they were but
vaguely conscious of the gong's soft warnings, though these were repeated
and protracted unusually. Finally the sound of a hearty voice, independent
and enraged, reached the pair. It came from the hall below.

"I says goo'-bye!" it called. "Da'ss all!"

Then the front door slammed.

"Why, what——" Mrs. Adams began.

They went down hurriedly to find out. Miss Perry informed them.

"I couldn't make her listen to reason," she said. "She rang the gong four
or five times and got to talking to herself; and then she went up to her room
and packed her bag. I told her she had no business to go out the front door,
anyhow."

Mrs. Adams took the news philosophically. "I thought she had something
like that in her eye when I paid her this morning, and I'm not surprised.
Well, we won't let Mr. Adams know anything's the matter till I get a new
one."

They lunched upon what the late incumbent had left chilling on the table,
and then Mrs. Adams prepared to wash the dishes; she would "have them
done in a jiffy," she said, cheerfully. But it was Alice who washed the dishes.

"I *don't* like to have you do that, Alice," her mother protested, following
her into the kitchen. "It roughens the hands, and when a girl has hands like
yours——"

"I know, mama." Alice looked troubled, but shook her head. "It can't be
helped this time; you'll need every minute to get that dress done."

Mrs. Adams went away lamenting, while Alice, no expert, began to splash
the plates and cups and saucers in the warm water. After a while, as she
worked, her eyes grew dreamy: she was making little gay-coloured pictures of
herself, unfounded prophecies of how she would look and what would happen to her that evening. She saw herself, charming and demure, wearing a
fluffy idealization of the dress her mother now determinedly struggled with
upstairs; she saw herself framed in a garlanded archway, the entrance to a
ballroom, and saw the people on the shining floor turning dramatically to
look at her; then from all points a rush of young men shouting for dances
with her; and she constructed a superb stranger, tall, dark, masterfully smiling, who swung her out of the clamouring group as the music began. She

saw herself dancing with him, saw the half-troubled smile she would give him; and she accurately smiled that smile as she rinsed the knives and forks.

These hopeful fragments of drama were not to be realized, she knew; but she played that they were true, and went on creating them. In all of them she wore or carried flowers—her mother's sorrow for her in this detail but made it the more important—and she saw herself glamorous with orchids; discarded these for an armful of long-stemmed, heavy roses; tossed them away for a great bouquet of white camellias; and so wandered down a lengthening hothouse gallery of floral beauty, all costly and beyond her reach except in such a wistful day-dream. And upon her present whole horizon, though she searched it earnestly, she could discover no figure of a sender of flowers.

Out of her fancies the desire for flowers to wear that night emerged definitely and became poignant; she began to feel that it might be particularly important to have them. "This might be the night!" She was still at the age to dream that the night of any dance may be the vital point in destiny. No matter how commonplace or disappointing other dance nights have been this one may bring the great meeting. The unknown magnifico may be there.

Alice was almost unaware of her own reveries in which this being appeared —reveries often so transitory that they developed and passed in a few seconds. And in some of them the being was not wholly a stranger; there were moments when he seemed to be composed of recognizable fragments of young men she knew—a smile she had liked, from one; the figure of another, the hair of another—and sometimes she thought he might be concealed, so to say, within the person of an actual acquaintance, someone she had never suspected of being the right seeker for her, someone who had never suspected that it was she who "waited" for him. Anything might reveal them to each other: a look, a turn of the head, a singular word—perhaps some flowers upon her breast or in her hand.

She wiped the dishes slowly, concluding the operation by dropping a saucer upon the floor and dreamily sweeping the fragments under the stove. She sighed and replaced the broom near a window, letting her glance wander over the small yard outside. The grass, repulsively besooted to the colour of coal-smoke all winter, had lately come to life again and now sparkled with green, in the midst of which a tiny shot of blue suddenly fixed her absent eyes. They remained upon it for several moments, becoming less absent.

It was a violet.

Alice ran upstairs, put on her hat, went outdoors and began to search out the violets. She found twenty-two, a bright omen—since the number was that of her years—but not enough violets. There were no more; she had ransacked every foot of the yard.

She looked dubiously at the little bunch in her hand, glanced at the lawn next door, which offered no favourable prospect; then went thoughtfully into the house, left her twenty-two violets in a bowl of water, and came quickly out again, her brow marked with a frown of decision. She went to a trolley-line and took a car to the outskirts of the city where a new park had been opened.

Here she resumed her search, but it was not an easily rewarded one, and for an hour after her arrival she found no violets. She walked conscientiously over the whole stretch of meadow, her eyes roving discontentedly; there was never a blue dot in the groomed expanse; but at last, as she came near the borders of an old grove of trees, left untouched by the municipal landscapers, the little flowers appeared, and she began to gather them. She picked them carefully, loosening the earth round each tiny plant, so as to bring the roots up with it, that it might live the longer; and she had brought a napkin, which she drenched at a hydrant, and kept loosely wrapped about the stems of her collection.

The turf was too damp for her to kneel; she worked patiently, stooping from the waist; and when she got home in a drizzle of rain at five o'clock her knees were tremulous with strain, her back ached, and she was tired all over, but she had three hundred violets. Her mother moaned when Alice showed them to her, fragrant in a basin of water.

"Oh, you *poor* child! To think of your having to work so hard to get things that other girls only need lift their little fingers for!"

"Never mind," said Alice, huskily. "I've got 'em and I *am* going to have a good time to-night!"

"You've just got to!" Mrs. Adams agreed, intensely sympathetic. "The Lord knows you deserve to, after picking all these violets, poor thing, and He wouldn't be mean enough to keep you from it. I may have to get dinner before I finish the dress, but I can get it done in a few minutes afterward, and it's going to look right pretty. Don't you worry about *that!* And with all these lovely violets——"

"I wonder——" Alice began, paused, then went on, fragmentarily: "I suppose—well, I wonder—do you suppose it would have been better policy to have told Walter before——"

"No," said her mother. "It would only have given him longer to grumble."

"But he might——"

"Don't worry," Mrs. Adams reassured her. "He'll be a little cross, but he won't be stubborn; just let me talk to him and don't you say anything at all, no matter what *he* says."

These references to Walter concerned some necessary manœuvres which took place at dinner, and were conducted by the mother, Alice having accepted her advice to sit in silence. Mrs. Adams began by laughing cheerfully. "I wonder how much longer it took me to cook this dinner than it does Walter to eat it?" she said. "Don't gobble, child! There's no hurry."

In contact with his own family Walter was no squanderer of words. "Is for me," he said. "Got date."

"I know you have, but there's plenty of time."

He smiled in benevolent pity. "*You* know, do you? If you made any coffee —don't bother if you didn't. Get some down-town." He seemed about to rise and depart; whereupon Alice, biting her lip, sent a panic-stricken glance at her mother.

But Mrs. Adams seemed not at all disturbed; and laughed again. "Why, what nonsense, Walter! I'll bring your coffee in a few minutes, but we're going to have dessert first."

"What sort?"

"Some lovely peaches."

"Doe' want 'ny canned peaches," said the frank Walter, moving back his chair. "G'-night."

"Walter! It doesn't begin till about nine o'clock at the earliest."

He paused, mystified. "What doesn't?"

"The dance."

"What dance?"

"Why, Mildred Palmer's dance, of course."

Walter laughed briefly. "What's that to me?"

"Why, you haven't forgotten it's *to-night*, have you?" Mrs. Adams cried. "What a boy!"

"I told you a week ago I wasn't going to that ole dance," he returned, frowning. "You heard me."

"Walter!" she exclaimed. "Of *course* you're going. I got your clothes all out this afternoon, and brushed them for you. They'll look very nice, and——"

"They won't look nice on *me*," he interrupted. "Got date down-town, I tell you."

"But of course you'll——"

"See here!" Walter said, decisively. "Don't get any wrong ideas in your head. I'm just as liable to go up to that ole dance at the Palmers' as I am to eat a couple of barrels of broken glass."

"But, Walter——"

Walter was beginning to be seriously annoyed. "Don't 'Walter' me! I'm no s'ciety snake. I wouldn't jazz with that Palmer crowd if they coaxed me with diamonds."

"Walter——"

"Didn't I tell you it's no use to 'Walter' me?" he demanded.

"My dear child——"

"Oh, Glory!"

At this Mrs. Adams abandoned her air of amusement, looked hurt, and glanced at the demure Miss Perry across the table. "I'm afraid Miss Perry won't think you have very good manners, Walter."

"You're right she won't," he agreed, grimly. "Not if I haf' to hear any more about me goin' to——"

But his mother interrupted him with some asperity: "It seems very strange that you always object to going anywhere among *our* friends, Walter."

"*Your* friends!" he said, and, rising from his chair, gave utterance to an

ironical laugh strictly monosyllabic. "*Your* friends!" he repeated, going to
the door. "Oh, yes! Certainly! Good-*night!*"

And looking back over his shoulder to offer a final brief view of his derisive face, he took himself out of the room.

Alice gasped: "Mama——"

"I'll stop him!" her mother responded, sharply; and hurried after the
truant, catching him at the front door with his hat and raincoat on.

"Walter——"

"Told you had a date down-town," he said, gruffly; and would have opened
the door, but she caught his arm and detained him.

"Walter, please come back and finish your dinner. When I take all the
trouble to cook it for you, I think you might at least——"

"Now, now!" he said. "That isn't what you're up to. You don't want to
make me eat; you want to make me listen."

"Well, you *must* listen!" She retained her grasp upon his arm, and made
it tighter. "Walter, please!" she entreated, her voice becoming tremulous.
"*Please* don't make me so much trouble!"

He drew back from her as far as her hold upon him permitted, and looked
at her sharply. "Look here!" he said. "I *get* you, all right! What's the matter
of Alice goin' to that party by herself?"

"She just *can't!*"

"Why not?"

"It makes things too *mean* for her, Walter. All the other girls have somebody to depend on after they get there."

"Well, why doesn't she have somebody?" he asked, testily. "Somebody besides *me*, I mean! Why hasn't somebody asked her to go? She ought to be
that popular, anyhow, I sh'd think—she *tries* enough!"

"I don't understand how you can be so hard," his mother wailed, huskily.
"You know why they don't run after her the way they do the other girls
she goes with, Walter. It's because we're poor, and she hasn't got any background."

" 'Background?' " Walter repeated. " 'Background?' What kind of talk is
that?"

"You *will* go with her to-night, Walter?" his mother pleaded, not stopping
to enlighten him. "You don't understand how hard things are for her and
how brave she is about them, or you *couldn't* be so selfish! It'd be more
than I can bear to see her disappointed to-night! She went clear out to
Belleview Park this afternoon, Walter, and spent hours and hours picking
violets to wear. You *will*——"

Walter's heart was not iron, and the episode of the violets may have
reached it. "Oh, *blub!*" he said, and flung his soft hat violently at the wall.

His mother beamed with delight. "*That's* a good boy, darling! You'll never
be sorry you——"

"Cut it out," he requested. "If I take her, will you pay for a taxi?"

"Oh, Walter!" And again Mrs. Adams showed distress. "Couldn't you?"

"No, I couldn't; I'm not goin' to throw away my good money like that, and you can't tell what time o' night it'll be before she's willin' to come home. What's the matter you payin' for one?"

"I haven't any money."

"Well, father——"

She shook her head dolefully. "I got some from him this morning, and I can't bother him for any more; it upsets him. He's *always* been so terribly close with money——"

"I guess he couldn't help that," Walter observed. "We're liable to go to the poorhouse the way it is. Well, what's the matter our walkin' to this rotten party?"

"In the rain, Walter?"

"Well, it's only a drizzle and we can take a streetcar to within a block of the house."

Again his mother shook her head. "It wouldn't do."

"Well, darn the luck, all *right!*" he consented, explosively. "I'll get her something to ride in. It means seventy-five cents."

"Why, Walter!" Mrs. Adams cried, much pleased. "Do you know how to get a cab for that little? How splendid!"

"'Tain't a cab," Walter informed her crossly. "It's a tin Lizzie, but you don't haf' to tell her what it is till I get her into it, do you?"

Mrs. Adams agreed that she didn't.

CHAPTER VI

Alice was busy with herself for two hours after dinner; but a little before nine o'clock she stood in front of her long mirror, completed, bright-eyed and solemn. Her hair, exquisitely arranged, gave all she asked of it; what artificialities in colour she had used upon her face were only bits of emphasis that made her prettiness the more distinct; and the dress, not rumpled by her mother's careful hours of work, was a white cloud of loveliness. Finally there were two triumphant bouquets of violets, each with the stems wrapped in tin-foil shrouded by a bow of purple chiffon; and one bouquet she wore at her waist and the other she carried in her hand.

Miss Perry, called in by a rapturous mother for the free treat of a look at this radiance, insisted that Alice was a vision. "Purely and simply a vision!" she said, meaning that no other definition whatever would satisfy her. "I never saw anybody look a vision if she don't look one to-night," the admiring nurse declared. "Her papa'll think the same I do about it. You see if he doesn't say she's purely and simply a vision."

Adams did not fulfil the prediction quite literally when Alice paid a brief visit to his room to "show" him and bid him good-night; but he chuckled feebly. "Well, well, well!" he said. "You look mighty fine—*mighty* fine!" And he waggled a bony finger at her two bouquets. "Why, Alice, who's your beau?"

"Never you mind!" she laughed, archly brushing his nose with the violets in her hand. "He treats me pretty well, doesn't he?"

"Must like to throw his money around! These violets smell mighty sweet, and they ought to, if they're going to a party with *you*. Have a good time, dearie."

"I mean to!" she cried; and she repeated this gaily, but with an emphasis expressing sharp determination as she left him. "I *mean* to!"

"What was he talking about?" her mother inquired, smoothing the rather worn and old evening wrap she had placed on Alice's bed. "What were you telling him you 'mean to?'"

Alice went back to her triple mirror for the last time, then stood before the long one. "That I mean to have a good time to-night," she said; and as she turned from her reflection to the wrap Mrs. Adams held up for her, "It looks as though I *could*, don't you think so?"

"You'll just be a queen to-night," her mother whispered in fond emotion. "You mustn't doubt yourself."

"Well, there's one thing," said Alice. "I think I do look nice enough to get along without having to dance with that Frank Dowling! All I ask is for it to happen just *once*; and if he comes near me to-night I'm going to treat him the way the other girls do. Do you suppose Walter's got the taxi out in front?"

"He—he's waiting down in the hall," Mrs. Adams answered, nervously; and she held up another garment to go over the wrap.

Alice frowned at it. "What's that, mama?"

"It's—it's your father's raincoat. I thought you'd put it on over——"

"But I won't need it in a taxicab."

"You will to get in and out, and you needn't take it into the Palmers'. You can leave it in the—in the—— It's drizzling, and you'll need it."

"Oh, well," Alice consented; and a few minutes later, as with Walter's assistance she climbed into the vehicle he had provided, she better understood her mother's solicitude.

"What on earth *is* this, Walter?" she asked.

"Never mind; it'll keep you dry enough with the top up," he returned, taking his seat beside her. Then for a time, as they went rather jerkily up the street, she was silent; but finally she repeated her question: "What *is* it, Walter?"

"What's what?"

"This—this *car*?"

"It's a ottomobile."

"I mean—what kind is it?"

"Haven't you got eyes?"

"It's too dark."

"It's a second-hand tin Lizzie," said Walter. "D'you know what that means? It means a flivver."

"Yes, Walter."

"Got 'ny 'bjections?"

"Why, no, dear," she said, placatively. "Is it yours, Walter? Have you bought it?"

"Me?" he laughed. "I couldn't buy a used wheelbarrow. I rent this sometimes when I'm goin' out among 'em. Costs me seventy-five cents and the price o' the gas."

"That seems very moderate."

"I guess it is! The feller owes me some money, and this is the only way I'd ever get it off him."

"Is he a garage-keeper?"

"Not exactly!" Walter uttered husky sounds of amusement. "You'll be just as happy, I guess, if you don't know who he is," he said.

His tone misgave her; and she said truthfully that she was content not to know who owned the car. "I joke sometimes about how you keep things to yourself," she added, "but I really never do pry in your affairs, Walter."

"Oh, no, you don't!"

"Indeed, I don't."

"Yes, you're mighty nice and cooing when you got me where you want me," he jeered. "Well, I just as soon tell you where I get this car."

"I'd just as soon you wouldn't, Walter," she said, hurriedly. "Please don't."

But Walter meant to tell her. "Why, there's nothin' exactly *criminal* about it," he said. "It belongs to old J. A. Lamb himself. He keeps it for their coon chauffeur. I rent it from him."

"From Mr. *Lamb?*"

"No; from the coon chauffeur."

"Walter!" she gasped.

"Sure I do! I can get it any night when the coon isn't goin' to use it himself. He's drivin' their limousine to-night—that little Henrietta Lamb's goin' to the party, no matter if her father *has* only been dead less'n a year!" He paused, then inquired: "Well, how d'you like it?"

She did not speak, and he began to be remorseful for having imparted so much information, though his way of expressing regret was his own. "Well, you *will* make the folks make me take you to parties!" he said. "I got to do it the best way I *can*, don't I?"

Then as she made no response, "Oh, the car's *clean* enough," he said. "This coon, he's as particular as any white man; you needn't worry about that." And as she still said nothing, he added gruffly, "I'd of had a better car if I could afforded it. You needn't get so upset about it."

"I don't understand—" she said in a low voice—"I don't understand how you know such people."

"Such people as who?"

"As—coloured chauffeurs."

"Oh, look here, now!" he protested, loudly. "Don't you know this is a democratic country?"

"Not quite that democratic, is it, Walter?"

"The trouble with you," he retorted, "you don't know there's anybody in town except just this silk-shirt crowd." He paused, seeming to await a refutation; but as none came, he expressed himself definitely: "They make me sick."

They were coming near their destination, and the glow of the big, brightly lighted house was seen before them in the wet night. Other cars, not like theirs, were approaching this center of brilliance; long triangles of light near the ground swept through the fine drizzle; small red tail-lights gleamed again from the moist pavement of the street; and, through the myriads of little glistening leaves along the curving driveway, glimpses were caught of lively colours moving in a white glare as the limousines released their occupants under the shelter of the porte-cochère.

Alice clutched Walter's arm in a panic; they were just at the driveway entrance. "Walter, we mustn't go in there."

"What's the matter?"

"Leave this awful car outside."

"Why, I——"

"Stop!" she insisted, vehemently. "You've got to! Go back!"

"Oh, Glory!"

The little car was between the entrance posts, but Walter backed it out, avoiding a collision with an impressive machine which swerved away from them and passed on toward the porte-cochère, showing a man's face grinning at the window as it went by. "Flivver runabout got the wrong number!" he said.

"Did he *see* us?" Alice cried.

"Did who see us?"

"Harvey Malone—in that foreign coupé."

"No; he couldn't tell who we were under this top," Walter assured her as he brought the little car to a standstill beside the curbstone, out in the street. "What's it matter if he did, the big fish?"

Alice responded with a loud sigh, and sat still.

"Well, want to go on back?" Walter inquired. "You bet I'm willing!"

"No."

"Well, then, what's the matter our drivin' on up to the porte-cochère? There's room for me to park just the other side of it."

"No, *no!*"

"What you expect to do? Sit *here* all night?"

"No, leave the car here."

"I don't care where we leave it," he said. "Sit still till I lock her, so none o' these millionaires around here'll run off with her." He got out with a padlock and chain; and, having put these in place, offered Alice his hand. "Come on, if you're ready."

"Wait," she said, and, divesting herself of the raincoat, handed it to Walter. "Please leave this with your things in the men's dressing-room, as if it
were an extra one of your own, Walter."

He nodded; she jumped out; and they scurried through the drizzle. As
they reached the porte-cochère she began to laugh airily, and spoke to the
impassive man in livery who stood there. "Joke on us!" she said, hurrying
by him toward the door of the house. "Our car broke down outside the gate."

The man remained impassive, though he responded with a faint gleam as
Walter, looking back at him, produced for his benefit a cynical distortion
of countenance which offered little confirmation of Alice's account of things.
Then the door was swiftly opened to the brother and sister; and they came
into a marble-floored hall, where a dozen sleeked young men lounged, smoked
cigarettes and fastened their gloves, as they waited for their ladies. Alice
nodded to one or another of these, and went quickly on, her face uplifted
and smiling; but Walter detained her at the door to which she hastened.

"Listen here," he said. "I suppose you want me to dance the first dance
with you——"

"If you please, Walter," she said, meekly.

"How long you goin' to hang around fixin' up in that dressin'-room?"

"I'll be out before you're ready yourself," she promised him; and kept her
word, she was so eager for her good time to begin. When he came for her,
they went down the hall to a corridor opening upon three great rooms which
had been thrown open together, with the furniture removed and the broad
floors waxed. At one end of the corridor musicians sat in a green grove, and
Walter, with some interest, turned toward these; but his sister, pressing his
arm, impelled him in the opposite direction.

"What's the matter now?" he asked. "That's Jazz Louie and his half-breed
bunch—three white and four mulatto. Let's——?"

"No, no," she whispered. "We must speak to Mildred and Mr. and Mrs.
Palmer."

" 'Speak' to 'em? I haven't got a thing to say to *those* berries!"

"Walter, won't you *please* behave?"

He seemed to consent, for the moment, at least, and suffered her to take
him down the corridor toward a floral bower where the hostess stood with
her father and mother. Other couples and groups were moving in the same
direction, carrying with them a hubbub of laughter and fragmentary chatter-
ings; and Alice, smiling all the time, greeted people on every side of her
eagerly—a little more eagerly than most of them responded—while Walter
nodded in a noncommittal manner to one or two, said nothing, and yawned
audibly, the last resource of a person who finds himself nervous in a false
situation. He repeated his yawn and was beginning another when a convulsive pressure upon his arm made him understand that he must abandon this
method of reassuring himself. They were close upon the floral bower.

Mildred was giving her hand to one and another of her guests as rapidly
as she could, passing them on to her father and mother, and at the same

time resisting the efforts of three or four detached bachelors who besought her to give over her duty in favour of the dance-music just beginning to blare.

She was a large, fair girl, with a kindness of eye somewhat withheld by an expression of fastidiousness; at first sight of her it was clear that she would never in her life do anything "incorrect," or wear anything "incorrect." But her correctness was of the finer sort, and had no air of being studied or achieved; conduct would never offer her a problem to be settled from a book of rules, for the rules were so deep within her that she was unconscious of them. And behind this perfection there was an even ampler perfection of what Mrs. Adams called "background." The big, rich, simple house was part of it, and Mildred's father and mother were part of it. They stood beside her, large, serene people, murmuring graciously and gently inclining their handsome heads as they gave their hands to the guests; and even the youngest and most ebullient of these took on a hushed mannerliness with a closer approach to the bower.

When the opportunity came for Alice and Walter to pass within this precinct, Alice, going first, leaned forward and whispered in Mildred's ear. "You *didn't* wear the maize Georgette! That's what I thought you were going to. But you look simply *darling!* And those *pearls*——"

Others were crowding decorously forward, anxious to be done with ceremony and get to the dancing; and Mildred did not prolong the intimacy of Alice's enthusiastic whispering. With a faint accession of colour and a smile tending somewhat in the direction of rigidity, she carried Alice's hand immediately onward to Mrs. Palmer's. Alice's own colour showed a little heightening as she accepted the suggestion thus implied; nor was that emotional tint in any wise decreased, a moment later, by an impression that Walter, in concluding the brief exchange of courtesies between himself and the stately Mr. Palmer, had again reassured himself with a yawn.

But she did not speak of it to Walter; she preferred not to confirm the impression and to leave in her mind a possible doubt that he had done it. He followed her out upon the waxed floor, said resignedly: "Well, come on," put his arm about her, and they began to dance.

Alice danced gracefully and well, but not so well as Walter. Of all the steps and runs, of all the whimsical turns and twirlings, of all the rhythmic swayings and dips commanded that season by such blarings as were the barbaric product, loud and wild, of the Jazz Louies and their half-breed bunches, the thin and sallow youth was a master. Upon his face could be seen contempt of the easy marvels he performed as he moved in swift precision from one smooth agility to another; and if some too-dainty or jealous cavalier complained that to be so much a stylist in dancing was "not quite like a gentleman," at least Walter's style was what the music called for. No other dancer in the room could be thought comparable to him. Alice told him so.

"It's wonderful!" she said. "And the mystery is, where you ever learned to *do* it! You never went to dancing-school, but there isn't a man in the room who can dance half so well. I don't see why, when you dance like this, you always make such a fuss about coming to parties."

He sounded his brief laugh, a jeering bark out of one side of the mouth, and swung her miraculously through a closing space between two other couples. "You know a lot about what goes on, don't you? You prob'ly think there's no other place to dance in this town except these frozen-face joints."

" 'Frozen face?' " she echoed, laughing. "Why, everybody's having a splendid time. Look at them."

"Oh, they holler loud enough," he said. "They do it to make each other think they're havin' a good time. You don't call that Palmer family frozen-face berries, I s'pose. No?"

"Certainly not. They're just dignified and——"

"Yeuh!" said Walter. "They're dignified, 'specially when you tried to whisper to Mildred to show how *in* with her you were, and she moved you on that way. *She's* a hot friend, isn't she!"

"She didn't mean anything by it. She——"

"Ole Palmer's a hearty, slap you-on-the-back ole berry," Walter interrupted; adding in a casual tone, "All I'd like, I'd like to hit him."

"Walter! By the way, you mustn't forget to ask Mildred for a dance before the evening is over."

"Me?" He produced the lop-sided appearance of his laugh, but without making it vocal. "You watch me do it!"

"She probably won't have one left, but you must ask her, anyway."

"Why must I?"

"Because, in the first place, you're supposed to, and, in the second place, she's my most intimate friend."

"Yeuh? Is she? I've heard you pull that 'most-intimate-friend' stuff often enough about her. What's *she* ever do to show she is?"

"Never mind. You really must ask her, Walter. I want you to; and I want you to ask several other girls afterwhile; I'll tell you who."

"Keep on wanting; it'll do you good."

"Oh, but you really——"

"Listen!" he said. "I'm just as liable to dance with any of these fairies as I am to buy a bucket o' rusty tacks and eat 'em. Forget it! Soon as I get rid of you I'm goin' back to that room where I left my hat and overcoat and smoke myself to death."

"Well," she said, a little ruefully, as the frenzy of Jazz Louie and his half-breeds was suddenly abated to silence, "you mustn't—you mustn't get rid of me *too* soon, Walter."

They stood near one of the wide doorways, remaining where they had stopped. Other couples, everywhere, joined one another, forming vivacious clusters, but none of these groups adopted the brother and sister, nor did any one appear to be hurrying in Alice's direction to ask her for the next dance. She looked about her, still maintaining that jubilance of look and manner she felt so necessary—for it is to the girls who are "having a good

time" that partners are attracted—and, in order to lend greater colour to her impersonation of a lively belle, she began to chatter loudly, bringing into play an accompaniment of frolicsome gesture. She brushed Walter's nose saucily with the bunch of violets in her hand, tapped him on the shoulder, shook her pretty forefinger in his face, flourished her arms, kept her shoulders moving, and laughed continuously as she spoke.

"You *naughty* old Walter!" she cried. "*Aren't* you ashamed to be such a wonderful dancer and then only dance with your own little sister! You could dance on the stage if you wanted to. Why, you could make your *fortune* that way! Why don't you? Wouldn't it be just lovely to have all the rows and rows of people clapping their hands and shouting, 'Hurrah! Hurrah, for Walter Adams! Hurrah! Hurrah! Hurrah'!"

He stood looking at her in stolid pity.

"Cut it out," he said. "You better be givin' some of these berries the eye so they'll ask you to dance."

She was not to be so easily checked, and laughed loudly, flourishing her violets in his face again. "You *would* like it; you know you would; you needn't pretend! Just think! A whole big audience shouting, 'Hurrah! *Hurrah! Hur*——'"

"The place 'll be pulled if you get any noisier," he interrupted, not ungently. "Besides, I'm no muley cow."

"A '*cow?*'" she laughed. "What on earth——"

"I can't eat dead violets," he explained. "So don't keep tryin' to make me do it."

This had the effect he desired, and subdued her; she abandoned her unsisterly coquetries, and looked beamingly about her, but her smile was more mechanical than it had been at first.

At home she had seemed beautiful; but here, where the other girls competed, things were not as they had been there, with only her mother and Miss Perry to give contrast. These crowds of other girls had all done their best, also, to look beautiful, though not one of them had worked so hard for such a consummation as Alice had. They did not need to; they did not need to get their mothers to make old dresses over; they did not need to hunt violets in the rain.

At home her dress had seemed beautiful; but that was different, too, where there were dozens of brilliant fabrics, fashioned in new ways—some of these new ways startling, which only made the wearers centers of interest and shocked no one. And Alice remembered that she had heard a girl say, not long before, "Oh, *organdie!* Nobody wears organdie for evening gowns except in midsummer." Alice had thought little of this; but as she looked about her and saw no organdie except her own, she found greater difficulty in keeping her smile as arch and spontaneous as she wished it. In fact, it was beginning to make her face ache a little.

Mildred came in from the corridor, heavily attended. She carried a great bouquet of violets laced with lilies-of-the-valley; and the violets were lusty, big purple things, their stems wrapped in cloth of gold, with silken cords dependent, ending in long tassels. She and her convoy passed near the two young Adamses; and it appeared that one of the convoy besought his hostess to permit "cutting in"; they were "doing it other places" of late, he urged; but he was denied and told to console himself by holding the bouquet, at intervals, until his third of the sixteenth dance should come. Alice looked dubiously at her own bouquet.

Suddenly she felt that the violets betrayed her; that any one who looked at them could see how rustic, how innocent of any florist's craft they were. "I can't eat dead violets," Walter said. The little wild flowers, dying indeed in the warm air, were drooping in a forlorn mass; and it seemed to her that whoever noticed them would guess that she had picked them herself. She decided to get rid of them.

Walter was becoming restive. "Look here!" he said. "Can't you flag one o' these long-tailed birds to take you on for the next dance? You came to have a good time; why don't you get busy and have it? I want to get out and smoke."

"You *mustn't* leave me, Walter," she whispered, hastily. "Somebody'll come for me before long, but until they do——"

"Well, couldn't you sit somewhere?"

"No, no! There isn't any one I could sit with."

"Well, why not? Look at those ole dames in the corners. What's the matter your tyin' up with some o' them for a while?"

"*Please*, Walter; no!"

In fact, that indomitable smile of hers was the more difficult to maintain because of these very elders to whom Walter referred. They were mothers of girls among the dancers, and they were there to fend and contrive for their offspring; to keep them in countenance through any trial; to lend them diplomacy in the carrying out of all enterprises; to be "background" for them; and in these essentially biological functionings to imitate their own matings and renew the excitement of their nuptial periods. Older men, husbands of these ladies and fathers of eligible girls, were also to be seen, most of them with Mr. Palmer in a billiard-room across the corridor.

Mr. and Mrs. Adams had not been invited. "Of course papa and mama just barely know Mildred Palmer," Alice thought, "and most of the other girls' fathers and mothers are old friends of Mr. and Mrs. Palmer, but I do think she might have *asked* papa and mama, anyway—she needn't have been afraid just to ask them; she knew they couldn't come." And her smiling lip twitched a little threateningly, as she concluded the silent monologue. "I suppose she thinks I ought to be glad enough she asked Walter!"

Walter was, in fact, rather noticeable. He was not Mildred's only guest to wear a short coat and to appear without gloves; but he was singular (at least in his present surroundings) on account of a kind of coiffuring he favoured, his hair having been shaped after what seemed a Mongol inspiration. Only upon the top of the head was actual hair perceived, the rest appearing to be nudity. And even more than by any difference in mode he was set apart by his look and manner, in which there seemed to be a brooding, secretive and jeering superiority; and this was most vividly expressed when he felt called upon for his loud, short, lop-sided laugh. Whenever he uttered it Alice laughed, too, as loudly as she could, to cover it.

"Well," he said. "How long we goin' to stand here? My feet are sproutin' roots."

Alice took his arm, and they began to walk aimlessly through the rooms, though she tried to look as if they had a definite destination, keeping her eyes eager and her lips parted;—people had called jovially to them from the distance, she meant to imply, and they were going to join these merry friends. She was still upon this ghostly errand when a furious outbreak of drums and saxophones sounded a prelude for the second dance.

Walter danced with her again, but he gave her a warning. "I don't want to leave you high and dry," he told her, "but I can't stand it. I got to get somewhere I don't haf' to hurt my eyes with these berries; I'll go blind if I got to look at any more of 'em. I'm goin' out to smoke as soon as the music begins the next time, and you better get fixed for it."

Alice tried to get fixed for it. As they danced she nodded sunnily to every man whose eye she caught, smiled her smile with the under lip caught between her teeth; but it was not until the end of the intermission after the dance that she saw help coming.

Across the room sat the globular lady she had encountered that morning, and beside the globular lady sat a round-headed, round-bodied girl; her daughter, at first glance. The family contour was also as evident a characteristic of the short young man who stood in front of Mrs. Dowling, engaged with her in a discussion which was not without evidences of an earnestness almost impassioned. Like Walter, he was declining to dance a third time with sister; he wished to go elsewhere.

Alice from a sidelong eye watched the controversy: she saw the globular young man glance toward her, over his shoulder; whereupon Mrs. Dowling, following this glance, gave Alice a look of open fury, became much more vehement in the argument, and even struck her knee with a round, fat fist for emphasis.

"I'm on my way," said Walter. "There's the music startin' up again, and I told you——"

She nodded gratefully. "It's all right—but come back before long, Walter."

The globular young man, red with annoyance, had torn himself from his family and was hastening across the room to her. "C'n I have this dance?"

"Why, you nice Frank Dowling!" Alice cried. "How lovely!"

CHAPTER VII

They danced. Mr. Dowling should have found other forms of exercise and pastime. Nature has not designed everyone for dancing, though sometimes those she has denied are the last to discover her niggardliness. But the round young man was at least vigorous enough—too much so, when his knees collided with Alice's—and he was too sturdy to be thrown off his feet, himself, or to allow his partner to fall when he tripped her. He held her up valiantly, and continued to beat a path through the crowd of other dancers by main force.

He paid no attention to anything suggested by the efforts of the musicians, and appeared to be unaware that there should have been some connection between what they were doing and what he was doing; but he may have listened to other music of his own, for his expression was of high content; he seemed to feel no doubt whatever that he was dancing. Alice kept as far away from him as under the circumstances she could; and when they stopped she glanced down, and found the execution of unseen manœuvres, within the protection of her skirt, helpful to one of her insteps and to the toes of both of her slippers.

Her cheery partner was paddling his rosy brows with a fine handkerchief. "That was great!" he said. "Let's go out and sit in the corridor; they've got some comfortable chairs out there."

"Well—let's not," she returned. "I believe I'd rather stay in here and look at the crowd."

"No; that isn't it," he said, chiding her with a waggish forefinger. "You think if you go out there you'll miss a chance of someone else asking you for the next dance, and so you'll have to give it to me."

"How absurd!" Then, after a look about her that revealed nothing encouraging, she added graciously, "You can have the next if you want it."

"Great!" he exclaimed, mechanically. "Now let's get out of here—out of *this* room, anyhow."

"Why? What's the matter with——"

"My mother," Mr. Dowling explained. "But don't look at her. She keeps motioning me to come and see after Ella, and I'm simply *not* going to do it, you see!"

Alice laughed. "I don't believe it's so much that," she said, and consented to walk with him to a point in the next room from which Mrs. Dowling's continuous signalling could not be seen. "Your mother hates me."

"Oh, no; I wouldn't say that. No, she don't," he protested, innocently. "She don't know you more than just to speak to, you see. So how could she?"

"Well, she does. I can tell."

A frown appeared upon his rounded brow. "No; I'll tell you the way she feels. It's like this: Ella isn't *too* popular, you know—it's hard to see why, because she's a right nice girl, in her way—and mother thinks I ought to look after her, you see. She thinks I ought to dance a whole lot with her myself, and stir up other fellows to dance with her—it's simply impossible to make mother understand you *can't* do that, you see. And then about me, you see, if she had her way I wouldn't get to dance with anybody at all except girls like Mildred Palmer and Henrietta Lamb. Mother wants to run my whole programme for me, you understand, but the trouble of it is—about girls like that, you see—well, I couldn't do what she wants, even if I wanted to myself, because you take those girls, and by the time I get Ella off my hands for a minute, why, their dances are always every last one taken, and where do I come in?"

Alice nodded, her amiability undamaged. "I see. So that's why you dance with me."

"No, I like to," he protested. "I'd rather dance with you than I do with those girls." And he added with a retrospective determination which showed that he had been through quite an experience with Mrs. Dowling in this matter, "I *told* mother I would, too!"

"Did it take all your courage, Frank?"

He looked at her shrewdly. "Now you're trying to tease me," he said. "I don't care; I *would* rather dance with you! In the first place, you're a perfectly beautiful dancer, you see, and in the second, a man feels a lot more comfortable with you than he does with them. Of course I know almost all the other fellows get along with those girls all right; but I don't waste any time on 'em I don't have to. *I* like people that are always cordial to everybody, you see—the way you are."

"Thank you," she said, thoughtfully.

"Oh, I *mean* it," he insisted. "There goes the band again. Shall we——?"

"Suppose we sit it out?" she suggested. "I believe I'd like to go out in the corridor, after all—it's pretty warm in here."

Assenting cheerfully, Dowling conducted her to a pair of easy-chairs within a secluding grove of box-trees, and when they came to this retreat they found Mildred Palmer just departing, under escort of a well-favoured gentleman about thirty. As these two walked slowly away, in the direction of the dancing-floor, they left it not to be doubted that they were on excellent terms with each other; Mildred was evidently willing to make their progress even slower, for she halted momentarily, once or twice; and her upward glances to her tall companion's face were of a gentle, almost blushing deference. Never before had Alice seen anything like this in her friend's manner.

"How queer!" she murmured.

"What's queer?" Dowling inquired as they sat down.

"Who was that man?"

"Haven't you met him?"

"I never saw him before. Who is he?"

"Why, it's this Arthur Russell."

"What Arthur Russell? I never heard of him."

Mr. Dowling was puzzled. "Why, *that's* funny! Only the last time I saw you, you were telling me how awfully well you knew Mildred Palmer."

"Why, certainly I do," Alice informed him. "She's my most intimate friend."

"That's what makes it seem so funny you haven't heard anything about this Russell, because everybody says even if she isn't engaged to him right now, she most likely will be before very long. I must say it looks a good deal that way to me, myself."

"What nonsense!" Alice exclaimed. "She's never even mentioned him to me."

The young man glanced at her dubiously and passed a finger over the tiny prong that dashingly composed the whole substance of his moustache. "Well, you see, Mildred *is* pretty reserved," he remarked. "This Russell is some kind of cousin of the Palmer family, I understand."

"He is?"

"Yes—second or third or something, the girls say. You see, my sister Ella hasn't got much to do at home, and don't read anything, or sew, or play solitaire, you see; and she hears about pretty much everything that goes on, you see. Well, Ella says a lot of the girls have been talking about Mildred and this Arthur Russell for quite a while back, you see. They were all wondering what he was going to look like, you see; because he only got here yesterday; and that proves she must have been talking to some of 'em, or else how——"

Alice laughed airily, but the pretty sound ended abruptly with an audible intake of breath. "Of course, while Mildred *is* my most intimate friend," she said, "I don't mean she tells me everything—and naturally she has other friends besides. What else did your sister say she told them about this Mr. Russell?"

"Well, it seems he's *very* well off; at least Henrietta Lamb told Ella he was. Ella says——"

Alice interrupted again, with an increased irritability. "Oh, never mind what Ella says! Let's find something better to talk about than Mr. Russell!"

"Well, *I'm* willing," Mr. Dowling assented, ruefully. "What you want to talk about?"

But this liberal offer found her unresponsive; she sat leaning back, silent, her arms along the arms of her chair, and her eyes, moist and bright, fixed upon a wide doorway where the dancers fluctuated. She was disquieted by more than Mildred's reserve, though reserve so marked had certainly the significance of a warning that Alice's definition, "my most intimate friend," lacked sanction. Indirect notice to this effect could not well have been more emphatic, but the sting of it was left for a later moment. Something else preoccupied Alice: she had just been surprised by an odd experience. At first sight of this Mr. Arthur Russell, she had said to herself instantly, in words as definite as if she spoke them aloud, though they seemed more like words spoken to her by some unknown person within her: "There! That's exactly the kind of looking man I'd like to marry!"

In the eyes of the restless and the longing, Providence often appears to be worse than inscrutable: an unreliable Omnipotence given to haphazard whimsies in dealing with its own creatures, choosing at random some among them to be rent with tragic deprivations and others to be petted with blessing upon blessing. In Alice's eyes, Mildred had been blessed enough; something ought to be left over, by this time, for another girl. The final touch to the heaping perfection of Christmas-in-everything for Mildred was that this Mr. Arthur Russell, good-looking, kind-looking, graceful, the perfect fiancé, should be also "*very* well off." Of course! These rich always married one another. And while the Mildreds danced with their Arthur Russells the best an outsider could do for herself was to sit with Frank Dowling—the one last course left her that was better than dancing with him.

"Well, what *do* you want to talk about?" he inquired.

"Nothing," she said. "Suppose we just sit, Frank." But a moment later she remembered something, and, with a sudden animation, began to prattle. She pointed to the musicians down the corridor. "Oh, look at them! Look at the leader! Aren't they *funny*? Someone told me they're called 'Jazz Louie and his half-breed bunch.' Isn't that just crazy? Don't you *love* it? Do watch them, Frank."

She continued to chatter, and, while thus keeping his glance away from herself, she detached the forlorn bouquet of dead violets from her dress and laid it gently beside the one she had carried. The latter already reposed in the obscurity selected for it at the base of one of the box-trees.

Then she was abruptly silent.

"You certainly are a funny girl," Dowling remarked. "You say you don't want to talk about anything at all, and all of a sudden you break out and talk a blue streak; and just about the time I begin to get interested in what you're saying you shut off! What's the matter with girls, anyhow, when they do things like that?"

"I don't know; we're just queer, I guess."

"I say so! Well, what'll we do *now*? Talk, or just sit?"

"Suppose we just sit some more."

"Anything to oblige," he assented. "I'm willing to sit as long as you like."

But even as he made his amiability clear in this matter, the peace was threatened—his mother came down the corridor like a rolling, ominous cloud. She was looking about her on all sides, in a fidget of annoyance, searching for him, and to his dismay she saw him. She immediately made a horrible face at his companion, beckoned to him imperiously with a dumpy arm, and shook her head reprovingly. The unfortunate young man tried to repulse her with an icy stare, but this effort having obtained little to encourage his feeble hope of driving her away, he shifted his chair so that his back was toward

her discomfiting pantomime. He should have known better, the instant result was Mrs. Dowling in motion at an impetuous waddle.

She entered the box-tree seclusion with the lower rotundities of her face hastily modelled into the resemblance of an over-benevolent smile—a contortion which neglected to spread its intended geniality upward to the exasperated eyes and anxious forehead.

"I think your mother wants to speak to you, Frank," Alice said, upon this advent.

Mrs. Dowling nodded to her. "Good evening, Miss Adams," she said. "I just thought as you and Frank weren't dancing you wouldn't mind my disturbing you——"

"Not at all," Alice murmured.

Mr. Dowling seemed of a different mind. "Well, what *do* you want?" he inquired, whereupon his mother struck him roguishly with her fan.

"Bad fellow!" She turned to Alice. "I'm sure you won't mind excusing him to let him do something for his old mother, Miss Adams."

"What *do* you want?" the son repeated.

"Two very nice things," Mrs. Dowling informed him. "Everybody is so anxious for Henrietta Lamb to have a pleasant evening, because it's the very first time she's been anywhere since her father's death, and of course her dear grandfather's an old friend of ours, and——"

"Well, well!" her son interrupted. "Miss Adams isn't interested in all this, mother."

"But Henrietta came to speak to Ella and me, and I told her you were so anxious to dance with her——"

"Here!" he cried. "Look here! I'd rather do my own——"

"Yes; that's just it," Mrs. Dowling explained. "I just thought it was such a good opportunity; and Henrietta said she had most of her dances taken, but she'd give you one if you asked her before they were all gone. So I thought you'd better see her as soon as possible."

Dowling's face had become rosy. "I refuse to do anything of the kind."

"Bad fellow!" said his mother, gaily. "I thought this would be the best time for you to see Henrietta, because it won't be long till all her dances are gone, and you've promised on your *word* to dance the next with Ella, and you mightn't have a chance to do it then. I'm sure Miss Adams won't mind if you——"

"Not at all," Alice said.

"Well, *I* mind!" he said. "I wish you *could* understand that when I want to dance with any girl I don't need my mother to ask her for me. I really *am* more than six years old!"

He spoke with too much vehemence, and Mrs. Dowling at once saw how to have her way. As with husbands and wives, so with many fathers and daughters, and so with some sons and mothers: the man will himself be cross in public and think nothing of it, nor will he greatly mind a little crossness on the part of the woman; but let her show agitation before any spectator, he is instantly reduced to a coward's slavery. Women understand that ancient weakness, of course; for it is one of their most important means of defense, but can be used ignobly.

Mrs. Dowling permitted a tremulousness to become audible in her voice. "It isn't very—very pleasant—to be talked to like that by your own son—before strangers!"

"Oh, my! Look here!" the stricken Dowling protested. "*I* didn't say anything, mother. I was just joking about how you never get over thinking I'm a little boy. I only——"

Mrs. Dowling continued: "I just thought I was doing you a little favour. I didn't think it would make you so angry."

"Mother, for goodness' sake! Miss Adams'll think——"

"I suppose," Mrs. Dowling interrupted, piteously, "I suppose it doesn't matter what *I* think!"

"Oh, gracious!"

Alice interfered; she perceived that the ruthless Mrs. Dowling meant to have her way. "I think you'd better go, Frank. Really."

"There!" his mother cried. "Miss Adams says so, herself! What more do you want?"

"Oh, gracious!" he lamented again, and, with a sick look over his shoulder at Alice, permitted his mother to take his arm and propel him away. Mrs. Dowling's spirits had strikingly recovered even before the pair passed from the corridor: she moved almost bouncingly beside her embittered son, and her eyes and all the convolutions of her abundant face were blithe.

Alice went in search of Walter, but without much hope of finding him. What he did with himself at frozen-face dances was one of his most successful mysteries, and her present excursion gave her no clue leading to its solution. When the musicians again lowered their instruments for an interval she had returned, alone, to her former seat within the partial shelter of the box-trees.

She had now to practise an art that affords but a limited variety of methods, even to the expert: the art of seeming to have an escort or partner when there is none. The practitioner must imply, merely by expression and attitude, that the supposed companion has left her for only a few moments, that she herself has sent him upon an errand; and, if possible, the minds of observers must be directed toward a conclusion that this errand of her devising is an amusing one; at all events, she is alone temporarily and of choice, not deserted. She awaits a devoted man who may return at any instant.

Other people desired to sit in Alice's nook, but discovered her in occupancy. She had moved the vacant chair closer to her own, and she sat with her arm extended so that her hand, holding her lace kerchief, rested upon the back of this second chair, claiming it. Such a preëmption, like that of a traveller's bag in the rack, was unquestionable; and, for additional evidence, sitting with her knees crossed, she kept one foot continuously moving a little,

in cadence with the other, which tapped the floor. Moreover, she added a
fine detail: her half-smile, with the under lip caught, seemed to struggle
against repression, as if she found the service engaging her absent companion
even more amusing than she would let him see when he returned: there
was jovial intrigue of some sort afoot, evidently. Her eyes, beaming with secret fun, were averted from intruders, but sometimes, when couples approached, seeking possession of the nook, her thoughts about the absentee
appeared to threaten her with outright laughter; and though one or two girls
looked at her skeptically, as they turned away, their escorts felt no such
doubts, and merely wondered what importantly funny affair Alice Adams
was engaged in. She had learned to do it perfectly.

She had learned it during the last two years; she was twenty when for
the first time she had the shock of finding herself without an applicant for
one of her dances. When she was sixteen "all the nice boys in town," as
her mother said, crowded the Adamses' small veranda and steps, or sat near
by, cross-legged on the lawn, on summer evenings; and at eighteen she had
replaced the boys with "the older men." By this time most of "the other
girls," her contemporaries, were away at school or college, and when they
came home to stay, they "came out"—that feeble revival of an ancient custom offering the maiden to the ceremonial inspection of the tribe. Alice neither went away nor "came out," and, in contrast with those who did, she
may have seemed to lack freshness of lustre—jewels are richest when revealed
all new in a white velvet box. And Alice may have been too eager to secure
new retainers, too kind in her efforts to keep the old ones. She had been
a belle too soon.

CHAPTER VIII

The device of the absentee partner has the defect that it cannot be employed
for longer than ten or fifteen minutes at a time, and it may not be repeated
more than twice in one evening: a single repetition, indeed, is weak, and
may prove a betrayal. Alice knew that her present performance could be
effective during only this interval between dances; and though her eyes were
guarded, she anxiously counted over the partnerless young men who lounged
together in the doorways within her view. Every one of them ought to have
asked her for dances, she thought, and although she might have been put
to it to give a reason why any of them "ought," her heart was hot with resentment against them.

For a girl who has been a belle, it is harder to live through these bad
times than it is for one who has never known anything better. Like a figure
of painted and brightly varnished wood, Ella Dowling sat against the wall
through dance after dance with glassy imperturbability; it was easier to be

wooden, Alice thought, if you had your mother with you, as Ella had. You were left with at least the shred of a pretense that you came to sit with your mother as a spectator, and not to offer yourself to be danced with by men who looked you over and rejected you—not for the first time. "Not for the first time": there lay a sting! Why had you thought this time might be different from the other times? Why had you broken your back picking those hundreds of violets?

Hating the fatuous young men in the doorways more bitterly for every instant that she had to maintain her tableau, the smiling Alice knew fierce impulses to spring to her feet and shout at them, "You *idiots!*" Hands in pockets, they lounged against the pilasters, or faced one another, laughing vaguely, each one of them seeming to Alice no more than so much mean beef in clothes. She wanted to tell them they were no better than that; and it seemed a cruel thing of heaven to let them go on believing themselves young lords. They were doing nothing, killing time. Wasn't she at her lowest value at least a means of killing time? Evidently the mean beeves thought not. And when one of them finally lounged across the corridor and spoke to her, he was the very one to whom she preferred her loneliness.

"Waiting for somebody, Lady Alicia?" he asked, negligently; and his easy burlesque of her name was like the familiarity of the rest of him. He was one of those full-bodied, grossly handsome men who are powerful and active, but never submit themselves to the rigour of becoming athletes, though they shoot and fish from expensive camps. Gloss is the most shining outward mark of the type. Nowadays these men no longer use brilliantine on their moustaches, but they have gloss bought from manicure-girls, from masseurs, and from automobile-makers; and their eyes, usually large, are glossy. None of this is allowed to interfere with business; these are "good business men," and often make large fortunes. They are men of imagination about two things —women and money, and, combining their imaginings about both, usually make a wise first marriage. Later, however, they are apt to imagine too much about some little woman without whom life seems duller than need be. They run away, leaving the first wife well enough dowered. They are never intentionally unkind to women, and in the end they usually make the mistake of thinking they have had their money's worth of life. Here was Mr. Harvey Malone, a young specimen in an earlier stage of development, trying to marry Henrietta Lamb, and now sauntering over to speak to Alice, as a time-killer before his next dance with Henrietta.

Alice made no response to his question, and he dropped lazily into the vacant chair, from which she sharply withdrew her hand. "I might as well use his chair till he comes, don't you think? You don't *mind*, do you, old girl?"

"Oh, no," Alice said. "It doesn't matter one way or the other. Please don't call me that."

"So that's how you feel?" Mr. Malone laughed indulgently, without much interest. "I've been meaning to come to see you for a long time—honestly I have—because I wanted to have a good talk with you about old times. I know you think it was funny, after the way I used to come to your house two or three times a week, and sometimes oftener—well, I don't blame you for being hurt, the way I stopped without explaining or anything. The truth is there wasn't any reason: I just happened to have a lot of important things to do and couldn't find the time. But I *am* going to call on you some evening —honestly I am. I don't wonder you think——"

"You're mistaken," Alice said. "I've never thought anything about it at all."

"Well, well!" he said, and looked at her languidly. "What's the use of being cross with this old man? He always means well." And, extending his arm, he would have given her a friendly pat upon the shoulder but she evaded it. "Well, well!" he said. "Seems to me you're getting awful tetchy! Don't you like your old friends any more?"

"Not all of them."

"Who's the new one?" he asked, teasingly. "Come on and tell us, Alice. Who is it you were holding this chair for?"

"Never mind."

"Well, all I've got to do is to sit here till he comes back; then I'll see who it is."

"He may not come back before you have to go."

"Guess you got me *that* time," Malone admitted, laughing as he rose. "They're tuning up, and I've got this dance. I *am* coming around to see you some evening." He moved away, calling back over his shoulder, "Honestly, I am!"

Alice did not look at him.

She had held her tableau as long as she could; it was time for her to abandon the box-trees; and she stepped forth frowning, as if a little annoyed with the absentee for being such a time upon her errand; whereupon the two chairs were instantly seized by a coquetting pair who intended to "sit out" the dance. She walked quickly down the broad corridor, turned into the broader hall, and hurriedly entered the dressing-room where she had left her wraps.

She stayed here as long as she could, pretending to arrange her hair at a mirror, then fidgeting with one of her slipper-buckles; but the intelligent elderly woman in charge of the room made an indefinite sojourn impracticable. "Perhaps I could help you with that buckle, Miss," she suggested, approaching. "Has it come loose?" Alice wrenched desperately; then it was loose. The competent woman, producing needle and thread, deftly made the buckle fast; and there was nothing for Alice to do but to express her gratitude and go.

She went to the door of the cloak-room opposite, where a coloured man stood watchfully in the doorway. "I wonder if you know which of the gentlemen is my brother, Mr. Walter Adams," she said.

"Yes'm; I know him."

"Could you tell me where he is?"

"No'm; I couldn't say."

"Well, if you see him, would you please tell him that his sister, Miss Adams, is looking for him and very anxious to speak to him?"

"Yes'm. Sho'ly, sho'ly!"

As she went away he stared after her and seemed to swell with some bursting emotion. In fact, it was too much for him, and he suddenly retired within the room, releasing strangulated laughter.

Walter remonstrated. Behind an excellent screen of coats and hats, in a remote part of the room, he was kneeling on the floor, engaged in a game of chance with a second coloured attendant; and the laughter became so vehement that it not only interfered with the pastime in hand, but threatened to attract frozen-face attention.

"I cain' he'p it, man," the laugher explained. "I cain' he'p it! You sut'n'y the beatin'es' white boy 'n 'is city!"

The dancers were swinging into an "encore" as Alice halted for an irresolute moment in a doorway. Across the room, a cluster of matrons sat chatting absently, their eyes on their dancing daughters; and Alice, finding a refugee's courage, dodged through the scurrying couples, seated herself in a chair on the outskirts of this colony of elders, and began to talk eagerly to the matron nearest her. The matron seemed unaccustomed to so much vivacity, and responded but dryly, whereupon Alice was more vivacious than ever; for she meant now to present the picture of a jolly girl too much interested in these wise older women to bother about every foolish young man who asked her for a dance.

Her matron was constrained to go so far as to supply a tolerant nod, now and then, in complement to the girl's animation, and Alice was grateful for the nods. In this fashion she supplemented the exhausted resources of the dressing-room and the box-tree nook; and lived through two more dances, when again Mr. Frank Dowling presented himself as a partner.

She needed no pretense to seek the dressing-room for repairs after that number; this time they were necessary and genuine. Dowling waited for her, and when she came out he explained for the fourth or fifth time how the accident had happened. "It was entirely those other people's fault," he said. "They got me in a kind of a corner, because neither of those fellows knows the least thing about guiding; they just jam ahead and expect everybody to get out of *their* way. It was Charlotte Thom's diamond crescent pin that got caught on your dress in the back and made such a——"

"Never mind," Alice said in a tired voice. "The maid fixed it so that she says it isn't very noticeable."

"Well, it isn't," he returned. "You could hardly tell there'd been anything the matter. Where do you want to go? Mother's been interfering in my affairs some more and I've got the next taken."

"I was sitting with Mrs. George Dresser. You might take me back there."

He left her with the matron, and Alice returned to her picture-making, so that once more, while two numbers passed, whoever cared to look was offered the sketch of a jolly, clever girl preoccupied with her elders. Then she found her friend Mildred standing before her, presenting Mr. Arthur Russell, who asked her to dance with him.

Alice looked uncertain, as though not sure what her engagements were; but her perplexity cleared; she nodded, and swung rhythmically away with the tall applicant. She was not grateful to her hostess for this alms. What a young hostess does with a fiancé, Alice thought, is to make him dance with the unpopular girls. She supposed that Mr. Arthur Russell had already danced with Ella Dowling.

The loan of a lover, under these circumstances, may be painful to the lessee, and Alice, smiling never more brightly, found nothing to say to Mr. Russell, though she thought he might have found something to say to her. "I wonder what Mildred told him," she thought. "Probably she said, 'Dearest, there's one more girl you've got to help me out with. You wouldn't like her much, but she dances well enough and she's having a rotten time. Nobody ever goes near her any more.'"

When the music stopped, Russell added his applause to the handclapping that encouraged the uproarious instruments to continue, and as they renewed the tumult, he said heartily, "That's splendid!"

Alice gave him a glance, necessarily at short range, and found his eyes kindly and pleased. Here was a friendly soul, it appeared, who probably "liked everybody." No doubt he had applauded for an "encore" when he danced with Ella Dowling, gave Ella the same genial look, and said, "That's splendid!"

When the "encore" was over, Alice spoke to him for the first time. "Mildred will be looking for you," she said. "I think you'd better take me back to where you found me."

He looked surprised. "Oh, if you——"

"I'm sure Mildred will be needing you," Alice said, and as she took his arm and they walked toward Mrs. Dresser, she thought it might be just possible to make a further use of the loan. "Oh, I wonder if you——" she began.

"Yes?" he said, quickly.

"You don't know my brother, Walter Adams," she said. "But he's somewhere—I think possibly he's in a smoking-room or some place where girls aren't expected, and if you wouldn't think it too much trouble to inquire——"

"I'll find him," Russell said, promptly. "Thank you so much for that dance. I'll bring your brother in a moment."

It was to be a long moment, Alice decided, presently. Mrs. Dresser had grown restive; and her nods and vague responses to her young dependent's gaieties were as meager as they could well be. Evidently the matron had no intention of appearing to her world in the light of a chaperone for Alice Adams; and she finally made this clear. With a word or two of excuse, breaking into something Alice was saying, she rose and went to sit next to Mildred's mother, who had become the nucleus of the cluster. So Alice was left very much against the wall, with short stretches of vacant chairs on each side of her. She had come to the end of her picture-making, and could only pretend that there was something amusing the matter with the arm of her chair.

She supposed that Mildred's Mr. Russell had forgotten Walter by this time. "I'm not even an intimate enough friend of Mildred's for him to have thought he ought to bother to tell me he couldn't find him," she thought. And then she saw Russell coming across the room toward her, with Walter beside him. She jumped up gaily.

"Oh, thank you!" she cried. "I know this naughty boy must have been terribly hard to find. Mildred'll *never* forgive me! I've put you to so much——"

"Not at all," he said, amiably, and went away, leaving the brother and sister together.

"Walter, let's dance just once more," Alice said, touching his arm placatively. "I thought—well, perhaps we might go home then."

But Walter's expression was that of a person upon whom an outrage has just been perpetrated. "No," he said. "We've stayed *this* long, I'm goin' to wait and see what they got to eat. And you look here!" He turned upon her angrily. "Don't you ever do that again!"

"Do what?"

"Send somebody after me that pokes his nose into every corner of the house till he finds me! 'Are you Mr. Walter Adams?' he says. I guess he must asked everybody in the place if they were Mr. Walter Adams! Well, I'll bet a few iron men you wouldn't send anybody to hunt for me again if you knew where he found me!"

"Where was it?"

Walter decided that her fit punishment was to know. "I was shootin' dice with those coons in the cloak-room."

"And he *saw* you?"

"Unless he was blind!" said Walter. "Come on, I'll dance this one more dance with you. Supper comes after that, and *then* we'll go home."

Mrs. Adams heard Alice's key turning in the front door and hurried down the stairs to meet her.

"Did you get wet coming in, darling?" she asked. "Did you have a good time?"

"Just lovely!" Alice said, cheerily; and after she had arranged the latch for Walter, who had gone to return the little car, she followed her mother upstairs and hummed a dance-tune on the way.

"Oh, I'm so glad you had a nice time," Mrs. Adams said, as they reached the door of her daughter's room together. "You *deserved* to, and it's lovely to think——"

But at this, without warning, Alice threw herself into her mother's arms, sobbing so loudly that in his room, close by, her father, half drowsing through the night, started to full wakefulness.

CHAPTER IX

On a morning, a week after this collapse of festal hopes, Mrs. Adams and her daughter were concluding a three-days' disturbance, the "Spring house-cleaning"—postponed until now by Adams's long illness—and Alice, on her knees before a chest of drawers, in her mother's room, paused thoughtfully after dusting a packet of letters wrapped in worn muslin. She called to her mother, who was scrubbing the floor of the hallway just beyond the open door,

"These old letters you had in the bottom drawer, weren't they some papa wrote you before you were married?"

Mrs. Adams laughed and said, "Yes. Just put 'em back where they were—or else up in the attic—anywhere you want to."

"Do you mind if I read one, mama?"

Mrs. Adams laughed again. "Oh, I guess you can if you want to. I expect they're pretty funny!"

Alice laughed in response, and chose the topmost letter of the packet. "My dear, beautiful girl," it began; and she stared at these singular words. They gave her a shock like that caused by overhearing some bewildering impropriety; and, having read them over to herself several times, she went on to experience other shocks.

MY DEAR, BEAUTIFUL GIRL:

This time yesterday I had a mighty bad case of blues because I had not had a word from you in two whole long days and when I do not hear from you every day things look mighty down in the mouth to me. Now it is all so different because your letter has arrived and besides I have got a piece of news I believe you will think as fine as I do. Darling, you will be surprised, so get ready to hear about a big effect on our future. It is this way. I had sort of a suspicion the head of the firm kind of took a fancy to me from the first when I went in there, and liked the way I attended to my work and so when he took me on this business trip with him I felt pretty sure of it and now it turns out I was about right. In return I guess I have got about the best boss in this world and I believe you will think so too. Yes, sweetheart, after the talk I have just had with him if J. A. Lamb asked me to cut my hand off for him I guess I would come pretty near doing it because what he says means the end of our waiting to be together. From New Years on he is going to put me in entire charge of the sundries dept. and what do you think is going to be my salary? Eleven hundred cool dollars a year ($1,100.00). That's all! Just only a cool eleven hundred per annum! Well, I guess that will show your mother whether I can take care of you or not. And oh how I would like to see your dear, beautiful, loving face when you get this news.

I would like to go out on the public streets and just dance and shout and it is all I can do to help doing it, especially when I know we will be talking it all over together this time next week, and oh my darling, now that your folks have no excuse for putting it off any longer we might be in our own little home before Xmas. Would you be glad?

Well, darling, this settles everything and makes our future just about as smooth for us as anybody could ask. I can hardly realize after all this waiting life's troubles are over for you and me and we have nothing to do but to enjoy the happiness granted us by this wonderful, beautiful thing we call life. I know I am not any poet and the one I tried to write about you the day of the picnic was fearful but the way I *think* about you is a poem.

Write me what you think of the news. I know but write me anyhow. I'll get it before we start home and I can be reading it over all the time on the train.

                                        Your always loving
                                                VIRGIL

The sound of her mother's diligent scrubbing in the hall came back slowly to Alice's hearing, as she restored the letter to the packet, wrapped the packet in its muslin covering, and returned it to the drawer. She had remained upon her knees while she read the letter; now she sank backward, sitting upon the floor with her hands behind her, an unconscious relaxing for better ease to think. Upon her face there had fallen a look of wonder.

For the first time she was vaguely perceiving that life is everlasting movement. Youth really believes what is running water to be a permanent crystallization and sees time fixed to a point: some people have dark hair, some people have blond hair, some people have gray hair. Until this moment, Alice had no conviction that there was a universe before she came into it. She had always thought of it as the background of herself: the moon was something to make her prettier on a summer night.

But this old letter, through which she saw still flickering an ancient starlight of young love, astounded her. Faintly before her it revealed the whole lives of her father and mother, who had been young, after all—they *really* had—and their youth was now so utterly passed from them that the picture of it, in the letter, was like a burlesque of them. And so she, herself, must pass to such changes, too, and all that now seemed vital to her would be nothing.

When her work was finished, that afternoon, she went into her father's room. His recovery had progressed well enough to permit the departure of Miss Perry; and Adams, wearing one of Mrs. Adams's wrappers over his nightgown, sat in a high-backed chair by a closed window. The weather was warm, but the closed window and the flannel wrapper had not sufficed him: round his shoulders he had an old crocheted scarf of Alice's; his legs were wrapped in a heavy comfort; and, with these swathings about him, and his eyes closed, his thin and grizzled head making but a slight indentation in the pillow supporting it, he looked old and little and queer.

Alice would have gone out softly, but without opening his eyes, he spoke to her: "Don't go, dearie. Come sit with the old man a little while."

She brought a chair near his. "I thought you were napping."

"No. I don't hardly ever do that. I just drift a little sometimes."

"How do you mean you drift, papa?"

He looked at her vaguely. "Oh, I don't know. Kind of pictures. They get a little mixed up—old times with times still ahead, like planning what to do, you know. That's as near a nap as I get—when the pictures mix up some. I suppose it's sort of drowsing."

She took one of his hands and stroked it. "What do you mean when you say you have pictures like 'planning what to do'?" she asked.

"I mean planning what to do when I get out and able to go to work again."

"But that doesn't need any planning," Alice said, quickly. "You're going back to your old place at Lamb's, of course."

Adams closed his eyes again, sighing heavily, but made no other response.

"Why, of *course* you are!" she cried. "What are you talking about?"

His head turned slowly toward her, revealing the eyes, open in a haggard stare. "I heard you the other night when you came from the party," he said. "I know what was the matter."

"Indeed, you don't," she assured him. "You don't know anything about it, because there wasn't anything the matter at all."

"Don't you suppose I heard you crying? What'd you cry for if there wasn't anything the matter?"

"Just nerves, papa. It wasn't anything else in the world."

"Never mind," he said. "Your mother told me."

"She promised me not to!"

At that Adams laughed mournfully. "It wouldn't be very likely I'd hear you so upset and not ask about it, even if she didn't come and tell me on her own hook. You needn't try to fool me; I tell you I know what was the matter."

"The only matter was I had a silly fit," Alice protested. "It did me good, too."

"How's that?"

"Because I've decided to do something about it, papa."

"That isn't the way your mother looks at it," Adams said, ruefully. "She thinks it's our place to do something about it. Well, I don't know—I don't know; everything seems so changed these days. You've always been a good daughter, Alice, and you ought to have as much as any of these girls you go with; she's convinced me she's right about *that*. The trouble is——" He faltered, apologetically, then went on, "I mean the question is—how to get it for you."

"No!" she cried. "I had no business to make such a fuss just because a lot of idiots didn't break their necks to get dances with me and because I got mortified about Walter—Walter *was* pretty terrible——"

"Oh, me, my!" Adams lamented. "I guess that's something we just have to leave work out itself. What you going to do with a boy nineteen or twenty years old that makes his own living? Can't whip him. Can't keep him locked up in the house. Just got to hope he'll learn better, I suppose."

"Of course he didn't want to go to the Palmers'," Alice explained, tolerantly—"and as mama and I made him take me, and he thought that was pretty selfish in me, why, he felt he had a right to amuse himself any way he could. Of course it was awful that this—that this Mr. Russell should——" In spite of her, the recollection choked her.

"Yes, it was awful," Adams agreed. "Just awful. Oh, me, my!"

But Alice recovered herself at once, and showed him a cheerful face. "Well, just a few years from now I probably won't even remember it! I believe hardly anything amounts to as much as we think it does at the time."

"Well—sometimes it don't."

"What I've been thinking, papa: it seems to me I ought to *do* something."

"What like?"

She looked dreamy, but was obviously serious as she told him: "Well, I mean I ought to be something besides just a kind of nobody. I ought to——" She paused.

"What, dearie?"

"Well—there's one thing I'd like to do. I'm sure I *could* do it, too."

"What?"

"I want to go on the stage: I know I could act."

At this, her father abruptly gave utterance to a feeble cackling of laughter; and when Alice, surprised and a little offended, pressed him for his reason, he tried to evade, saying, "Nothing, dearie. I just thought of something." But she persisted until he had to explain.

"It made me think of your mother's sister, your Aunt Flora, that died when you were little," he said. "She was always telling how she was going on the stage, and talking about how she was certain she'd make a great actress, and all so on; and one day your mother broke out and said *she* ought 'a' gone on the stage, herself, because she always knew she had the talent for it— and, well, they got into kind of a spat about which one'd make the best actress. I had to go out in the hall to laugh!"

"Maybe you were wrong," Alice said, gravely. "If they both felt it, why wouldn't that look as if there was talent in the family? I've *always* thought——"

"No, dearie," he said, with a final chuckle. "Your mother and Flora weren't different from a good many others. I expect ninety per cent. of all the women I ever knew were just sure they'd be mighty fine actresses if they ever got the chance. Well, I guess it's a good thing; they enjoy thinking about it and it don't do anybody any harm."

Alice was piqued. For several days she had thought almost continuously of a career to be won by her own genius. Not that she planned details, or concerned herself with first steps; her picturings overleaped all that. Principally, she saw her name great on all the bill-boards of that unkind city, and herself, unchanged in age but glamorous with fame and Paris clothes, returning in a private car. No doubt the pleasantest development of her vision was a dialogue with Mildred; and this became so real that, as she projected it, Alice assumed the proper expressions for both parties to it, formed words with her lips, and even spoke some of them aloud. "No, I haven't forgotten you, Mrs. Russell. I remember you quite pleasantly, in fact. You were a Miss Palmer, I recall, in those funny old days. Very kind of you, I'm shaw. I appreciate your eagerness to do something for me in your

own little home. As you say, a reception *would* renew my acquaintanceship
with many old friends—but I'm shaw you won't mind my mentioning that
I don't find much inspiration in these provincials. I really must ask you not
to press me. An artist's time is not her own, though of course I could hardly
expect you to understand——"

Thus Alice illuminated the dull time; but she retired from the interview
with her father still manfully displaying an outward cheerfulness, while depression grew heavier within, as if she had eaten soggy cake. Her father
knew nothing whatever of the stage, and she was aware of his ignorance, yet
for some reason his innocently skeptical amusement reduced her bright
project almost to nothing. Something like this always happened, it seemed;
she was continually making these illuminations, all gay with gildings and
colourings; and then as soon as anybody else so much as glanced at them—
even her father, who loved her—the pretty designs were stricken with a deso-
lating pallor. "Is this *life?*" Alice wondered, not doubting that the question
was original and all her own. "Is it life to spend your time imagining things
that aren't so, and never will be? Beautiful things happen to other people;
why should I be the only one they never *can* happen to?"

The mood lasted overnight; and was still upon her the next afternoon
when an errand for her father took her down-town. Adams had decided to
begin smoking again, and Alice felt rather degraded, as well as embarrassed,
when she went into the large shop her father had named, and asked for the
cheap tobacco he used in his pipe. She fell back upon an air of amused
indulgence, hoping thus to suggest that her purchase was made for some
faithful old retainer, now infirm; and although the calmness of the clerk who
served her called for no such elaboration of her sketch, she ornamented it
with a little laugh and with the remark, as she dropped the package into her
coat-pocket, "I'm sure it'll please him; they tell me it's the kind he likes."

Still playing Lady Bountiful, smiling to herself in anticipation of the joy
she was bringing to the simple old negro or Irish follower of the family, she
left the shop; but as she came out upon the crowded pavement her smile
vanished quickly.

Next to the door of the tobacco-shop, there was the open entrance to a
stairway, and, above this rather bleak and dark aperture, a sign-board displayed in begrimed gilt letters the information that Frincke's Business College occupied the upper floors of the building. Furthermore, Frincke here
publicly offered "personal instruction and training in practical mathematics,
bookkeeping, and all branches of the business life, including stenography,
typewriting, etc."

Alice halted for a moment, frowning at this signboard as though it were
something surprising and distasteful which she had never seen before. Yet
it was conspicuous in a busy quarter; she almost always passed it when she
came down-town, and never without noticing it. Nor was this the first time
she had paused to lift toward it that same glance of vague misgiving.

The building was not what the changeful city defined as a modern one, and the dusty wooden stairway, as seen from the pavement, disappeared upward into a smoky darkness. So would the footsteps of a girl ascending there lead to a hideous obscurity, Alice thought; an obscurity as dreary and as permanent as death. And like dry leaves falling about her she saw her wintry imaginings in the May air: pretty girls turning into withered creatures as they worked at typing-machines; old maids "taking dictation" from men with double chins; Alice saw old maids of a dozen different kinds "taking dictation." Her mind's eye was crowded with them, as it always was when she passed that stairway entrance; and though they were all different from one another, all of them looked a little like herself.

She hated the place, and yet she seldom hurried by it or averted her eyes. It had an unpleasant fascination for her, and a mysterious reproach, which she did not seek to fathom. She walked on thoughtfully to-day; and when, at the next corner, she turned into the street that led toward home, she was given a surprise. Arthur Russell came rapidly from behind her, lifting his hat as she saw him.

"Are you walking north, Miss Adams?" he asked. "Do you mind if I walk with you?"

She was not delighted, but seemed so. "How charming!" she cried, giving him a little flourish of the shapely hands; and then, because she wondered if he had seen her coming out of the tobacco-shop, she laughed and added, "I've just been on the most ridiculous errand!"

"What was that?"

"To order some cigars for my father. He's been quite ill, poor man, and he's so particular—but what in the world do I know about cigars?"

Russell laughed. "Well, what do you know about 'em? Did you select by the price?"

"Mercy, no!" she exclaimed, and added, with an afterthought, "Of course he wrote down the name of the kind he wanted and I gave it to the shopman. I could never have pronounced it."

CHAPTER X

In her pocket as she spoke her hand rested upon the little sack of tobacco, which responded accusingly to the touch of her restless fingers; and she found time to wonder why she was building up this fiction for Mr. Arthur Russell. His discovery of Walter's device for whiling away the dull evening had shamed and distressed her; but she would have suffered no less if almost any other had been the discoverer. In this gentleman, after hearing that he was Mildred's Mr. Arthur Russell, Alice felt not the slightest "personal interest"; and there was yet to develop in her life such a thing as an interest not personal. At twenty-two this state of affairs is not unique.

So far as Alice was concerned Russell might have worn a placard, "Engaged." She looked upon him as diners entering a restaurant look upon tables marked "Reserved": the glance, slightly discontented, passes on at once. Or so the eye of a prospector wanders querulously over staked and established claims on the mountainside, and seeks the virgin land beyond; unless, indeed, the prospector be dishonest. But Alice was no claim-jumper —so long as the notice of ownership was plainly posted.

Though she was indifferent now, habit ruled her: and, at the very time she wondered why she created fictitious cigars for her father, she was also regretting that she had not boldly carried her Malacca stick down-town with her. Her vivacity increased automatically.

"Perhaps the clerk thought you wanted the cigars for yourself," Russell suggested. "He may have taken you for a Spanish countess."

"I'm sure he did!" Alice agreed, gaily; and she hummed 'a bar or two of "La Paloma," snapping her fingers as castanets, and swaying her body a little, to suggest the accepted stencil of a "Spanish Dancer." "Would you have taken me for one, Mr. Russell?" she asked, as she concluded the impersonation.

"I? Why, yes," he said. "I'd take you for anything you wanted me to."

"Why, what a speech!" she cried, and, laughing, gave him a quick glance in which there glimmered some real surprise. He was looking at her quizzically, but with the liveliest appreciation. Her surprise increased; and she was glad that he had joined her.

To be seen walking with such a companion added to her pleasure. She would have described him as "altogether quite stunning-looking"; and she liked his tall, dark thinness, his gray clothes, his soft hat, and his clean brown shoes; she liked his easy swing of the stick he carried.

"Shouldn't I have said it?" he asked. "Would you rather not be taken for a Spanish countess?"

"That isn't it," she explained. "You said——"

"I said I'd take you for whatever you wanted me to. Isn't that all right?"

"It would all depend, wouldn't it?"

"Of course it would depend on what you wanted."

"Oh, no!" she laughed. "It might depend on a lot of things."

"Such as?"

"Well——" She hesitated, having the mischievous impulse to say, "Such as Mildred!" But she decided to omit this reference, and became serious, remembering Russell's service to her at Mildred's house. "Speaking of what I want to be taken for," she said;—"I've been wondering ever since the other night what you did take me for! You must have taken me for the sister of a professional gambler, I'm afraid!"

Russell's look of kindness was the truth about him, she was to discover; and he reassured her now by the promptness of his friendly chuckle. "Then your young brother told you where I found him, did he? I kept my face straight at the time, but I laughed afterward—to myself. It struck me as original, to say the least: his amusing himself with those darkies."

"Walter *is* original," Alice said; and, having adopted this new view of her brother's eccentricities, she impulsively went on to make it more plausible. "He's a very odd boy, and I was afraid you'd misunderstand. He tells wonderful 'darky stories,' and he'll do anything to draw coloured people out and make them talk; and that's what he was doing at Mildred's when you found him for me—he says he wins their confidence by playing dice with them. In the family we think he'll probably write about them some day. He's rather literary."

"Are you?" Russell asked, smiling.

"I? Oh——" She paused, lifting both hands in a charming gesture of helplessness. "Oh, I'm just—me!"

His glance followed the lightly waved hands with keen approval, then rose to the lively and colourful face, with its hazel eyes, its small and pretty nose, and the lip-caught smile which seemed the climax of her decorative transition. Never had he seen a creature so plastic or so wistful.

Here was a contrast to his cousin Mildred, who was not wistful, and controlled any impulses toward plasticity, if she had them. "By George!" he said. "But you *are* different!"

With that, there leaped in her such an impulse of roguish gallantry as she could never resist. She turned her head, and, laughing and bright-eyed, looked him full in the face.

"From whom?" she cried.

"From—everybody!" he said. "Are you a mind-reader?"

"Why?"

"How did you know I was thinking you were different from my cousin, Mildred Palmer?"

"What makes you think I *did* know it?"

"Nonsense!" he said. "You knew what I was thinking and I knew you knew."

"Yes," she said with cool humour. "How intimate that seems to make us all at once!"

Russell left no doubt that he was delighted with these gaieties of hers. "By George!" he exclaimed again. "I thought you were this sort of girl the first moment I saw you!"

"What sort of girl? Didn't Mildred tell you what sort of girl I am when she asked you to dance with me?"

"She didn't ask me to dance with you—I'd been looking at you. You were talking to some old ladies, and I asked Mildred who you were."

"Oh, so Mildred *didn't*——" Alice checked herself. "Who did she tell you I was?"

"She just said you were a Miss Adams, so I——"

" 'A' Miss Adams?" Alice interrupted.

"Yes. Then I said I'd like to meet you."

"I see. You thought you'd save me from the old ladies."

"No. I thought I'd save myself from some of the girls Mildred was getting me to dance with. There was a Miss Dowling——"

"Poor man!" Alice said, gently, and her impulsive thought was that Mildred had taken few chances, and that as a matter of self-defense her carefulness might have been well founded. This Mr. Arthur Russell was a much more responsive person than one had supposed.

"So, Mr. Russell, you don't know anything about me except what you thought when you first saw me?"

"Yes, I know I was right when I thought it."

"You haven't told me what you thought."

"I thought you were like what you *are* like."

"Not very definite, is it? I'm afraid you shed more light a minute or so ago, when you said how different from Mildred you thought I was. That *was* definite, unfortunately!"

"I didn't say it," Russell explained. "I thought it, and you read my mind. That's the sort of girl I thought you were—one that could read a man's mind. Why do you say 'unfortunately' you're not like Mildred?"

Alice's smooth gesture seemed to sketch Mildred. "Because she's perfect —why, she's *perfectly* perfect! She never makes a mistake, and everybody looks up to her—oh, yes, we all fairly adore her! She's like some big, noble, cold statue—'way above the rest of us—and she hardly ever does anything mean or treacherous. Of all the girls I know I believe she's played the fewest really petty tricks. She's——"

Russell interrupted; he looked perplexed. "You say she's perfectly perfect, but that she does play some——"

Alice laughed, as if at his sweet innocence. "Men are so funny!" she informed him. "Of course girls *all* do mean things sometimes. My own career's just one long brazen smirch of 'em! What I mean is, Mildred's perfectly perfect compared to the rest of us."

"I see," he said, and seemed to need a moment or two of thoughtfulness. Then he inquired, "What sort of treacherous things do *you* do?"

"I? Oh, the very worst kind! Most people bore me—particularly the men in this town—and I show it."

"But I shouldn't call that treacherous, exactly."

"Well, *they* do," Alice laughed. "It's made me a terribly unpopular character! I do a lot of things they hate. For instance, at a dance I'd a lot rather find some clever old woman and talk to her than dance with nine-tenths of these nonentities. I usually do it, too."

"But you danced as if you liked it. You danced better than any other girl I——"

"This flattery of yours doesn't quite turn my head, Mr. Russell," Alice interrupted. "Particularly since Mildred only gave you Ella Dowling to compare with me!"

"Oh, no," he insisted. "There were others—and of course Mildred, herself."

"Oh, of course, yes. I forgot that. Well——" She paused, then added, "I certainly *ought* to dance well."

"Why is it so much a duty?"

"When I think of the dancing-teachers and the expense to papa! All sorts of fancy instructors—I suppose that's what daughters have fathers for, though, isn't it? To throw money away on them?"

"You don't——" Russell began, and his look was one of alarm. "You haven't taken up——"

She understood his apprehension and responded merrily, "Oh, murder, no! You mean you're afraid I break out sometimes in a piece of cheesecloth and run around a fountain thirty times, and then, for an encore, show how much like snakes I can make my arms look."

"I *said* you were a mind-reader!" he exclaimed. "That's exactly what I was pretending to be afraid you might do."

"'Pretending?' That's nicer of you. No; it's not my mania."

"What is?"

"Oh, nothing in particular that I know of just now. Of course I've had the usual one: the one that every girl goes through."

"What's that?"

"Good heavens, Mr. Russell, you can't expect me to believe you're really a man of the world if you don't know that every girl has a time in her life when she's positive she's divinely talented for the stage! It's the only universal rule about women that hasn't got an exception. I don't mean we all want to go on the stage, but we all think we'd be wonderful if we did. Even Mildred. Oh, she wouldn't confess it to you: you'd have to know her a great deal better than any man can ever know her to find out."

"I see," he said. "Girls are always telling us we can't know them. I wonder if you——"

She took up his thought before he expressed it, and again he was fascinated by her quickness, which indeed seemed to him almost telepathic. "Oh, but *don't* we know one another, though!" she cried. "Such things we have to keep secret—things that go on right before *your* eyes!"

"Why don't some of you tell us?" he asked.

"We can't tell you."

"Too much honour?"

"No. Not even too much honour among thieves, Mr. Russell. We don't tell you about our tricks against one another because we know it wouldn't make any impression on you. The tricks aren't played against you, and you have a soft side for cats with lovely manners!"

"What about your tricks against us?"

"Oh, those!" Alice laughed. "We think they're rather cute!"

"Bravo!" he cried, and hammered the ferrule of his stick upon the pavement.

"What's the applause for?"

"For you. What you said was like running up the black flag to the masthead."

"Oh, no. It was just a modest little sign in a pretty flower-bed: 'Gentlemen, beware!'"

"I see I must," he said, gallantly.

"Thanks! But I mean, beware of the whole bloomin' garden!" Then, picking up a thread that had almost disappeared: "You needn't think you'll ever find out whether I'm right about Mildred's not being an exception by asking her," she said. "She won't tell you: she's not the sort that ever makes a confession."

But Russell had not followed her shift to the former topic. "'Mildred's not being an exception?'" he said, vaguely. "I don't——"

"An exception about thinking she could be a wonderful thing on the stage if she only cared to. If you asked her I'm pretty sure she'd say, 'What nonsense!' Mildred's the dearest, finest thing anywhere, but you won't find out many things about her by asking her."

Russell's expression became more serious, as it did whenever his cousin was made their topic. "You think not?" he said. "You think she's——"

"No. But it's not because she isn't sincere exactly. It's only because she has such a lot to live up to. She has to live up to being a girl on the grand style—to herself, I mean, of course." And without pausing Alice rippled on, "You ought to have seen *me* when I had the stage-fever! I used to play 'Juliet' all alone in my room." She lifted her arms in graceful entreaty, pleading musically,

> "O, swear not by the moon, the inconstant moon,
>   That monthly changes in her circled orb,
>   Lest thy love prove——"

She broke off abruptly with a little flourish, snapping thumb and finger of each outstretched hand, then laughed and said, "Papa used to make such fun of me! Thank heaven, I was only fifteen; I was all over it by the next year."

"No wonder you had the fever," Russell observed. "You do it beautifully. Why didn't you finish the line?"

"Which one? 'Lest thy love prove likewise variable'? Juliet was saying it to a *man*, you know. She seems to have been ready to worry about his constancy pretty early in their affair!"

Her companion was again thoughtful. "Yes," he said, seeming to be rather irksomely impressed with Alice's suggestion. "Yes; it does appear so."

Alice glanced at his serious face, and yielded to an audacious temptation. "You mustn't take it so hard," she said, flippantly. "It isn't about you: it's only about Romeo and Juliet."

"See here!" he exclaimed. "You aren't at your mind-reading again, are you? There are times when it won't do, you know!"

She leaned toward him a little, as if companionably: they were walking slowly, and this geniality of hers brought her shoulder in light contact with his for a moment. "Do you dislike my mind-reading?" she asked, and, across their two just touching shoulders, gave him her sudden look of smiling wistfulness. "Do you hate it?"

He shook his head. "No, I don't," he said, gravely. "It's quite—pleasant. But I think it says, 'Gentlemen, beware!' "

She instantly moved away from him, with the lawless and frank laugh of one who is delighted to be caught in a piece of hypocrisy. "How lovely!" she cried. Then she pointed ahead. "Our walk is nearly over. We're coming to the foolish little house where I live. It's a queer little place, but my father's so attached to it the family have about given up hope of getting him to build a real house farther out. He doesn't mind our being extravagant about anything else, but he won't let us alter one single thing about his precious little old house. Well!" She halted, and gave him her hand. "Adieu!"

"I couldn't," he began; hesitated, then asked: "I couldn't come in with you for a little while?"

"Not now," she said, quickly. "You can come——" She paused.

"When?"

"Almost any time." She turned and walked slowly up the path, but he waited. "You can come in the evening if you like," she called back to him over her shoulder.

"Soon?"

"As soon as you like!" She waved her hand; then ran indoors and watched him from a window as he went up the street. He walked rapidly, a fine, easy figure, swinging his stick in a way that suggested exhilaration. Alice, staring after him through the irregular apertures of a lace curtain, showed no similar buoyancy. Upon the instant she closed the door all sparkle left her: she had become at once the simple and sometimes troubled girl her family knew.

"What's going on out there?" her mother asked, approaching from the dining-room.

"Oh, nothing," Alice said, indifferently, as she turned away. "That Mr. Russell met me down-town and walked up with me."

"Mr. Russell? Oh, the one that's engaged to Mildred?"

"Well—I don't know for certain. He didn't seem so much like an engaged man to me." And she added, in the tone of thoughtful preoccupation: "Anyhow—not so terribly!"

Then she ran upstairs, gave her father his tobacco, filled his pipe for him, and petted him as he lighted it.

CHAPTER XI

After that, she went to her room and sat down before her three-leafed mirror. There was where she nearly always sat when she came into her room, if she had nothing in mind to do. She went to that chair as naturally as a dog goes to his corner.

She leaned forward, observing her profile; gravity seemed to be her mood. But after a long, almost motionless scrutiny, she began to produce dramatic sketches upon that ever-ready stage, her countenance: she showed gaiety, satire, doubt, gentleness, appreciation of a companion and love-in-hiding—all studied in profile first, then repeated for a "three-quarter view." Subsequently she ran through them, facing herself in full.

In this manner she outlined a playful scenario for her next interview with Arthur Russell; but grew solemn again, thinking of the impression she had already sought to give him. She had no twinges for any underminings of her "most intimate friend"—in fact, she felt that her work on a new portrait of Mildred for Mr. Russell had been honest and accurate. But why had it been her instinct to show him an Alice Adams who didn't exist?

Almost everything she had said to him was upon spontaneous impulse, springing to her lips on the instant; yet it all seemed to have been founded upon a careful design, as if some hidden self kept such designs in stock and handed them up to her, ready-made, to be used for its own purpose. What appeared to be the desired result was a false-coloured image in Russell's mind; but if he liked that image he wouldn't be liking Alice Adams; nor would anything he thought about the image be a thought about her. Nevertheless, she knew she would go on with her false, fancy colourings of this nothing as soon as she saw him again; she had just been practising them. "What's the idea?" she wondered. "What makes me tell such lies? Why shouldn't I be just myself?" And then she thought, "But which one is myself?"

Her eyes dwelt on the solemn eyes in the mirror; and her lips, disquieted by a deepening wonder, parted to whisper:

"Who in the world are you?"

The apparition before her had obeyed her like an alert slave, but now, as she subsided to a complete stillness, that aspect changed to the old mockery with which mirrors avenge their wrongs. The nucleus of some queer thing seemed to gather and shape itself behind the nothingness of the reflected eyes until it became almost an actual strange presence. If it could be identified, perhaps the presence was that of the hidden designer who handed up the false, ready-made pictures, and, for unknown purposes, made Alice exhibit them; but whatever it was, she suddenly found it monkey-like and terrifying. In a flutter she jumped up and went to another part of the room.

A moment or two later she was whistling softly as she hung her light coat over a wooden triangle in her closet, and her musing now was quainter than the experience that led to it; for what she thought was this, "I certainly am a queer girl!" She took a little pride in so much originality, believing herself probably the only person in the world to have such thoughts as had been hers since she entered the room, and the first to be disturbed by a strange presence in the mirror. In fact, the effect of the tiny episode became apparent in that look of preoccupied complacency to be seen for a time upon any girl who has found reason to suspect that she is a being without counterpart.

This slight glow, still faintly radiant, was observed across the dinner-table by Walter, but he misinterpreted it. "What *you* lookin' so self-satisfied about?" he inquired, and added in his knowing way, "I saw you, all right, cutie!"

"Where'd you see me?"

"Down-town."

"This afternoon, you mean, Walter?"

"Yes, 'this afternoon, I mean, Walter,' " he returned, burlesquing her voice at least happily enough to please himself; for he laughed applausively. "Oh, you never saw me! I passed you close enough to pull a tooth, but you were awful busy. I never did see anybody as busy as you get, Alice, when you're towin' a barge. My, but you keep your hands goin'! Looked like the air was full of 'em! That's why I'm onto why you look so tickled this evening; I saw you with that big fish."

Mrs. Adams laughed benevolently; she was not displeased with this rallying. "Well, what of it, Walter?" she asked. "If you happen to see your sister on the street when some nice young man is being attentive to her——"

Walter barked and then cackled. "Whoa, Sal!" he said. "You got the parts mixed. It's little Alice that was 'being attentive.' I know the big fish she was attentive to, all right, too."

"Yes," his sister retorted, quietly. "I should think you might have recognized him, Walter."

Walter looked annoyed. "Still harpin' on *that!*" he complained. "The kind of women I like, if they get sore they just hit you somewhere on the face and then they're through. By the way, I heard this Russell was supposed to be your dear, old, sweet friend Mildred's steady. What you doin' walkin' as close to him as all that?"

Mrs. Adams addressed her son in gentle reproof, "Why Walter!"

"Oh, never mind, mama," Alice said. "To the horrid all things are horrid."

"Get out!" Walter protested, carelessly. "I heard all about this Russell down at the shop. Young Joe Lamb's such a talker I wonder he don't ruin his grandfather's business; he keeps all us cheap help standin' round listening to him nine-tenths of our time. Well, Joe told me this Russell's some kin or other to the Palmer family, and he's got some little money of his own, and he's puttin' it into ole Palmer's trust company and Palmer's goin' to make him a vice-president of the company. Sort of a keep-the-money-in-the-family arrangement, Joe Lamb says."

Mrs. Adams looked thoughtful. "I don't see——" she began.

"Why, this Russell's supposed to be tied up to Mildred," her son explained. "When ole Palmer dies this Russell will be his son-in-law, and all he'll haf' to do'll be to barely lift his feet and step into the ole man's shoes. It's certainly a mighty fat hand-me-out for this Russell! You better lay off o' there, Alice. Pick somebody that's got less to lose and you'll make a better showing."

Mrs. Adams's air of thoughtfulness had not departed. "But you say this Mr. Russell is well off on his own account, Walter."

"Oh, Joe Lamb says he's got some little of his own. Didn't know how much."

"Well, then——"

Walter laughed his laugh. "Cut it out," he bade her. "Alice wouldn't run in fourth place."

Alice had been looking at him in a detached way, as though estimating the value of a specimen in a collection not her own. "Yes," she said, indifferently. "You *really* are vulgar, Walter."

He had finished his meal; and, rising, he came round the table to her and patted her good-naturedly on the shoulder. "Good ole Allie!" he said. "*Honest*, you wouldn't run in fourth place. If I was you I'd never even start in the class. That frozen-face gang will rule you off the track soon as they see your colours."

"Walter!" his mother said again.

"Well, ain't I her brother?" he returned, seeming to be entirely serious and direct, for the moment, at least. "*I* like the ole girl all right. Fact is, sometimes I'm kind of sorry for her."

"But what's it all *about*?" Alice cried. "Simply because you met me downtown with a man I never saw but once before and just barely know! Why all this palaver?"

"'Why?'" he repeated, grinning. "Well, I've seen you start before, you know!" He went to the door, and paused. "I got no date to-night. Take you to the movies, you care to go."

She declined crisply. "No, thanks!"

"Come on," he said, as pleasantly as he knew how. "Give me a chance to show you a better time than we had up at that frozen-face joint. I'll get you some chop suey afterward."

"No, thanks!"

"All right," he responded and waved a flippant adieu. "As the barber says, 'The better the advice, the worse it's wasted!' Good-*night!*"

Alice shrugged her shoulders; but a moment or two later, as the jar of the carelessly slammed front door went through the house, she shook her head, reconsidering. "Perhaps I ought to have gone with him. It might have kept him away from whatever dreadful people are his friends—at least for one night."

"Oh, I'm sure Walter's a *good* boy," Mrs. Adams said, soothingly; and this was what she almost always said when either her husband or Alice expressed such misgivings. "He's odd, and he's picked up right queer manners; but that's only because we haven't given him advantages like the other young men. But I'm sure he's a *good* boy."

She reverted to the subject a little later, while she washed the dishes and Alice wiped them. "Of course Walter could take his place with the other nice boys of the town even yet," she said. "I mean, if we could afford to help him financially. They all belong to the country clubs and have cars and——"

"Let's don't go into that any more, mama," the daughter begged her. "What's the use?"

"It *could* be of use," Mrs. Adams insisted. "It could if your father——"

"But papa *can't*."

"Yes, he can."

"But how can he? He told me a man of his age *can't* give up a business he's been in practically all his life, and just go groping about for something that might never turn up at all. I think he's right about it, too, of course!"

Mrs. Adams splashed among the plates with a new vigour heightened by an old bitterness. "Oh, yes," she said. "He talks that way; but he knows better."

"How could he 'know better,' mama?"

"*He* knows how!"

"But what does he know?"

Mrs. Adams tossed her head. "You don't suppose I'm such a fool I'd be urging him to give up something for nothing, do you, Alice? Do you suppose I'd want him to just go 'groping around' like he was telling you? That would be crazy, of course. Little as his work at Lamb's brings in, I wouldn't be so silly as to ask him to give it up just on a *chance* he could find something else. Good gracious, Alice, you must give me credit for a little intelligence once in a while!"

Alice was puzzled. "But what else could there be except a chance? I don't see——"

"Well, *I* do," her mother interrupted, decisively. "That man could make us all well off right now if he wanted to. We could have been rich long ago if he'd ever really felt as he ought to about his family."

"What! Why, how could——"

"You know how as well as I do," Mrs. Adams said, crossly. "I guess you haven't forgotten how he treated me about it the Sunday before he got sick."

She went on with her work, putting into it a sudden violence inspired by the recollection; but Alice, enlightened, gave utterance to a laugh of lugubrious derision. "Oh, the *glue* factory again!" she cried. "How silly!" And she renewed her laughter.

So often do the great projects of parents appear ignominious to their children. Mrs. Adams's conception of a glue factory as a fairy godmother of this family was an absurd old story which Alice had never taken seriously. She remembered that when she was about fifteen her mother began now and then to say something to Adams about a "glue factory," rather timidly, and as a vague suggestion, but never without irritating him. Then, for years, the preposterous subject had not been mentioned; possibly because of some explosion on the part of Adams, when his daughter had not been present. But during the last year Mrs. Adams had quietly gone back to these old hints, reviving them at intervals and also reviving her husband's irritation. Alice's bored impression was that her mother wanted him to found, or buy, or do something, or other, about a glue factory; and that he considered the proposal so impracticable as to be insulting. The parental conversations took place when neither Alice nor Walter was at hand, but sometimes Alice had come in upon the conclusion of one, to find her father in a shouting mood, and shocking the air behind him with profane monosyllables as he departed. Mrs. Adams would be left quiet and troubled; and when Alice, sympathizing with the goaded man, inquired of her mother why these tiresome bickerings had been renewed, she always got the brooding and cryptic answer, "He could do it—if he wanted to." Alice failed to comprehend the desirability of a glue factory—to her mind a father engaged in a glue factory lacked impressiveness; had no advantage over a father employed by Lamb and Company; and she supposed that Adams knew better than her mother whether such an enterprise would be profitable or not. Emphatically, he thought it would not, for she had heard him shouting at the end of one of these painful interviews, "You can keep up your dang talk till *you* die and *I* die, but I'll never make one God's cent that way!"

There had been a culmination. Returning from church on the Sunday preceding the collapse with which Adams's illness had begun, Alice found her mother downstairs, weeping and intimidated, while her father's stamping footsteps were loudly audible as he strode up and down his room overhead. So were his endless repetitions of invective loudly audible: "That woman! Oh, that woman! Oh, that danged woman!"

Mrs. Adams admitted to her daughter that it was "the old glue factory" and that her husband's wildness had frightened her into a "solemn promise" never to mention the subject again so long as she had breath. Alice laughed. The "glue factory" idea was not only a bore, but ridiculous, and her mother's evident seriousness about it one of those inexplicable vagaries we sometimes discover in the people we know best. But this Sunday rampage appeared to be the end of it, and when Adams came down to dinner, an hour later, he was unusually cheerful. Alice was glad he had gone wild enough to settle the glue factory once and for all; and she had ceased to think of the episode long before Friday of that week, when Adams was brought home in the middle of the afternoon by his old employer, the "great J. A. Lamb," in the latter's car.

During the long illness the "glue factory" was completely forgotten, by

Alice at least; and her laugh was rueful as well as derisive now, in the kitchen, when she realized that her mother's mind again dwelt upon this abandoned nuisance. "I thought you'd got over all that nonsense, mama," she said.

Mrs. Adams smiled, pathetically. "Of course you think it's nonsense, dearie. Young people think everything's nonsense that they don't know anything about."

"Good gracious!" Alice cried. "I should think I used to hear enough about that horrible old glue factory to know something about it!"

"No," her mother returned patiently. "You've never heard anything about it at all."

"I haven't?"

"No. Your father and I didn't discuss it before you children. All you ever heard was when he'd get in such a rage, after we'd been speaking of it, that he couldn't control himself when you came in. Wasn't I always quiet? Did I ever go on talking about it?"

"No; perhaps not. But you're talking about it now, mama, after you promised never to mention it again."

"I promised not to mention it to your father," said Mrs. Adams, gently. "I haven't mentioned it to him, have I?"

"Ah, but if you mention it to me I'm afraid you *will* mention it to him. You always do speak of things that you have on your mind, and you might get papa all stirred up again about——" Alice paused, a light of divination flickering in her eyes. "Oh!" she cried. "I *see!*"

"What do you see?"

"You *have* been at him about it!"

"Not one single word!"

"No!" Alice cried. "Not a *word*, but that's what you've meant all along! You haven't spoken the words to him, but all this urging him to change, to 'find something better to go into'—it's all been about nothing on earth but your foolish old glue factory that you know upsets him, and you gave your solemn word never to speak to him about again! You didn't say it, but you meant it—and he *knows* that's what you meant! Oh, mama!"

Mrs. Adams, with her hands still automatically at work in the flooded dishpan, turned to face her daughter. "Alice," she said, tremulously, "what do I ask for myself?"

"What?"

"I say, What do I ask for myself? Do you suppose *I* want anything? Don't you know I'd be perfectly content on your father's present income if I were the only person to be considered? What do I care about any pleasure for myself? I'd be willing never to have a maid again; I don't mind doing the work. If we didn't have any children I'd be glad to do your father's cooking and the housework and the washing and ironing, too, for the rest of my life. I wouldn't care. I'm a poor cook and a poor housekeeper; I don't do anything well; but it would be good enough for just him and me. I wouldn't ever utter one word of com——"

"Oh, goodness!" Alice lamented. "What *is* it all about?"

"It's about this," said Mrs. Adams, swallowing. "You and Walter are a new generation and you ought to have the same as the rest of the new generation get. Poor Walter—asking you to go to the movies and a Chinese restaurant: the best he had to offer! Don't you suppose I see how the poor boy is deteriorating? Don't you suppose I know what *you* have to go through, Alice? And when I think of that man upstairs——" The agitated voice grew louder. "When I think of him and know that nothing in the world but his *stubbornness* keeps my children from having all they want and what they *ought* to have, do you suppose I'm going to hold myself bound to keep to the absolute letter of a silly promise he got from me by behaving like a crazy man? I can't! I can't do it! No mother could sit by and see him lock up a horn of plenty like that in his closet when the children were starving!"

"Oh, goodness, goodness me!" Alice protested. "We aren't precisely 'starving,' are we?"

Mrs. Adams began to weep. "It's just the same. Didn't I see how flushed and pretty you looked, this afternoon, after you'd been walking with this young man that's come here? Do you suppose he'd *look* at a girl like Mildred Palmer if you had what you ought to have? Do you suppose he'd be going into business with her father if *your* father——"

"Good heavens, mama; you're worse than Walter: I just barely know the man! *Don't* be so absurd!"

"Yes, I'm always 'absurd,'" Mrs. Adams moaned. "All I can do is cry, while your father sits upstairs, and his horn of plenty——"

But Alice interrupted with a peal of desperate laughter. "Oh, that 'horn of plenty!' Do come down to earth, mama. How can you call a *glue* factory, that doesn't exist except in your mind, a 'horn of plenty'? Do let's be a little rational!"

"It *could* be a horn of plenty," the tearful Mrs. Adams insisted. "It could! You don't understand a thing about it."

"Well, I'm willing," Alice said, with tired skepticism. "Make me understand, then. Where'd you ever get the idea?"

Mrs. Adams withdrew her hands from the water, dried them on a towel, and then wiped her eyes with a handkerchief. "Your father could make a fortune if he wanted to," she said, quietly. "At least, I don't say a fortune, but anyhow a great deal more than he does make."

"Yes, I've heard that before, mama, and you think he could make it out of a glue factory. What I'm asking is: How?"

"How? Why, by making glue and selling it. Don't you know how bad most glue is when you try to mend anything? A good glue is one of the rarest things there is; and it would just sell itself, once it got started. Well, your father knows how to make as good a glue as there is in the world."

Alice was not interested. "What of it? I suppose probably anybody could make it if they wanted to."

"I *said* you didn't know anything about it. Nobody else could make it. Your father knows a formula for making it."

"What of that?"

"It's a secret formula. It isn't even down on paper. It's worth any amount of money."

" 'Any amount?' " Alice said, remaining incredulous. "Why hasn't papa sold it then?"

"Just because he's too stubborn to do anything with it at all!"

"How did papa get it?"

"He got it before you were born, just after we were married. I didn't think much about it then: it wasn't till you were growing up and I saw how much we needed money that I——"

"Yes, but how did papa get it?" Alice began to feel a little more curious about this possible buried treasure. "Did he invent it?"

"Partly," Mrs. Adams said, looking somewhat preoccupied. "He and another man invented it."

"Then maybe the other man——"

"He's dead."

"Then his family——"

"I don't think he left any family," Mrs. Adams said. "Anyhow, it belongs to your father. At least it belongs to him as much as it does to any one else. He's got an absolutely perfect right to do anything he wants to with it, and it would make us all comfortable if he'd do what I want him to—and he *knows* it would, too!"

Alice shook her head pityingly. "Poor mama!" she said. "Of course he knows it wouldn't do anything of the kind, or else he'd have done it long ago."

"He would, you say?" her mother cried. "That only shows how little you know him!"

"Poor mama!" Alice said again, soothingly. "If papa were like what you say he is, he'd be—why, he'd be crazy!"

Mrs. Adams agreed with a vehemence near passion. "You're right about him for once: that's just what he is! He sits up there in his stubbornness and lets us slave here in the kitchen when if he wanted to—if he'd so much as lift his little finger——"

"Oh, come, now!" Alice laughed. "You can't build even a glue factory with just one little finger."

Mrs. Adams seemed about to reply that finding fault with a figure of speech was beside the point; but a ringing of the front door bell forestalled the retort. "Now, who do you suppose that is?" she wondered aloud; then her face brightened. "Ah—did Mr. Russell ask if he could——"

"No, he wouldn't be coming this evening," Alice said. "Probably it's the great J. A. Lamb: he usually stops for a minute on Thursdays to ask how papa's getting along. I'll go."

She tossed her apron off, and as she went through the house her expression was thoughtful. She was thinking vaguely about the glue factory and wondering if there might be "something in it" after all. If her mother was right about the rich possibilities of Adams's secret—but that was as far as Alice's speculations upon the matter went at this time: they were checked, partly by the thought that her father probably hadn't enough money for such an enterprise, and partly by the fact that she had arrived at the front door.

CHAPTER XII

The fine old gentleman revealed when she opened the door was probably the last great merchant in America to wear the chin beard. White as white frost, it was trimmed short with exquisite precision, while his upper lip and the lower expanses of his cheeks were clean and rosy from fresh shaving. With this trim white chin beard, the white waistcoat, the white tie, the suit of fine gray cloth, the broad and brilliantly polished black shoes, and the wide-brimmed gray felt hat, here was a man who had found his style in the seventies of the last century, and thenceforth kept it. Files of old magazines of that period might show him, in woodcut, as, "Type of Boston Merchant"; Nast might have drawn him as an honest statesman. He was eighty, hale and sturdy, not aged; and his quick blue eyes, still unflecked, and as brisk as a boy's, saw everything.

"Well, well, well!" he said, heartily. "You haven't lost any of your good looks since last week, I see, Miss Alice, so I guess I'm to take it you haven't been worrying over your daddy. The young feller's getting along all right, is he?"

"He's much better; he's sitting up, Mr. Lamb. Won't you come in?"

"Well, I don't know but I might." He turned to call toward twin disks of light at the curb, "Be out in a minute, Billy"; and the silhouette of a chauffeur standing beside a car could be seen to salute in response, as the old gentleman stepped into the hall. "You don't suppose your daddy's receiving callers yet, is he?"

"He's a good deal stronger than he was when you were here last week, but I'm afraid he's not very presentable, though."

" 'Presentable?' " The old man echoed her jovially. "Pshaw! I've seen lots of sick folks. I know what they look like and how they love to kind of nest in among a pile of old blankets and wrappers. Don't you worry about that, Miss Alice, if you think he'd like to see me."

"Of course he would—if——" Alice hesitated; then said quickly, "Of course he'd love to see you and he's quite able to, if you care to come up."

She ran up the stairs ahead of him, and had time to snatch the crocheted wrap from her father's shoulders. Swathed as usual, he was sitting beside a

table, reading the evening paper; but when his employer appeared in the doorway he half rose as if to come forward in greeting.

"Sit still!" the old gentleman shouted. "What do you mean? Don't you know you're weak as a cat? D'you think a man can be sick as long as you have and *not* be weak as a cat? What you trying to do the polite with *me* for?"

Adams gratefully protracted the handshake that accompanied these inquiries. "This is certainly mighty fine of you, Mr. Lamb," he said. "I guess Alice has told you how much our whole family appreciate your coming here so regularly to see how this old bag o' bones was getting along. Haven't you, Alice?"

"Yes, papa," she said; and turned to go out, but Lamb checked her.

"Stay right here, Miss Alice; I'm not even going to sit down. I know how it upsets sick folks when people outside the family come in for the first time."

"*You* don't upset me," Adams said. "I'll feel a lot better for getting a glimpse of you, Mr. Lamb."

The visitor's laugh was husky, but hearty and reassuring, like his voice in speaking. "That's the way all my boys blarney me, Miss Alice," he said. "They think I'll make the work lighter on 'em if they can get me kind of flattered up. You just tell your daddy it's no use; he doesn't get on *my* soft side, pretending he likes to see me even when he's sick."

"Oh, I'm not so sick any more," Adams said. "I expect to be back in my place ten days from now at the longest."

"Well, now, don't hurry it, Virgil; don't hurry it. You take your time; take your time."

This brought to Adams's lips a feeble smile not lacking in a kind of vanity, as feeble. "Why?" he asked. "I suppose you think my department runs itself down there, do you?"

His employer's response was another husky laugh. "Well, well, well!" he cried, and patted Adams's shoulder with a strong pink hand. "Listen to this young feller, Miss Alice, will you! He thinks we can't get along without him a minute! Yes, sir, this daddy of yours believes the whole works 'll just take and run down if he isn't there to keep 'em wound up. I always suspected he thought a good deal of himself, and now I know he does!"

Adams looked troubled. "Well, I don't like to feel that my salary's going on with me not earning it."

"Listen to him, Miss Alice! Wouldn't you think, now, he'd let me be the one to worry about that? Why, on my word, if your daddy had his way, *I* wouldn't be anywhere. He'd take all my worrying and everything else off my shoulders and shove me right out of Lamb and Company! He would!"

"It seems to me I've been soldiering on you a pretty long while, Mr. Lamb," the convalescent said, querulously. "I don't feel right about it; but I'll be back in ten days. You'll see."

The old man took his hand in parting. "All right; we'll see, Virgil. Of course we do need you, seriously speaking; but we don't need you so bad we'll let you come down there before you're fully fit and able." He went to the door. "You hear, Miss Alice? That's what I wanted to make the old feller understand, and what I want you to kind of enforce on him. The old place is there waiting for him, and it'd wait ten years if it took him that long to get good and well. You see that he remembers it, Miss Alice!"

She went down the stairs with him, and he continued to impress this upon her until he had gone out of the front door. And even after that, the husky voice called back from the darkness, as he went to his car, "Don't forget, Miss Alice; let him take his own time. We always want him, but we want him to get good and well first. Good-night, good-night, young lady!"

When she closed the door her mother came from the farther end of the "living-room," where there was no light; and Alice turned to her.

"I can't help liking that old man, mama," she said. "He always sounds so —well, so solid and honest and friendly! I do like him."

But Mrs. Adams failed in sympathy upon this point. "He didn't say anything about raising your father's salary, did he?" she asked, dryly.

"No."

"No. I thought not."

She would have said more, but Alice, indisposed to listen, began to whistle, ran up the stairs, and went to sit with her father. She found him bright-eyed with the excitement a first caller brings into a slow convalescence: his cheeks showed actual hints of colour; and he was smiling tremulously as he filled and lit his pipe. She brought the crocheted scarf and put it about his shoulders again, then took a chair near him.

"I believe seeing Mr. Lamb did do you good, papa," she said. "I sort of thought it might, and that's why I let him come up. You really look a little like your old self again."

Adams exhaled a breathy "Ha!" with the smoke from his pipe as he waved the match to extinguish it. "That's fine," he said. "The smoke I had before dinner didn't taste the way it used to, and I kind of wondered if I'd lost my liking for tobacco, but this one seems to be all right. You bet it did me good to see J. A. Lamb! He's the biggest man that's ever lived in this town or ever will live here; and you can take all the Governors and Senators or anything they've raised here, and put 'em in a pot with him, and they won't come out one-two-three alongside o' him! And to think as big a man as that, with all his interests and everything he's got on his mind—to think he'd never let anything prevent him from coming here once every week to ask how I was getting along, and then walk right upstairs and kind of *call* on me, as it were—well, it makes me sort of feel as if I wasn't so much of a nobody, so to speak, as your mother seems to like to make out sometimes."

"How foolish, papa! Of *course* you're not 'a nobody.'"

Adams chuckled faintly upon his pipe-stem, what vanity he had seeming to be further stimulated by his daughter's applause. "I guess there aren't a whole lot of people in this town that could claim J. A. showed that much interest in 'em," he said. "Of course I don't set up to believe it's all because

of merit, or anything like that. He'd do the same for anybody else that'd
been with the company as long as I have, but still it *is* something to be with
the company that long and have him show he appreciates it."

"Yes, indeed, it is, papa."

"Yes, sir," Adams said, reflectively. "Yes, sir, I guess that's so. And besides,
it all goes to show the kind of a man he is. Simon pure, that's what that man
is, Alice. Simon pure! There's never been anybody work for him that didn't
respect him more than they did any other man in the world, I guess. And
when you work for him you know he respects you, too. Right from the start
you get the feeling that J. A. puts absolute confidence in you; and that's
mighty stimulating: it makes you want to show him he hasn't misplaced it.
There's great big moral values to the way a man like him gets you to feeling
about your relations with the business: it ain't all just dollars and cents—
not by any means!"

He was silent for a time, then returned with increasing enthusiasm to
this theme, and Alice was glad to see so much renewal of life in him; he
had not spoken with a like cheerful vigour since before his illness. The visit
of his idolized great man had indeed been good for him, putting new spirit
into him: and liveliness of the body followed that of the spirit. His improvement carried over the night: he slept well and awoke late, declaring that he
was "pretty near a well man and ready for business right now." Moreover,
having slept again in the afternoon, he dressed and went down to dinner,
leaning but lightly on Alice, who conducted him.

"My! but you and your mother have been at it with your scrubbing and
dusting!" he said, as they came through the "living-room." "I don't know I
ever did see the house so spick and span before!" His glance fell upon a few
carnations in a vase, and he chuckled admiringly. "Flowers, too! So *that's*
what you coaxed that dollar and a half out o' me for, this morning!"

Other embellishments brought forth his comment when he had taken his
old seat at the head of the small dinner-table. "Why, I declare, Alice!" he
exclaimed. "I been so busy looking at all the spick-and-spanishness after the
house-cleaning, and the flowers out in the parlour—'living-room' I suppose you
want me to call it, if I just *got* to be fashionable—I been so busy studying over
all this so-and-so, I declare I never noticed *you* till this minute! My, but you
are all dressed up! What's goin' on? What's it about: you so all dressed up,
and flowers in the parlour and everything?"

"Don't you see, papa? It's in honour of your coming downstairs again, of
course."

"Oh, so that's it," he said. "I never would 'a' thought of that, I guess."

But Walter looked sidelong at his father, and gave forth his sly and knowing laugh. "Neither would I!" he said.

Adams lifted his eyebrows jocosely. "You're jealous, are you, sonny? You
don't want the old man to think our young lady'd make so much fuss over
him, do you?"

"Go on thinkin' it's over you," Walter retorted, amused. "Go on and think it. It'll do you good."

"Of course I'll think it," Adams said. "It isn't anybody's birthday. Certainly the decorations are on account of me coming downstairs. Didn't you hear Alice say so?"

"Sure, I heard her say so."

"Well, then——"

Walter interrupted him with a little music. Looking shrewdly at Alice, he sang:

> "I was walkin' out on Monday with my sweet thing.
> She's my neat thing,
> My sweet thing:
> I'll go round on Tuesday night to see her.
> Oh, how we'll spoon——"

"Walter!" his mother cried. "*Where* do you learn such vulgar songs?" However, she seemed not greatly displeased with him, and laughed as she spoke.

"So that's it, Alice!" said Adams. "Playing the hypocrite with your old man, are you? It's some new beau, is it?"

"I only wish it were," she said, calmly. "No. It's just what I said: it's all for you, dear."

"Don't let her con you," Walter advised his father. "She's got expectations. You hang around downstairs a while after dinner and you'll see."

But the prophecy failed, though Adams went to his own room without waiting to test it. No one came.

Alice stayed in the "living-room" until half-past nine, when she went slowly upstairs. Her mother, almost tearful, met her at the top, and whispered, "You mustn't mind, dearie."

"Mustn't mind what?" Alice asked, and then, as she went on her way, laughed scornfully. "What utter nonsense!" she said.

Next day she cut the stems of the rather scant show of carnations and refreshed them with new water. At dinner, her father, still in high spirits, observed that she had again "dressed up" in honour of his second descent of the stairs; and Walter repeated his fragment of objectionable song; but these jocularities were rendered pointless by the eventless evening that followed; and in the morning the carnations began to appear tarnished and flaccid. Alice gave them a long look, then threw them away; and neither Walter nor her father was inspired to any rallying by her plain costume for that evening. Mrs. Adams was visibly depressed.

When Alice finished helping her mother with the dishes, she went outdoors and sat upon the steps of the little front veranda. The night, gentle with warm air from the south, surrounded her pleasantly, and the perpetual smoke was thinner. Now that the furnaces of dwelling-houses were no longer fired, life in that city had begun to be less like life in a railway tunnel; people were aware of summer in the air, and in the thickened foliage of the shade-trees, and in the sky. Stars were unveiled by the passing of the denser smoke fogs, and to-night they could be seen clearly; they looked warm and near. Other girls sat upon verandas and stoops in Alice's street, cheerful as young fishermen along the banks of a stream.

Alice could hear them from time to time; thin sopranos persistent in laughter that fell dismally upon her ears. She had set no lines or nets herself, and what she had of "expectations," as Walter called them, were vanished. For Alice was experienced; and one of the conclusions she drew from her experience was that when a man says, "I'd take you for anything you wanted me to," he may mean it or he may not; but, if he does, he will not postpone the first opportunity to say something more. Little affairs, once begun, must be warmed quickly; for if they cool they are dead.

But Alice was not thinking of Arthur Russell. When she tossed away the carnations she likewise tossed away her thoughts of that young man. She had been like a boy who sees upon the street, some distance before him, a bit of something round and glittering, a possible dime. He hopes it is a dime, and, until he comes near enough to make sure, he plays that it is a dime. In his mind he has an adventure with it: he buys something delightful. If he picks it up, discovering only some tin-foil which has happened upon a round shape, he feels a sinking. A dulness falls upon him.

So Alice was dull with the loss of an adventure; and when the laughter of other girls reached her, intermittently, she had not sprightliness enough left in her to be envious of their gaiety. Besides, these neighbours were ineligible even for her envy, being of another caste; they could never know a dance at the Palmers', except remotely, through a newspaper. Their laughter was for the encouragement of snappy young men of the stores and offices down-town, clerks, bookkeepers, what not—some of them probably graduates of Frincke's Business College.

Then, as she recalled that dark portal, with its dusty stairway mounting between close walls to disappear in the upper shadows, her mind drew back as from a doorway to Purgatory. Nevertheless, it was a picture often in her reverie; and sometimes it came suddenly, without sequence, into the midst of her other thoughts, as if it leaped up among them from a lower darkness; and when it arrived it wanted to stay. So a traveller, still roaming the world afar, sometimes broods without apparent reason upon his family burial lot: "I wonder if I shall end there."

The foreboding passed abruptly, with a jerk of her breath, as the street-lamp revealed a tall and easy figure approaching from the north, swinging a stick in time to its stride. She had given Russell up—and he came.

"What luck for me!" he exclaimed. "To find you alone!"

Alice gave him her hand for an instant, not otherwise moving. "I'm glad it happened so," she said. "Let's stay out here, shall we? Do you think it's too provincial to sit on a girl's front steps with her?"

" 'Provincial?' Why, it's the very best of our institutions," he returned, taking his place beside her. "At least, I think so to-night."

"Thanks! Is that practise for other nights somewhere else?"

"No," he laughed. "The practising all led up to this. Did I come too soon?"

"No," she replied, gravely. "Just in time!"

"I'm glad to be so accurate; I've spent two evenings wanting to come, Miss Adams, instead of doing what I was doing."

"What was that?"

"Dinners. Large and long dinners. Your fellow-citizens are immensely hospitable to a newcomer."

"Oh, no," Alice said. "We don't do it for everybody. Didn't you find yourself charmed?"

"One was a men's dinner," he explained. "Mr. Palmer seemed to think I ought to be shown to the principal business men."

"What was the other dinner?"

"My cousin Mildred gave it."

"Oh, *did* she!" Alice said, sharply, but she recovered herself in the same instant, and laughed. "She wanted to show you to the principal business women, I suppose."

"I don't know. At all events, I shouldn't give myself out to be so much fêted by your 'fellow-citizens,' after all, seeing these were both done by my relatives, the Palmers. However, there are others to follow, I'm afraid. I was wondering—I hoped maybe you'd be coming to some of them. Aren't you?"

"I rather doubt it," Alice said, slowly. "Mildred's dance was almost the only evening I've gone out since my father's illness began. He seemed better that day; so I went. He was better the other day when he wanted those cigars. He's very much up and down." She paused. "I'd almost forgotten that Mildred is your cousin."

"Not a very near one," he explained. "Mr. Palmer's father was my great-uncle."

"Still, of course you are related."

"Yes; that distantly."

Alice said placidly, "It's quite an advantage."

He agreed. "Yes. It is."

"No," she said, in the same placid tone. "I mean for Mildred."

"I don't see——"

She laughed. "No. You wouldn't. I mean it's an advantage over the rest of us who might like to compete for some of your time; and the worst of it is we can't accuse her of being unfair about it. We can't prove she showed any trickiness in having you for a cousin. Whatever else she might plan to do with you, she didn't plan that. So the rest of us must just bear it!"

"The 'rest of you!'" he laughed. "It's going to mean a great deal of suffering!"

Alice resumed her placid tone. "You're staying at the Palmers', aren't you?"

"No, not now. I've taken an apartment. I'm going to live here; I'm permanent. Didn't I tell you?"

"I think I'd heard somewhere that you were," she said. "Do you think
you'll like living here?"

"How can one tell?"

"If I were in your place I think I should be able to tell, Mr. Russell."

"How?"

"Why, good gracious!" she cried. "Haven't you got the most perfect creature in town for your—your cousin? *She* expects to make you like living here,
doesn't she? How could you keep from liking it, even if you tried not to,
under the circumstances?"

"Well, you see, there's such a lot of circumstances," he explained; "I'm
not sure I'll like getting back into a business again. I suppose most of the
men of my age in the country have been going through the same experience:
the War left us with a considerable restlessness of spirit."

"You were in the War?" she asked, quickly, and as quickly answered herself, "Of course you were!"

"I was a left-over; they only let me out about four months ago," he said.
"It's quite a shake-up trying to settle down again."

"You were in France, then?"

"Oh, yes; but I didn't get up to the front much—only two or three times,
and then just for a day or so. I was in the transportation service."

"You were an officer, of course."

"Yes," he said. "They let me play I was a major."

"I guessed a major," she said. "You'd always be pretty grand, of course."

Russell was amused. "Well, you see," he informed her, "as it happened,
we had at least several other majors in our army. Why would I always be
something 'pretty grand?'"

"You're related to the Palmers. Don't you notice they always affect the
pretty grand?"

"Then you think I'm only one of their affectations, I take it."

"Yes, you seem to be the most successful one they've got!" Alice said,
lightly. "You certainly do belong to them." And she laughed as if at something hidden from him. "Don't you?"

"But you've just excused me for that," he protested. "You said nobody
could be blamed for my being their third cousin. What a contradictory girl
you are!"

Alice shook her head. "Let's keep away from the kind of girl I am."

"No," he said. "That's just what I came here to talk about."

She shook her head again. "Let's keep first to the kind of man you are.
I'm glad you were in the War."

"Why?"

"Oh, I don't know." She was quiet a moment, for she was thinking that
here she spoke the truth: his service put about him a little glamour that
helped to please her with him. She had been pleased with him during their

walk; pleased with him on his own account; and now that pleasure was growing keener. She looked at him, and though the light in which she saw him was little more than starlight, she saw that he was looking steadily at her with a kindly and smiling seriousness. All at once it seemed to her that the night air was sweeter to breathe, as if a distant fragrance of new blossoms had been blown to her. She smiled back to him, and said, "Well, what kind of man are you?"

"I don't know; I've often wondered," he replied. "What kind of girl are you?"

"Don't you remember? I told you the other day. I'm just me!"

"But who is that?"

"You forget everything," said Alice. "You told me what kind of a girl I am. You seemed to think you'd taken quite a fancy to me from the very first."

"So I did," he agreed, heartily.

"But how quickly you forgot it!"

"Oh, no. I only want *you* to say what kind of a girl you are."

She mocked him. " 'I don't know; I've often wondered!' What kind of a girl does Mildred tell you I am? What has she said about me since she told you I was 'a Miss Adams?' "

"I don't know; I haven't asked her."

"Then *don't* ask her," Alice said, quickly.

"Why?"

"Because she's such a perfect creature and I'm such an imperfect one. Perfect creatures have the most perfect way of ruining the imperfect ones."

"But then they wouldn't be perfect. Not if they——"

"Oh, yes, they remain perfectly perfect," she assured him. "That's because they never go into details. They're not so vulgar as to come right out and *tell* that you've been in jail for stealing chickens. They just look absent-minded and say in a low voice, 'Oh, very; but I scarcely think you'd like her particularly'; and then begin to talk of something else right away."

His smile had disappeared. "Yes," he said, somewhat ruefully. "That does sound like Mildred. You certainly do seem to know her! Do you know everybody as well as that?"

"Not myself," Alice said. "I don't know myself at all. I got to wondering about that—about who I was—the other day after you walked home with me."

He uttered an exclamation, and added, explaining it, "You do give a man a chance to be fatuous, though! As if it were walking home with me that made you wonder about yourself!"

"It was," Alice informed him, coolly. "I was wondering what I wanted to make you think of me, in case I should ever happen to see you again."

This audacity appeared to take his breath. "By George!" he cried.

"You mustn't be astonished," she said. "What I decided then was that I would probably never dare to be just myself with you—not if I cared to have you want to see me again—and yet here I am, just being myself after all!"

"You *are* the cheeriest series of shocks," Russell exclaimed, whereupon Alice added to the series.

"Tell me: Is it a good policy for me to follow with you?" she asked, and he found the mockery in her voice delightful. "Would you advise me to offer you shocks as a sort of vacation from suavity?"

"Suavity" was yet another sketch of Mildred; a recognizable one, or it would not have been humorous. In Alice's hands, so dexterous in this work, her statuesque friend was becoming as ridiculous as a fine figure of wax left to the mercies of a satirist.

But the lively young sculptress knew better than to overdo: what she did must appear to spring all from mirth; so she laughed as if unwillingly, and said, "I *mustn't* laugh at Mildred! In the first place, she's your—your cousin. And in the second place, she's not meant to be funny; it isn't right to laugh at really splendid people who take themselves seriously. In the third place, you won't come again if I do."

"Don't be sure of that," Russell said, "whatever you do."

" 'Whatever I do?' " she echoed. "That sounds as if you thought I *could* be terrific! Be careful; there's one thing I could do that would keep you away."

"What's that?"

"I could tell you not to come," she said. "I wonder if I ought to."

"Why do you wonder if you 'ought to?' "

"Don't you guess?"

"No."

"Then let's both be mysteries to each other," she suggested. "I mystify you because I wonder, and you mystify me because you don't guess why I wonder. We'll let it go at that, shall we?"

"Very well; so long as it's certain that you *don't* tell me not to come again."

"I'll not tell you that—yet," she said. "In fact——" She paused, reflecting, with her head to one side. "In fact, I won't tell you not to come, probably, until I see that's what you want me to tell you. I'll let you out easily—and I'll be sure to see it. Even before you do, perhaps."

"That arrangement suits me," Russell returned, and his voice held no trace of jocularity: he had become serious. "It suits me better if you're enough in earnest to mean that I can come—oh, not whenever I want to; I don't expect so much!—but if you mean that I can see you pretty often."

"Of course I'm in earnest," she said. "But before I say you can come 'pretty often,' I'd like to know how much of my time you'd need if you did come 'whenever you want to'; and of course you wouldn't dare make any answer to that question except one. Wouldn't you let me have Thursdays out?"

"No, no," he protested. "I want to know. Will you let me come pretty often?"

"Lean toward me a little," Alice said. "I want you to understand." And as he obediently bent his head near hers, she inclined toward him as if to whisper; then, in a half-shout, she cried,

"Y*es!*"

He clapped his hands. "By George!" he said. "What a girl you are!"

"Why?"

"Well, for the first reason, because you have such gaieties as that one. I should think your father would actually like being ill, just to be in the house with you all the time."

"You mean by that," Alice inquired, "I keep my family cheerful with my amusing little ways?"

"Yes. Don't you?"

"There were only boys in your family, weren't there, Mr. Russell?"

"I was an only child, unfortunately."

"Yes," she said. "I see you hadn't any sisters."

For a moment he puzzled over her meaning, then saw it, and was more delighted with her than ever. "I can answer a question of yours, now, that I couldn't a while ago."

"Yes, I know," she returned, quietly.

"But how could you know?"

"It's the question I asked you about whether you were going to like living here," she said. "You're about to tell me that now you know you *will* like it."

"More telepathy!" he exclaimed. "Yes, that was it, precisely. I suppose the same thing's been said to you so many times that you——"

"No, it hasn't," Alice said, a little confused for the moment. "Not at all. I meant——" She paused, then asked in a gentle voice, "Would you really like to know?"

"Yes."

"Well, then, I was only afraid you didn't mean it."

"See here," he said. "I did mean it. I told you it was being pretty difficult for me to settle down to things again. Well, it's more difficult than you know, but I think I can pull through in fair spirits if I can see a girl like you 'pretty often.'"

"All right," she said, in a business-like tone. "I've told you that you can if you want to."

"I do want to," he assured her. "I do, indeed!"

"How often is 'pretty often,' Mr. Russell?"

"Would you walk with me sometimes? To-morrow?"

"Sometimes. Not to-morrow. The day after."

"That's splendid!" he said. "You'll walk with me day after to-morrow, and the night after that I'll see you at Miss Lamb's dance, won't I?"

But this fell rather chillingly upon Alice. "Miss Lamb's dance? Which Miss Lamb?" she asked.

"I don't know—it's the one that's just coming out of mourning."

"Oh, Henrietta—yes. Is her dance so soon? I'd forgotten."

"You'll be there, won't you?" he asked. "Please say you're going."

Alice did not respond at once, and he urged her again: "Please do promise you'll be there."

"No, I can't promise anything," she said, slowly. "You see, for one thing, papa might not be well enough."

"But if he is?" said Russell. "If he is you'll surely come, won't you? Or, perhaps——" He hesitated, then went on quickly, "I don't know the rules in this place yet, and different places have different rules; but do you have to have a chaperone, or don't girls just go to dances with the men sometimes? If they do, would you—would you let me take you?"

Alice was startled. "Good gracious!"

"What's the matter?"

"Don't you think your relatives—— Aren't you expected to go with Mildred —and Mrs. Palmer?"

"Not necessarily. It doesn't matter what I might be expected to do," he said. "Will you go with me?"

"I—— No; I couldn't."

"Why not?"

"I can't. I'm not going."

"But why?"

"Papa's not really any better," Alice said, huskily. "I'm too worried about him to go to a dance." Her voice sounded emotional, genuinely enough; there was something almost like a sob in it. "Let's talk of other things, please."

He acquiesced gently; but Mrs. Adams, who had been listening to the conversation at the open window, just overhead, did not hear him. She had correctly interpreted the sob in Alice's voice, and, trembling with sudden anger, she rose from her knees, and went fiercely to her husband's room.

CHAPTER XIII

He had not undressed, and he sat beside the table, smoking his pipe and reading his newspaper. Upon his forehead the lines in that old pattern, the historical map of his troubles, had grown a little vaguer lately; relaxed by the complacency of a man who not only finds his health restored, but sees the days before him promising once more a familiar routine that he has always liked to follow.

As his wife came in, closing the door behind her, he looked up cheerfully. "Well, mother," he said, "what's the news downstairs?"

"That's what I came to tell you," she informed him, grimly.

Adams lowered his newspaper to his knee and peered over his spectacles at her. She had remained by the door, standing, and the great greenish shadow of the small lamp-shade upon his table revealed her but dubiously. "Isn't everything all right?" he asked. "What's the matter?"

"Don't worry: I'm going to tell you," she said, her grimness not relaxed.

"There's matter enough, Virgil Adams. Matter enough to make me sick of being alive!"

With that, the markings on his brows began to emerge again in all their sharpness; the old pattern reappeared. "Oh, my, my!" he lamented. "I thought maybe we were all going to settle down to a little peace for a while. What's it about now?"

"It's about Alice. Did you think it was about *me* or anything for *myself*?"

Like some ready old machine, always in order, his irritability responded immediately and automatically to her emotion. "How in thunder could I think what it's about, or who it's for? *Say* it, and get it over!"

"Oh, I'll 'say' it," she promised, ominously. "What I've come to ask you is, How much longer do you expect me to put up with that old man and his doings?"

"Whose doings? What old man?"

She came at him, fiercely accusing. "You know well enough what old man, Virgil Adams! That old man who was here the other night."

"Mr. Lamb?"

"Yes; 'Mister Lamb!' " She mocked his voice. "What other old man would I be likely to mean, except J. A. Lamb?"

"What's he been doing now?" her husband inquired, satirically. "Where'd you get something new against him since the last time you——"

"Just this!" she cried. "The other night when that man was here, if I'd known how he was going to make my child suffer, I'd never have let him set his foot in my house."

Adams leaned back in his chair as though her absurdity had eased his mind. "Oh, I see," he said. "You've just gone plain crazy. That's the only explanation of such talk, and it suits the case."

"Hasn't that man made us all suffer every day of our lives?" she demanded. "I'd like to know why it is that my life and my children's lives have to be sacrificed to him?"

"How are they 'sacrificed' to him?"

"Because you keep on working for him! Because you keep on letting him hand out whatever miserable little pittance he chooses to give you; that's why! It's as if he were some horrible old Juggernaut and I had to see my children's own father throwing them under the wheels to keep him satisfied."

"I won't hear any more such stuff!" Lifting his paper, Adams affected to read.

"You'd better listen to me," she admonished him. "You might be sorry you didn't, in case he ever tried to set foot in my house again! I might tell him to his face what I think of him."

At this, Adams slapped the newspaper down upon his knee. "Oh, the devil! What's it matter what you think of him?"

"It had better matter to you!" she cried. "Do you suppose I'm going to submit forever to him and his family and what they're doing to my child?"

"What are he and his family doing to 'your child?' "

Mrs. Adams came out with it. "That snippy little Henrietta Lamb has always snubbed Alice every time she's ever had the chance. She's followed the lead of the other girls; they've always all of 'em been jealous of Alice because she dared to try and be happy, and because she's slowier and better-looking than they are, even though you do give her only about thirty-five cents a year to do it on! They've all done everything on earth they could to drive the young men away from her and belittle her to 'em; and this mean little Henrietta Lamb's been the worst of the whole crowd to Alice, every time she could see a chance."

"What for?" Adams asked, incredulously. "Why should she or anybody else pick on Alice?"

" 'Why?' 'What for?' " his wife repeated with a greater vehemence. "Do *you* ask me such a thing as that? Do *you* really want to know?"

"Yes; I'd want to know—I would if I believed it."

"Then I'll tell you," she said in a cold fury. "It's on account of *you*, Virgil, and nothing else in the world."

He hooted at her. "Oh, yes! These girls don't like *me*, so they pick on Alice."

"Quit your palavering and evading," she said. "A crowd of girls like that, when they get a pretty girl like Alice among them, they act just like wild beasts. They'll tear her to pieces, or else they'll chase her and run her out, because they know if she had half a chance she'd outshine 'em. They can't do that to a girl like Mildred Palmer because she's got money and family to back her. Now you listen to me, Virgil Adams: the way the world is now, money *is* family. Alice would have just as much 'family' as any of 'em—every single bit—if you hadn't fallen behind in the race."

"How did I——"

"Yes, you did!" she cried. "Twenty-five years ago when we were starting and this town was smaller, you and I could have gone with any of 'em if we'd tried hard enough. Look at the people we knew then that do hold their heads up alongside of anybody in this town! *Why* can they? Because the men of those families made money and gave their children everything that makes life worth living! Why can't we hold *our* heads up? Because those men passed you in the race. They went up the ladder, and you—you're still a clerk down at that old hole!"

"You leave that out, please," he said. "I thought you were going to tell me something Henrietta Lamb had done to our Alice."

"You *bet* I'm going to tell you," she assured him, vehemently. "But first I'm telling *why* she does it. It's because you've never given Alice any backing nor any background, and they all know they can do anything they like to her with perfect impunity. If she had the hundredth part of what *they* have to fall back on she'd have made 'em sing a mighty different song long ago!"

"How would she?"

"Oh, my heavens, but you're slow!" Mrs. Adams moaned. "Look here! You remember how practically all the nicest boys in this town used to come here a few years ago. Why, they were all crazy over her; and the girls *had* to be nice to her then. Look at the difference now! There'll be a whole month go by and not a young man come to call on her, let alone send her candy or flowers, or ever think of *taking* her any place—and yet she's prettier and brighter than she was when they used to come. It isn't the child's fault she couldn't hold 'em, is it? Poor thing, *she* tried hard enough! I suppose you'd say it was her fault, though."

"No; I wouldn't."

"Then whose fault is it?"

"Oh, mine, mine," he said, wearily. "I drove the young men away, of course."

"You might as well have driven 'em, Virgil. It amounts to just the same thing."

"How does it?"

"Because as they got older a good many of 'em began to think more about money; that's one thing. Money's at the bottom of it all, for that matter. Look at these country clubs and all such things: the other girls' families belong and we don't, and Alice don't; and she can't go unless somebody takes her, and nobody does any more. Look at the other girls' houses, and then look at our house, so shabby and old-fashioned she'd be pretty near ashamed to ask anybody to come in and sit down nowadays! Look at her clothes—oh, yes; you think you shelled out a lot for that little coat of hers and the hat and skirt she got last March; but it's nothing. Some of these girls nowadays spend more than your whole salary on their clothes. And what jewellery has she got? A plated watch and two or three little pins and rings of the kind people's maids wouldn't wear now. Good Lord, Virgil Adams, wake up! Don't sit there and tell me you don't know things like this mean *suffering* for the child!"

He had begun to rub his hands wretchedly back and forth over his bony knees, as if in that way he somewhat alleviated the tedium caused by her racking voice. "Oh, my, my!" he muttered. "*Oh*, my, my!"

"Yes, I should think you *would* say 'Oh, my, my!'" she took him up, loudly. "That doesn't help things much! If you ever wanted to *do* anything about it, the poor child might see some gleam of hope in her life. You don't *care* for her, that's the trouble; you don't care a single thing about her."

"I don't?"

"No; you don't. Why, even with your miserable little salary you could have given her more than you have. You're the closest man I ever knew: it's like pulling teeth to get a dollar out of you for her, now and then, and yet you hide some away, every month or so, in some wretched little investment or other. You——"

"Look here, now," he interrupted, angrily. "You look here! If I didn't put a little by whenever I could, in a bond or something, where would you be if anything happened to me? The insurance doctors never passed me; *you* know that. Haven't we got to have *something* to fall back on?"

"Yes, we have!" she cried. "We ought to have something to go on with right now, too, when we need it. Do you suppose these snippets would treat Alice the way they do if she could afford to *entertain?* They leave her out of their dinners and dances simply because they know she can't give any dinners and dances to leave them out of! They know she can't get *even,* and that's the whole story! That's why Henrietta Lamb's done this thing to her now."

Adams had gone back to his rubbing of his knees. "Oh, my, my!" he said. "*What* thing?"

She told him. "Your dear, grand, old Mister Lamb's Henrietta has sent out invitations for a large party—a *large* one. Everybody that is anybody in this town is asked, you can be sure. There's a very fine young man, a Mr. Russell, has just come to town, and he's interested in Alice, and he's asked her to go to this dance with him. Well, Alice can't accept. She can't go with him, though she'd give anything in the world to do it. Do you understand? The reason she can't is because Henrietta Lamb hasn't invited her. Do you want to know why Henrietta hasn't invited her? It's because she knows Alice can't get even, and because she thinks Alice ought to be snubbed like this on account of only being the daughter of one of her grandfather's clerks. I *hope* you understand!"

"Oh, my, my!" he said. "*Oh,* my, my!"

"That's your sweet old employer," his wife cried, tauntingly. "That's your dear, kind, grand old Mister Lamb! Alice has been left out of a good many smaller things, like big dinners and little dances, but this is just the same as serving her notice that she's out of everything! And it's all done by your dear, grand old——"

"Look here!" Adams exclaimed. "I don't want to hear any more of that! You can't hold him responsible for everything his grandchildren do, I guess! He probably doesn't know a thing about it. You don't suppose he's troubling *his* head over——"

But she burst out at him passionately. "Suppose *you* trouble *your* head about it! You'd better, Virgil Adams! You'd better, unless you want to see your child just dry up into a miserable old maid! She's still young and she has a chance for happiness, if she had a father that didn't bring a millstone to hang around her neck, instead of what he ought to give her! You just wait till you die and God asks you what you had in your breast instead of a heart!"

"Oh, my, my!" he groaned. "What's my heart got to do with it?"

"Nothing! You haven't got one or you'd give her what she needed. Am I asking anything you *can't* do? You know better; you know I'm not!"

At this he sat suddenly rigid, his troubled hands ceasing to rub his knees; and he looked at her fixedly. "Now, tell me," he said, slowly. "Just what *are* you asking?"

"You know!" she sobbed.

"You mean you've broken your word never to speak of *that* to me again?"

"What do *I* care for my word?" she cried, and, sinking to the floor at his feet, rocked herself back and forth there. "Do you suppose I'll let my 'word' keep me from struggling for a little happiness for my children? It won't, I tell you; it won't! I'll struggle for that till I die! I will, till I die—till I die!"

He rubbed his head now instead of his knees, and, shaking all over, he got up and began with uncertain steps to pace the floor. "Hell, hell, hell!" he said. "I've got to go through *that* again!"

"Yes, you have!" she sobbed. "Till I die."

"Yes; that's what you been after all the time I was getting well."

"Yes, I have, and I'll keep on till I die!"

"A fine wife for a man," he said. "Beggin' a man to be a dirty dog!"

"No! To be a *man*—and I'll keep on till I die!"

Adams again fell back upon his last solace: he walked, half staggering, up and down the room, swearing in a rhythmic repetition.

His wife had repetitions of her own, and she kept at them in a voice that rose to a higher and higher pitch, like the sound of an old well-pump. "Till I die! Till I die! Till I *die!*"

She ended in a scream; and Alice, coming up the stairs, thanked heaven that Russell had gone. She ran to her father's door and went in.

Adams looked at her, and gesticulated shakily at the convulsive figure on the floor. "Can you get her out of here?"

Alice helped Mrs. Adams to her feet; and the stricken woman threw her arms passionately about her daughter.

"Get her out!" Adams said, harshly; then cried, "Wait!"

Alice, moving toward the door, halted, and looked at him blankly, over her mother's shoulder. "What is it, papa?"

He stretched out his arm and pointed at her. "She says—she says you have a mean life, Alice."

"No, papa."

Mrs. Adams turned in her daughter's arms. "Do you hear her lie? Couldn't you be as brave as she is, Virgil?"

"Are you lying, Alice?" he asked. "Do you have a mean time?"

"No, papa."

He came toward her. "Look at me!" he said. "Things like this dance now—is that so hard to bear?"

Alice tried to say, "No, papa," again, but she couldn't. Suddenly and in spite of herself she began to cry.

"Do you hear her?" his wife sobbed. "Now do you——"

He waved at them fiercely. "Get out of here!" he said. "Both of you! Get out of here!"

As they went, he dropped in his chair and bent far forward, so that his haggard face was concealed from them. Then, as Alice closed the door, he began to rub his knees again, muttering, "Oh, my, my! *Oh*, my, my!"

CHAPTER XIV

There shone a jovial sun overhead on the appointed "day after to-morrow"; a day not cool yet of a temperature friendly to walkers; and the air, powdered with sunshine, had so much life in it that it seemed to sparkle. To Arthur Russell this was a day like a gay companion who pleased him well; but the gay companion at his side pleased him even better. She looked her prettiest, chattered her wittiest, smiled her wistfulest, and delighted him with all together.

"You look so happy it's easy to see your father's taken a good turn," he told her.

"Yes; he has this afternoon, at least," she said. "I might have other reasons for looking cheerful, though."

"For instance?"

"Exactly!" she said, giving him a sweet look just enough mocked by her laughter. "For instance!"

"Well, go on," he begged.

"Isn't it expected?" she asked.

"Of you, you mean?"

"No," she returned. "For you, I mean!"

In this style, which uses a word for any meaning that quick look and colourful gesture care to endow it with, she was an expert; and she carried it merrily on, leaving him at liberty (one of the great values of the style) to choose as he would how much or how little she meant. He was content to supply mere cues, for although he had little coquetry of his own, he had lately begun to find that the only interesting moments in his life were those during which Alice Adams coquetted with him. Happily, these obliging moments extended themselves to cover all the time he spent with her. However serious she might seem, whatever appeared to be her topic, all was thou-and-I.

He planned for more of it, seeing otherwise a dull evening ahead; and reverted, afterwhile, to a forbidden subject. "About that dance at Miss Lamb's—since your father's so much better——"

She flushed a little. "Now, now!" she chided him. "We agreed not to say any more about that."

"Yes, but since he *is* better——"

Alice shook her head. "He won't be better to-morrow. He always has a bad day after a good one—especially after such a good one as this is."

"But if this time it should be different," Russell persisted; "wouldn't you be willing to come—if he's better by to-morrow evening? Why not wait and decide at the last minute?"

She waved her hands airily. "What a pother!" she cried. "What does it matter whether poor little Alice Adams goes to a dance or not?"

"Well, I thought I'd made it clear that it looks fairly bleak to me if you don't go."

"Oh, yes!" she jeered.

"It's the simple truth," he insisted. "I don't care a great deal about dances these days; and if you aren't going to be there——"

"You could stay away," she suggested. "You wouldn't!"

"Unfortunately, I can't. I'm afraid I'm supposed to be the excuse. Miss Lamb, in her capacity as a friend of my relatives——"

"Oh, she's giving it for *you!* I see! On Mildred's account you mean?"

At that his face showed an increase of colour. "I suppose just on account of my being a cousin of Mildred's and of——"

"Of course! You'll have a beautiful time, too. Henrietta'll see that you have somebody to dance with besides Miss Dowling, poor man!"

"But what I want somebody to see is that I dance with you! And perhaps your father——"

"Wait!" she said, frowning as if she debated whether or not to tell him something of import; then, seeming to decide affirmatively, she asked: "Would you really like to know the truth about it?"

"If it isn't too unflattering."

"It hasn't anything to do with you at all," she said. "Of course I'd like to go with you and to dance with you—though you don't seem to realize that you wouldn't be permitted much time with me."

"Oh, yes, I——"

"Never mind!" she laughed. "Of course you wouldn't. But even if papa should be better to-morrow, I doubt if I'd go. In fact, I know I wouldn't. There's another reason besides papa."

"Is there?"

"Yes. The truth is, I don't get on with Henrietta Lamb. As a matter of fact, I dislike her, and of course that means she dislikes me. I should never think of asking her to anything *I* gave, and I really wonder she asks me to things *she* gives." This was a new inspiration; and Alice, beginning to see her way out of a perplexity, wished that she had thought of it earlier: she should have told him from the first that she and Henrietta had a feud, and consequently exchanged no invitations. Moreover, there was another thing to beset her with little anxieties: she might better not have told him from the first, as she had indeed told him by intimation, that she was the pampered daughter of an indulgent father, presumably able to indulge her; for now she must elaborately keep to the part. Veracity is usually simple; and its opposite, to be successful, should be as simple; but practitioners of the opposite are most often impulsive, like Alice; and, like her, they become enmeshed in elaborations.

"It wouldn't be very nice for me to go to her house," Alice went on, "when I wouldn't want her in mine. I've never admired her. I've always thought she was lacking in some things most people are supposed to be equipped with— for instance, a certain feeling about the death of a father who was always pretty decent to his daughter. Henrietta's father died just eleven months and twenty-seven days before your cousin's dance, but she couldn't stick out those few last days and make it a year; she was there." Alice stopped, then laughed ruefully, exclaiming, "But this is dreadful of me!"

"Is it?"

"Blackguarding her to you when she's giving a big party for you! Just the way Henrietta would blackguard me to you—heaven knows what she *wouldn't* say if she talked about me to you! It would be fair, of course, but—well, I'd rather she didn't!" And with that, Alice let her pretty hand, in its white glove, rest upon his arm for a moment; and he looked down at it, not unmoved to see it there. "I want to be unfair about just this," she said, letting a troubled laughter tremble through her appealing voice as she spoke. "I won't take advantage of her with anybody, except just—you! I'd a little rather you didn't hear anybody blackguard me, and, if you don't mind—could you promise not to give Henrietta the chance?"

It was charmingly done, with a humorous, faint pathos altogether genuine; and Russell found himself suddenly wanting to shout at her, "Oh, you *dear!*" Nothing else seemed adequate; but he controlled the impulse in favour of something more conservative. "Imagine any one speaking unkindly of you —not praising you!"

"Who *has* praised me to you?" she asked, quickly.

"I haven't talked about you with any one; but if I did, I know they'd——"

"No, no!" she cried, and went on, again accompanying her words with little tremulous runs of laughter. "You don't understand this town yet. You'll be surprised when you do; we're different. We talk about one another fearfully! Haven't I just proved it, the way I've been going for Henrietta? Of course I didn't say anything really very terrible about her, but that's only because I don't follow that practise the way most of the others do. They don't stop with the worst of the truth they can find: they make *up* things—yes, they really do! And, oh, I'd *rather* they didn't make up things about me—to you!"

"What difference would it make if they did?" he inquired, cheerfully. "I'd know they weren't true."

"Even if you did know that, they'd make a difference," she said. "Oh, yes, they would! It's too bad, but we don't like anything quite so well that's had specks on it, even if we've wiped the specks off;—it's just that much spoiled, and some things are all spoiled the instant they're the least bit spoiled. What a man thinks about a girl, for instance. Do you want to have what you think about me spoiled, Mr. Russell?"

"Oh, but that's already far beyond reach," he said, lightly.

"But it can't be!" she protested.

"Why not?"

"Because it never can be. Men don't change their minds about one another often: they make it quite an event when they do, and talk about it as if something important had happened. But a girl only has to go down-town with a shoe-string unfastened, and every man who sees her will change his mind about her. Don't you know that's true?"

"Not of myself, I think."

"There!" she cried. "That's precisely what every man in the world would say!"

"So you wouldn't trust me?"

"Well—I'll be awfully worried if you give 'em a chance to tell you that I'm too lazy to tie my shoe-strings!"

He laughed delightedly. "Is that what they do say?" he asked.

"Just about! Whatever they hope will get results." She shook her head wisely. "Oh, yes; we do that here!"

"But I don't mind loose shoe-strings," he said. "Not if they're yours."

"They'll find out what you do mind."

"But suppose," he said, looking at her whimsically; "suppose I wouldn't mind anything—so long as it's yours?"

She curtsied. "Oh, pretty enough! But a girl who's talked about has a weakness that's often a fatal one."

"What is it?"

"It's this: when she's talked about she isn't *there*. That's how they kill her."

"I'm afraid I don't follow you."

"Don't you see? If Henrietta—or Mildred—or any of 'em—or some of their mothers—oh, we *all* do it! Well, if any of 'em told you I didn't tie my shoe-strings, and if I were there, so that you could see me, you'd know it wasn't true. Even if I were sitting so that you couldn't see my feet, and couldn't tell whether the strings were tied or not just then, still you could look at me, and see that I wasn't the sort of girl to neglect my shoe-strings. But that isn't the way it happens: they'll get at you when I'm nowhere around and can't remind you of the sort of girl I really am."

"But you don't do that," he complained. "You don't remind me—you don't even tell me—the sort of girl you really are! I'd like to know."

"Let's be serious then," she said, and looked serious enough herself. "Would you honestly like to know?"

"Yes."

"Well, then, you must be careful."

" 'Careful?' " The word amused him.

"I mean careful not to get me mixed up," she said. "Careful not to mix up the girl you might hear somebody talking about with the me I honestly try to make you see. If you do get those two mixed up—well, the whole show'll be spoiled!"

"What makes you think so?"

"Because it's——" She checked herself, having begun to speak too impulsively; and she was disturbed, realizing in what tricky stuff she dealt. What had been on her lips to say was, "Because it's happened before!" She changed to, "Because it's so easy to spoil anything—easiest of all to spoil anything that's pleasant."

"That might depend."

"No; it's so. And if you care at all about—about knowing a girl who'd like someone to know her——"

"Just 'someone?' That's disappointing."

"Well—you," she said.

"Tell me how 'careful' you want me to be, then!"

"Well, don't you think it would be nice if you didn't give anybody the chance to talk about me the way—the way I've just been talking about Henrietta Lamb?"

With that they laughed together, and he said,

"You may be cutting me off from a great deal of information, you know."

"Yes," Alice admitted. "Somebody might begin to praise me to you, too; so it's dangerous to ask you to change the subject if I ever happen to be mentioned. But after all——" She paused.

" 'After all' isn't the end of a thought, is it?"

"Sometimes it is of a girl's thought; I suppose men are neater about their thoughts, and always finish 'em. It isn't the end of the thought I had then, though."

"What is the end of it?"

She looked at him impulsively. "Oh, it's foolish," she said, and she laughed as laughs one who proposes something probably impossible. "But *wouldn't* it be pleasant if two people could ever just keep themselves to themselves, so far as they two were concerned? I mean, if they could just manage to be friends without people talking about it, or talking to *them* about it?"

"I suppose that might be rather difficult," he said, more amused than impressed by her idea.

"I don't know: it might be done," she returned, hopefully. "Especially in a town of this size; it's grown so it's quite a huge place these days. People can keep themselves to themselves in a big place better, you know. For instance, nobody knows that you and I are taking a walk together today."

"How absurd, when here we are on exhibition!"

"No; we aren't."

"We aren't?"

"Not a bit of it!" she laughed. "We were the other day, when you walked home with me, but anybody could tell that had just happened by chance, on account of your overtaking me; people can always see things like that. But we're not on exhibition now. Look where I've led you!"

Amused and a little bewildered, he looked up and down the street, which was one of gaunt-faced apartment-houses, old, sooty, frame boarding-houses, small groceries and drug-stores, laundries and one-room plumbers' shops, with the sign of a clairvoyant here and there.

"You see?" she said. "I've been leading you without your knowing it. Of course that's because you're new to the town, and you give yourself up to the guidance of an old citizen."

"I'm not so sure, Miss Adams. It might mean that I don't care where I follow so long as I follow you."

"Very well," she said. "I'd like you to keep on following me—at least long enough for me to show you that there's something nicer ahead of us than this dingy street."

"Is that figurative?" he asked.

"Might be!" she returned, gaily. "There's a pretty little park at the end, but it's very proletarian, and nobody you and I know will be more likely to see us there than on this street."

"What an imagination you have!" he exclaimed. "You turn our proper little walk into a Parisian adventure."

She looked at him in what seemed to be a momentary grave puzzlement. "Perhaps you feel that a Parisian adventure mightn't please your—your relatives?"

"Why, no," he returned. "You seem to think of them oftener than I do."

This appeared to amuse Alice, or at least to please her, for she laughed. "Then I can afford to quit thinking of them, I suppose. It's only that I used to be quite a friend of Mildred's—but there! we needn't to go into that. I've never been a friend of Henrietta Lamb's, though, and I almost wish she weren't taking such pains to be a friend of yours."

"Oh, but she's not. It's all on account of——"

"On Mildred's account," Alice finished this for him, coolly. "Yes, of course."

"It's on account of the two families," he was at pains to explain, a little awkwardly. "It's because I'm a relative of the Palmers, and the Palmers and the Lambs seem to be old family friends."

"Something the Adamses certainly are not," Alice said. "Not with either of 'em; particularly not with the Lambs!" And here, scarce aware of what impelled her, she returned to her former elaborations and colourings. "You see, the differences between Henrietta and me aren't entirely personal: I couldn't go to her house even if I liked her. The Lambs and Adamses don't get on with each other, and we've just about come to the breaking-point as it happens."

"I hope it's nothing to bother you."

"Why? A lot of things bother me."

"I'm sorry they do," he said, and seemed simply to mean it.

She nodded gratefully. "That's nice of you, Mr. Russell. It helps. The break between the Adamses and the Lambs is a pretty bothersome thing. It's been coming on a long time." She sighed deeply, and the sigh was half genuine; this half being for her father, but the other half probably belonged to her instinctive rendering of Juliet Capulet, daughter to a warring house. "I hate it all so!" she added.

"Of course you must."

"I suppose most quarrels between families are on account of business," she said. "That's why they're so sordid. Certainly the Lambs seem a sordid lot to me, though of course I'm biased." And with that she began to sketch a history of the commercial antagonism that had risen between the Adamses and the Lambs.

The sketching was spontaneous and dramatic. Mathematics had no part in it; nor was there accurate definition of Mr. Adams's relation to the institution of Lamb and Company. The point was clouded, in fact; though that might easily be set down to the general haziness of young ladies confronted with the mysteries of trade or commerce. Mr. Adams either had been a vague sort of junior member of the firm, it appeared, or else he should have been made some such thing; at all events, he was an old mainstay of the business; and he, as much as any Lamb, had helped to build up the prosperity of the company. But at last, tired of providing so much intelligence and energy for which other people took profit greater than his own, he had decided to leave the company and found a business entirely for himself. The Lambs were going to be enraged when they learned what was afoot.

Such was the impression, a little misted, wrought by Alice's quick narrative. But there was dolorous fact behind it: Adams had succumbed.

His wife, grave and nervous, rather than triumphant, in success, had told their daughter that the great J. A. would be furious and possibly vindictive. Adams was afraid of him, she said.

"But what for, mama?" Alice asked, since this seemed a turn of affairs out of reason. "What in the world has Mr. Lamb to do with papa's leaving the company to set up for himself? What right has he to be angry about it? If he's such a friend as he claims to be, I should think he'd be glad—that is, if the glue factory turns out well. What will he be angry for?"

Mrs. Adams gave Alice an uneasy glance, hesitated, and then explained that a resignation from Lamb's had always been looked upon, especially by "that old man," as treachery. You were supposed to die in the service, she said bitterly, and her daughter, a little mystified, accepted this explanation. Adams had not spoken to her of his surrender; he seemed not inclined to speak to her at all, or to any one.

Alice was not serious too long, and she began to laugh as she came to the end of her decorative sketch. "After all, the whole thing is perfectly ridiculous," she said. "In fact, it's *funny!* That's on account of what papa's going to throw over the Lamb business *for!* To save your life you couldn't imagine what he's going to do!"

"I won't try, then," Russell assented.

"It takes all the romance out of *me*," she laughed. "You'll never go for a Parisian walk with me again, after I tell you what I'll be heiress to." They had come to the entrance of the little park; and, as Alice had said, it was a pretty place, especially on a day so radiant. Trees of the oldest forest stood there, hale and serene over the trim, bright grass; and the proletarians had not come from their factories at this hour; only a few mothers and their babies were to be seen, here and there, in the shade. "I think I'll postpone telling you about it till we get nearly home again," Alice said, as they began to saunter down one of the gravelled paths. "There's a bench beside a spring farther on; we can sit there and talk about a lot of things—things not so sticky as my dowry's going to be."

" 'Sticky?' " he echoed. "What in the world——"

She laughed despairingly.

"A glue factory!"

Then he laughed, too, as much from friendliness as from amusement; and she remembered to tell him that the project of a glue factory was still "an Adams secret." It would be known soon, however, she added; and the whole Lamb connection would probably begin saying all sorts of things, heaven knew what!

Thus Alice built her walls of flimsy, working always gaily, or with at least the air of gaiety; and even as she rattled on, there was somewhere in her mind a constant little wonder. Everything she said seemed to be necessary to support something else she had said. How had it happened? She found herself telling him that since her father had decided on making so great a change in his ways, she and her mother hoped at last to persuade him to give up that "foolish little house" he had been so obstinate about; and she checked herself abruptly on this declivity just as she was about to slide into a remark concerning her own preference for a "country place." Discretion caught her in time; and something else, in company with discretion, caught her, for she stopped short in her talk and blushed.

They had taken possession of the bench beside the spring, by this time; and Russell, his elbow on the back of the bench and his chin on his hand, the better to look at her, had no guess at the cause of the blush, but was content to find it lovely. At his first sight of Alice she had seemed pretty in the particular way of being pretty that he happened to like best; and, with every moment he spent with her, this prettiness appeared to increase. He felt that he could not look at her enough: his gaze followed the fluttering of the graceful hands in almost continual gesture as she talked; then lifted happily to the vivacious face again. She charmed him.

After her abrupt pause, she sighed, then looked at him with her eyebrows lifted in a comedy appeal. "You haven't said you wouldn't give Henrietta the chance," she said, in the softest voice that can still have a little laugh running in it.

He was puzzled. "Give Henrietta the chance?"

"You know! You'll let me keep on being unfair, won't you? Not give the other girls a chance to get even?"

He promised, heartily.

CHAPTER XV

Alice had said that no one who knew either Russell or herself would be likely to see them in the park or upon the dingy street; but although they returned by that same ungenteel thoroughfare they were seen by a person who knew them both. Also, with some surprise on the part of Russell, and something more poignant than surprise for Alice, they saw this person.

All of the dingy street was ugly, but the greater part of it appeared to be honest. The two pedestrians came upon a block or two, however, where it offered suggestions of a less upright character, like a steady enough workingman with a naughty book sticking out of his pocket. Three or four dim shops, a single story in height, exhibited foul signboards, yet fair enough so far as the wording went; one proclaiming a tobacconist, one a junk-dealer, one a dispenser of "soft drinks and cigars." The most credulous would have doubted these signboards; for the craft of the modern tradesman is exerted to lure indoors the passing glance, since if the glance is pleased the feet may follow; but this alleged tobacconist and his neighbours had long been fond of dust on their windows, evidently, and shades were pulled far down on the glass of their doors. Thus the public eye, small of pupil in the light of the open street, was intentionally not invited to the dusky interiors. Something different from mere lack of enterprise was apparent; and the signboards

might have been omitted; they were pains thrown away, since it was plain
to the world that the business parts of these shops were the brighter back
rooms implied by the dark front rooms; and that the commerce there was
in perilous new liquors and in dice and rough girls.

Nothing could have been more innocent than the serenity with which
these wicked little places revealed themselves for what they were; and, bound
by this final tie of guilelessness, they stood together in a row which ended
with a companionable barber-shop, much like them. Beyond was a series of
soot-harried frame two-story houses, once part of a cheerful neighbourhood
when the town was middle-aged and settled, and not old and growing. These
houses, all carrying the label, "Rooms," had the worried look of vacancy that
houses have when they are too full of everybody without being anybody's
home; and there was, too, a surreptitious air about them, as if, like the false
little shops, they advertised something by concealing it.

One of them—the one next to the barber-shop—had across its front an
ample, jig-sawed veranda, where aforetime, no doubt, the father of a family
had fanned himself with a palm-leaf fan on Sunday afternoons, watching the
surreys go by, and where his daughter listened to mandolins and badinage
on starlit evenings; but, although youth still held the veranda, both the youth
and the veranda were in decay. The four or five young men who lounged
there this afternoon were of a type known to shady pool-parlours. Hats found
no favour with them; all of them wore caps; and their tight clothes, apparently
from a common source, showed a vivacious fancy for oblique pockets, false
belts, and Easter-egg colourings. Another thing common to the group was
the expression of eye and mouth; and Alice, in the midst of her other
thoughts, had a distasteful thought about this.

The veranda was within a dozen feet of the sidewalk, and as she and her
escort came nearer, she took note of the young men, her face hardening a
little, even before she suspected there might be a resemblance between them
and any one she knew. Then she observed that each of these loungers wore
not for the occasion, but as of habit, a look of furtively amused contempt;
the mouth smiled to one side as if not to dislodge a cigarette, while the eyes
kept languidly superior. All at once Alice was reminded of Walter; and the
slight frown caused by this idea had just begun to darken her forehead when
Walter himself stepped out of the open door of the house and appeared upon
the veranda. Upon his head was a new straw hat, and in his hand was a
Malacca stick with an ivory top, for Alice had finally decided against it for
herself and had given it to him. His mood was lively: he twirled the stick
through his fingers like a drum-major's baton, and whistled loudly.

Moreover, he was indeed accompanied. With him was a thin girl who had
made a violent black-and-white poster of herself: black dress, black flimsy
boa, black stockings, white slippers, great black hat down upon the black
eyes; and beneath the hat a curve of cheek and chin made white as white-
wash, and in strong bilateral motion with gum.

The loungers on the veranda were familiars of the pair; hailed them with cacklings; and one began to sing, in a voice all tin:

> "Then my skirt, Sal, and me did go
> Right straight to the moving-pitcher show.
> *Oh*, you bashful vamp!"

The girl laughed airily. "God, but you guys are wise!" she said. "Come on, Wallie."

Walter stared at his sister; then grinned faintly, and nodded at Russell as the latter lifted his hat in salutation. Alice uttered an incoherent syllable of exclamation, and, as she began to walk faster, she bit her lip hard, not in order to look wistful, this time, but to help her keep tears of anger from her eyes.

Russell laughed cheerfully. "Your brother certainly seems to have found the place for 'colour' to-day," he said. "That girl's talk must be full of it."

But Alice had forgotten the colour she herself had used in accounting for Walter's peculiarities, and she did not understand. "What?" she said, huskily.

"Don't you remember telling me about him? How he was going to write, probably, and would go anywhere to pick up types and get them to talk?"

She kept her eyes ahead, and said sharply, "I think his literary tastes scarcely cover *this* case!"

"Don't be too sure. He didn't look at all disconcerted. He didn't seem to mind your seeing him."

"That's all the worse, isn't it?"

"Why, no," her friend said, genially. "It means he didn't consider that he was engaged in anything out of the way. You can't expect to understand everything boys do at his age; they do all sorts of queer things, and outgrow them. Your brother evidently has a taste for queer people, and very likely he's been at least half sincere when he's made you believe he had a literary motive behind it. We all go through——"

"Thanks, Mr. Russell," she interrupted. "Let's don't say any more."

He looked at her flushed face and enlarged eyes; and he liked her all the better for her indignation: this was how good sisters ought to feel, he thought, failing to understand that most of what she felt was not about Walter. He ventured only a word more. "Try not to mind it so much; it really doesn't amount to anything."

She shook her head, and they went on in silence; she did not look at him again until they stopped before her own house. Then she gave him only one glimpse of her eyes before she looked down. "It's spoiled, isn't it?" she said, in a low voice.

"What's 'spoiled?'"

"Our walk—well, everything. Somehow it always—is."

"'Always is' what?" he asked.

"Spoiled," she said.

He laughed at that; but without looking at him she suddenly offered him her hand, and, as he took it, he felt a hurried, violent pressure upon his fingers, as if she meant to thank him almost passionately for being kind. She was gone before he could speak to her again.

In her room, with the door locked, she did not go to her mirror, but to her bed, flinging herself face down, not caring how far the pillows put her hat awry. Sheer grief had followed her anger; grief for the calamitous end of her bright afternoon, grief for the "end of everything," as she thought then. Nevertheless, she gradually grew more composed, and, when her mother tapped on the door presently, let her in. Mrs. Adams looked at her with quick apprehension.

"Oh, poor child! Wasn't he—"

Alice told her. "You see how it—how it made me look, mama," she quavered, having concluded her narrative. "I'd tried to cover up Walter's awfulness at the dance with that story about his being 'literary,' but no story was big enough to cover this up—and oh! it must make him think I tell stories about other things!"

"No, no, no!" Mrs. Adams protested. "Don't you see? At the worst, all *he* could think is that Walter told stories to you about why he likes to be with such dreadful people, and you believed them. That's all *he'd* think; don't you see?"

Alice's wet eyes began to show a little hopefulness. "You honestly think it might be that way, mama?"

"Why, from what you've told me he said, I *know* it's that way. Didn't he say he wanted to come again?"

"N-no," Alice said, uncertainly. "But I think he will. At least I begin to think so now. He—" She stopped.

"From all you tell me, he seems to be a very desirable young man," Mrs. Adams said, primly.

Her daughter was silent for several moments; then new tears gathered upon her downcast lashes. "He's just—dear!" she faltered.

Mrs. Adams nodded. "He's told you he isn't engaged, hasn't he?"

"No. But I know he isn't. Maybe when he first came here he was near it, but I know he's not."

"I guess Mildred Palmer would *like* him to be, all right!" Mrs. Adams was frank enough to say, rather triumphantly; and Alice, with a lowered head, murmured:

"Anybody—would."

The words were all but inaudible.

"Don't you worry," her mother said, and patted her on the shoulder. "Everything will come out all right; don't you fear, Alice. Can't you see that beside any other girl in town you're just a perfect *queen?* Do you think any young man that wasn't prejudiced, or something, would need more than just one look to—"

But Alice moved away from the caressing hand. "Never mind, mama. I

wonder he looks at me at all. And if he does again, after seeing my brother
with those horrible people——"

"Now, now!" Mrs. Adams interrupted, expostulating mournfully. "I'm sure
Walter's a *good* boy——"

"You are?" Alice cried, with a sudden vigour. "You *are?*"

"I'm sure he's *good*, yes—and if he isn't, it's not his fault. It's mine."

"What nonsense!"

"No, it's true," Mrs. Adams lamented. "I tried to bring him up to be good,
God knows; and when he was little he was the best boy I ever saw. When
he came from Sunday-school he'd always run to me and we'd go over the
lesson together; and he let me come in his room at night to hear his prayers
almost until he was sixteen. Most boys won't do that with their mothers—
not nearly that long. I tried so hard to bring him up right—but if anything's
gone wrong it's my fault."

"How could it be? You've just said——"

"It's because I didn't make your father take this—this new step earlier.
Then Walter might have had all the advantages that other——"

"Oh, mama, *please!*" Alice begged her. "Let's don't go over all that again.
Isn't it more important to think what's to be done about him? Is he going
to be allowed to go on disgracing us as he does?"

Mrs. Adams sighed profoundly. "I don't know what to do," she confessed,
unhappily. "Your father's so upset about—about this new step he's taking—
I don't feel as if we ought to——"

"No, no!" Alice cried. "Papa mustn't be distressed with this, on top of
everything else. But *something's* got to be done about Walter."

"What can be?" her mother asked, helplessly. "What can be?"

Alice admitted that she didn't know.

At dinner, an hour later, Walter's habitually veiled glance lifted, now and
then, to touch her furtively;—he was waiting, as he would have said, for her
to "spring it"; and he had prepared a brief and sincere defense to the effect
that he made his own living, and would like to inquire whose business it was
to offer intrusive comment upon his private conduct. But she said nothing,
while his father and mother were as silent as she. Walter concluded that
there was to be no attack, but changed his mind when his father, who ate
only a little, and broodingly at that, rose to leave the table and spoke to him.

"Walter," he said, "when you've finished I wish you'd come up to my room.
I got something I want to say to you."

Walter shot a hard look at his apathetic sister, then turned to his father.
"Make it to-morrow," he said. "This is Satad'y night and I got a date."

"No," Adams said, frowning. "You come up before you go out. It's important."

"All right; I've had all I want to eat," Walter returned. "I got a few minutes. Make it quick."

He followed his father upstairs, and when they were in the room together Adams shut the door, sat down, and began to rub his knees.

"Rheumatism?" the boy inquired, slyly. "That what you want to talk to me about?"

"No." But Adams did not go on; he seemed to be in difficulties for words, and Walter decided to help him.

"Hop ahead and spring it," he said. "Get it off your mind: I'll tell the world *I* should worry! You aren't goin' to bother *me* any, so why bother yourself? Alice hopped home and told you she saw me playin' around with some pretty gay-lookin' berries and you——"

"Alice?" his father said, obviously surprised. "It's nothing about Alice."

"Didn't she tell you——"

"I haven't talked with her all day."

"Oh, I see," Walter said. "She told mother and mother told you."

"No, neither of 'em have told me anything. What was there to tell?"

Walter laughed. "Oh, it's nothin'," he said. "I was just startin' out to buy a girl friend o' mine a rhinestone buckle I lost to her on a bet, this afternoon, and Alice came along with that big Russell fish; and I thought she looked sore. She expects me to like the kind she likes, and I don't like 'em. I thought she'd prob'ly got you all stirred up about it."

"No, no," his father said, peevishly. "I don't know anything about it, and I don't care to know anything about it. I want to talk to you about something important."

Then, as he was again silent, Walter said, "Well, *talk* about it; I'm listening."

"It's this," Adams began, heavily. "It's about me going into this glue business. Your mother's told you, hasn't she?"

"She said you were goin' to leave the old place down-town and start a glue factory. That's all I know about it; I got my own affairs to 'tend to."

"Well, this is your affair," his father said, frowning. "You can't stay with Lamb and Company."

Walter looked a little startled. "What you mean, I can't? Why not?"

"You've got to help me," Adams explained slowly; and he frowned more deeply, as if the interview were growing increasingly laborious for him. "It's going to be a big pull to get this business on its feet."

"Yes!" Walter exclaimed with a sharp skepticism. "I should say it was!" He stared at his father incredulously. "Look here; aren't you just a little bit sudden, the way you're goin' about things? You've let mother shove you a little too fast, haven't you? Do you know anything about what it means to set up a new business these days?"

"Yes, I know all about it," Adams said. "About this business, I do."

"How do you?"

"Because I made a long study of it. I'm not afraid of going about it the wrong way; but it's a hard job and you'll have to put in all whatever sense and strength you've got."

Walter began to breathe quickly, and his lips were agitated; then he set them obstinately. "Oh, I will," he said.

"Yes, you will," Adams returned, not noticing that his son's inflection was satiric. "It's going to take every bit of energy in your body, and all the energy I got left in mine, and every cent of the little I've saved, besides something I'll have to raise on this house. I'm going right at it, now I've got to; and you'll have to quit Lamb's by the end of next week."

"Oh, I will?" Walter's voice grew louder, and there was a shrillness in it. "I got to quit Lamb's the end of next week, have I?" He stepped forward, angrily. "Listen!" he said. "I'm not walkin' out o' Lamb's, see? I'm not quittin' down there: I stay with 'em, see?"

Adams looked up at him, astonished. "You'll leave there next Saturday," he said. "I've got to have you."

"You don't anything o' the kind," Walter told him, sharply. "Do you expect to pay me anything?"

"I'd pay you about what you been getting down there."

"Then pay somebody else; I don't know anything about glue. You get somebody else."

"No. You've got to——"

Walter cut him off with the utmost vehemence. "Don't tell me what I got to do! I know what I got to do better'n you, I guess! I stay at Lamb's, see?"

Adams rose angrily. "You'll do what I tell you. You can't stay down there."

"Why can't I?"

"Because I won't let you."

"Listen! Keep on not lettin' me: I'll be there just the same."

At that his father broke into a sour laughter. "They won't let you, Walter! They won't have you down there after they find out I'm going."

"Why won't they? You don't think they're goin' to be all shot to pieces over losin' you, do you?"

"I tell you they won't let you stay," his father insisted, loudly.

"Why, what do they care whether you go or not?"

"They'll care enough to fire you, my boy!"

"Look here, then; show me why."

"They'll do it!"

"Yes," Walter jeered; "you keep sayin' they will, but when I ask you to show me why, you keep sayin' they will! That makes little headway with me, I can tell you!"

Adams groaned, and, rubbing his head, began to pace the floor. Walter's refusal was something he had not anticipated; and he felt the weakness of his own attempt to meet it: he seemed powerless to do anything but utter angry words, which, as Walter said, made little headway. "Oh, my, my!" he muttered. "Oh, my, my!"

Walter, usually sallow, had grown pale: he watched his father narrowly, and now took a sudden resolution. "Look here," he said. "When you say

Lamb's is likely to fire me because you're goin' to quit, you talk like the people that have to be locked up. I don't know where you get such things in your head; Lamb and Company won't know you're gone. Listen: I can stay there long as I want to. But I'll tell you what I'll do: make it worth my while and I'll hook up with your old glue factory, after all."

Adams stopped his pacing abruptly, and stared at him. " 'Make it worth your while?' What you mean?"

"I got a good use for three hundred dollars right now," Walter said. "Let me have it and I'll quit Lamb's to work for you. Don't let me have it and I *swear* I won't!"

"Are you crazy?"

"Is everybody crazy that needs three hundred dollars?"

"Yes," Adams said. "They are if they ask *me* for it, when I got to stretch every cent I can lay my hands on to make it look like a dollar!"

"You won't do it?"

Adams burst out at him. "You little fool! If I had three hundred dollars to throw away, besides the pay I expected to give you, haven't you got sense enough to see I could hire a man worth three hundred dollars more to me than you'd be? It's a *fine* time to ask me for three hundred dollars, isn't it! What *for*? Rhinestone buckles to throw around on your 'girl friends?' Shame on you! Ask me to *bribe* you to help yourself and your own family!"

"I'll give you a last chance," Walter said. "Either you do what I want, or I won't do what you want. Don't ask me again after this, because——"

Adams interrupted him fiercely. " 'Ask you again!' Don't worry about that, my boy! All I ask you is to get out o' my room."

"Look here," Walter said, quietly; and his lopsided smile distorted his livid cheek. "Look here: I expect *you* wouldn't give me three hundred dollars to save my life, would you?"

"You make me sick," Adams said, in his bitterness. "Get out of here."

Walter went out, whistling; and Adams drooped into his old chair again as the door closed. "*Oh*, my, my!" he groaned. "Oh, Lordy, Lordy! The way of the transgressor——"

CHAPTER XVI

He meant his own transgression and his own way; for Walter's stubborn refusal appeared to Adams just then as one of the inexplicable but righteous besettings he must encounter in following that way. "Oh, Lordy, Lord!" he groaned, and then, as resentment moved him—"That dang boy! Dang idiot!" Yet he knew himself for a greater idiot because he had not been able to tell Walter the truth. He could not bring himself to do it, nor even to state his case in its best terms; and that was because he felt that even in its best terms the case was a bad one.

Of all his regrets the greatest was that in a moment of vanity and tenderness, twenty-five years ago, he had told his young wife a business secret. He had wanted to show how important her husband was becoming, and how much the head of the universe, J. A. Lamb, trusted to his integrity and ability. The great man had an idea: he thought of "branching out a little," he told Adams confidentially, and there were possibilities of profit in glue.

What he wanted was a liquid glue to be put into little bottles and sold cheaply. "The kind of thing that sells itself," he said; "the kind of thing that pays its own small way as it goes along, until it has profits enough to begin advertising it right. Everybody has to use glue, and if I make mine convenient and cheap, everybody'll buy mine. But it's got to be glue that'll *stick*; it's got to be the best; and if we find how to make it we've got to keep it a big secret, of course, or anybody can steal it from us. There was a man here last month; he knew a formula he wanted to sell me, 'sight unseen'; but he was in such a hurry I got suspicious, and I found he'd managed to steal it, working for the big packers in their glue-works. We've got to find a better glue than that, anyhow. I'm going to set you and Campbell at it. You're a practical, wide-awake young feller, and Campbell's a mighty good chemist; I guess you two boys ought to make something happen."

His guess was shrewd enough. Working in a shed a little way outside the town, where their cheery employer visited them sometimes to study their malodorous stews, the two young men found what Lamb had set them to find. But Campbell was thoughtful over the discovery. "Look here," he said. "Why ain't this just about yours and mine? After all, it may be Lamb's money that's paid for the stuff we've used, but it hasn't cost much."

"But he pays *us*," Adams remonstrated, horrified by his companion's idea. "He paid us to do it. It belongs absolutely to him."

"Oh, I know he *thinks* it does," Campbell admitted, plaintively. "I suppose we've got to let him take it. It's not patentable, and he'll have to do pretty well by us when he starts his factory, because he's got to depend on us to run the making of the stuff so that the workmen can't get onto the process. You better ask him the same salary I do, and mine's going to be high."

But the high salary, thus pleasantly imagined, was never paid. Campbell died of typhoid fever, that summer, leaving Adams and his employer the only possessors of the formula, an unwritten one; and Adams, pleased to think himself more important to the great man than ever, told his wife that there could be little doubt of his being put in sole charge of the prospective glue-works. Unfortunately, the enterprise remained prospective.

Its projector had already become "inveigled into another side-line," as he told Adams. One of his sons had persuaded him to take up a "cough-lozenge," to be called the "Jalamb Balm Trochee"; and the lozenge did well enough to amuse Mr. Lamb and occupy his spare time, which was really about all he had asked of the glue project. He had "all the *money* anybody ought to want," he said, when Adams urged him; and he could "start up this little glue side-line" at any time; the formula was safe in their two heads.

At intervals Adams would seek opportunity to speak of "the little glue side-line" to his patron, and to suggest that the years were passing; but Lamb, petting other hobbies, had lost interest. "Oh, I'll start it up some day, maybe. If I don't, I may turn it over to my heirs: it's always an asset, worth something or other, of course. We'll probably take it up some day, though, you and I."

The sun persistently declined to rise on that day, and, as time went on, Adams saw that his rather timid urgings bored his employer, and he ceased to bring up the subject. Lamb apparently forgot all about glue, but Adams discovered that unfortunately there was someone else who remembered it.

"It's really *yours*," she argued, that painful day when for the first time she suggested his using his knowledge for the benefit of himself and his family. "Mr. Campbell might have had a right to part of it, but he died and didn't leave any kin, so it belongs to you."

"Suppose J. A. Lamb hired me to saw some wood," Adams said. "Would the sticks belong to me?"

"He hasn't got any right to take your invention and bury it," she protested. "What good is it doing him if he doesn't *do* anything with it? What good is it doing *anybody*? None in the world! And what harm would it do him if you went ahead and did this for yourself and for your children? None in the world! And what could he do to you if he *was* old pig enough to get angry with you for doing it? He couldn't do a single thing, and you've admitted he couldn't, yourself. So what's your reason for depriving your children and your wife of the benefits you know you could give 'em?"

"Nothing but decency," he answered; and she had her reply ready for that. It seemed to him that, strive as he would, he could not reach her mind with even the plainest language; while everything that she said to him, with such vehemence, sounded like so much obstinate gibberish. Over and over he pressed her with the same illustration, on the point of ownership, though he thought he was varying it.

"Suppose he hired me to build him a house: would that be *my* house?"

"He didn't hire you to build him a house. You and Campbell invented——"

"Look here: suppose you give a cook a soup-bone and some vegetables, and pay her to make you a soup: has she got a right to take and sell it? You know better!"

"I know *one* thing: if that old man tried to keep your own invention from you he's no better than a robber!"

They never found any point of contact in all their passionate discussions of this ethical question; and the question was no more settled between them, now that Adams had succumbed, than it had ever been. But at least the wrangling about it was over: they were grave together, almost silent, and an uneasiness prevailed with her as much as with him.

He had already been out of the house, to walk about the small green yard;

and on Monday afternoon he sent for a taxicab and went down-town, but kept a long way from the "wholesale section," where stood the formidable old oblong pile of Lamb and Company. He arranged for the sale of the bonds he had laid away, and for placing a mortgage upon his house; and on his way home, after five o'clock, he went to see an old friend, a man whose term of service with Lamb and Company was even a little longer than his own.

This veteran, returned from the day's work, was sitting in front of the apartment house where he lived, but when the cab stopped at the curb he rose and came forward, offering a jocular greeting. "Well, well, Virgil Adams! I always thought you had a sporty streak in you. Travel in your own hired private automobile nowadays, do you? Pamperin' yourself because you're still layin' off sick, I expect."

"Oh, I'm well enough again, Charley Lohr," Adams said, as he got out and shook hands. Then, telling the driver to wait, he took his friend's arm, walked to the bench with him, and sat down. "I been practically well for some time," he said. "I'm fixin' to get into harness again."

"Bein' sick has certainly produced a change of heart in you," his friend laughed. "You're the last man I ever expected to see blowin' yourself—or anybody else—to a taxicab! For that matter, I never heard of you bein' in *any* kind of a cab, 'less'n it might be when you been pall-bearer for somebody. What's come over you?"

"Well, I got to turn over a new leaf, and that's a fact," Adams said. "I got a lot to do, and the only way to accomplish it, it's got to be done soon, or I won't have anything to live on while I'm doing it."

"What you talkin' about? What you got to do except to get strong enough to come back to the old place?"

"Well——" Adams paused, then coughed, and said slowly, "Fact is, Charley Lohr, I been thinking likely I wouldn't come back."

"What! What you talkin' about?"

"No," said Adams. "I been thinking I might likely kind of branch out on my own account."

"Well, I'll be doggoned!" Old Charley Lohr was amazed; he ruffled up his gray moustache with thumb and forefinger, leaving his mouth open beneath, like a dark cave under a tangled wintry thicket. "Why, that's the doggonedest thing I ever heard!" he said. "I already am the oldest inhabitant down there, but if you go, there won't be anybody else of the old generation at all. What on earth you thinkin' of goin' into?"

"Well," said Adams, "I rather you didn't mention it till I get started—of course anybody'll know what it is by then—but I *have* been kind of planning to put a liquid glue on the market."

His friend, still ruffling the gray moustache upward, stared at him in frowning perplexity. "Glue?" he said. "*Glue!*"

"Yes. I been sort of milling over the idea of taking up something like that."

"Handlin' it for some firm, you mean?"

"No. Making it. Sort of a glue-works likely."

Lohr continued to frown. "Let me think," he said. "Didn't the ole man have some such idea once, himself?"

Adams leaned forward, rubbing his knees; and he coughed again before he spoke. "Well, yes. Fact is, he did. That is to say, a mighty long while ago he did."

"I remember," said Lohr. "He never said anything about it that I know of; but seems to me I recollect we had sort of a rumour around the place how you and that man—le's see, wasn't his name Campbell, that died of typhoid fever? Yes, that was it, Campbell. Didn't the ole man have you and Campbell workin' sort of private on some glue proposition or other?"

"Yes, he did." Adams nodded. "I found out a good deal about glue then, too."

"Been workin' on it since, I suppose?"

"Yes. Kept it in my mind and studied out new things about it."

Lohr looked serious. "Well, but see here," he said. "I hope it ain't anything the ole man'll think might infringe on whatever he had you doin' for *him*. You know how he is: broad-minded, liberal, free-handed man as walks this earth, and if he thought he owed you a cent he'd sell his right hand for a pork-chop to pay it, if that was the only way; but if he got the idea anybody was tryin' to get the better of him, he'd sell *both* his hands, if he had to, to keep 'em from doin' it. Yes, at eighty, he would! Not that I mean I think you might be tryin' to get the better of him, Virg. You're a mighty close ole codger, but such a thing ain't in you. What I mean: I hope there ain't any chance for the ole man to *think* you might be——"

"Oh, no," Adams interrupted. "As a matter of fact, I don't believe he'll ever think about it at all, and if he did he wouldn't have any real right to feel offended at me: the process I'm going to use is one I expect to change and improve a lot different from the one Campbell and I worked on for him."

"Well, that's good," said Lohr. "Of course you know what you're up to: you're old enough, God knows!" He laughed ruefully. "My, but it will seem funny to me—down there with you gone! I expect you and I both been gettin' to be pretty much dead-wood in the place, the way the young fellows look at it, and the only one that'd miss either of us would be the other one! Have you told the ole man yet?"

"Well——" Adams spoke laboriously. "No. No, I haven't. I thought—well, that's what I wanted to see you about."

"What can I do?"

"I thought I'd write him a letter and get you to hand it to him for me."

"My soul!" his friend exclaimed. "Why on earth don't you just go down there and tell him?"

Adams became pitiably embarrassed. He stammered, coughed, stammered again, wrinkling his face so deeply he seemed about to weep; but finally he contrived to utter an apologetic laugh. "I ought to do that, of course; but in some way or other I just don't seem to be able to—to manage it."

"Why in the world not?" the mystified Lohr inquired.

"I could hardly tell you—'less'n it is to say that when you been with one boss all your life it's so—so kind of embarrassing—to quit him, I just can't make up my mind to go and speak to him about it. No; I got it in my head a letter's the only satisfactory way to do it, and I thought I'd ask you to hand it to him."

"Well, of course I don't mind doin' that for you," Lohr said, mildly. "But why in the world don't you just mail it to him?"

"Well, I'll tell you," Adams returned. "You know, like that, it'd have to go through a clerk and that secretary of his, and I don't know who all. There's a couple of kind of delicate points I want to put in it: for instance, I want to explain to him how much improvement and so on I'm going to introduce on the old process I helped to work out with Campbell when we were working for him, so't he'll understand it's a different article and no infringement at all. Then there's another thing: you see all during while I was sick he had my salary paid to me—it amounts to considerable, I was on my back so long. Under the circumstances, because I'm quitting, I don't feel as if I ought to accept it, and so I'll have a check for him in the letter to cover it, and I want to be sure he knows it, and gets it personally. If it had to go through a lot of other people, the way it would if I put it in the mail, why, you can't tell. So what I thought: if you'd hand it to him for me, and maybe if he happened to read it right then, or anything, it might be you'd notice whatever he'd happen to say about it—and you could tell me afterward."

"All right," Lohr said. "Certainly if you'd rather do it that way, I'll hand it to him and tell you what he says; that is, if he says anything and I hear him. Got it written?"

"No; I'll send it around to you last of the week." Adams moved toward his taxicab. "Don't say anything to anybody about it, Charley, especially till after that."

"All right."

"And, Charley, I'll be mighty obliged to you," Adams said, and came back to shake hands in farewell. "There's one thing more you might do—if you'd ever happen to feel like it." He kept his eyes rather vaguely fixed on a point above his friend's head as he spoke, and his voice was not well controlled. "I been—I been down there a good many years and I may not 'a' been so much use lately as I was at first, but I always *tried* to do my best for the old firm. If anything turned out so's they *did* kind of take offense with me, down there, why, just say a good word for me—if you'd happen to feel like it, maybe."

Old Charley Lohr assured him that he would speak a good word if opportunity became available; then, after the cab had driven away, he went up to his small apartment on the third floor and muttered ruminatively until his wife inquired what he was talking to himself about.

"Ole Virg Adams," he told her. "He's out again after his long spell of sickness, and the way it looks to me he'd better stayed in bed."

"You mean he still looks too bad to be out?"

"Oh, I expect he's gettin' his *health* back," Lohr said, frowning.

"Then what's the matter with him? You mean he's lost his mind?"

"My goodness, but women do jump at conclusions!" he exclaimed.

"Well," said Mrs. Lohr, "what other conclusion did you leave me to jump at?"

Her husband explained with a little heat: "People can have a sickness that *affects* their mind, can't they? Their mind can get some affected without bein' *lost*, can't it?"

"Then you mean the poor man's mind does seem affected?"

"Why, no; I'd scarcely go as far as that," Lohr said, inconsistently, and declined to be more definite.

Adams devoted the latter part of that evening to the composition of his letter—a disquieting task not completed when, at eleven o'clock, he heard his daughter coming up the stairs. She was singing to herself in a low, sweet voice, and Adams paused to listen incredulously, with his pen lifted and his mouth open, as if he heard the strangest sound in the world. Then he set down the pen upon a blotter, went to his door, and opened it, looking out at her as she came.

"Well, dearie, you seem to be feeling pretty good," he said. "What you been doing?"

"Just sitting out on the front steps, papa."

"All alone, I suppose."

"No. Mr. Russell called."

"Oh, he did?" Adams pretended to be surprised. "What all could you and he find to talk about till this hour o' the night?"

She laughed gaily. "You don't know me, papa!"

"How's that?"

"You've never found out that I always do all the talking."

"Didn't you let him get a word in all evening?"

"Oh, yes; every now and then."

Adams took her hand and petted it. "Well, what did he say?"

Alice gave him a radiant look and kissed him. "Not what you think!" she laughed; then slapped his cheek with saucy affection, pirouetted across the narrow hall and into her own room, and curtsied to him as she closed her door.

Adams went back to his writing with a lighter heart; for since Alice was born she had been to him the apple of his eye, his own phrase in thinking of her; and what he was doing now was for her. He smiled as he picked up his pen to begin a new draft of the painful letter; but presently he looked puzzled. After all, she could be happy just as things were, it seemed. Then why had he taken what his wife called "this new step," which he had so long resisted?

He could only sigh and wonder. "Life works out pretty peculiarly," he thought; for he couldn't go back now, though the reason he couldn't was not clearly apparent. He had to go ahead.

CHAPTER XVII

He was out in his taxicab again the next morning, and by noon he had secured what he wanted.

It was curiously significant that he worked so quickly. All the years during which his wife had pressed him toward his present shift he had sworn to himself, as well as to her, that he would never yield; and yet when he did yield he had no plans to make, because he found them already prepared and worked out in detail in his mind; as if he had long contemplated the "step" he believed himself incapable of taking.

Sometimes he had thought of improving his income by exchanging his little collection of bonds for a "small rental property," if he could find "a good buy"; and he had spent many of his spare hours rambling over the enormously spreading city and its purlieus, looking for the ideal "buy." It remained unattainable, so far as he was concerned; but he found other things.

Not twice a crow's mile from his own house there was a dismal and slummish quarter, a decayed "industrial district" of earlier days. Most of the industries were small; some of them died, perishing of bankruptcy or fire; and a few had moved, leaving their shells. Of the relics, the best was a brick building which had been the largest and most important factory in the quarter: it had been injured by a long vacancy almost as serious as a fire, in effect, and Adams had often guessed at the sum needed to put it in repair.

When he passed it, he would look at it with an interest which he supposed detached and idly speculative. "That'd be just the thing," he thought. "If a fellow had money enough, and took a notion to set up some new business on a big scale, this would be a pretty good place—to make glue, for instance, if that wasn't out of the question, of course. It would take a lot of money, though; a great deal too much for *me* to expect to handle—even if I'd ever dream of doing such a thing."

Opposite the dismantled factory was a muddy, open lot of two acres or so, and near the middle of the lot, a long brick shed stood in a desolate abandonment, not happily decorated by old coatings of theatrical and medicinal advertisements. But the brick shed had two wooden ells, and, though both shed and ells were of a single story, here was empty space enough for a modest enterprise—"space enough for almost anything, to start with," Adams thought, as he walked through the low buildings, one day, when he was prospecting in that section. "Yes, I suppose I *could* swing this," he thought. "If the process belonged to me, say, instead of being out of the question because it isn't my property—or if I was the kind of man to do such a thing anyhow, here would be something I could probably get hold of pretty cheap. They'd want a lot of money for a lease on that big building over the way—but this, why, I should think it'd be practically nothing at all."

Then, by chance, meeting an agent he knew, he made inquiries—merely to satisfy a casual curiosity, he thought—and he found matters much as he had supposed, except that the owners of the big building did not wish to let, but to sell it, and this at a price so exorbitant that Adams laughed. But the long brick shed in the great muddy lot was for sale or to let, or "pretty near to be given away," he learned, if anybody would take it.

Adams took it now, though without seeing that he had been destined to take it, and that some dreary wizard in the back of his head had foreseen all along that he would take it, and planned to be ready. He drove in his taxicab to look the place over again, then down-town to arrange for a lease; and came home to lunch with his wife and daughter. Things were "moving," he told them.

He boasted a little of having acted so decisively, and said that since the dang thing had to be done, it was "going to be done *right!*" He was almost cheerful, in a feverish way, and when the cab came for him again, soon after lunch, he explained that he intended not only to get things done right, but also to "get 'em done quick!" Alice, following him to the front door, looked at him anxiously and asked if she couldn't help. He laughed at her grimly.

"Then let me go along with you in the cab," she begged. "You don't look able to start in so hard, papa, just when you're barely beginning to get your strength back. Do let me go with you and see if I can't help—or at least take care of you if you should get to feeling badly."

He declined, but upon pressure let her put a tiny bottle of spirits of ammonia in his pocket, and promised to make use of it if he "felt faint or anything." Then he was off again; and the next morning had men at work in his sheds, though the wages he had to pay frightened him.

He directed the workmen in every detail, hurrying them by example and exhortations, and receiving, in consequence, several declarations of independence, as well as one resignation, which took effect immediately. "Yous capitalusts seem to think a man's got nothin' to do but break his back p'doosin' wealth fer yous to squander," the resigning person loudly complained. "You look out: the toiler's day is a-comin', and it ain't so fur off, neither!" But the capitalist was already out of hearing, gone to find a man to take this orator's place.

By the end of the week, Adams felt that he had moved satisfactorily forward in his preparations for the simple equipment he needed; but he hated the pause of Sunday. He didn't *want* any rest, he told Alice impatiently, when she suggested that the idle day might be good for him.

Late that afternoon he walked over to the apartment house where old Charley Lohr lived, and gave his friend the letter he wanted the head of Lamb and Company to receive "personally." "I'll take it as a mighty great favour in you to hand it to him personally, Charley," he said, in parting. "And you won't forget, in case he says anything about it—and remember if you ever do get a chance to put in a good word for me later, you know——"

Old Charley promised to remember, and, when Mrs. Lohr came out of the "kitchenette," after the door closed, he said thoughtfully, "Just skin and bones."

"You mean Mr. Adams is?" Mrs. Lohr inquired.

"Who'd you think I meant?" he returned. "One o' these partridges in the wall-paper?"

"Did he look so badly?"

"Looked kind of distracted to *me*," her husband replied. "These little thin fellers can stand a heap sometimes, though. He'll be over here again Monday."

"Did he say he would?"

"No," said Lohr. "But he will. You'll see. He'll be over to find out what the big boss says when I give him this letter. Expect I'd be kind of anxious, myself, if I was him."

"Why would you? What's Mr. Adams doing to be so anxious about?"

Lohr's expression became one of reserve, the look of a man who has found that when he speaks his inner thoughts his wife jumps too far to conclusions. "Oh, nothing," he said. "Of course any man starting up a new business is bound to be pretty nervous a while. He'll be over here to-morrow evening, all right; you'll see."

The prediction was fulfilled: Adams arrived just after Mrs. Lohr had removed the dinner dishes to her "kitchenette"; but Lohr had little information to give his caller.

"He didn't say a word, Virgil; nary a word. I took it into his office and handed it to him, and he just sat and read it; that's all. I kind of stood around as long as I could, but he was sittin' at his desk with his side to me, and he never turned around full toward me, as it were, so I couldn't hardly even tell anything. All I know: he just read it."

"Well, but see here," Adams began, nervously. "Well——"

"Well what, Virg?"

"Well, but what did he say when he *did* speak?"

"He didn't speak. Not so long I was in there, anyhow. He just sat there and read it. Read kind of slow. Then, when he came to the end, he turned back and started to read it all over again. By that time there was three or four other men standin' around in the office waitin' to speak to him, and I had to go."

Adams sighed, and stared at the floor, irresolute. "Well, I'll be getting along back home then, I guess, Charley. So you're sure you couldn't tell anything what he might have thought about it, then?"

"Not a thing in the world. I've told you all I know, Virg."

"I guess so, I guess so," Adams said, mournfully. "I feel mighty obliged to you, Charley Lohr; mighty obliged. Good-night to you." And he departed, sighing in perplexity.

On his way home, preoccupied with many thoughts, he walked so slowly that once or twice he stopped and stood motionless for a few moments, without being aware of it; and when he reached the juncture of the sidewalk with the short brick path that led to his own front door, he stopped again, and stood for more than a minute. "Ah, I wish I knew," he whispered, plaintively. "I do wish I knew what he thought about it."

He was roused by a laugh that came lightly from the little veranda near by. "Papa!" Alice called gaily. "What *are* you standing there muttering to yourself about?"

"Oh, are you there, dearie?" he said, and came up the path. A tall figure rose from a chair on the veranda.

"Papa, this is Mr. Russell."

The two men shook hands, Adams saying, "Pleased to make your acquaintance," as they looked at each other in the faint light diffused through the opaque glass in the upper part of the door. Adams's impression was of a strong and tall young man, fashionable but gentle; and Russell's was of a dried, little old business man with a grizzled moustache, worried bright eyes, shapeless dark clothes, and a homely manner.

"Nice evening," Adams said further, as their hands parted. "Nice time o' year it is, but we don't always have as good weather as this; that's the trouble of it. Well——" He went to the door. "Well—I bid you good evening," he said, and retired within the house.

Alice laughed. "He's the old-fashionedest man in town, I suppose—and frightfully impressed with *you*, I could see!"

"What nonsense!" said Russell. "How could anybody be impressed with me?"

"Why not? Because you're quiet? Good gracious! Don't you know that you're the *most* impressive sort? We chatterers spend all our time playing to you quiet people."

"Yes; we're only the audience."

"'Only!'" she echoed. "Why, we live for you, and we can't live without you."

"I wish you couldn't," said Russell. "That would be a new experience for both of us, wouldn't it?"

"It might be a rather bleak one for me," she answered, lightly. "I'm afraid I'll miss these summer evenings with you when they're over. I'll miss them enough, thanks!"

"Do they have to be over some time?" he asked.

"Oh, everything's over *some* time, isn't it?"

Russell laughed at her. "Don't let's look so far ahead as that," he said. "We don't need to be already thinking of the cemetery, do we?"

"I didn't," she said, shaking her head. "Our summer evenings will be over before then, Mr. Russell."

"Why?" he asked.

"Good heavens!" she said. "*There's* laconic eloquence: almost a proposal in a single word! Never mind, I shan't hold you to it. But to answer you: well, I'm always looking ahead, and somehow I usually see about how things are coming out."

"Yes," he said. "I suppose most of us do; at least it seems as if we did, because we so seldom feel surprised by the way they do come out. But maybe that's only because life isn't like a play in a theatre, and most things come about so gradually we get used to them."

"No, I'm sure I can see quite a long way ahead," she insisted, gravely. "And it doesn't seem to me as if our summer evenings could last very long. Something'll interfere—somebody will, I mean—they'll *say* something——"

"What if they do?"

She moved her shoulders in a little apprehensive shiver. "It'll change you," she said. "I'm just sure something spiteful's going to happen to me. You'll feel differently about—things."

"Now, isn't that an idea!" he exclaimed.

"It will," she insisted. "I know something spiteful's going to happen!"

"You seem possessed by a notion not a bit flattering to me," he remarked.

"Oh, but isn't it? That's just what it is! Why isn't it?"

"Because it implies that I'm made of such soft material the slightest breeze will mess me all up. I'm not so like that as I evidently appear; and if it's true that we're afraid other people will do the things we'd be most likely to do ourselves, it seems to me that I ought to be the one to be afraid. I ought to be afraid that somebody may say something about me to you that will make you believe I'm a professional forger."

"No. We both know they won't," she said. "We both know you're the sort of person everybody in the world says nice things about." She lifted her hand to silence him as he laughed at this. "Oh, of course you are! I think perhaps you're a little flirtatious—most quiet men have that one sly way with 'em—oh, yes, they do! But you happen to be the kind of man everybody loves to praise. And if you weren't, *I* shouldn't hear anything terrible about you. I told you I was unpopular: I don't see anybody at all any more. The only man except you who's been to see me in a month is that fearful little fat Frank Dowling, and I sent word to *him* I wasn't home. Nobody'd tell me of your wickedness, you see."

"Then let me break some news to you," Russell said. "Nobody would tell me of yours, either. Nobody's even mentioned you to me."

She burlesqued a cry of anguish. "That *is* obscurity! I suppose I'm too apt to forget that they say the population's about half a million nowadays. There *are* other people to talk about, you feel, then?"

"None that I want to," he said. "But I should think the size of the place might relieve your mind of what seems to insist on burdening it. Besides, I'd rather you thought me a better man than you do."

"What kind of a man do I think you are?"

"The kind affected by what's said about people instead of by what they do themselves."

"Aren't you?"

"No, I'm not," he said. "If you want our summer evenings to be over you'll have to drive me away yourself."

"Nobody else could?"

"No."

She was silent, leaning forward, with her elbows on her knees and her clasped hands against her lips. Then, not moving, she said softly:

"Well—I won't!"

She was silent again, and he said nothing, but looked at her, seeming to be content with looking. Her attitude was one only a graceful person should assume, but she was graceful; and, in the wan light, which made a prettily shaped mist of her, she had beauty. Perhaps it was beauty of the hour, and of the love scene almost made into form by what they had both just said, but she had it; and though beauty of the hour passes, he who sees it will long remember it and the hour when it came.

"What are you thinking of?" he asked.

She leaned back in her chair and did not answer at once. Then she said: "I don't know; I doubt if I was thinking of anything. It seems to me I wasn't. I think I was just being sort of sadly happy just then."

"Were you? Was it 'sadly,' too?"

"Don't you know?" she said. "It seems to me that only little children can be just happily happy. I think when we get older our happiest moments are like the one I had just then: it's as if we heard strains of minor music running through them—oh, so sweet, but oh, so sad!"

"But what makes it sad for *you*?"

"I don't know," she said, in a lighter tone. "Perhaps it's a kind of useless foreboding I seem to have pretty often. It may be that—or it may be poor papa."

"You *are* a funny, delightful girl, though!" Russell laughed. "When your father's so well again that he goes out walking in the evenings!"

"He does too much walking," Alice said. "Too much altogether, over at his new plant. But there isn't any stopping him." She laughed and shook her head. "When a man gets an ambition to be a multimillionaire his family don't appear to have much weight with him. He'll walk all he wants to, in spite of them."

"I suppose so," Russell said, absently; then he leaned forward. "I wish I could understand better why you were 'sadly' happy."

Meanwhile, as Alice shed what further light she could on this point, the man ambitious to be a "multimillionaire" was indeed walking too much for his own good. He had gone to bed, hoping to sleep well and rise early for a long day's work, but he could not rest, and now, in his nightgown and slippers, he was pacing the floor of his room.

"I wish I *did* know," he thought, over and over. "I *do* wish I knew how he feels about it."

CHAPTER XVIII

That was a thought almost continuously in his mind, even when he was hardest at work; and, as the days went on and he could not free himself, he became querulous about it. "I guess I'm the biggest dang fool alive," he told his wife as they sat together one evening. "I got plenty else to bother me, without worrying my head off about what *he* thinks. I can't help what he thinks; it's too late for that. So why should I keep pestering myself about it?"

"It'll wear off, Virgil," Mrs. Adams said, reassuringly. She was gentle and sympathetic with him, and for the first time in many years he would come to sit with her and talk, when he had finished his day's work. He had told her, evading her eye, "Oh, I don't blame you. You didn't get after me to do this on your own account; you couldn't help it."

"Yes; but it don't wear off," he complained. "This afternoon I was showing the men how I wanted my vats to go, and I caught my fool self standing there saying to my fool self, 'It's funny I don't hear how he feels about it from *some*body.' I was saying it aloud, almost—and it *is* funny I don't hear anything!"

"Well, you see what it means, don't you, Virgil? It only means he hasn't said anything to anybody about it. Don't you think you're getting kind of morbid over it?"

"Maybe, maybe," he muttered.

"Why, yes," she said, briskly. "You don't realize what a little bit of a thing all this is to him. It's been a long, long while since the last time you even mentioned glue to him, and he's probably forgotten everything about it."

"You're off your base; it isn't like him to forget things," Adams returned, peevishly. "He may seem to forget 'em, but he don't."

"But he's not thinking about this, or you'd have heard from him before now."

Her husband shook his head. "Ah, that's just it!" he said. "Why *haven't* I heard from him?"

"It's all your morbidness, Virgil. Look at Walter: if Mr. Lamb held this up against you, would he still let Walter stay there? Wouldn't he have discharged Walter if he felt angry with you?"

"That dang boy!" Adams said. "If he *wanted* to come with me now, I wouldn't hardly let him. What do you suppose makes him so bull-headed?"

"But hasn't he a right to choose for himself?" she asked. "I suppose he feels he ought to stick to what he thinks is sure pay. As soon as he sees that you're going to succeed with the glue-works he'll want to be with you quick enough."

"Well, he better get a little sense in his head," Adams returned, crossly. "He wanted me to pay him a three-hundred-dollar bonus in advance, when anybody with a grain of common sense knows I need every penny I can lay my hands on!"

"Never mind," she said. "He'll come around later and be glad of the chance."

"He'll have to beg for it then! *I* won't ask him again."

"Oh, Walter will come out all right; you needn't worry. And don't you see that Mr. Lamb's not discharging him means there's no hard feeling against you, Virgil?"

"I can't make it out at all," he said, frowning. "The only thing I can *think* it means is that J. A. Lamb is so fair-minded—and of course he *is* one of the fair-mindedest men alive—I suppose that's the reason he hasn't fired Walter. He may know," Adams concluded, morosely—"he may know that's just another thing to make me feel all the meaner: keeping my boy there on a salary after I've done him an injury."

"Now, now!" she said, trying to comfort him. "You couldn't do anybody an injury to save your life, and everybody knows it."

"Well, anybody ought to know I wouldn't *want* to do an injury, but this world isn't built so't we can do just what we want." He paused, reflecting. "Of course there may be one explanation of why Walter's still there: J. A. maybe hasn't noticed that he *is* there. There's so many I expect he hardly knows him by sight."

"Well, just do quit thinking about it," she urged him. "It only bothers you without doing any good. Don't you know that?"

"Don't I, though!" he laughed, feebly. "I know it better'n anybody! How funny that is: when you know thinking about a thing only pesters you without helping anything at all, and yet you keep right on pestering yourself with it!"

"But *why?*" she said. "What's the use when you know you haven't done anything wrong, Virgil? You said yourself you were going to improve the process so much it would be different from the old one, and you'd *really* have a right to it."

Adams had persuaded himself of this when he yielded; he had found it necessary to persuade himself of it—though there was a part of him, of course, that remained unpersuaded; and this discomfiting part of him was what made his present trouble. "Yes, I know," he said. "That's true, but I can't quite seem to get away from the fact that the principle of the process is a good deal the same—well, it's more'n that; it's just *about* the same as the one he hired Campbell and me to work out for him. Truth is, nobody could tell the difference, and I don't know as there *is* any difference except in these improvements I'm making. Of course, the improvements do give me pretty near a perfect right to it, as a person might say; and that's one of the things I thought of putting in my letter to him; but I was afraid he'd just think I was trying to make up excuses, so I left it out. I kind of worried all the time I was writing that letter, because if he thought I *was* just making up excuses, why, it might set him just so much more against me."

Ever since Mrs. Adams had found that she was to have her way, the depths of her eyes had been troubled by a continuous uneasiness; and, although she knew it was there, and sometimes veiled it by keeping the revealing eyes averted from her husband and children, she could not always cover it under that assumption of absent-mindedness. The uneasy look became vivid, and her voice was slightly tremulous now, as she said, "But what if he *should* be against you—although I don't believe he is, of course—you told me he couldn't *do* anything to you, Virgil."

"No," he said, slowly. "I can't see how he could do anything. It was just a secret, not a patent; the thing ain't patentable. I've tried to think what he could do—supposing he was to want to—but I can't figure out anything at all that would be any harm to me. There isn't any way in the world it could be made a question of law. Only thing he could do'd be to *tell* people his side of it, and set 'em against me. I been kind of waiting for that to happen, all along."

She looked somewhat relieved. "So did I expect it," she said. "I was dreading it most on Alice's account: it might have—well, young men are so easily influenced and all. But so far as the business is concerned, what if Mr. Lamb did talk? That wouldn't amount to much. It wouldn't affect the business; not to hurt. And, besides, he isn't even doing that."

"No; anyhow not yet, it seems." And Adams sighed again, wistfully. "But I *would* give a good deal to know what he thinks!"

Before his surrender he had always supposed that if he did such an unthinkable thing as to seize upon the glue process for himself, what he would feel must be an overpowering shame. But shame is the rarest thing in the world: what he felt was this unremittent curiosity about his old employer's thoughts. It was an obsession, yet he did not want to hear what Lamb "thought" from Lamb himself, for Adams had a second obsession, and this was his dread of meeting the old man face to face. Such an encounter could happen only by chance and unexpectedly; since Adams would have avoided any deliberate meeting, so long as his legs had strength to carry him, even if Lamb came to the house to see him. But people do meet unexpectedly; and when Adams had to be down-town he kept away from the "wholesale district." One day he did see Lamb, as the latter went by in his car, impassive, going home to lunch; and Adams, in the crowd at a corner, knew that the old man had not seen him. Nevertheless, in a streetcar, on the way back to his sheds, an hour later, he was still subject to little shivering seizures of horror.

He worked unceasingly, seeming to keep at it even in his sleep, for he always woke in the midst of a planning and estimating that must have been going on in his mind before consciousness of himself returned. Moreover, the work, thus urged, went rapidly, in spite of the high wages he had to pay his labourers for their short hours. "It eats money," he complained, and, in fact, by the time his vats and boilers were in place it had eaten almost all he could supply; but in addition to his equipment he now owned a stock of "raw material," raw indeed; and when operations should be a little further along he was confident his banker would be willing to "carry" him.

Six weeks from the day he had obtained his lease he began his glue-making. The terrible smells came out of the sheds and went writhing like snakes all through that quarter of the town. A smiling man, strolling and breathing the air with satisfaction, would turn a corner and smile no more, but hurry. However, coloured people had almost all the dwellings of this old section to themselves; and although even they were troubled, there was recompense for them. Being philosophic about what appeared to them as in the order of nature, they sought neither escape nor redress, and soon learned to bear what the wind brought them. They even made use of it to enrich those figures of speech with which the native impulses of coloured people decorate their communications: they flavoured metaphor, simile, and invective with it; and thus may be said to have enjoyed it. But the man who produced it took a hot bath as soon as he reached his home the evening of that first day when his manufacturing began. Then he put on fresh clothes; but after dinner he seemed to be haunted, and asked his wife if she "noticed anything."

She laughed and inquired what he meant.

"Seems to me as if that glue-works smell hadn't quit hanging to me," he explained. "Don't you notice it?"

"No! What an idea!"

He laughed, too, but uneasily; and told her he was sure "the dang glue smell" was somehow sticking to him. Later, he went outdoors and walked up and down the small yard in the dusk; but now and then he stood still, with his head lifted, and sniffed the air suspiciously. "Can you smell it?" he called to Alice, who sat upon the veranda, prettily dressed and waiting in a reverie.

"Smell what, papa?"

"That dang glue-works."

She did the same thing her mother had done: laughed, and said, "No! How foolish! Why, papa, it's over two miles from here!"

"You don't get it at all?" he insisted.

"The idea! The air is lovely to-night, papa."

The air did not seem lovely to him, for he was positive that he detected the taint. He wondered how far it carried, and if J. A. Lamb would smell it, too, out on his own lawn a mile to the north; and if he did, would he guess what it was? Then Adams laughed at himself for such nonsense; but could not rid his nostrils of their disgust. To him the whole town seemed to smell of his glue-works.

Nevertheless, the glue was making, and his sheds were busy. "Guess we're stirrin' up this ole neighbourhood with more than the smell," his foreman remarked one morning.

"How's that?" Adams inquired.

"That great big, enormous ole dead butterine factory across the street from our lot," the man said. "Nothin' like settin' an example to bring real estate to life. That place is full o' carpenters startin' in to make a regular buildin' of it again. Guess you ought to have the credit of it, because you was the first man in ten years to see any possibilities in this neighbourhood."

Adams was pleased, and, going out to see for himself, heard a great hammering and sawing from within the building; while carpenters were just emerging gingerly upon the dangerous roof. He walked out over the dried mud of his deep lot, crossed the street, and spoke genially to a workman who was removing the broken glass of a window on the ground floor.

"Here! What's all this howdy-do over here?"

"Goin' to fix her all up, I guess," the workman said. "Big job it is, too."

"Sh' think it would be."

"Yes, sir; a pretty big job—a pretty big job. Got men at it on all four floors and on the roof. They're doin' it *right*."

"Who's doing it?"

"Lord! I d' know. Some o' these here big manufacturing corporations, I guess."

"What's it going to be?"

"They tell *me*," the workman answered—"they tell *me* she's goin' to be a butterine factory again. Anyways, I hope she won't be anything to smell like that glue-works you got over there—not while *I'm* workin' around her, anyways!"

"That smell's all right," Adams said. "You soon get used to it."

"You do?" The man appeared incredulous. "Listen! I was over in France: it's a good thing them Dutchmen never thought of it; we'd of had to quit!"

Adams laughed, and went back to his sheds. "I guess my foreman was right," he told his wife, that evening, with a little satisfaction. "As soon as one man shows enterprise enough to found an industry in a broken-down neighbourhood, somebody else is sure to follow. I kind of like the look of it: it'll help make our place seem sort of more busy and prosperous when it comes to getting a loan from the bank—and I got to get one mighty soon, too. I did think some that if things go as well as there's every reason to think they *ought* to, I might want to spread out and maybe get hold of that old factory myself; but I hardly expected to be able to handle a proposition of that size before two or three years from now, and anyhow there's room enough on the lot I got, if we need more buildings some day. Things are going about as fine as I could ask: I hired some girls to-day to do the bottling—coloured girls along about sixteen to twenty years old. Afterwhile, I expect to get a machine to put the stuff in the little bottles, when we begin to get good returns; but half a dozen of these coloured girls can do it all right now, by hand. We're getting to have really quite a little plant over there: yes, sir, quite a regular little plant!"

He chuckled, and at this cheerful sound, of a kind his wife had almost forgotten he was capable of producing, she ventured to put her hand upon his arm. They had gone outdoors, after dinner, taking two chairs with them, and were sitting through the late twilight together, keeping well away from the "front porch," which was not yet occupied, however. Alice was in her room changing her dress.

"Well, honey," Mrs. Adams said, taking confidence not only to put her hand upon his arm, but to revive this disused endearment;—"it's grand to have you so optimistic. Maybe some time you'll admit I was right, after all. Everything's going so well, it seems a pity you didn't take this—this step—long ago. Don't you think maybe so, Virgil?"

"Well—if I was ever going to, I don't know but I might as well of. I got to admit the proposition begins to look pretty good: I know the stuff'll sell, and I can't see a thing in the world to stop it. It does look good, and if—if——" He paused.

"If what?" she said, suddenly anxious.

He laughed plaintively, as if confessing a superstition. "It's funny—well, it's mighty funny about that smell. I've got so used to it at the plant I never seem to notice it at all over there. It's only when I get away. Honestly, can't you notice——?"

"Virgil!" She lifted her hand to strike his arm chidingly. "Do quit harping on that nonsense!"

"Oh, of course it don't amount to anything," he said. "A person can stand a good deal of just smell. It don't *worry* me any."

"I should think not—especially as there isn't any."

"Well," he said, "I feel pretty fair over the whole thing—a lot better'n I ever expected to, anyhow. I don't know as there's any reason I shouldn't tell you so."

She was deeply pleased with this acknowledgment, and her voice had tenderness in it as she responded: "There, honey! Didn't I always say you'd be glad if you did it?"

Embarrassed, he coughed loudly, then filled his pipe and lit it. "Well," he said, slowly, "it's a puzzle. Yes, sir, it's a puzzle."

"What is?"

"Pretty much everything, I guess."

As he spoke, a song came to them from a lighted window over their heads. Then the window darkened abruptly, but the song continued as Alice went down through the house to wait on the little veranda. "*Mi chiamo Mimi,*" she sang, and in her voice throbbed something almost startling in its sweetness. Her father and mother listened, not speaking until the song stopped with the click of the wire screen at the front door as Alice came out.

"My!" said her father. "How sweet she does sing! I don't know as I ever heard her voice sound nicer than it did just then."

"There's something that makes it sound that way," his wife told him.

"I suppose so," he said, sighing. "I suppose so. You think——"

"She's just terribly in love with him!"

"I expect that's the way it ought to be," he said, then drew upon his pipe for reflection, and became murmurous with the symptoms of melancholy laughter. "It don't make things less of a puzzle, though, does it?"

"In what way, Virgil?"

"Why, here," he said—"here we go through all this muck and moil to help fix things nicer for her at home, and what's it all amount to? Seems like she's just gone ahead the way she'd 'a' gone anyhow; and *now*, I suppose, getting ready to up and leave us! Ain't that a puzzle to you? It is to me."

"Oh, but things haven't gone that far yet."

"Why, you just said——"

She gave a little cry of protest. "Oh, they aren't *engaged* yet. Of course they *will* be; he's just as much interested in her as she is in him, but——"

"Well, what's the trouble then?"

"You *are* a simple old fellow!" his wife exclaimed, and then rose from her chair. "That reminds me," she said.

"What of?" he asked. "What's my being simple remind you of?"

"Nothing!" she laughed. "It wasn't you that reminded me. It was just something that's been on my mind. I don't believe he's actually ever been inside our house!"

"Hasn't he?"

"I actually don't believe he ever has," she said. "Of course we must——" She paused, debating.

"We must what?"

"I guess I better talk to Alice about it right now," she said. "He don't usually come for about half an hour yet; I guess I've got time." And with that she walked away, leaving him to his puzzles.

CHAPTER XIX

Alice was softly crooning to herself as her mother turned the corner of the house and approached through the dusk.

"Isn't it the most *beautiful* evening!" the daughter said. "*Why* can't summer last all year? Did you ever know a lovelier twilight than this, mama?"

Mrs. Adams laughed, and answered, "Not since I was your age, I expect."

Alice was wistful at once. "Don't they stay beautiful after my age?"

"Well, it's not the same thing."

"Isn't it? Not—ever?"

"You may have a different kind from mine," the mother said, a little sadly. "I think you will, Alice. You deserve——"

"No, I don't. I don't deserve anything, and I know it. But I'm getting a great deal these days—more than I ever dreamed *could* come to me. I'm—I'm pretty happy, mama!"

"Dearie!" Her mother would have kissed her, but Alice drew away.

"Oh, I don't mean——" She laughed nervously. "I wasn't meaning to tell you I'm *engaged*, mama. We're not. I mean—oh! things seem pretty beautiful in spite of all I've done to spoil 'em."

"You?" Mrs. Adams cried, incredulously. "What have you done to spoil anything?"

"Little things," Alice said. "A thousand little silly—oh, what's the use? He's so honestly what he is—just simple and good and intelligent—I feel a tricky mess beside him! I don't see why he likes me; and sometimes I'm afraid he wouldn't if he knew me."

"He'd just worship you," said the fond mother. "And the more he knew you, the more he'd worship you."

Alice shook her head. "He's not the worshiping kind. Not like that at all. He's more——"

But Mrs. Adams was not interested in this analysis, and she interrupted briskly, "Of course it's time your father and I showed some interest in him. I was just saying I actually don't believe he's ever been inside the house."

"No," Alice said, musingly; "that's true: I don't believe he has. Except when we've walked in the evening we've always sat out here, even those two times when it was drizzly. It's so much nicer."

"We'll have to do *something* or other, of course," her mother said.

"What like?"

"I was thinking——" Mrs. Adams paused. "Well, of course we could hardly put off asking him to dinner, or something, much longer."

Alice was not enthusiastic; so far from it, indeed, that there was a melancholy alarm in her voice. "Oh, mama, must we? Do you think so?"

"Yes, I do. I really do."

"Couldn't we—well, couldn't we wait?"

"It looks queer," Mrs. Adams said. "It isn't the thing at all for a young man to come as much as he does, and never more than just barely meet your father and mother. No. We ought to do something."

"But a dinner!" Alice objected. "In the first place, there isn't anybody I want to ask. There isn't anybody I *would* ask."

"I didn't mean trying to give a big dinner," her mother explained. "I just mean having him to dinner. That mulatto woman, Malena Burns, goes out by the day, and she could bring a waitress. We can get some flowers for the table and some to put in the living-room. We might just as well go ahead and do it to-morrow as any other time; because your father's in a fine mood, and I saw Malena this afternoon and told her I might want her soon. She said she didn't have any engagements this week, and I can let her know to-night. Suppose when he comes you ask him for to-morrow, Alice. Everything'll be very nice, I'm sure. Don't worry about it."

"Well—but——" Alice was uncertain.

"But don't you see, it looks so queer, not to do *something*?" her mother urged. "It looks so kind of poverty-stricken. We really oughtn't to wait any longer."

Alice assented, though not with a good heart. "Very well, I'll ask him, if you think we've got to."

"That matter's settled then," Mrs. Adams said. "I'll go telephone Malena, and then I'll tell your father about it."

But when she went back to her husband, she found him in an excited state of mind, and Walter standing before him in the darkness. Adams was almost shouting, so great was his vehemence.

"Hush, hush!" his wife implored, as she came near them. "They'll hear you out on the front porch!"

"I don't care who hears me," Adams said, harshly, though he tempered his loudness. "Do you want to know what this boy's asking me for? I thought he'd maybe come to tell me he'd got a little sense in his head at last, and a little decency about what's due his family! I thought he was going to ask me to take him into my plant. No, ma'am; *that's* not what he wants!"

"No, it isn't," Walter said. In the darkness his face could not be seen; he stood motionless, in what seemed an apathetic attitude; and he spoke quietly, "No," he repeated. "That isn't what I want."

"You stay down at that place," Adams went on, hotly, "instead of trying to be a little use to your family; and the only reason you're *allowed* to stay there is because Mr. Lamb's never happened to notice you *are* still there! You just wait——"

"You're off," Walter said, in the same quiet way. "He knows I'm there. He spoke to me yesterday: he asked me how I was getting along with my work."

"He did?" Adams said, seeming not to believe him.

"Yes. He did."

"What else did he say, Walter?" Mrs. Adams asked quickly.

"Nothin'. Just walked on."

"I don't believe he knew who you were," Adams declared.

"Think not? He called me 'Walter Adams.' "

At this Adams was silent; and Walter, after waiting a moment, said:

"Well, are you going to do anything about me? About what I told you I got to have?"

"What is it, Walter?" his mother asked, since Adams did not speak.

Walter cleared his throat, and replied in a tone as quiet as that he had used before, though with a slight huskiness, "I got to have three hundred and fifty dollars. You better get him to give it to me if you can."

Adams found his voice. "Yes," he said, bitterly. "That's all he asks! He won't do anything I ask *him* to, and in return he asks me for three hundred and fifty dollars! That's all!"

"What in the world!" Mrs. Adams exclaimed. "What *for*, Walter?"

"I got to have it," Walter said.

"But what *for*?"

His quiet huskiness did not alter. "I got to have it."

"But can't you tell us——"

"I got to have it."

"That's all you can get out of him," Adams said. "He seems to think it'll bring him in three hundred and fifty dollars!"

A faint tremulousness became evident in the husky voice. "Haven't you got it?"

"No, I haven't got it!" his father answered. "And I've got to go to a bank for more than my pay-roll next week. Do you think I'm a mint?"

"I don't understand what you mean, Walter," Mrs. Adams interposed, perplexed and distressed. "If your father had the money, of course he'd need every cent of it, especially just now, and, anyhow, you could scarcely expect him to give it to you, unless you told us what you want with it. But he hasn't got it."

"All right," Walter said; and after standing a moment more, in silence, he added, impersonally, "I don't see as you ever did anything much for me, anyhow—either of you."

Then, as if this were his valedictory, he turned his back upon them, walked away quickly, and was at once lost to their sight in the darkness.

"There's a fine boy to've had the trouble of raising!" Adams grumbled. "Just crazy, that's all."

"What in the world do you suppose he wants all that money for?" his wife said, wonderingly. "I can't imagine what he could do with it. I wonder——" She paused. "I wonder if he——"

"If he what?" Adams prompted her irritably.

"If he could have bad—associates."

"God knows!" said Adams. "I don't! It just looks to me like he had something in him I don't understand. You can't keep your eye on a boy all the time in a city this size, not a boy Walter's age. You got a girl pretty much in the house, but a boy'll follow his nature. I don't know what to do with him!"

Mrs. Adams brightened a little. "He'll come out all right," she said. "I'm sure he will. I'm sure he'd never be anything really bad: and he'll come around all right about the glue-works, too; you'll see. Of course every young man wants money—it doesn't prove he's doing anything wrong just because he asks you for it."

"No. All it proves to me is that he hasn't got good sense—asking me for three hundred and fifty dollars, when he knows as well as you do the position I'm in! If I wanted to, I couldn't hardly let him have three hundred and fifty cents, let alone dollars!"

"I'm afraid you'll have to let me have that much—and maybe a little more," she ventured, timidly; and she told him of her plans for the morrow. He objected vehemently.

"Oh, but Alice has probably asked him by this time," Mrs. Adams said. "It really must be done, Virgil: you don't want him to think she's ashamed of us, do you?"

"Well, go ahead, but just let me stay away," he begged. "Of course I expect to undergo a kind of talk with him, when he gets ready to say something to us about Alice, but I do hate to have to sit through a fashionable dinner."

"Why, it isn't going to bother you," she said; "just one young man as a guest."

"Yes, I know; but you want to have all this fancy cookin'; and I see well enough you're going to get that old dress suit out of the cedar chest in the attic, and try to make me put it on me."

"I do think you better, Virgil."

"I hope the moths have got in it," he said. "Last time I wore it was to the banquet, and it was pretty old then. Of course I didn't mind wearing it to the banquet so much, because that was what you might call quite an occasion." He spoke with some reminiscent complacency; "the banquet," an affair now five years past, having provided the one time in his life when he had been so distinguished among his fellow-citizens as to receive an invitation to be present, with some seven hundred others, at the annual eating and speech-making of the city's Chamber of Commerce. "Anyhow, as you say, I think it would look foolish of me to wear a dress suit for just one young man," he went on protesting, feebly. "What's the use of all so much howdy-do, anyway? You don't expect him to believe we put on all that style every night, do you? Is that what you're after?"

"Well, we want him to think we live nicely," she admitted.

"So that's it!" he said, querulously. "You want him to think that's our regular gait, do you? Well, he'll know better about me, no matter how you fix me up, because he saw me in my regular suit the evening she introduced me to him, and he could tell anyway I'm not one of these moving-picture sporting-men that's always got a dress suit on. Besides, you and Alice certainly have some idea he'll come *again*, haven't you? If they get things settled between 'em he'll be around the house and to meals most any time, won't he? You don't hardly expect to put on style all the time, I guess. Well, he'll see then that this kind of thing was all show-off and bluff, won't he? What about it?"

"Oh, well, by *that* time——" She left the sentence unfinished, as if absently. "You could let us have a little money for to-morrow, couldn't you, honey?"

"Oh, I reckon, I reckon," he mumbled. "A girl like Alice is some comfort: she don't come around acting as if she'd commit suicide if she didn't get three hundred and fifty dollars in the next five minutes. I expect I can spare five or six dollars for your show-off if I got to."

However, she finally obtained fifteen before his bedtime; and the next morning "went to market" after breakfast, leaving Alice to make the beds. Walter had not yet come downstairs. "You had better call him," Mrs. Adams said, as she departed with a big basket on her arm. "I expect he's pretty sleepy; he was out so late last night I didn't hear him come in, though I kept awake till after midnight, listening for him. Tell him he'll be late to work if he doesn't hurry; and see that he drinks his coffee, even if he hasn't time for anything else. And when Malena comes, get her started in the kitchen: show

her where everything is." She waved her hand, as she set out for a corner
where the cars stopped. "Everything'll be lovely. Don't forget about Walter."

Nevertheless, Alice forgot about Walter for a few minutes. She closed the
door, went into the "living-room" absently, and stared vaguely at one of the
old brown-plush rocking-chairs there. Upon her forehead were the little
shadows of an apprehensive reverie, and her thoughts overlapped one another
in a fretful jumble. "What will he think? These old chairs—they're hideous.
I'll scrub those soot-streaks on the columns: it won't do any good, though.
That long crack in the column—nothing can help it. What will he think of
papa? I hope mama won't talk too much. When he thinks of Mildred's house,
or of Henrietta's, or any of 'em, beside this—— She said she'd buy plenty of
roses; that ought to help some. Nothing could be done about these horrible
chairs: can't take 'em up in the attic—a room's got to have chairs! Might
have rented some. No; if he ever comes again he'd see they weren't here. 'If
he ever comes again'—oh, it won't be *that* bad! But it won't be what he expects. I'm responsible for what he expects: he expects just what the airs I've
put on have made him expect. What did I want to pose so to him for—as
if papa were a wealthy man and all that? What *will* he think? The photograph
of the Colosseum's a rather good thing, though. It helps some—as if we'd
bought it in Rome perhaps. I hope he'll think so; he believes I've been
abroad, of course. The other night he said, 'You remember the feeling you
get in the Sainte-Chapelle'—There's another lie of mine, not saying I didn't
remember because I'd never been there. What makes me do it? Papa *must*
wear his evening clothes. But Walter——"

With that she recalled her mother's admonition, and went upstairs to
Walter's door. She tapped upon it with her fingers.

"Time to get up, Walter. The rest of us had breakfast over half an hour
ago, and it's nearly eight o'clock. You'll be late. Hurry down and I'll have
some coffee and toast ready for you." There came no sound from within the
room, so she rapped louder.

"Wake up, Walter!"

She called and rapped again, without getting any response, and then, finding that the door yielded to her, opened it and went in. Walter was not there.

He had been there, however; had slept upon the bed, though not inside
the covers; and Alice supposed he must have come home so late that he had
been too sleepy to take off his clothes. Near the foot of the bed was a shallow
closet where he kept his "other suit" and his evening clothes; and the door
stood open, showing a bare wall. Nothing whatever was in the closet, and
Alice was rather surprised at this for a moment. "That's queer," she murmured; and then she decided that when he woke he found the clothes he
had slept in "so mussy" he had put on his "other suit," and had gone out
before breakfast with the mussed clothes to have them pressed, taking his
evening things with them. Satisfied with this explanation, and failing to observe that it did not account for the absence of shoes from the closet floor,
she nodded absently, "Yes, that must be it"; and, when her mother returned,

told her that Walter had probably breakfasted down-town. They did not delay over this; the coloured woman had arrived, and the basket's disclosures were important.

"I stopped at Worlig's on the way back," said Mrs. Adams, flushed with hurry and excitement. "I bought a can of caviar there. I thought we'd have little sandwiches brought into the 'living-room' before dinner, the way you said they did when you went to that dinner at the——"

"But I think that was to go with cocktails, mama, and of course we haven't——"

"No," Mrs. Adams said. "Still, I think it would be nice. We can make them look very dainty, on a tray, and the waitress can bring them in. I thought we'd have the soup already on the table; and we can walk right out as soon as we have the sandwiches, so it won't get cold. Then, after the soup, Malena says she can make sweetbread patés with mushrooms: and for the meat course we'll have larded fillet. Malena's really a fancy cook, you know, and she says she can do anything like that to perfection. We'll have peas with the fillet, and potato balls and Brussels sprouts. Brussels sprouts are fashionable now, they told me at market. Then will come the chicken salad, and after that the ice-cream—she's going to make an angel-food cake to go with it —and then coffee and crackers and a new kind of cheese I got at Worlig's, he says is very fine."

Alice was alarmed. "Don't you think perhaps it's too much, mama?"

"It's better to have too much than too little," her mother said, cheerfully. "We don't want him to think we're the kind that skimp. Lord knows we have to enough, though, most of the time! Get the flowers in water, child. I bought 'em at market because they're so much cheaper there, but they'll keep fresh and nice. You fix 'em any way you want. Hurry! It's got to be a busy day."

She had bought three dozen little roses. Alice took them and began to arrange them in vases, keeping the stems separated as far as possible so that the clumps would look larger. She put half a dozen in each of three vases in the "living-room," placing one vase on the table in the center of the room, and one at each end of the mantelpiece. Then she took the rest of the roses to the dining-room; but she postponed the arrangement of them until the table should be set, just before dinner. She was thoughtful; planning to dry the stems and lay them on the tablecloth like a vine of roses running in a delicate design, if she found that the dozen and a half she had left were enough for that. If they weren't she would arrange them in a vase.

She looked a long time at the little roses in the basin of water, where she had put them; then she sighed, and went away to heavier tasks, while her mother worked in the kitchen with Malena. Alice dusted the "living-room" and the dining-room vigorously, though all the time with a look that grew more and more pensive; and having dusted everything, she wiped the furniture; rubbed it hard. After that, she washed the floors and the woodwork.

Emerging from the kitchen at noon, Mrs. Adams found her daughter on

hands and knees, scrubbing the bases of the columns between the hall and
the "living-room."

"Now, dearie," she said, "you mustn't tire yourself out, and you'd better
come and eat something. Your father said he'd get a bite down-town to-day
—he was going down to the bank—and Walter eats down-town all the time
lately, so I thought we wouldn't bother to set the table for lunch. Come on
and we'll have something in the kitchen."

"No," Alice said, dully, as she went on with her work. "I don't want anything."

Her mother came closer to her. "Why, what's the matter?" she asked,
briskly. "You seem kind of pale, to me; and you don't look—you don't look
happy."

"Well——" Alice began, uncertainly, but said no more.

"See here!" Mrs. Adams exclaimed. "This is all just for you! You ought
to be *enjoying* it. Why, it's the first time we've—we've entertained in I don't
know how long! I guess it's almost since we had that little party when you
were eighteen. What's the matter with you?"

"Nothing. I don't know."

"But, dearie, aren't you looking *forward* to this evening?"

The girl looked up, showing a pallid and solemn face. "Oh, yes, of course,"
she said, and tried to smile. "Of course we had to do it—I do think it'll be
nice. Of course I'm looking forward to it."

CHAPTER XX

She was indeed "looking forward" to that evening, but in a cloud of apprehension; and, although she could never have guessed it, this was the simultaneous condition of another person—none other than the guest for whose
pleasure so much cooking and scrubbing seemed to be necessary. Moreover,
Mr. Arthur Russell's premonitions were no product of mere coincidence;
neither had any magical sympathy produced them. His state of mind was
rather the result of rougher undercurrents which had all the time been running beneath the surface of a romantic friendship.

Never shrewder than when she analyzed the gentlemen, Alice did not libel
him when she said he was one of those quiet men who are a bit flirtatious,
by which she meant that he was a bit "susceptible," the same thing—and he
had proved himself susceptible to Alice upon his first sight of her. "There!"
he said to himself. "Who's that?" And in the crowd of girls at his cousin's
dance, all strangers to him, she was the one he wanted to know.

Since then, his summer evenings with her had been as secluded as if, for
three hours after the falling of dusk, they two had drawn apart from the
world to some dear bower of their own. The little veranda was that glamor-

ous nook, with a faint golden light falling through the glass of the closed door upon Alice, and darkness elsewhere, except for the one round globe of the street lamp at the corner. The people who passed along the sidewalk, now and then, were only shadows with voices, moving vaguely under the maple trees that loomed in obscure contours against the stars. So, as the two sat together, the back of the world was the wall and closed door behind them; and Russell, when he was away from Alice, always thought of her as sitting there before the closed door. A glamour was about her thus, and a spell upon him; but he had a formless anxiety never put into words: all the pictures of her in his mind stopped at the closed door.

He had another anxiety; and, for the greater part, this was of her own creating. She had too often asked him (no matter how gaily) what he heard about her; too often begged him not to hear anything. Then, hoping to forestall whatever he might hear, she had been at too great pains to account for it, to discredit and mock it; and, though he laughed at her for this, telling her truthfully he did not even hear her mentioned, the everlasting irony that deals with all such human forefendings prevailed.

Lately, he had half confessed to her what a nervousness she had produced. "You make me dread the day when I'll hear somebody speaking of you. You're getting me so upset about it that if I ever hear anybody so much as say the name 'Alice Adams,' I'll run!" The confession was but half of one because he laughed; and she took it for an assurance of loyalty in the form of burlesque. She misunderstood: he laughed, but his nervousness was genuine.

After any stroke of events, whether a happy one or a catastrophe, we see that the materials for it were a long time gathering, and the only marvel is that the stroke was not prophesied. What bore the air of fatal coincidence may remain fatal indeed, to this later view; but, with the haphazard aspect dispelled, there is left for scrutiny the same ancient hint from the Infinite to the effect that since events have never yet failed to be law-abiding, perhaps it were well for us to deduce that they will continue to be so until further notice.

. . . On the day that was to open the closed door in the background of his pictures of Alice, Russell lunched with his relatives. There were but the four people, Russell and Mildred and her mother and father, in the great, cool dining-room. Arched French windows, shaded by awnings, admitted a mellow light and looked out upon a green lawn ending in a long conservatory, which revealed through its glass panes a carnival of plants in luxuriant blossom. From his seat at the table, Russell glanced out at this pretty display, and informed his cousins that he was surprised. "You have such a glorious spread of flowers all over the house," he said, "I didn't suppose you'd have any left out yonder. In fact, I didn't know there were so many splendid flowers in the world."

Mrs. Palmer, large, calm, fair, like her daughter, responded with a mild reproach: "That's because you haven't been cousinly enough to get used to them, Arthur. You've almost taught us to forget what you look like."

In defense Russell waved a hand toward her husband. "You see, he's begun to keep me so hard at work——"

But Mr. Palmer declined the responsibility. "Up to four or five in the afternoon, perhaps," he said. "After that, the young gentleman is as much a stranger to me as he is to my family. I've been wondering who she could be."

"When a man's preoccupied there must be a lady then?" Russell inquired.

"That seems to be the view of your sex," Mrs. Palmer suggested. "It was my husband who said it, not Mildred or I."

Mildred smiled faintly. "Papa may be singular in his ideas; they may come entirely from his own experience, and have nothing to do with Arthur."

"Thank you, Mildred," her cousin said, bowing to her gratefully. "You seem to understand my character—and your father's quite as well!"

However, Mildred remained grave in the face of this customary pleasantry, not because the old jest, worn round, like what preceded it, rolled in an old groove, but because of some preoccupation of her own. Her faint smile had disappeared, and, as her cousin's glance met hers, she looked down; yet not before he had seen in her eyes the flicker of something like a question—a question both poignant and dismayed. He may have understood it; for his own smile vanished at once in favour of a reciprocal solemnity.

"You see, Arthur," Mrs. Palmer said, "Mildred is always a good cousin. She and I stand by you, even if you do stay away from us for weeks and weeks." Then, observing that he appeared to be so occupied with a bunch of iced grapes upon his plate that he had not heard her, she began to talk to her husband, asking him what was "going on down-town."

Arthur continued to eat his grapes, but he ventured to look again at Mildred after a few moments. She, also, appeared to be occupied with a bunch of grapes though she ate none, and only pulled them from their stems. She sat straight, her features as composed and pure as those of a new marble saint in a cathedral niche; yet her downcast eyes seemed to conceal many thoughts; and her cousin, against his will, was more aware of what these thoughts might be than of the leisurely conversation between her father and mother. All at once, however, he heard something that startled him, and he listened—and here was the effect of all Alice's forefendings; he listened from the first with a sinking heart.

Mr. Palmer, mildly amused by what he was telling his wife, had just spoken the words, "this Virgil Adams." What he had said was, "this Virgil Adams—that's the man's name. Queer case."

"Who told you?" Mrs. Palmer inquired, not much interested.

"Alfred Lamb," her husband answered. "He was laughing about his father, at the club. You see the old gentleman takes a great pride in his judgment of men, and always boasted to his sons that he'd never in his life made a mistake in trusting the wrong man. Now Alfred and James Albert, Junior, think they have a great joke on him; and they've twitted him so much about it he'll scarcely speak to them. From the first, Alfred says, the old chap's only repartee was, 'You wait and you'll see!' And they've asked him so often to show them what they're going to see that he won't say anything at all!"

"He's a funny old fellow," Mrs. Palmer observed. "But he's so shrewd I can't imagine his being deceived for such a long time. Twenty years, you said?"

"Yes, longer than that, I understand. It appears when this man—this Adams—was a young clerk, the old gentleman trusted him with one of his business secrets, a glue process that Mr. Lamb had spent some money to get hold of. The old chap thought this Adams was going to have quite a future with the Lamb concern, and of course never dreamed he was dishonest. Alfred says this Adams hasn't been of any real use for years, and they should have let him go as dead wood, but the old gentleman wouldn't hear of it, and insisted on his being kept on the payroll; so they just decided to look on it as a sort of pension. Well, one morning last March the man had an attack of some sort down there, and Mr. Lamb got his own car out and went home with him, himself, and worried about him and went to see him no end, all the time he was ill."

"He would," Mrs. Palmer said, approvingly. "He's a kind-hearted creature, that old man."

Her husband laughed. "Alfred says he thinks his kind-heartedness is about cured! It seems that as soon as the man got well again he deliberately walked off with the old gentleman's glue secret. Just calmly stole it! Alfred says he believes that if he had a stroke in the office now, himself, his father wouldn't lift a finger to help him!"

Mrs. Palmer repeated the name to herself thoughtfully. " 'Adams'—'Virgil Adams.' You said his name was Virgil Adams?"

"Yes."

She looked at her daughter. "Why, you know who that is, Mildred," she said, casually. "It's that Alice Adams's father, isn't it? Wasn't his name Virgil Adams?"

"I think it is," Mildred said.

Mrs. Palmer turned toward her husband. "You've seen this Alice Adams here. Mr. Lamb's pet swindler must be her father."

Mr. Palmer passed a smooth hand over his neat gray hair, which was not disturbed by this effort to stimulate recollection. "Oh, yes," he said. "Of course—certainly. Quite a good-looking girl—one of Mildred's friends. How queer!"

Mildred looked up, as if in a little alarm, but did not speak. Her mother set matters straight. "Fathers *are* amusing," she said smilingly to Russell, who was looking at her, though how fixedly she did not notice; for she turned from him at once to enlighten her husband. "Every girl who meets Mildred, and tries to push the acquaintance by coming here until the poor child has to hide, isn't a *friend* of hers, my dear!"

Mildred's eyes were downcast again, and a faint colour rose in her cheeks. "Oh, I shouldn't put it quite that way about Alice Adams," she said, in a low voice. "I saw something of her for a time. She's not unattractive—in a way."

Mrs. Palmer settled the whole case of Alice carelessly. "A pushing sort of girl," she said. "A very pushing little person."

"I——" Mildred began; and, after hesitating, concluded, "I rather dropped her."

"Fortunate you've done so," her father remarked, cheerfully. "Especially since various members of the Lamb connection are here frequently. They mightn't think you'd show great tact in having her about the place." He laughed, and turned to his cousin. "All this isn't very interesting to poor Arthur. How terrible people are with a newcomer in a town; they talk as if he knew all about everybody!"

"But we don't know anything about these queer people, ourselves," said Mrs. Palmer. "We know something about the girl, of course—she used to be a bit *too* conspicuous, in fact! However, as you say, we might find a subject more interesting for Arthur." She smiled whimsically upon the young man. "Tell the truth," she said. "Don't you fairly detest going into business with that tyrant yonder?"

"What? Yes—I beg your pardon!" he stammered.

"You were right," Mrs. Palmer said to her husband. "You've bored him so, talking about thievish clerks, he can't even answer an honest question."

But Russell was beginning to recover his outward composure. "Try me again," he said. "I'm afraid I was thinking of something else."

This was the best he found to say. There was a part of him that wanted to protest and deny, but he had not heat enough, in the chill that had come upon him. Here was the first "mention" of Alice, and with it the reason why it was the first: Mr. Palmer had difficulty in recalling her, and she happened to be spoken of, only because her father's betrayal of a benefactor's trust had been so peculiarly atrocious that, in the view of the benefactor's family, it contained enough of the element of humour to warrant a mild laugh at a club. There was the deadliness of the story: its lack of malice, even of resentment. Deadlier still were Mrs. Palmer's phrases: "a pushing sort of girl," "a very pushing little person," and "used to be a bit *too* conspicuous, in fact." But she spoke placidly and by chance; being as obviously without unkindly motive as Mr. Palmer was when he related the cause of Alfred Lamb's amusement. Her opinion of the obscure young lady momentarily her topic had been expressed, moreover, to her husband, and at her own table. She sat there, large, kind, serene—a protest might astonish but could not change her; and Russell, crumpling in his strained fingers the lace-edged little web of a napkin on his knee, found heart enough to grow red, but not enough to challenge her.

She noticed his colour, and attributed it to the embarrassment of a scrupulously gallant gentleman caught in a lapse of attention to a lady. "Don't be disturbed," she said, benevolently. "People aren't expected to listen all the time to their relatives. A high colour's very becoming to you, Arthur; but it really isn't necessary between cousins. You can always be informal enough with us to listen only when you care to."

His complexion continued to be ruddier than usual, however, throughout the meal, and was still somewhat tinted when Mrs. Palmer rose. "The man's bringing you cigarettes here," she said, nodding to the two gentlemen. "We'll give you a chance to do the sordid kind of talking we know you really like. Afterwhile, Mildred will show you what's in bloom in the hothouse, if you wish, Arthur."

Mildred followed her, and, when they were alone in another of the spacious rooms, went to a window and looked out, while her mother seated herself near the center of the room in a gilt armchair, mellowed with old Aubusson tapestry. Mrs. Palmer looked thoughtfully at her daughter's back, but did not speak to her until coffee had been brought for them.

"Thanks," Mildred said, not turning, "I don't care for any coffee, I believe."

"No?" Mrs. Palmer said, gently. "I'm afraid our good-looking cousin won't think you're very talkative, Mildred. You spoke only about twice at lunch. I shouldn't care for him to get the idea you're piqued because he's come here so little lately, should you?"

"No, I shouldn't," Mildred answered in a low voice, and with that she turned quickly, and came to sit near her mother. "But it's what I am afraid of! Mama, did you notice how red he got?"

"You mean when he was caught not listening to a question of mine? Yes; it's very becoming to him."

"Mama, I don't think that was the reason. I don't think it was because he wasn't listening, I mean."

"No?"

"I think his colour and his not listening came from the same reason," Mildred said, and although she had come to sit near her mother, she did not look at her. "I think it happened because you and papa——" She stopped.

"Yes?" Mrs. Palmer said, good-naturedly, to prompt her. "Your father and I did something embarrassing?"

"Mama, it was because of those things that came out about Alice Adams."

"How could that bother Arthur? Does he know her?"

"Don't you remember?" the daughter asked. "The day after my dance I mentioned how odd I thought it was in him—I was a little disappointed in him. I'd been seeing that he met everybody, of course, but she was the only girl *he* asked to meet; and he did it as soon as he noticed her. I hadn't meant to have him meet her—in fact, I was rather sorry I'd felt I had to ask her, because she—oh, well, she's the sort that 'tries for the new man,' if she has half a chance; and sometimes they seem quite fascinated—for a time, that is. I thought Arthur was above all that; or at the very least I gave him credit for being too sophisticated."

"I see," Mrs. Palmer said, thoughtfully. "I remember now that you spoke of it. You said it seemed a little peculiar, but of course it really wasn't: a 'new man' has nothing to go by, except his own first impressions. You can't blame poor Arthur—she's quite a piquant looking little person. You think he's seen something of her since then?"

Mildred nodded slowly. "I never dreamed such a thing till yesterday, and even then I rather doubted it—till he got so red, just now! I was surprised when he asked to meet her, but he just danced with her once and didn't mention her afterward; I forgot all about it—in fact, I virtually forgot all about *her*. I'd seen quite a little of her—"

"Yes," said Mrs. Palmer. "She did keep coming here!"

"But I'd just about decided that it really wouldn't do," Mildred went on. "She isn't—well, I didn't admire her."

"No," her mother assented, and evidently followed a direct connection of thought in a speech apparently irrelevant. "I understand the young Malone wants to marry Henrietta. I hope she won't; he seems rather a gross type of person."

"Oh, he's just one," Mildred said. "I don't know that he and Alice Adams were ever engaged—she never told me so. She may not have been engaged to any of them; she was just enough among the other girls to get talked about—and one of the reasons I felt a little inclined to be nice to her was that they seemed to be rather edging her out of the circle. It wasn't long before I saw they were right, though. I happened to mention I was going to give a dance and she pretended to take it as a matter of course that I meant to invite her brother—at least, I thought she pretended; she may have really believed it. At any rate, I had to send him a card; but I didn't intend to be let in for that sort of thing again, of course. She's what you said, 'pushing'; though I'm awfully sorry you said it."

"Why shouldn't I have said it, my dear?"

"Of course I didn't say 'shouldn't,'" Mildred explained, gravely. "I meant only that I'm sorry it happened."

"Yes; but why?"

"Mama"—Mildred turned to her, leaning forward and speaking in a lowered voice—"Mama, at first the change was so little it seemed as if Arthur hardly knew it himself. He'd been lovely to me always, and he was still lovely to me—but—oh, well, you've understood—after my dance it was more as if it was just his nature and his training to be lovely to me, as he would be to everyone—a kind of politeness. He'd never said he *cared* for me, but after that I could see he didn't. It was clear—after that. I didn't know what had happened; I couldn't think of anything I'd done. Mama—it was Alice Adams."

Mrs. Palmer set her little coffee-cup upon the table beside her, calmly following her own motion with her eyes, and not seeming to realize with what serious entreaty her daughter's gaze was fixed upon her. Mildred repeated the last sentence of her revelation, and introduced a stress of insistence.

"Mama, it *was* Alice Adams!"

But Mrs. Palmer declined to be greatly impressed, so far as her appearance went, at least; and to emphasize her refusal, she smiled indulgently. "What makes you think so?"

"Henrietta told me yesterday."

At this Mrs. Palmer permitted herself to laugh softly aloud. "Good heavens! Is Henrietta a soothsayer? Or is she Arthur's particular *confidante?*"

"No. Ella Dowling told her."

Mrs. Palmer's laughter continued. "Now we have it!" she exclaimed. "It's a game of gossip: Arthur tells Ella, Ella tells Henrietta, and Henrietta tells——"

"Don't laugh, please, mama," Mildred begged. "Of course Arthur didn't tell anybody. It's roundabout enough, but it's true. I know it! I hadn't quite believed it, but I knew it was true when he got so red. He looked—oh, for a second or so he looked—stricken! He thought I didn't notice it. Mama, he's been to see her almost every evening lately. They take long walks together. That's why he hasn't been here."

Of Mrs. Palmer's laughter there was left only her indulgent smile, which she had not allowed to vanish. "Well, what of it?" she said.

"Mama!"

"Yes," said Mrs. Palmer. "What of it?"

"But don't you see?" Mildred's well-tutored voice, though modulated and repressed even in her present emotion, nevertheless had a tendency to quaver. "It's true. Frank Dowling was going to see her one evening and he saw Arthur sitting on the stoop with her, and didn't go in. And Ella used to go to school with a girl who lives across the street from her. She told Ella——"

"Oh, I understand," Mrs. Palmer interrupted. "Suppose he does go there. My dear, I said, 'What of it?' "

"I don't see what you mean, mama. I'm so afraid he might think we knew about it, and that you and papa said those things about her and her father on that account—as if we abused them because he goes there instead of coming here."

"Nonsense!" Mrs. Palmer rose, went to a window, and, turning there, stood with her back to it, facing her daughter and looking at her cheerfully. "Nonsense, my dear! It was perfectly clear that she was mentioned by accident, and so was her father. What an extraordinary man! If Arthur makes friends with people like that, he certainly knows better than to expect to hear favourable opinions of them. Besides, it's only a little passing thing with him."

"Mama! When he goes there almost every——"

"Yes," Mrs. Palmer said, dryly. "It seems to me I've heard somewhere that other young men have gone there 'almost every!' She doesn't last, apparently. Arthur's gallant, and he's impressionable—but he's fastidious, and fastidiousness is always the check on impressionableness. A girl belongs to her family, too—and this one does especially, it strikes me! Arthur's very sensible; he sees more than you'd think."

Mildred looked at her hopefully. "Then you don't believe he's likely to imagine we said those things of her in any meaning way?"

At this, Mrs. Palmer laughed again. "There's one thing you seem not to have noticed, Mildred."

"What's that?"

"It seems to have escaped your attention that he never said a word."

"Mightn't that mean——?" Mildred began, but she stopped.

"No, it mightn't," her mother replied, comprehending easily. "On the contrary, it might mean that instead of his feeling it too deeply to speak, he was getting a little illumination."

Mildred rose and came to her. "Why do you suppose he never told us he went there? Do you think he's—do you think he's pleased with her, and yet ashamed of it? Why do you suppose he's never spoken of it?"

"Ah, that," Mrs. Palmer said;—"that might possibly be her own doing. If it is, she's well paid by what your father and I said, because we wouldn't have said it if we'd known that Arthur——" She checked herself quickly. Looking over her daughter's shoulder, she saw the two gentlemen coming from the corridor toward the wide doorway of the room; and she greeted them cheerfully. "If you've finished with each other for a while," she added, "Arthur may find it a relief to put his thoughts on something prettier than a trust company—and more fragrant."

Arthur came to Mildred.

"Your mother said at lunch that perhaps you'd——"

"I didn't say 'perhaps,' Arthur," Mrs. Palmer interrupted, to correct him. "I said she would. If you care to see and smell those lovely things out yonder, she'll show them to you. Run along, children!"

Half an hour later, glancing from a window, she saw them come from the hothouses and slowly cross the lawn. Arthur had a fine rose in his buttonhole and looked profoundly thoughtful.

CHAPTER XXI

That morning and noon had been warm, though the stirrings of a feeble breeze made weather not flagrantly intemperate; but at about three o'clock in the afternoon there came out of the southwest a heat like an affliction sent upon an accursed people, and the air was soon dead of it. Dripping negro ditch-diggers whooped with satires praising hell and hot weather, as the tossing shovels flickered up to the street level, where sluggish male pedestrians carried coats upon hot arms, and fanned themselves with straw hats, or, remaining covered, wore soaked handkerchiefs between scalp and straw. Clerks drooped in silent, big department stores; stenographers in offices kept as close to electric fans as the intervening bulk of their employers would let them; guests in hotels left the lobbies and went to lie unclad upon their beds; while in hospitals the patients murmured querulously against the heat, and perhaps against some noisy motorist who strove to feel the air by splitting it, not troubled by any foreboding that he, too, that hour next week, might need quiet near a hospital. The "hot spell" was a true spell, one upon men's spirits; for it was so hot that, in suburban outskirts, golfers crept slowly back over the low undulations of their club lands, abandoning their matches and returning to shelter.

Even on such a day, sizzling work had to be done, as in winter. There were glowing furnaces to be stoked, liquid metals to be poured; but such tasks found seasoned men standing to them; and in all the city probably no brave soul challenged the heat more gamely than Mrs. Adams did, when, in a corner of her small and fiery kitchen, where all day long her hired African immune cooked fiercely, she pressed her husband's evening clothes with a hot iron. No doubt she risked her life, but she risked it cheerfully in so good and necessary a service for him. She would have given her life for him at any time, and both his and her own for her children.

Unconscious of her own heroism, she was surprised to find herself rather faint when she finished her ironing. However, she took heart to believe that the clothes looked better, in spite of one or two scorched places; and she carried them upstairs to her husband's room before increasing blindness forced her to grope for the nearest chair. Then trying to rise and walk, without having sufficiently recovered, she had to sit down again; but after a little while she was able to get upon her feet; and, keeping her hand against the wall, moved successfully to the door of her own room. Here she wavered; might have gone down, had she not been stimulated by the thought of how much depended upon her;—she made a final great effort, and floundered across the room to her bureau, where she kept some simple restoratives. They served her need, or her faith in them did; and she returned to her work.

She went down the stairs, keeping a still tremulous hand upon the rail; but she smiled brightly when Alice looked up from below, where the woodwork was again being tormented with superfluous attentions.

"Alice, *don't!*" her mother said, commiseratingly. "You did all that this morning and it looks lovely. What's the use of wearing yourself out on it? You ought to be lying down, so's to look fresh for to-night."

"Hadn't you better lie down yourself?" the daughter returned. "Are you ill, mama?"

"Certainly not. What in the world makes you think so?"

"You look pretty pale," Alice said, and sighed heavily. "It makes me ashamed, having you work so hard—for me."

"How foolish! I think it's fun, getting ready to entertain a little again, like this. I only wish it hadn't turned so hot: I'm afraid your poor father'll suffer—his things are pretty heavy, I noticed. Well, it'll do him good to bear something for style's sake this once, anyhow!" She laughed, and coming to Alice, bent down and kissed her. "Dearie," she said, tenderly, "wouldn't you please slip upstairs now and take just a little teeny nap to please your mother?"

But Alice responded only by moving her head slowly, in token of refusal.

"Do!" Mrs. Adams urged. "You don't want to look worn out, do you?"

"I'll *look* all right," Alice said, huskily. "Do you like the way I've arranged the furniture now? I've tried all the different ways it'll go."

"It's lovely," her mother said, admiringly. "I thought the last way you had it was pretty, too. But you know best; I never knew anybody with so much taste. If you'd only just quit now, and take a little rest——"

"There'd hardly be time, even if I wanted to; it's after five—but I couldn't; really, I couldn't. How do you think we can manage about Walter—to see that he wears his evening things, I mean?"

Mrs. Adams pondered. "I'm afraid he'll make a lot of objections, on account of the weather and everything. I wish we'd had a chance to tell him last night or this morning. I'd have telephoned to him this afternoon except —well, I scarcely like to call him up at that place, since your father——"

"No, of course not, mama."

"If Walter gets home late," Mrs. Adams went on, "I'll just slip out and speak to him, in case Mr. Russell's here before he comes. I'll just tell him he's *got* to hurry and get his things on."

"Maybe he won't come home to dinner," Alice suggested, rather hopefully. "Sometimes he doesn't."

"No; I think he'll be here. When he doesn't come he usually telephones by this time to say not to wait for him; he's very thoughtful about that. Well, it really is getting late: I must go and tell her she ought to be preparing her fillet. Dearie, *do* rest a little."

"You'd much better do that yourself," Alice called after her, but Mrs. Adams shook her head cheerily, not pausing on her way to the fiery kitchen.

Alice continued her useless labours for a time; then carried her bucket to the head of the cellar stairway, where she left it upon the top step; and, closing the door, returned to the "living-room." Again she changed the positions of the old plush rocking-chairs, moving them into the corners where she thought they might be least noticeable; and while thus engaged she was startled by a loud ringing of the door-bell. For a moment her face was panic-stricken, and she stood staring; then she realized that Russell would not arrive for another hour, at the earliest, and recovering her equipoise, went to the door.

Waiting there, in a languid attitude, was a young coloured woman, with a small bundle under her arm and something malleable in her mouth. "Listen," she said. "You folks expectin' a coloured lady?"

"No," said Alice. "Especially not at the front door."

"Listen," the coloured woman said again. "Listen. Say, listen. Ain't they another coloured lady awready here by the day? Listen. Ain't Miz Malena Burns here by the day this evenin'? Say, listen. This the number house she give *me*."

"Are you the waitress?" Alice asked dismally.

"Yes'm, if Malena here."

"Malena is here," Alice said, and hesitated; but she decided not to send the waitress to the back door, it might be a risk. She let her in. "What's your name?"

"Me? I'm name' Gertrude. Miss Gertrude Collamus."

"Did you bring a cap and apron?"

Gertrude took the little bundle from under her arm. "Yes'm. I'm all fix'."

"I've already set the table," Alice said. "I'll show you what we want done." She led the way to the dining-room, and, after offering some instruction there, received by Gertrude with languor and a slowly moving jaw, she took her into the kitchen, where the cap and apron were put on. The effect was not fortunate; Gertrude's eyes were noticeably bloodshot, an affliction made more apparent by the white cap; and Alice drew her mother apart, whispering anxiously,

"Do you suppose it's too late to get someone else?"

"I'm afraid it is," Mrs. Adams said. "Malena says it was hard enough to get her! You have to pay them so much that they only work when they feel like it."

"Mama, could you ask her to wear her cap straighter? Every time she moves her head she gets it on one side, and her skirt's too long behind and too short in front—and oh, I've *never* seen such *feet!*" Alice laughed desolately. "And she *must* quit that terrible chewing!"

"Never mind; I'll get to work with her. I'll straighten her out all I can, dearie; don't worry." Mrs. Adams patted her daughter's shoulder encouragingly. "Now *you* can't do another thing, and if you don't run and begin dressing you won't be ready. It'll only take me a minute to dress, myself, and I'll be down long before you will. Run, darling! I'll look after everything."

Alice nodded vaguely, went up to her room, and, after only a moment with her mirror, brought from her closet the dress of white organdie she had worn the night when she met Russell for the first time. She laid it carefully upon her bed, and began to make ready to put it on. Her mother came in, half an hour later, to "fasten" her.

"*I'm* all dressed," Mrs. Adams said, briskly. "Of course it doesn't matter. He won't know what the rest of us even look like: How could he? I know I'm an old *sight*, but all I want is to look respectable. Do I?"

"You look like the best woman in the world; that's all!" Alice said, with a little gulp.

Her mother laughed and gave her a final scrutiny. "You might use just a tiny bit more colour, dearie—I'm afraid the excitement's made you a little pale. And you *must* brighten up! There's sort of a look in your eyes as if you'd got in a trance and couldn't get out. You've had it all day. I must run: your father wants me to help him with his studs. Walter hasn't come yet, but

I'll look after him; don't worry. And you better *hurry*, dearie, if you're going to take any time fixing the flowers on the table."

She departed, while Alice sat at the mirror again, to follow her advice concerning a "tiny bit more colour." Before she had finished, her father knocked at the door, and, when she responded, came in. He was dressed in the clothes his wife had pressed; but he had lost substantially in weight since they were made for him; no one would have thought that they had been pressed. They hung from him voluminously, seeming to be the clothes of a larger man.

"Your mother's gone downstairs," he said, in a voice of distress. "One of the buttonholes in my shirt is too large and I can't keep the dang thing fastened. I don't know what to do about it! I only got one other white shirt, and it's kind of ruined: I tried it before I did this one. Do you s'pose you could do anything?"

"I'll see," she said.

"My collar's got a frayed edge," he complained, as she examined his troublesome shirt. "It's a good deal like wearing a saw; but I expect it'll wilt down flat pretty soon, and not bother me long. I'm liable to wilt down flat, myself, I expect; I don't know as I remember any such hot night in the last ten or twelve years." He lifted his head and sniffed the flaccid air, which was laden with a heavy odour. "My, but that smell is pretty strong!" he said.

"Stand still, please, papa," Alice begged him. "I can't see what's the matter if you move around. How absurd you are about your old glue smell, papa! There isn't a vestige of it, of course."

"I didn't mean glue," he informed her. "I mean cabbage. Is that fashionable now, to have cabbage when there's company for dinner?"

"That isn't cabbage, papa. It's Brussels sprouts."

"Oh, is it? I don't mind it much, because it keeps that glue smell off me, but it's fairly strong. I expect you don't notice it so much because you been in the house with it all along, and got used to it while it was growing."

"It is pretty dreadful," Alice said. "Are all the windows open downstairs?"

"I'll go down and see, if you'll just fix that hole up for me."

"I'm afraid I can't," she said. "Not unless you take your shirt off and bring it to me. I'll have to sew the hole smaller."

"Oh, well, I'll go ask your mother to——"

"No," said Alice. "She's got everything on her hands. Run and take it off. Hurry, papa; I've got to arrange the flowers on the table before he comes."

He went away, and came back presently, half undressed, bringing the shirt. "There's *one* comfort," he remarked, pensively, as she worked. "I've got that collar off—for a while, anyway. I wish I could go to table like this; I could stand it a good deal better. Do you seem to be making any headway with the dang thing?"

"I think probably I can——"

Downstairs the door-bell rang, and Alice's arms jerked with the shock.

"Golly!" her father said. "Did you stick your finger with that fool needle?"

She gave him a blank stare. "He's come!"

She was not mistaken, for, upon the little veranda, Russell stood facing the closed door at last. However, it remained closed for a considerable time after he rang. Inside the house the warning summons of the bell was immediately followed by another sound, audible to Alice and her father as a crash preceding a series of muffled falls. Then came a distant voice, bitter in complaint.

"Oh, Lord!" said Adams. "What's that?"

Alice went to the top of the front stairs, and her mother appeared in the hall below.

"Mama!"

Mrs. Adams looked up. "It's all right," she said, in a loud whisper. "Gertrude fell down the cellar stairs. Somebody left a bucket there, and——" She was interrupted by a gasp from Alice, and hastened to reassure her. "Don't worry, dearie. She may limp a little, but——"

Adams leaned over the banisters. "Did she break anything?" he asked.

"Hush!" his wife whispered. "No. She seems upset and angry about it, more than anything else; but she's rubbing herself, and she'll be all right in time to bring in the little sandwiches. Alice! Those flowers!"

"I know, mama. But——"

"Hurry!" Mrs. Adams warned her. "Both of you hurry! I *must* let him in!"

She turned to the door, smiling cordially, even before she opened it. "Do come right in, Mr. Russell," she said, loudly, lifting her voice for additional warning to those above. "I'm *so* glad to receive you informally, this way, in our own little home. There's a hat-rack here under the stairway," she continued, as Russell, murmuring some response, came into the hall. "I'm afraid you'll think it's almost *too* informal, my coming to the door, but unfortunately our housemaid's just had a little accident—oh, nothing to mention! I just thought we better not keep you waiting any longer. Will you step into our 'living-room,' please?"

She led the way between the two small columns, and seated herself in one of the plush rocking-chairs, selecting it because Alice had once pointed out that the chairs, themselves, were less noticeable when they had people sitting in them. "Do sit down, Mr. Russell; it's so very warm it's really quite a trial just to stand up!"

"Thank you," he said, as he took a seat. "Yes. It is quite warm." And this seemed to be the extent of his responsiveness for the moment. He was grave, rather pale; and Mrs. Adams's impression of him, as she formed it then, was of "a distinguished-looking young man, really elegant in the best sense of the word, but timid and formal when he first meets you." She beamed upon him, and used with everything she said a continuous accompaniment of laughter, meaningless except that it was meant to convey cordiality. "Of course we *do* have a great deal of warm weather," she informed him. "I'm glad it's so much cooler in the house than it is outdoors."

"Yes," he said. "It is pleasanter indoors." And, stopping with this single untruth, he permitted himself the briefest glance about the room; then his eyes returned to his smiling hostess.

"Most people make a great fuss about hot weather," she said. "The only person I know who doesn't mind the heat the way other people do is Alice. She always seems as cool as if we had a breeze blowing, no matter how hot it is. But then she's so amiable she never minds anything. It's just her character. She's always been that way since she was a little child; always the same to everybody, high and low. I think character's the most important thing in the world, after all, don't you, Mr. Russell?"

"Yes," he said solemnly; and touched his bedewed white forehead with a handkerchief.

"Indeed it is," she agreed with herself, never failing to continue her murmur of laughter. "That's what I've always told Alice; but she never sees anything good in herself, and she just laughs at me when I praise her. She sees good in everybody *else* in the world, no matter how unworthy they are, or how they behave toward *her*; but she always underestimates herself. From the time she was a little child she was always that way. When some other little girl would behave selfishly or meanly toward her, do you think she'd come and tell me? Never a word to anybody! The little thing was too proud! She was the same way about school. The teacher had to tell me when she took a prize; she'd bring it home and keep it in her room without a word about it to her father and mother. Now, Walter was just the other way. Walter would——" But here Mrs. Adams checked herself, though she increased the volume of her laughter. "How silly of me!" she exclaimed. "I expect you know how mothers *are*, though, Mr. Russell. Give us a chance and we'll talk about our children forever! Alice would feel terribly if she knew how I've been going on about her to you."

In this Mrs. Adams was right, though she did not herself suspect it, and upon an almost inaudible word or two from him she went on with her topic. "Of course my excuse is that few mothers have a daughter like Alice. I suppose we all think the same way about our children, but *some* of us must be right when we feel we've got the best. Don't you think so?"

"Yes. Yes, indeed."

"I'm sure *I* am!" she laughed. "I'll let the others speak for themselves." She paused reflectively. "No; I think a mother knows when she's got a treasure in her family. If she *hasn't* got one, she'll pretend she has, maybe; but if she has, she knows it. I certainly know *I* have. She's always been what people call 'the joy of the household'—always cheerful, no matter what went wrong, and always ready to smooth things over with some bright, witty saying. You must be sure not to *tell* we've had this little chat about her—she'd just be furious with me—but she *is* such a dear child! You won't tell her, will you?"

"No," he said, and again applied the handkerchief to his forehead for an instant. "No, I'll——" He paused, and finished lamely: "I'll—not tell her."

Thus reassured, Mrs. Adams set before him some details of her daughter's popularity at sixteen, dwelling upon Alice's impartiality among her young suitors: "She never could *bear* to hurt their feelings, and always treated all of them just alike. About half a dozen of them were just *bound* to marry her! Naturally, her father and I considered any such idea ridiculous; she was too young, of course."

Thus the mother went on with her biographical sketches, while the pale young man sat facing her under the hard overhead light of a white globe, set to the ceiling; and listened without interrupting. She was glad to have the chance to tell him a few things about Alice he might not have guessed for himself, and, indeed, she had planned to find such an opportunity, if she could; but this was getting to be altogether too much of one, she felt. As time passed, she was like an actor who must improvise to keep the audience from perceiving that his fellow-players have missed their cues; but her anxiety was not betrayed to the still listener; she had a valiant soul.

Alice, meanwhile, had arranged her little roses on the table in as many ways, probably, as there were blossoms; and she was still at it when her father arrived in the dining-room by way of the back stairs and the kitchen.

"It's pulled out again," he said. "But I guess there's no help for it now; it's too late, and anyway it lets some air into me when it bulges. I can sit so's it won't be noticed much, I expect. Isn't it time you quit bothering about the looks of the table? Your mother's been talking to him about half an hour now, and I had the idea he came on your account, not hers. Hadn't you better go and——"

"Just a minute," Alice said, piteously. "Do *you* think it looks all right?"

"The flowers? Fine! Hadn't you better leave 'em the way they are, though?"

"Just a minute," she begged again. "Just *one* minute, papa!" And she exchanged a rose in front of Russell's plate for one that seemed to her a little larger.

"You better come on," Adams said, moving to the door.

"Just *one* more second, papa." She shook her head, lamenting. "Oh, I wish we'd rented some silver!"

"Why?"

"Because so much of the plating has rubbed off a lot of it. *Just* a second, papa." And as she spoke she hastily went round the table, gathering the knives and forks and spoons that she thought had their plating best preserved, and exchanging them for more damaged pieces at Russell's place. "There!" she sighed, finally. "Now I'll come." But at the door she paused to look back dubiously, over her shoulder.

"What's the matter now?"

"The roses. I believe after all I shouldn't have tried that vine effect; I ought to have kept them in water, in the vase. It's so hot, they already begin to look a little wilted, out on the dry tablecloth like that. I believe I'll——"

"Why, look here, Alice!" he remonstrated, as she seemed disposed to turn back. "Everything'll burn up on the stove if you keep on——"

"Oh, well," she said, "the vase was terribly ugly; I can't do any better.

We'll go in." But with her hand on the door-knob she paused. "No, papa. We mustn't go in by this door. It might look as if——"

"As if what?"

"Never mind," she said. "Let's go the other way."

"I don't see what difference it makes," he grumbled, but nevertheless followed her through the kitchen, and up the back stairs then through the upper hallway. At the top of the front stairs she paused for a moment, drawing a deep breath and then, before her father's puzzled eyes, a transformation came upon her. Her shoulders, like her eyelids, had been drooping, but now she threw her head back: the shoulders straightened, and the lashes lifted over sparkling eyes; vivacity came to her whole body in a flash; and she tripped down the steps, with her pretty hands rising in time to the lilting little tune she had begun to hum.

At the foot of the stairs, one of those pretty hands extended itself at full arm's length toward Russell, and continued to be extended until it reached his own hand as he came to meet her. "How terrible of me!" she exclaimed. "To be so late coming down! And papa, too—I think you know each other."

Her father was advancing toward the young man, expecting to shake hands with him, but Alice stood between them, and Russell, a little flushed, bowed to him gravely over her shoulder, without looking at him; whereupon Adams, slightly disconcerted, put his hands in his pockets and turned to his wife.

"I guess dinner's more'n ready," he said. "We better go sit down."

But she shook her head at him fiercely, "Wait!" she whispered.

"What for? For Walter?"

"No; he can't be coming," she returned, hurriedly, and again warned him by a shake of her head. "Be quiet!"

"Oh, well——" he muttered.

"Sit down!"

He was thoroughly mystified, but obeyed her gesture and went to the rocking-chair in the opposite corner, where he sat down, and, with an expression of meek inquiry, awaited events.

Meanwhile, Alice prattled on: "It's really not a fault of mine, being tardy. The shameful truth is I was trying to hurry papa. He's incorrigible: he stays so late at his terrible old factory—terrible *new* factory, I should say. I hope you don't *hate* us for making you dine with us in such fearful weather! I'm nearly dying of the heat, myself, so you have a fellow-sufferer, if that pleases you. Why is it we always bear things better if we think other people have to stand them, too?" And she added, with an excited laugh: "*Silly* of us, don't you think?"

Gertrude had just made her entrance from the dining-room, bearing a tray. She came slowly, with an air of resentment; and her skirt still needed adjusting, while her lower jaw moved at intervals, though not now upon any substance, but reminiscently, of habit. She halted before Adams, facing him.

He looked plaintive. "What you want o' me?" he asked.

For response, she extended the tray toward him with a gesture of indifference; but he still appeared to be puzzled. "What in the world——?" he began, then caught his wife's eye, and had presence of mind enough to take a damp and plastic sandwich from the tray. "Well, I'll *try* one," he said, but a moment later, as he fulfilled this promise, an expression of intense dislike came upon his features, and he would have returned the sandwich to Gertrude. However, as she had crossed the room to Mrs. Adams he checked the gesture, and sat helplessly, with the sandwich in his hand. He made another effort to get rid of it as the waitress passed him, on her way back to the dining-room, but she appeared not to observe him, and he continued to be troubled by it.

Alice was a loyal daughter. "These are delicious, mama," she said; and turning to Russell, "You missed it; you should have taken one. Too bad we couldn't have offered you what ought to go with it, of course, but——"

She was interrupted by the second entrance of Gertrude, who announced, "Dinner serve'," and retired from view.

"Well, well!" Adams said, rising from his chair, with relief. "That's good! Let's go see if we can eat it." And as the little group moved toward the open door of the dining-room he disposed of his sandwich by dropping it in the empty fireplace.

Alice, glancing back over her shoulder, was the only one who saw him, and she shuddered in spite of herself. Then, seeing that he looked at her entreatingly, as if he wanted to explain that he was doing the best he could, she smiled upon him sunnily, and began to chatter to Russell again.

CHAPTER XXII

Alice kept her sprightly chatter going when they sat down, though the temperature of the room and the sight of hot soup might have discouraged a less determined gaiety. Moreover, there were details as unpropitious as the heat: the expiring roses expressed not beauty but pathos, and what faint odour they exhaled was no rival to the lusty emanations of the Brussels sprouts; at the head of the table, Adams, sitting low in his chair, appeared to be unable to flatten the uprising wave of his starched bosom; and Gertrude's manner and expression were of a recognizable hostility during the long period of vain waiting for the cups of soup to be emptied. Only Mrs. Adams made any progress in this direction; the others merely feinting, now and then lifting their spoons as if they intended to do something with them.

Alice's talk was little more than cheerful sound, but, to fill a desolate interval, served its purpose; and her mother supported her with every faithful cooings of applausive laughter. "What a funny thing weather is!" the girl ran on. "Yesterday it was cool—angels had charge of it—and to-day they had an engagement somewhere else, so the devil saw his chance and started to move the equator to the North Pole; but by the time he got half-way, he thought of something else he wanted to do, and went off; and left the equator here, right on top of *us!* I wish he'd come back and get it!"

"Why, Alice dear!" her mother cried, fondly. "What an imagination! Not a very pious one, I'm afraid Mr. Russell might think, though!" Here she gave Gertrude a hidden signal to remove the soup; but, as there was no response, she had to make the signal more conspicuous. Gertrude was leaning against the wall, her chin moving like a slow pendulum, her streaked eyes fixed mutinously upon Russell. Mrs. Adams nodded several times, increasing the emphasis of her gesture, while Alice talked briskly; but the brooding waitress continued to brood. A faint snap of the fingers failed to disturb her; nor was a covert hissing whisper of avail, and Mrs. Adams was beginning to show signs of strain when her daughter relieved her.

"Imagine our trying to eat anything so hot as soup on a night like this!" Alice laughed. "What *could* have been in the cook's mind not to give us something iced and jellied instead? Of course it's because she's equatorial, herself, originally, and only feels at home when Mr. Satan moves it north." She looked round at Gertrude, who stood behind her. "Do take this dreadful soup away!"

Thus directly addressed, Gertrude yielded her attention, though unwillingly, and as if she decided only by a hair's weight not to revolt, instead. However, she finally set herself in slow motion; but overlooked the supposed head of the table, seeming to be unaware of the sweltering little man who sat there. As she disappeared toward the kitchen with but three of the cups upon her tray he turned to look plaintively after her, and ventured an attempt to recall her.

"Here!" he said, in a low voice. "Here, you!"

"What is it, Virgil?" his wife asked.

"What's her name?"

Mrs. Adams gave him a glance of sudden panic, and, seeing that the guest of the evening was not looking at her, but down at the white cloth before him, she frowned hard, and shook her head.

Unfortunately Alice was not observing her mother, and asked, innocently: "What's whose name, papa?"

"Why, this young darky woman," he explained. "She left mine."

"Never mind," Alice laughed. "There's hope for you, papa. She hasn't gone forever!"

"I don't know about that," he said, not content with this impulsive assurance. "She *looked* like she is." And his remark, considered as a prediction, had begun to seem warranted before Gertrude's return with china preliminary to the next stage of the banquet.

Alice proved herself equal to the long gap, and rattled on through it with a spirit richly justifying her mother's praise of her as "always ready to smooth things over"; for here was more than long delay to be smoothed over. She smoothed over her father and mother for Russell; and she smoothed over him for them, though he did not know it, and remained unaware of what he owed her. With all this, throughout her prattlings, the girl's bright eyes kept seeking his with an eager gaiety, which but little veiled both interrogation and entreaty—as if she asked: "Is it too much for you? Can't you bear it? Won't you *please* bear it? I would for you. Won't you give me a sign that it's all right?"

He looked at her but fleetingly, and seemed to suffer from the heat, in spite of every manly effort not to wipe his brow too often. His colour, after rising when he greeted Alice and her father, had departed, leaving him again moistly pallid; a condition arising from discomfort, no doubt, but, considered as a decoration, almost poetically becoming to him. Not less becoming was the faint, kindly smile, which showed his wish to express amusement and approval; and yet it was a smile rather strained and plaintive, as if he, like Adams, could only do the best he could.

He pleased Adams, who thought him a fine young man, and decidedly the quietest that Alice had ever shown to her family. In her father's opinion this was no small merit; and it was to Russell's credit, too, that he showed embarrassment upon this first intimate presentation; here was an applicant with both reserve and modesty. "So far, he seems to be first rate—a mighty fine young man," Adams thought; and, prompted by no wish to part from Alice but by reminiscences of apparent candidates less pleasing, he added, "At last!"

Alice's liveliness never flagged. Her smoothing over of things was an almost continuous performance, and had to be. Yet, while she chattered through the hot and heavy courses, the questions she asked herself were as continuous as the performance, and as poignant as what her eyes seemed to be asking Russell. Why had she not prevailed over her mother's fear of being "skimpy?" Had she been, indeed, as her mother said she looked, "in a trance?" But above all: What was the matter with *him?* What had happened? For she told herself with painful humour that something even worse than this dinner must be "the matter with him."

The small room, suffocated with the odour of boiled sprouts, grew hotter and hotter as more and more food appeared, slowly borne in, between deathly long waits, by the resentful, loud-breathing Gertrude. And while Alice still sought Russell's glance, and read the look upon his face a dozen different ways, fearing all of them; and while the straggling little flowers died upon the stained cloth, she felt her heart grow as heavy as the food, and wondered that it did not die like the roses.

With the arrival of coffee, the host bestirred himself to make known a hospitable regret, "By George!" he said. "I meant to buy some cigars." He addressed himself apologetically to the guest. "I don't know what I was thinking about, to forget to bring some home with me. I don't use 'em myself —unless somebody hands me one, you might say. I've always been a pipe-smoker, pure and simple, but I ought to remembered for kind of an occasion like this."

"Not at all," Russell said. "I'm not smoking at all lately; but when I do, I'm like you, and smoke a pipe."

Alice started, remembering what she had told him when he overtook her on her way from the tobacconist's; but, after a moment, looking at him, she decided that he must have forgotten it. If he had remembered, she thought, he could not have helped glancing at her. On the contrary, he seemed more at ease, just then, than he had since they sat down, for he was favouring her father with a thoughtful attention as Adams responded to the introduction of a man's topic into the conversation at last. "Well, Mr. Russell, I guess you're right, at that. I don't say but what cigars may be all right for a man that can afford 'em, if he likes 'em better than a pipe, but you take a good old pipe now——"

He continued, and was getting well into the eulogium customarily provoked by this theme, when there came an interruption: the door-bell rang, and he paused inquiringly, rather surprised.

Mrs. Adams spoke to Gertrude in an undertone:

"Just say, 'Not at home.'"

"What?"

"If it's callers, just say we're not at home."

Gertrude spoke out freely: "You mean you astin' me to 'tend you' front do' fer you?"

She seemed both incredulous and affronted, but Mrs. Adams persisted, though somewhat apprehensively. "Yes. Hurry—uh—please. Just say we're not at home—if you please."

Again Gertrude obviously hesitated between compliance and revolt, and again the meeker course fortunately prevailed with her. She gave Mrs. Adams a stare, grimly derisive, then departed. When she came back she said:

"He say he wait."

"But I told you to tell anybody we were not at home," Mrs. Adams returned. "Who is it?"

"Say he name Mr. Law."

"We don't know any Mr. Law."

"Yes'm; he know you. Say he anxious to speak Mr. Adams. Say he wait."

"Tell him Mr. Adams is engaged."

"Hold on a minute," Adams intervened. "Law? No. I don't know any Mr. Law. You sure you got the name right?"

"Say he name Law," Gertrude replied, looking at the ceiling to express her fatigue. "Law. 'S all he tell me; 's all I know."

Adams frowned. "Law," he said. "Wasn't it maybe 'Lohr?'"

"Law," Gertrude repeated. "'S all he tell me; 's all I know."

"What's he look like?"

"He ain't much," she said. "'Bout you' age; got brustly white moustache, nice eye-glasses."

"It's Charley Lohr!" Adams exclaimed. "I'll go see what he wants."

"But, Virgil," his wife remonstrated, "do finish your coffee; he might stay all evening. Maybe he's come to call."

Adams laughed. "He isn't much of a caller, I expect. Don't worry: I'll take him up to my room." And turning toward Russell, "Ah—if you'll just excuse me," he said; and went out to his visitor.

When he had gone, Mrs. Adams finished her coffee, and, having glanced intelligently from her guest to her daughter, she rose. "I think perhaps I ought to go and shake hands with Mr. Lohr, myself," she said, adding in explanation to Russell, as she reached the door, "He's an old friend of my husband's and it's a very long time since he's been here."

Alice nodded and smiled to her brightly, but upon the closing of the door, the smile vanished; all her liveliness disappeared; and with this change of expression her complexion itself appeared to change, so that her rouge became obvious, for she was pale beneath it. However, Russell did not see the alteration, for he did not look at her; and it was but a momentary lapse—the vacation of a tired girl, who for ten seconds lets herself look as she feels. Then she shot her vivacity back into place as by some powerful spring.

"Penny for your thoughts!" she cried, and tossed one of the wilted roses at him, across the table. "I'll bid more than a penny; I'll bid tuppence—no, a poor little dead rose—a rose for your thoughts, Mr. Arthur Russell! What are they?"

He shook his head. "I'm afraid I haven't any."

"No, of course not," she said. "Who could have thoughts in weather like this? Will you *ever* forgive us?"

"What for?"

"Making you eat such a heavy dinner—I mean *look* at such a heavy dinner, because you certainly didn't do more than look at it—on such a night! But the crime draws to a close, and you can begin to cheer up!" She laughed gaily, and, rising, moved to the door. "Let's go in the other room; your fearful duty is almost done, and you can run home as soon as you want to. That's what you're dying to do."

"Not at all," he said in a voice so feeble that she laughed aloud.

"Good gracious!" she cried. "I hadn't realized it was *that* bad!"

For this, though he contrived to laugh, he seemed to have no verbal retort whatever; but followed her into the "living-room," where she stopped and turned, facing him.

"Has it really been so frightful?" she asked.

"Why, of course not. Not at all."

"Of course yes, though, you mean!"

"Not at all. It's been most kind of your mother and father and you."

"Do you know," she said, "you've never once looked at me for more than a second at a time the whole evening? And it seemed to me I looked rather nice to-night, too!"

"You always do," he murmured.

"I don't see how you know," she returned; and then stepping closer to him, spoke with gentle solicitude: "Tell me: you're really feeling wretchedly, aren't you? I know you've got a fearful headache, or something. Tell me!"

"Not at all."

"You are ill—I'm sure of it."

"Not at all."

"On your word?"

"I'm really quite all right."

"But if you are——" she began; and then, looking at him with a desperate sweetness, as if this were her last resource to rouse him, "What's the matter, little boy?" she said with lisping tenderness. "Tell auntie!"

It was a mistake, for he seemed to flinch, and to lean backward, however, slightly. She turned away instantly, with a flippant lift and drop of both hands. "Oh, my dear!" she laughed. "I won't eat you!"

And as the discomfited young man watched her, seeming able to lift his eyes, now that her back was turned, she went to the front door and pushed open the screen. "Let's go out on the porch," she said. "Where we belong!"

Then, when he had followed her out, and they were seated, "Isn't this better?" she asked. "Don't you feel more like yourself out here?"

He began a murmur: "Not at——"

But she cut him off sharply: "Please don't say 'Not at all' again!"

"I'm sorry."

"You do seem sorry about something," she said. "What is it? Isn't it time you were telling me what's the matter?"

"Nothing. Indeed nothing's the matter. Of course one *is* rather affected by such weather as this. It may make one a little quieter than usual, of course."

She sighed, and let the tired muscles of her face rest. Under the hard lights, indoors, they had served her until they ached, and it was a luxury to feel that in the darkness no grimacings need call upon them.

"Of course, if you won't tell me——" she said.

"I can only assure you there's nothing to tell."

"I know what an ugly little house it is," she said. "Maybe it was the furniture—or mama's vases that upset you. Or was it mama herself—or papa?"

"Nothing 'upset' me."

At that she uttered a monosyllable of doubting laughter. "I wonder why you say that."

"Because it's so."

"No. It's because you're too kind, or too conscientious, or too embarrassed—anyhow too something—to tell me." She leaned forward, elbows on knees and chin in hands, in the reflective attitude she knew how to make graceful. "I have a feeling that you're not going to tell me," she said, slowly. "Yes—even that you're never going to tell me. I wonder—I wonder——"

"Yes? What do you wonder?"

"I was just thinking—I wonder if they haven't done it, after all."

"I don't understand."

"I wonder," she went on, still slowly, and in a voice of reflection, "I wonder who *has* been talking about me to you, after all? Isn't that it?"

"Not at——" he began, but checked himself and substituted another form of denial. "Nothing is 'it.'"

"Are you sure?"

"Why, yes."

"How curious!" she said.

"Why?"

"Because all evening you've been so utterly different."

"But in this weather——"

"No. That wouldn't make you afraid to look at me all evening!"

"But I did look at you. Often."

"No. Not really a *look*."

"But I'm looking at you now."

"Yes—in the dark!" she said. "No—the weather might make you even quieter than usual, but it wouldn't strike you so nearly dumb. No—and it wouldn't make you seem to be under such a strain—as if you thought only of escape!"

"But I haven't——"

"You shouldn't," she interrupted, gently. "There's nothing you have to escape from, you know. You aren't committed to—to this friendship."

"I'm sorry you think——" he began, but did not complete the fragment.

She took it up. "You're sorry I think you're so different, you mean to say, don't you? Never mind: that's what you did mean to say, but you couldn't finish it because you're not good at deceiving."

"Oh, no," he protested, feebly. "I'm not deceiving. I'm——"

"Never mind," she said again. "You're sorry I think you're so different—and all in one day—since last night. Yes, your voice *sounds* sorry, too. It sounds sorrier than it would just because of my thinking something you could change my mind about in a minute—so it means you're sorry you *are* different."

"No—I——"

But disregarding the faint denial, "Never mind," she said. "Do you remember one night when you told me that nothing anybody else could do would ever keep you from coming here? That if you—if you left me—it would be because I drove you away myself?"

"Yes," he said, huskily. "It was true."

"Are you sure?"

"Indeed I am," he answered in a low voice, but with conviction.

"Then——" She paused. "Well—but I haven't driven you away."

"No."

"And yet you've gone," she said, quietly.

"Do I seem so stupid as all that?"

"You know what I mean." She leaned back in her chair again, and her

hands, inactive for once, lay motionless in her lap. When she spoke it was in a rueful whisper:

"I wonder if I *have* driven you away?"

"You've done nothing—nothing at all," he said.

"I wonder——" she said once more, but she stopped. In her mind she was going back over their time together since the first meeting—fragments of talk, moments of silence, little things of no importance, little things that might be important; moonshine, sunshine, starlight; and her thoughts zigzagged among the jumbling memories; but, as if she made for herself a picture of all these fragments, throwing them upon the canvas haphazard, she saw them all just touched with the one tainting quality that gave them coherence, the faint, false haze she had put over this friendship by her own pretendings. And, if this terrible dinner, or anything, or everything, had shown that saffron tint in its true colour to the man at her side, last night almost a lover, then she had indeed of herself driven him away, and might well feel that she was lost.

"Do you know?" she said, suddenly, in a clear, loud voice. "I have the strangest feeling. I feel as if I were going to be with you only about five minutes more in all the rest of my life!"

"Why, no," he said. "Of course I'm coming to see you—often. I——"

"No," she interrupted. "I've never had a feeling like this before. It's—it's just *so*; that's all! You're *going*—why, you're never coming here again!" She stood up, abruptly, beginning to tremble all over. "Why, it's *finished*, isn't it?" she said, and her trembling was manifest now in her voice. "Why, it's all *over*, isn't it? Why, yes!"

He had risen as she did. "I'm afraid you're awfully tired and nervous," he said. "I really ought to be going."

"Yes, of *course* you ought," she cried, despairingly. "There's nothing else for you to do. When anything's spoiled, people *can't* do anything but run away from it. So good-bye!"

"At least," he returned, huskily, "we'll only—only say good-night."

Then, as moving to go, he stumbled upon the veranda steps, "Your *hat!*" she cried. "I'd like to keep it for a souvenir, but I'm afraid you need it!"

She ran into the hall and brought his straw hat from the chair where he had left it. "You poor thing!" she said, with quavering laughter. "Don't you know you can't go without your hat?"

Then, as they faced each other for the short moment which both of them knew would be the last of all their veranda moments, Alice's broken laughter grew louder. "What a thing to say!" she cried. "What a romantic parting—talking about *hats!*"

Her laughter continued as he turned away, but other sounds came from within the house, clearly audible with the opening of a door upstairs—a long and wailing cry of lamentation in the voice of Mrs. Adams. Russell paused at the steps, uncertain, but Alice waved to him to go on.

"Oh, don't bother," she said. "We have lots of that in this funny little old house! Good-bye!"

And as he went down the steps, she ran back into the house and closed the door heavily behind her.

CHAPTER XXIII

Her mother's wailing could still be heard from overhead, though more faintly; and old Charley Lohr was coming down the stairs alone.

He looked at Alice compassionately. "I was just comin' to suggest maybe you'd excuse yourself from your company," he said. "Your mother was bound not to disturb you, and tried her best to keep you from hearin' how she's takin' on, but I thought probably you better see to her."

"Yes, I'll come. What's the matter?"

"Well," he said, "*I* only stepped over to offer my sympathy and services, as it were. *I* thought of course you folks knew all about it. Fact is, it was in the evening paper—just a little bit of an item on the back page, of course."

"What is it?"

He coughed. "Well, it ain't anything so terrible," he said. "Fact is, your brother Walter's got in a little trouble—well, I suppose you might call it quite a good deal of trouble. Fact is, he's quite considerable short in his accounts down at Lamb and Company."

Alice ran up the stairs and into her father's room, where Mrs. Adams threw herself into her daughter's arms. "Is he gone?" she sobbed. "He didn't hear me, did he? I tried so hard——"

Alice patted the heaving shoulders her arms enclosed. "No, no," she said. "He didn't hear you—it wouldn't have mattered—he doesn't matter anyway."

"Oh, *poor* Walter!" The mother cried. "Oh, the *poor* boy! Poor, poor Walter! Poor, poor, poor, *poor*——"

"Hush, dear, hush!" Alice tried to soothe her, but the lament could not be abated, and from the other side of the room a repetition in a different spirit was as continuous. Adams paced furiously there, pounding his fist into his left palm as he strode. "The dang boy!" he said. "Dang little fool! Dang idiot! Dang fool! Whyn't he *tell* me, the dang little fool?"

"He *did!*" Mrs. Adams sobbed. "He *did* tell you, and you wouldn't *give* it to him."

"He *did*, did he?" Adams shouted at her. "What he begged me for was money to run away with! He never dreamed of putting back what he took. What the dangnation you talking about—accusing me!"

"He *needed* it," she said. "He needed it to run away with! How could he expect to *live*, after he got away, if he didn't have a little money? Oh, poor, poor, *poor* Walter! Poor, poor, poor——"

She went back to this repetition; and Adams went back to his own, then paused, seeing his old friend standing in the hallway outside the open door.

"Ah—I'll just be goin', I guess, Virgil," Lohr said. "I don't see as there's any use my tryin' to say any more. I'll do anything you want me to, you understand."

"Wait a minute," Adams said, and, groaning, came and went down the stairs with him. "You say you didn't see the old man at all?"

"No, I don't know a thing about what he's going to do," Lohr said, as they reached the lower floor. "Not a thing. But look here, Virgil, I don't see as this calls for you and your wife to take on so hard about—anyhow not as hard as the way you've started."

"No," Adams gulped. "It always seems that way to the other party that's only looking on!"

"Oh, well, I know that, of course," old Charley returned, soothingly. "But look here, Virgil: they *may* not catch the boy; they didn't even seem to be sure what train he made, and if they do get him, why, the ole man might decide not to prosecute if——"

"*Him?*" Adams cried, interrupting. "Him not prosecute? Why, that's what he's been waiting for, all along! He thinks my boy and me both cheated him! Why, he was just letting Walter walk into a trap! Didn't you say they'd been suspecting him for some time back? Didn't you say they'd been watching him and were just about fixing to arrest him?"

"Yes, I know," said Lohr; "but you can't tell, especially if you raise the money and pay it back."

"Every cent!" Adams vociferated. "Every last penny! I can raise it—I *got* to raise it! I'm going to put a loan on my factory to-morrow. Oh, I'll get it for him, you tell him! Every last penny!"

"Well, ole feller, you just try and get quieted down some now." Charley held out his hand in parting. "You and your wife just quiet down some. You *ain't* the healthiest man in the world, you know, and you already been under quite some strain before this happened. You want to take care of yourself for the sake of your wife and that sweet little girl upstairs, you know. Now, good-night," he finished, stepping out upon the veranda. "You send for me if there's anything I can do."

"Do?" Adams echoed. "There ain't anything *anybody* can do!" And then, as his old friend went down the path to the sidewalk, he called after him, "You tell him I'll pay him every last cent! Every last, dang, dirty *penny!*"

He slammed the door and went rapidly up the stairs, talking loudly to himself. "Every dang, last, dirty penny! Thinks *everybody* in this family wants to steal from him, does he? Thinks we're *all* yellow, does he? I'll show him!" And he came into his own room vociferating, "Every last, dang, dirty penny!"

Mrs. Adams had collapsed, and Alice had put her upon his bed, where she lay tossing convulsively and sobbing, "Oh, *poor* Walter!" over and over, but after a time she varied the sorry tune. "Oh, poor Alice!" she moaned, clinging to her daughter's hand. "Oh, poor, *poor* Alice—to have *this* come on the night of your dinner—just when everything seemed to be going so well—at last—oh, poor, poor, *poor*——"

"Hush!" Alice said, sharply. "Don't say 'poor Alice!' I'm all right."

"You *must* be!" her mother cried, clutching her. "You've just *got* to be! *One* of us has got to be all right—surely God wouldn't mind just *one* of us being all right—that wouldn't hurt Him——"

"Hush, hush, mother! Hush!"

But Mrs. Adams only clutched her the more tightly. "He seemed *such* a nice young man, dearie! He may not see this in the paper—Mr. Lohr said it was just a little bit of an item—he *may* not see it, dearie——"

Then her anguish went back to Walter again; and to his needs as a fugitive —she had meant to repair his underwear, but had postponed doing so, and her neglect now appeared to be a detail as lamentable as the calamity itself. She could neither be stilled upon it, nor herself exhaust its urgings to self-reproach, though she finally took up another theme temporarily. Upon an unusually violent outbreak of her husband's, in denunciation of the runaway, she cried out faintly that he was cruel; and further wearied her broken voice with details of Walter's beauty as a baby, and of his bedtime pieties throughout his infancy.

So the hot night wore on. Three had struck before Mrs. Adams was got to bed; and Alice, returning to her own room, could hear her father's bare feet thudding back and forth after that. "Poor papa!" she whispered in helpless imitation of her mother. "Poor papa! Poor mama! Poor Walter! Poor all of us!"

She fell asleep, after a time, while from across the hall the bare feet still thudded over their changeless route; and she woke at seven, hearing Adams pass her door, shod. In her wrapper she ran out into the hallway and found him descending the stairs.

"Papa!"

"Hush," he said, and looked up at her with reddened eyes. "Don't wake your mother."

"I won't," she whispered. "How about you? You haven't slept any at all!"

"Yes, I did. I got some sleep. I'm going over to the works now. I got to throw some figures together to show the bank. Don't worry: I'll get things fixed up. You go back to bed. Good-bye."

"Wait!" she bade him sharply.

"What for?"

"You've got to have some breakfast."

"Don't want 'ny."

"You wait!" she said, imperiously, and disappeared to return almost at once. "I can cook in my bedroom slippers," she explained, "but I don't believe I could in my bare feet!"

Descending softly, she made him wait in the dining-room until she brought him toast and eggs and coffee. "Eat!" she said. "And I'm going to telephone for a taxicab to take you, if you think you've really got to go."

"No, I'm going to walk—I *want* to walk."

She shook her head anxiously. "You don't look able. You've walked all night."

"No, I didn't," he returned. "I tell you I got some sleep. I got all I wanted anyhow."

"But, papa——"

"Here!" he interrupted, looking up at her suddenly and setting down his cup of coffee. "Look here! What about this Mr. Russell? I forgot all about him. What about him?"

Her lip trembled a little, but she controlled it before she spoke. "Well, what about him, papa?" she asked, calmly enough.

"Well, we could hardly——" Adams paused, frowning heavily. "We could hardly expect he wouldn't hear something about all this."

"Yes; of course he'll hear it, papa."

"Well?"

"Well, what?" she asked, gently.

"You don't think he'd be the—the cheap kind it'd make a difference with, of course."

"Oh, no; he isn't cheap. It won't make any difference with him."

Adams suffered a profound sigh to escape him. "Well—I'm glad of that, anyway."

"The difference," she explained—"the difference was made without his hearing anything about Walter. He doesn't know about *that* yet."

"Well, what does he know about?"

"Only," she said, "about me."

"What you mean by that, Alice?" he asked, helplessly.

"Never mind," she said. "It's nothing beside the real trouble we're in— I'll tell you some time. You eat your eggs and toast; you can't keep going on just coffee."

"I can't eat any eggs and toast," he objected, rising. "I can't."

"Then wait till I can bring you something else."

"No," he said, irritably. "I won't do it! I don't want any dang food! And look here"—he spoke sharply to stop her, as she went toward the telephone —"I don't want any dang taxi, either! You look after your mother when she wakes up. I got to be at *work!*"

And though she followed him to the front door, entreating, he could not be stayed or hindered. He went through the quiet morning streets at a rickety, rapid gait, swinging his old straw hat in his hands, and whispering angrily to himself as he went. His grizzled hair, not trimmed for a month, blew back from his damp forehead in the warm breeze; his reddened eyes stared hard at nothing from under blinking lids; and one side of his face twitched startlingly from time to time;—children might have run from him, or mocked him.

When he had come into that fallen quarter his industry had partly revived and wholly made odorous, a negro woman, leaning upon her whitewashed gate, gazed after him and chuckled for the benefit of a gossiping
friend in the next tiny yard. "Oh, good Satan! Wha'ssa matter that ole glue
man?"

"Who? Him?" the neighbour inquired. "What he do now?"

"Talkin' to his ole se'f!" the first explained, joyously. "Look like gone distracted—ole glue man!"

Adams's legs had grown more uncertain with his hard walk, and he stumbled heavily as he crossed the baked mud of his broad lot, but cared little
for that, was almost unaware of it, in fact. Thus his eyes saw as little as his
body felt, and so he failed to observe something that would have given him
additional light upon an old phrase that already meant quite enough for him.

There are in the wide world people who have never learned its meaning;
but most are either young or beautifully unobservant who remain wholly unaware of the inner poignancies the words convey: "a rain of misfortunes." It
is a boiling rain, seemingly whimsical in its choice of spots whereon to fall;
and, so far as mortal eye can tell, neither the just nor the unjust may hope
to avoid it, or need worry themselves by expecting it. It had selected the
Adams family for its scaldings; no question.

The glue-works foreman, standing in the doorway of the brick shed, observed his employer's eccentric approach, and doubtfully stroked a whiskered
chin. "Well, they ain't no putticular use gettin' so upset over it," he said, as
Adams came up. "When a thing happens, why, it happens, and that's all
there is to it. When a thing's so, why, it's so. All you can do about it is think
if there's anything you *can* do; and that's what you better be doin' with this
case."

Adams halted, and seemed to gape at him. "What—case?" he said, with
difficulty. "Was it in the morning papers, too?"

"No, it ain't in no morning papers. My land! It don't need to be in no
papers; look at the *size* of it!"

"The size of what?"

"Why, great God!" the foreman exclaimed. "He ain't even seen it. Look!
Look yonder!"

Adams stared vaguely at the man's outstretched hand and pointing forefinger, then turned and saw a great sign upon the façade of the big factory
building across the street. The letters were large enough to be read two blocks
away.

"AFTER THE FIFTEENTH OF NEXT MONTH
THIS BUILDING WILL BE OCCUPIED BY
THE J. A. LAMB LIQUID GLUE CO. INC."

A gray touring-car had just come to rest before the principal entrance of
the building, and J. A. Lamb himself descended from it. He glanced over

toward the humble rival of his projected great industry, saw his old clerk, and immediately walked across the street and the lot to speak to him.

"Well, Adams," he said, in his husky, cheerful voice, "how's your glue-works?"

Adams uttered an inarticulate sound, and lifted the hand that held his hat as if to make a protestive gesture, but failed to carry it out; and his arm sank limp at his side. The foreman, however, seemed to feel that something ought to be said.

"Our glue-works, hell!" he remarked. "I guess we won't *have* no glue-works over here—not very long, if we got to compete with the sized thing you got over there!"

Lamb chuckled. "I kind of had some such notion," he said. "You see, Virgil, I couldn't exactly let you walk off with it like swallering a pat o' butter, now, could I? It didn't look exactly reasonable to expect me to let go like that, now, did it?"

Adams found a half-choked voice somewhere in his throat. "Do you—would you step into my office a minute, Mr. Lamb?"

"Why, certainly I'm willing to have a little talk with you," the old gentleman said, as he followed his former employee indoors, and he added, "I feel a lot more like it than I did before I got *that* up, over yonder, Virgil!"

Adams threw open the door of the rough room he called his office, having as justification for this title little more than the fact that he had a telephone there and a deal table that served as a desk. "Just step into the office, please," he said.

Lamb glanced at the desk, at the kitchen chair before it, at the telephone, and at the partition walls built of old boards, some covered with ancient paint and some merely weatherbeaten, the salvage of a house-wrecker; and he smiled broadly. "So these arc your offices, are they?" he asked. "You expect to do quite a business here, I guess, don't you, Virgil?"

Adams turned upon him a stricken and tortured face. "Have you seen Charley Lohr since last night, Mr. Lamb?"

"No; I haven't seen Charley."

"Well, I told him to tell you," Adams began;—"I told him I'd pay you——"

"Pay me what you expect to make out o' glue, you mean, Virgil?"

"No," Adams said, swallowing. "I mean what my boy owes you. That's what I told Charley to tell you. I told him to tell you I'd pay you every last——"

"Well, well!" the old gentleman interrupted, testily. "I don't know anything about that."

"I'm expecting to pay you," Adams went on, swallowing again, painfully. "I was expecting to do it out of a loan I thought I could get on my glue-works."

The old gentleman lifted his frosted eyebrows. "Oh, out o' the *glue*-works? You expected to raise money on the glue-works, did you?"

At that, Adams's agitation increased prodigiously. "How'd you *think* I expected to pay you?" he said. "Did you think I expected to get money on my own old bones?" He slapped himself harshly upon the chest and legs. "Do you think a bank'll lend money on a man's ribs and his broken-down old knee-bones? They won't do it! You got to have some *business* prospects to show 'em, if you haven't got any property nor securities; and what business prospects have I got now, with that sign of yours up over yonder? Why, you don't need to make an *ounce* o' glue; your sign's fixed *me* without your doing another lick! *That's* all you had to do; just put your sign up! You needn't to——"

"Just let me tell you something, Virgil Adams," the old man interrupted, harshly. "I got just one right important thing to tell you before we talk any further business, and that's this: there's some few men in this town made their money in off-colour ways, but there aren't many; and those there are have had to be a darn sight slicker than you know how to be, or ever *will* know how to be! Yes, sir, and they none of them had the little gumption to try to make it out of a man that had the spirit not to let 'em, and the *strength* not to let 'em! I know what *you* thought. 'Here,' you said to yourself, 'here's this ole fool J. A. Lamb; he's kind of worn out and in his second childhood like; I can put it over on him, without his ever——'"

"I did not!" Adams shouted. "A great deal *you* know about my feelings and all what I said to myself! There's one thing I want to tell *you*, and that's what I'm saying to myself *now*, and what my feelings are this *minute!*"

He struck the table a great blow with his thin fist, and shook the damaged knuckles in the air. "I just want to tell you, whatever I did feel, I don't feel *mean* any more; not to-day, I don't. There's a meaner man in this world than *I* am, Mr. Lamb!"

"Oh, so you feel better about yourself to-day, do you, Virgil?"

"You bet I do! You worked till you got me where you want me; and I wouldn't do that to another man, no matter what he did to me! I wouldn't——"

"What you talkin' about! How've I 'got you where I want you?'"

"Ain't it plain enough?" Adams cried. "You even got me where I can't raise the money to pay back what my boy owes you! Do you suppose anybody's fool enough to let me have a cent on this business after one look at what you got over there across the road?"

"No, I don't."

"No, you don't," Adams echoed, hoarsely. "What's more, you knew my house was mortgaged, and my——"

"I did not," Lamb interrupted, angrily. "What do *I* care about your house?"

"What's the use your talking like that?" Adams cried. "You got me where I can't even raise the money to pay what my boy owes the company, so't I can't show any reason to stop the prosecution and keep him out the penitentiary. That's where you worked till you got *me!*"

"What!" Lamb shouted. "You accuse me of——"

"'Accuse you?' What am I telling you? Do you think I got no *eyes?*" And

Adams hammered the table again. "Why, you knew the boy was weak——"

"I did not!"

"Listen: you kept him there after you got mad at my leaving the way I did. You kept him there after you suspected him; and you had him watched; you let him go on; just waited to catch him and ruin him!"

"You're crazy!" the old man bellowed. "I didn't know there was anything against the boy till last night. You're *crazy*, I say!"

Adams looked it. With his hair disordered over his haggard forehead and bloodshot eyes; with his bruised hands pounding the table and flying in a hundred wild and absurd gestures, while his feet shuffled constantly to preserve his balance upon staggering legs, he was the picture of a man with a mind gone to rags.

"Maybe I *am* crazy!" he cried, his voice breaking and quavering. "Maybe I am, but I wouldn't stand there and taunt a man with it if I'd done to him what you've done to me! Just look at me: I worked all my life for you, and what I did when I quit never harmed you—it didn't make two cents' worth o' difference in your life and it looked like it'd mean all the difference in the world to my family—and now look what you've *done* to me for it! I tell you, Mr. Lamb, there never was a man looked up to another man the way I looked up to you the whole o' my life, but I don't look up to you any more! You think you got a fine day of it now, riding up in your automobile to look at that sign—and then over here at my poor little works that you've ruined. But listen to me just this one last time!" The cracking voice broke into falsetto, and the gesticulating hands fluttered uncontrollably. "Just you listen!" he panted. "You think I did you a bad turn, and now you got me ruined for it, and you got my works ruined, and my family ruined; and if anybody'd 'a' told me this time last year I'd ever say such a thing to you I'd called him a dang liar, but I *do* say it: I say you've acted toward me like—like a—a dog-gone mean—man!"

His voice, exhausted, like his body, was just able to do him this final service; then he sank, crumpled, into the chair by the table, his chin down hard upon his chest.

"I tell you, you're crazy!" Lamb said again. "I never in the world——" But he checked himself, staring in sudden perplexity at his accuser. "Look here!" he said. "What's the matter of you? Have you got another of those——?" He put his hand upon Adams's shoulder, which jerked feebly under the touch.

The old man went to the door and called to the foreman.

"Here!" he said. "Run and tell my chauffeur to bring my car over here. Tell him to drive right up over the sidewalk and across the lot. Tell him to hurry!"

So, it happened, the great J. A. Lamb a second time brought his former clerk home, stricken and almost inanimate.

CHAPTER XXIV

About five o'clock that afternoon, the old gentleman came back to Adams's house; and when Alice opened the door, he nodded, walked into the "living-room" without speaking; then stood frowning as if he hesitated to decide some perplexing question.

"Well, how is he now?" he asked, finally.

"The doctor was here again a little while ago; he thinks papa's coming through it. He's pretty sure he will."

"Something like the way it was last spring?"

"Yes."

"Not a bit of sense to it!" Lamb said, gruffly. "When he was getting well the other time the doctor told me it wasn't a regular stroke, so to speak—this 'cerebral effusion' thing. Said there wasn't any particular reason for your father to expect he'd ever have another attack, if he'd take a little care of himself. Said he could consider himself well as anybody else long as he did that."

"Yes. But he didn't do it!"

Lamb nodded, sighed aloud, and crossed the room to a chair. "I guess not," he said, as he sat down. "Bustin' his health up over his glue-works, I expect."

"Yes."

"I guess so; I guess so." Then he looked up at her with a glimmer of anxiety in his eyes. "Has he came to yet?"

"Yes. He's talked a little. His mind's clear; he spoke to mama and me—and to Miss Perry." Alice laughed sadly. "We were lucky enough to get her back, but papa didn't seem to think it was lucky. When he recognized her he said, 'Oh, my goodness, 'tisn't *you*, is it!' "

"Well, that's a good sign, if he's getting a little cross. Did he—did he happen to say anything—for instance, about me?"

This question, awkwardly delivered, had the effect of removing the girl's pallor; rosy tints came quickly upon her cheeks. "He—yes, he did," she said. "Naturally, he's troubled about—about——" She stopped.

"About your brother, maybe?"

"Yes, about making up the——"

"Here, now," Lamb said, uncomfortably, as she stopped again. "Listen, young lady; let's don't talk about that just yet. I want to ask you: you understand all about this glue business, I expect, don't you?"

"I'm not sure. I only know——"

"Let me tell you," he interrupted, impatiently. "I'll tell you all about it in two words. The process belonged to me, and your father up and walked off with it; there's no getting around *that* much, anyhow."

"Isn't there?" Alice stared at him. "I think you're mistaken, Mr. Lamb. Didn't papa improve it so that it virtually belonged to him?"

There was a spark in the old blue eyes at this. "What?" he cried. "Is that the way he got around it? Why, in all my life I never heard of such a——" But he left the sentence unfinished; the testiness went out of his husky voice and the anger out of his eyes. "Well, I expect maybe that was the way of it," he said. "Anyhow, it's right for you to stand up for your father; and if you think he had a right to it——"

"But he did!" she cried.

"I expect so," the old man returned, pacifically. "I expect so, probably. Anyhow, it's a question that's neither here nor there, right now. What I was thinking of saying—well, did your father happen to let out that he and I had words this morning?"

"No."

"Well, we did." He sighed and shook his head. "Your father—well, he used some pretty hard expressions toward me, young lady. They weren't *so*, I'm glad to say, but he used 'em to me, and the worst of it was he believed 'em. Well, I been thinking it over, and I thought I'd just have a kind of little talk with you to set matters straight, so to speak."

"Yes, Mr. Lamb."

"For instance," he said, "it's like this. Now, I hope you won't think I mean any indelicacy, but you take your brother's case, since we got to mention it, why, your father had the whole thing worked out in his mind about as wrong as anybody ever got anything. If I'd acted the way your father thought I did about that, why, somebody just ought to take me out and shoot me! Do *you* know what that man thought?"

"I'm not sure."

He frowned at her, and asked, "Well, what do you think about it?"

"I don't know," she said. "I don't believe I think anything at all about anything to-day."

"Well, well," he returned; "I expect not; I expect not. You kind of look to me as if you ought to be in bed yourself, young lady."

"Oh, no."

"I guess you mean 'Oh, yes'; and I won't keep you long, but there's something we got to get fixed up, and I'd rather talk to you than I would to your mother, because you're a smart girl and always friendly; and I want to be sure I'm understood. Now, listen."

"I will," Alice promised, smiling faintly.

"I never even hardly noticed your brother was still working for me," he explained, earnestly. "I never thought anything about it. My sons sort of tried to tease me about the way your father—about his taking up this glue business, so to speak—and one day Albert, Junior, asked me if I felt all right about your brother's staying there after that, and I told him—well, I just asked him to shut up. If the boy wanted to stay there, I didn't consider it my business to send him away on account of any feeling I had toward his father; not as long as he did his work right—and the report showed he did. Well, as it happens, it looks now as if he stayed because he *had* to; he couldn't quit because he'd 'a' been found out if he did. Well, he'd been covering up his shortage for a considerable time—and do you know what your father practically charged me with about that?"

"No, Mr. Lamb."

In his resentment, the old gentleman's ruddy face became ruddier and his husky voice huskier. "Thinks I kept the boy there because I suspected him! Thinks I did it to get even with *him!* Do I look to *you* like a man that'd do such a thing?"

"No," she said, gently. "I don't think you would."

"No!" he exclaimed. "Nor *he* wouldn't think so if he was himself; he's known me too long. But he must been sort of brooding over this whole business—I mean before Walter's trouble—he must been taking it to heart pretty hard for some time back. He thought I didn't think much of him any more —and I expect he maybe wondered some what I was going to *do*—and there's nothing worse'n that state of mind to make a man suspicious of all kinds of meanness. Well, he practically stood up there and accused me to my face of fixing things so't he couldn't ever raise the money to settle for Walter and ask us not to prosecute. That's the state of mind your father's brooding got him into, young lady—charging me with a trick like that!"

"I'm sorry," she said. "I know you'd never——"

The old man slapped his sturdy knee, angrily. "Why, that dang fool of a Virgil Adams!" he exclaimed. "He wouldn't even give me a chance to talk; and he got me so mad I couldn't hardly talk, anyway! He might 'a' known from the first I wasn't going to let him walk in and beat me out of my own —that is, he might 'a' known I wouldn't let him get ahead of me in a business matter—not with my boys twitting me about it every few minutes! But to talk to me the way he did this morning—well, he was out of his head; that's all! Now, wait just a minute," he interposed, as she seemed about to speak. "In the first place, we aren't going to push this case against your brother. I believe in the law, all right, and business men got to protect themselves; but in a case like this, where restitution's made by the family, why, I expect it's just as well sometimes to use a little influence and let matters drop. Of course your brother'll have to keep out o' this state; that's all."

"But—you said——" she faltered.

"Yes. What'd I say?"

"You said, 'where restitution's made by the family.' That's what seemed to trouble papa so terribly, because—because restitution couldn't——"

"Why, yes, it could. That's what I'm here to talk to you about."

"I don't see——"

"I'm going to *tell* you, ain't I?" he said, gruffly. "Just hold your horses a minute, please." He coughed, rose from his chair, walked up and down the room, then halted before her. "It's like this," he said. "After I brought your father home, this morning, there was one of the things he told me, when he was going for me, over yonder—it kind of stuck in my craw. It was something about all this glue controversy not meaning anything to me in particular, and meaning a whole heap to him and his family. Well, he was wrong about that two ways. The first one was, it did mean a good deal to me to have him go back on me after so many years. I don't need to say any more about it, except just to tell you it meant quite a little more to me than you'd think, maybe. The other way he was wrong is, that how much a thing means to one man and how little it means to another ain't the right way to look at a business matter."

"I suppose it isn't, Mr. Lamb."

"No," he said. "It isn't. It's not the right way to look at anything. Yes, and your father knows it as well as I do, when he's in his right mind; and I expect that's one of the reasons he got so mad at me—but anyhow, I couldn't help thinking about how much all this thing *had* maybe meant to him;—as I say, it kind of stuck in my craw. I want you to tell him something from me, and I want you to go and tell him right off, if he's able and willing to listen. You tell him I got kind of a notion he was pushed into this thing by circumstances, and tell him I've lived long enough to know that circumstances can beat the best of us—you tell him I said 'the *best* of us.' Tell him I haven't got a bit of feeling against him—not any more—and tell him I came here to ask him not to have any against me."

"Yes, Mr. Lamb."

"Tell him I said——" The old man paused abruptly and Alice was surprised, in a dull and tired way, when she saw that his lips had begun to twitch and his eyelids to blink; but he recovered himself almost at once, and continued: "I want him to remember, 'Forgive us our transgressions, as we forgive those that transgress against us'; and if he and I been transgressing against each other, why, tell him I think it's time we *quit* such foolishness!"

He coughed again, smiled heartily upon her, and walked toward the door; then turned back to her with an exclamation: "Well, if I ain't an old fool!"

"What is it?" she asked.

"Why, I forgot what we were just talking about! Your father wants to settle for Walter's deficit. Tell him we'll be glad to accept it; but of course we don't expect him to clean the matter up until he's able to talk business again."

Alice stared at him blankly enough for him to perceive that further explanations were necessary. "It's like this," he said. "You see, if your father decided to keep his works going over yonder, I don't say but he might give us some little competition for a time, 'specially as he's got the start on us and about ready for the market. Then I was figuring we could use his plant —it's small, but it'd be to our benefit to have the use of it—and he's got a lease on that big lot; it may come in handy for us if we want to expand some. Well, I'd prefer to make a deal with him as quietly as possible—no good in every Tom, Dick and Harry hearing about things like this—but I figured he could sell out to me for a little something more'n enough to cover the mortgage he put on this house, and Walter's deficit, too—*that* don't amount to much in dollars and cents. The way I figure it, I could offer him about ninety-three hundred dollars as a total—or say ninety-three hundred and fifty—and if he feels like accepting, why, I'll send a confidential man up here with the papers soon's your father's able to look 'em over. You tell him, will you, and ask him if he sees his way to accepting that figure?"

"Yes," Alice said; and now her own lips twitched, while her eyes filled so that she saw but a blurred image of the old man, who held out his hand in parting. "I'll tell him. Thank you."

He shook her hand hastily. "Well, let's just keep it kind of quiet," he said, at the door. "No good in every Tom, Dick and Harry knowing all what goes on in town! You telephone me when your papa's ready to go over the papers —and call me up at my house to-night, will you? Let me hear how he's feeling?"

"I will," she said, and through her grateful tears gave him a smile almost radiant. "He'll be better, Mr. Lamb. We all will."

CHAPTER XXV

One morning, that autumn, Mrs. Adams came into Alice's room, and found her completing a sober toilet for the street; moreover, the expression revealed in her mirror was harmonious with the business-like severity of her attire. "What makes you look so cross, dearie?" the mother asked. "Couldn't you find anything nicer to wear than that plain old dark dress?"

"I don't believe I'm cross," the girl said, absently. "I believe I'm just thinking. Isn't it about time?"

"Time for what?"

"Time for thinking—for me, I mean?"

Disregarding this, Mrs. Adams looked her over thoughtfully. "I can't see why you don't wear more colour," she said. "At your age it's becoming and proper, too. Anyhow, when you're going on the street, I think you ought to look just as gay and lively as you can manage. You want to show 'em you've got some spunk!"

"How do you mean, mama?"

"I mean about Walter's running away and the mess your father made of his business. It would help to show 'em you're holding up your head just the same."

"Show whom!"

"All these other girls that——"

"Not I!" Alice laughed shortly, shaking her head. "I've quit dressing at them, and if they saw me they wouldn't think what you want 'em to. It's funny; but we don't often make people think what we want 'em to, mama.

You do thus and so; and you tell yourself, 'Now, seeing me do thus and so, people will naturally think this and that'; but they don't. They think something else—usually just what you *don't* want 'em to. I suppose about the only good in pretending is the fun we get out of fooling ourselves that we fool somebody."

"Well, but it wouldn't be pretending. You ought to let people see you're still holding your head up because you *are*. You wouldn't want that Mildred Palmer to think you're cast down about—well, you know you wouldn't want *her* not to think you're holding your head up, would you?"

"She wouldn't know whether I am or not, mama." Alice bit her lip, then smiled faintly as she said: "Anyhow, I'm not thinking about my head in that way—not this morning, I'm not."

Mrs. Adams dropped the subject casually. "Are you going down-town?" she inquired.

"Yes."

"What for?"

"Just something I want to see about. I'll tell you when I come back. Anything you want me to do?"

"No; I guess not to-day. I thought you might look for a rug, but I'd rather go with you to select it. We'll have to get a new rug for your father's room, I expect."

"I'm glad you think so, mama. I don't suppose he's ever even noticed it, but that old rug of his—well, really!"

"I didn't mean for him," her mother explained, thoughtfully. "No; he don't mind it, and he'd likely make a fuss if we changed it on his account. No; what I meant—we'll have to put your father in Walter's room. He won't mind, I don't expect—not much."

"No, I suppose not," Alice agreed, rather sadly. "I heard the bell awhile ago. Was it somebody about that?"

"Yes; just before I came upstairs. Mrs. Lohr gave him a note to me, and he was really a very pleasant-looking young man. A *very* pleasant-looking young man," Mrs. Adams repeated with increased animation and a thoughtful glance at her daughter. "He's a Mr. Will Dickson; he has a first-rate position with the gas works, Mrs. Lohr says, and he's fully able to afford a nice room. So if you and I double up in here, then with that young married couple in my room, and this Mr. Dickson in your father's, we'll just about have things settled. I thought maybe I could make one more place at table, too, so that with the other people from outside we'd be serving eleven altogether. You see if I have to pay this cook twelve dollars a week—it can't be helped, I guess—well, one more would certainly help toward a profit. Of course it's a terribly worrying thing to see how we *will* come out. Don't you suppose we could squeeze in one more?"

"I suppose it *could* be managed; yes."

Mrs. Adams brightened. "I'm sure it'll be pleasant having that young married couple in the house—and especially this Mr. Will Dickson. He seemed very much of a gentleman, and anxious to get settled in good surroundings. I was very favourably impressed with him in every way; and he explained to me about his name; it seems it isn't William, it's just 'Will'; his parents had him christened that way. It's curious." She paused, and then, with an effort to seem casual, which veiled nothing from her daughter: "It's *quite* curious," she said again. "But it's rather attractive and different, don't you think?"

"Poor mama!" Alice laughed compassionately. "Poor mama!"

"He is, though," Mrs. Adams maintained. "He's *very* much of a gentleman, unless I'm no judge of appearances; and it'll really be nice to have him in the house."

"No doubt," Alice said, as she opened her door to depart. "I don't suppose we'll mind having any of 'em as much as we thought we would. Good-bye."

But her mother detained her, catching her by the arm. "Alice, you do hate it, don't you!"

"No," the girl said, quickly. "There wasn't anything else to do."

Mrs. Adams became emotional at once: her face cried tragedy, and her voice misfortune. "There *might* have been something else to do! Oh, Alice, you gave your father bad advice when you upheld him in taking a miserable little ninety-three hundred and fifty from that old wretch! If your father'd just had the gumption to hold out, they'd have had to pay him anything he asked. If he'd just had the gumption and a little manly *courage*——"

"Hush!" Alice whispered, for her mother's voice grew louder. "Hush! He'll hear you, mama."

"Could he hear me too often?" the embittered lady asked. "If he'd listened to me at the right time, would we have to be taking in boarders and sinking *down* in the scale at the end of our lives, instead of going *up?* You were both wrong; we didn't need to be so panicky—that was just what that old man wanted: to scare us and buy us out for nothing! If your father'd just listened to me then, or if for once in his life he'd just been half a *man*——"

Alice put her hand over her mother's mouth. "You mustn't! He *will* hear you!"

But from the other side of Adams's closed door his voice came querulously. "Oh, I *hear* her, all right!"

"You see, mama?" Alice said, and, as Mrs. Adams turned away, weeping, the daughter sighed; then went in to speak to her father.

He was in his old chair by the table, with a pillow behind his head, but the crocheted scarf and Mrs. Adams's wrapper swathed him no more; he wore a dressing-gown his wife had bought for him, and was smoking his pipe. "The old story, is it?" he said, as Alice came in. "The same, same old story! Well, well! Has she gone?"

"Yes, papa."

"Got your hat on," he said. "Where you going?"

"I'm going down-town on an errand of my own. Is there anything you want, papa?"

"Yes, there is." He smiled at her. "I wish you'd sit down a while and talk to me—unless your errand——"

"No," she said, taking a chair near him. "I was just going down to see about some arrangements I was making for myself. There's no hurry."

"What arrangements for yourself, dearie?"

"I'll tell you afterwards—after I find out something about 'em myself."

"All right," he said, indulgently. "Keep your secrets; keep your secrets." He paused, drew musingly upon his pipe, and shook his head. "Funny—the way your mother looks at things! For the matter o' that, everything's pretty funny, I expect, if you stop to think about it. For instance, let her say all she likes, but we were pushed right spang to the wall, if J. A. Lamb hadn't taken it into his head to make that offer for the works; and there's one of the things I been thinking about lately, Alice: thinking about how funny they work out."

"What did you think about it, papa!"

"Well, I've seen it happen in other people's lives, time and time again; and now it's happened in ours. You think you're going to be pushed right up against the wall; you can't see any way out, or any hope at all; you think you're *gone*—and then something you never counted on turns up; and, while maybe you never do get back to where you used to be, yet somehow you kind of squirm out of being right *spang* against the wall. You keep on going —maybe you can't go much, but you do go a little. See what I mean?"

"Yes. I understand, dear."

"Yes, I'm afraid you do," he said. "Too bad! You oughtn't to understand it at your age. It seems to me a good deal as if the Lord really meant for the young people to have the good times, and for the old to have the troubles; and when anybody as young as you has trouble there's a big mistake somewhere."

"Oh, no!" she protested.

But he persisted whimsically in this view of divine error: "Yes, it does look a good deal that way. But of course we can't tell; we're never certain about anything—not about anything at all. Sometimes I look at it another way, though. Sometimes it looks to me as if a body's troubles came on him mainly because he hadn't had sense enough to know how not to have any— as if his troubles were kind of like a boy's getting kept in after school by the teacher, to give him discipline, or something or other. But, my, my! We don't learn easy!" He chuckled mournfully. "Not to learn how to live till we're about ready to die, it certainly seems to me dang tough!"

"Then I wouldn't brood on such a notion, papa," she said.

" 'Brood?' No!" he returned. "I just kind o' mull it over." He chuckled again, sighed, and then, not looking at her, he said, "That Mr. Russell—your mother tells me he hasn't been here again—not since——"

"No," she said, quietly, as Adams paused. "He never came again."

"Well, but maybe——"

"No," she said. "There isn't any 'maybe.' I told him good-bye that night, papa. It was before he knew about Walter—I told you."

"Well, well," Adams said. "Young people are entitled to their own privacy; I don't want to pry." He emptied his pipe into a chipped saucer on the table beside him, laid the pipe aside, and reverted to a former topic. "Speaking of dying——"

"Well, but we weren't!" Alice protested.

"Yes, about not knowing how to live till you're through living—and *then* maybe not!" he said, chuckling at his own determined pessimism. "I see I'm pretty old because I talk this way—I remember my grandmother saying things a good deal like all what I'm saying now; I used to hear her at it when I was a young fellow—she was a right gloomy old lady, I remember. Well, anyhow, it reminds me: I want to get on my feet again as soon as I can; I got to look around and find something to go into."

Alice shook her head gently. "But, papa, he told you——"

"Never mind throwing that dang doctor up at me!" Adams interrupted, peevishly. "He said I'd be good for *some* kind of light job—if I could find just the right thing. 'Where there wouldn't be either any physical or mental strain,' he said. Well, I got to find something like that. Anyway, I'll feel better if I can just get out *looking* for it."

"But, papa, I'm afraid you won't find it, and you'll be disappointed."

"Well, I want to hunt around and *see*, anyhow."

Alice patted his hand. "You must just be contented, papa. Everything's going to be all right, and you mustn't get to worrying about doing anything. We own this house—it's all clear—and you've taken care of mama and me all our lives; now it's our turn."

"No, sir!" he said, querulously. "I don't like the idea of being the landlady's husband around a boarding-house; it goes against my gizzard. *I* know: makes out the bills for his wife Sunday mornings—works with a screw-driver on somebody's bureau drawer sometimes—'tends the furnace maybe—one the boarders gives him a cigar now and then. That's a *fine* life to look forward to! No, sir; I don't want to finish as a landlady's husband!"

Alice looked grave; for she knew the sketch was but too accurately prophetic in every probability. "But, papa," she said, to console him, "don't you think maybe there isn't such a thing as a 'finish,' after all! You say perhaps we don't learn to live till we die—but maybe that's how it is *after* we die, too—just learning some more, the way we do here, and maybe through trouble again, even after that."

"Oh, it might be," he sighed. "I expect so."

"Well, then," she said, "what's the use of talking about a 'finish?' We do keep looking ahead to things as if they'd finish something, but when we get *to* them, they don't finish anything. They're just part of going on. I'll tell you—I looked ahead all summer to something I was afraid of, and I said to myself, 'Well, if that happens, I'm finished!' But it wasn't so, papa. It

did happen, and nothing's finished; I'm going on, just the same—only——"
She stopped and blushed.

"Only what?" he asked.

"Well——" She blushed more deeply, then jumped up, and, standing be-fore him, caught both his hands in hers. "Well, don't you think, since we do have to go on, we ought at least to have learned some sense about how to do it?"

He looked up at her adoringly.

"What *I* think," he said, and his voice trembled;—"I think you're the smartest girl in the world! I wouldn't trade you for the whole kit-and-boodle of 'em!"

But as this folly of his threatened to make her tearful, she kissed him hastily, and went forth upon her errand.

Since the night of the tragic-comic dinner she had not seen Russell, nor caught even the remotest chance glimpse of him; and it was curious that she should encounter him as she went upon such an errand as now engaged her. At a corner, not far from that tobacconist's shop she had just left when he overtook her and walked with her for the first time, she met him to-day. He turned the corner, coming toward her, and they were face to face; where-upon that engaging face of Russell's was instantly reddened, but Alice's re-mained serene.

She stopped short, though; and so did he; then she smiled brightly as she put out her hand.

"Why, Mr. Russell!"

"I'm so—I'm so glad to have this—this chance," he stammered. "I've wanted to tell you—it's just that going into a new undertaking—this business life—one doesn't get to do a great many things he'd like to. I hope you'll let me call again some time, if I can."

"Yes, do!" she said, cordially, and then, with a quick nod, went briskly on.

She breathed more rapidly, but knew that he could not have detected it, and she took some pride in herself for the way she had met this little crisis. But to have met it with such easy courage meant to her something more reassuring than a momentary pride in the serenity she had shown. For she found that what she had resolved in her inmost heart was now really true: she was "through with all that!"

She walked on, but more slowly, for the tobacconist's shop was not far from her now—and, beyond it, that portal of doom, Frincke's Business College. Already Alice could read the begrimed gilt letters of the sign; and although they had spelled destiny never with a more painful imminence than just then, an old habit of dramatizing herself still prevailed with her.

There came into her mind a whimsical comparison of her fate with that of the heroine in a French romance she had read long ago and remembered well, for she had cried over it. The story ended with the heroine's taking the veil after a death blow to love; and the final scene again became vivid to Alice, for a moment. Again, as when she had read and wept, she seemed herself to stand among the great shadows in the cathedral nave; smelled the smoky incense on the enclosed air, and heard the solemn pulses of the organ. She remembered how the novice's father knelt, trembling, beside a pillar of gray stone; how the faithless lover watched and shivered behind the statue of a saint; how stifled sobs and outcries were heard when the novice came to the altar; and how a shaft of light struck through the rose-window, enveloping her in an amber glow.

It was the vision of a moment only, and for no longer than a moment did Alice tell herself that the romance provided a prettier way of taking the veil than she had chosen, and that a faithless lover, shaking with remorse behind a saint's statue, was a greater solace than one left on a street corner protesting that he'd like to call some time—if he could! Her pity for herself vanished more reluctantly; but she shook it off and tried to smile at it, and at her romantic recollections—at all of them. She had something important to think of.

She passed the tobacconist's, and before her was that dark entrance to the wooden stairway leading up to Frincke's Business College—the very doorway she had always looked upon as the end of youth and the end of hope.

How often she had gone by here, hating the dreary obscurity of that stairway; how often she had thought of this obscurity as something lying in wait to obliterate the footsteps of any girl who should ascend into the smoky darkness above! Never had she passed without those ominous imaginings of hers: pretty girls turning into old maids "taking dictation"—old maids of a dozen different types, yet all looking a little like herself.

Well, she was here at last! She looked up and down the street quickly, and then, with a little heave of the shoulders, she went bravely in, under the sign, and began to climb the wooden steps. Half-way up the shadows were heaviest, but after that the place began to seem brighter. There was an open window overhead somewhere, she found, and the steps at the top were gay with sunshine.

The One-Hundred-Dollar Bill

The new one-hundred-dollar bill, clean and green, freshening the heart with the colour of springtime, slid over the glass of the teller's counter and passed under his grille to a fat hand, dingy on the knuckles, but brightened by a flawed diamond. This interesting hand was a part of one of those men who seem to have too much fattened muscle for their clothes: his shoulders distended his overcoat; his calves strained the sprightly checked cloth, a little soiled, of his trousers; his short neck bulged above the glossy collar. His hat, round and black as a pot, and appropriately small, he wore slightly obliqued; while under its curled brim his small eyes twinkled surreptitiously between those upper and nether puffs of flesh that mark the too faithful practitioner of unhallowed gaieties. Such was the first individual owner of the new one-hundred-dollar bill, and he at once did what might have been expected of him.

Moving away from the teller's grille, he made a cylindrical packet of bills smaller in value—"ones" and "fives"—then placed round them, as a wrapper, the beautiful one-hundred-dollar bill, snapped a rubber band over it; and the desired inference was plain: a roll all of hundred-dollar bills, inside as well as outside. Something more was plain, too: obviously the man's small head had a sportive plan in it, for the twinkle between his eye-puffs hinted of liquor in the offing and lively women impressed by a show of masterly riches. Here, in brief, was a man who meant to make a night of it; who would feast, dazzle, compel deference, and be loved. For money gives power, and power is loved; no doubt he would be loved. He was happy, and went out of the bank believing that money is made for joy.

So little should we be certain of our happiness in this world: the splendid one-hundred-dollar bill was taken from him untimely, before nightfall that very evening. At the corner of two busy streets he parted with it to the law, though in a mood of excruciating reluctance and only after a cold-blooded threatening on the part of the lawyer. This latter walked away thoughtfully, with the one-hundred-dollar bill, now not quite so clean, in his pocket.

Collinson was the lawyer's name, and in years he was only twenty-eight,

but already had the slightly harried appearance that marks the young husband who begins to suspect that the better part of his life has been his
bachelorhood. His dark, ready-made clothes, his twice-soled shoes and his
hair, which was too long for a neat and businesslike aspect, were symptoms
of necessary economy; but he did not wear the eager look of a man who
saves to "get on for himself": Collinson's look was that of an employed man
who only deepens his rut with his pacing of it.

An employed man he was, indeed; a lawyer without much hope of ever
seeing his name on the door or on the letters of the firm that employed
him, and his most important work was the collection of small debts. This
one-hundred-dollar bill now in his pocket was such a collection, small to the
firm and the client, though of a noble size to himself and the long-pursued
debtor from whom he had just collected it.

The banks were closed; so was the office, for it was six o'clock, and Collinson was on his way home when by chance he encountered the debtor: there
was nothing to do but to keep the bill over night. This was no hardship,
however, as he had a faint pleasure in the unfamiliar experience of walking
home with such a thing in his pocket; and he felt a little important by proxy
when he thought of it.

Upon the city the November evening had come down dark and moist,
holding the smoke nearer the ground and enveloping the buildings in a soil-
ing black mist. Lighted windows and street lamps appeared and disappeared
in the altering thicknesses of fog, but at intervals, as Collinson walked on
northward, he passed a small shop, or a cluster of shops, where the light was
close to him and bright, and at one of these oases of illumination he lingered
a moment, with a thought to buy a toy in the window for his three-year-
old little girl. The toy was a gaily coloured acrobatic monkey that willingly
climbed up and down a string, and he knew that the "baby," as he and his
wife still called their child, would scream with delight at the sight of it.
He hesitated, staring into the window rather longingly, and wondering if he
ought to make such a purchase. He had twelve dollars of his own in his
pocket, but the toy was marked "35 cents" and he decided he could not
afford it. So he sighed and went on, turning presently into a darker street.

Here the air was like that of a busy freight-yard, thick with coal-dust and
at times almost unbreathable so that Collinson was glad to get out of it
even though the exchange was for the early-evening smells of the cheap
apartment house where he lived.

His own "kitchenette" was contributing its share, he found, the baby was
crying over some inward perplexity not to be explained; and his wife, pretty
and a little frowzy, was as usual, and as he had expected. That is to say, he
found her irritated by cooking, bored by the baby, and puzzled by the dull
life she led. Other women, it appeared, had happy and luxurious homes,
and, during the malnutritious dinner she had prepared, she mentioned
many such women by name, laying particular stress upon the achievements
of their husbands. Why should she ("alone," as she put it) lead the life she

did in one room and a kitchenette, without even being able to afford to go to the movies more than once or twice a month? Mrs. Theodore Thompson's husband had bought a perfectly beautiful little sedan automobile; he gave his wife everything she wanted. Mrs. Will Gregory had merely mentioned that her old Hudson seal coat was wearing a little, and her husband had instantly said, "What'll a new one come to, girlie? Four or five hundred? Run and get it!" Why were other women's husbands like that—and why, oh, why! was hers like *this*? An eavesdropper might well have deduced from Mrs. Collinson's harangue that her husband owned somewhere a storehouse containing all the good things she wanted and that he withheld them from her out of his perverse wilfulness. Moreover, he did not greatly help his case by protesting that the gratification of her desires was beyond his powers.

"My goodness!" he said. "You talk as if I had sedans and sealskin coats and theatre tickets *on* me! Well, I haven't; that's all!"

"Then go out and get 'em!" she said fiercely. "Go out and get 'em!"

"What with?" he inquired. "I have twelve dollars in my pocket, and a balance of seventeen dollars at the bank; that's twenty-nine. I get twenty-five from the office day after to-morrow—Saturday; that makes fifty-four; but we have to pay forty-five for rent on Monday; so that'll leave us nine dollars. Shall I buy you a sedan and a sealskin coat on Tuesday out of the nine?"

Mrs. Collinson began to weep a little. "The old, old story!" she said. "Six long, long years it's been going on now! I ask you how much you've got, and you say, 'Nine dollars,' or 'Seven dollars,' or 'Four dollars'; and once it was sixty-five cents! Sixty-five cents; that's what we have to live on! Sixty-five cents!"

"Oh, hush!" he said wearily.

"Hadn't you better hush a little yourself?" she retorted. "You come home with twelve dollars in your pocket and tell your wife to hush! That's nice! Why can't you do what decent men do?"

"What's that?"

"Why, give their wives something to live for. What do you give me, I'd like to know! Look at the clothes I wear, please!"

"Well, it's your own fault," he muttered.

"What did you say? Did you say it's my fault I wear clothes any woman I know wouldn't be *seen* in?"

"Yes, I did. If you hadn't made me get you that platinum ring——"

"What!" she cried, and flourished her hand at him across the table. "Look at it! It's platinum, yes; but look at the stone in it, about the size of a pin-head, so't I'm ashamed to wear it when any of my friends see me! A hundred and sixteen dollars is what this magnificent ring cost you, and how long did I have to beg before I got even *that* little out of you? And it's the best thing I own and the only thing I ever did get out of you!"

"Oh, Lordy!" he moaned.

"I wish you'd seen Charlie Loomis looking at this ring to-day," she said, with a desolate laugh. "He happened to notice it, and I saw him keep glancing at it, and I wish you'd seen Charlie Loomis's expression!"

Collinson's own expression became noticeable upon her introduction of this name; he stared at her gravely until he completed the mastication of one of the indigestibles she had set before him; then he put down his fork and said:

"So you saw Charlie Loomis again to-day. Where?"

"Oh, my!" she sighed. "Have we got to go over all that again?"

"Over all what?"

"Over all the fuss you made the last time I mentioned Charlie's name. I thought we settled it you were going to be a little more sensible about him."

"Yes," Collinson returned. "I was going to be more sensible about him, because you were going to be more sensible about him. Wasn't that the agreement?"

She gave him a hard glance, tossed her head so that the curls of her bobbed hair fluttered prettily, and with satiric mimicry repeated his question: "'Agreement! Wasn't that the agreement?' Oh, my, but you do make me tired, talking about 'agreements'! As if it was a crime my going to a vaudeville matinée with a man kind enough to notice that my husband never takes me anywhere!"

"Did you go to a vaudeville with him to-day?"

"No, I didn't!" she said. "I was talking about the time when you made such a fuss. I didn't go anywhere with him to-day."

"I'm glad to hear it," Collinson said. "I wouldn't have stood for it."

"Oh, you wouldn't?" she cried, and added a shrill laugh as further comment. "You 'wouldn't have stood for it'! How very, very dreadful!"

"Never mind," he returned doggedly. "We went over all that the last time, and you understand me: I'll have no more foolishness about Charlie Loomis."

"How nice of you! He's a friend of yours; you go with him yourself; but your wife mustn't even look at him just because he happens to be the one man that amuses her a little. That's fine!"

"Never mind," Collinson said again. "You say you saw him to-day. I want to know where."

"Suppose I don't choose to tell you."

"You'd better tell me, I think."

"Do you? I've got to answer for every minute of my day, do I?"

"I want to know where you saw Charlie Loomis."

She tossed her curls again, and laughed. "Isn't it funny!" she said. "Just because I like a man, he's the one person I can't have anything to do with! Just because he's kind and jolly and amusing and I like his jokes and his thoughtfulness toward a woman, when he's with her, I'm not to be allowed to see him at all! But my *husband*—oh, that's entirely different! *He* can go out with Charlie whenever he likes and have a good time, while I stay home and wash the dishes! Oh, it's a lovely life!"

"Where did you see him to-day?"

Instead of answering his question, she looked at him plaintively, and allowed tears to shine along her lower eyelids. "Why do you treat me like this?" she asked in a feeble voice. "Why can't I have a man friend if I want to? I do like Charlie Loomis. I do like him——"

"Yes! That's what I noticed!"

"Well, but what's the good of always insulting me about him? He has time on his hands of afternoons, and so have I. Our janitor's wife is crazy about the baby and just adores to have me leave her in their flat—the longer the better. Why shouldn't I go to a matinée or a picture-show sometimes with Charlie? Why should I just have to sit around instead of going out and having a nice time when he wants me to?"

"I want to know where you saw him to-day!"

Mrs. Collinson jumped up. "You make me sick!" she said, and began to clear away the dishes.

"I want to know where——"

"Oh, hush up!" she cried. "He came here to leave a note for you."

"Oh," said her husband. "I beg your pardon. That's different."

"How sweet of you!"

"Where's the note, please?"

She took it from her pocket and tossed it to him. "So long as it's a note for *you* it's all right, of course!" she said. "I wonder what you'd do if he'd written one to me!"

"Never mind," said Collinson, and read the note.

DEAR COLLIE: Dave and Smithie and Old Bill and Sammy Hoag and maybe Steinie and Sol are coming over to the shack about eight-thirt. Home brew and the old pastime. You know! Don't fail.—CHARLIE.

"You've read this, of course," Collinson said. "The envelope wasn't sealed."

"I have not," his wife returned, covering the prevarication with a cold dignity. "I'm not in the habit of reading other peoples's correspondence, thank you! I suppose you think I do so because you'd never hesitate to read any note *I* get; but I don't do everything you do, you see!"

"Well, you can read it now," he said, and gave her the note.

Her eyes swept the writing briefly, and she made a sound of wonderment, as if amazed to find herself so true a prophet. "And the words weren't more than out of mouth! *You* can go and have a grand party right in his flat, while your wife stays home and gets the baby to bed and washes the dishes!"

"I'm not going."

"Oh, no!" she said mockingly. "I suppose not! I see you missing one of Charlie's stag-parties!"

"I'll miss this one."

But it was not to Mrs. Collinson's purpose that he should miss the party; she wished him to be as intimate as possible with the debonair Charlie Loomis; and so, after carrying some dishes into the kitchenette in meditative silence, she reappeared with a changed manner. She went to her husband, gave him a shy little pat on the shoulder and laughed good-naturedly. "Of course you'll go," she said. "I do think you're silly about my never going out with him when it would give me a little innocent pleasure and when you're not home to take me, yourself; but I wasn't really in such terrible earnest, all I said. You work hard the whole time, honey, and the only pleasure you ever do have, it's when you get a chance to go to one of these little penny-ante stag-parties. You haven't been to one for ever so long, and you never stay after twelve; it's really all right with me. I want you to go."

"Oh, no," said Collinson. "It's only penny-ante, but I couldn't afford to lose anything at all."

"But you never do. You always win a little."

"I know," he said. "I've figured out I'm about sixteen dollars ahead at penny-ante on the whole year. I cleaned up seven dollars and sixty cents at Charlie's last party; but of course my luck might change, and we couldn't afford it."

"If you did lose, it'd only be a few cents," she said. "What's the difference, if it gives you a little fun? You'll work all the better if you go out and enjoy yourself once in a while."

"Well, if you really look at it that way, I'll go."

"That's right, dear," she said, smiling. "Better put on a fresh collar and your other suit, hadn't you?"

"I suppose so," he assented, and began to make the changes she suggested. He went about them in a leisurely way, played with the baby at intervals, while Mrs. Collinson sang cheerfully over her work; and when he had completed his toilet, it was time for him to go. She came in from the kitchenette, kissed him, and then looked up into his eyes, letting him see a fond and brightly amiable expression.

"There, honey," she said. "Run along and have a nice time. Then maybe you'll be a little more sensible about some of *my* little pleasures."

He held the one-hundred-dollar bill, folded, in his hand, meaning to leave it with her, but as she spoke a sudden recurrence of suspicion made him forget his purpose. "Look here," he said. "I'm not making any bargain with you. You talk as if you thought I was going to let you run around to vaude-villes with Charlie because you let me go to this party. Is that your idea?"

It was, indeed, precisely Mrs. Collinson's idea, and she was instantly angered enough to admit it in her retort. "Oh, aren't you *mean!*" she cried. "I might know better than to look for any fairness in a man like you!"

"See here——"

"Oh, hush up!" she said. "Shame on you! Go on to your party!" With that she put both hands upon his breast, and pushed him toward the door.

"I won't go. I'll stay here."

"You will, too, go!" she cried shrewishly. "I don't want to look at you around here all evening. It'd make me sick to look at a man without an ounce of fairness in his whole mean little body!"

"All right," said Collinson, violently, "I *will* go!"

"Yes! Get out of my sight!"

And he did, taking the one-hundred-dollar bill with him to the penny-ante poker party.

The gay Mr. Charlie Loomis called his apartment "the shack" in jocular depreciation of its beauty and luxury, but he regarded it as a perfect thing, and in one way it was; for it was perfectly in the family likeness of a thousand such "shacks." It had a ceiling with false beams, walls of green burlap spotted with coloured "coaching prints," brown shelves supporting pewter plates and mugs, "mission" chairs, a leather couch with violet cushions, silver-framed photographs of lady-friends and officer-friends, a droplight of pink-shot imitation alabaster, a papier-mâché skull tobacco-jar among moving-picture magazines on the round card-table; and, of course, the final Charlie Loomis touch—a Japanese man-servant.

The master of all this was one of those neat, stoutish young men with fat, round heads, sleek, fair hair, immaculate, pale complexions and infirm little pink mouths—in fact, he was of the type that may suggest to the student of resemblances a fastidious and excessively clean white pig with transparent ears. Nevertheless, Charlie Loomis was of a free-handed habit in some matters, being particularly indulgent to pretty women and their children. He spoke of the latter as "the kiddies," of course, and liked to call their mothers "kiddo," or "girlie." One of his greatest pleasures was to tell a woman that she was "the dearest, bravest little girlie in the world." Naturally he was a welcome guest in many households, and would often bring a really magnificent toy to the child of some friend whose wife he was courting. Moreover, at thirty-three, he had already done well enough in business to take things easily, and he liked to give these little card-parties, not for gain, but for pastime. He was cautious and disliked high stakes in a game of chance.

That is to say, he disliked the possibility of losing enough money to annoy him, though of course he set forth his principles as resting upon a more gallant and unselfish basis. "I don't consider it hospitality to have any man go out o' my shack sore," he was wont to say. "Myself, I'm a bachelor and got no obligations; I'll shoot any man that can afford it for anything he wants to. Trouble is, you never can tell when a man *can't* afford it, or what harm his losin' might mean to the little girlie at home and the kiddies. No, boys, penny-ante and ten-cent limit is the highest we go in this ole shack. Penny-ante and a few steins of the ole home-brew that hasn't got a divorce in a barrel of it!"

Penny-ante and the ole home-brew had been in festal operation for half an hour when the morose Collinson arrived this evening. Mr. Loomis and his guests sat about the round table under the alabaster droplight; their coats were off; cigars were worn at the deliberative poker angle; colourful chips and cards glistened on the cloth; one of the players wore a green shade over his eyes; and all in all, here was a little poker party for a lithograph. To complete the picture, several of the players continued to concentrate upon their closely held cards, and paid no attention to the newcomer or to their host's lively greeting of him.

"Ole Collie, b'gosh!" Mr. Loomis shouted, humorously affecting the bucolic. "Here's your vacant cheer; stack all stuck out for you 'n' ever'thin'! Set daown, neighbour, an' Smithie'll deal you in, next hand. What made you so late? Helpin' the little girlie at home get the kiddy to bed? That's a great kiddy of yours, Collie. I got a little Christmas gift for her I'm goin' to bring around some day soon. Yes, sir, that's a great little kiddy Collie's got over at his place, boys."

Collinson took the chair that had been left for him, counted his chips, and then as the playing of a "hand" still preoccupied three of the company, he picked up a silver dollar that lay upon the table near him. "What's this?" he asked. "A side bet? Or did somebody just leave it here for me?"

"Yes; for you to look at," Mr. Loomis explained. "It's Smithie's."

"What's wrong with it?"

"Nothin'. Smithie was just showin' it to us. Look at it."

Collinson turned the coin over and saw a tiny inscription that had been lined into the silver with a point of steel. "'Luck,'" he read;—"'Luck hurry back to me!'" Then he spoke to the owner of this marked dollar. "I suppose you put that on there, Smithie, to help make sure of getting our money to-night."

But Smithie shook his head, which was a large, gaunt head, as it happened —a head fronted with a sallow face shaped much like a coffin, but inconsistently genial in expression. "No," he said. "It just came in over my counter this afternoon, and I noticed it when I was checkin' up the day's cash. Funny, ain't it: 'Luck hurry back to me!'"

"Who do you suppose marked that on it?" Collinson said thoughtfully.

"Golly!" his host exclaimed. "It won't do you much good to wonder about that!"

Collinson frowned, continuing to stare at the marked dollar. "I guess not, but really I should like to know."

"I would, too," Smithie said. "I been thinkin' about it. Might 'a' been somebody in Seattle or somebody in Ipswich, Mass., or New Orleans or St. Paul. How you goin' to tell? Might 'a' been a woman; might 'a' been a man. The way I guess it out, this poor boob, whoever he was, well, prob'ly he'd had good times for a while, and maybe carried this dollar for a kind of pocket piece, the way some people do, you know. Then he got in trouble—or she did, whichever it was—and got flat broke and had to spend this last dollar he had—for something to eat, most likely. Well, he thought a while before he spent it, and the way I guess it out, he said to himself, he said, 'Well,' he said, 'most of the good luck I've enjoyed lately,' he said, 'it's been while I had this dollar on me. I got to kiss 'em good-bye now, good luck and good dollar together; but maybe I'll get 'em both back some day, so I'll just mark the wish on the dollar, like this: Luck hurry back to me! That'll help some, maybe, and anyhow I'll *know* my luck dollar if I ever do get it back.' That's the way I guess it out, anyhow. It's funny how some people like to believe luck depends on some little thing like that."

"Yes, it is," Collinson assented, still brooding over the coin.

The philosophic Smithie extended his arm across the table, collecting the cards to deal them, for the "hand" was finished. "Yes, sir, it's funny," he repeated. "Nobody knows exactly what luck is, but the way I guess it out, it lays in a man's *believin'* he's in luck, and some little object like this makes him kind of concentrate his mind on thinkin' he's goin' to be lucky, because of course you often *know* you're goin' to win, and then you do win. You don't win when you *want* to win, or when you need to; you win when you *believe* you'll win. I don't know who was the dummy that said, 'Money's the root of all evil'; but I guess he didn't have *too* much sense! I suppose if some man killed some other man for a dollar, the poor fish that said that would let the man out and send the dollar to the chair. No, sir; money's just as good as it is bad; and it'll come your way if you *feel* it will; so you take this marked dollar o' mine——"

But here this garrulous and discursive guest was interrupted by immoderate protests from several of his colleagues. "Cut it out!" "My Lord!" "Do something!" "Smith*ie*! Are you ever goin' to *deal*?"

"I'm goin' to shuffle first," he responded, suiting the action to the word, though with deliberation, and at the same time continuing his discourse. "It's a mighty interesting thing, a piece o' money. You take this dollar, now: Who's it belonged to? Where's it been? What different kind o' funny things has it been spent for sometimes? What funny kind of secrets do you suppose it could 'a' heard if it had ears? Good people have had it and bad people have had it: why, a dollar could tell more about the human race—why, it could tell *all* about it!"

"I guess it couldn't tell all about the way you're dealin' these cards," said the man with the green shade. "You're mixin' things all up."

"I'll straighten 'em all out then," said Smithie cheerfully. "I knew of a twenty-dollar bill once; a pickpocket prob'ly threw it in the gutter to keep from havin' it found on him when they searched him, but anyway a woman I knew found it and sent it to her young sister out in Michigan to take some music lessons with, and the sister was so excited she took this bill out of the letter and kissed it. That's where they thought she got the germ she died of a couple o' weeks later, and the undertaker got the twenty-dollar bill, and got robbed of it the same night. Nobody knows where it went then. They say, 'Money talks.' Golly! If it *could* talk, what couldn't it tell? Nobody'd be safe. *I* got this dollar now, but who's it goin' to belong to next, and what'll *he* do with it? And then after *that*! Why for years and years and years it'll go on from one pocket to another, in a millionaire's house one day, in some burglar's flat the next, maybe, and in one person's hand money'll do good, likely, and in another's it'll do harm. We all *want* money; but some say it's a bad thing, like that dummy I was talkin' about. Lordy! Goodness or badness, I'll take all anybody——"

He was interrupted again, and with increased vehemence. Collinson, who sat next to him, complied with the demand to "ante up," then placed the dollar near his little cylinders of chips, and looked at his cards. They proved unencouraging, and he turned to his neighbour. "I'd sort of like to have that marked dollar, Smithie," he said. "I'll give you a paper dollar and a nickel for it."

But Smithie laughed, shook his head, and slid the coin over toward his own chips. "No, sir. I'm goin' to keep it—awhile, anyway."

"So you do think it'll bring you luck, after all!"

"No. But I'll hold onto it for this evening, anyhow."

"Not if we clean you out, you won't," said Charlie Loomis. "You know the rules o' the ole shack: only cash goes in *this* game; no I. O. U. stuff ever went here or ever will. Tell you what I'll do, though, before you lose it: I'll give you a dollar and a quarter for your ole silver dollar, Smithie."

"Oh, you want it, too, do you? I guess I can spot what sort of luck *you* want it for, Charlie."

"Well, Mr. Bones, what sort of luck do I want it for?"

"*You* win, Smithie," one of the other players said. "We all know what sort o' luck ole Charlie wants your dollar for—he wants it for luck with the dames."

"Well, I might," Charlie admitted, not displeased. "I haven't been so lucky that way lately—not so dog-*gone* lucky!"

All of his guests, except one, laughed at this; but Collinson frowned, still staring at the marked dollar. For a reason he could not have put into words just then, it began to seem almost vitally important to him to own this coin if he could, and to prevent Charlie Loomis from getting possession of it. The jibe, "He wants it for luck with the dames," rankled in Collinson's mind: somehow it seemed to refer to his wife.

"I'll tell you what I'll do, Smithie," he said. "I'll bet two dollars against that dollar of yours that I hold a higher hand next deal than you do."

"Here! Here!" Charlie remonstrated. "Shack rules! Ten-cent limit."

"That's only for the game," Collinson said, turning upon his host with a sudden sharpness. "This is an outside bet between Smithie and me. Will you do it, Smithie? Where's your sporting spirit?"

So liberal a proposal at once roused the spirit to which it appealed. "Well, I might, if some o' the others'll come in too, and make it really worth my while."

"I'm in," the host responded with prompt inconsistency; and others of the party, it appeared, were desirous of owning the talisman. They laughed and said it was "crazy stuff," yet they all "came in," and, for the first time in the history of this "shack," what Mr. Loomis called "real money" was seen upon the table as a stake. It was won, and the silver dollar with it, by the largest and oldest of the gamesters, a fat man with a walrus moustache that inevitably made him known in this circle as "Old Bill." He smiled condescendingly, and would have put the dollar in his pocket with the "real money," but Mr. Loomis protested.

"Here! What you doin'?" he shouted, catching Old Bill by the arm. "Put that dollar back on the table."

"What for?"

"What for? Why, we're goin' to play for it again. Here's two dollars against it I beat you on the next hand."

"No," said Old Bill calmly. "It's worth more than two dollars to me. It's worth five."

"Well, five then," his host returned. "I want that dollar!"

"So do I," said Collinson. "I'll put in five dollars if you do."

"Anybody else in?" Old Bill inquired, dropping the coin on the table; and all of the others again "came in." Old Bill won again; but once more Charlie Loomis prevented him from putting the silver dollar in his pocket.

"Come on now!" Mr. Loomis exclaimed. "Anybody else but me in on this for five dollars next time?"

"I am," said Collinson, swallowing with a dry throat; and he set forth all that remained to him of his twelve dollars. In return he received a pair of deuces, and the jubilant Charlie won.

He was vainglorious in his triumph. "Didn't that little luck piece just keep on tryin' to find the right man?" he cried, and read the inscription loudly. " 'Luck hurry back to me!' Righto! You're home where you belong, girlie! Now we'll settle down to our reg'lar little game again."

"Oh, no," said Old Bill. "You wouldn't let me keep it. Put it out there and play for it again."

"I won't. She's mine now."

"I want my luck piece back myself," said Smithie. "Put it out and play for it. You made Old Bill."

"I won't do it."

"Yes, you will," Collinson said, and he spoke without geniality. "You put it out there."

"Oh, yes, I will," Mr. Loomis returned mockingly. "I will for ten dollars."

"Not I," said Old Bill. "Five is foolish enough." And Smithie agreed with him. "Nor me!"

"All right, then. If you're afraid of ten, I keep it. I thought the ten'd scare you."

"Put that dollar on the table," Collinson said. "I'll put ten against it."

There was a little commotion among these mild gamesters; and someone said, "You're crazy, Collie. What do you want to do that for?"

"I don't care," said Collinson. "That dollar's already cost me enough, and I'm going after it."

"Well, you see, I want it, too," Charlie Loomis retorted cheerfully; and he appealed to the others. "I'm not askin' him to put up ten against it, am I?"

"Maybe not," Old Bill assented. "But how long is this thing goin' to keep on? It's already balled our game all up, and if we keep on foolin' with these side bets, why, what's the use?"

"My goodness!" the host exclaimed. "*I'm* not pushin' this thing, am I? I don't want to risk my good old luck piece, do I? It's Collie that's crazy to go on, ain't it?" He laughed. "He hasn't showed his money yet, though, I notice, and this ole shack is run on strickly cash principles. I don't believe he's got ten dollars more on him!"

"Oh, yes, I have."

"Let's see it then."

Collinson's nostrils distended a little; but he said nothing, fumbled in his pocket, and then tossed the one-hundred-dollar bill, rather crumpled, upon the table.

"Great heavens!" shouted Old Bill. "Call the doctor: I'm all of a swoon!"

"Look at what's spilled over our nice clean table!" another said, in an awed voice. "Did you claim he didn't have *ten* on him, Charlie?"

"Well, it's nice to look at," Smithie observed. "But I'm with Old Bill. How long are you two goin' to keep this thing goin'? If Collie wins the luck piece, I suppose Charlie'll bet him fifteen against it, and then——"

"No, I won't," Charlie interrupted. "Ten's the limit."

"Goin' to keep on bettin' ten against it all night?"

"No," said Charlie. "I tell you what I'll do with you, Collinson; we both of us seem kind o' set on this luck piece, and you're already out some on it. I'll give you a square chance at it and at catchin' even. It's twenty minutes after nine. I'll keep on these side bets with you till ten o'clock, but when my clock hits ten, we're through, and the one that's got it then keeps it, and no more foolin'. You want to do that, or quit now? I'm game either way."

"Go ahead and deal," said Collinson. "Whichever one of us has it at ten o'clock, it's his, and we quit."

But when the little clock on Charlie's green-painted mantel shelf struck ten, the luck piece was Charlie's and with it an overwhelming lien on the one-hundred-dollar bill. He put both in his pocket; "Remember this ain't my fault; it was you that insisted," he said, and handed Collinson four five-dollar bills as change.

Old Bill, platonically interested, discovered that his cigar was sparkless, applied a match, and casually set forth his opinion. "Well, I guess that was about as poor a way of spendin' eighty dollars as I ever saw, but it all goes to show there's truth in the old motto that anything at all can happen in any poker game! That was a mighty nice hundred-dollar bill you had on you, Collie; but it's like what Smithie said: a piece o' money goes hoppin' around from one person to another—*it* don't care!—and yours has gone and hopped to Charlie. The question is, Who's it goin' to hop to next?" He paused to laugh, glanced over the cards that had been dealt him, and concluded: "My guess is 't some good-lookin' woman 'll prob'ly get a pretty fair chunk o' that hundred-dollar bill out o' Charlie. Well, let's settle down to the ole army game."

They settled down to it, and by twelve o'clock (the invariable closing hour of these pastimes in the old shack) Collinson had lost four dollars and thirty cents more. He was commiserated by his fellow gamesters as they put on their coats and overcoats, preparing to leave the hot little room. They shook their heads, laughed ruefully in sympathy, and told him he oughtn't to carry hundred-dollar bills upon his person when he went out among friends. Old Bill made what is sometimes called an unfortunate remark.

"Don't worry about Collie," he said jocosely. "That hundred-dollar bill prob'ly belonged to some rich client of his."

"What!" Collinson said, staring.

"Never mind, Collie; I wasn't in earnest," the joker explained. "Of course I didn't mean it."

"Well, you oughtn't to say it," Collinson protested. "People say a thing like that about a man in a joking way, but other people hear it sometimes and don't know he's joking, and a story gets started."

"My goodness, but you're serious!" Old Bill exclaimed. "You look like you had a misery in your chest, as the rubes say; and I don't blame you! Get on out in the fresh night air and you'll feel better."

He was mistaken, however; the night air failed to improve Collinson's spirits as he walked home alone through the dark and chilly streets. There was indeed a misery in his chest, where stirred a sensation vaguely nauseating; his hands were tremulous and his knees infirm as he walked. In his mind was a confusion of pictures and sounds, echoes from Charlie Loomis's shack: he could not clear his mind's eye of the one-hundred-dollar bill; and its likeness, as it lay crumpled on the green cloth under the droplight, haunted and hurt him as a face in a coffin haunts and hurts the new mourner. Bits of Smithie's discursiveness resounded in his mind's ear, keeping him from thinking. "In one person's hands money'll do good likely, and in another's it'll do harm."—"The dummy that said, 'Money's the root of all evil!'"

It seemed to Collinson then that money was the root of all evil and the root of all good, the root and branch of all life, indeed. With money, his wife would have been amiable, not needing gay bachelors to take her to vaudevilles. Her need of money was the true foundation of the jealousy that had sent him out morose and reckless to-night; of the jealousy that had made it seem, when he gambled with Charlie Loomis for the luck dollar, as though they really gambled for luck with her.

It still seemed to him that they had gambled for luck with her: Charlie had wanted the talisman, as Smithie said, in order to believe in his luck— his luck with women—and therefore actually be lucky with them; and Charlie had won. But as Collinson plodded homeward in the chilly midnight, his shoulders sagging and his head drooping, he began to wonder how he could have risked money that belonged to another man. What on earth had made him do what he had done? Was it the mood his wife had set him in as he went out that evening? No; he had gone out feeling like that often enough, and nothing had happened.

Something had brought this trouble on him, he thought; for it appeared to

Collinson that he had been an automaton, having nothing to do with his own actions. He must bear the responsibility for them; but he had not willed them. If the one-hundred-dollar bill had not happened to be in his pocket—— That was it! And at the thought he mumbled desolately to himself: "I'd been all right if it hadn't been for that." If the one-hundred-dollar bill had not happened to be in his pocket, he'd have been "all right." The one-hundred-dollar bill had done this to him. And Smithie's romancing again came back to him: "In one person's hands money'll do good, likely; in another's it'll do harm." It was the money that did harm or good, not the person; and the money in his hands had done this harm to himself.

He had to deliver a hundred dollars at the office in the morning, somehow, for he dared not take the risk of the client's meeting the debtor. There was a balance of seventeen dollars in his bank, and he could pawn his watch for twenty-five, as he knew well enough, by experience. That would leave fifty-eight dollars to be paid, and there was only one way to get it. His wife would have to let him pawn her ring. She'd *have* to!

Without any difficulty he could guess what she would say and do when he told her of his necessity: and he knew that never in her life would she forego the advantage over him she would gain from it. He knew, too, what stipulations she would make, and he had to face the fact that he was in no position to reject them. The one-hundred-dollar bill had cost him the last vestiges of mastery in his own house; and Charlie Loomis had really won not only the bill and the luck, but the privilege of taking Collinson's wife to vaudevilles. But it all came back to the same conclusion: the one-hundred-dollar bill had done it to him. "What kind of a thing *is* this life?" Collinson mumbled to himself, finding matters wholly perplexing in a world made into tragedy at the caprice of a little oblong slip of paper.

Then, as he went on his way to wake his wife and face her with the soothing proposal to pawn her ring early the next morning, something happened to Collinson. Of itself the thing that happened was nothing, but he was aware of his folly as if it stood upon a mountain top against the sun—and so he gathered knowledge of himself and a little of the wisdom that is called better than happiness.

His way was now the same as upon the latter stretch of his walk home from the office that evening. The smoke fog had cleared, and the air was clean with a night wind that moved briskly from the west; in all the long street there was only one window lighted, but it was sharply outlined now, and fell as a bright rhomboid upon the pavement before Collinson. When he came to it he paused at the hint of an inward impulse he did not think to trace; and, frowning, he perceived that this was the same shop window that had detained him on his homeward way, when he had thought of buying a toy for the baby.

The toy was still there in the bright window; the gay little acrobatic monkey that would climb up or down a red string as the string slacked or straightened; but Collinson's eye fixed itself upon the card marked with the price: "35 cents."

He stared and stared. "Thirty-five cents!" he said to himself. "Thirty-five cents!"

Then suddenly he burst into loud and prolonged laughter.

The sound was startling in the quiet night, and roused the interest of a meditative policeman who stood in the darkened doorway of the next shop. He stepped out, not unfriendly.

"What *you* havin' such a good time over, this hour o' the night?" he inquired. "What's all the joke?"

Collinson pointed to the window. "It's that monkey on the string," he said. "Something about it struck me as mighty funny!"

So, with a better spirit, he turned away, still laughing, and went home to face his wife.

Mary Smith

Henry Millick Chester, rising early from intermittent slumbers, found himself the first of the crowded Pullman to make a toilet in the men's smoke-and-wash-room, and so had the place to himself—an advantage of high dramatic value to a person of his age and temperament, on account of the mirrors which, set at various angles, afford a fine view of the profile. Henry Millick Chester, scouring cinders and stickiness from his eyes and rouging his ears with honest friction, enriched himself of this too unfamiliar opportunity. He smiled and was warmly interested in the results of his smile in reflection, particularly in some pleasant alterations it effected upon an outline of the cheek usually invisible to the bearer. He smiled graciously, then he smiled sardonically. Other smiles he offered—the tender smile, the forbidding smile, the austere and the seductive, the haughty and the pleading, the mordant and the compassionate, the tolerant but incredulous smile of a man of the world, and the cold, ascetic smile that shows a woman that her shallow soul has been read all too easily—pastimes abandoned only with the purely decorative application of shaving lather to his girlish chin. However, as his unbeetling brow was left unobscured, he was able to pursue his physiognomical researches and to produce for his continued enlightenment a versatile repertory of frowns—the stern, the quizzical, the bitter, the treacherous, the bold, the agonized, the inquisitive, the ducal, and the frown of the husband who says: "I forgive you. Go!" A few minutes later Mr. Chester, abruptly pausing in the operation of fastening his collar, bent a sudden, passionate interest upon his right forearm without apparent cause and with the air of never having seen it until that moment. He clenched his fingers tightly, producing a slight stringiness above the wrist, then crooked his elbow with intensity, noting this enormous effect in all the mirrors. Regretfully, he let his shirt-sleeves fall and veil the rare but private beauties just discovered, rested his left hand negligently upon his hip, extended his right in a gesture of flawlessly aristocratic grace, and, with a slight inclination of his head, uttered aloud these simple but befitting words: "I thank ye, my good people." T' yoong Maister was greeting the loyal tenantry who acclaimed his return to

Fielding Manor, a flowered progress thoroughly incomprehensible to the Pullman porter whose transfixed eye—glazed upon an old-gold face intruded through the narrow doorway—Mr. Chester encountered in the glass above the nickeled washbasins. The Libyan withdrew in a cloud of silence, and t' yoong Maister, flushing somewhat, resumed his toilet with annoyed precision and no more embroidery. He had yesterday completed his sophomore year; the brushes he applied to his now adult locks were those of a junior. And with a man's age had come a man's cares and responsibilities. Several long years had rolled away since for the last time he had made himself sick on a train in a club-car orgy of cubebs and sarsaparilla pop.

Zigzagging through shoe-bordered aisles of sleepers in morning dishevelment, he sought the dining car, where the steward escorted him to an end table for two. He would have assumed his seat with that air of negligent hauteur which was his chosen manner for public appearances, had not the train, taking a curve at high speed, heaved him into the undesirable embrace of an elderly man breakfasting across the aisle. "Keep your feet, sonny; keep your feet," said this barbarian, little witting that he addressed a member of the nineteen-something prom. committee. People at the next table laughed genially, and Mr. Chester, muttering a word of hostile apology, catapulted into his assigned place, his cheeks hot with the triple outrage.

He relieved himself a little by the icy repulsion with which he countered the cordial advances of the waiter, who took his order and wished him a good morning, hoped he had slept well, declared the weather delightful and, unanswered, yet preserved his beautiful courtesy unimpaired. When this humble ambassador had departed on his mission to the kitchen Henry Millick Chester, unwarrantably persuaded that all eyes were searching his every inch and angle—an impression not uncharacteristic of his years—gazed out of the window with an indifference which would have been obtrusive if any of the other breakfasters had happened to notice it. The chill exclusiveness of his expression was a rebuke to such prying members of the proletariat as might be striving to read his thoughts, and barred his fellow passengers from every privilege to his consideration. The intensely reserved gentleman was occupied with interests which were the perquisites of only his few existing peers in birth, position, and intelligence, none of whom, patently, was in that car.

He looked freezingly upon the abashed landscape, which fled in shame; nor was that wintry stare relaxed when the steward placed someone opposite him at the little table. Nay, our frosty scholar now intensified the bleakness of his isolation, retiring quite to the pole in reproval of this too close intrusion. He resolutely denied the existence of his vis-à-vis, refused consciousness of its humanity, even of its sex, and then inconsistently began to perspire with the horrible impression that it was glaring at him fixedly. It was a dreadful feeling. He felt himself growing red, and coughed vehemently to afford the public an explanation of his change of colour. At last, his suffering grown unendurable, he desperately turned his eyes full upon the newcomer. She was not looking at him at all, but down at the edge of the white cloth on her own side of the table; and she was the very prettiest girl he had ever seen in his life.

She was about his own age. Her prettiness was definitely extreme, and its fair delicacy was complete and without any imperfection whatever. She was dressed in pleasant shades of tan and brown. A brown veil misted the rim of her hat, tan gloves were folded back from her wrists; and they, and all she wore, were fresh and trim and ungrimed by the dusty journey. She was charming. Henry Millick Chester's first gasping appraisal of her was perfectly accurate, for she *was* a peach—or a rose, or anything that is dewy and fresh and delectable. She was indeed some smooth. She was the smoothest thing in the world, and the world knows it!

She looked up.

Henry Millick Chester was lost.

At the same instant that the gone feeling came over him she dropped her eyes again to the edge of the table. Who can tell if she knew what she had done?

The conversation began with appalling formalities, which preluded the most convenient placing of a sugar bowl and the replenishing of an exhausted salt cellar. Then the weather, spurned as the placative offering of the gentle waiter, fell from the lips of the princess in words of diamonds and rubies and pearls. Our Henry took up the weather where she left it; he put it to its utmost; he went forward with it, prophesying weather; he went backward with it, recalling weather; he spun it out and out, while she agreed to all he said, until this overworked weather got so stringy that each obscurely felt it to be hideous. The thread broke; fragments wandered in the air for a few moments, but disappeared; a desperate propriety descended, and they fell into silence over their eggs.

Frantically Mr. Chester searched his mind for some means to pursue the celestial encounter. According to the rules, something ought to happen that would reveal her as Patricia Beekman, the sister of his roommate, Schuyler Beekman, and to-night he should be handing the imperturbable Dawkins a wire to send: "My dear Schuyler, I married your sister this afternoon." But it seemed unlikely, because his roommate's name was Jake Schmulze, and Jake lived in Cedar Rapids; and, besides, this train wasn't coming from or going to Palm Beach—it was going to St. Louis eventually, and now hustled earnestly across the placid and largely unbutlered plains of Ohio.

Often—as everyone knows—people have been lost to each other forever through the lack of a word, and few have realized this more poignantly than our Henry, as he helplessly suffered the precious minutes to accumulate vacancy. True, he had thought of something to say, yet he abandoned it. Probably he was wiser to wait, as what he thought of saying was: "Will you be my wife?" It might seem premature, he feared.

The strain was relieved by a heavenly accident which saved the life of a romance near perishing at birth. That charming girl, relaxing slightly in her

chair, made some small, indefinite, and entirely ladylike movement of rest-
fulness that reached its gentle culmination upon the two feet of Mr. Chester
which, obviously mistaken for structural adjuncts of the table, were thereby
glorified and became beautiful on the mountains. He was not the man to
criticise the remarkable ignorance of dining-car table architecture thus displayed, nor did he in any wise resent being mistaken up to the ankles for
metal or wood. No. The light pressure of her small heels hardly indented
the stout toes of his brown shoes; the soles of her slippers reposed upon his
two insteps, and rapture shook his soul to its foundations, while the ineffable
girl gazed lustrously out of the window, the clear serenity of her brilliant eyes
making plain her complete unconsciousness of the nature of what added to
her new comfort.

A terrific blush sizzled all over him, and to conceal its visible area he bent
low to his coffee. She was unaware. He was transported, she—to his eyes—
transfigured. Glamour diffused itself about her, sprayed about them both
like showers of impalpable gold-dust, and filled the humble dining car—it
filled the whole world. Transformed, seraphic waiters passed up and down
the aisle in a sort of obscure radiance. A nimbus hovered faintly above the
brown veil; a sacred luminosity was exhaled by the very tablecloth, where an
angel's pointed fingers drummed absently.

It would be uncharitable to believe that a spirit of retaliation inspired the
elderly and now replete man across the aisle, and yet, when he rose, he fell
upon the neck of Henry as Henry had fallen upon his, and the shock of it
jarred four shoes from the acute neighbourliness of their juxtaposition. The
accursed graybeard, giggling in his senility, passed on; but that angel leaped
backward in her chair while her beautiful eyes, wide open, stunned, her
beautiful mouth, wide open, incredulous, gave proof that horror can look
bewitching.

"Murder!" she gasped. "Were those your *feet?*"

And as he could compass no articulate reply, she grew as pink as he, murmured inaudibly, and stared at him in wider and wilder amazement.

"It—it didn't hurt," he finally managed to stammer.

At this she covered her blushes with her two hands and began to gurgle
and shake with laughter. She laughed and laughed and laughed. It became a
paroxysm. He laughed, too, because she laughed. Other passengers looked at
them and laughed. The waiters laughed; they approved—coloured waiters always approve of laughter—and a merry spirit went abroad in the car.

At last she controlled herself long enough to ask:

"But what did you think of me?"

"It—it didn't hurt," he repeated idiotically, to his own mortification, for
he passionately aspired to say something airy and winsome; but, as he
couldn't think of anything like that, he had to let it go. "Oh, not at all," he
added feebly.

However, "though not so deep as a well," it served, 'twas enough, for she
began to laugh again, and there loomed no further barrier in the way of

acquaintance. Therefore it was pleasantly without constraint, and indeed as a matter of course, that he dropped into a chair beside her half an hour later, in the observation car; and something in the way she let the *Illustrated London News* slide into the vacant chair on the other side of her might have suggested that she expected him.

"I was still wondering what you must have thought of me."

This gave him an opportunity, because he had thought out a belated reply for the first time she had said it. Hence, quick as a flash, he made the dashing rejoinder:

"It wasn't so much what I thought of you, but what I thought of myself—I thought I was in heaven!"

She must have known what pretty sounds her laughter made. She laughed a great deal. She even had a way of laughing in the middle of some of her words, and it gave them a kind of ripple. There are girls who naturally laugh like that; others learn to; a few won't, and some can't. It isn't fair to the ones that can't.

"But you oughtn't to tell me that," she said.

It was in the middle of "oughtn't" that she rippled. A pen cannot express it, neither can a typewriter, and no one has yet invented a way of writing with a flute; but the effect on Henry shows what a wonderful ripple it was. Henry trembled. From this moment she had only to ripple to make Henry tremble. Henry was more in love than he had been at breakfast. Henry was a Goner.

"Why oughtn't I to?" he demanded with white intensity. "If anything's true, it's right to tell it, isn't it? I believe that everybody has a right to tell the truth, don't you?"

"Ye-es——"

"You take the case of a man that's in love," said this rather precipitate gentleman; "isn't it right for him to——"

"But suppose," she interrupted, becoming instantly serious with the introduction of the great topic—"Suppose he isn't *really* in love. Don't you think there are very few cases of people truly and deeply caring for each other?"

"There are men," he said firmly, "who know how to love truly and deeply, and could never in their lives care for anybody but the one woman they have picked out. I don't say all men feel that way; I don't think they do. But there are a few that are capable of it." The seats in an observation car are usually near neighbours, and it happened that the brown cuff of a tan sleeve, extended reposefully on the arm of her chair, just touched the back of his hand, which rested on the arm of his. This ethereally light contact continued. She had no apparent cognizance of it, but a vibrant thrill passed through him, and possibly quite a hearty little fire might have been built under him without his perceiving good cause for moving. He shook, gulped, and added: "I am!"

"But how could you be sure of that," she said thoughtfully, "until you tried?" And as he seemed about to answer, perhaps too impulsively, she checked him with a smiling, "At your age!"

"You don't know how old I am. I'm older than you!"

"How old are you?"

"Twenty-one next March."

"What day?"

"The seventh."

"That is singular!"

"Why?"

"Because," she began in a low tone and with full recognition of the solemn import of the revelation—"Because my birthday is only one day after yours. I was twenty years old the eighth of last March."

"By George!" The exclamation came from him, husky with awe.

There was a fateful silence.

"Yes, I was born on the eighth," she said slowly.

"And me on the seventh!" At such a time no man is a purist.

"It is strange," she said.

"Strange! I came into the world just one day before you did!"

They looked at each other curiously, deeply stirred. Coincidence could not account for these birthdays of theirs, nor chance for their meeting on a train "like this." Henry Millick Chester was breathless. The mysteries were glimpsed. No doubt was possible—he and the wondrous creature at his side were meant for each other, intended from the beginning of eternity.

She dropped her eyes slowly from his, but he was satisfied that she had felt the marvel precisely as he had felt it.

"Don't you think," she said gently, "that a girl has seen more of the world at twenty than a man?"

Mr. Chester well wished to linger upon the subject of birthdays; however, the line of original research suggested by her question was alluring also. "Yes —and no," he answered with admirable impartiality. "In some ways, yes. In some ways, no. For instance, you take the case of a man that's in love——"

"Well," interrupted the lady, "I think, for instance, that a girl understands men better at twenty than men do women."

"It may be," he admitted, nodding. "I like to think about the deeper things like this sometimes."

"So do I. I think they're interesting," she said with that perfect sympathy of understanding which he believed she was destined to extend to him always and in all things. "Life itself is interesting. Don't you think so?"

"I think it's the most interesting subject there can be. Real life, that is, though—not just on the surface. Now, for instance, you take the case of a man that's in——"

"Do you go in much for reading?" she asked.

"Sure. But as I was saying, you take——"

"I think reading gives us so many ideas, don't you?"

"Yes. I get a lot out of it. I——"

"I do, too. I try to read only the best things," she said. "I don't believe in reading everything, and there's so much to read nowadays that isn't really good."

"Who do you think," he inquired with deference, "is the best author now?"

It was not a question to be settled quite offhand; she delayed her answer slightly, then, with a gravity appropriate to the literary occasion, temporized: "Well, since Victor Hugo is dead, it's hard to say just who is the best."

"Yes, it is," he agreed. "We get that in the English course in college. There aren't any great authors any more. I expect probably Swinburne's the best."

She hesitated. "Perhaps; but more as a poet."

He assented. "Yes, that's so. I expect he would be classed more as a poet. Come to think of it, I believe he's dead, too. I'm not sure, though; maybe it was Beerbohm Tree—somebody like that. I've forgotten; but, anyway, it doesn't matter. I didn't mean poetry; I meant who do you think writes the best books? Mrs. Humphry Ward?"

"Yes, she's good, and so's Henry James."

"I've never read anything by Henry James. I guess I'll read some of his this summer. What's the best one to begin on?"

The exquisite pink of her cheeks extended its area almost imperceptibly. "Oh, any one. They're all pretty good. Do you care for Nature?"

"Sure thing," he returned quickly. "Do you?"

"I love it!"

"So do I. I can't do much for mathematics, though."

"Br-r!" She shivered prettily. "I hate it!"

"So do I. I can't give astronomy a whole lot, either."

She turned a softly reproachful inquiry upon him. "Oh, don't you love to look at the stars?"

In horror lest the entrancing being think him a brute, he responded with breathless haste: "Oh, rath-er-r! To look at 'em, sure thing! I meant astronomy in college; that's mostly math, you know—just figures. But stars to look at—of course that's different. Why, I look up at 'em for hours sometimes!" He believed what he was saying. "I look up at 'em, and think and think and think——"

"So do I." Her voice was low and hushed; there was something almost holy in the sound of it, and a delicate glow suffused her lovely, upraised face— like that picture of Saint Cecilia, he thought. "Oh, I love the stars! And music—and flowers——"

"And birds," he added automatically in a tone that, could it by some miracle have been heard at home, would have laid his nine-year-old brother flat on the floor in a might-be mortal swoon.

A sweet warmth centred in the upper part of his diaphragm and softly filtered throughout him. The delicious future held no doubts or shadows for him. It was assured. He and this perfect woman had absolutely identical tastes; their abhorrences and their enthusiasms marched together; they would never know a difference in all their lives to come. Destiny unrolled before him a shining pathway which they two would walk hand-in-hand through the summer days to a calm and serene autumn, respected and admired by the world, but finding ever their greatest and most sacred joy in the light of each other's eyes—that light none other than the other could evoke.

Could it be possible, he wondered, that he was the same callow boy who but yesterday pranced and exulted in the "pee-rade" of the new juniors! How absurd and purposeless that old life seemed; how far away, how futile, and how childish! Well, it was over, finished. By this time to-morrow he would have begun his business career.

Back in the old life, he had expected to go through a law school after graduating from college, subsequently to enter his father's office. That meant five years before even beginning to practice, an idea merely laughable now. There was a men's furnishing store on a popular corner at home; it was an establishment which had always attracted him, and what pleasanter way to plow the road to success than through acres of variously woven fabrics, richly coloured silks, delicate linens, silver mountings and odorous leathers, in congenial association with neckties, walking-sticks, hosiery, and stickpins? He would be at home a few hours hence, and he would not delay. After lunch he would go boldly to his father and say: "Father, I have reached man's estate and I have put away childish things. I have made up my mind upon a certain matter and you will only waste time by any effort to alter this, my firm determination. Father, I here and now relinquish all legal ambitions, for the reason that a mercantile career is more suited to my inclinations and my abilities. Father, I have met the one and only woman I can ever care for, and I intend to make her my wife. Father, you have always dealt squarely with me; I will deal squarely with you. I ask you the simple question: Will you or will you not advance me the funds to purchase an interest in Paul H. Hoy & Company's Men's Outfitting Establishment? If you will not, then I shall seek help elsewhere."

Waking dreams are as swift, sometimes, as the other kind—which, we hear, thread mazes so labyrinthine "between the opening and the closing of a door"; and a twenty-year-old fancy, fermenting in the inclosure of a six-and-seven-eighth plaid cap, effervesces with a power of sizzling and sparkling and popping.

"I believe I love music best of all," said the girl dreamily.

"Do you play?" he asked, and his tone and look were those of one who watches at the sick-bed of a valued child.

"Yes, a little."

"I love the piano." He was untroubled by any remorse for what he and some of his gang had done only two days since to a previously fine instrument in his dormitory entry. He had forgotten the dead past in his present vision, which was of a luxurious room in a spacious mansion, and a tired man of affairs coming quietly into that room—from a conference at which he had consolidated the haberdashery trade of the world—and sinking noiselessly upon a rich divan, while a beautiful woman in a dress of brown and tan, her hair slightly silvered, played to him through the twilight upon a grand piano, the only other sound in the great house being the softly murmurous voices of perfectly trained children being put to bed in a distant nursery upstairs.

"I like the stage, too," she said. "Don't you?"

"You know! Did you see The Tinkle-Dingle Girl?"

"Yes. I liked it."

"It's a peach show." He spoke with warranted authority. During the university term just finished he had gone eight times to New York, and had enriched his critical perceptions of music and the drama by ten visits to The Tinkle-Dingle Girl, two of his excursions having fallen on matinee days. "Those big birds that played the comedy parts were funny birds, weren't they?"

"The tramp and the brewer? Yes. Awfully funny."

"We'll go lots to the theatre!" He spoke eagerly and with superb simplicity, quite without consciousness that he was skipping much that would usually be thought necessarily intermediate. An enchanting vision engrossed his mind's eye. He saw himself night after night at The Tinkle-Dingle Girl, his lovely wife beside him—growing matronly, perhaps, but slenderly matronly—with a grace of years that only added to her beauty, and always wearing tan gloves and a brown veil.

The bewilderment of her expression was perhaps justified.

"What!"

At this he realized the import of what he had said and what, in a measure, it did assume. He became pinkish, then pink, then more pink; and so did she. Paralyzed, the blushing pair looked at each other throughout this duet in colour, something like a glint of alarm beginning to show through the wide astonishment in her eyes; and with the perception of this he was assailed by an acute perturbation. He had spoken thoughtlessly, even hastily, he feared; he should have given her more time. Would she rise now with chilling dignity and leave him, it might be forever? Was he to lose her just when he had found her? He shuddered at the ghastly abyss of loneliness disclosed by the possibility. But this was only the darkest moment before a radiance that shot heavenward like the flaming javelins of an equatorial sunrise.

Her eyes lowered slowly till the long, brown lashes shadowed the rose-coloured cheek and the fall of her glance came to rest upon the arms of their two chairs, where the edge of her coat sleeve just touched the knuckle of his little finger. Two people were passing in front of them; there was no one who could see; and with a lightning-swift impulse she turned her wrist and for a half second, while his heart stopped beating, touched all his fingers with her own, then as quickly withdrew her hand and turned as far away from him as the position of her chair permitted.

It was a caress of incredible brevity, and so fleeting, so airy, that it was little more than a touch of light itself, like the faint quick light from a flying star one might just glimpse on one's hand as it passed. But in our pleasant world important things have resulted from touches as evanescent as that. Nature has its uses for the ineffable.

Blazing with glory, dumb with rapture, Henry Millick Chester felt his heart rebound to its work, while his withheld breath upheaved in a gulp that half suffocated him. Thus, blinded by the revelation of the stupefying beauty of life, he sat through a heaven-stricken interval, and time was of no moment. Gradually he began to perceive, in the midst of the effulgence which surrounded the next chair like a bright mist, the adorable contour of a shoulder in a tan coat and the ravishing outline of a rosy cheek that belonged to this divine girl who was his.

By and by he became dreamily aware of other objects beyond that cheek and that shoulder, of a fat man and his fat wife on the opposite side of the car near the end. Unmistakably they were man and wife, but it seemed to Henry that they had no reason to be—such people had no right to be married. They had no obvious right to exist at all; certainly they had no right whatever to exist in that car. Their relation to each other had become a sickening commonplace, the bleakness of it as hideously evident as their overfed convexity. It was visible that they looked upon each other as inevitable nuisances which had to be tolerated. They were horrible. Had Love ever known these people? It was unthinkable! For lips such as theirs to have pronounced the name of the god would have been blasphemy; for those fat hands ever to have touched, desecration! Henry hated the despicable pair.

All at once his emotion changed: he did not hate them, he pitied them. From an immense height he looked down with compassion upon their wretched condition. He pitied everybody except himself and the roseate being beside him; they floated together upon a tiny golden cloud, alone in the vast sky at an immeasurable altitude above the squalid universe. A wave of pity for the rest of mankind flooded over him, but most of all he pitied that miserable, sodden, befleshed old married couple.

He was dimly aware of a change that came over these fat people, a strangeness; but he never did realize that at this crisis his eyes, fixed intently upon them and aided by his plastic countenance, had expressed his feelings and sentiments, regarding them in the most lively and vivid way. For at the moment when the stout gentleman laid his paper down, preparatory to infuriated inquiry, both he and his wife were expunged from Henry's consciousness forever and were seen of him thenceforth no more than if they had been ether and not solid flesh. The exquisite girl had been pretending to pick a thread out of her left sleeve with her right hand—but now at last she leaned back in her chair and again turned her face partly toward Henry. Her under lip was caught in slightly beneath her upper teeth, as if she had been doing something that possibly she oughtn't to be doing, and though the pause in the conversation had been protracted—it is impossible to calculate how long —her charming features were still becomingly overspread with rose. She looked toward her rapt companion, not at him, and her eyes were preoccupied, tender, and faintly embarrassed.

The pause continued.

He leaned a little closer to her. And he looked at her and looked at her and looked at her. At intervals his lips moved as if he were speaking, and yet he was thinking wordlessly. Leaning thus toward her, his gaze and attitude had all the intensity of one who watches a ninth-inning tie in the deciding game of a championship series. And as he looked and looked and looked, the fat man and his wife, quite unaware of their impalpability, also looked and looked and looked in grateful fascination.

"Did you——" Henry Millick Chester finally spoke these words in a voice he had borrowed, evidently from a stranger, for it did not fit his throat and was so deep that it disappeared—it seemed to fall down a coal-hole and ended in a dusty choke. "Did you——" he began again, two octaves higher, and immediately squeaked out. He said "Did you" five times before he subjugated the other two words.

"Did you—mean that?"

"What?" Her own voice was so low that he divined rather than heard what she said. He leaned even a little closer—and the fat man nudged his wife, who elbowed his thumb out of her side morbidly: she wasn't missing anything.

"Did you—did you mean that?"

"Mean what?"

"That!"

"I don't know what you mean."

"When you—when you—oh, you know!"

"No, I don't."

"When you—when you took my hand."

"I!"

With sudden, complete self-possession she turned quickly to face him, giving him a look of half-shocked, half-amused astonishment.

"When I took your hand?" she repeated incredulously. "What are you saying?"

"You—you know," he stammered. "A while ago when—when—you—you——"

"I didn't do anything of the kind!" Impending indignation began to cloud the delicate face ominously. "Why in the world should I?"

"But you——"

"I didn't!" She cut him off sharply. "I couldn't. Why, it wouldn't have been nice! What made you dream I would do a thing like that? How dare you imagine such things!"

At first dumfounded, then appalled, he took the long, swift, sickening descent from his golden cloud with his mouth open, but it snapped tight at the bump with which he struck the earth. He lay prone, dismayed, abject. The lovely witch could have made him believe anything; at least it is the fact that for a moment she made him believe he had imagined that angelic little caress; and perhaps it was the sight of his utter subjection that melted her. For she flashed upon him suddenly with a dazing smile, and then, blushing again but more deeply than before, her whole attitude admitting and yielding, she offered full and amazing confession, her delicious laugh rippling tremulously throughout every word of it.

"It must have been an accident—partly!"

"I love you!" he shouted.

The translucent fat man and his wife groped for each other feverishly, and a coloured porter touched Henry Millick Chester on the shoulder.

"Be in Richmon' less'n fi' minutes now," said the porter. He tapped the youth's shoulder twice more; it is his office to awaken the rapt dreamer. "Richmon', In'iana, less'n fi' minutes now," he repeated more slowly.

Henry gave him a stunned and dishevelled "What?"

"You get off Richmon', don't you?"

"What of it? We haven't passed Dayton yet."

"Yessuh, long 'go. Pass' Dayton eight-fifty. Be in Richmon' mighty quick now."

The porter appeared to be a malicious liar. Henry appealed pitifully to the girl.

"But we haven't passed Dayton?"

"Yes, just after you sat down by me. We stopped several minutes."

"Yessuh. Train don't stop no minutes in Richmon' though," said the porter with a hard laugh, waving his little broom at some outlying freight cars they were passing. "Gittin' in now. I got you' bag on platfawm."

"I don't want to be brushed," Henry said, almost sobbing. "For heaven's sake, get out!"

Porters expect anything. This one went away solemnly without even lifting his eyebrows.

The brakes were going on.

One class of railway tragedies is never recorded, though it is the most numerous of all and fills the longest list of heartbreaks; the statics ignore it, yet no train ever leaves its shed, or moves, that is not party to it. It is time and overtime that the safety-device inventors should turn their best attention to it, so that the happy day may come at last when we shall see our common carriers equipped with something to prevent these lovers' partings.

The train began to slow down.

Henry Millick Chester got waveringly to his feet; she rose at the same time and stood beside him.

"I am no boy," he began, hardly knowing what he said, but automatically quoting a fragment from his forthcoming address to his father. "I have reached man's estate and I have met the only——" He stopped short with an exclamation of horror. "You—you haven't even told me your name!"

"My name?" the girl said, a little startled.

"Yes! And your address!"

"I'm not on my way home now," she said. "I've been visiting in New York and I'm going to St. Louis to make another visit."

"But your name!"

She gave him an odd glance of mockery, a little troubled.

"You mightn't like my name!"

"Oh, please, please!"

"Besides, do you think it's quite proper for me to——"

"Oh, please! To talk of that now! Please!" The train had stopped.

The glint of a sudden decision shone in the lovely eyes. "I'll write it for you so you won't forget."

She went quickly to the writing desk at the end of the compartment, he with her, the eyes of the fat man and his wife following them like two pairs of searchlights swung by the same mechanism.

"And where you live," urged Henry. "I shall write to you every day." He drew a long, deep breath and threw back his head. "Till the day—the day when I come for you."

"Don't look over my shoulder." She laughed shyly, wrote hurriedly upon a loose sheet, placed it in an envelope, sealed the envelope, and then, as he reached to take it, withheld it tantalizingly. "No. It's my name and where I live, but you can't have it. Not till you've promised not to open it until the train is clear out of the station."

Outside the window sounded the twice-repeated "Awl aboh-oh," and far ahead a fatal bell was clanging.

"I promise," he gulped.

"Then take it!"

With a strange, new-born masterfulness he made a sudden impetuous gesture and lifted both the precious envelope and the fingers that inclosed it to his lips. Then he turned and dashed to the forward end of the car where a porter remained untipped as Henry leaped from the already rapidly moving steps of the car to the ground. Instantly the wonderful girl was drawn past him, leaning and waving from the railed rear platform whither she had run for this farewell. And in the swift last look that they exchanged there was in her still-flushing, lovely face a light of tenderness and of laughter, of kindness and of something like a fleeting regret.

The train gained momentum, skimming onward and away, the end of the observation car dwindling and condensing into itself like a magician's disappearing card, while a white handkerchief, waving from the platform, quickly became an infinitesimal shred of white—and then there was nothing. The girl was gone.

Probably Henry Millick Chester owes his life to the fact that there are no gates between the station building and the tracks at Richmond. For gates and a ticket-clipping official might have delayed Henry's father in the barely successful dash he made to drag from the path of a backing local a boy wholly lost to the outward world in a state of helpless puzzlement, which already threatened to become permanent as he stared and stared at a sheet of railway notepaper whereon was written in a charming hand:

Mary Smith, Chicago, Ill.

"Dolling"

At five o'clock upon a February afternoon the commodious rooms on the lower floor of Mrs. Cromwell's big house resounded with all the noise that a hundred women unaided by firearms could make. A hundred men, gathered in a similar social manner, if that were possible, might either be quiet or produce a few uproariously bellowing groups, a matter depending upon the presence or absence of noisy individuals; but a hundred habitually soft-voiced women, brought together for a brief enjoyment of one another's society and a trifling incidental repast, must almost inevitably abandon themselves to that vocal rioting ultimately so helpful to the incomes of the "nerve specialists."

The strain, of course, is not put upon the nerves by the overpitched voices alone. At times during Mrs. Cromwell's "tea" the face of almost every woman in the house was distressed by the expression of caressive animation maintained upon it. The most conscientious of the guests held this expression upon their faces from the moment they entered the house until they left it; they went about from room to room, from group to group, shouting indomitably; and, without an instant's relaxation, kept a sweet archness frozen upon their faces, no matter how those valiant faces ached.

Men may not flatter themselves in believing it is for them that women most ardently sculpture their expressions. A class of women has traduced the rest: those women who are languid where there are no men. The women at Mrs. Cromwell's "tea," with not a man in sight, so consistently moulded their faces that the invitations might well have read, "From Four to Six: a Ladies' Masque."

What gave most truly the colour of a masquerade was the unmasking. This, of course, was never general, nor at any time simultaneous, except with two or three; yet, here and there, withdrawn a little to the side of a room, or near a corner, ladies might be seen who wore no expression at all, or else looked jaded or even frostily observant of the show. Sometimes clubs of two seemed to form temporarily, the members unmasking to each other, exhibiting their real faces in confidence, and joining in criticism of the maskers about them. At such times, if a third lady approached, the two would immediately resume their masks and bob and beam; then they might seem to elect her to membership; whereupon all three would drop their masks, shout gravely, close to one another's ears, then presently separate, masking again in facial shapings designed to picture universal love and jaunty humour.

But among the hundred merrymakers there was one of whom it could not be said that she was masked; yet, strange to tell, neither could it be said of her that she was not masked; for either she wore no mask at all or wore one always. Her face at Mrs. Cromwell's was precisely as it was when seen anywhere else; though where it seemed most appropriately surrounded was in church.

Calm, pale, the chin uplifted a little, with the slant of the head always more toward heaven than earth, this angelic face was borne high by the straight throat and slender figure like the oriflamme upon its staff; and so it passed through the crowd of shouting women, seeming to move in a spiritual light that fell upon them and illuminated them, yet illuminated most the uplifted face that was its source. Moreover, upon the lips the exquisite promise of a smile was continuously hinted; and the hint foreshadowed how fine the smile would be: how gentle, though a little martyred by life, and how bravely tolerant.

The beholder waited for this promised heavenly smile, but waited in vain. "You always think she's just going to until you see her often enough to find she never does," a broad-shouldered matron explained to two of her friends at Mrs. Cromwell's. The three had formed one of the little clubs for a temporary unmasking and were lookers-on for the moment. "It's an old worn-out kind of thing to say," the sturdy matron continued;—"but I never can resist applying it to her. Nobody can ever possibly be so good as Mrs. Leslie Braithwaite looks. I'll even risk saying that nobody can ever possibly be so good as she seems to behave!"

"Oh, Mrs. Dodge!" one of the others exclaimed. "But isn't behaviour the final proof? My husband says conduct is the only test of character."

"He doesn't know what he's talking about," the brusque Mrs. Dodge returned. "When we do anything noble, it's in spite of our true character; that's what makes it a noble thing to do. I've lived next door to that woman for five years, and, though I seldom exchange more than a word with her, I can't help having her in my sight pretty often. She always looks noble and she always sounds noble. Even when she says, 'Isn't it a lovely day,' she sounds noble—and, for my part, I'm sick and tired of her nobility!"

"But my husband says——"

"I don't care what Mr. Battle says," Mrs. Dodge interrupted. "The woman's a nuisance!"

"To me," said the third of the group, gravely, "that sounds almost like sacrilege. I've always felt that even though Mrs. Leslie Braithwaite is still quite a young woman, she's the focus of spiritual life for this whole community. I think the people here generally look upon her as the finest inspiration we have among us."

"I know they do," Mrs. Dodge said, irritably. "That's one reason I think she's a pest. People are always trying to live up to her, and it makes cowards and hypocrites of 'em. Look at her now!"

Mrs. Braithwaite had reached the hostess, who was shouting in concert with several new arrivals; but when Mrs. Braithwaite appeared, the voices of all this group were somewhat lowered (though they could not be lowered much and hope to be audible) and, what was more remarkable, Mrs. Cromwell's expression and her manner were instantly altered perceptibly:—so were the expressions and manners of the others about her, as Mrs. Dodge vindictively pointed out.

"Look at that!" she said. "Every one of those poor geese is trying to look like *her*;—they feel they have to seem as noble as she is! Instinctively they're all trying to take on her hushed sweetness. Nobody dares be natural anywhere near her."

"But that's because of the affection people feel for her," Mrs. Battle explained. "Don't you feel——"

"Affection your grandmother!" the brusque lady interrupted. "What are you talking about?"

"Well, reverence, then. Perhaps that's the better word for the feeling people have about her. They know how much of her life she gives to good works. She's at the head of——"

"Yes, she certainly is!" Mrs. Dodge agreed, bitterly. "She's the head and front of every uplifting movement among us. You can't open your mail without finding benefit tickets you have to buy for some good cause she's chairman of. She's always the girl that passes the hat: she's the one that makes us feel like selfish dogs if we don't give till it hurts! She's the star collector, all right!"

"Well, oughtn't we to be grateful that she takes such duties upon herself?"

"Do we ever omit any of our gratitude? Why, the papers are full of it: 'It is the sense of this committee that, except for the noble, unflagging, and self-sacrificing devotion of Mrs. Leslie Braithwaite, this fund could never have reached the generous dimensions necessary for the carrying on of this work. Therefore, be it resolved that the thanks of this entire organization'—and so forth. And, as a matter by the way, you never hear whether she gave any of the fund herself."

"She gives time. She gives energy. Mr. Battle says, 'Who gives himself gives all.' Mrs. Braithwaite gives herself."

"Yes, she does," Mrs. Dodge agreed. "It's her form of recreation!"

Her two auditors stared at her incredulously, so that she could plainly see how shocked they were; but, before either of them spoke, a beautiful change in look and manner came upon them. Both of them elevated their chins a little, so that their faces slanted more toward heaven than toward earth; both of them seemed about to smile angelically, but stopped just short of smiling; a purified softness came into their eyes; and, altogether, by means of various other subtle little manifestations, the two ladies began to look noble.

Mrs. Dodge had turned her back toward the group about the hostess, but without looking round she understood what the change in her two companions portended. "Good-bye, ladies of Shalott," she said. "The curse has come upon you!" And she moved away, just as the ennobled two stepped forward to meet Mrs. Leslie Braithwaite in her approach to them.

"Clever of me!" Mrs. Dodge thought, with some bitterness. "Getting myself the reputation of a 'dangerous woman'!" For she understood well enough that she would do no injury to Mrs. Braithwaite in attacking her;—on the contrary, the injury would inevitably be to the assailant; and yet Mrs. Dodge could not forbear from a little boomerang practice at this shining and impervious mark. The reason, unfortunately, was personal, as most reasons are: Mrs. Dodge had come to the "tea" in an acute state of irritation that had been increasing since morning. In fact, she had begun the day with a breakfast-table argument of which Mrs. Braithwaite was the subject.

Mr. Dodge made the unfortunate admission that he had recently sent Mrs. Braithwaite a check for a hundred dollars, his subscription to the Workers' Welfare League; and he was forced into subsequent admissions: he had no interest in the Workers' Welfare League, and could give no reason for sending a check to it except that Mrs. Braithwaite had written him appealing for a subscription. She was sure he wouldn't like to miss the chance to aid in so splendid a movement, she said. Now, as Mrs. Braithwaite had previously written twice to Mrs. Dodge in almost the same words, and as Mrs. Dodge had twice replied declining to make a donation, the argument (so to call it) on Mrs. Dodge's part was a heated one. It availed her husband little to protest that he had never heard of Mrs. Braithwaite's appeals to his wife; Mrs. Dodge was too greatly incensed to be reasonable.

Later in the day she was remorseful, realizing that she had taken poor Mr. Dodge for her anvil because he was within reach, and what she really wanted to hammer wasn't. Her remorse applied itself strictly to her husband, however, and she had none for her feeling toward the lady next door. Mrs. Dodge and her neighbour had never discovered any point of congeniality: Mrs. Braithwaite's high serenity, which Mrs. Dodge called suavity, was of so paradoxical a smoothness that Mrs. Dodge said it "rubbed the wrong way from the start." The uncongeniality had increased with time until it became a settled dislike, so far as Mrs. Dodge was concerned; and now, after Mrs. Leslie Braithwaite's successful appeal to Mr. Dodge for what Mr. Dodge's wife had refused, the dislike was rankling itself into a culmination not unlike an actual and lusty hatred.

Mrs. Dodge realized her own condition;—she knew hatred is bad for the hater; but she could not master the continuous anger within her. Fascinated, she watched Mrs. Leslie Braithwaite at the "tea"; could not help watching her, although, as the victim of this fascination admitted to herself in so many words, the sight was "poison" to her. Nor was the poison alleviated by the effect of Mrs. Braithwaite upon the other guests: everywhere the angelic presence moved about the capacious rooms it was preceded and followed by deference. And when Mrs. Braithwaite joined a woman or a group of women, Mrs. Dodge marked with a hot eye how that woman or group of women straightway hushed a little and looked noble.

Mrs. Dodge went home early. "I oughtn't to have come," she told her hostess, confidentially, in parting. "I try to be a Christian sometimes, but this is one of the days when I think Nero was right."

"But what——"

"I may tell you—some day," Mrs. Dodge promised, and gloomily went her way.

At dinner that evening she was grim, softening little when her husband plaintively resumed his defence. Lily inquired why her mother was of so dread a countenance.

"Me," Mr. Dodge explained. "It began at breakfast before you were up, and it's the old culprit, Lily."

"I guessed that much," Lily said, cheerfully. "I haven't been falling in love with anybody foolish for three or four months now; and that's the only thing I ever do to make her look like this, so I knew it must be you. What you been up to?"

"Aiding in good causes," he answered, sighing. "She hates me for helping the Workers, Lily. Our next-door neighbour appealed to Cæsar, over your mother's head. I've explained two or three hundred times that I didn't know there'd been any previous request to her; but she hates my wicked plotting just the same."

"No. I only hate your weakness," Mrs. Dodge said, not relaxing her severity. "You were so eager to please that woman you couldn't even wait to consult your wife. Her writing to you and ignoring what I'd twice written her was the rudest thing I've ever had done to me, and your donation puts you in the position of approving of it. She did it because she's furious with me and so——"

But Lily interrupted her. "Mamma!" she exclaimed. "Why, you're talking just ridiculously! Everybody knows Mrs. Braithwaite couldn't be 'furious.' Not with anybody!"

"Couldn't she? Then why did she do such an insulting thing to me? Don't you suppose she knows it's insulting to show she can get a poor silly husband to do something his wife has declined to do? Is there a cattier trick in the whole cattish repertoire? She did it because she's the slyest puss in this community and she knows I know it, and hates me for it!"

Lily stared in the blankest surprise. "Why, it just sounds like anarchy!" she cried. "I never heard you break out like that before except when you were talking about some boy I liked! When did you get this way about Mrs. Leslie Braithwaite?"

"I've never liked her," Mrs. Dodge said. "Never! I've always suspected she was a whited sepulchre, and now I've got proof of it."

"Proof? That's quite a strong word, Lydia," Mr. Dodge reminded her.

"Thank you!" she said. "I mean exactly what I'm saying. Mrs. Braithwaite did this thing to me out of deliberate spitefulness; and she did it because she knows what I think of her."

"But you said you had 'proof' that she's a 'whited sepulchre,'" he said. "The word 'proof'——"

"May we assume that it means reliable evidence reliably confirmed?" Mrs. Dodge asked, with satirical politeness. "Suppose you've done something disgraceful and another person happens to know you did it. Then suppose you play a nasty trick on this other person. Wouldn't it be proof that you hate him because he knows you did the disgraceful thing?"

"I'm afraid I don't follow you," Mr. Dodge said, uncomfortably. "When did I ever do this disgraceful thing you're talking about? If it's actually disgraceful to subscribe a hundred dollars to the Workers——"

"I'm not talking of that," his wife said. "I'll try to put it within reach of your intellect. Suppose I know Mrs. Braithwaite to be a whited sepulchre; then if she does an insulting thing to me, isn't that proof she's furious with me for finding her out?"

"No," he answered. "It might incline one to think that she resented your poor opinion of her, but it doesn't prove anything at all."

"Doesn't it? You wouldn't say so if you knew what I know!"

Lily's eyes widened in hopeful eagerness.

"How exciting!" she cried. "Mamma, *what* do you know about Mrs. Braithwaite?"

"Never mind!"

"But you said——"

"I said, 'Never mind'!"

"But I do mind!" Lily insisted. "You haven't got any right to get a person's interest all worked up like that and then just say, 'Never mind'!"

"That's all I *shall* say, however," Mrs. Dodge informed her stubbornly, and kept to her word, though Lily continued to press her until the meal was over. Mr. Dodge made no effort to aid his daughter in obtaining the revelation she sought;—he appeared to be superior to the curiosity that impelled her; but this appearance of superiority may have been only an appearance: he may have foreseen that his wife would presently be a little more explicit about what she had implied against their neighbour.

In fact, Lily had no sooner gone forth upon some youthful junketing, immediately after dinner, than symptoms of forthcoming revelation were manifested. Mr. Dodge's physician allowed him one cigar a day, and it had just begun to scent the library.

"I suppose, of course, you're condemning me for a reckless talker," Mrs.

Dodge said. "You assume that I'm willing to hint slander against a woman with only my own injury for a basis, instead of facts."

"On the contrary, Lydia," he returned, mildly, "I know you wouldn't have said what you did unless you have something serious to found it on."

Probably she was a little mollified, but she did not show it. "So you give me that much credit?" she asked, sourly. "I imagine it's because you're just as curious as Lily and hope to hear what I wouldn't tell her. Well, I'm not going to gratify your curiosity."

"No?" He picked up a magazine from the table beside his chair, and began to turn over the pages. "Oh, very well!"

"I *am* going to tell you *something*, though," she said. "It's because I think you ought to be told at least *part* of what I know. It may be good for you."

"For me?" he inquired, calmly, though he well understood what she was going to say next.

"Yes; you might find it wiser to consult your wife next time, even when you're dealing with people you think are saints."

"Why, I don't think Mrs. Braithwaite's a saint," he protested. "She *looks* rather like one—a pretty one, too—and the general report is that she *is* one; but I don't know anything more than that about her. She happens to be a neighbour; but we've never had the slightest intimacy with her and her husband. We've never been in their house or they in ours; I bow to her when I see her and sometimes exchange a few words with her across the hedge between our two yards, usually about the weather. I don't think anything about her at all."

"Then it's time you did," Mrs. Dodge said with prompt inconsistency.

"All right. What do you want me to think about her, Lydia?"

"Nothing!" she said, sharply. "Oh, laugh if you want to! I'll tell you just this much: I found out something about her by pure accident; and I decided I'd never tell anybody in the world—not even you. I'm not the kind of person to wreck anybody's life exactly; and I decided just to bury what I happened to find out. What's more, I'd have kept it *all* buried if she'd had sense enough to let me alone. I wouldn't even have told you that I know something about her."

"It's something really serious?"

" 'Serious'?" she said. "No, it's not 'serious.' It's ruinous."

Mr. Dodge released a sound from his mouth. "Whee-ew!" Whistled, not spoken, it was his characteristic token that he found himself impressed. "You've certainly followed the right course, Lydia. Mrs. Leslie Braithwaite's standing isn't just a high one; it's lofty. I shouldn't care to be the person who blasts that statue off its pedestal;—sometimes statues crush the blasters when they fall. I'm glad you kept your information to yourself." He paused, and then, being morally but an ordinary man, he added, "Not—not that I see any particular harm in your confiding in my discretion in such a matter."

"Didn't I explain I'm not confiding in your discretion?" Mrs. Dodge returned. "Lately, I don't believe you have any. I've told you this much so that next time you won't be so hasty in sending checks to women who are merely using you to annoy your wife."

He sighed. "There's where you puzzle me, Lydia. If you found out something ruinous about Mrs. Braithwaite, as you say, and if she knows you did —you intimated she knows it, I think?"

"Absolutely."

"Then I should think you'd be the last person in the world she'd want to annoy. I should think she'd do everything on earth to please you and placate you. She'd want to keep you from telling. That's the weak point in your theory, Lydia."

"It isn't a theory. I'm speaking of facts."

"But if she knows you're aware of what might ruin her," he insisted, "she would naturally be afraid of you. Then why would she do a thing that might infuriate you?"

"Because she's a woman," said Mrs. Dodge. "And that's something you'll never understand!"

"But even a woman would behave with some remnants of caution, under the circumstances, wouldn't she?"

"Some women might. Mrs. Braithwaite doesn't because she's so sure of her lofty position she thinks she can deliberately insult me and I won't dare to do anything about it. She wanted to show me that she isn't afraid of me."

Mr. Dodge looked thoughtfully at that point upon his long cigar where a slender ring of red glow intervened between the adhering gray ash and the brown tobacco. "Well, at least she shows a fiery heart," he said. "In a way, you'd have to consider her action quite the sporting thing. You mean she's sent you a kind of declaration of war, don't you?"

"If you want to look at it that way. I don't myself. I take it just as she meant it, and that's as a deliberate insult."

"But it isn't an 'insult' if she only meant it to show she isn't afraid of you, Lydia."

"It is, though," Mrs. Dodge insisted. "What she means is derision of me. It's the same as if she said: 'Here's a slap in the face for you. I have the satisfaction of humiliating you as your punishment for knowing what you do know about me, and you can't retaliate, because you aren't important enough to be able to injure me!' It's just the same as if she'd said those words to me."

"It seems quite a message," he observed. "Of course, I can't grasp it myself because I haven't any conception of this ruinous proceeding of hers. You were the only witness, I assume?"

"There was a third person present," Mrs. Dodge said, stiffly. "But not as a witness."

"Then what was the third person present doing?"

Mrs. Dodge looked at him with severity, as if she reproved him for tempting her to do something wrong; then she took from a basket in her lap a square piece of partly embroidered linen and gave it her attention, not relaxing this preoccupation where her husband began to repeat his question.

"What was the third person——"

"I heard you," Mrs. Dodge interrupted, frowning at her embroidery. "If I told you that much I'd be virtually telling the whole thing; and I've decided not to do that, even under her deliberate provocation. If I let myself be provoked into telling, I'd be as small as she is, so you needn't hope to get another word out of me on the subject. The only answer I'll make to your question is that the third person present was not her husband."

"Oh!" Mr. Dodge said, loudly, and, in his sudden enlightenment, whistled "Whee-ew!" again. "So *that's* it!"

"Not at all," she said. "You needn't jump to conclusions, and you'll never know anything more about it from me. The only way you could ever know about it would be through her husband's making a fuss and its getting into the papers or something."

"I see," Mr. Dodge said, apparently not much discouraged. "And, since it's something he hasn't *yet* made any fuss about, it's evidently because he doesn't know."

"*He!*" Mrs. Dodge cried, and, in her scorn of Mrs. Leslie Braithwaite's consort, dropped the embroidery into the basket and stared fiercely at Mr. Dodge; though it was really at an invisible Mr. Braithwaite that she directed this glare of hers. Apparently the unfortunate gentleman was one of those mere husbands whose existence seems either to amuse or to incense the wives of more dominant men: Mrs. Dodge certainly appeared to be incensed. "That miserable little pale shadow of a man!" she cried. "His name's Leslie Braithwaite, but do you ever hear him spoken of except as 'Mrs. Leslie Braithwaite's husband'? He goes down to his little brass-rod works at eight o'clock every morning and gets money for her until six in the evening. Then he comes home and works on the account books of her uplifts until bedtime. If they go out, he stands around with her wrap over his arm and doesn't speak unless you ask him a question. If you do, he begins his answer by saying, 'My wife informs me'—How could that poor little creature know anything about anything?"

"But *you* know," Mr. Dodge persisted. "You *do* know, do you, Lydia?"

"I know what I know," she replied, and resumed her preoccupation with the embroidery.

"But you couldn't substantiate it by another witness, I take it," he said, musingly. "That is, she feels safe against you because if you should ever decide to tell what you know, she would deny it and put you in the position of an accuser without proofs. It would simply be your word against hers, and she'd have the sympathy that goes to the party attacked and also the advantage of her wide reputation for lofty character and——"

"Go on," his wife interrupted. "Amuse yourself all you like; you'll not find out another thing from me. Perhaps, if you should ever spend the morning at home digging around in our flower border along the hedge between her yard and ours, you might happen to hear her talking to her chauffeur, and in that case you might get to know something more. Otherwise, I don't see how you ever will."

"Lydia!"

"What?"

"I'm not going to dig in any flower border! I'm not going to spy around any hedge just to——"

"Neither did I!" she cried, indignantly. "Did you ever know me to do any spying?"

"Certainly not. But you said——"

"I said 'If you *happen* to.' You don't suppose I hid and listened deliberately? I was down on my hands and knees planting tulip bulbs, and the thick hedge was between us. That's how it happened, and why, she never *dreamed* anybody was near her. I didn't even hear her come in that part of the yard until I heard her speaking right by me, on the other side of the hedge. Please don't be quite so quick to think your wife would be willing to spy on another woman."

"I didn't," Mr. Dodge protested, hastily. "What did she say to the chauffeur?"

"That," his wife replied, severely, "is something you'll never hear from me!"

"From whom shall I hear it, then?"

"I've just told you how you might hear it," she said, plying her needle and seeming to give it all her attention.

"But I can't spend my time in the tulip bed, Lydia."

"That's not what I meant. I said, 'If her husband ever makes such a fuss that it gets into the papers.' "

"If he does, I might find out what she said to the chauffeur?"

"Oh, maybe," Mrs. Dodge said; and she gave him a sidelong glance of some sharpness, then quickly seemed to be busy again with her work.

"I don't make it out at all," the puzzled gentleman complained. "Apparently you overheard Mrs. Braithwaite saying something to her chauffeur that would be ruinous to her if it were known—something that might cause her husband to make a public uproar if he had heard it himself. Is that it?"

Mrs. Dodge began to hum fragmentarily to herself and seemed concerned with nothing in the world except the selection of a proper spool of thread from her basket.

"Is that it, Lydia?"

"You'll never find out from me," she said, searching anxiously through the basket. "Anyhow, I shouldn't think you'd need to ask such simple questions."

"So that *is* it! What you heard her say to her chauffeur would ruin her if people knew about it. Was she talking to the chauffeur about her husband?"

"Good gracious!" Mrs. Dodge cried, derisively. "What would she be talking to anybody about *that* poor little thing for? She never does. I don't believe anybody ever heard her mention him in her life!"

"Then was she talking to the chauffeur about some other man?"

"Of all the ideas! If a woman were in love with a man not her husband, do you think she'd tell her servants about it? Besides, they've only had this chauffeur about two weeks. Have you noticed him?"

"Yes," said Mr. Dodge. "I've seen him sitting in their car in front of the house several times, and I was quite struck with him. He seemed to be not only one of the handsomest young men I ever saw, but to have rather the look of a gentleman."

"So?" Mrs. Dodge said, inquiringly; and her tone was the more significant because of her appearing to be wholly preoccupied with her work-basket. "You noticed *that*, did you?"

"You don't mean to say——"

"I don't mean to say anything at all," she interrupted, crisply. "I've told you that often enough for you to begin to understand it."

"All right, I do. Well, when she'd said whatever she did say to the chauffeur, what happened?"

"Oh, that," she returned, "I'm perfectly willing to tell you. I got up and looked at her over the hedge. I wasn't going to stay there and listen—and I certainly wasn't going to crawl away on my hands and knees! I just looked at her quietly and turned away and came into the house."

"What did she do?"

"She was absolutely disconcerted. Her face just seemed to go all to pieces; —it didn't look like *her* face at all. She was frightened to death, and I never saw anything plainer. That's one reason she hates me so—because I saw her looking so afraid of me and she couldn't help it. Of course, as soon as I got into the house I looked out through the lace curtains at a window—you could hardly expect me not to—and I saw her just going back into her own house by the side door. She'd braced up and looked all stained-glass Joan of Arc again by that time."

Mr. Dodge sat waggling his head and muttering in wonder. "Of all the curious things!" he said. "Human nature is so everlastingly full of oddities it's always turning up new ones that you sit and stare at and can't believe are real. There they are, right before your eyes, and yet they're incredible. What did she say to the chauffeur?"

"No, no," Mrs. Dodge said, reprovingly. "That's what I *can't* tell you." And she added, "I should think you could guess it, anyhow."

"Was there——" He paused a moment, pondering. "Did she use any specially marked terms of endearment in addressing him?"

"No," Mrs. Dodge replied, returning her attention to her work;—"not terms."

"Oh," he said. "Just one term, then. She used a single term of endearment in addressing him. Is that correct?"

Again Mrs. Dodge became musical: she hummed a cheerful tune, but her face was overcast with a dour solemnity.

"So she did!" her husband exclaimed. "Did she call him 'dear'?"

"No, she didn't."

" 'Dearest'?"

"No, she didn't."

"Not," he said, incredulously, "not—'*darling*'?"

Mrs. Dodge instantly resumed her humming.

"By George!" her husband cried. "Why, that's just awful! What else did she say to him besides calling him 'darling'?"

"I didn't say she said anything else," Mrs. Dodge returned, primly. "The rest wasn't so important, anyhow, and she was speaking in a low voice. I thought the rest of it was, 'Rosemary, that's for remembrance.' I couldn't be sure because I didn't hear it distinctly."

"But you *did* distinctly hear her call him 'darling'?"

"What I heard distinctly," Mrs. Dodge replied, "I heard distinctly."

"So what Mrs. Leslie Braithwaite said to the chauffeur was this: 'Rosemary, that's for remembrance, darling'?"

"You must draw your own conclusions," she advised him, severely.

"I do—rather!" he returned, and in a marvelling tone slowly pronounced their neighbour's name, "Mrs. Leslie Braithwaite! Of all the women in the world, Mrs. Leslie Braithwaite! And when you rose up, and she saw you, she just went all to pieces and didn't say a word?"

"I told you."

"What did the handsome chauffeur do?"

"Just stood there."

"It's beyond anything!" Mr. Dodge's amazement was not abated;—he shook his head and uttered groaning sounds of pessimistic wonderment. "I suppose the true meaning of the saying, 'It's the unexpected that happens,' is that life is always teaching us to accept the incredible. How long ago was it?"

"A week ago yesterday."

"Have you seen her since?"

"I never talk to her or she to me. We say, 'How do you do? What lovely weather!' and that's all we ever do say. We haven't even any neighbourly contact through congenial servants, because of our having coloured people; —hers are white. I haven't caught a glimpse of her since it happened until this afternoon, when she came to Mrs. Cromwell's tea. Of course, she knew I was looking at her, and she knew perfectly what I was thinking—particularly about her insult to me in making such a goose of my husband."

"But, Lydia——"

"She was having the time of her life over that!"

"Well," he said, reflectively, "leaving out the question of whether or not I was a goose especially, and considering her without personal bias, I must say that under the circumstances she's shown a mighty picturesque intricacy of character, as well as a pretty dashing kind of hardihood. If, as you believe, she sent her note to me as really a derisive taunt—a gauntlet flung at you with mocking laughter—and all the while she knows you know of her philandering with a good-looking varlet——"

"She's a bad woman!" Mrs. Dodge exclaimed, angrily. "That's all there is to it, and you needn't be so poetical about her!"

"Good gracious, Lydia, I wasn't——"

"Never mind! We can talk of her just as well without any references to gauntlets and mocking laughter and varlets. That is, if you insist upon talking about her at all. For my part, I prefer just to keep her entirely out of my mind."

"Very well," he assented, meekly. "I don't know that I can keep anything so singular out of my mind; but I won't speak of it if it annoys you. What else shall we talk of?"

"Anything in the world except that detestable woman," Mrs. Dodge replied. Then, after some moments of silence over her embroidery, she added abruptly, "Of course, *you* don't think she's detestable!"

"I only said——"

"'Picturesque' was what you said. 'Dashing' was another thing you said. You're quite fascinated with her derisive gauntlets and her mocking laughter! Dear *me*, if that isn't like men!"

"But I only——"

"Oh, murder!" Mrs. Dodge moaned, interrupting him. "I thought you said you weren't going to *talk* about her any more!"

At this he showed spirit enough to laugh. "You know well enough we're both going to keep on talking about her, Lydia. What do you intend to do?"

"About what?" Mrs. Dodge looked surprised. "About *her*, you mean? Why, naturally, I intend to keep on doing what I have been doing, and that's nothing whatever except to hold my peace;—I don't descend to the level of feuds with intriguing women. She gave me a clew, though, this afternoon."

"What sort of a clew, Lydia?"

"I don't suppose a man could understand, but I'll try to give you a glimmering. When she wrote that note to you, there was one thing she hadn't thought of. She thought of it this afternoon at that tea: it struck her all of a sudden that I could make things a little unpleasant for her if I took the notion to. She just happened to remember that Mrs. Cromwell is my most intimate friend, and that she is the grandest old rock-bottomed mountain this community can boast. That woman all at once remembered, and got afraid I might tell my friends."

"How do you know she did?"

"That's what a man couldn't see. I knew it by a lot of little things I couldn't put into words if I tried, but principally I knew it by watching her manner with Mrs. Cromwell."

"You mean she tried to ingratiate herself?" he asked. "Her manner was more winsome or flattering than usual?"

"No, not exactly. Not so open—you couldn't understand—but it was perfectly clear to me she was having the time of her life thinking of what she'd done to me through my husband's weakness, when all at once she thought of my influence with the Cromwells. Well, she's afraid of it, and it made her wish she hadn't gone quite so far with me. She'd give a whole lot to-night, I'll wager, if she'd been just a little less picturesque with her gauntlet throwing and her mocking laughter! You asked me what I was going to do and I told you 'Nothing.' But *she'll* do something. She's afraid, and she'll make a move of some sort. You'll see."

"But what? What could she do?"

"I don't know, but you'll see. You'll see before long, too."

"Well, I'm inclined to hope so," he said. "It would certainly be interesting; but I doubt her making any move at all. I'm afraid you won't turn out to be a good prophet."

On the contrary, he himself was a poor prophet; for sometimes destiny seems to juggle miraculously with coincidences in order to attract our attention to the undiscovered laws that produce them. In fact, Mr. Dodge was so poor a prophet—and so near to intentional burlesque are the manners of destiny in its coincidence juggling—that at this moment Mrs. Leslie Braithwaite's husband had just rung the Dodges' front-door bell. Two minutes later a mulatto housemaid appeared in the doorway of the library and produced a sensational effect merely by saying, "Mrs. Braithwaite and Mr. Braithwaite is calling. I showed 'em into the drawing-room."

She withdrew, and the staggered couple, after an interval of incoherent whispering, went forth to welcome their guests.

Mrs. Braithwaite was superb;—at least, that was Mr. Dodge's impersonal conception of her. Never before had he seen sainthood so suavely combined with a piquant beauty, nor an evening gown of dull red silk and black lace so exquisitely invested with an angelic presence. For to-night this lady looked not only noble, she looked charming; and either his wife had made a grotesque mistake or he stood before an actress unmatched in his experience. She began talking at once, in her serene and sweet contralto voice—a beautiful voice, delicately hushed and almost imperceptibly precise in its pronunciation. "It seemed to us really rather absurd, Mrs. Dodge, that you and your husband should be our next-door neighbours for so long without even having set foot in our house or we in yours. And as Mr. Dodge has lately been so generous to my poor little Workers' Welfare League—the unhappy creatures do need help so, and the ladies of the committee were so touched by your kindness, Mr. Dodge—we thought we'd just make that an excuse to call, even thus informally and for only a few minutes. We wanted to express the thanks of the League, of course, and we thought it was about time to say we aren't really so unneighbourly as we may have seemed—and we hope you aren't, either!"

"No, indeed," Mr. Dodge responded with a hasty glance of sidelong uneasiness at his wife. Her large face was red and rather dismayingly fierce as she sat stiffly in the stiffest chair in the Dodges' white-walled, cold, and rigidly symmetrical drawing-room; but she said, "No, indeed," too, though not so heartily as her husband did. In fact, she said it grimly; yet he was relieved, for her expression made him fear that she would say nothing at all.

"One of the things I find to regret about modern existence," Mrs. Braithwaite continued, in her beautiful voice, "is the disappearance of neighbourliness even in a quiet suburban life like yours and ours. Of course, this is anything but a new thought, yet how concretely our two houses have illustrated it! So it did seem time, at last, to break the ice, especially as I have good reason to think that just these last few days you must have been thinking of me as quite a naughty person, Mrs. Dodge."

Mrs. Dodge stared at her; appeared to stare not only with astounded eyes but with a slowly opening mouth. "What? What did you say?" she asked, huskily.

"I'm afraid you've been thinking of me as rather naughty," the serene caller said, and her ever promised smile seemed a little more emphatically promised than it had been. "I ought to confess to you that as a collector for my poor little Workers' League I'm terribly unscrupulous. It's such a struggling little organization, and the need of help is so frightfully pressing, I may as well admit I haven't any scruples at all how I get money for it. Yet, of course, I know I ought to apologize for asking Mr. Dodge to contribute to a cause that you didn't feel particularly interested in yourself."

"Oh!" Mrs. Dodge said, and to her husband's consternation she added formidably: "Is *that* what you're talking about!"

No disastrous effect was visible, however. Mrs. Braithwaite nodded sunnily. "I'm sure you'll forgive me for the sake of the happiness the money brought to a pitiful little family—the father hasn't had any work for eight months; there are four young children and one just born. If you could see their joy when——"

"I dare say!" Mrs. Dodge interrupted. "I'm glad it did *some* good!"

"I was sure you'd feel so." Mrs. Braithwaite glanced gently at her host, whose face was a remarkable study of geniality in conflict with apprehension; —then her gaze returned to her hostess. "I wanted to make my peace not only for myself," she added, "but for your husband. I'm sure you're going to forgive him, Mrs. Dodge."

Innocently, Mr. Dodge supposed this to be intended as a kindly effort on his behalf and in the general interests of amiability. He was surprised, therefore, and his apprehensions of an outbreak on the part of his wife were little abated, when he perceived that its effect upon her was far from placative. Her ample figure seemed to swell; she was red but grew redder; her action in breathing became not only visible but noticeable; to his appalled vision she seemed about to snort forth sparks. For several perilous moments she did not speak;—then, after compressing her lips tightly, she said: "Mr. Dodge sent you his check upon my direction, of course. Naturally, he consulted me. I told him that since you had twice solicited me for a subscription it would be best for us to send you some money and be done with it."

Mrs. Braithwaite uttered a soothing sound as of amused relief. "That's so much nicer," she said. "I was afraid you might have been annoyed with both of us—with both poor Mr. Dodge and myself—but that exculpates us. I'm so very glad." She turned to the perturbed host. "I was *so* afraid I'd involved you, Mr. Dodge—perhaps quite beyond forgiveness."

"Not at all—not at all," he said, removing his gaze with difficulty from his wife's face. "Oh, no. Everything—everything's been perfectly pleasant," he floundered, and Mrs. Dodge's expression did not reassure him that he was saying the right thing. "Perfectly—pleasant," he repeated, feebly.

"I *so* hoped it would be," Mrs. Braithwaite said. "I hoped Mrs. Dodge wouldn't be *very* hard on you for aiding in such a good cause."

"No," he returned, nervously. "No, she—she wasn't. She proved to be entirely—ah—amiable, of course." And again he was dismayed by Mrs. Dodge's expression.

"Of course," Mrs. Braithwaite agreed, sunnily, with only the quickest and sweetest little fling of a glance at her hostess, "I was *sure* she'd forgive you. Well, at any rate, we've both made our peace with her now and established the *entente cordiale*, I hope." She turned toward her husband and spoke his name gently, in the tone that is none the less a command to the obedient follower: "Leslie." It was apparently her permission for him to prepare himself for departure; but it may also have been a signal or command for him to do something else;—Mr. Dodge noticed that it brought an oddly plaintive look into the eyes of the small and dark Braithwaite.

Throughout the brief but strained interview he had been sitting in one of the Dodges' rigid chairs as quietly as if he had been a well-behaved little son of Mrs. Braithwaite's, brought along to make a call upon grown people. He was slender as well as short; of a delicate, almost fragile, appearance; and in company habitually so silent, so self-obliterative that it might well have been a matter of doubt whether he was profoundly secretive or of an overwhelming timidity. But as he sat in the Dodges' slim black chair, himself rather like that chair, with his trim, thin little black legs primly uncrossed and his small black back straight and stiff, there were suggestions that he was more secretive than timid. Under his eyes were semicircles of darkness, as if part of what he secreted might have been a recent anguish, either physical or mental. Moreover, if he had been in reality the well-trained little boy his manners during this short evening call had suggested, those semicircles under his eyes would have told of anguish so acute that the little boy had wept.

When his wife said "Leslie," he swallowed; there came into his eyes the odd and plaintive look his host had noticed—it was the look now not of a good little boy but of a good little dog, obedient in a painful task set by the adored master—and he stood up immediately.

"We really must be running," his wife said, rising, too. "This was just our funny little effort to break the ice. I do hope it has, and that you'll both come in to see us some evening. I *do* hope you'll *both* come." She put an almost imperceptible stress on the word "both" as she moved toward the door; then said "Leslie" again. He was still standing beside his chair.

"Ah—" he said; then paused and coughed. "I—I wonder——"

"Yes?" his host said, encouragingly.

"I—that is, I was going to say, by the way, I wonder if you happen to know of a good chauffeur, Mr. Dodge."

At this, Mrs. Dodge's breathing became audible as well as visible, there fell a moment of such silence.

"A—a chauffeur? No," Mr. Dodge said. "No, I don't think I do. We haven't one ourselves; we do our own driving. A chauffeur? No. I'm afraid I don't know of any."

"I see," Braithwaite returned. "I just happened to ask. We've—ah—lost the man we've had lately. He was a very good driver and we haven't anybody to take his place."

Mrs. Dodge spoke sepulchrally as she rose from her chair. "That's too bad," she said, and, to her husband's relief, stopped there, adding nothing.

"Yes," Braithwaite assented. "He was a very good driver indeed; but he was a college graduate and only yesterday he found another position, tutoring, and left us. He was a very good man—Dolling."

"What?" Mr. Dodge said. "Who?"

"Dolling," Braithwaite replied; and followed his wife to the door. "I just happened to mention his name: Dolling. I—I didn't address you as 'darling,' Mr. Dodge, though I see how you might easily have thought I did. The man's name was Dolling. I shouldn't like you to think I'd take the liberty of calling *you*——"

But here he was interrupted by such an uproarious shout of laughter from his host that his final words were lost. Mr. Dodge's laughter continued, though it was interspersed with hearty expressions of hospitality and parting cheer, until the callers had passed the outer threshold and the door had closed behind them. Then the hilarious gentleman returned from the hall to face a wife who found nothing in the world, just then, a laughing matter.

"The worst thing you did," she assured him, "was to be so fascinated that you told her I'd been amiable to you about your sending that check—just after I said I knew all about it *before* you sent it and had *told* you to send it! That was a pleasant position to put your wife in, wasn't it?"

"Lydia!" he shouted, still outrageous in his mirth. "Let's forget that part of it and remember only Dolling!"

"All right," she said, and her angry eyes flashed. "Suppose his name *was* Dolling. What was she talking to him about rosemary and remembrance for?"

"I don't know, and it doesn't seem important. The only thing I can get my mind on is your keeping to yourself so solemnly the scandalous romance of Dolling!" And becoming more respectably sober, for a time, he asked her: "Don't you really see a little fun in it, Lydia?"

"What!" she cried. "Do you? After you saw that wretched little man of hers stand up there and recite his lesson like a trained monkey? Did you look at *her* while he was performing? She stood in the doorway and held the whip-lash over him till he finished! And if this idol of yours is so innocent and pure, why did she go all to pieces the way she did when she saw me that morning by the hedge?"

"Why, don't you see?" he cried. "Of course she saw you thought she'd called the man 'darling'! She knew you didn't know his name was Dolling. Isn't it plain to you *yet*?"

"No!" his wife said, vehemently. "It isn't plain to me and it never will be!"

Against all reason she persisted in a sinister interpretation of her lovely neighbour's conduct;—never would Mrs. Dodge admit that Mr. Dodge had the right of the matter, and after a time she complained that she found his continued interest in it "pretty tiresome."

"You keep bringing it up," she said, "because you think you've had a wretched little triumph over me. It's one of those things that never can be settled either way, and I don't care to talk of it any more. If you want to occupy your spare thoughts I have a topic to offer you."

"What topic?"

Mrs. Dodge shook her head in a certain way. "Lily."

"Oh, dear me!" he said. "It isn't happening again?"

She informed him that it was, indeed. Lily's extreme affections were once more engaged. "We're in for it!" was the mother's preface as she began the revelation; and, when she concluded, her husband sorrowfully agreed with her.

"It's awful now and will be worse," he said; and thus his "spare thoughts" became but too thoroughly occupied. In his growing anxiety over his daughter, he ceased to think of his neighbours;—the handsome chauffeur passed from his mind. Then abruptly, one day, as the wandering searchlight of a harboured ship may startlingly clarify some obscure thing upon the shore, a chance conjuncture illuminated for him most strangely the episode of Dolling.

He was lunching with a younger member of his firm in a canyon restaurant downtown, and his attention happened to become concentrated upon a debonair young man who had finished his lunch and was now engaged in affable discussion with the pretty cashier. He was one of those young men, sometimes encountered, who have not only a strong masculine beauty, but the look of talent, with both the beauty and the talent belittled by an irresponsible twinkle of the eye. Standing below the level of the cashier's desk, which was upon a platform, there was something about him that suggested a laughing Romeo; and, in response, the cashier was evidently not unwilling to play a flippant Juliet. She tossed her head at him, tapped his cheek with a pencil, chattering eagerly; she blushed, laughed, and at last looked yearningly after him as he went away. Mr. Dodge also looked; for the young man was Dolling, once Mrs. Leslie Braithwaite's chauffeur.

"Fine little bit of comedy, that," the junior member of Mr. Dodge's firm remarked, across their small table. "Talked her into giving him credit for his lunch. She'll have to make it up out of her own pocket until he pays her. Of course, he's done it before, and she knows him. Characteristic of that fellow;—he's a great hand to put it over with the girls!"

"Do you know him, Williams?" Mr. Dodge asked, a little interested.

"Know him? Lord, yes! He was in my class at college till he got fired in sophomore year. Every now and then he comes to me and I have to stake him. He's a reporter just now; but it's always the same—whether he's working or not, he never has any money. He can do anything: act, sing, break horses, drive an airplane, any kind of newspaper work—publishes poetry in the papers sometimes, and he's not such a bad poet, either, at that. But he's just one of these natural-born drifters—too good looking and too restless. He never holds a job more than a couple of months."

"I suppose not," Mr. Dodge said, absently. "I suppose he's tried a good many."

"Rather!" Williams exclaimed. "I've got him I don't know how many, myself. The last time I did he was pretty well down and out, and the best I could get for him was a chauffeur's job for a little cuss I happened to know in the brass trade—Braithwaite. Lives out your way somewhere, I think. O'Boyle *took* it all right; it was chauff or starve!"

"I beg your pardon. Who took what?"

"O'Boyle," said Williams. "Charlie O'Boyle, the man we're talking about —the chap that was just conning the cashier yonder. I was telling you he took a job as chauffeur for a family out your way in the suburbs."

"Yes, I understood," Mr. Dodge returned, with more gravity than Williams expected as a tribute to this casual narrative. "You said this O'Boyle became a chauffeur to some people named Braithwaite and that you obtained the position for him. I merely wondered—I suppose when you recommended this O'Boyle to Mr. Braithwaite you—ah—you mentioned his name? I mean to say: you introduced O'Boyle as O'Boyle."

"Well, naturally," Williams replied, surprised and a little nettled. "Why wouldn't I? I wouldn't expect people to take on a man for a family job like that and not tell 'em his *name*, would I? I don't see what you——"

"Nothing," Mr. Dodge said, hurriedly. "Nothing at all. It was a ridiculous question. My mind was wandering to other things, or I shouldn't have asked it. We'd better get down to business, I suppose."

But that was something his wandering mind refused to do; nor would it under any consideration or pressure "get down to business" during the rest of that afternoon. He went home early, and, walking from his suburban station in the first twilight of a gray but rainless November day, arrived at his own gate just as the Braithwaites' closed car drew up at the curb before the next house.

An elderly negro chauffeur climbed down rustily from his seat at the wheel and opened the shining door; Mrs. Braithwaite stepped gracefully down, and, with her lovely saint's face uplifted above dark furs, she crossed the pavement, entered the low iron gateway, and walked up the wide stone path that led through the lawn to the house. On the opposite side of the street a group of impressed women stopped to stare, grateful for the favouring chance that gave them this glimpse of the great lady.

Mr. Braithwaite descended from the car and followed his wife toward the house. He did not overtake her and walk beside her; but his insignificant legs beneath his overcoat kept his small feet moving in neat short steps a little way behind her.

Meanwhile, the pausing neighbour gazed at them and his open mouth showed how he pondered. It was not upon this strange woman, a little of whose strangeness had so lately been revealed to him, that he pondered most, nor about her that he most profoundly wondered. For, strange as the woman seemed to him, far stranger seemed the little creature pattering so faithfully behind her up the walk.

In so helpless a fidelity Mr. Dodge felt something touching; and perhaps, too, he felt that men must keep men's secrets. At all events, he made a high resolve. It would be hard on Mrs. Dodge, even unfair to her; but then and there he made up his mind that for the sake of Mrs. Leslie Braithwaite's husband he would never tell anybody—and of all the world he would never tell Mrs. Dodge—what he had learned that day about Mrs. Leslie Braithwaite's husband's loyalty.

Mrs. Protheroe

When Alonzo Rawson took his seat as the Senator from Stackpole in the upper branch of the General Assembly of the State, an expression of pleasure and of greatness appeared to be permanently imprinted upon his countenance. He felt that if he had not quite arrived at all which he meant to make his own, at least he had emerged upon the arena where he was to win it, and he looked about him for a few other strong spirits with whom to construct a focus of power which should control the senate. The young man had not long to look, for within a week after the beginning of the session these others showed themselves to his view, rising above the general level of mediocrity and timidity, party-leaders and chiefs of faction, men who were on their feet continually, speaking half-a-dozen times a day, freely and loudly. To these, and that house at large, he felt it necessary to introduce himself by a speech which must prove him one of the elect, and he awaited impatiently an opening.

Alonzo had no timidity himself. He was not one of those who first try their voices on motions to adjourn, written in form and handed out to novices by presiding officers and leaders. He was too conscious of his own gifts, and he had been "accustomed to speaking" ever since his days in the Stackpole City Seminary. He was under the impression, also, that his appearance alone would command attention from his colleagues and the gallery. He was tall; his hair was long, with a rich waviness, rippling over both brow and collar, and he had, by years of endeavour, succeeded in moulding his features to present an aspect of stern and thoughtful majesty whenever he "spoke."

The opportunity to show his fellows that new greatness was among them delayed not overlong, and Senator Rawson arose, long and bony in his best clothes, to address the senate with a huge voice in denunciation of the "Sunday Baseball Bill," then upon second reading. The classical references, which, as a born orator, he felt it necessary to introduce, were received with acclamations which the gavel of the Lieutenant-Governor had no power to still.

"What led to the De-cline and Fall of the Roman Empire?" he exclaimed. "I await an answer from the advocates of this *de*-generate measure! I *demand*

an answer from them! Let me hear from them on *that* subject! Why don't
they speak up? They can't give one. Not because they ain't familiar with
history, no sir! That's not the reason! It's because they *daren't*, because their
answer would have to go on record *against* 'em! Don't any of you try to raise
it against me that I ain't speakin' to the point, for I tell you that when you
encourage Sunday Baseball, or any kind of Sabbath-breakin' on Sunday,
you're tryin' to start this State on the downward path that beset Rome! *I'll*
tell you what ruined it. The Roman Empire started out to be the greatest
nation on earth, and they had a good start, too, just like the United States
has got to-day. *Then* what happened to 'em? Why, them old ancient fellers
got more interested in athletic games and gladiatorial combats and racing
and all kinds of out-door sports, and bettin' on 'em, than they were in oratory, or literature, or charitable institutions and good works of all kinds. At
first they were moderate and the country was prosperous. But six days in the
week wouldn't content 'em, and they went at it all the time, so that at last
they gave up the seventh day to their sports, the way this bill wants *us* to
do, and from that time on the result was *de*-generacy and *de*-gredation! You
better remember *that* lesson, my friends, and don't try to sink this State to
the level of Rome!"

When Alonzo Rawson wiped his dampened brow, and dropped into his
chair, he was satisfied to the core of his heart with the effect of his maiden
effort. There was not one eye in the place that was not fixed upon him and
shining with surprise and delight, while the kindly Lieutenant-Governor, his
face very red, rapped for order. The young senator across the aisle leaned
over and shook Alonzo's hand excitedly.

"That was beautiful, Senator Rawson!" he whispered. "I'm *for* the bill,
but I can respect a masterly opponent."

"I thank you, Senator Truslow," Alonzo returned graciously. "I am glad to
have your good opinion, Senator."

"You have it, Senator," said Truslow enthusiastically. "I hope you intend
to speak often?"

"I do, Senator. I intend to make myself heard," the other answered
gravely, "upon all questions of moment."

"You will fill a great place among us, Senator!"

Then Alonzo Rawson wondered if he had not underestimated his neighbour across the aisle; he had formed an opinion of Truslow as one of small
account and no power, for he had observed that, although this was Truslow's
second term, he had not once demanded recognition nor attempted to take
part in a debate. Instead, he seemed to spend most of his time frittering
over some desk work, though now and then he walked up and down the aisles
talking in a low voice to various senators. How such a man could have been
elected at all, Alonzo failed to understand. Also, Truslow was physically inconsequent, in his colleague's estimation—"a little insignificant, dudish kind
of a man," he had thought; one whom he would have darkly suspected of
cigarettes had he not been dumbfounded to behold Truslow smoking an old

black pipe in the lobby. The Senator from Stackpole had looked over the other's clothes with a disapproval that amounted to bitterness. Truslow's attire reminded him of pictures in New York magazines, or the dress of boys newly home from college, he didn't know which, but he did know that it was contemptible. Consequently, after receiving the young man's congratulations, Alonzo was conscious of the keenest surprise at his own feeling that there might be something in him after all.

He decided to look him over again, more carefully to take the measure of one who had shown himself so frankly an admirer. Waiting, therefore, a few moments until he felt sure that Truslow's gaze had ceased to rest upon himself, he turned to bend a surreptitious but piercing scrutiny upon his neighbour. His glance, however, sweeping across Truslow's shoulder toward the face, suddenly encountered another pair of eyes beyond, so intently fixed upon himself that he started. The clash was like two search-lights meeting —and the glorious brown eyes that shot into Alonzo's were not the eyes of Truslow.

Truslow's desk was upon the outer aisle, and along the wall were placed comfortable leather chairs and settees, originally intended for the use of members of the upper house, but nearly always occupied by their wives and daughters, or "lady-lobbyists," or other women spectators. Leaning back with extraordinary grace, in the chair nearest Truslow, sat the handsomest woman Alonzo had ever seen in his life. Her long coat of soft grey fur was unrecognizable to him in connection with any familiar breed of squirrel; her broad flat hat of the same fur was wound with a grey veil, underneath which her heavy brown hair seemed to exhale a mysterious glow, and never, not even in a lithograph, had he seen features so regular or a skin so clear! And to look into her eyes seemed to Alonzo like diving deep into clear water and turning to stare up at the light.

His own eyes fell first. In the breathless awkwardness that beset him they seemed to stumble shamefully down to his desk, like a country-boy getting back to his seat after a thrashing on the teacher's platform. For the lady's gaze, profoundly liquid as it was, had not been friendly.

Alonzo Rawson had neither the habit of petty analysis, nor the inclination toward it; yet there arose within him a wonder at his own emotion, at its strangeness and the violent reaction of it. A moment ago his soul had been steeped in satisfaction over the figure he had cut with his speech and the extreme enthusiasm which had been accorded it—an extraordinarily pleasant feeling: suddenly this was gone, and in its place he found himself almost choking with a dazed sense of having been scathed, and at the same time understood in a way in which he did not understand himself. And yet—he and this most unusual lady had been so mutually conscious of each other in their mysterious interchange that he felt almost acquainted with her. Why, then, should his head be hot with resentment? Nobody had *said* anything to him!

He seized upon the fattest of the expensive books supplied to him by the

State, opened it with emphasis and began not to read it, with abysmal abstraction, tinglingly alert to the circumstance that Truslow was holding a low-toned but lively conversation with the unknown. Her laugh came to him, at once musical, quiet, and of a quality which irritated him into saying bitterly to himself that he guessed there was just as much refinement in Stackpole as there was in the Capital City, and just as many old families! The clerk calling his vote upon the "Baseball Bill" at that moment, he roared "No!" in a tone which was profane. It seemed to him that he was avenging himself upon somebody for something and it gave him a great deal of satisfaction.

He returned immediately to his imitation of Archimedes, only relaxing the intensity of his attention to the text (which blurred into jargon before his fixed gaze) when he heard that light laugh again. He pursed his lips, looked up at the ceiling as if slightly puzzled by some profound question beyond the reach of womankind; solved it almost immediately, and, setting his hand to pen and paper, wrote the capital letter "O" several hundred times on note-paper furnished by the State. So oblivious was he, apparently, to everything but the question of statecraft which occupied him, that he did not even look up when the morning's session was adjourned and the lawmakers began to pass noisily out, until Truslow stretched an arm across the aisle and touched him upon the shoulder.

"In a moment, Senator!" answered Alonzo in his deepest chest tones. He made it a very short moment, indeed, for he had a wild, breath-taking suspicion of what was coming.

"I want you to meet Mrs. Protheroe, Senator," said Truslow, rising, as Rawson, after folding his writings with infinite care, placed them in his breast pocket.

"I am pleased to make your acquaintance, ma'am," Alonzo said in a loud, firm voice, as he got to his feet, though the place grew vague about him when the lady stretched a charming, slender, gloved hand to him across Truslow's desk. He gave it several solemn shakes.

"We shouldn't have disturbed you, perhaps?" she asked, smiling radiantly upon him. "You were at some important work, I'm afraid."

He met her eyes again, and their beauty and the thoughtful kindliness of them fairly took his breath. "I am the chairman, ma'am," he replied, swallowing, "of the committee on drains and dikes."

"I knew it was something of great moment," she said gravely, "but I was anxious to tell you that I was interested in your speech."

A few minutes later, without knowing how he had got his hat and coat from the cloak-room, Alonzo Rawson found himself walking slowly through the marble vistas of the State-house to the great outer doors with the lady and Truslow. They were talking inconsequently of the weather, and of various legislators, but Alonzo did not know it. He vaguely formed replies to her questions and he hardly realized what the questions were; he was too stirringly conscious of the rich quiet of her voice and of the caress of the grey fur of her cloak when the back of his hand touched it—rather accidentally—now and then, as they moved on together.

It was a cold, quick air to which they emerged and Alonzo, daring to look at her, found that she had pulled the veil down over her face, the colour of which, in the keen wind, was like that of June roses seen through morning mists. At the curb a long, low, rakish black automobile was in waiting, the driver a mere indistinguishable cylinder of fur.

Truslow, opening the little door of the tonneau, offered his hand to the lady. "Come over to the club, Senator, and lunch with me," he said. "Mrs. Protheroe won't mind dropping us there on her way."

That was an eerie ride for Alonzo, whose feet were falling upon strange places. His pulses jumped and his eyes swam with the tears of unlawful speed, but his big ungloved hand tingled not with the cold so much as with the touch of that divine grey fur upon his little finger.

"You intend to make many speeches, Mr. Truslow tells me," he heard the rich voice saying.

"Yes ma'am," he summoned himself to answer. "I expect I will. Yes ma'am." He paused, and then repeated, "Yes ma'am."

She looked at him for a moment. "But you will do some work, too, won't you?" she asked slowly.

Her intention in this passed by Alonzo at the time. "Yes, ma'am," he answered. "The committee work interests me greatly, especially drains and dikes."

"I have heard," she said, as if searching his opinion, "that almost as much is accomplished in the committee-rooms as on the floor? There—and in the lobby and in the hotels and clubs?"

"I don't have much to do with that!" he returned quickly. "I guess none of them lobbyists will get much out of me! I even sent back all their railroad tickets. They needn't come near me!"

After a pause which she may have filled with unexpressed admiration, she ventured, almost timidly: "Do you remember that it was said that Napoleon once attributed the secret of his power over other men to one quality?"

"I am an admirer of Napoleon," returned the Senator from Stackpole. "I admire all great men."

"He said that he held men by his reserve."

"It can be done," observed Alonzo, and stopped, feeling that it was more reserved to add nothing to the sentence.

"But I suppose that such a policy," she smiled upon him inquiringly, "wouldn't have helped him much with women?"

"No," he agreed immediately. "My opinion is that a man ought to tell a *good* woman everything. What is more sacred than—"

The car, turning a corner much too quickly, performed a gymnastic squirm about an unexpected street-car and the speech ended in a gasp, as Alonzo, not of his own volition, half rose and pressed his cheek closely against hers. Instantaneous as it was, his heart leaped violently, but not with fear. Could all the things of his life that had seemed beautiful have been compressed into one instant, it would not have brought him even the suggestion of the wild shock of joy of that one, wherein he knew the glamorous perfume of Mrs. Protheroe's brown hair and felt her cold cheek firm against his, with only the grey veil between.

"I'm afraid this driver of mine will kill me some day," she said, laughing and composedly straightening her hat. "Do you care for big machines?"

"Yes ma'am," he answered huskily. "I haven't been in many."

"Then I'll take you again," said Mrs. Protheroe. "If you like I'll come down to the State-house and take you out for a run in the country."

"When?" said the lost young man, staring at her with his mouth open. "When?"

"Saturday afternoon if you like. I'll be there at two."

They were in front of the club and Truslow had already jumped out. Mrs. Protheroe gave him her hand and they exchanged a glance significant of something more than a friendly good-bye. Indeed, one might have hazarded that there was something almost businesslike about it. The confused Senator from Stackpole, climbing out reluctantly, observed it not, nor could he have understood even if he had seen, that delicate signal which passed between his two companions.

When he was upon the ground Mrs. Protheroe extended her hand without speaking, but her lips formed the word, "Saturday." Then she was carried away quickly, while Alonzo, his heart hammering, stood looking after her, borne into a strange world, the touch of the grey fur upon his little finger, the odour of her hair faintly about him, one side of his face red, the other pale.

"To-day is Wednesday," he said, half aloud.

"Come on, Senator." Truslow took his arm and turned him toward the club doors.

The other looked upon his new friend vaguely. "Why, I forgot to thank her for the ride," he said.

"You'll have other chances, Senator," Truslow assured him. "Mrs. Protheroe has a hobby for studying politics and she expects to come down often. She has plenty of time—she's a widow, you know."

"I hope you didn't think," exclaimed Alonzo indignantly, "that I thought she was a married woman!"

After lunch they walked back to the State-house together, Truslow regarding his thoughtful companion with sidelong whimsicalness. Mrs. Protheroe's question, suggestive of a difference between work and speechmaking, had recurred to Alonzo, and he had determined to make himself felt, off the floor as well as upon it. He set to this with a fine energy, that afternoon, in his committee-room, and the Senator from Stackpole knew his subject. On drains and dikes he had no equal. He spoke convincingly to his colleagues of the committee upon every bill that was before them, and he compelled their humblest respect. He went earnestly at it, indeed, and sat very late that night, in his room at a near-by boarding house, studying bills, trying to keep his mind upon them and not to think of his strange morning and of Saturday. Finally his neighbour in the next room, Senator Ezra Trumbull, long abed, was awakened by his praying and groaned slightly. Trumbull meant to speak to Rawson about his prayers, for Trumbull was an early one to bed and they woke him every night. The partition was flimsy and Alonzo addressed his Maker in the loud voice of those accustomed to talking across wide out-of-door spaces. Trumbull considered it especially unnecessary in the city; though, as a citizen of a county which loved but little his neighbour's district, he felt that in Stackpole there was good reason for a person to shout his prayers at the top of his voice and even then have small chance to carry through the distance. Still, it was a delicate matter to mention and he put it off from day to day.

Thursday passed slowly for Alonzo Rawson, nor was his voice lifted in debate. There was little but routine; and the main interest of the chamber was in the lobbying that was being done upon the "Sunday Baseball Bill" which had passed to its third reading and would come up for final disposition within a fortnight. This was the measure which Alonzo had set his heart upon defeating. It was a simple enough bill: it provided, in substance, that baseball might be played on Sunday by professionals in the State capital, which was proud of its league team. Naturally, it was denounced by clergymen, and deputations of ministers and committees from women's religious societies were constantly arriving at the State-house to protest against its passage. The Senator from Stackpole reassured all of these with whom he talked, and was one of their staunchest allies and supporters. He was active in leading the wavering among his colleagues, or even the inimical, out to meet and face the deputations. It was in this occupation that he was engaged, on Friday afternoon, when he received a shock.

A committee of women from a church society was waiting in the corridor, and he had rounded up a reluctant half-dozen senators and led them forth to be interrogated as to their intentions regarding the bill. The committee and the lawmakers soon distributed themselves into little argumentative clumps, and Alonzo found himself in the centre of these, with one of the ladies who had unfortunately—but, in her enthusiasm, without misgivings—begun a reproachful appeal to an advocate of the bill whose name was Goldstein.

"Senator Goldstein," she exclaimed, "I could not believe it when I heard that you were in favour of this measure! I have heard my husband speak in the highest terms of your old father. May I ask you what *he* thinks of it? If you voted for the desecration of Sunday by a low baseball game, could you dare go home and face that good old man?"

"Yes, madam," said Goldstein mildly; "we are *both* Jews."

A low laugh rippled out from near-by, and Alonzo, turning almost violently, beheld his lady of the furs. She was leaning back against a broad pilaster, her hands sweeping the same big coat behind her, her face turned toward him, but her eyes, sparklingly delighted, resting upon Goldstein. Under the broad fur hat she made a picture as enraging, to Alonzo Rawson, as it was bewitching. She appeared not to see him, to be quite unconscious of him—and he believed it. Truslow and five or six members of both houses were about her, and they all seemed to be bending eagerly toward her. Alonzo was furious with her.

Her laugh lingered upon the air for a moment, then her glance swept round the other way, omitting the Senator from Stackpole, who, immediately putting into practice a reserve which would have astonished Napoleon, swung about and quitted the deputation without a word of farewell or explanation. He turned into the cloak-room and paced the floor for three minutes with a malevolence which awed the coloured attendants into not brushing his coat; but, when he returned to the corridor, cautious inquiries addressed to the tobacconist elicited the information that the handsome lady with Senator Truslow had departed.

Truslow himself had not gone. He was lounging in his seat when Alonzo returned and was genially talkative. The latter refrained from replying in kind, not altogether out of reserve, but more because of a dim suspicion (which rose within him, the third time Truslow called him "Senator" in one sentence) that his first opinion of the young man as a light-minded person might have been correct.

There was no session the following afternoon, but Alonzo watched the street from the windows of his committee-room, which overlooked the splendid breadth of stone steps leading down from the great doors to the pavement. There were some big bookcases in the room, whose glass doors served as mirrors in which he more and more sternly regarded the soft image of an entirely new grey satin tie, while the conviction grew within him that (arguing from her behaviour of the previous day) she would not come, and that the Stackpole girls were nobler by far at heart than many who might wear a king's-ransom's-worth of jewels round their throats at the opera-house in a large city. This sentiment was heartily confirmed by the clock when it marked half-past two. He faced the bookcase doors and struck his breast, his open hand falling across the grey tie with tragic violence; after which, turning for the last time to the windows, he uttered a loud exclamation and, laying hands upon an ulster and a grey felt hat, each as new as the satin tie, ran hurriedly from the room. The black automobile was waiting.

"I thought it possible you might see me from a window," said Mrs. Protheroe as he opened the little door.

"I was just coming out," he returned, gasping for breath. "I thought—from yesterday—you'd probably forgotten."

"Why 'from yesterday'?" she asked.

"I thought—I thought—" He faltered to a stop as the full glorious sense of her presence overcame him. She wore the same veil.

"You thought I did not see you yesterday in the corridor?"

"I thought you might have acted more—more—"

"More cordially?"

"Well," he said, looking down at his hands, "more like you knew we'd been introduced."

At that she sat silent, looking away from him, and he, daring a quick glance at her, found that he might let his eyes remain upon her face. That was a dangerous place for eyes to rest, yet Alonzo Rawson was anxious for the risk. The car flew along the even asphalt on its way to the country like a wild goose on a long slant of wind, and, with his foolish fury melted inexplicably into honey, Alonzo looked at her—and looked at her—till he would have given an arm for another quick corner and a street-car to send his cheek against that veiled, cold cheek of hers again. It was not until they reached the alternate vacant lots and bleak Queen Anne cottages of the city's ragged edge that she broke the silence.

"You were talking to some one else," she said almost inaudibly.

"Yes ma'am, Goldstein, but—"

"Oh, no!" She turned toward him, lifting her hand. "You were quite the lion among ladies."

"I don't know what you mean, Mrs. Protheroe," he said, truthfully.

"What were you talking to all those women about?"

"It was about the 'Sunday Baseball Bill.'"

"Ah! The bill you attacked in your speech, last Wednesday?"

"Yes ma'am."

"I hear you haven't made any speeches since then," she said indifferently.

"No ma'am," he answered gently. "I kind of got the idea that I'd better lay low for a while, at first, and get in some quiet hard work."

"I understand. You are a man of intensely reserved nature."

"With men," said Alonzo, "I am. With ladies I am not so much so. I think a good woman ought to be told—"

"But you are interested," she interrupted, "in defeating that bill?"

"Yes ma'am," he returned. "It is an iniquitous measure."

"Why?"

"Mrs. Protheroe!" he exclaimed, taken aback. "I thought all the ladies were against it. My own mother wrote to me from Stackpole that she'd rather see me in my grave than votin' for such a bill, and I'd rather see myself there!"

"But are you sure that you understand it?"

"I only know it desecrates the Sabbath. That's enough for me!"

She leaned toward him and his breath came quickly.

"No. You're wrong," she said, and rested the tips of her fingers upon his sleeve.

"I don't understand why—why you say that," he faltered. "It sounds kind of—surprising to me—"

"Listen," she said. "Perhaps Mr. Truslow told you that I am studying such things. I do not want to be an idle woman; I want to be of use to the world, even if it must be only in small ways."

"I think that is a noble ambition!" he exclaimed. "I think all good women ought—"

"Wait," she interrupted gently. "Now, that bill is a worthy one, though it astonishes you to hear me say so. Perhaps you don't understand the conditions. Sunday is the labouring-man's only day of recreation—and what recreation is he offered?"

"He ought to go to church," said Alonzo promptly.

"But the fact is that he doesn't—not often—not at *all* in the afternoon. Wouldn't it be well to give him some wholesome way of employing his Sunday afternoons? This bill provides for just that, and it keeps him away from drinking too, for it forbids the sale of liquor on the grounds."

"Yes, I know," said Alonzo plaintively. "But it ain't *right!* I was raised to respect the Sabbath and—"

"Ah, that's what you should do! You think I could believe in anything that wouldn't make it better and more sacred?"

"Oh, no, ma'am!" he cried reproachfully. "It's only that I don't see—"

"I am telling you." She lifted her veil and let him have the full dazzle of her beauty. "Do you know that many thousands of labouring people spend their Sundays drinking and carousing about the low country road-houses because the game is played at such places on Sunday? They go there because they never get a chance to see it played in the city. And don't you understand that there would be no Sunday liquor trade, no working-men poisoning themselves every seventh day in the low groggeries, as hundreds of them do now, if they had something to see that would interest them?—something as wholesome and fine as this sport would be, under the conditions of this bill; something to keep them in the open air, something to bring a little gaiety into their dull lives!" Her voice had grown louder and it shook a little, with a rising emotion, though its sweetness was only the more poignant. "Oh, my dear Senator," she cried, "don't you *see* how wrong you are? Don't you want to *help* these poor people?"

Her fingers, which had tightened upon his sleeve, relaxed and she leaned back, pulling the veil down over her face as if wishing to conceal from him that her lips trembled slightly; then resting her arm upon the leather cushions, she turned her head away from him, staring fixedly into the gaunt beech woods lining the country road along which they were now coursing. For a time she heard nothing from him, and the only sound was the monotonous chug of the machine.

"I suppose you think it rather shocking to hear a woman talking practically of such commonplace things," she said at last, in a cold voice, just loud enough to be heard.

"No ma'am," he said huskily.

"Then what *do* you think?" she cried, turning toward him again with a quick imperious gesture.

"I think I'd better go back to Stackpole," he answered very slowly, "and resign my job. I don't see as I've got any business in the Legislature."

"I don't understand you."

He shook his head mournfully. "It's a simple enough matter. I've studied out a good many bills and talked 'em over and I've picked up some influence and—"

"I know you have," she interrupted eagerly. "Mr. Truslow says that the members of your drains-and-dikes committee follow your vote on every bill."

"Yes ma'am," said Alonzo Rawson meekly, "but I expect they oughtn't to. I've had a lesson this afternoon."

"You mean to say—"

"I mean that I didn't know what I was doing about that baseball bill. I was just pig-headedly goin' ahead against it, not knowing nothing about the conditions, and it took a lady to show me what they were. I would have done a wrong thing if you hadn't stopped me."

"You mean," she cried, her splendid eyes widening with excitement and delight; "you mean that you—that you—"

"I mean that I will vote for the bill!" He struck his clenched fist upon his knee. "I come to the Legislature to do *right!*"

"You will, ah, you *will* do right in this!" Mrs. Protheroe thrust up her veil again and her face was flushed and radiant with triumph. "And you'll work, and you'll make a speech for the bill?"

At this the righteous exaltation began rather abruptly to simmer down in the soul of Alonzo Rawson. He saw the consequences of too violently reversing, and knew how difficult they might be to face.

"Well, not—not exactly," he said weakly. "I expect our best plan would be for me to lay kind of low and not say any more about the bill at all. Of course, I'll quit workin' against it; and on the roll-call I'll edge up close to the clerk and say 'Aye' so that only him'll hear me. That's done every day —and I—well, I don't just exactly like to come out too publicly for it, after my speech and all I've done against it."

She looked at him sharply for a short second, and then offered him her hand and said: "Let's shake hands *now*, on the vote. Think what a triumph it is for me to know that I helped to show you the right."

"Yes ma'am," he answered confusedly, too much occupied with shaking her hand to know what he said. She spoke one word in an undertone to the driver and the machine took the very shortest way back to the city.

After this excursion, several days passed, before Mrs. Protheroe came to the State-house again. Rawson was bending over the desk of Senator Josephus Battle, the white-bearded leader of the opposition to the "Sunday Baseball Bill," and was explaining to him the intricacies of a certain drainage measure, when Battle, whose attention had wandered, plucked his sleeve and whispered:

"If you want to see a mighty pretty woman that's doin' no good here, look behind you, over there in the chair by the big fireplace at the back of the room."

Alonzo looked.

It was she whose counterpart had been in his dream's eye every moment of the dragging days which had been vacant of her living presence. A number of his colleagues were hanging over her almost idiotically; her face was gay and her voice came to his ears, as he turned, with the accent of her cadenced laughter running through her talk like a chime of tiny bells flitting through a strain of music.

"This is the third time she's been here," said Battle, rubbing his beard the wrong way. "She's lobbyin' for that infernal Sabbath-Desecration bill, but we'll beat her, my son."

"Have you made her acquaintance, Senator?" asked Alonzo stiffly.

"No, sir, and I don't want to. But I knew her father—the slickest old beat and the smoothest talker that ever waltzed up the pike. She married rich; her husband left her a lot of real estate around here, but she spends most of her time away. Whatever struck her to come down and lobby for that bill I don't know—yet—but I will! Truslow's helping her to help himself; he's got stock in the company that runs the baseball team, but what she's up to—well, I'll bet there's a nigger in the woodpile *some*where!"

"I expect there's a lot of talk like that!" said Alonzo, red with anger, and taking up his papers abruptly.

"Yes, *sir!*" said Battle emphatically, utterly misunderstanding the other's tone and manner. "Don't you worry, my son. We'll kill that venomous bill right here in this chamber! We'll kill it so dead that it won't make one flop after the axe hits it. You and me and some others'll tend to *that!* Let her work that pretty face and those eyes of hers all she wants to! I'm keepin' a little lookout, too—and I'll—"

He broke off, for the angry and perturbed Alonzo had left him and gone to his own desk. Battle, slightly surprised, rubbed his beard the wrong way and sauntered out to the lobby to muse over a cigar. Alonzo, loathing Battle with a great loathing, formed bitter phrases concerning that vicious-minded old gentleman, while for a moment he affected to be setting his desk in order. Then he walked slowly up the aisle, conscious of a roaring in his ears (though not aware how red they were) as he approached the semicircle about her.

He paused within three feet of her in a sudden panic of timidity, and then, to his consternation, she looked him squarely in the face, over the shoulders of two of the group, and the only sign of recognition that she exhibited was a slight frown of unmistakable repulsion, which appeared between her handsome eyebrows.

It was very swift; only Alonzo saw it; the others had no eyes for anything but her, and were not aware of his presence behind them, for she did not even pause in what she was saying.

Alonzo walked slowly away with the wormwood in his heart. He had not grown up among the young people of Stackpole without similar experiences, but it had been his youthful boast that no girl had ever "stopped speaking" to him without reason, or "cut a dance" with him and afterward found opportunity to repeat the indignity.

"What have I *done* to *her?*" was perhaps the hottest cry of his bruised soul, for the mystery was as great as the sting of it.

It was no balm upon that sting to see her pass him at the top of the outer steps, half an hour later, on the arm of that one of his colleagues who had been called the "best-dressed man in the Legislature." She swept by him without a sign, laughing that same laugh at some sally of her escort, and they got into the black automobile together and were whirled away and out of sight by the impassive bundle of furs who manipulated the wheel.

For the rest of that afternoon and the whole of that night no man, woman, or child heard the voice of Alonzo Rawson, for he spoke to none. He came not to the evening meal, nor was he seen by any who had his acquaintance. He entered his room at about midnight, and Trumbull was awakened by his neighbour's overturning a chair. No match was struck, however, and Trumbull was relieved to think that the Senator from Stackpole intended going directly to bed without troubling to light the gas, and that his prayers would soon be over. Such was not the case, for no other sound came from the room, nor were Alonzo's prayers uttered that night, though the unhappy statesman in the next apartment could not get to sleep for several hours on account of his nervous expectancy of them.

After this, as the day approached upon which hung the fate of the bill which Mr. Josephus Battle was fighting, Mrs. Protheroe came to the Senate Chamber nearly every morning and afternoon. Not once did she appear to be conscious of Alonzo Rawson's presence, nor once did he allow his eyes to delay upon her, though it cannot be truthfully said that he did not always know when she came, when she left, and with whom she stood or sat or talked. He evaded all mention or discussion of the bill or of Mrs. Protheroe; avoided Truslow (who, strangely enough, was avoiding *him*) and, spending upon drains and dikes all the energy that he could manage to concentrate, burned the midnight oil and rubbed salt into his wounds to such marked effect that by the evening of the Governor's Reception—upon the morning following which the mooted bill was to come up—he offered an impression so haggard and worn that an actor might have studied him for a make-up as a young statesman going into a decline.

Nevertheless, he dressed with great care and bitterness, and placed the fragrant blossom of a geranium—taken from a plant belonging to his landlady—in the lapel of his long coat before he set out.

And yet, when he came down the Governor's broad stairs, and wandered through the big rooms, with the glare of lights above him and the shouting of the guests ringing in his ears, a sense of emptiness beset him; the crowded place seemed vacant and without meaning. Even the noise sounded hollow and remote—and why had he bothered about the geranium? He hated her and would never look at her again—but why was she not there?

By-and-by, he found himself standing against a wall, where he had been pushed by the press of people. He was wondering drearily what he was to do with a clean plate and a napkin which a courteous negro had handed him, half-an-hour earlier, when he felt a quick jerk at his sleeve. It was Truslow, who had worked his way along the wall and who now, standing on tiptoe, spoke rapidly but cautiously, close to his ear.

"Senator, be quick," he said sharply, at the same time alert to see that they were unobserved. "Mrs. Protheroe wants to speak to you at once. You'll find her near the big palms under the stairway in the hall."

He was gone—he had wormed his way half across the room—before the other, in his simple amazement could answer. When Alonzo at last found a word, it was only a monosyllable, which, with his accompanying action, left a matron of years, who was at that moment being pressed fondly to his side, in a state of mind almost as dumbfounded as his own. *"Here!"* was all he said as he pressed the plate and napkin into her hand and departed forcibly for the hall, leaving a spectacular wreckage of trains behind him.

The upward flight of the stairway left a space underneath, upon which, as it was screened (save for a narrow entrance) by a thicket of palms, the crowd had not encroached. Here were placed a divan and a couple of chairs; there was shade from the glare of gas, and the light was dim and cool. Mrs. Protheroe had risen from the divan when Alonzo entered this grotto, and stood waiting for him.

He stopped in the green entrance-way with a quick exclamation.

She did not seem the same woman who had put such slights upon him, this tall, white vision of silk, with the summery scarf falling from her shoulders. His great wrath melted at the sight of her; the pain of his racked pride, which had been so hot in his breast, gave way to a species of fear. She seemed not a human being, but a white spirit of beauty and goodness who stood before him, extending two fine arms to him in long, white gloves.

She left him to his trance for a moment, then seized both his hands in hers and cried to him in her rapturous, low voice: "Ah, Senator, you have come! I *knew* you understood!"

"Yes ma'am," he whispered chokily.

She drew him to one of the chairs and sank gracefully down upon the divan near him.

"Mr. Truslow was so afraid you wouldn't," she went on rapidly, "but I was sure. You see I didn't want anybody to suspect that I had any influence with you. I didn't want them to know, even, that I'd talked to you. It all came to me after the first day that we met. You see I've believed in you, in your power and in your reserve, from the first. I want all that you do to seem to come from yourself and not from me or any one else. Oh, I *believe* in great, strong men who stand upon their own feet and conquer the world for themselves! That's *your* way, Senator Rawson. So, you see, as they think I'm lobbying for the bill, I wanted them to believe that your speech for it to-morrow comes from your own great, strong mind and heart and your sense of right, and not from any suggestion of mine."

"My speech!" he stammered.

"Oh, I know," she cried; "I know you think I don't believe much in speeches, and I don't ordinarily, but a few, simple, straightforward and vigorous words from you, to-morrow, may carry the bill through. You've made such *progress*, you've been so *reserved*, that you'll carry great weight—and there are three votes of the drains-and-dikes that are against us now, but will follow yours absolutely. Do you think I would have 'cut' *you* if it hadn't been *best?*"

"But I—"

"Oh, I know you didn't actually promise me to speak, that day. But I knew you would when the time came! I knew that a man of power goes over *all* obstacles, once his sense of *right* is aroused! I *knew*—I never doubted it, that once *you* felt a thing to be right you would strike for it, with all your great strength—at all costs—at all—"

"I can't—I—I—can't!" he whispered nervously. "Don't you see—don't you see—I—"

She leaned toward him, lifting her face close to his. She was so near him that the faint odour of her hair came to him again, and once more the unfortunate Senator from Stackpole risked a meeting of his eyes with hers, and saw the light shining far down in their depths.

At this moment the shadow of a portly man who was stroking his beard the wrong way projected itself upon them from the narrow, green entrance to the grotto. Neither of them perceived it.

Senator Josephus Battle passed on, but when Alonzo Rawson emerged, a few moments later, he was pledged to utter a few simple, straightforward and vigorous words in favour of the bill. And—let the shame fall upon the head of the scribe who tells it—he had kissed Mrs. Protheroe!

The fight upon the "Sunday Baseball Bill," the next morning, was the warmest of that part of the session, though for a while the reporters were disappointed. They were waiting for Senator Battle, who was famous among them for the vituperative vigour of his attacks and for the kind of personalities which made valuable copy. And yet, until the debate was almost over, he contented himself with going quietly up and down the aisles, whispering to the occupants of the desks, and writing and sending a multitude of notes to his colleagues. Meanwhile, the orators upon both sides harangued their fellows, the lobby, the unpolitical audience, and the patient presiding officer to no effect, so far as votes went. The general impression was that it would be close.

Alonzo Rawson sat, bent over his desk, his eyes fixed with gentle steadiness upon Mrs. Protheroe, who occupied the chair wherein he had first seen her. A senator of the opposition was finishing his denunciation, when she turned and nodded almost imperceptibly to the young man.

He gave her one last look of pathetic tenderness and rose.

"The Senator from Stackpole!"

"I want," Alonzo began, in his big voice: "I want to say a few simple, straightforward but vigorous words about this bill. You may remember I spoke against it on its second reading—"

"You did *that!*" shouted Senator Battle suddenly.

"I want to say now," the Senator from Stackpole continued, "that at that time I hadn't studied the subject sufficiently. I didn't know the conditions of the case, nor the facts, but since then a great light has broke in upon me—"

"I should say it had! I saw it break!" was Senator Battle's second violent interruption.

When order was restored, Alonzo, who had become very pale, summoned his voice again. "I think we'd ought to take into consideration that Sunday is the working-man's only day of recreation and not drive him into low groggeries, but give him a chance in the open air to indulge his love of wholesome sport—"

"Such as the ancient Romans enjoyed!" interposed Battle vindictively.

"No, sir!" Alonzo wheeled upon him, stung to the quick. "Such a sport as free-born Americans and *only* free-born Americans can play in this wide world—the American game of baseball, in which no other nation of the *Earth* is our equal!"

This was a point scored and the cheering lasted two minutes. Then the orator resumed:

"I say: 'Give the working-man a chance!' Is his life a happy one? You know it ain't! Give him his one day. *Don't* spoil it for him with your laws—he's only got one! I'm not goin' to take up any more of your time, but if there's anybody here who thinks my well-considered opinion worth following I say: '*Vote for this bill.*' It is right and virtuous and ennobling, and it ought to be passed! I say: '*Vote for it.*'"

The reporters decided that the Senator from Stackpole had "wakened things up." The gavel rapped a long time before the chamber quieted down, and when it did, Josephus Battle was on his feet and had obtained the recognition of the chair.

"I wish to say, right here," he began, with a rasping leisureliness, "that I hope no member of this honoured body will take my remarks as personal or unparliamentary—*but*"—he raised a big forefinger and shook it with menace at the presiding officer, at the same time suddenly lifting his voice to an unprintable shriek—"I say to *you*, sir, that the song of the siren has been *heard* in the land, and the call of Delilah has been answered! When the Senator from Stackpole rose in this chamber, less than three weeks ago, and denounced this iniquitous measure, I heard him with pleasure—we *all* heard him with pleasure—*and* respect! In spite of his youth and the poor quality of his expression, *we* listened to him. *We* knew he was sincere! What has caused the change in him? What *has*, I ask? I shall not tell you, upon this floor, but I've taken mighty good care to let most of you know, during the morning, either by word of mouth or by *note* of hand! Especially those of you of the

drains-and-dikes and others who might follow this young Samson, whose
locks have been shore! *I've* told you all about that, and more—*I've* told you
the *inside* history of some *facts* about the bill that I will not make public,
because I am too confident of our strength to defeat this devilish measure,
and prefer to let our vote speak our opinion of it! Let me not detain you
longer. *I* thank you!"

Long before he had finished, the Senator from Stackpole was being held
down in his chair by Truslow and several senators whose seats were adjacent;
and the vote was taken amid an uproar of shouting and confusion. When
the clerk managed to proclaim the result over all other noises, the bill was
shown to be defeated and "killed," by a majority of five votes.

A few minutes later, Alonzo Rawson, his neckwear disordered and his face
white with rage, stumbled out of the great doors upon the trail of Battle,
who had quietly hurried away to his hotel for lunch as soon as he had voted.

The black automobile was vanishing round a corner. Truslow stood upon
the edge of the pavement staring after it ruefully:

"Where is Mrs. Protheroe?" gasped the Senator from Stackpole.

"She's gone," said the other.

"Gone where?"

"Gone back to Paris. She sails day after to-morrow. She just had time
enough to catch her train for New York after waiting to hear how the vote
went. She told me to tell you good-bye, and that she was sorry. Don't stare
at me, Rawson! I guess we're in the same boat!—Where are you going?"
he finished abruptly.

Alonzo swung by him and started across the street. "To find Battle!" the
hoarse answer came back.

The conquering Josephus was leaning meditatively upon the counter of the
cigar-stand of his hotel when Alonzo found him. He took one look at the
latter's face and backed to the wall, tightening his grasp upon the heavy-
headed ebony cane it was his habit to carry, a habit upon which he now
congratulated himself.

But his precautions were needless. Alonzo stopped out of reaching distance.

"You tell me," he said in a breaking voice; "you tell me what you meant
about Delilah and sirens and Samsons and inside facts! You tell me!"

"You wild ass of the prairies," said Battle, "I saw you last night behind
them pa'ms! But don't you think I told it—or ever will! I just passed the
word around that she'd argued you into her way of thinkin', same as she
had a good many others. And as for the rest of it, I found out where the
nigger in the woodpile was, and I handed that out, too. Don't you take it
hard, my son, but I told you her husband left her a good deal of land around
here. She owns the ground that they use for the baseball park, and her lease
would be worth considerable more if they could have got the right to play
on Sundays!"

Senator Trumbull sat up straight, in bed, that night, and, for the first time during his martyrdom, listened with no impatience to the prayer which fell upon his ears.

"O Lord Almighty," through the flimsy partition came the voice of Alonzo Rawson, quaveringly, but with growing strength: "Aid Thou me to see my way more clear! I find it hard to tell right from wrong, and I find myself beset with tangled wires. O God, I feel that I am ignorant, and fall into many devices. These are strange paths wherein Thou hast set my feet, but I feel that through Thy help, and through great anguish, I am learning!"

Mrs. Dodge, Mrs. Cromwell and
Mrs. Roderick Brooks Battle

We learned in childhood that appearances are deceitful, and our subsequent scrambling about upon this whirling globe has convinced many of us that the most deceptive of all appearances are those of peace. The gentlest looking liquor upon the laboratory shelves was what removed the east wing of the Chemical Corporation's building on Christmas morning; it was the stillest Sunday noon of a drowsy August when, without even the courtesy of a little introductory sputtering, the gas works blew up; and both of these disturbances were thought to be peculiarly outrageous because of the previous sweet aspects that prevented any one from expecting trouble. Yet those aspects, like the flat calm of the summer of 1914, should have warned people of experience that outbreaks were impending.

What could offer to mortal eye a picture of more secure placidity than three smiling ladies walking homeward together after a club meeting? The particular three in mind, moreover, were in a visibly prosperous condition of life; for, although the afternoon was brightly cold, their furs afforded proof of expenditures with which any moderate woman would be satisfied, and their walk led them into the most luxurious stretch of the long thoroughfare that was called the handsome suburb's finest street. The three addressed one another in the caressively amiable tones that so strikingly characterize the élite of their sex in converse; and their topic, which had been that of the club paper, was impersonal. In fact, it was more than impersonal, it was celestial. "Sweetness and Light: Essay. Mrs. Roderick Brooks Battle"—these were the words printed in the club's year book beneath the date of that meeting, and Mrs. Roderick Brooks Battle was the youngest of the three placid ladies.

"You're all so sweet to say such lovely things about it," she said, as they walked slowly along. "I only wish I deserved them, but of course, as everyone must have guessed, it was all Mr. Battle. I don't suppose I could write a single connected paragraph without his telling me how, and if he hadn't kept helping me I just wouldn't have been ready with any paper at all. Never in the world!"

"Oh, yes, you would, Amelia," the elder of the two other ladies assured her. "For instance, dear, that beautiful thought about the 'bravery of silence'—about how much nobler it is never to answer an attack—I thought it was the finest thought in the whole paper, and I'm sure that was your own and not your husband's, Amelia."

"Oh, no, Mrs. Cromwell," Mrs. Battle returned, and although her manner was deferential to the older woman she seemed to be gently shocked;—her voice became a little protesting. "I could never in the world have experienced a thought like that just by myself. It was every bit Mr. Battle's. In fact, he almost as much as dictated that whole paragraph to me, word for word. It seemed a shame for me to sit up there and appear to take the credit for it; but I knew, of course, that everybody who knows us the least bit intimately would understand I could never write anything and it was all Mr. Battle."

"My dear, you'll never persuade us of it," the third lady said. "There were thoughts in your paper so characteristically feminine that no one but a woman could possibly——"

"Oh, but *he* could!" Mrs. Battle interrupted with an eagerness that was more than audible, for it showed itself vividly in her brightened eyes and the sudden glow of pink beneath them. "That's one of the most wonderful things about Mr. Battle: his intellect is just as feminine as it is masculine, Mrs. Dodge. He's absolutely—well, the only way I can express it is in his own words. Mr. Battle says no one can be great who isn't universal in his thinking. And you see that's where he excels so immensely;—Mr. Battle is absolutely universal in his thinking. It seems to me it's one of the great causes of Mr. Battle's success; he not only has the most powerful reasoning faculties I ever knew in any man but he's absolutely gifted with a woman's intuition." She paused to utter a little murmur of fond laughter, as if she herself had so long and helplessly marvelled over Mr. Battle that she tolerantly found other people's incredulous amazement at his prodigiousness natural but amusing. "You see, an intellect like Mr. Battle's can't be comprehended from knowing other men, Mrs. Dodge," she added. "Other men look at things simply in a masculine way, of course. Mr. Battle says that's only seeing half. Mr. Battle says women live on one hemisphere of a globe and men on the other, and neither can look round the circle, but from the stars the whole globe is seen—so that's why we should keep our eyes among the stars! I wanted to work that thought into my paper, too. Isn't it beautiful, the idea of keeping our eyes among the stars? But he said there wasn't a logical opening for it, so I didn't. Mr. Battle says we should never use a thought that doesn't find its own logical place. That is, not in writing, he says. But don't you think it's wonderful—that idea of the globe and the two hemispheres and all?"

"Lovely," Mrs. Dodge agreed. "Yet I don't see how it proves Mr. Battle has a feminine mind."

"Oh, but I don't mean just that alone," Mrs. Battle returned eagerly. "It's the thousand and one things in my daily contact with him that prove it. Of course, I know how hard it must be for other women to understand. I suppose no one could hope to realize what Mr. Battle's mind is like at all without the great privilege of being married to him."

"And that," Mrs. Cromwell remarked, "has been denied to so many of us, my dear!"

Mrs. Dodge laughed a little brusquely, but the consort of the marvellous Battle was herself so marvellous that she merely looked preoccupied. "I know," she said, gravely, while Mrs. Dodge and Mrs. Cromwell stared with widening eyes, first at her and then at each other. "How often I've thought of it!" she went on, her own eyes fixed earnestly upon the distance where, in perspective, the two curbs of the long, straight street appeared to meet. "It grows stranger and stranger to me how such a miracle could have happened to a commonplace little woman like me! I never shall understand why I should have been the one selected."

Thereupon, having arrived at her own gate, it was with this thought that she left them. From the gate a path of mottled flagstones led through a smooth and snowy lawn to a house upon which the architect had chastely indulged his Latin pleasure in stucco and wrought iron; and as Mrs. Battle took her way over the flagstones she received from her two friends renewed congratulations upon her essay, as well as expressions of parting endearment; and she replied to these cheerfully; but all the while the glowing, serious eyes of the eager little brown-haired woman remained preoccupied with the miracle she had mentioned.

Mrs. Cromwell and Mrs. Dodge went on their way with some solemnity, and were silent until the closing door of the stucco house let them know they were out of earshot. Then Mrs. Cromwell, using a hushed voice, inquired: "Do you suppose she ever had a painting made of the Annunciation?"

"The Annunciation?" Mrs. Dodge did not follow her.

"Yes. When the miracle was announced to her that she should be the wife of Roderick Brooks Battle. Of course, she must have been forewarned by an angel that she was 'the one selected.' If Battle had just walked in and proposed to her it would have been too much for her!"

"I know one thing," Mrs. Dodge said, emphatically. "I've stood just about as much of her everlasting 'Mr. Battle says' as I intend to! You can't go anywhere and get away from it; you can hear it over all the chatter at a dinner; you can hear it over fifty women gabbing at a tea—'Mr. Battle says this,' 'Mr. Battle says that,' 'Mr. Battle says this and that'! When Belloni was singing at the Fortnightly Afternoon Music last week you could hear her 'Mr. Battle says' to all the women around her, even during that loud Puccini suite, and she treed Belloni on his way out, after the concert, to tell him Mr. Battle's theory of music. She hadn't listened to a note the man sang, and Belloni understands about two words of English, but Amelia kept right on Mr. Battle-saysing for half an hour! For my part, I've had all I can stand of it, and I'm about ready to do something about it!"

"I don't see just what one could do," Mrs. Cromwell said, laughing vaguely.

"*I* do!" her companion returned. Then both were silent for a few thoughtful moments and wore the air of people who have introduced a subject upon which they are not yet quite warm enough to speak plainly. Mrs. Cromwell evidently decided to slide away from it, for the time being, at least. "I don't think Amelia's looking well," she said. "She's rather lost her looks these last few years, I'm afraid. She seems pretty worn and thin to me;—she's getting a kind of skimpy look."

"What else could you expect? She's made herself the man's slave ever since they were married. She was his valet, his cook, and his washerwoman night and day for years. I wonder how many times actually and literally she's blacked his boots for him! How could you expect her *not* to get worn out and skimpy looking?"

"Oh, I know," Mrs. Cromwell admitted;—"but all that was in their struggling days, and she certainly doesn't need to do such things now. I hear he has twenty or thirty houses to build this year, and just lately an immense contract for two new office buildings. Besides, he's generous with her; she dresses well enough nowadays."

"Yes," Mrs. Dodge said, grimly. "They'd both see to that for *his* credit; but if he comes in with wet feet you needn't tell me she doesn't get down on her knees before him and take off his shoes herself. I know her! Yes, and I know him, too! Rich or poor, she'd be his valet and errand girl just the same as she always was."

"Perhaps," said Mrs. Cromwell. "But it seems to me her most important office for him is the one she's just been filling."

"Press agent? I should say so! She may stop blacking his boots, but she'll never stop that. It's just why she makes me so confounded tired, too! She thinks she's the only woman that ever got married!"

"Amelia *is* rather that way," the other said, musingly. "She certainly never seems to realize that any of the rest of us have husbands of our own."

" 'Mr. Battle can't be comprehended from knowing other men!' " Here Mrs. Dodge somewhat bitterly mimicked the unfortunate Amelia's eager voice. " 'Other men look at things in simply a masculine way!' 'I know how hard it must be for other women to understand a god like my husband just from knowing their own poor little imitation husbands!' "

"Oh, no," Mrs. Cromwell protested. "She didn't quite say that."

"But isn't it what she meant? Isn't it exactly what she felt?"

"Well—perhaps."

"It does make me tired!" Mrs. Dodge said, vigorously, and with the repetition she began to be more than vigorous. Under the spell of that rancour which increases in people when they mull over their injuries, she began to be indignant. "For one thing, outside of the shamelessness of it, some of the rest of us could just possibly find a few enthusiastic things to say of our husbands if we didn't have some regard for not boring one another to death! I've got a fairly good husband of my own I'd like to mention once in a while, but——"

"But, of course, you'll never get the chance," Mrs. Cromwell interrupted. "Not if Amelia's in your neighbourhood when you attempt it."

"What I *can't* understand, though," Mrs. Dodge went on, "is her never having the slightest suspicion what a nuisance it is. I should think the man himself would stop her."

But Mrs. Cromwell laughed and shook her head. "In the first place, of course, he agrees with her. He thinks Amelia's just stating facts—facts that ought to be known. In the second, don't you suppose he understands how useful her press-agenting is to him?"

"But it isn't. It makes us all sick of him."

"Oh, it may have that effect on you and me, Lydia, but I really wonder——" Mrs. Cromwell paused, frowning seriously, then continued: "Of course, he'd never take such a view of it. He instinctively knows it's useful, but he'd never take the view of it that——"

"The view of it that what?" Mrs. Dodge inquired, as her friend paused again.

"Why, that it may be actually the principal reason for his success. When he left the firm that employed him as a draughtsman and started out for himself, with not a thing coming in for him to do, don't you remember that even then everybody had the impression, somehow, that he was a genius and going to do wonders when the chance came? How do you suppose that got to be the general impression except through Amelia's touting it about? And then, when he *did* put up a few little houses, don't you remember hearing it said that they represented the first real Architecture with a capital 'A' ever seen in the whole city? Now, almost nobody really *knows* anything about architecture, though we all *talk* about it as glibly as if we did, and pretty soon—don't you remember?—we were all raving over those little houses of Roderick Brooks Battle's. What do you suppose made us rave? We must have been wrong, because Amelia says now that Battle thinks those first houses of his were 'rather bad'—he's 'grown so tremendously in his art.' Well, since they were bad, what except Amelia made us think then that they were superb? And look at what's happened to Battle these last few years. In spite of Amelia's boring us to death about him, isn't it true that there's somehow a wide impression that he's a great man? Of course there is!"

"And yet," Mrs. Dodge interposed, "he's not done anything that proves it. Battle's a good architect, certainly, but there are others as good, and he's not a bit better as an architect than Mr. Cromwell is as a lawyer or than my husband is as a consulting engineer."

"Not a bit," Mrs. Cromwell echoed, carrying on the thought she had been following. "But Mr. Dodge and Mr. Cromwell haven't had anybody to go about, day after day for years, proclaiming them and building up a legend about them. Nobody has any idea that they're great men, poor things! Don't you see where that puts you and me, Lydia?"

"No, I don't."

"My dear!" Mrs. Cromwell exclaimed. "Why, even Battle himself didn't know that he was a great man until he married Amelia and *she* believed he was—and *told* him he was—and started her long career of going about making everybody else sort of believe it, too."

"I think it's simply her own form of egoism," said the emphatic Mrs. Dodge. "She'd have done exactly the same whoever she married."

"Precisely! It's Amelia's way of being in love—she's a born idolizer. But you didn't answer me when I asked you where that puts *us*."

"You and me?" Mrs. Dodge inquired, frowning.

"Don't you see, if she'd married my husband, for instance, instead of Battle, everybody'd be having the impression by this time that Mr. Cromwell is a great man? He'd have felt that way himself, too, and I'm afraid it would give him a great deal of pleasure. Haven't we failed as wives when we see what Amelia's done for *her* husband?"

"What an idea!" The two ladies had been walking slowly as they talked; —now they came to a halt at their parting place before Mrs. Cromwell's house, which was an important, even imposing, structure of the type called Georgian, and in handsome conventional solidity not unlike the lady who lived in it. Across the broad street was a newer house, one just finished, a pinkish stucco interpretation of Mediterranean gaiety, and so fresh of colour that it seemed rather a showpiece, not yet actually inhabited though glamoured with brocaded curtains and transplanted arbor vitæ into the theatrical semblance of a dwelling in use. Mrs. Dodge glanced across at it with an expression of disfavour. "I call the whole thing perfectly disgusting!" she said.

Mrs. Cromwell also looked at the new house; then she shook her head. "It's painful, rather," she said, and evidently referred to something more than the house itself.

"Outright disgusting!" her friend insisted. "I suppose he's there as much as ever?"

"Oh, yes. Rather more."

"Well, I'll say one thing," Mrs. Dodge declared; "Amelia Battle won't get any sympathy from me!"

"Sympathy? My dear, you don't suppose she dreams she needs *sympathy!* Doesn't she show the rest of us every day how she pities us because we're not married to Roderick Brooks Battle?"

"Yes, and that's what makes me so furious. But she *will* need sympathy,"

Mrs. Dodge persisted, with a dark glance at the new house across the street. "She will when she knows about that!"

"But maybe she'll never know."

"What!" Mrs. Dodge laughed scornfully. "My dear, when a woman builds a man into a god he's going to assume the privileges of a god."

"And behave like the devil?"

"Just that," Mrs. Dodge returned, grimly. "Especially when his idolater has burnt up her youth on his altar and her friends begin to notice she's getting a skimpy look. What chance has a skimpy-looking slave against a glittering widow rich enough to build a new house every time she wants to have tête-à-têtes with a godlike architect?"

"But she's only built one," Mrs. Cromwell cried, protesting.

"So far!" her pessimistic companion said; then laughed at her own extravagance, and became serious again. "I think Amelia ought to know."

"Oh, no!"

"Yes, she ought," Mrs. Dodge insisted. "In the first place, she ought to be saved from making herself so horribly ridiculous. Of course, she's always been ridiculous; but the way she raves about him when *he's* raving about another woman—why, it's *too* ridiculous! In the second place, if she knew something about the Mrs. Sylvester affair now it might help her to bear a terrific jolt later."

"What terrific jolt, Lydia?"

"If he leaves her," Mrs. Dodge said, gravely. "If Mrs. Sylvester decides to make him a permanent fixture. Men do these things nowadays, you know."

"Yes, I know they do." Mrs. Cromwell looked as serious as her friend did, though her seriousness was more sympathetically a troubled one than Mrs. Dodge's. "Poor Amelia! To wear her youth out making a man into such a brilliant figure that a woman of the Sylvester type might consider him worth while taking away from her——"

"*Look!*" Mrs. Dodge interrupted in a thrilled voice.

A balustraded stone terrace crossed the façade of the new house, and two people emerged from a green door and appeared upon the terrace. One was a man whose youthful figure made a pleasing accompaniment to a fine and scholarly head;—he produced, moreover, an impression of success and distinction obvious to the first glance of a stranger, though what was most of all obvious about him at the present moment was his devoted, even tender, attention to the woman at his side. She was a tall and graceful laughing creature, so sparklingly pretty as to approach the contours and colours of a Beauty. Her rippling hair glimmered with a Venetian ruddiness, and the blue of her twinkling eyes was so vivid that a little flash of it shot clear across the street and was perceptible to the two observant women as brightest azure.

Upon her lovely head she had a little sable hat, and, over a dress of which only a bit of gray silk could be glimpsed at throat and ankle, she wore a sable coat of the kind and dimensions staggering to moderate millionaires. She had the happy and triumphant look of a woman confident through experience that no slightest wish of hers would ever be denied by anybody, herself distinctly included; and, all in all, she was dazzling, spoiled, charming, and fearless.

Certainly she had no fear of the two observant women, neither of their opinion nor of what she might give them cause to tell;—that sparkle of azure she sent across the intervening street was so carelessly amused it was derisive, like the half nod to them with which she accompanied it. She and her companion walked closely together, absorbed in what they were saying, her hand upon his arm; and, when they came to the terrace steps, where a closed foreign car waited, with a handsome young chauffeur at the wheel and a twin of him at attention beside the door, she did a thing that Mrs. Dodge and Mrs. Cromwell took to be final and decisive.

Her companion had evidently offered some light pleasantry or witticism at which she took humorous offense, for she removed her white-gloved hand from his arm and struck him several times playfully upon the shoulder—but with the last blow allowed her hand to remain where it was; and, although she might have implied that it was to aid her movement into the car, the white fingers could still be seen remaining upon the shoulder of the man's brown overcoat as he, moving instantly after her, took his seat beside her in the gray velvet interior. Thus, what appeared to be a playful gesture protracted itself into a caress, and a caress of no great novelty to the participants.

At least, it was so interpreted across the street, where Mrs. Dodge gave utterance to a sound vocal but incoherent, and Mrs. Cromwell said "Oh, *my!*" in a husky whisper. The French car glided by them, passing them as they openly stared at it, or indeed glared at it, and a moment later it was far down the street, leaving them to turn their glares upon each other.

"That settles it," Mrs. Dodge gasped. "It ought to have been a gondola."

"A gondola?"

"A Doge's wife carrying on with a fool poet or something;—she always has that air to me. What a comedy!"

Mrs. Cromwell shook her head; her expression was of grief and shock. "It's tragedy, Lydia."

"Just as you choose to look at it. The practical point of view is that it's going to happen to Amelia, and pretty soon, too! Some day before long that man's going to walk in and tell her she's got to step aside and let him marry somebody else. Doesn't what we just saw prove it? That woman did it deliberately in our faces, and she knows we're friends of his wife's. She deliberately showed us she didn't care what we saw. And as for him——"

"He didn't see us, I think," Mrs. Cromwell murmured.

"*See* us? He wouldn't have seen Amelia herself if she'd been with us—and she might have been! That's why I say she ought to know."

"Oh, I don't think I'd like to——"

"*Somebody* ought to," Mrs. Dodge said, firmly. "Somebody ought to tell her, and right away, at that."

"Oh, but——"

"Oughtn't she to be given the chance to prepare herself for what's coming to her?" Mrs. Dodge asked, testily. "She's made that man think he's Napoleon, and so she's going to get what Napoleon's wife got. I think she ought to be warned at once, and a true friend would see to it."

In genuine distress, Mrs. Cromwell shrank from the idea. "Oh, but I could never——"

"Somebody's *got* to," Mrs. Dodge insisted, implacably. "If you won't, then somebody else."

"Oh, but you—you wouldn't take such a responsibility, would you? You—you *wouldn't*, would you, Lydia?"

The severe matron, Lydia Dodge, thus flutteringly questioned, looked more severe than ever. "I shouldn't care to take such a burden on my shoulders," she said. "Looking after my own burdens is quite enough for me, and it's time I was on my way to them." She moved in departure, but when she had gone a little way, spoke over her shoulder, "*Some*body's got to, though! Good-bye."

Mrs. Cromwell, murmuring a response, entered her own domain and walked slowly up the wide brick path; then halted, turned irresolutely, and glanced to where her friend marched northward upon the pavement. To Mrs. Cromwell the outlines of Mrs. Dodge, thus firmly moving on, expressed something formidable and imminent. "But, Lydia——" the hesitant lady said, impulsively, though she knew that Lydia was already too distant to hear her. Mrs. Cromwell took an uncertain step or two, as if to follow and remonstrate, but paused, turned again, and went slowly into her house.

A kind-hearted soul, and in a state of sympathetic distress for Amelia Battle, she was beset by compassion and perplexity during what remained of the afternoon; and her husband and daughters found her so preoccupied at the dinner table that they accused her of concealing a headache. But by this time what she concealed was an acute anxiety; she feared that Lydia's sense of duty might lead to action, and that the action might be precipitate and destructive. For Mrs. Cromwell knew well enough that Amelia's slavery was Amelia's paradise—the only paradise Amelia knew how to build for herself —and paradises are, of all structures, the most perilously fragile.

Mrs. Cromwell was the more fearful because, being a woman, she understood that more than a sense of duty would impel Lydia to action: Lydia herself might interpret her action as the prompting of duty, but the vital incentive was likely to be something much more human; for within the race is a profound willingness to see a proud head lowered, particularly if that head be one that has displayed its pride. Amelia had displayed hers too long and too gallingly for Lydia's patience;—Lydia had "really *meant* it," Mrs. Cromwell thought, recalling the fierceness of Mrs. Dodge's "I've had all I can stand of it!" that afternoon. A sense of duty with gall behind it is indeed to be feared; and the end of Mrs. Cromwell's anxieties was the conclusion that Amelia's paradise of slavery was more imminently threatened by the virtuous Lydia than by that gorgeous pagan, Mrs. Sylvester.

The troubled lady began to wish devoutly that the sight of Mrs. Sylvester caressing Mr. Battle had not shocked her into a fluttering and indecisive state of mind;—she should have discussed the event more calmly with Lydia; should have argued against anything precipitate;—and so, as soon as she could, after her preoccupied dinner, she went to the telephone and gave Mrs. Dodge's number.

Mr. and Mrs. Dodge were dining in town, she was informed; they were going to the theatre afterward and were not expected to return until midnight. This blank wall at once increased Mrs. Cromwell's inward disturbance, for she was a woman readily tortured by her imagination; and in her mind she began to design terrible pictures of what might now be happening in the house of the Battles. Until she went to the telephone she thought it unlikely that Lydia had acted with such promptness; but after receiving through the instrument the information that no information was to be had for the present, Mrs. Cromwell became certain that Mrs. Dodge had already destroyed Amelia's peace of mind.

She went away from the telephone, then came back to it, and again sat before the little table that bore it; but she did not at once put its miraculous powers into operation. Instead, she sat staring at it, afraid to employ it, while her imaginings became more piteous and more horrifying. Amelia had no talk except "Mr. Battle says"; she had no thought except "Mr. Battle thinks"; she had no life at all except as part of her husband's life; and if that were taken away from her, what was left? She had made no existence whatever of her own and for herself, and if brought to believe that she had lost him, she was annihilated.

If the great Battle merely died, Amelia could live on, as widows of the illustrious sometimes do, to be his monument continually reinscribed with mourning tributes; but if a Venetian beauty carried him off in a gondola, Amelia would be so extinct that the act of self-destruction might well be thought gratuitous;—and yet Mrs. Cromwell's imagination pictured Amelia in the grisly details of its commission by all the usual processes. She saw Amelia drown herself variously; saw her with a razor, with a pistol, with a rope, with poison, with a hat-pin.

Naturally, it became impossible to endure such pictures, and Mrs. Cromwell tremulously picked up the telephone, paused before releasing the curved nickel prong, but did release it, and when a woman's voice addressed her, "What number, please?" she returned the breathless inquiry: "Is that you, Amelia?" Then she apologized, pronounced a number, and was presently greeted by the response: "Mr. Roderick Battle's residence. Who is it, please?"

"Mrs. Cromwell. May I speak to Mrs. Battle?"

"I think so, ma'am."

In the interval of silence Mrs. Cromwell muttered, "I *think* so" to herself. The maid wasn't certain;—that was bad; for it might indicate a state of prostration.

"Yes?" said the little voice in the telephone. "Is it Mrs. Cromwell?"

Mrs. Cromwell with a great effort assumed her most smiling and reassuring expression. "Amelia? Is it you, Amelia?"

"Yes."

"I just wanted to tell you again what a lovely impression your essay made on me, dear. I've been thinking of it ever since, and I felt you might like to know it."

"Thank you, Mrs. Cromwell."

"Lydia Dodge and I kept on talking about it after you left us this afternoon," Mrs. Cromwell continued, beaming fondly upon the air above the telephone. "We both said we thought it was the best paper ever read at the club. I—I just wondered if—if Lydia called you up to tell you so, too. Did she?"

"No. No, she didn't call me up."

"Oh, didn't she? I just thought she might have because she was so enthusiastic."

"No. She didn't."

Mrs. Cromwell listened intently, seeking to detect emotion that might indicate Amelia's state of mind, but Amelia's voice revealed nothing whatever. It was one of those voices obscured and dwindled by the telephone into dry little metallic sounds; language was communicated, but nothing more, and a telegram from her would have conveyed as much personal revelation. "No, Mrs. Dodge didn't call me up," she said again.

Mrs. Cromwell offered some manifestations of mirth, though she intended them to express a tender cordiality rather than amusement; and the facial sweetness with which she was favouring the air before her became less strained; a strong sense of relief was easing her. "Well, I just thought Lydia *might*, you know," she said, continuing to ripple her gentle laughter into the mouthpiece. "She was so enthusiastic, I just thought——"

"No, she didn't call me up," the small voice in the telephone interrupted.

"Well, I'm gl——" But Mrs. Cromwell checked herself sharply, having begun too impulsively. "I hope I'm not keeping you from anything you were doing," she said hastily, to change the subject.

"No, I'm all alone. Mr. Battle is spending the evening with Mrs. Sylvester."

"What!" Mrs. Cromwell exclaimed, and her almost convivial expression disappeared instantly; her face became a sculpture of features only. "He is?"

"Yes. He's finishing the interior of her new house. With important clients like that he always interprets them into their houses you know. He makes a study of their personalities."

"I—see!" Mrs. Cromwell said. Then, recovering herself, she was able to nod pleasantly and beam again, though now her beaming was rigidly automatic. "Well, I mustn't keep you. I just wanted to tell you again how immensely we all admired your beautiful essay, and I thought possibly Lydia might have called you up to say so, too, because she fairly raved over it when we were——"

"No." The metallic small voice said; and it informed her for the fourth time: "She didn't call me up." Then it added: "She came here."

"No!" Mrs. Cromwell cried.

"Yes. She came here," the voice in the instrument repeated.

"She *did?*"

"Yes. Just before dinner. She came to see me."

"Oh, my!" Mrs. Cromwell murmured. "What did she say?"

"She was in great trouble about Mr. Dodge."

"What?"

"She was in a tragic state," the impersonal voice replied with perfect distinctness. "She was in a tragic state about her husband."

"About John *Dodge?*" Mrs. Cromwell cried.

"Yes. She was hurried and didn't have time to tell me any details, because they had a dinner engagement in town, and he kept telephoning her they'd be disgraced if she didn't come home and dress; but that's what she came to see me about. It seems he's been misbehaving himself over some fascinating and unscrupulous woman, and Mrs. Dodge thinks he probably intends to ask for a divorce and abandon her. She was in a most upset state over it, of course."

"*Amelia!*" Mrs. Cromwell shouted the name at the mouthpiece.

"Yes. Isn't it distressing?" was the response. "Of course, I won't mention it to anybody but you. I supposed you knew all about it since you're her most intimate friend."

Mrs. Cromwell made an effort to speak coherently. "Let me try to understand you," she said. "You say that Lydia Dodge came to you this afternoon——"

"It was really evening," the voice interrupted, in correction. "Almost seven. And their engagement was in town at half past. That's why he kept calling her up so excitedly."

"And she told you," Mrs. Cromwell continued, "Lydia Dodge told you that her husband, John Dodge, was philandering with——"

"There was no doubt about it whatever," the voice interrupted. "Some friends of hers had seen an actual caress exchanged between Mr. Dodge and the other woman."

"*What!*"

"Yes. That's what she told me."

"Wait!" Mrs. Cromwell begged. "Lydia Dodge told you that John Dodge——"

"Yes," the voice of Amelia Battle replied colourlessly in the telephone. "It seems too tragic, and it was such a shock to me—I never dreamed that people of forty or fifty had troubles like that—but it was what she came here to tell me. Of course, she didn't have time to tell me much, because she was so upset and Mr. Dodge was in such a hurry for her to come home. I never dreamed there was anything but peace and happiness between them, did you?"

"No, I didn't," gasped Mrs. Cromwell. "But Amelia——"

"That's all I know about it, I'm afraid."

"Amelia——"

"Probably she'll talk about it to you pretty soon," Amelia said, at the other end of the wire. "I'm surprised she didn't tell you before she did me; you really know her so much better than I do. I'm afraid I'll have to go now. One of Mr. Battle's assistants has just come in and I'm doing some work with him. It was lovely of you to call me up about the little essay, but, of course, that was *all* Mr. Battle. Good-night."

Mrs. Cromwell sat staring at the empty mechanism in her hand until it rattled irritably, warning her to replace it upon its prong.

She had a restless night, for she repeatedly woke up with a start, her eyes opening widely in the darkness of her bedroom; and each time this happened she made the same muffled and incomplete exclamation: "Well, of all——!" Her condition was still as exclamatory as it was anxiously expectant when, just after her nine-o'clock breakfast the next morning, she went to her Georgian drawing-room window and beheld the sterling figure of Mrs. Dodge in the act of hurrying from the sidewalk to the Georgian doorway. Mrs. Cromwell ran to admit her; brought her quickly into the drawing room. "Lydia!" she cried. "What on earth *happened?*" For, even if telephones had never been invented, the early caller's expression would have made it plain that there had been a happening.

"I'd have called you up last night," the perturbed Lydia began;—"but we didn't get back till one o'clock, and it was too late. In all my life I never had such an experience!"

"You don't mean at the theatre or——"

"No!" Mrs. Dodge returned, indignantly. "I mean with that woman!"

"With Amelia?"

"With Amelia Battle."

"But *tell* me," Mrs. Cromwell implored. "My dear, I've been in such a state of perplexity——"

"Perplexity!" her friend echoed scornfully, and demanded: "What sort of state do you think *I've* been in? My dear, I went to her."

"To Amelia?"

"To Amelia Battle," Mrs. Dodge said. "I went straight home after I left you yesterday; but I kept thinking about what we'd seen——"

"You mean——" Mrs. Cromwell paused, and glanced nervously through the glass of the broad-paned window beside which she and her guest had seated themselves. Her troubled eyes came to rest upon the pinkish Italian villa across the street. "You mean what we saw—over there?"

"I mean what was virtually an embrace between Roderick Brooks Battle and Mrs. Sylvester under our eyes," Mrs. Dodge said angrily. "And she looked us square in the face just before she did it! I also mean that both of them showed by their manner that such caresses were absolutely familiar and habitual—and that was all *I* needed to prove that the talk about them was only too well founded. So, when I'd thought it over and over—Oh, I didn't act in haste!—I decided it was somebody's absolute *duty* to prepare Amelia for what I plainly saw was coming to her. Did you ever see anything show more proprietorship than Mrs. Sylvester's fondling of that man's shoulder? So, as you had declared *you* wouldn't go, and although it was late, and Mr. Dodge and I had an important dinner engagement, I made up my mind it had to be done immediately and I went."

"But what did you *tell* her?" Mrs. Cromwell implored.

"Never," said Mrs. Dodge, "never in my life have I had such an experience! I tried to begin tactfully; I didn't want to give her a shock, and so I tried to begin and lead up to it; but it was difficult to begin at all, because I'd scarcely sat down before she told me my husband had got home and had telephoned to see if I'd reached her house, and he'd left word for me to come straight back home because he was afraid we'd be late for the dinner—and all the time I was trying to talk to her, her maid kept coming in to say he was calling up again, and then I'd have to go and *beseech* him to let me alone for a minute —but he wouldn't——"

Mrs. Cromwell was unable to wait in patience through these preliminaries. "Lydia! What did you *tell* her?"

"I'm trying to explain it as well as I can, please," her guest returned, irritably. "If I didn't explain how crazily my husband kept behaving you couldn't possibly understand. He'd got it into his head that we *had* to be at this dinner on time, because it was with some people who have large mining interests and——"

"Lydia, *what* did you——"

"I told you I tried to be tactful," said Mrs. Dodge. "I tried to lead up to it, and I'll tell you exactly what I said, though with that awful telephone interrupting every minute it was hard to say *anything* connectedly! First, I told her what a deep regard both of us had for her."

"Both of you? You mean you and your husband, Lydia?"

"No, you and me. It was necessary to mention you, of course, because of what we saw yesterday."

"Oh," said Mrs. Cromwell. "Well, go on."

"I told her," Mrs. Dodge continued, complying. "I said nobody could have her interests more at heart than you and I did, and that was why I had come. She thanked me, but I noticed a change in her manner right there. I thought she looked at me in a kind of bright-eyed way, as if she were on her guard and suspicious. I *thought* she looked like that, and now I'm *sure* she did. I said, 'Amelia, I want to put a little problem to you, just to see if you think I've done right in coming.' She said, 'Yes, Mrs. Dodge,' and asked me what the problem was."

"And what was it, Lydia?"

"My dear, will you let me tell you? I said in the kindest way, I said, 'Amelia, just for a moment let us suppose that my husband were not true to me; suppose he might even be planning to set me aside so that he could marry another woman; and suppose that two women friends of mine, who had my interests dearly at heart, had seen him with this other woman; and suppose her to be a fascinating woman, and that my friends saw with their own eyes that my husband felt her fascination so deeply that anybody could tell in an instant he was actually in love with her;—and, *more* than that,' I said, 'suppose that these friends of mine saw my husband actually exchanging a caress with this woman, and saw him go off driving with her, with her hand on his shoulder and he showing that he liked it there and was used to having it there;—Amelia,' I said, 'Amelia, what would you think about the question of duty for those two friends of mine who had seen such a thing? Amelia,' I said, 'wouldn't you think it was the true duty of one or the other of them to come and tell me and warn me and give me time to prepare myself?' That's what I said to her."

"And what did she——"

"She jumped right up and came and threw her arms around me," said Mrs. Dodge in a strained voice. "I never had such an experience in my life!"

"But what did she *say?*"

"She said, 'You poor *thing!*'" Mrs. Dodge explained irascibly. "She didn't 'say' it, either; she shouted it, and she kept on shouting it over and over. 'You poor *thing!*' And when she wasn't saying that, she was saying she'd never *dreamed* Mr. Dodge was that sort of a man, and she made such a commotion I was afraid the neighbours would hear her!"

"But why didn't you——"

"I *did!*" Mrs. Dodge returned passionately. "I told her a *hundred* times I didn't mean Mr. Dodge; but she never gave me a chance to finish a word I began; she just kept taking on about what a terrible thing it must be for me, and how dreadful it was to think of Mr. Dodge misbehaving like that —I tell you I never in my *life* had such an experience!"

"But why didn't you *make* her listen, at least long enough to——"

Mrs. Dodge's look was that of a person badgered to desperation. "I *couldn't!* Every time I opened my mouth she shouted louder than I did! She'd say, 'You poor thing!' again, or some more about Mr. Dodge, or she'd want to know if I didn't need ammonia or camphor, or she'd offer to make beef *tea* for me! And every minute my husband was making an idiot of himself ringing the Battles' telephone again. You don't seem to understand what sort of an experience it was at *all!* I tell you when I finally had to leave the house she was standing on their front steps shouting after me that she'd never tell anybody a thing about Mr. Dodge unless I wanted her to!"

"It's so queer!" Mrs. Cromwell said, bewildered more than ever. "If I'd been in your place I know I'd never have come away without making her understand I meant her husband, not mine!"

"'Making her understand!'" Mrs. Dodge repeated, mocking her friend's voice—so considerable was her bitterness. "You goose! You don't suppose she didn't understand *that*, do you?"

"You don't think——"

"Absolutely! She had been expecting it to happen."

"What to happen?"

"Somebody's coming to warn her about Mrs. Sylvester. She did the whole thing deliberately. Absolutely! She understood I was talking about Battle as well as you do now. Of course," said Mrs. Dodge, "of *course* she understood!"

Then both ladies seemed to ponder, and for a time uttered various sounds of marvelling; but suddenly Mrs. Cromwell, whose glance had wandered to the window, straightened herself to an attentive rigidity. Her guest's glance followed hers, and instantly became fixed; but neither lady spoke, for a sharply outlined coincidence was before them, casting a spell upon them and holding them fascinated.

Across the street a French car entered the driveway of the stucco house, and a Venetian Beauty descended, wrapped in ermine too glorious for the time and occasion. Out of the green door of the house eagerly came upon the balustraded terrace a dark man, poetic and scholarly in appearance, dressed scrupulously and with a gardenia, like a bridegroom's flower, in his coat. In his hand he held an architect's blue print; but for him and for the azure-eyed lady in ermine this blue print seemed not more important, nor less, than that book in which the two lovers of Rimini read no more one day. They glanced but absently at the blue print; then the man let it dangle from his hand while he looked into the lady's eyes and she into his; and they talked with ineffable gentleness together.

Here was an Italian episode most romantic in its elements: a Renaissance terrace for the trysting place of a Renaissance widow and a great man, two who met and made love under the spying eyes of female *sbirri* lurking in a window opposite; but it was Amelia Battle who made the romantic episode into a realistic coincidence. In a vehicle needful of cleansing and polish she appeared from down the long street, sitting in the attentive attitude necessary for the proper guidance of what bore her, and wearing (as Mrs. Cromwell hoarsely informed Mrs. Dodge) "her market clothes." That she was returning from a market there could be no doubt; Amelia had herself this touch of the Renaissance, but a Renaissance late, northern, and robust. Both of the rear windows of her diligent vehicle framed still-life studies to lure the brush of sixteenth- and seventeenth-century lowland painters: the green tops of sheaved celery nodded there; fat turnips reposed in baskets; purple ragged plumes of beets pressed softly against the glass; jugs that suggested buttermilk and cider, perhaps both, snugly neighboured the hearty vegetables, and made plain to all that the good wife in the forward seat had a providing heart for her man and her household.

The ladies in the Georgian window were truly among those who cared to look. "Oh, *my!*" Mrs. Cromwell whispered.

Amelia stopped her market machine and jumped out in her market clothes at the foot of the driveway, where stood Mrs. Sylvester's French car in the care of its two magnificent young men. There was an amiable briskness, cheerful and friendly, in the air with which Amelia trotted up the terrace steps and joined the romantic couple standing beside the balustrade. The three entered into converse.

Mrs. Cromwell and Mrs. Dodge became even more breathless; and then, with amazement, and perhaps a little natural disappointment, they saw that the conversation was not acrimonious—at least, not outwardly so. They marked that Amelia, smiling, took the lead in it, and that she at once set her hand upon her husband's arm—and in a manner of ownership so masterful and complete that the proprietorship assumed by Mrs. Sylvester in the same gesture, the preceding day, seemed in comparison the temporary claim of a mere borrower. And Mrs. Cromwell marked also a kind of feebleness in the attitude of the Venetian Beauty: Mrs. Sylvester was smiling politely, but there was a disturbed petulance in her smile. Suddenly Mrs. Cromwell perceived that beside Amelia, for all Amelia's skimpiness, Mrs. Sylvester looked ineffective. With that, glancing at the sturdy figure of Lydia Dodge, Mrs. Cromwell came to the conclusion that since Amelia had been too much for Lydia, Amelia would certainly be too much for Mrs. Sylvester.

"Look!" said Lydia.

Amelia and her husband were leaving the terrace together. Battle walked to the "sedan" with her and held the door open for her; she climbed to the driver's seat and seemed to wait, with assurance, for him to do more than hold the door. And at this moment the seriousness of his expression was so emphasized that it was easily visible to the Georgian window, though only his profile was given to its view as he looked back, over his shoulder, at the glazing smile of the lady upon the terrace. He seemed to waver, hesitating; and then, somewhat bleakly, he climbed into the "sedan" beside his wife.

"*Open it!*" Mrs. Dodge was struggling with a catch of the Georgian window.

"What for?"

"She's shouting again! I've *got* to hear her!" Mrs. Dodge panted; and the window yielded to her exertions.

Amelia's attitude showed that she was encouraging her machine to begin operations, while at the same time she was calling parting words to Mrs. Sylvester. "Good-bye!" Amelia shouted. "Mr. Battle says he's been *so* inspired by your sympathy in his work! Mr. Battle says that's *so* necessary to an architect! Mr. Battle says *no* artist can ever even *hope* to do anything great without it! Mr. Battle says——"

But here, under the urging of her foot, the engine burst into a shattering uproar: ague seized the car with a bitter grip; convulsive impulses of the apparatus to leap at random were succeeded by more decorous ideas, and then the "sedan" moved mildly forward; the vegetables nodded affably in the windows, and the Battles were borne from sight.

"I see," said Lydia Dodge, moving back to her chair. "I understand now."

"You understand what?" her hostess inquired, brusquely, as she closed the Georgian window.

"I understand what I just saw. I can't tell you exactly how or why, but it was plainly *there*—in Roderick Brooks Battle's look, in his slightest gesture. We were absolutely mistaken to think it possible. He'll never ask Amelia to step aside: he'll never leave her. And however much he philanders, *she'll* never leave *him*, either. She'll go straight on the way she's always gone. *He's* shown us that, and *she's* shown us that."

"Well, then," Mrs. Cromwell inquired; "why is it? You say you understand."

"It's because he knows that between his Venetian romance and his press agent he's got to take the press agent. He's had sense enough to see he mightn't be a great man at all without his press agent—and he'd rather keep on being a great man. And Amelia knows she's getting too skimpy-looking to get a chance to make a great man out of anybody *else*; so she wouldn't let me tell her about him, because she's going to stick to him!"

At this Mrs. Cromwell made gestures of negation and horror, though in the back of her mind, at that moment, she was recalling her yesterday's thought that Lydia's sense of duty was really Lydia's pique. "Lydia Dodge!" she cried, "I won't listen to you! Don't you know you're taking the lowest, unchristianest, vilest possible view of human nature?"

Mrs. Dodge looked guilty, but she decided to offer a plea in excuse. "Well, I suppose that may be true," she said. "But sometimes it does seem about the only way to understand people!"

Great Men's Sons

•

Mme. Bernhardt and M. Coquelin were playing "L'Aiglon." Toward the end of the second act people began to slide down in their seats, shift their elbows, or casually rub their eyes; by the close of the third, most of the taller gentlemen were sitting on the small of their backs with their knees as high as decorum permitted, and many were openly coughing; but when the fourth came to an end, active resistance ceased, hopelessness prevailed, the attitudes were those of the stricken field, and the over-crowded house was like a college chapel during an interminable compulsory lecture. Here and there—but most rarely—one saw an eager woman with bright eyes, head bent forward and body spellbound, still enchantedly following the course of the play. Between the acts the orchestra pattered ragtime and inanities from the new comic operas, while the audience in general took some heart. When the play was over, we were all enthusiastic; though our admiration, however vehement in the words employed to express it, was somewhat subdued as to the accompanying manner, which consisted, mainly, of sighs and resigned murmurs. In the lobby a thin old man with a grizzled chin-beard dropped his hand lightly on my shoulder, and greeted me in a tone of plaintive inquiry:

"Well, son?"

Turning, I recognized a patron of my early youth, in whose woodshed I had smoked my first cigar, an old friend whom I had not seen for years; and to find him there, with his long, dust-coloured coat, his black string tie and rusty hat, brushed on every side by opera cloaks and feathers, was a rich surprise, warming the cockles of my heart. His name is Tom Martin; he lives in a small country town, where he commands the trade in Dry Goods and Men's Clothing; his speech is pitched in a high key, is very slow, sometimes whines faintly; and he always calls me "Son."

"What in the world!" I exclaimed, as we shook hands.

"Well," he drawled, "I dunno why I shouldn't be as meetropolitan as anybody. I come over on the afternoon accommodation for the show. Let's you and me make a night of it. What say, son?"

"What did you think of the play?" I asked, as we turned up the street toward the club.

"I think they done it about as well as they could."

"That all?"

"Well," he rejoined with solemnity, "there was a heap *of* it, wasn't there!"

We talked of other things, then, until such time as we found ourselves seated by a small table at the club, old Tom somewhat uneasily regarding a twisted cigar he was smoking and plainly confounded by the "carbonated" syphon, for which, indeed, he had no use in the world. We had been joined by little Fiderson, the youngest member of the club, whose whole nervous person jerkily sparkled "L'Aiglon" enthusiasm.

"Such an evening!" he cried, in his little spiky voice. "Mr. Martin, it does one good to realize that our country towns are sending representatives to us when we have such things; that they wish to get in touch with what is greatest in Art. They should do it often. To think that a journey of only seventy miles brings into your life the magnificence of Rostand's point of view made living fire by the genius of a Bernhardt and a Coquelin!"

"Yes," said Mr. Martin, with a curious helplessness, after an ensuing pause, which I refused to break, "yes, sir, they seemed to be doing it about as well as they could."

Fiderson gasped slightly. "It was magnificent! Those two great artists! But over all the play—the play! Romance new-born; poesy marching with victorious banners; a great spirit breathing! Like 'Cyrano'—the birth-mark of immortality on this work!"

There was another pause, after which old Tom turned slowly to me, and said: "Homer Tibbs's opened up a cigar-stand at the deepo. Carries a line of candy, magazines, and fruit, too. Home's a hustler."

Fiderson passed his hand through his hair.

"That death scene!" he exlaimed at me, giving Martin up as a log accidentally rolled in from the woods. "I thought that after 'Wagram' I could feel nothing more; emotion was exhausted; but then came that magnificent death! It was tragedy made ecstatic; pathos made into music; the grandeur of a gentle spirit, conquered physically but morally unconquerable! Goethe's 'More Light' outshone!"

Old Tom's eyes followed the smoke of his perplexing cigar along its heavy strata in the still air of the room, as he inquired if I remembered Orlando T. Bickner's boy, Mel. I had never heard of him, and said so.

"No, I expect not," rejoined Martin. "Prob'ly you wouldn't; Bickner was governor along in *my* early days, and I reckon he ain't hardly more than jest a name to you two. But *we* kind of thought he was the biggest man this country had ever seen, or was goin' to see, and he *was* a big man. He made one president, and could have been it himself, instead, if he'd be'n willing to do a kind of underhand trick, but I expect without it he was about as big a man as anybody'd care to be; governor, senator, secretary of state—and just owned his party! And, my law!—the whole earth bowin' down to him; torchlight processions and sky-rockets when he come home in the night; bands and cannon if his train got in, daytime; home-folks so proud of him they couldn't see; everybody's hat off; and all the most important men in the country following at his heels—a country, too, that'd put up consider'ble of a comparison with everything Napoleon had when he'd licked 'em all, over there.

"Of course he had enemies, and, of course, year by year, they got to be more of 'em, and they finally downed him for good; and like other public men so fixed, he didn't live long after that. He had a son, Melville, mighty likable young fellow, studyin' law when his paw died. I was livin' in their town then, and I knowed Mel Bickner pretty well; he was consider'ble of a man.

"I don't know as I ever heard him speak of that's bein' the reason, but I expect it may've be'n partly in the hope of carryin' out some of his paw's notions, Mel tried hard to git into politics; but the old man's local enemies jumped on every move he made, and his friends wouldn't help any; you can't tell why, except that it generally *is* thataway. Folks always like to laugh at a great man's son and say *he* can't amount to anything. Of course that comes partly from fellows like that ornery little cuss we saw to-night, thinkin' they're a good deal because somebody else done something, and the somebody else happened to be their paw; and the women run after 'em, and they git low-down like he was, and so on."

"Mr. Martin," interrupted Fiderson, with indignation, "will you kindly inform me in what way 'L'Aiglon' was 'low-down'?"

"Well, sir, didn't that huntin'-lodge appointment kind of put you in mind of a camp-meetin' scandal?" returned old Tom quietly. "It did me."

"But—"

"Well, sir, I can't say as I understood the French of it, but I read the book in English before I come up, and it seemed to me he was pretty much of a low-down boy; yet I wanted to see how they'd make him out; hearin' it was thought, the country over, to be such a great *play*; though to tell the truth all I could tell about *that* was that every line seemed to end in 'awze'; and 't they all talked in rhyme, and it did strike me as kind of enervatin' to be expected to believe that people could keep it up that long; and that it wasn't only the boy that never quit on the subject of himself and his folks, but pretty near any of 'em, if he'd git the chanst, did the same thing, so't almost I sort of wondered if Rostand wasn't that kind."

"Go on with Melville Bickner," said I.

"What do you expect," retorted Mr. Martin with a vindictive gleam in his eye, "when you give a man one of these here spiral staircase cigars? Old Peter himself couldn't keep straight along one subject if he tackled a cigar like this. Well, sir, I always thought Mel had a mighty mean time of it. He had to take care of his mother and two sisters, his little brother and an aunt that lived with them; and there was mighty little to do it on; big men don't usually leave much but debts, and in this country, of course, a man can't eat and spend long on his paw's reputation, like that little Dook of Reishtod—"

"I beg to tell you, Mr. Martin—" Fiderson began hotly.

Martin waved his bony hand soothingly.

"Oh, I know; they was money in his mother's family, and they give him his vit'als and clothes, and plenty, too. *His* paw didn't leave much either—though he'd stole more than Boss Tweed. I suppose—and, just lookin' at things from the point of what they'd *earned*, his maw's folks had stole a good deal, too; or else you can say they were a kind of public charity; old Metternich, by what I can learn, bein' the only one in the whole possetucky of 'em that really *did* anything to deserve his salary—" Mr. Martin broke off suddenly, observing that I was about to speak, and continued:

"Mel didn't git much law practice, jest about enough to keep the house goin' and pay taxes. He kept workin' for the party jest the same and jest as cheerfully as if it didn't turn him down hard every time he tried to git anything for himself. They lived some ways out from town; and he sold the horses to keep the little brother in school, one winter, and used to walk in to his office and out again, twice a day, over the worst roads in the State, rain or shine, snow, sleet, or wind, without any overcoat; and he got kind of a skimpy, froze-up look to him that lasted clean through summer. He worked like a mule, that boy did, jest barely makin' ends meet. He had to quit runnin' with the girls and goin' to parties and everything like that; and I expect it may have been some hard to do; for if they ever *was* a boy loved to dance and be gay, and up to anything in the line of fun and junketin' round, it was Mel Bickner. He had a laugh I can hear yet—made you feel friendly to everybody you saw; feel like stoppin' the next man you met and shakin' hands and havin' a joke with him.

"Mel was engaged to Jane Grandis when Governor Bickner died. He had to go and tell her to take somebody else—it was the only thing to do. He couldn't give Jane anything but his poverty, and she wasn't used to it. They say she offered to come to him anyway, but he wouldn't hear of it, and no more would he let her wait for him; told her she mustn't grow into an old maid, lonely, and still waitin' for the lightning to strike him—that is, his luck to come; and actually advised her to take 'Gene Callender, who'd be'n pressin' pretty close to Mel for her before the engagement. The boy didn't talk to her this way with tears in his eyes and mourning and groaning. No, sir! It was done *cheerful*; and so much so that Jane never *was* quite sure afterwerds whether Mel wasn't kind of glad to git rid of her or not. Fact is, they say she quit speakin' to him. Mel *knowed*; a state of puzzlement or even a good *mad's* a mighty sight better than bein' all harrowed up and grief-stricken. And he never give her—nor any one else—a chanst to be sorry for him. His maw was the only one heard him walk the floor nights, and after he found out she could hear him he walked in his socks.

"Yes, sir! Meet that boy on the street, or go up in his office, you'd think that he was the gayest feller in town. I tell you there wasn't anything pathetic about Mel Bickner! He didn't believe in it. And at home he had a funny story every evening of the world, about something 'd happened during the day; and 'd whistle to the guitar, or git his maw into a game of cards with his aunt and the girls. La! that boy didn't believe in no house of mourning. He'd be up at four in the morning, hoein' up their old garden; raised garden-truck for their table, sparrowgrass and sweet corn—yes, and roses, too; always had the house full of roses in June-time; never *was* a house sweeter-smellin' to go into.

"Mel was what I call a useful citizen. As I said, I knowed him well. I don't recollect I ever heard him speak of himself, nor yet of his father but once—for *that*, I reckon, he jest couldn't; and for himself; I don't believe it ever occurred to him.

"And he was a *smart* boy. Now, you take it, all in all, a boy can't be as smart as Mel was, and work as hard as he did, and not *git* somewhere—in this State, anyway! And so, about the fifth year, things took a sudden change for him; his father's enemies and his own friends, both, had to jest about own they was beat. The crowd that had been running the conventions and keepin' their own men in all the offices, had got to be pretty unpopular, and they had the sense to see that they'd have to branch out and connect up with some mighty good men, jest to keep the party in power. Well, sir, Mel had got to be about the most popular and respected man in the county. Then one day I met him on the street; he was on his way to buy an overcoat, and he was lookin' skimpier and more froze-up and genialer than ever. It was March, and up to jest that time things had be'n hardest of all for Mel. I walked around to the store with him, and he was mighty happy; goin' to send his mother north in the summer, and the girls were goin' to have a party, and Bob, his little brother, could go to the best school in the country in the fall. Things had come his way at last, and that very morning the crowd had called him in and told him they were goin' to run him for county clerk.

"Well, sir, the next evening I heard Mel was sick. Seein' him only the day before on the street, out and well, I didn't think anything of it—thought prob'ly a cold or something like that; but in the morning I heard the doctor said he was likely to die. Of course I couldn't hardly believe it; thing like that never *does* seem possible, but they all said it was true, and there wasn't anybody on the street that day that didn't look blue or talked about anything else. Nobody seemed to know what was the matter with him exactly, and I reckon the doctor did jest the wrong thing for it. Near as I can make out, it was what they call appendicitis nowadays, and had come on him in the night.

"Along in the afternoon I went out there to see if there was anything I could do. You know what a house in that condition is like. Old Fes Bainbridge, who was some sort of a relation, and me sat on the stairs together outside Mel's room. We could hear his voice, clear and strong and hearty as ever. He was out of pain; and he had to die with the full flush of health and strength on him, and he knowed it. Not *wantin'* to go, through the waste and wear of a long sickness, but with all the ties of life clinchin' him here, and success jest comin'. We heard him speak of us, amongst others, old Fes and me; wanted 'em to be sure not fergit to tell me to remember to vote fer

Fillmore if the ground-hog saw his shadow election year, which was an old joke I always had with him. He was awful worried about his mother, though he tried not to show it, and when the minister wanted to pray fer him, we heard him say, 'No, sir, you pray fer my mamma!' That was the only thing that was different from his usual way of speakin'; he called his mother 'mamma,' and he wouldn't let 'em pray fer him neither; not once; all the time he could spare for their prayin' was put in fer her.

"He called in old Fes to tell him all about his life insurance. He'd carried a heavy load of it, and it was all paid up; and the sweat it must have took to do it you'd hardly like to think about. He give directions about everything as careful and painstaking as any day of his life. He asked to speak to Fes alone a minute, and later I helped Fes do what he told him. 'Cousin Fes,' he says, 'it's bad weather, but I expect mother'll want all the flowers taken out to the cemetery and you better let her have her way. But there wouldn't be any good of their stayin' there; snowed on, like as not. I wish you'd wait till after she's come away, and git a wagon and take 'em in to the hospital. You can fix up the anchors and so forth so they won't look like funeral flowers.'

"About an hour later his mother broke out with a scream, sobbin' and cryin', and he tried to quiet her by tellin' over one of their old-time family funny stories; it made her worse, so he quit. 'Oh, Mel,' she says, 'you'll be with your father—'

"I don't know as Mel had much of a belief in a hereafter; certainly he wasn't a great church-goer. 'Well,' he says, mighty slow, but hearty and smiling, too, 'if I see father, I—guess—I'll—be—pretty—well—fixed!' Then he jest lay still, tryin' to quiet her and pettin' her head. And so—that's the way he went."

Fiderson made one of his impatient little gestures, but Mr. Martin drowned his first words with a loud fit of coughing.

"Well, sir," he observed, "I read that 'Leglong' book down home; and I heard two or three countries, and especially ourn, had gone middling crazy over it; it seemed kind of funny that *we* should, too, so I thought I better come up and see it for myself, how it *was*, on the stage, where you could *look* at it; and—I expect they done it as well as they could. But when that little boy, that'd always had his board and clothes and education free, saw that he'd jest about talked himself to death, and called for the press notices about his christening to be read to him to soothe his last spasms—why, I wasn't overly put in mind of Melville Bickner."

Mr. Martin's train left for Plattsville at two in the morning. Little Fiderson and I escorted him to the station. As the old fellow waved us good-bye from within the gates, Fiderson turned and said:

"Just the type of sodden-headed old pioneer that you couldn't hope to make understand a beautiful thing like 'L'Aiglon' in a thousand years. I thought it better not to try, didn't you?"

Stella Crozier

Any middle-aged native of our overgrowing and smoky city can tell you the fairy story of George Crozier's fortune. Of course, in one sense it wouldn't be thought a fairy story, because it is true. What made it seem magical to us was that a fortune of such size could be acquired by one of ourselves.

We were used to reading of people in New York who were worth as much as George Crozier; but to have for a fellow townsman so overwhelming a millionaire—a man we every day saw familiarly upon our own streets—seemed incredible enough to be a little necromantic. Fairies or Fates appeared to have singled this one of us out, set him apart and gilded him with a glorious light; even Crozier's old cronies and neighbours couldn't help showing greater deference to him than they did to their more ordinarily successful friends; and as for the manner of the general townsmen with him, it was as close to an awed reverence as the self-respect of a free citizenry permits.

This magical gilding of Crozier emitted illuminations that glowed upon all his possessions; but the things most personal to him were those most magnetically aureate. His house, emanating gold dust in the afternoon sunshine, hushed the voices of people driving by, but long held their passing faces toward it. His car at the curbstone before the Crozier Building brought pedestrians to stop and gaze, though never to stand quite close to it. In the eyes of bank clerks who saw Crozier's hat upon a desk while he talked with the president, that hat was a thing vivid with significance; and among the commonalty even his Negro servants held a curious prestige because of their daily access to his person.

Most personal of all to him, and most warmly gilded by the illumination, was, of course, his only child, his daughter, Stella; for Crozier was a widower before the gilding began. Stella grew up with the growing illumination, and by the time she was of marriageable age, she was the very centre of it, as glowing as Crozier himself. Not only her young contemporaries were conscious of Stella's glow; her elders proved as eager. When she went to a reception or tea where older women were, they hurried to gather about her, chattering, seeming to be made merry in that gold light she shed; and the first to reach her, when she came in, was usually a bishop's wife.

For Stella was a philanthropist, though she didn't look like one. She was a small girl, with curled fair hair, a small white face and one of those small mouths that seem to have lately eaten too much candy and to suspect everyone of intending to offer it more. This pampered and disapproving look of hers wasn't temporary; it was her characteristic expression; so no one could believe that great riches made Stella Crozier bloomingly happy. She appeared to have no outright joys whatever, though she undoubtedly took a pale and withholding kind of pleasure in the jewels she bought, and she usually wore such massive and important ones that she could have looked in place only at a coronation. Yet even her great emeralds were tainted with discontent for her; she bargained sharply with her jewellers and always in the end was sure that they had overcharged her.

It was so with her philanthropies; she bargained about them, too, and was seldom satisfied that someone wasn't cheating her. In her benevolence she followed an unyielding principle—so she called it—and never gave anything without qualification and restriction. If the Mercy Hospital Board would raise thirty thousand dollars for the new ward, Stella would give fifteen thousand; but the fund must be called the Crozier Foundation, and the patients admitted should be strictly limited to sufferers from spinal disorders.

Moreover, Stella always had a cause or two of her own for which she was, in turn, soliciting money. Something would strike her imagination and she'd organize a fund for it and make us all feel that our public duty required us to subscribe to it. At the time she gave the fifteen thousand dollars to the Mercy Hospital she was interested in a ten-year-old girl with a pretty voice. Stella liked to hear the child sing and said that such a voice ought to be cultivated; so she went about with a subscription list, which she had headed with a promise of several hundred dollars in case the rest should be subscribed and thus collected the five thousand she thought necessary. The members of the Mercy Hospital Board all had to put their names down for Stella's Musical Education Fund before she subscribed to the new ward. She spent a large part of her time raising money for her causes; she hadn't much else to do, and no doubt she did a great deal of good.

But the truth is, she was what we called "close." She herself could easily have given the money she raised; and, as we say, she'd never have known the difference. When she was twenty her father had made a trust fund for her that gave her independent means greater than those of any other person in the city—except Crozier himself, of course—and even though she bought for herself everything that she could possibly imagine she wanted, she didn't spend a fifth of her income. This closeness of hers was a curious thing, though thoughtful old citizens sometimes accounted for it by the fact that her mother worried a great deal about Crozier's putting all his eggs in one basket, as he did when he acquired the basis of his later great fortune. That was the year Stella was born, and they said Mrs. Crozier died as much of worry over money as she did of Stella.

One peculiar symptom of Stella's closeness was talked about more critically than the others were. That is to say, it was talked about among the families intimate with the Croziers—for of course it is by our nearest friends that we are most talked about—and this was her treatment of her cousin, Lucy Pauls.

Lucy was the same age that Stella was, and smallish like Stella, but much prettier. Of course, Lucy's being the prettier wasn't noticed usually; and probably Stella herself never knew it, for she had Lucy with her a great deal of the time, not exactly as a companion but as a background assistant; Lucy was naturally quiet and seemed to make no effort to appear more than a kind of congenial attendant in waiting on her cousin. She was a cousin on Stella's mother's side, not really related to Crozier; and that was probably why he hadn't made any stable provision for her as he had for all his own relatives.

But we who knew the Croziers well often asked one another the question: Why didn't Stella herself make some such provision for her cousin? Lucy was an orphan; her father hadn't left her anything at all; and at twenty-five she found herself overlooked by the boys she'd grown up with. They were busy marrying other girls or laying siege to Stella; and for all the attention any of them paid to Lucy, she might as well have been furniture. Young men are likely to look upon background features as neuter, and being pretty and intelligent didn't help Lucy to appear anything but neuter as long as she was background. It seemed in a fair way to become a permanent position for her; but the trouble was that it didn't carry a salary with it. True, it sometimes brought her a dress or wrap that Stella had worn and Lucy could make over for herself; and Stella took her once or twice to New York or Hot Springs for a fortnight, and at Christmas gave her a string of crystal beads, or a small amethyst pin, or a prettily bound book, perhaps; but for the actual means to pay the weekly bills in the boarding house where she lived, Lucy had to turn elsewhere.

She had a fairly easy small position as a sort of librarian for the chamber of commerce, and it gave her time to study stenography and wait on Stella. Also, her stenography helped her to look after Stella's correspondence, which was large and called for the service of a professional secretary; but Stella wouldn't have one, because, she said, she didn't want to be burdened with a secretary. It was Mary Buell who explained what Stella really meant by this. Mary Buell lived next door to the great lawn-girt villa Crozier had built on the site of the old quiet house he had formerly lived in. Mary was thirty-four and charming; she hadn't married, and I have heard her called "a complete gossip," the word "complete" implying that she had no other occupation. Of course, her own definition of herself was different. She said she resembled that pleasant French Academician who at seventy regarded his curiosity about other people as a proper justification for still going on living. "Like him,

I'm really an interpreter," Mary explained. "Life needs a few of us to look on and reveal our neighbours to one another."

"What Stella Crozier means by the burden of having a secretary," Mary said to me one day—I am her cousin and often go to her for interpretations—"what Stella really means is that she doesn't see the use of burdening herself with paying a secretary when she can just as well get Lucy to do the work for nothing. Wouldn't you think she'd do something substantial for that girl? Wouldn't you think that if she couldn't be generous enough to set aside a thousandth part of her property to give Lucy a little independence, she'd at least pay her a salary for the work she gets out of her? Not Stella Crozier! Here's a burlesque situation for you: Lucy gives Stella hundreds of times more than what Stella gives Lucy, and it is Stella who is dependent on Lucy—she has Lucy do a great deal more for her than anyone suspects—and yet people generally believe that Stella does all the giving and that Lucy's a poor dependent on Stella's benevolence. This world is the most absurd place!"

"What is it that Stella has Lucy do that the rest of us don't suspect? You don't mean—well, underhanded, do you, Mary?"

She looked doubtful. "Not exactly—not in a feminine sense, at least. You might call it sly—no, secret. Secret from men, at least."

"But what is it?"

My cousin laughed wisely. "To understand that you'd have to understand Stella better than you do; you probably wouldn't believe me if I'd tell you."

"You might try. What is it I don't understand about Stella? I know she's close, of course——"

Mary Buell interrupted me; she uttered a little cry of triumph. "Ah! But you don't understand why she's close!"

"I suppose she was born so."

"That explains only that she's always been what she is now," Mary returned. "What you can't understand is that Stella Crozier has never in her life had to do anything she didn't want to, and that's one reason she's nothing in the world but a sample bit of human female nature in the raw. You can't understand it because you couldn't understand what such a bit of nature is. Only another female—and a very intelligent one—could understand the full meaning of that."

"All right," I said. "What is the unsuspected thing that Stella makes Lucy Pauls do?"

Mary looked at me whimsically; she evidently deliberated within her; then she became serious. "I wonder if a man could possibly see it," she said musingly. "If the thing were under your very eyes and you were looking straight at it, I wonder if you could see it."

"Give me a chance to look at it and I'll tell you whether or not I see it, Mary," I answered.

"I?" she said. "I have nothing to do with it. It's Stella and Lucy. As a matter of fact, they'll put it under your eyes this very evening. You're going there to dinner, aren't you?"

"Yes. Aren't you?"

"Of course," Mary said thoughtfully, then looked at me in a skeptical sharp way she had. "Have you ever taken the pains to read a dinner properly?"

"'Read'?" I inquired. "My impression is that dinners are usually——"

"Usually eaten?" she interrupted, with satire. "Cookery interests you to that extent? You go out to dinner for the purpose of taking nourishment simultaneously with other people, do you? Seems rather a trivial sort of imbecility to me. And as for making and listening to verbal noises as part of your duty during the process, you don't find babble very stimulating, do you? Some people say they go to dinners because it's a way of developing good talk, but for that I found long ago I'd do a great deal better at a lecture. At twenty I thought dinners were part of the settings of courtship; at twenty-five I thought they were a penalty for living as a social person; but at twenty-eight I discovered they were meant to be read, and after that discovery they became my favourite revel. I recommend the habit to you; it's as good as a play. In fact, that's what it actually is, often enough."

"But about the secret things you say Stella makes Lucy Pauls do for her——"

"Those secret things will be under your very eyes to-night, I told you," Mary interrupted. "If you have any talent at all as a dinner reader, you couldn't have a fairer opportunity to show it than this evening will offer you, and you'll discover for yourself what it is that Lucy does; you can bring me home afterward and I'll tell you whether you're right or not. The main thing for you to remember is that it's all very simple and in words of one syllable."

"You mean that Stella——" I began; but she cut me off.

"I mean you must do your own reading. If you read what I read, then it will be all right for us to talk about it; but if I should merely tell you what I read I'd be no better than the ordinary gossip literal-minded people sometimes say I am."

She frowned virtuously as she spoke, and although I urged her a little she remained firmly noncommittal. I had to find out what I could for myself at the Croziers' dinner. Mary had challenged me, so to say, and besides, I was sharply curious—a state of mind for which no one need apologize since Mary's discovery that curiosity as a justification for living has the sanction of that fine authority, the French Academy.

The dinner table was a roseate oval plateau within the setting of the long and lofty ivory-coloured Crozier dining room, where laughed down upon us the Boucher panels Crozier's architect had made him buy. It was one of those rooms that are decorative to the most commonplace occupants, for even these become glamoured by the noble background into the semblance of portraits finer than the sitters. The Crozier dining room, moreover, was peculiarly becoming to the pale but able-bodied Crozier himself—a personage not lacking in grizzled grandee distinction anywhere, and at the head of his own table as imposing as he was untalkative. For that matter, any table at which he sat would have seemed his own and his seat the head of it, though he said nothing, or, indeed, partly because he said nothing. He had that talent for saying nothing which sometimes makes impressive men prodigious. At his right sat the ostensible reason for the repast, Mrs. Strumer Greene, comely, blonde, statuesque in figure though not in manner, no resident of our city, but an old friend of Crozier's. Her husband had been his associate in commercial enterprises upon the seaboard; she had inherited an interest in these and twice before had travelled this far to confer with Crozier upon the business. Evidently, this time he had felt that she was recovered enough from her bereavement to be offered a dinner, and in plain truth she appeared more than convalescent.

At times she chattered gaily to her host, at other times was humorously confidential and whispered to him; she touched his arm affectionately and even patted his hand. I thought she affected playfully to coquet with him in so far as it is possible for anybody to pretend to coquet with a familiar old friend; and this comedy seemed to be her effort to do her share, as principal guest, in enlivening the table. Crozier in the same spirit appeared to look upon her kittenishness benignly; but it was plain that I should find no clue to Mary Buell's meaning here. If I was to read this dinner I must look elsewhere.

Naturally, the elsewhere to look was in the first place at Stella, and in the second, at Lucy. Stella sat languid behind a collection of her most staggering jewels at the other end of the table—it was impossible not to look at them before you looked at her. She seemed more than usually a little thing, unimportant herself, like the unnoted staff of a spectacular banner; the gems were fastened to her, it is true, but their bedazzlings appeared to be their own and disconnected from her. Moreover, the young man who sat beside her apparently shared this disconnection, although he, too, was supposedly hers, being, in fact, her betrothed.

This was young Garvey of the Garvey Refrigerator dynasty, a business mildly prosperous under his grandfather and affluent now, so that young Garvey appeared to be the nearest thing to an appropriate alliance for the Crozier heiress that our community afforded. He had been the great desirable for every girl's mother in the town, though, of course, none of them continued any hope after he began to look toward Stella Crozier. He was any mother's beau ideal for a daughter's husband, this well-favoured young man whose judgment and energy were already known to be respected by his father and uncles. Nothing praiseworthy appeared to lack in him; he was both a devoted figure in the life of his church and a manly one upon the polo field.

Stella had taken him rather in the manner of taking the best thing in sight as naturally one of her possessions, but to-night he appeared to be more an adjunct of Mary Buell's, for he talked continually with Mary and not at all with Stella. I concluded, however, that this might be partly because engaged persons often say little to each other when on display and partly because Stella had little to say to him. She was almost as silent as her father; but where his benignity encouraged Mrs. Greene's gaieties, Stella's languid distrustfulness of expression, habitual with her and not relaxed in favour of the genial occasion, encouraged nothing.

My reading made no progress with her, though I caught a glimpse of what seemed a kind of peevish urgency in her glances at Lucy, who was unaware, I thought, both of the glances and the urgency in them. Lucy appeared to be too busy, indeed, with the gentleman upon her left to have time for anything else. She sat directly across the table from me, and I was glad she did; for this was one of those surprising evenings that sometimes befall a pretty woman, apparently by chance, making her beautiful. There was a warmth upon Lucy Pauls that came near radiance, and whatever she had done to the pinkish brocaded gown she wore—without doubt a discarded one of Stella's —she had made it a rosy charm upon her. No one could have taken her for a poor relation or a background cousin; she was all alight and the air seemed bright about her.

The favoured gentleman next her, naturally beaming in the rays she shed upon him, was Atwill Daily. I knew him pretty well and marvelled that Lucy found him inspiring; he seemed to me a good enough old soul, as we say, but certainly no spark of white fire. He worked faithfully, took care of his mother and sister, with whom he lived, did welfare work two evenings every week, read musical reviews, never missed a concert, was amiable, hopeful, mildly handsome in a prematurely baldish way, and talked copiously about whatever had no importance.

Since with all his fluency he never said anything not already frequently said and Lucy was notoriously intelligent, I felt an increasing astonishment at her ardent attention to his discourse and at the elation she visibly derived from it. In the general fanfare their actual words were obscure to my ears, but no one could question that here was a couple for whom the occasion made a happy and congenial opportunity. Such was my conclusion—a tame one for a neophyte reader of dinners, and no clue to the secret doings of Lucy Pauls under the compulsion of her cousin. Certainly Stella was not making Lucy enjoy talking to Atwill Daily.

Mary had said the secret would be placed before my very eyes and had intimated that I must look, not for subtle undercurrents, but for something obvious and simple. What I saw, however, proved altogether too simple, being nothing at all. Nobody did anything significant; nothing happened. Of course, what I watched for most alertly was anything that Lucy might do upon a hint from Stella; but during the whole evening Lucy did only two things that any suggestion of Stella's might be thought to account for, and both of these things were so casual that it would have been absurd to see anything sly or hidden behind them.

The first happened when coffee was brought to the table. Crozier always had a separate service for himself—he relished an infamous kind of thick Turkish coffee, a strangling brown mush that nobody else could endure. It was made at the table for him, usually by Stella, in the silver machine that was placed before her to-night; but the guest of special honour intervened. "Do let me make it," Mrs. Strumer Greene begged. "I understand Turkish coffee and I'd dearly love to show your father my own pet little way of brewing it."

The instrument was sent to her and she had the attention of the table while she brightly operated. No timidity bothered her as she thus became the centre of the stage; on the contrary, the centre seemed to her taste, for she bloomed at once into the playful ingénue, and her demonstrations were those of the cozy housewife at work for the master. "You do it thus and so, you see," she said in this honeyed manner. "And now you take off the top of the silver furnace, you see, and shovel in all the coal—like this." So she humorously dramatized the powdered coffee and the compartment it was to occupy. "Then you pour in the water that's to keep the coal from catching fire, you see—and then you stir it and stir it with the beautiful silver coal shovel, you see—like this—and after that you close the furnace again. Then you listen and listen till you hear, oh, the loveliest bubbling sounds inside! And when you do, then you can give the sultan his coffee. No!" She made chastising gestures with a spoon, beating Crozier's sleeve with it—he had extended his hand toward the cup in waiting. "No! Be patient. The lovely bubbling sound hasn't come yet. Listen! Ah—now it has!"

She filled the cup; gave it to Crozier; he drank; and his daughter, after observing his face, said quietly, "Never mind, Papa." She nodded to Lucy. "Lucy, perhaps you'd better——"

Lucy sat near Crozier's end of the table and next but one to Mrs. Greene. Atwill Daily was the intervening guest, and, following the direction of a slight gesture from Stella, passed the coffee machine on its tray to his right-hand neighbour. "Just a minute, Cousin George," Lucy said quietly.

Mrs. Greene protested merrily, beating Crozier again with the spoon. "What! Make a face over the first perfect Turkish coffee he ever tasted? An Arab sheik taught me how to make it, in the Souks at Tunis. Don't dare tell me it isn't delicious! I'll show you!" And to prove her point the merry widow seized upon the cup she had prepared for Crozier and too quickly drank from it.

Too quickly, because the Souks at Tunis furnish no experience of the rancid mystery that Crozier preferred as coffee. Mrs. Greene's face at once showed a terrible perplexity. A problem engrossed her, and for a moment it was evident that she could not decide which of two courses, both heroic, to follow. She chose the one internally disastrous, swallowed what she had so lightly invited within the portal of her lips, and then, being a brave woman, commanded those well-pencilled lips to the semblance of a smile.

"There!" she said; but the word was something gasplike.

"Get her to drink some water," Lucy said in an undertone to Daily, who obeyed as far as he was able; but Mrs. Greene, with a little pettishness, pushed away the crystal goblet he offered her.

"Please, Mr. Daily!" she said. "I'm quite able to lift my own glass if I need it, thank you!" Then she recovered herself enough to beat Crozier again with the spoon. "How dare you laugh at me?"

That seemed to me a mistaken interpretation of Crozier's expression; he was waiting for his coffee in some impatience. "Well, Lucy," he said, "if you don't mind——"

"It's ready," she returned, filling a fresh cup, which Daily passed to him; and she added, "I think the lovely bubbling was all right this time."

A breath of laughter irresistibly forced itself into her voice as she spoke, and she had evidently intended an undertone in the ear of Atwill Daily, for she showed distress when a surreptitious giggle went about the table. "Oh, dear!" she said. "I didn't know everybody was listening. Mrs. Greene, I certainly didn't mean you to hear me. You must forgive me."

"Not at all." The maturer lady nodded graciously, and though her cheeks showed a suffusion of colour, it may have been due more to what she had swallowed than to Lucy's too impulsive mockery. "Not at all. I'm still convinced that my own little silvery bubbling was the loveliest; but I suppose I'll have to learn how to produce yours if I'm ever to be allowed to use this particular machine again." She turned to Crozier, chiding him amiably: "Treacherous person!"

He laughed, benign again; for he had his coffee. It pleased him, and ceased to be interesting to his guests, who were already prattling in couples. I tried to catch Mary Buell's eye, but couldn't, as she was on my side of the table and talking with young Garvey. What I meant my own eye to ask hers, severely, was the question: "Is this one of the secret things Stella has Lucy do for her? Making Crozier's coffee?" Naturally, Lucy knew how, since she was so much in attendance on her cousin as to be almost part of the household; and the reason Stella asked her to make it to-night was obvious: to avoid the little bother of having the machine brought back to the other end of the table. What could anyone read in so shapeless a triviality? I began to be annoyed with Mary Buell and her mysteries.

The other thing that Lucy did because Stella asked her came later in the evening. We had been forming haphazard groups in the drawing room, that vastness of rose brocade and dark marble; Stella went to the piano and strummed, talking meanwhile with Atwill Daily, to whom she offered the other half of the piano bench on which she sat. Her strumming evidently reminded our host of his chief guest's accomplishment; for he brought her to the piano and waved Stella and Daily away.

"Mrs. Strumer Greene has most kindly consented to sing for us," he said, and we were at once hushed in deference. Mrs. Greene was known to possess a voice; in fact, we had been told that she would have sought an operatic career except for her late husband's persistent opposition. How successful her search might have been I did not find myself competent to say; but I have heard opera singers whose singing gave me less pleasure than Mrs. Greene's.

She settled herself upon the piano bench, making an impressive figure there; for if she appeared a little opulent of contour, she had also the authority of what is massive. She performed a double feat, playing elaborate accompaniments excellently; and the company was brought to a state of almost genuine enthusiasm, in spite of the fact that her selections were somewhat above our heads. What she gave us was from the new school in music, her composers all being the most puzzling moderns, so that I am afraid we guessed badly at the meanings and found much of the sound mere commotion. On the other hand, we could not doubt that the singer herself knew distinctly what it was all about.

Her voice was large, sure, elastic, and, at some of the crises, even exhilarating. Thus, although most of us were in doubt about when she had finished one or two of the songs, and so misplaced some flutterings of applause—and although we found ourselves disturbed, too, for something creditable to say when she more definitely concluded—nevertheless, all in all, Mrs. Greene's entertainment had the quality and achieved the success proper to a guest of honour's display of talent in Crozier's architect's great drawing room. Mary Buell helped matters along, of course; she sat forward, glowing, made the necessary exclamations or audible breathings of wonder, and could be trusted to inquire, "What was that last marvellous thing?"

Mrs. Greene took her honours without either modesty or vainglory; she was pleased, flushed, bright eyed, a little triumphant, but showed no peacockery. "I'm delighted, of course, if your friends liked it, George," she said to Crozier when he came to thank her as she rose from the bench. Then she turned aside with him, her hand upon his arm.

Stella had moved to a corner of the room with Atwill Daily. Now she called to her cousin. "Lucy, sing something."

Lucy looked startled. "Good gracious! The only song I ever sing is a joke, and you know it well enough, Stella."

"I don't care. Sing it."

"But surely not just after——"

"Yes," Stella insisted. "Don't be so stubborn."

Mrs. Greene glanced amusedly over her shoulder to add a gracious entreaty. "Won't you sing, Miss Pauls? I didn't know that you——"

"I don't," Lucy said, blushing. "The only song I know is an old sentimental absurdity." Her voice broke in a choke of lamenting laughter. "It's 'In the Gloaming.'"

"Don't talk so much about it," Stella called. "Sit down and sing it."

Lucy still protested: "What a horrible idea, Stella! Do you want to make me ridiculous? Do you think Mrs. Greene could bear to hear it? Probably she was fond of 'In the Gloaming' when she was a little girl and it was new enough for her nurse to sing it to her, but since then——"

Mrs. Greene interrupted, laughing good-naturedly: "I'm afraid it wasn't quite new when I was a little girl; but I'm still capable of bearing it—I should say enjoying it even, if you'll sing it, Miss Pauls."

"Lucy!" Stella called sharply. "Quit making all that fuss and do as we say."

"Won't you?" Crozier said. "I still like it, Lucy."

With a gesture Lucy disclaimed responsibility for the consequences, went to the piano and obediently began to sing. She had a warm little quaint voice with a frequent plaintive quavering in it like the quavering in the voice of a nine-year-old child who sings on exhibition at a family reunion; and the stringy accompaniment she played—three or four makeshift chords for which her fingers always groped—was as piteous. After the sophisticated offerings of Mrs. Strumer Greene and the swinging easy power of Mrs. Greene's voice, poor Lucy's "In the Gloaming" was like something ignoble. What made it worse, Lucy herself seemed to suffer an accompanying discredit; she should not have consented to sing even under protest, for the protest did not save her from a personal diminution.

All that evening, until she sang, she had appeared charming; but an exhibition so naïve as this made her appear too naïve indeed. And when, having begun, she seemed unable to stop, and went on to a second stanza, we were troubled by our polite facial expressions; to keep them plausible we could only cease to look at her. For my part, the sympathetic shame human beings feel under such circumstances made me unable to look directly at any of my fellow listeners; but the sidelong vision we get with even an averted eye gave me an impression of their attitudes. In this manner I was aware that Stella was still peevish but less languid beside Atwill Daily; that Atwill, being musical—though inarticulately—was distressed; that Crozier had stretched himself in a chair and dreamily regarded the ceiling; that Mrs. Greene, seated close to him, struggled with a severely threatening mirth; and that Mary Buell was excited.

Mary's excitement was the plainest of all to me, and yet the most obscure. "Dramatizing cobwebs!" I thought, angry with her and guessing—accurately —that she would later say to me, "What! You didn't even understand why Stella made her sing?"

Poor Lucy! "In the Gloaming" broke up the evening early. As she finished we produced a semblance of applausive murmuring—though not all of us were that game. Atwill Daily did nothing but stare incredulously at this disgraced dinner partner of his with whom he had lately been so congenial at the table, and almost immediately there was a general rising for departure. Lucy understood too well what had given us one of those impulses that disperse companies of people to their homes, and she assured us she would not sing again; but though we feebly laughed with her, she knew that her apologetic humour at her own expense did not redeem her.

"I'd like to tell you what I think of your idea of dinner reading," I said to Mary Buell when we were outside. "I won't, though, because I always make it a point to be careful of your feelings."

In the moonlight she turned her head and stared at me. "Good heavens! You don't mean to tell me you didn't see it!"

"I saw whatever was to be seen. I don't see things with my imagination, you know, Mary."

"No. You don't even realize that's the only way anybody ever sees anything," she said scornfully. "Do you mean to tell me you don't even know why Lucy sang?"

"Certainly I do. I suppose she sang because Crozier asked her to."

"Because he did?" Mary cried.

"Yes. She didn't do it until he asked her. She was still refusing Stella until Crozier spoke too."

"You goose! Stella got her to do it, just as she got her to make that coffee."

"Suppose she did. There wasn't any surreptitious secret, sly——"

"Oh, you poor lamb!" Mary interrupted, loftily despairing of me. We had reached her door and said nothing further till we were in the library, where she went to the grate and poked a dead fire as she spoke. "I couldn't have believed it! That even a man could go through so exciting an evening and never see——"

" 'Exciting'?" I laughed.

"You saw a struggle between two women for a man. You saw another struggle between three women over another man. That's part of what you saw—and you saw nothing!"

Mary's brightened eyes were wide; her voice was vehement and her colour high; and then, as I sat down and again laughed at her, she became furious with me. "Imbecile male gigglings!" she cried. "That's all you know how to do when you've been looking on at the crises of five lives!"

"Five? Is that all?"

"Six lives," she said. "I forgot one. You saw the crises of six lives, not five."

"Couldn't you make it seven, Mary?"

"Stop laughing!" she commanded. "You don't realize what a lack it exposes. It isn't becoming."

I tried to obey. "Give me a chance. I've just been to an altogether commonplace dinner where nothing happened—unless you call poor Lucy's mistaken vocalizings something—and you tell me that I was a witness of convulsions in the lives of six people and that I saw two sets of women's struggles——"

"You did," Mary said. "I gave you the key to all of it this afternoon, when I told you to read in words of one syllable and that Stella Crozier was just raw human female nature."

"Indeed?" I said. "Was that why she asked Lucy to make Crozier's coffee?"

Mary dropped the poker noisily into an iron rack and swung round upon me. "I can't stand it," she said. "I'm going to make you see the whole thing." She sat down, facing me. "Look here! When you met Mrs. Strumer Greene, before we went into dinner, what did you think of her?"

"I thought she was a handsome, worldly person of fashion—what the Eighteenth Century called 'a fine woman.' "

"At the beginning of the evening you thought her a proper person to be the second Mrs. Crozier, for instance."

"Why not?" I said. "In case Crozier felt that way."

"Exactly. What's your idea of Mrs. Strumer Greene now, when the evening is over?"

"Now? Well, I have rather a different impression of her. I have an idea that at times she might be—well, almost silly."

"So! What did you think about Lucy Pauls when she was having such a good time with Atwill Daily at the table?"

"I thought she was a Lucy I'd never seen before—a radiant stranger among us."

"Exactly! And what do you think of Lucy now?"

"Poor girl!" I said. "She ought never to have done it. Those things are fatal; I'm afraid I'll never be able to look at her again without thinking of the exhibition she made of herself at the piano."

"Then the result of the evening," Mary said sharply, "is that two women are discredited with you?"

"In a way—yes."

"Who did the discrediting?"

"They did, themselves. Lucy certainly wasn't compelled to sing, but she did; and Mrs. Greene made herself look foolish over that coffee."

"She did nothing of the kind," my cousin said. "Stella did it by making Lucy Pauls do it. When Mrs. Greene was here three months ago George Crozier showed his interest in her; he went to see her when he was in New York a little later, and he talked about her when he came home; Stella decided the woman was getting dangerous."

"Why dangerous? Why shouldn't Crozier marry again if he wants to?"

"He should, but that little white-faced brute of his will never let him," Mary said; and her bitterness was that of a looker-on, not on her own account. She had no desire to marry Crozier, or anybody, as I well knew. "Stella Crozier is a little brute," she went on. "Stella is the heart's essence of green. Only over her dead body will one penny of her father's fortune ever get into anybody else's hands; and while she lives George Crozier's not going to be allowed to marry again. Every eligible widow and all the spinsters, except me, in this town have had hopes of him, I think; but Stella's beaten them all. She discredits them with him one after the other, and, when she can, she uses Lucy Pauls to do it. Lucy is just so much furniture around the house to Crozier; she's always been there and is a sort of Stella's shadow—a nothing. So, when even this nothing, this shadow, this chair of a girl, does something well that another woman does ill, the other woman looks like thirty cents. And Stella's never used Lucy better than she did to-night."

"I'm afraid you'll have to be more definite," I said. "How and when did Stella——"

"Didn't she fairly leap to it when poor Mrs. Greene gave her the chance she'd been waiting for and made a mess indeed of Crozier's coffee? Stella showed her father that even furniture could do it better! Lucy did her sly little part well, the poor slave! Did you miss her mockery of Mrs. Greene—about the 'lovely bubbling'?"

"You think Lucy said that deliberately instead of irresistibly?"

"She said it obediently," Mary answered. "She had to do it because she knew what Stella wanted, and Stella's got her into the habit of complete subjection. Well, what did Mrs. Greene do to meet that attack on her? The woman knew she'd been attacked by the two cousins; I suppose you admit that now, don't you?"

"I thought she took it very well."

"She did more than take it well. She put on her big show. You may not have realized how superbly she sang, but nobody needed to be musical to see how stunning she looked at the piano. She knew it, of course, just as well as she knew a man like Crozier might very well decide that such a fine duchessy showpiece was just the thing he needs to complete his big showy house and his showy, lonely life. Stella knocked the show to flinders. She made Lucy sing right afterward and utterly spoiled Mrs. Greene."

"What! It was Lucy who was spoiled."

"No," Mary said. "Not with everyone. You didn't look carefully at George Crozier. He was impressed by Mrs. Greene's music; but Stella knows that he's like most business men about such things. What he really likes is 'Sweet Genevieve,' and he hates anything he doesn't understand. Mrs. Greene had made him almost forget that, but Stella reminded him. 'In the Gloaming' in a little child's voice like Lucy's is his real style. Stella threw it at Mrs. Greene to-night and finished her. Poor Lucy! She was tragic."

"She was at least pitiful," I said.

"She was tragic, I tell you! What she did involved a sacrifice. I told you that you'd seen a struggle of three women over a man—we've just been talking about that—and another struggle of two women for another man. It's one of the most atrocious things I ever knew!"

She spoke with a wrathfulness that at least was proof of her conviction; and in a meek voice I asked her to be more explicit. "I'll try to see it if you show me."

"I think Stella Crozier ought to be hanged," she said. "Lucy and Atwill Daily sat directly across from you at the table. Of course, you're used to thinking of Lucy as background—out of it so far as men are concerned—but if you'd been a stranger and had watched that couple opposite you, you'd have thought they were lovers. Wouldn't you?"

"I suppose I should."

"You'd have been right," Mary said. "That's exactly what they were. Atwill Daily has been seeking Lucy out lately as much as he possibly could. It's been her first chance to marry and she wanted to take it, poor thing! Background furniture mightn't get another chance—ever. Stella ruined it all to-night. Atwill is musical—at least he thinks he is—and 'In the Gloaming' finished Lucy for him. Did you see his face when she was at the piano?"

But at this I protested. "You do run away with yourself! You've just been telling me that Stella made Lucy sing in order to upset Mrs. Greene with Crozier, and now you——"

"I do indeed," Mary insisted with emphasis. "That pallid little brute must have come as near happiness over it as she could ever come over anything. She did two vicious things at one stroke."

"But why should she spoil Lucy? She certainly isn't wantonly destructive."

"Listen," Mary said. "Stella's never cared anything at all about the man she's engaged to. She took him because almost all the other girls' mothers wanted him; but she's had that mild pleasure and it's palled. Suddenly it appears that her unregarded handmaiden has the most interesting-looking cavalier in town as a prospective suitor."

"Atwill Daily! Why, he isn't interesting looking. He isn't even——"

"Women think so," Mary said with superiority. "In regard to the appearance and charm of men, women have a different eye—you'll save time by thinking of that simply as an inexplicable fact. To us Atwill Daily is the most interesting-looking man in town; we don't care whether or not he's the handsomest. What's more, he doesn't shine in a general conversation, but when he becomes personal with a lady he's quite another matter; naturally, you couldn't know anything about that. Well, what does Stella Crozier do when she suddenly discovers that he's in a fair way to be owned by her slave? I can't tell you what she feels, because some recesses of that niggardly little bosom are secrets to me; but I can tell you what she's decided to do. She's decided to take away this one desirable possession of her cousin's and own it herself."

"But there's Garvey; Stella's engaged to him."

"He's the sixth I was talking about," Mary said. "I mean his was the sixth life that came to a crisis to-night. Stella will toss him back to the girls' mothers."

At this I ventured to laugh again. "And for Atwill Daily! You say she's avaricious, and yet she's going to throw away a pearl for a paste diamond. Garvey's worth a thousand of Atwill."

"But Atwill has one overwhelming value: He belongs to another girl. What's absolutely unbearable to Stella is that the other girl is the wearer of her old dresses."

"Perhaps I could come nearer understanding that than I could another mystery in your drama," I said. "Lucy certainly knew, herself, what an exhibition her singing made of her; she showed how miserably she knew it. Then why did she let Stella make her sing? Answer that and I'll believe your whole preposterous theory."

Mary frowned. "Lucy struggled, but she had to give in. It was in line with her job of discrediting Mrs. Greene, and she has the long habit of doing for Stella. She and Stella weren't eight years old when Stella began being the 'rich little girl' and Lucy the 'poor relation.' Stella's put that over her all her life and she put it over her to-night as she always has. Don't you see?"

"No." I got up to go. "Not if Lucy cares for Atwill Daily or wants to marry

him. Force of habit wouldn't make her lose the most important thing in her
life. Lucy's too intelligent. She may be Stella's slave, but she's never been
Stella's fool. And on that one point your whole structure collapses, Mary."

"It doesn't," she said sharply, rising to face me. "I'm speaking of facts;
I'm not building a structure. I'm absolutely right about the whole thing,
and you'll soon see that I am."

"How soon?"

"Within three months."

"Very well. If I don't see you proved right within three months——"

"Two!" she said. "Within two months even you will know that I speak the
truth of Stella Crozier. Two!"

We didn't have to wait that long. Mrs. Strumer Greene, vanishing upon
the third day after her performance at the Croziers', left behind her the
rumour of a Sicilian destination; and, that the dispersal of the dinner party
might not lack in spaciousness, another member of it was shortly afterward
announced as intended for the Argentine. Young Garvey was to establish a
Garvey Refrigerator branch in Buenos Aires; would remain there in charge
for a year—or more, if necessary—and he was to sail accompanied by experts
but not by a bride. Stella had balked at South America; her father needed
her and she could not leave him; she would faithfully await her lover's return.

Two weeks after he sailed she was quietly married to Atwill Daily in the
new cathedral, which must have looked grandly unpeopled, since the only
witnesses were a best friend of the groom, the bride's father, Lucy, and Mary
Buell. What Mary really represented as a witness was General Publicity, I
think, though ostensibly she was there in her character of next-door neighbour; and when I heard of the event I was ready to admit that she had
astonished me. I kept away from her, however, because when she is freshly in
triumph she is sometimes less charming than I like to find her, and a readiness to admit astonishment does not mean that one is ready to be trampled
upon.

When I did go again to her house it was on a wintry afternoon several
weeks later; and as I reached her gate I caught a glimpse of two of the six
figures involved in the undoubted crises of the dinner I had failed to read.

A heavy closed car rolled out of Crozier's driveway and turned townward
upon the thoroughfare. Travelling bags were visible in front with the chauffeur; Crozier, in brown tweeds, sat within the glossy inclosure, and beside
him, Lucy Pauls, apparently taking dictation from him as they drove.

"Taking more than dictation," I thought, deducing that Lucy was taking
her cousin's place in Stella's absence, on guard for Stella against all widows
and spinsters, and adding a little secretarial work to boot. Evidently the hon-
eymooners had not returned, or Stella would have been going to the station
with her father, as she always did.

Here I was wrong, for I found her in Mary Buell's living room. Moreover,
I found her there in tears, and almost, though not quite, upon Mary's shoul-

der. Even before I turned to retire I had time for some flickerings of thought upon this singularity. Mary so loved her own interpreting that she would have offered solace to Judas himself in order to get something out of him to interpret. This I knew; but why do troubled ladies so often bring their tragic confidences to recognized gossipers? Is it because that there they are surest of the tokens of sympathy, or is it because what they really want, sometimes, is to get their confidences made known?

The question was in my mind as I mumbled something and went back to the door I had too hastily entered; but Stella's sobbing became instantly turbulent. "No, no!" she said, and made detaining gestures. "You're a neighbour too. Don't go. I want you to know. Wait a minute."

She meant that she needed a minute to compose herself, and she spent it with a sodden little handkerchief upon her eyes and nose. Mary sat silent, looking at her, though she spared me a queer side glance that puzzled me. Mary was excited, of course; but what I could not understand was the lack of even a surreptitious triumph in this quick half look at me. There was bafflement in it, as if some of her reading had been mistaken or her predicting had gone wrong, perhaps. I hoped so.

Stella asked me, in a watery voice, "You haven't heard what's just happened?"

"No. I didn't even know you'd come home."

"Home!" she sobbed. "To think I'd ever come home like this! It isn't home any more. I thought it was—I always thought it was my home until I got Papa's telegram, yesterday morning." She turned to Mary. "I started back twenty minutes after I got the telegram. I left my trunks—everything. Atwill was out on the hotel golf links. Of course, he would be! I left a note and the telegram for him; I suppose he'll get here sometime to-day. He wouldn't have been any use though."

Thus she spoke of her bridegroom, and her tone was that of a woman married for years and long accustomed to her husband's inadequacy. "He wouldn't have known how to help me. It does seem too awful!"

"You shouldn't think of it like that," Mary said. "You're not looking at it sensibly, Stella."

"I'm not?" Stella cried, and she rose from her chair, clenching the small wet handkerchief tightly in both hands. "I've had my father taken away from me—I've had my very home taken away from me—I've had everything I care for in this disgusting world taken away from me—and you tell me it isn't awful! Maybe you'll tell me she isn't awful?"

"She isn't that," Mary said, and in her voice I caught a note of wondering admiration. "She's certainly shown herself much more adroit and calculating than anybody would have dreamed she was; and yet, after all, she only——"

"She only!" Stella echoed, in fiercest mockery. "Only! She's only plotted and planned and sneaked and tricked and played false to every human decency for years and years; that's all she's 'only' done! You were at that dinner we gave to Mrs. Greene—you both were—and you saw what the little snake

did. Poor Mrs. Greene! I'd a thousand times rather have had her. I'd give anything in the world if I could undo what was done that night. What that little snake did to Mrs. Greene is what she's done to other nice women that liked Papa before; and all the time I thought she was only helping me to guard him! And I—blind! Blind and trusting all this time! When I got his telegram I saw the whole hideous thing—I'd never dreamed it. I had hysterics four times on the train. Who wouldn't?"

"What for?" I said.

She almost screamed. "What for? I'll never speak to him again! I hate him! Oh, how I hate him for his spinelessness! I hate him for that almost as much as I hate her treachery. All the time she was just playing with me; she made me think she liked Atwill. She did! She pretended to be excited over him so that I'd never suspect what she was excited over. I absolutely believed she wanted Atwill. I told Papa she'd done that; I told him so before her the instant I got to the house this noon. Do you think it did any good? Did it stop him? He had the minister in the library and just took her in there with him and locked the door and left me outside. I've taken care of him and nursed him and watched over him every minute of my life since my mother died, and that's what he did to me! Locked me out of the room while he was doing that ghastly, treacherous, wicked thing!"

"What wicked thing?" I asked. "What is it your father's done, Stella?"

Her voice became an outright shriek. "What's he done? He's married Lucy Pauls! Two hours ago, while I beat and beat and beat on the door till my knuckles bled, and they wouldn't let me in!"

"What?"

"See!" she cried. "Look! Look what I did to stop them!"

Then, sobbing, she stretched forth her little hands and showed me the marks upon them. I beheld the signs that had been lacking to me before. In those tiny wounds upon helpless hands that had beaten a closed door I beheld and comprehended the whole life of Stella Crozier.

Penrod

CHAPTER I

A BOY AND HIS DOG

Penrod sat morosely upon the back fence and gazed with envy at Duke, his wistful dog.

A bitter soul dominated the various curved and angular surfaces known by a careless world as the face of Penrod Schofield. Except in solitude, that face was almost always cryptic and emotionless; for Penrod had come into his twelfth year wearing an expression carefully trained to be inscrutable. Since the world was sure to misunderstand everything, mere defensive instinct prompted him to give it as little as possible to lay hold upon. Nothing is more impenetrable than the face of a boy who has learned this, and Penrod's was habitually as fathomless as the depth of his hatred this morning for the literary activities of Mrs. Lora Rewbush—an almost universally respected fellow citizen, a lady of charitable and poetic inclinations, and one of his own mother's most intimate friends.

Mrs. Lora Rewbush had written something which she called "The Children's Pageant of the Table Round," and it was to be performed in public that very afternoon at the Women's Arts and Guild Hall for the benefit of the Coloured Infants' Betterment Society. And if any flavour of sweetness remained in the nature of Penrod Schofield after the dismal trials of the school-week just past, that problematic, infinitesimal remnant was made pungent acid by the imminence of his destiny to form a prominent feature of the spectacle, and to declaim the loathsome sentiments of a character named upon the programme the Child Sir Lancelot.

After each rehearsal he had plotted escape, and only ten days earlier there had been a glimmer of light: Mrs. Lora Rewbush caught a very bad cold, and it was hoped it might develop into pneumonia; but she recovered

so quickly that not even a rehearsal of the Children's Pageant was postponed. Darkness closed in. Penrod had rather vaguely debated plans for a self-mutilation such as would make his appearance as the Child Sir Lancelot inexpedient on public grounds; it was a heroic and attractive thought, but the results of some extremely sketchy preliminary experiments caused him to abandon it.

There was no escape; and at last his hour was hard upon him. Therefore he brooded on the fence and gazed with envy at his wistful Duke.

The dog's name was undescriptive of his person, which was obviously the result of a singular series of mésalliances. He wore a grizzled moustache and indefinite whiskers; he was small and shabby, and looked like an old postman. Penrod envied Duke because he was sure Duke would never be compelled to be a Child Sir Lancelot. He thought a dog free and unshackled to go or come as the wind listeth. Penrod forgot the life he led Duke.

There was a long soliloquy upon the fence, a plaintive monologue without words: the boy's thoughts were adjectives, but they were expressed by a running film of pictures in his mind's eye, morbidly prophetic of the hideosities before him. Finally he spoke aloud, with such spleen that Duke rose from his haunches and lifted one ear in keen anxiety.

> "'I hight Sir Lancelot du Lake, the Child,
> Gentul-hearted, meek, and mild.

What though I'm *but* a littul child,
Gentul-hearted, meek, and——'   *Oof!*"

All of this except "oof" was a quotation from the Child Sir Lancelot, as
conceived by Mrs. Lora Rewbush. Choking upon it, Penrod slid down from
the fence, and with slow and thoughtful steps entered a one-storied wing of
the stable, consisting of a single apartment, floored with cement and used as
a storeroom for broken bric-à-brac, old paint-buckets, decayed garden-hose,
worn-out carpets, dead furniture, and other condemned odds and ends not
yet considered hopeless enough to be given away.

In one corner stood a large box, a part of the building itself: it was eight
feet high and open at the top, and it had been constructed as a sawdust
magazine from which was drawn material for the horse's bed in a stall on
the other side of the partition. The big box, so high and towerlike, so commodious, so suggestive, had ceased to fulfil its legitimate function; though,
providentially, it had been at least half full of sawdust when the horse died.
Two years had gone by since that passing; an interregnum in transportation
during which Penrod's father was "thinking" (he explained sometimes) of an
automobile. Meanwhile, the gifted and generous sawdust-box had served brilliantly in war and peace: it was Penrod's stronghold.

There was a partially defaced sign upon the front wall of the box; the
donjon-keep had known mercantile impulses:

The O. K. RaBiT Co.
PENROD ScHoFiELD AND CO.
iNQuiRE FOR PRicEs

This was a venture of the preceding vacation, and had netted, at one
time, an accrued and owed profit of $1.38. Prospects had been brightest on
the very eve of cataclysm. The storeroom was locked and guarded, but twenty-
seven rabbits and Belgian hares, old and young, had perished here on a
single night—through no human agency, but in a foray of cats, the besiegers
treacherously tunnelling up through the sawdust from the small aperture
which opened into the stall beyond the partition. Commerce has its martyrs.

Penrod climbed upon a barrel, stood on tiptoe, grasped the rim of the
box; then, using a knot-hole as a stirrup, threw one leg over the top, drew himself up, and dropped within. Standing upon the packed sawdust, he was just
tall enough to see over the top.

Duke had not followed him into the storeroom, but remained near the
open doorway in a concave and pessimistic attitude. Penrod felt in a dark
corner of the box and laid hands upon a simple apparatus consisting of an
old bushel-basket with a few yards of clothes-line tied to each of its handles.
He passed the ends of the lines over a big spool, which revolved upon an
axle of wire suspended from a beam overhead, and, with the aid of this
improvised pulley, lowered the empty basket until it came to rest in an up-

right position upon the floor of the storeroom at the foot of the sawdust-box.

"Eleva-ter!" shouted Penrod. "Ting-ting!"

Duke, old and intelligently apprehensive, approached slowly, in a semi-circular manner, deprecatingly, but with courtesy. He pawed the basket deli-cately; then, as if that were all his master had expected of him, uttered one bright bark, sat down, and looked up triumphantly. His hypocrisy was shal-low: many a horrible quarter of an hour had taught him his duty in this matter.

"El-e-*vay*-ter!" shouted Penrod sternly. "You want me to come down there *to* you?"

Duke looked suddenly haggard. He pawed the basket feebly again and, upon another outburst from on high, prostrated himself flat. Again threat-ened, he gave a superb impersonation of a worm.

"You get in that el-e-VAY-ter!"

Reckless with despair, Duke jumped into the basket, landing in a dishev-elled posture, which he did not alter until he had been drawn up and poured out upon the floor of sawdust with the box. There, shuddering, he lay in doughnut shape and presently slumbered.

It was dark in the box, a condition that might have been remedied by sliding back a small wooden panel on runners, which would have let in am-ple light from the alley; but Penrod Schofield had more interesting means of illumination. He knelt, and from a former soap-box, in a corner, took a lantern without a chimney, and a large oil-can, the leak in the latter being so nearly imperceptible that its banishment from household use had seemed to Penrod as inexplicable as it was providential.

He shook the lantern near his ear: nothing splashed; there was no sound but a dry clinking. But there was plenty of kerosene in the can; and he filled the lantern, striking a match to illumine the operation. Then he lit the lan-tern and hung it upon a nail against the wall. The sawdust floor was slightly impregnated with oil, and the open flame quivered in suggestive proximity to the side of the box; however, some rather deep charrings of the plank against which the lantern hung offered evidence that the arrangement was by no means a new one, and indicated at least a possibility of no fatality occurring this time.

Next, Penrod turned up the surface of the sawdust in another corner of the floor, and drew forth a cigar-box in which were half a dozen cigarettes, made of hayseed and thick brown wrapping paper, a lead-pencil, an eraser, and a small note-book, the cover of which was labelled in his own hand-writing:

"English Grammar. Penrod Schofield. Room 6, Ward School Nomber Seventh."

The first page of this book was purely academic; but the study of English undefiled terminated with a slight jar at the top of the second: "Nor must an adverb be used to modif——"

Immediately followed:

"HARoLD RAMoREZ THE RoADAGENT
OR WiLD LiFE AMoNG THE
ROCKY MTS."

And the subsequent entries in the book appeared to have little concern with Room 6, Ward School Nomber Seventh.

CHAPTER II

ROMANCE

The author of "Harold Ramorez," etc., lit one of the hayseed cigarettes, seated himself comfortably, with his back against the wall and his right shoulder just under the lantern, elevated his knees to support the note-book, turned to a blank page, and wrote, slowly and earnestly:

"CHAPITER THE SIXTH"

He took a knife from his pocket, and, broodingly, his eyes upon the inward embryos of vision, sharpened his pencil. After that, he extended a foot and meditatively rubbed Duke's back with the side of his shoe. Creation, with Penrod, did not leap, full-armed, from the brain; but finally he began to produce. He wrote very slowly at first, and then with increasing rapidity; faster and faster, gathering momentum and growing more and more fevered as he sped, till at last the true fire came, without which no lamp of real literature may be made to burn.

Mr. Wilson reched for his gun but our hero had him covred and soon said Well I guess you don't come any of that on me my freind.

Well what makes you so sure about it sneered the other bitting his lip so savageley that the blood ran. You are nothing but a common Roadagent any way and I do not propose to be bafled by such, Ramorez laughed at this and kep Mr. Wilson covred by his ottomatick

Soon the two men were struggling together in the deathroes but soon Mr Wilson got him bound and gaged his mouth and went away for awhile leavin our hero, it was dark and he writhd at his bonds writhing on the floor wile the rats came out of their holes and bit him and vernim got all over him from the floor of that helish spot but soon he managed to push the gag out of his mouth with the end of his toungeu and got all his bonds off

Soon Mr Wilson came back to tant him with his helpless condition flowed by his gang of detectives and they said Oh look at Ramorez sneering at his plight and

tanted him with his helpless condition because Ramorez had put the bonds back
sos he would look the same but could throw them off him when he wanted to
Just look at him now sneered they. To hear him talk you would thought he was hot
stuff and they said Look at him now, him that was going to do so much, Oh I would
not like to be in his fix

Soon Harold got mad at this and jumped up with blasing eyes throwin off his bonds
like they were air Ha Ha sneered he I guess you better not talk so much next time.
Soon there flowed another awful struggle and siezin his ottomatick back from Mr
Wilson he shot two of the detectives through the heart Bing Bing went the ottomatick and two more went to meet their Maker only two detectives left now and so
he stabbed one and the scondrel went to meet his Maker for now our hero was
fighting for his very life. It was dark in there now for night had falen and a terrible
view met the eye Blood was just all over everything and the rats were eatin the
dead men.

Soon our hero manged to get his back to the wall for he was fighting for his very
life now and shot Mr Wilson through the abodmen Oh said Mr Wilson you——
—— —— (*The dashes are Penrod's.*)

Mr Wilson stagerd back vile oaths soilin his lips for he was in pain Why you——
——you sneered he I will get you yet—— ——you Harold Ramorez

The remainin scondrel had an ax which he came near our heros head with but
missed him and ramand stuck in the wall Our heros amunition was exhaused what
was he to do, the remanin scondrel would soon get his ax lose so our hero sprung
forward and bit him till his teeth met in the flech for now our hero was fighting for
his very life. At this the remanin scondrel also cursed and swore vile oaths. Oh
sneered he—— —— ——you Harold Ramorez what did you bite me for Yes sneered
Mr Wilson also and he has shot me in the abdomen too the——

Soon they were both cursin and reviln him together Why you—— —— —— ——
——sneered they what did you want to injure us for——you Harold Ramorez you
have not got any sence and you think you are so much but you are no better than
anybody else and you are a—— —— —— —— —— ——

Soon our hero could stand this no longer. If you could learn to act like gentlmen
said he I would not do any more to you now and your low vile exppresions have not
got any effect on me only to injure your own self when you go to meet your Maker
Oh I guess you have had enogh for one day and I think you have learned a lesson
and will not soon atemp to beard Harold Ramorez again so with a tantig laugh he
cooly lit a cigarrete and takin the keys of the cell from Mr Wilson poket went on out

Soon Mr Wilson and the wonded detective manged to bind up their wonds and
got up off the floor—— ——it I will have that dasstads life now sneered they if we
have to swing for it—— —— —— ——him he shall not eccape us again the low
down—— —— —— —— ——

Chapiter seventh

A mule train of heavily laden burros laden with gold from the mines was to be
seen wondering among the highest clifts and gorgs of the Rocky Mts and a tall man
with a long silken mustash and a cartigde belt could be heard cursin vile oaths because he well knew this was the lair of Harold Ramorez Why—— —— ——you
you—— —— —— ——mules you sneered he because the poor mules were not able
to go any quicker —— you I will show you Why —— —— —— —— —— —— it
sneered he his oaths growing viler and viler I will whip you—— —— —— —— ——
—— ——you sos you will not be able to walk for a week—— ——you you mean old
—— —— —— —— —— —— —— ——mules you

Scarcly had the vile words left his lips when——

"Penrod!"

It was his mother's voice, calling from the back porch.

Simultaneously, the noon whistles began to blow, far and near; and the romancer in the sawdust-box, summoned prosaically from steep mountain passes above the clouds, paused with stubby pencil halfway from lip to knee. His eyes were shining: there was a rapt sweetness in his gaze. As he wrote, his burden had grown lighter; thoughts of Mrs. Lora Rewbush had almost left him; and in particular as he recounted (even by the chaste dash) the annoyed expressions of Mr. Wilson, the wounded detective, and the silken moustached mule-driver, he had felt mysteriously relieved concerning the Child Sir Lancelot. Altogether he looked a better and a brighter boy.

"Pen-*rod!*"

The rapt look faded slowly. He sighed, but moved not.

"Penrod! We're having lunch early just on your account, so you'll have plenty of time to be dressed for the pageant. Hurry!"

There was silence in Penrod's aerie.

"*Pen*-rod!"

Mrs. Schofield's voice sounded nearer, indicating a threatened approach. Penrod bestirred himself: he blew out the lantern, and shouted plaintively:

"Well, ain't I coming fast's I can?"

"Do hurry," returned the voice, withdrawing; and the kitchen door could be heard to close.

Languidly, Penrod proceeded to set his house in order.

Replacing his manuscript and pencil in the cigar-box, he carefully buried the box in the sawdust, put the lantern and oil-can back in the soap-box, adjusted the elevator for the reception of Duke, and, in no uncertain tone, invited the devoted animal to enter.

Duke stretched himself amiably, affecting not to hear; and when this pretence became so obvious that even a dog could keep it up no longer, sat down in a corner, facing it, his back to his master, and his head perpendicular, nose upward, supported by the convergence of the two walls. This, from a dog, is the last word, the *comble* of the immutable. Penrod commanded, stormed, tried gentleness; persuaded with honeyed words and pictured rewards. Duke's eyes looked backward; otherwise he moved not. Time elapsed. Penrod stooped to flattery, finally to insincere caresses; then, losing patience spouted sudden threats. Duke remained immovable, frozen fast to his great gesture of implacable despair.

A footstep sounded on the threshold of the storeroom.

"Penrod, come down from that box this instant!"

"Ma'am?"

"Are you up in that sawdust-box again?" As Mrs. Schofield had just heard her son's voice issue from the box, and also, as she knew he was there anyhow, her question must have been put for oratorical purposes only. "Because if you are," she continued promptly, "I'm going to ask your papa not to let you play there any——"

Penrod's forehead, his eyes, the tops of his ears, and most of his hair, became visible to her at the top of the box. "I ain't 'playing!'" he said indignantly.

"Well, what *are* you doing?"

"Just coming down," he replied, in a grieved but patient tone.

"Then why don't you *come?*"

"I got Duke here. I got to get him *down,* haven't I? You don't suppose I want to leave a poor dog in here to starve, do you?"

"Well, hand him down over the side to me. Let me——"

"I'll get him down all right," said Penrod. "I got him up here, and I guess I can get him down!"

"Well then, *do* it!"

"I will if you'll let me alone. If you'll go on back to the house I promise to be there inside of two minutes. Honest!"

He put extreme urgency into this, and his mother turned toward the house. "If you're not there in two minutes——"

"I will be!"

After her departure, Penrod expended some finalities of eloquence upon Duke, then disgustedly gathered him up in his arms, dumped him into the basket and, shouting sternly, "All in for the ground floor—step back there, madam—all ready, Jim!" lowered dog and basket to the floor of the store-room. Duke sprang out in tumultuous relief, and bestowed frantic affection upon his master as the latter slid down from the box.

Penrod dusted himself sketchily, experiencing a sense of satisfaction, dulled by the overhanging afternoon, perhaps, but perceptible: he had the feeling of one who has been true to a cause. The operation of the elevator was unsinful and, save for the shock to Duke's nervous system, it was harmless; but Penrod could not possibly have brought himself to exhibit it in the presence of his mother or any other grown person in the world. The reasons for secrecy were undefined; at least, Penrod did not define them.

CHAPTER III

THE COSTUME

After lunch his mother and his sister Margaret, a pretty girl of nineteen, dressed him for the sacrifice. They stood him near his mother's bedroom window and did what they would to him.

During the earlier anguishes of the process he was mute, exceeding the pathos of the stricken calf in the shambles; but a student of eyes might have perceived in his soul the premonitory symptoms of a sinister uprising. At a rehearsal (in citizens' clothes) attended by mothers and grown-up sisters, Mrs. Lora Rewbush had announced that she wished the costuming to be "as medieval and artistic as possible." Otherwise, and as to details, she said, she would leave the costumes entirely to the good taste of the children's parents. Mrs. Schofield and Margaret were no archæologists, but they knew that their taste was as good as that of other mothers and sisters concerned; so with perfect confidence they had planned and executed a costume for Penrod; and the only misgiving they felt was connected with the tractability of the Child Sir Lancelot himself.

Stripped to his underwear, he had been made to wash himself vehemently; then they began by shrouding his legs in a pair of silk stockings, once blue but now mostly whitish. Upon Penrod they visibly surpassed mere ampleness; but they were long, and it required only a rather loose imagination to assume that they were tights.

The upper part of his body was next concealed from view by a garment so peculiar that its description becomes difficult. In 1886, Mrs. Schofield, then unmarried, had worn at her "coming-out party" a dress of vivid salmon silk which had been remodelled after her marriage to accord with various epochs of fashion until a final, unskilful campaign at a dye-house had left it in a condition certain to attract much attention to the wearer. Mrs. Schofield had considered giving it to Della, the cook; but had decided not to do so, because you never could tell how Della was going to take things, and cooks were scarce.

It may have been the word "medieval" (in Mrs. Lora Rewbush's rich phrase) which had inspired the idea for a last conspicuous usefulness; at all events, the bodice of that once salmon dress, somewhat modified and moderated, now took a position, for its farewell appearance in society, upon the back, breast, and arms of the Child Sir Lancelot.

The area thus costumed ceased at the waist, leaving a Jaeger-like and unmedieval gap thence to the tops of the stockings. The inventive genius of woman triumphantly bridged it, but in a manner which imposes upon history almost insuperable delicacies of narration. Penrod's father was an old-fashioned man: the twentieth century had failed to shake his faith in red flannel for cold weather; and it was while Mrs. Schofield was putting away her husband's winter underwear that she perceived how hopelessly one of the elder specimens had dwindled; and simultaneously she received the inspiration which resulted in a pair of trunks for the Child Sir Lancelot, and added an earnest bit of colour, as well as a genuine touch of the Middle Ages, to his costume. Reversed, fore to aft, with the greater part of the legs cut off, and strips of silver braid covering the seams, this garment, she felt, was not traceable to its original source.

When it had been placed upon Penrod, the stockings were attached to it by a system of safety-pins, not very perceptible at a distance. Next, after being severely warned against stooping, Penrod got his feet into the slippers he wore to dancing-school—"patent-leather pumps" now decorated with large pink rosettes.

"If I can't stoop," he began, smoulderingly, "I'd like to know how'm I goin' to kneel in the pag——"

"You must *manage!*" This, uttered through pins, was evidently thought to be sufficient.

They fastened some ruching about his slender neck, pinned ribbons at random all over him, and then Margaret thickly powdered his hair.

"Oh, yes, that's all right," she said, replying to a question put by her mother. "They always powdered their hair in Colonial times."

"It doesn't seem right to me—exactly," objected Mrs. Schofield, gently. "Sir Lancelot must have been ever so long before Colonial times."

"That doesn't matter," Margaret reassured her. "Nobody'll know the difference—Mrs. Lora Rewbush least of all. I don't think she knows a thing about it, though, of course, she does write splendidly and the words of the pageant are just beautiful. Stand still, Penrod!" (The author of "Harold Ramorez" had moved convulsively.) "Besides, powdered hair's always becoming. Look at him. You'd hardly know it was Penrod!"

The pride and admiration with which she pronounced this undeniable truth might have been thought tactless, but Penrod, not analytical, found his spirits somewhat elevated. No mirror was in his range of vision and, though he had submitted to cursory measurements of his person a week earlier, he had no previous acquaintance with the costume. He began to form a not unpleasing mental picture of his appearance, something somewhere between the portraits of George Washington and a vivid memory of Miss Julia Marlowe at a matinée of "Twelfth Night."

He was additionally cheered by a sword which had been borrowed from a neighbour, who was a Knight of Pythias. Finally there was a mantle, an old golf cape of Margaret's. Fluffy polka-dots of white cotton had been sewed to it generously; also it was ornamented with a large cross of red flannel, suggested by the picture of a Crusader in a newspaper advertisement. The mantle was fastened to Penrod's shoulder (that is, to the shoulder of Mrs. Schofield's ex-bodice) by means of large safety-pins, and arranged to hang down behind him, touching his heels, but obscuring nowise the glory of his façade. Then, at last, he was allowed to step before a mirror.

It was a full-length glass, and the worst immediately happened. It might have been a little less violent, perhaps, if Penrod's expectations had not been so richly and poetically idealized; but as things were, the revolt was volcanic. Victor Hugo's account of the fight with the devil-fish, in "Toilers of the Sea," encourages a belief that, had Hugo lived and increased in power, he might have been equal to a proper recital of the half hour which followed Penrod's first sight of himself as the Child Sir Lancelot. But Mr. Wilson himself, dastard but eloquent foe of Harold Ramorez, could not have expressed, with all the vile dashes at his command, the sentiments which animated Penrod's bosom when the instantaneous and unalterable conviction descended upon him that he was intended by his loved ones to make a public spectacle of himself in his sister's stockings and part of an old dress of his mother's.

To him these familiar things were not disguised at all; there seemed no possibility that the whole world would not know them at a glance. The stockings were worse than the bodice. He had been assured that these could not be recognized, but, seeing them in the mirror, he was sure that no human eye could fail at first glance to detect the difference between himself and the former purposes of these stockings. Fold, wrinkle, and void shrieked their history with a hundred tongues, invoking earthquake, eclipse, and blue ruin. The frantic youth's final submission was obtained only after a painful telephonic conversation between himself and his father, the latter having been called up and upon, by the exhausted Mrs. Schofield, to subjugate his offspring by wire.

The two ladies made all possible haste, after this, to deliver Penrod into the hands of Mrs. Lora Rewbush; nevertheless, they found opportunity to exchange earnest congratulations upon his not having recognized the humble but serviceable paternal garment now brilliant about the Lancelotish middle. Altogether, they felt that the costume was a success. Penrod looked like nothing ever remotely imagined by Sir Thomas Malory or Alfred Tennyson; —for that matter, he looked like nothing ever before seen on earth; but as Mrs. Schofield and Margaret took their places in the audience at the Women's Arts and Guild Hall, the anxiety they felt concerning Penrod's elocutionary and gesticular powers, so soon to be put to public test, was pleasantly tempered by their satisfaction that, owing to their efforts, his outward appearance would be a credit to the family.

CHAPTER IV

DESPERATION

The Child Sir Lancelot found himself in a large anteroom behind the stage —a room crowded with excited children, all about equally medieval and artistic. Penrod was less conspicuous than he thought himself, but he was so preoccupied with his own shame, steeling his nerves to meet the first inevitable taunting reference to his sister's stockings, that he failed to perceive there were others present in much of his own unmanned condition. Retiring to a corner, immediately upon his entrance, he managed to unfasten the mantle at the shoulders, and, drawing it round him, pinned it again at his throat so that it concealed the rest of his costume. This permitted a temporary relief, but increased his horror of the moment when, in pursuance of the action of the "pageant," the sheltering garment must be cast aside.

Some of the other child knights were also keeping their mantles close about them. A few of the envied opulent swung brilliant fabrics from their shoulders airily, showing off hired splendours from a professional costumer's stock, while one or two were insulting examples of parental indulgence, particularly little Maurice Levy, the Child Sir Galahad. This shrinking person went clamorously about, making it known everywhere that the best tailor in town had been dazzled by a great sum into constructing his costume. It consisted of blue velvet knickerbockers, a white satin waistcoat, and a beautifully cut little swallow-tailed coat with pearl buttons. The medieval and artistic triumph was completed by a mantle of yellow velvet, and little white boots, sporting gold tassels.

All this radiance paused in a brilliant career and addressed the Child Sir Lancelot, gathering an immediately formed semicircular audience of little girls. Woman was ever the trailer of magnificence.

"What *you* got on?" inquired Mr. Levy, after dispensing information. "What you got on under that ole golf cape?"

Penrod looked upon him coldly. At other times his questioner would have approached him with deference, even with apprehension. But to-day the Child Sir Galahad was somewhat intoxicated with the power of his own beauty.

"What *you* got on?" he repeated.

"Oh, nothin'," said Penrod, with an indifference assumed at great cost to his nervous system.

The elate Maurice was inspired to set up as a wit. "Then you're nakid!" he shouted exultantly. "Penrod Schofield says he hasn't got nothin' on under that ole golf cape! He's nakid! He's nakid."

The indelicate little girls giggled delightedly, and a javelin pierced the inwards of Penrod when he saw that the Child Elaine, amber-curled and beautiful Marjorie Jones, lifted golden laughter to the horrid jest.

Other boys and girls came flocking to the uproar. "He's nakid, he's nakid!" shrieked the Child Sir Galahad. "Penrod Schofield's nakid! He's *na-a-a-kid!*"

"Hush, hush!" said Mrs. Lora Rewbush, pushing her way into the group. "Remember, we are all little knights and ladies to-day. Little knights and ladies of the Table Round would not make so much noise. Now children, we must begin to take our places on the stage. Is everybody here?"

Penrod made his escape under cover of this diversion: he slid behind Mrs. Lora Rewbush, and being near a door, opened it unnoticed and went out quickly, closing it behind him. He found himself in a narrow and vacant hallway which led to a door marked "Janitor's Room."

Burning with outrage, heart-sick at the sweet, cold-blooded laughter of Marjorie Jones, Penrod rested his elbows upon a window-sill and speculated upon the effects of a leap from the second story. One of the reasons he gave it up was his desire to live on Maurice Levy's account: already he was forming educational plans for the Child Sir Galahad.

A stout man in blue overalls passed through the hallway muttering to himself petulantly. "I reckon they'll find that hall hot enough *now!*" he said, conveying to Penrod an impression that some too feminine women had sent him upon an unreasonable errand to the furnace. He went into the Janitor's Room and, emerging a moment later, minus the overalls, passed Penrod again with a bass rumble—"Dern 'em!" it seemed he said—and made a gloomy exit by the door at the upper end of the hallway.

The conglomerate and delicate rustle of a large, mannerly audience was heard as the janitor opened and closed the door; and stage-fright seized the boy. The orchestra began an overture, and, at that, Penrod, trembling violently, tiptoed down the hall into the Janitor's Room. It was a cul-de-sac: There was no outlet save by the way he had come.

Despairingly he doffed his mantle and looked down upon himself for a last sickening assurance that the stockings were as obviously and disgracefully Margaret's as they had seemed in the mirror at home. For a moment he was encouraged: perhaps he was no worse than some of the other boys. Then he noticed that a safety-pin had opened; one of those connecting the stockings with his trunks. He sat down to fasten it and his eye fell for the first time with particular attention upon the trunks. Until this instant he had been preoccupied with the stockings.

Slowly recognition dawned in his eyes.

The Schofields' house stood on a corner at the intersection of two main-travelled streets; the fence was low, and the publicity obtained by the washable portion of the family apparel, on Mondays, had often been painful to Penrod; for boys have a peculiar sensitiveness in these matters. A plain, matter-of-fact washerwoman, employed by Mrs. Schofield, never left anything to the imagination of the passer-by; and of all her calm display the scarlet flaunting of his father's winter wear had most abashed Penrod. One day Marjorie Jones, all gold and starch, had passed when the dreadful things were on the line: Penrod had hidden himself, shuddering. The whole town, he was convinced, knew these garments intimately and derisively.

And now, as he sat in the janitor's chair, the horrible and paralyzing recognition came. He had not an instant's doubt that every fellow actor, as well as every soul in the audience, would recognize what his mother and sister had put upon him. For as the awful truth became plain to himself it seemed blazoned to the world; and far, far louder than the stockings, the trunks did fairly bellow the grisly secret: *whose* they were and WHAT they were!

Most people have suffered in a dream the experience of finding themselves very inadequately clad in the midst of a crowd of well-dressed people, and such dreamers' sensations are comparable to Penrod's, though faintly, because Penrod was awake and in much too full possession of the most active capacities for anguish.

A human male whose dress has been damaged, or reveals some vital lack, suffers from a hideous and shameful loneliness which makes every second absolutely unbearable until he is again as others of his sex and species; and there is no act or sin whatever too desperate for him in his struggle to attain that condition. Also, there is absolutely no embarrassment possible to a woman which is comparable to that of a man under corresponding circumstances; and in this a boy is a man. Gazing upon the ghastly trunks, the stricken Penrod felt that he was a degree worse than nude; and a great horror of himself filled his soul.

"Penrod Schofield!"

The door into the hallway opened, and a voice demanded him. He could not be seen from the hallway, but the hue and the cry was up; and he knew he must be taken. It was only a question of seconds. He huddled in his chair.

"Penrod Schofield!" cried Mrs. Lora Rewbush angrily.

The distracted boy rose and, as he did so, a long pin sank deep into his back. He extracted it frenziedly, which brought to his ears a protracted and sonorous ripping, too easily located by a final gesture of horror.

"Penrod Schofield!" Mrs. Lora Rewbush had come out into the hallway.

And now, in this extremity, when all seemed lost indeed, particularly including honour, the dilating eye of the outlaw fell upon the blue overalls which the janitor had left hanging upon a peg.

Inspiration and action were almost simultaneous.

CHAPTER V

THE PAGEANT OF THE TABLE ROUND

"Penrod!" Mrs. Lora Rewbush stood in the doorway, indignantly gazing upon a Child Sir Lancelot mantled to the heels. "Do you know that you have kept an audience of five hundred people waiting for ten minutes?" She, also, detained the five hundred while she spake further.

"Well," said Penrod contentedly, as he followed her toward the buzzing stage, "I was just sitting there thinking."

Two minutes later the curtain rose on a medieval castle hall richly done in the new stage-craft made in Germany and consisting of pink and blue cheesecloth. The Child King Arthur and the Child Queen Guinevere were disclosed upon thrones, with the Child Elaine and many other celebrities in attendance; while about fifteen Child Knights were seated at a dining-room table round, which was covered with a large Oriental rug, and displayed (for the knights' refreshment) a banquet service of silver loving-cups and trophies, borrowed from the Country Club and some local automobile manufacturers.

In addition to this splendour, potted plants and palms have seldom been

more lavishly used in any castle on the stage or off. The footlights were aided
by a "spot-light" from the rear of the hall; and the children were revealed in
a blaze of glory.

A hushed, multitudinous "O-oh" of admiration came from the decorous
and delighted audience. Then the children sang feebly:

> "Chuldrun of the Tabul Round,
> Lit-tul knights and ladies we.
> Let our voy-siz all resound
> Faith and hope and charitee!"

The Child King Arthur rose, extended his sceptre with the decisive gesture
of a semaphore, and spake:

> "Each littul knight and lady born
> Has noble deeds to perform
> In thee child-world of shivullree,
> No matter how small his share may be.
> Let each advance and tell in turn
> What claim has each to knighthood earn."

The Child Sir Mordred, the villain of this piece, rose in his place at the
table round, and piped the only lines ever written by Mrs. Lora Rewbush
which Penrod Schofield could have pronounced without loathing. Georgie
Bassett, a really angelic boy, had been selected for the rôle of Mordred. His
perfect conduct had earned for him the sardonic sobriquet, "The Little Gentleman," among his boy acquaintances. (Naturally he had no friends.) Hence
the other boys supposed that he had been selected for the wicked Mordred
as a reward of virtue. He declaimed serenely:

> "I hight Sir Mordred the Child, and I teach
> Lessons of selfishest evil, and reach
> Out into darkness. Thoughtless, unkind,
> And ruthless is Mordred, and unrefined."

The Child Mordred was properly rebuked and denied the accolade,
though, like the others, he seemed to have assumed the title already. He
made a plotter's exit. Whereupon Maurice Levy rose, bowed, announced
that he highted the Child Sir Galahad, and continued with perfect sang-
froid:

> "I am the purest of the pure.
> I have but kindest thoughts each day.
> I give my riches to the poor,
> And follow in the Master's way."

This elicited tokens of approval from the Child King Arthur, and he bade Maurice "stand forth" and come near the throne, a command obeyed with the easy grace of conscious merit.

It was Penrod's turn. He stepped back from his chair, the table between him and the audience, and began in a high, breathless monotone:

> "I hight Sir Lancelot du Lake, the Child,
>   Gentul-hearted, meek, and mild.
> What though I'm *but* a littul child,
>   Gentul-heartud, meek, and mild,
> I do my share though but—though but——"

Penrod paused and gulped. The voice of Mrs. Lora Rewbush was heard from the wings, prompting irritably, and the Child Sir Lancelot repeated:

> "I do my share though but—though but a tot,
>   I pray you knight Sir Lancelot!"

This also met the royal favour, and Penrod was bidden to join Sir Galahad at the throne. As he crossed the stage, Mrs. Schofield whispered to Margaret:

"That boy! He's unpinned his mantle and fixed it to cover his whole costume. After we worked so hard to make it becoming!"

"Never mind; he'll have to take the cape off in a minute," returned Margaret. She leaned forward suddenly, narrowing her eyes to see better. "What *is* that thing hanging about his left ankle?" she whispered uneasily. "How queer! He must have got tangled in something."

"Where?" asked Mrs. Schofield, in alarm.

"His left foot. It makes him stumble. Don't you see? It looks—it looks like an elephant's foot!"

The Child Sir Lancelot and the Child Sir Galahad clasped hands before their Child King. Penrod was conscious of a great uplift; in a moment he would have to throw aside his mantle, but even so he was protected and sheltered in the human garment of a man. His stage-fright had passed, for the audience was but an indistinguishable blur of darkness beyond the dazzling lights. His most repulsive speech (that in which he proclaimed himself a "tot") was over and done with; and now at last the small, moist hand of the Child Sir Galahad lay within his own. Craftily his brown fingers stole from Maurice's palm to the wrist. The two boys declaimed in concert:

> "We are two chuldrun of the Tabul Round
>   Strewing kindness all a-round.
> With love and good deeds striving ever for the best,
>   May our littul efforts e'er be blest.
> Two littul hearts we offer. See
> United in love, faith, hope, and char—*Ow!*"

The conclusion of the duet was marred. The Child Sir Galahad suddenly stiffened, and, uttering an irrepressible shriek of anguish, gave a brief exhibition of the contortionist's art. (*"He's twistin' my wrist! Dern you, leggo!"*)

The voice of Mrs. Lora Rewbush was again heard from the wings; it sounded bloodthirsty. Penrod released his victim; and the Child King Arthur, somewhat disconcerted, extended his sceptre and, with the assistance of the enraged prompter, said:

> "Sweet child-friends of the Tabul Round,
>   In brotherly love and kindness abound,
>   Sir Lancelot, you have spoken well,
>   Sir Galahad, too, as clear as bell.
> So now pray doff your mantles gay.
> You shall be knighted this very day."

And Penrod doffed his mantle.

Simultaneously, a thick and vasty gasp came from the audience, as from five hundred bathers in a wholly unexpected surf. This gasp was punctuated irregularly, over the auditorium, by imperfectly subdued screams both of dismay and incredulous joy, and by two dismal shrieks. Altogether it was an extraordinary sound, a sound never to be forgotten by any one who heard it. It was almost as unforgettable as the sight which caused it; the word "sight" being here used in its vernacular sense, for Penrod, standing unmantled and revealed in all the medieval and artistic glory of the janitor's blue overalls, falls within its meaning.

The janitor was a heavy man, and his overalls, upon Penrod, were merely oceanic. The boy was at once swaddled and lost within their blue gulfs and vast saggings; and the left leg, too hastily rolled up, had descended with a distinctively elephantine effect, as Margaret had observed. Certainly, the Child Sir Lancelot was at least a sight.

It is probable that a great many in that hall must have had, even then, a consciousness that they were looking on at History in the Making. A supreme act is recognizable at sight: it bears the birthmark of immortality. But Penrod, that marvellous boy, had begun to declaim, even with the gesture of flinging off his mantle for the accolade:

> "I first, the Child Sir Lancelot du Lake,
>   Will volunteer to knighthood take,
>   And kneeling here before your throne
>   I vow to——"

He finished his speech unheard. The audience had recovered breath, but had lost self-control, and there ensued something later described by a participant as a sort of cultured riot.

The actors in the "pageant" were not so dumfounded by Penrod's costume as might have been expected. A few precocious geniuses perceived that the overalls were the Child Lancelot's own comment on maternal intentions; and these were profoundly impressed: they regarded him with the grisly admiration of young and ambitious criminals for a jailmate about to be distinguished by hanging. But most of the children simply took it to be the case (a little strange, but not startling) that Penrod's mother had dressed him like that—which is pathetic. They tried to go on with the "pageant."

They made a brief, manful effort. But the irrepressible outbursts from the audience bewildered them; every time Sir Lancelot du Lake the Child opened his mouth, the great, shadowy house fell into an uproar, and the children into confusion. Strong women and brave girls in the audience went out into the lobby, shrieking and clinging to one another. Others remained, rocking in their seats, helpless and spent. The neighbourhood of Mrs. Schofield and Margaret became, tactfully, a desert. Friends of the author went behind the scenes and encountered a hitherto unknown phase of Mrs. Lora Rewbush; they said, afterward, that she hardly seemed to know what she was doing. She begged to be left alone somewhere with Penrod Schofield, for just a little while.

They led her away.

CHAPTER VI

EVENING

The sun was setting behind the back fence (though at a considerable distance) as Penrod Schofield approached that fence and looked thoughtfully up at the top of it, apparently having in mind some purpose to climb up and sit there. Debating this, he passed his fingers gently up and down the backs of his legs; and then something seemed to decide him not to sit anywhere. He leaned against the fence, sighed profoundly, and gazed at Duke, his wistful dog.

The sigh was reminiscent: episodes of simple pathos were passing before his inward eye. About the most painful was the vision of lovely Marjorie Jones, weeping with rage as the Child Sir Lancelot was dragged, insatiate, from the prostrate and howling Child Sir Galahad, after an onslaught delivered the precise instant the curtain began to fall upon the demoralized "pageant." And then—oh, pangs! oh, woman!—she slapped at the ruffian's cheek, as he was led past her by a resentful janitor; and turning, flung her arms round the Child Sir Galahad's neck.

"*Penrod Schofield, don't you dare ever speak to me again as long as you live!*" Maurice's little white boots and gold tassels had done their work.

At home the late Child Sir Lancelot was consigned to a locked clothes-closet pending the arrival of his father. Mr. Schofield came and, shortly after, there was put into practice an old patriarchal custom. It is a custom of inconceivable antiquity: probably primordial, certainly prehistoric, but still in vogue in some remaining citadels of the ancient simplicities of the Republic.

And now, therefore, in the dusk, Penrod leaned against the fence and sighed.

His case is comparable to that of an adult who could have survived a similar experience. Looking back to the sawdust-box, fancy pictures this comparable adult a serious and inventive writer engaged in congenial literary activities in a private retreat. We see this period marked by the creation of some of the most virile passages of a Work dealing exclusively in red corpuscles and huge primal impulses. We see this thoughtful man dragged from his calm seclusion to a horrifying publicity; forced to adopt the stage and, himself a writer, compelled to exploit the repulsive sentiments of an author not only personally distasteful to him but whose whole method and school in *belles lettres* he despises.

We see him reduced by desperation and modesty to stealing a pair of overalls. We conceive him to have ruined, then, his own reputation, and to have utterly disgraced his family; next, to have engaged in the *duello* and to have been spurned by his lady-love, thus lost to him (according to her own declaration) forever. Finally, we must behold: imprisonment by the authorities; the third degree—and flagellation.

We conceive our man decided that his career had been perhaps too eventful. Yet Penrod had condensed all of it into eight hours.

It appears that he had at least some shadowy perception of a recent fulness of life, for, as he leaned against the fence, gazing upon his wistful Duke, he sighed again and murmured aloud:

"*Well, hasn't this been a day!*"

But in a little while a star came out, freshly lighted, from the highest part of the sky, and Penrod, looking up, noticed it casually and a little drowsily. He yawned. Then he sighed once more, but not reminiscently: evening had come; the day was over.

It was a sigh of pure *ennui*.

CHAPTER VII

EVILS OF DRINK

Next day, Penrod acquired a dime by a simple and antique process which was without doubt sometimes practised by the boys of Babylon. When the teacher of his class in Sunday-school requested the weekly contribution, Penrod, fumbling honestly (at first) in the wrong pockets, managed to look so embarrassed that the gentle lady told him not to mind, and said she was often forgetful herself. She was so sweet about it that, looking into the future, Penrod began to feel confident of a small but regular income.

At the close of the afternoon services he did not go home, but proceeded to squander the funds just withheld from China upon an orgy of the most pungently forbidden description. In a Drug Emporium, near the church, he purchased a five-cent sack of candy consisting for the most part of the heavily flavoured hoofs of horned cattle, but undeniably substantial, and so generously capable of resisting solution that the purchaser must needs be avaricious beyond reason who did not realize his money's worth.

Equipped with this collation, Penrod contributed his remaining nickel to a picture show, countenanced upon the seventh day by the legal but not the moral authorities. Here, in cozy darkness, he placidly insulted his liver with jaw-breaker upon jaw-breaker from the paper sack, and in a surfeit of content watched the silent actors on the screen.

One film made a lasting impression upon him. It depicted with relentless pathos the drunkard's progress; beginning with his conversion to beer in the company of loose travelling men; pursuing him through an inexplicable lapse into evening clothes and the society of some remarkably painful ladies, next, exhibiting the effects of alcohol on the victim's domestic disposition, the unfortunate man was seen in the act of striking his wife and, subsequently, his pleading baby daughter with an abnormally heavy walking-stick. Their flight—through the snow—to seek the protection of a relative was shown, and finally, the drunkard's picturesque behaviour at the portals of a madhouse.

So fascinated was Penrod that he postponed his departure until this film came round again, by which time he had finished his unnatural repast and almost, but not quite, decided against following the profession of a drunkard when he grew up.

Emerging, satiated, from the theatre, a public timepiece before a jeweller's shop confronted him with an unexpected dial and imminent perplexities. How was he to explain at home these hours of dalliance? There was a steadfast rule that he return direct from Sunday-school; and Sunday rules were important, because on that day there was his father, always at home and at hand, perilously ready for action. One of the hardest conditions of boyhood is the almost continuous strain put upon the powers of invention by the constant and harassing necessity for explanations of every natural act.

Proceeding homeward through the deepening twilight as rapidly as possible, at a gait half skip and half canter, Penrod made up his mind in what manner he would account for his long delay, and, as he drew nearer, rehearsed in words the opening passage of his defence.

"Now see here," he determined to begin; "I do not wished to be blamed for things I couldn't help, nor any other boy. I was going along the street by a cottage and a lady put her head out of the window and said her husband was drunk and whipping her and her little girl, and she asked me wouldn't

I come in and help hold him. So I went in and tried to get hold of this drunken lady's husband where he was whipping their baby daughter, but he wouldn't pay any attention, and I *told* her I ought to be getting home, but she kep' on askin' me to stay——"

At this point he reached the corner of his own yard, where a coincidence not only checked the rehearsal of his eloquence but happily obviated all occasion for it. A cab from the station drew up in front of the gate, and there descended a troubled lady in black and a fragile little girl about three. Mrs. Schofield rushed from the house and enfolded both in hospitable arms.

They were Penrod's Aunt Clara and cousin, also Clara, from Dayton, Illinois, and in the flurry of their arrival everybody forgot to put Penrod to the question. It is doubtful, however, if he felt any relief; there may have been even a slight, unconscious disappointment not altogether dissimilar to that of an actor deprived of a good part.

In the course of some really necessary preparations for dinner he stepped from the bathroom into the pink-and-white bedchamber of his sister, and addressed her rather thickly through a towel.

"When'd mamma find out Aunt Clara and Cousin Clara were coming?"

"Not till she saw them from the window. She just happened to look out as they drove up. Aunt Clara telegraphed this morning, but it wasn't delivered."

"How long they goin' to stay?"

"I don't know."

Penrod ceased to rub his shining face, and thoughtfully tossed the towel through the bathroom door. "Uncle John won't try to make 'em come back home, I guess, will he?" (Uncle John was Aunt Clara's husband, a successful manufacturer of stoves, and his lifelong regret was that he had not entered the Baptist ministry.) "He'll let 'em stay here quietly, won't he?"

"What *are* you talking about?" demanded Margaret, turning from her mirror. "Uncle John sent them here. Why shouldn't he let them stay?"

Penrod looked crestfallen. "Then he hasn't taken to drink?"

"Certainly not!" She emphasized the denial with a pretty peal of soprano laughter.

"Then why," asked her brother gloomily, "why did Aunt Clara look so worried when she got here?"

"Good gracious! Don't people worry about anything except somebody's drinking? Where did you get such an idea?"

"Well," he persisted, "you don't *know* it ain't that."

She laughed again, whole-heartedly. "Poor Uncle John! He won't even allow grape juice or ginger ale in his house. They came because they were afraid little Clara might catch the measles. She's very delicate, and there's such an epidemic of measles among the children over in Dayton the schools had to be closed. Uncle John got so worried that last night he dreamed about it; and this morning he couldn't stand it any longer and packed them off over here, though he thinks it's wicked to travel on Sunday. And Aunt

Clara was worried when she got here because they'd forgotten to check her trunk and it will have to be sent by express. Now what in the name of the common sense put it into your head that Uncle John had taken to——"

"Oh, nothing." He turned lifelessly away and went downstairs, a new-born hope dying in his bosom. Life seems so needlessly dull sometimes.

CHAPTER VIII

SCHOOL

Next morning, when he had once more resumed the dreadful burden of education, it seemed infinitely duller. And yet what pleasanter sight is there than a schoolroom well filled with children of those sprouting years just before the 'teens? The casual visitor, gazing from the teacher's platform upon these busy little heads, needs only a blunted memory to experience the most agreeable and exhilarating sensations. Still, for the greater part, the children are unconscious of the happiness of their condition; for nothing is more pathetically true than that we "never know when we are well off." The boys in a public school are less aware of their happy state than are the girls; and of all the boys in his room, probably Penrod himself had the least appreciation of his felicity.

He sat staring at an open page of a textbook, but not studying; not even reading; not even thinking. Nor was he lost in a reverie: his mind's eye was shut, as his physical eye might well have been, for the optic nerve, flaccid with *ennui*, conveyed nothing whatever of the printed page upon which the orb of vision was partially focused. Penrod was doing something very unusual and rare, something almost never accomplished except by coloured people or by a boy in school on a spring day: he was doing really nothing at all. He was merely a state of being.

From the street a sound stole in through the open window, and abhorring Nature began to fill the vacuum called Penrod Schofield; for the sound was the spring song of a mouth-organ, coming down the sidewalk. The windows were intentionally above the level of the eyes of the seated pupils; but the picture of the musician was plain to Penrod, painted for him by a quality in the runs and trills, partaking of the oboe, of the calliope, and of cats in anguish; an excruciating sweetness obtained only by the wallowing, walloping yellow-pink palm of a hand whose back was Congo black and shiny. The music came down the street and passed beneath the window, accompanied by the care-free shuffling of a pair of old shoes scuffing syncopations on the cement sidewalk. It passed into the distance; became faint and blurred; was gone. Emotion stirred in Penrod a great and poignant desire, but (perhaps fortunately) no fairy godmother made her appearance. Otherwise Penrod would have gone down the street in a black skin, playing the mouthorgan, and an unprepared coloured youth would have found himself enjoying educational advantages for which he had no ambition whatever.

Roused from perfect apathy, the boy cast about the schoolroom an eye wearied to nausea by the perpetual vision of the neat teacher upon the platform, the backs of the heads of the pupils in front of him, and the monotonous stretches of blackboard threateningly defaced by arithmetical formulæ and other insignia of torture. Above the blackboard, the walls of the high room were of white plaster—white with the qualified whiteness of old snow in a soft coal town. This dismal expanse was broken by four lithographic portraits, votive offerings of a thoughtful publisher. The portraits were of good and great men, kind men; men who loved children. Their faces were noble and benevolent. But the lithographs offered the only rest for the eyes of children fatigued by the everlasting sameness of the schoolroom. Long day after long day, interminable week in and interminable week out, vast month on vast month, the pupils sat with those four portraits beaming kindness down upon them. The faces became permanent in the consciousness of the children; they became an obsession—in and out of school the children were never free of them. The four faces haunted the minds of children falling asleep; they hung upon the minds of children waking at night; they rose forebodingly in the minds of children waking in the morning; they became monstrously alive in the minds of children lying sick of fever. Never, while the children of that schoolroom lived, would they be able to forget one detail of the four lithographs: the hand of Longfellow was fixed, for them, forever, in his beard. And by a simple and unconscious association of ideas, Penrod Schofield was accumulating an antipathy for the gentle Longfellow and for James Russell Lowell and for Oliver Wendell Holmes and for John Greenleaf Whittier, which would never permit him to peruse a work of one of those great New Englanders without a feeling of personal resentment.

His eyes fell slowly and inimically from the brow of Whittier to the braid of reddish hair belonging to Victorine Riordan, the little octoroon girl who sat directly in front of him. Victorine's back was as familiar to Penrod as the necktie of Oliver Wendell Holmes. So was her gayly coloured plaid waist. He hated the waist as he hated Victorine herself, without knowing why. Enforced companionship in large quantities and on an equal basis between the sexes appears to sterilize the affections, and schoolroom romances are few.

Victorine's hair was thick, and the brickish glints in it were beautiful, but Penrod was very tired of it. A tiny knot of green ribbon finished off the braid and kept it from unravelling; and beneath the ribbon there was a final wisp of hair which was just long enough to repose upon Penrod's desk when Victorine leaned back in her seat. It was there now. Thoughtfully, he took the braid between thumb and forefinger, and, without disturbing Victorine, dipped the end of it and the green ribbon into the ink-well of his desk. He brought hair and ribbon forth dripping purple ink, and partially dried them on a blotter, though, a moment later when Victorine leaned forward, they were still able to add a few picturesque touches to the plaid waist.

Rudolph Krauss, across the aisle from Penrod, watched the operation with protuberant eyes, fascinated. Inspired to imitation, he took a piece of chalk from his pocket and wrote "RATS" across the shoulder-blades of the boy in front of him, then looked across appealingly to Penrod for tokens of congratulation. Penrod yawned. It may not be denied that at times he appeared to be a very self-centred boy.

CHAPTER IX

SOARING

Half the members of the class passed out to a recitation-room, the empurpled Victorine among them, and Miss Spence started the remaining half through the ordeal of trial by mathematics. Several boys and girls were sent to the blackboard, and Penrod, spared for the moment, followed their operations a little while with his eyes, but not with his mind; then, sinking deeper in his seat, limply abandoned the effort. His eyes remained open, but saw nothing; the routine of the arithmetic lesson reached his ears in familiar, meaningless sounds, but he heard nothing; and yet, this time, he was profoundly occupied. He had drifted away from the painful land of facts, and floated now in a new sea of fancy which he had just discovered.

Maturity forgets the marvellous realness of a boy's day-dreams, how colourful they glow, rosy and living, and how opaque the curtain closing down between the dreamer and the actual world. That curtain is almost soundproof, too, and causes more throat-trouble among parents than is suspected.

The nervous monotony of the schoolroom inspires a sometimes unbearable longing for something astonishing to happen, and as every boy's fundamental desire is to do something astonishing himself, so as to be the centre of all human interest and awe, it was natural that Penrod should discover in fancy the delightful secret of self-levitation. He found, in this curious series of imaginings, during the lesson in arithmetic, that the atmosphere may be navigated as by a swimmer under water, but with infinitely greater ease and with perfect comfort in breathing. In his mind he extended his arms gracefully, at a level with his shoulders, and delicately paddled the air with his hands, which at once caused him to be drawn up out of his seat and elevated gently to a position about midway between the floor and the ceiling, where he came to an equilibrium and floated; a sensation not the less exquisite because of the screams of his fellow pupils, appalled by the miracle. Miss Spence herself was amazed and frightened, but he only smiled down carelessly upon her when she commanded him to return to earth; and then, when she climbed upon a desk to pull him down, he quietly paddled himself a little higher, leaving his toes just out of her reach. Next, he swam through a few slow somersaults to show his mastery of the new art, and, with the shouting of the dumfounded scholars ringing in his ears, turned on his side and floated swiftly out of the window, immediately rising above the housetops, while people in the street below him shrieked, and a trolley car stopped dead in wonder.

With almost no exertion he paddled himself, many yards at a stroke, to the girls' private school where Marjorie Jones was a pupil—Marjorie Jones of the amber curls and the golden voice! Long before the "Pageant of the Table Round," she had offered Penrod a hundred proofs that she considered him wholly undesirable and ineligible. At the Friday Afternoon Dancing Class she consistently incited and led the laughter at him whenever Professor Bartet singled him out for admonition in matters of feet and decorum. And but yesterday she had chid him for his slavish lack of memory in daring to offer her a greeting on the way to Sunday-school. "Well! I expect you must forgot I told you never to speak to me again! If I was a boy, I'd be too proud to come hanging around people that don't speak to me, even if I *was* the Worst Boy in Town!" So she flouted him. But now, as he floated in through the window of her classroom and swam gently along the ceiling like an escaped toy balloon, she fell upon her knees beside her little desk, and, lifting up her arms toward him, cried with love and admiration:

"Oh, Penrod!"

He negligently kicked a globe from the high chandelier, and, smiling coldly, floated out through the hall to the front steps of the school, while Marjorie followed, imploring him to grant her one kind look.

In the street an enormous crowd had gathered, headed by Miss Spence and a brass band; and a cheer from a hundred thousand throats shook the very ground as Penrod swam overhead. Marjorie knelt upon the steps and watched adoringly while Penrod took the drum-major's baton and, performing sinuous evolutions above the crowd, led the band. Then he threw the baton so high that it disappeared from sight; but he went swiftly after it, a double delight, for he had not only the delicious sensation of rocketing safely up and up into the blue sky, but also that of standing in the crowd below, watching and admiring himself as he dwindled to a speck, disappeared and then, emerging from a cloud, came speeding down, with the baton in his hand, to the level of the treetops, where he beat time for the band and the vast throng and Marjorie Jones, who all united in the "Star-spangled Banner" in honour of his aerial achievements. It was a great moment.

It was a great moment, but something seemed to threaten it. The face of Miss Spence looking up from the crowd grew too vivid—unpleasantly vivid. She was beckoning him and shouting, "Come down, Penrod Schofield!

Penrod Schofield, come down here!" He could hear her above the band and the singing of the multitude; she seemed intent on spoiling everything. Marjorie Jones was weeping to show how sorry she was that she had formerly slighted him, and throwing kisses to prove that she loved him; but Miss Spence kept jumping between him and Marjorie, incessantly calling his name.

He grew more and more irritated with her; he was the most important person in the world and was engaged in proving it to Marjorie Jones and the whole city, and yet Miss Spence seemed to feel she still had the right to order him about as she did in the old days when he was an ordinary schoolboy. He was furious; he was sure she wanted him to do something disagreeable. It seemed to him that she had screamed "Penrod Schofield!" thousands of times.

From the beginning of his aerial experiments in his own schoolroom, he had not opened his lips, knowing somehow that one of the requirements for air floating is perfect silence on the part of the floater; but, finally, irritated beyond measure by Miss Spence's clamorous insistence, he was unable to restrain an indignant rebuke—and immediately came to earth with a frightful bump.

Miss Spence—in the flesh—had directed toward the physical body of the absent Penrod an inquiry as to the fractional consequences of dividing seventeen apples, fairly, among three boys, and she was surprised and displeased to receive no answer although to the best of her knowledge and belief, he was looking fixedly at her. She repeated her question crisply, without visible effect; then summoned him by name with increasing asperity. Twice she called him, while all his fellow pupils turned to stare at the gazing boy. She advanced a step from the platform.

"Penrod Schofield!"

"Oh, my goodness!" he shouted suddenly. "Can't you keep still a *minute?*"

CHAPTER X

UNCLE JOHN

Miss Spence gasped. So did the pupils. The whole room filled with a swelling conglomerate "*O-o-o-o-h!*"

As for Penrod himself, the walls reeled with the shock. He sat with his mouth open, a mere lump of stupefaction. For the appalling words that he had hurled at the teacher were as inexplicable to him as to any other who heard them.

Nothing is more treacherous than the human mind; nothing else so loves to play the Iscariot. Even when patiently bullied into a semblance of order and training, it may prove but a base and shifty servant. And Penrod's mind was not his servant; it was a master, with the April wind's whims; and it had just played him a diabolical trick. The very jolt with which he came back to the schoolroom in the midst of his fancied flight jarred his day-dream utterly out of him; and he sat, open-mouthed in horror at what he had said.

The unanimous gasp of awe was protracted. Miss Spence, however, finally recovered her breath, and, returning deliberately to the platform, faced the school. "And then, for a little while," as pathetic stories sometimes recount, "everything was very still." It was so still, in fact, that Penrod's newborn notoriety could almost be heard growing. This grisly silence was at last broken by the teacher.

"Penrod Schofield, stand up!"

The miserable child obeyed.

"What did you mean by speaking to me in that way?"

He hung his head, raked the floor with the side of his shoe, swayed, swallowed, looked suddenly at his hands with the air of never having seen them before, then clasped them behind him. The school shivered in ecstatic horror, every fascinated eye upon him; yet there was not a soul in the room but was profoundly grateful to him for the sensation—including the offended teacher herself. Unhappily, all this gratitude was unconscious and altogether different from the kind which results in testimonials and loving-cups. On the contrary!

"Penrod Schofield!"

He gulped.

"Answer me at once! Why did you speak to me like that?"

"I was——" He choked, unable to continue.

"Speak out!"

"I was just—thinking," he managed to stammer.

"That will not do," she returned sharply. "I wish to know immediately why you spoke as you did."

The stricken Penrod answered helplessly:

"Because I was just thinking."

Upon the very rack he could have offered no ampler truthful explanation. It was all he knew about it.

"Thinking what?"

"Just thinking."

Miss Spence's expression gave evidence that her power of self-restraint was undergoing a remarkable test. However, after taking counsel with herself, she commanded:

"Come here!"

He shuffled forward, and she placed a chair upon the platform near her own.

"Sit there!"

Then (but not at all as if nothing had happened), she continued the lesson in arithmetic. Spiritually the children may have learned a lesson in very small fractions indeed as they gazed at the fragment of sin before them on the stool of penitence. They all stared at him attentively with hard and passionately interested eyes, in which there was never one trace of pity. It cannot be said with precision that he writhed; his movement was more a slow, continuous squirm, effected with a ghastly assumption of languid indifference; while his gaze, in the effort to escape the marble-hearted glare of his schoolmates, affixed itself with apparent permanence to the waistcoat button of James Russell Lowell just above the "U" in "Russell."

Classes came and classes went, grilling him with eyes. Newcomers received the story of the crime in darkling whispers; and the outcast sat and sat and sat, and squirmed and squirmed and squirmed. (He did one or two things with his spine which a professional contortionist would have observed with real interest.) And all this while of freezing suspense was but the criminal's detention awaiting trial. A known punishment may be anticipated with some measure of equanimity; at least, the prisoner may prepare himself to undergo it; but the unknown looms more monstrous for every attempt to guess it. Penrod's crime was unique; there were no rules to aid him in estimating the vengeance to fall upon him for it. What seemed most probable was that he would be expelled from the schools in the presence of his family, the mayor, and council, and afterward whipped by his father upon the State House steps, with the entire city as audience by invitation of the authorities.

Noon came. The rows of children filed out, every head turning for a last unpleasingly speculative look at the outlaw. Then Miss Spence closed the door into the cloakroom and that into the big hall, and came and sat at her desk, near Penrod. The tramping of feet outside, the shrill calls and shouting and the changing voices of the older boys ceased to be heard—and there was silence. Penrod, still affecting to be occupied with Lowell, was conscious that Miss Spence looked at him intently.

"Penrod," she said gravely, "what excuse have you to offer before I report your case to the principal?"

The word "principal" struck him to the vitals. Grand Inquisitor, Grand Khan, Sultan, Emperor, Tsar, Cæsar Augustus—these are comparable. He stopped squirming instantly, and sat rigid.

"I want an answer. Why did you shout those words at me?"

"Well," he murmured, "I was just—thinking."

"Thinking what?" she asked sharply.

"I don't know."

"That won't do!"

He took his left ankle in his right hand and regarded it helplessly.

"That won't do, Penrod Schofield," she repeated severely. "If that is all the excuse you have to offer I shall report your case this instant!"

And she rose with fatal intent.

But Penrod was one of those whom the precipice inspires. "Well, I *have* got an excuse."

"Well"—she paused impatiently—"what is it?"

He had not an idea, but he felt one coming, and replied automatically, in a plaintive tone:

"I guess anybody that had been through what *I* had to go through, last night, would think they had an excuse."

Miss Spence resumed her seat, though with the air of being ready to leap from it instantly.

"What has last night to do with your insolence to me this morning?"

"Well, I guess you'd see," he returned, emphasizing the plaintive note, "if you knew what *I* know."

"Now, Penrod," she said, in a kinder voice, "I have a high regard for your mother and father, and it would hurt me to distress them, but you must either tell me what was the matter with you or I'll have to take you to Mrs. Houston."

"Well, ain't I going to?" he cried, spurred by the dread name. "It's because I didn't sleep last night."

"Were you ill?" The question was put with some dryness.

He felt the dryness. "No'm; I wasn't."

"Then if someone in your family was so ill that even you were kept up all night, how does it happen they let you come to school this morning?"

"It wasn't illness," he returned, shaking his head mournfully. "It was lots worse'n anybody's being sick. It was—it was—well, it was jest awful."

"*What* was?" He remarked with anxiety the incredulity in her tone.

"It was about Aunt Clara," he said.

"Your Aunt Clara!" she repeated. "Do you mean your mother's sister who married Mr. Farry of Dayton, Illinois?"

"Yes—Uncle John," returned Penrod sorrowfully. "The trouble was about him."

Miss Spence frowned a frown which he rightly interpreted as one of continued suspicion. "She and I were in school together," she said. "I used to know her very well, and I've always heard her married life was entirely happy. I don't——"

"Yes, it was," he interrupted, "until last year when Uncle John took to running with travelling men——"

"What?"

"Yes'm." He nodded solemnly. "That was what started it. At first he was a good, kind husband, but these travelling men would coax him into a saloon on his way home from work, and they got him to drinking beer and then ales, wines, liquors, and cigars——"

"Penrod!"

"Ma'am?"

"I'm not inquiring into your Aunt Clara's private affairs; I'm asking you if you have anything to say which would palliate——"

"That's what I'm tryin' to *tell* you about, Miss Spence," he pleaded,—"if you'd jest only let me. When Aunt Clara and her little baby daughter got to our house last night——"

"You say Mrs. Farry is visiting your mother?"

"Yes'm—not just visiting—you see, she *had* to come. Well of course, little baby Clara, she was so bruised up and mauled, where he'd been hittin' her with his cane——"

"You mean that your uncle had done such a thing as *that!*" exclaimed Miss Spence, suddenly disarmed by this scandal.

"Yes'm, and mamma and Margaret had to sit up all night nursin' little Clara—and *Aunt* Clara was in such a state *somebody* had to keep talkin' to *her*, and there wasn't anybody but me to do it, so I——"

"But where was your father?" she cried.

"Ma'am?"

"Where was your father while——"

"Oh—papa?" Penrod paused, reflected; then brightened. "Why, he was down at the train, waitin' to see if Uncle John would try to follow 'em and make 'em come home so's he could persecute 'em some more. I wanted to do that, but they said if he did come I mightn't be strong enough to hold him and——" The brave lad paused again, modestly. Miss Spence's expression was encouraging. Her eyes were wide with astonishment, and there may have been in them, also, the mingled beginnings of admiration and self-reproach. Penrod, warming to his work, felt safer every moment.

"And so," he continued, "I had to sit up with Aunt Clara. She had some pretty big bruises, too, and I had to——"

"But why didn't they send for a doctor?" However, this question was only a flicker of dying incredulity.

"Oh, they didn't want any *doctor*," exclaimed the inspired realist promptly. "They don't want anybody to *hear* about it because Uncle John might reform—and then where'd he be if everybody knew he'd been a drunkard and whipped his wife and baby daughter?"

"Oh!" said Miss Spence.

"You see, he used to be upright as anybody," he went on explanatively. "It all begun——"

"Began, Penrod."

"Yes'm. It all commenced from the first day he let those travelling men coax him into the saloon." Penrod narrated the downfall of his Uncle John at length. In detail he was nothing short of plethoric; and incident followed incident, sketched with such vividness, such abundance of colour, and such verisimilitude to a drunkard's life as a drunkard's life should be, that had Miss Spence possessed the rather chilling attributes of William J. Burns himself, the last trace of skepticism must have vanished from her mind. Besides, there are two things that will be believed of any man whatsoever, and one of them is that he has taken to drink. And in every sense it was a moving picture which, with simple but eloquent words, the virtuous Penrod set before his teacher.

His eloquence increased with what it fed on; and as with the eloquence so with self-reproach in the gentle bosom of the teacher. She cleared her throat with difficulty once or twice, during his description of his ministering night with Aunt Clara. "And I said to her, 'Why, Aunt Clara, what's the use of takin' on so about it?' And I said, 'Now, Aunt Clara, all the crying in the world can't make things any better.' And then she'd just keep catchin' hold of me, and sob and kind of holler, and I'd say, 'Don't cry, Aunt Clara —please don't cry.'"

Then, under the influence of some fragmentary survivals of the respectable portion of his Sunday adventures, his theme became more exalted; and, only partially misquoting a phrase from a psalm, he related how he had made it of comfort to Aunt Clara, and how he had besought her to seek Higher guidance in her trouble.

The surprising thing about a structure such as Penrod was erecting is that the taller it becomes the more ornamentation it will stand. Gifted boys have this faculty of building magnificence upon cobwebs—Penrod was gifted. Under the spell of his really great performance, Miss Spence gazed more and more sweetly upon the prodigy of spiritual beauty and goodness before her, until at last, when Penrod came to the explanation of his "just thinking," she was forced to turn her head away.

"You mean, dear," she said gently, "that you were all worn out and hardly knew what you were saying?"

"Yes'm."

"And you were thinking about all those dreadful things so hard that you forgot where you were?"

"I was thinking," he said simply, "how to save Uncle John."

And the end of it for this mighty boy was that the teacher kissed him!

CHAPTER XI

FIDELITY OF A LITTLE DOG

The returning students, that afternoon, observed that Penrod's desk was vacant—and nothing could have been more impressive than that sinister mere emptiness. The accepted theory was that Penrod had been arrested. How breathtaking, then, the sensation when, at the beginning of the second hour, he strolled in with inimitable carelessness and, rubbing his eyes, somewhat noticeably in the manner of one who has snatched an hour of much needed sleep, took his place as if nothing in particular had happened. This, at first supposed to be a superhuman exhibition of sheer audacity, became but the more dumfounding when Miss Spence—looking up from her desk—greeted him with a pleasant little nod. Even after school, Penrod gave numerous maddened investigators no relief. All he would consent to say was:

"Oh, I just *talked* to her."

A mystification not entirely unconnected with the one thus produced was manifested at his own family dinner-table the following evening. Aunt Clara had been out rather late, and came to the table after the rest were seated. She wore a puzzled expression.

"Do you ever see Mary Spence nowadays?" she inquired, as she unfolded her napkin, addressing Mrs. Schofield. Penrod abruptly set down his soup-spoon and gazed at his aunt with flattering attention.

"Yes; sometimes," said Mrs. Schofield. "She's Penrod's teacher."

"Is she?" said Mrs. Farry. "Do you—" She paused. "Do people think her a little—queer, these days?"

"Why, no," returned her sister. "What makes you say that?"

"She has acquired a very odd manner," said Mrs. Farry decidedly. "At least, she seemed odd to *me*. I met her at the corner just before I got to the house, a few minutes ago, and after we'd said howdy-do to each other, she kept hold of my hand and looked as though she was going to cry. She seemed to be trying to say something, and choking——"

"But I don't think that's so very queer, Clara. She knew you in school, didn't she?"

"Yes, but——"

"And she hadn't seen you for so many years, I think it's perfectly natural she——"

"Wait! She stood there squeezing my hand, and struggling to get her voice —and I got really embarrassed—and then finally she said, in a kind of tearful whisper, 'Be of good cheer—this trial will pass!'"

"How queer!" exclaimed Margaret.

Penrod sighed, and returned somewhat absently to his soup.

"Well, I don't know," said Mrs. Schofield thoughtfully. "Of course she's heard about the outbreak of measles in Dayton, since they had to close the schools, and she knows you live there——"

"But doesn't it seem a *very* exaggerated way," suggested Margaret, "to talk about measles?"

"Wait!" begged Aunt Clara. "After she said that, she said something even queerer, and then put her handkerchief to her eyes and hurried away."

Penrod laid down his spoon again and moved his chair slightly back from the table. A spirit of prophecy was upon him: he knew that someone was going to ask a question which he felt might better remain unspoken.

"What *was* the other thing she said?" Mr. Schofield inquired, thus immediately fulfilling his son's premonition.

"She said," returned Mrs. Farry slowly, looking about the table, "she said, 'I know that Penrod is a great, great comfort to you!'"

There was a general exclamation of surprise. It was a singular thing, and in no manner may it be considered complimentary to Penrod, that this speech of Miss Spence's should have immediately confirmed Mrs. Farry's doubts about her in the minds of all his family.

Mr. Schofield shook his head pityingly.

"I'm afraid she's a goner," he went so far as to say.

"Of all the weird ideas!" cried Margaret.

"I never heard anything like it in my life!" Mrs. Schofield exclaimed. "Was that *all* she said?"

"Every word!"

Penrod again resumed attention to his soup. His mother looked at him curiously, and then, struck by a sudden thought, gathered the glances of the adults of the table by a significant movement of the head, and, by another, conveyed an admonition to drop the subject until later. Miss Spence was Penrod's teacher: it was better, for many reasons, not to discuss the subject of her queerness before him. This was Mrs. Schofield's thought at the time. Later she had another, and it kept her awake.

The next afternoon, Mr. Schofield, returning at five o'clock from the cares of the day, found the house deserted, and sat down to read his evening paper in what appeared to be an uninhabited apartment known to its own world as the "drawing-room." A sneeze, unexpected both to him and the owner, informed him of the presence of another person.

"Where are you, Penrod?" the parent asked, looking about.

"Here," said Penrod meekly.

Stooping, Mr. Schofield discovered his son squatting under the piano, near an open window—his wistful Duke lying beside him.

"What are you doing there?"

"Me?"

"Why under the piano?"

"Well," the boy returned, with grave sweetness, "I was just kind of sitting here—thinking."

"All right." Mr. Schofield, rather touched, returned to the digestion of a murder, his back once more to the piano; and Penrod silently drew from beneath his jacket (where he had slipped it simultaneously with the sneeze) a paper-backed volume entitled: "Slimsy, the Sioux City Squealer, or, 'Not Guilty, Your Honor.'"

In this manner the reading-club continued in peace, absorbed, contented, the world well forgot—until a sudden, violently irritated slam-bang of the front door startled the members; and Mrs. Schofield burst into the room and threw herself into a chair, moaning.

"What's the matter, mamma?" asked her husband laying aside his paper.

"Henry Passloe Schofield," returned the lady, "I don't know what *is* to be done with that boy; I do *not!*"

"You mean Penrod?"

"Who else could I mean?" She sat up, exasperated, to stare at him. "Henry Passloe Schofield, you've got to take this matter in your hands—it's beyond me!"

"Well, what has he——"

"Last night I got to thinking," she began rapidly, "about what Clara told us—thank Heaven she and Margaret and little Clara have gone to tea at Cousin Charlotte's!—but they'll be home soon—about what she said about Miss Spence——"

"You mean about Penrod's being a comfort?"

"Yes, and I kept thinking and thinking and thinking about it till I couldn't stand it any——"

"By *George!*" shouted Mr. Schofield startlingly, stooping to look under the piano. A statement that he had suddenly remembered his son's presence would be lacking in accuracy, for the highly sensitized Penrod was, in fact, no longer present. No more was Duke, his faithful dog.

"What's the matter?"

"Nothing," he returned, striding to the open window and looking out. "Go on."

"Oh," she moaned, "it must be kept from Clara—and I'll never hold up my head again if John Farry ever hears of it!"

"Hears of *what?*"

"Well, I just couldn't stand it, I got so curious; and I thought of course if Miss Spence *had* become a little unbalanced it was my duty to know it, as Penrod's mother and she his teacher; so I thought I would just call on her at her apartment after school and have a chat and see—and I did and—oh——"

"Well?"

"I've just come from there, and she told me—she told me! Oh, I've *never* known anything like this!"

"*What* did she tell you?"

Mrs. Schofield, making a great effort, managed to assume a temporary appearance of calm. "Henry," she said solemnly, "bear this in mind: whatever you do to Penrod, it must be done in some place when Clara won't hear it. But the first thing to do is to find him."

Within view of the window from which Mr. Schofield was gazing was the closed door of the storeroom in the stable, and just outside this door Duke was performing a most engaging trick.

His young master had taught Duke to "sit up and beg" when he wanted anything, and if that didn't get it, to "speak." Duke was facing the closed door and sitting up and begging, and now he also spoke—in a loud, clear bark.

There was an open transom over the door, and from this descended—hurled by an unseen agency—a can half filled with old paint.

It caught the small besieger of the door on his thoroughly surprised right ear, encouraged him to some remarkable acrobatics, and turned large portions of him a dull blue. Allowing only a moment to perplexity, and deciding, after a single and evidently unappetizing experiment, not to cleanse himself of paint, the loyal animal resumed his quaint, upright posture.

Mr. Schofield seated himself on the window-sill, whence he could keep in view that pathetic picture of unrequited love.

"Go on with your story, mamma," he said. "I think I can find Penrod when we want him."

And a few minutes later he added, "And I think I know the place to do it in."

Again the faithful voice of Duke was heard, pleading outside the bolted door.

CHAPTER XII

MISS RENNSDALE ACCEPTS

"One-Two-Three; one-two-three—glide!" said Professor Bartet, emphasizing his instructions by a brisk collision of his palms at "glide." "One-two-three; one-two-three—glide!"

The school week was over, at last, but Penrod's troubles were not.

Round and round the ballroom went the seventeen struggling little couples of the Friday Afternoon Dancing Class. Round and round went their reflections with them, swimming rhythmically in the polished, dark floor—white and blue and pink for the girls; black, with dabs of white, for the white-collared, white-gloved boys; and sparks and slivers of high light everywhere as the glistening pumps flickered along the surface like a school of flying fish. Every small pink face—with one exception—was painstaking and set for duty. It was a conscientious little merry-go-round.

"One-two-three; one-two-three—glide! One-two-three; one-two-three—glide! One-two-th—Ha! Mister Penrod Schofield, you lose the step. Your left foot! No, no! This is the left! See—like me! Now again! One-two-three; one-two-three—glide! Better! Much better! Again! One-two-three; one-two-three—gl—Stop! Mr. Penrod Schofield, this dancing class is provided by the kind parents of the pupilses as much to learn the mannerss of good societies as to dance. You think you shall ever see a gentleman in good societies to tickle his partner in the dance till she say Ouch? Never! I assure you it is not done. Again! Now then! Piano, please! One-two-three; one-two-three—glide! Mr. Penrod Schofield, your right foot—your right foot! No, no! Stop!"

The merry-go-round came to a standstill.

"Mr. Penrod Schofield and partner"—Professor Bartet wiped his brow—"will you kindly observe me? One-two-three—glide! So! Now then—no; you will please keep your places, ladies and gentlemen. Mr. Penrod Schofield, I would puttickly like your attention; this is for you!"

"Pickin' on me again!" murmured the smouldering Penrod to his small, unsympathetic partner. "Can't let me alone a minute!"

"Mister Georgie Bassett, please step to the centre," said the professor.

Mr. Bassett complied with modest alacrity.

"Teacher's pet!" whispered Penrod hoarsely. He had nothing but contempt for Georgie Bassett. The parents, guardians, aunts, uncles, cousins, governesses, housemaids, cooks, chauffeurs and coachmen, appertaining to the members of the dancing class, all dwelt in the same part of town and shared certain communal theories; and among the most firmly established was that which maintained Georgie Bassett to be the Best Boy in Town. Contrariwise, the unfortunate Penrod, largely because of his recent dazzling but disastrous attempts to control forces far beyond him, had been given a clear title as the Worst Boy in Town. (Population, 135,000.) To precisely what degree his reputation was the product of his own energies cannot be calculated. It was Marjorie Jones who first applied the description, in its definite simplicity, the day after the "pageant," and, possibly, her frequent and effusive repetitions of it, even upon wholly irrelevant occasions, had something to do with its prompt and quite perfect acceptance by the community.

"Miss Rennsdale will please do me the fafer to be Mr. Georgie Bassett's partner for one moment," said Professor Bartet. "Mr. Penrod Schofield will please give his attention. Miss Rennsdale and Mister Bassett, obliche me, if you please. Others please watch. Piano, please! Now then!"

Miss Rennsdale, aged eight—the youngest lady in the class—and Mr. Georgie Bassett one-two-three-glided with consummate technique for the better education of Penrod Schofield. It is possible that amber-curled, beautiful Marjorie felt that she, rather than Miss Rennsdale, might have been selected as the example of perfection—or perhaps her remark was only woman.

"Stopping everybody for that boy!" said Marjorie.

Penrod, across the circle from her, heard distinctly—nay, he was obviously intended to hear; but over a scorched heart he preserved a stoic front. Whereupon Marjorie whispered derisively in the ear of her partner, Maurice Levy, who wore a pearl pin in his tie.

"Again, please, everybody—ladies and gentlemen!" cried Professor Bartet. "Mister Penrod Schofield, if you please, pay puttickly attention! Piano, please! Now then!"

The lesson proceeded. At the close of the hour Professor Bartet stepped to the centre of the room and clapped his hands for attention.

"Ladies and gentlemen, if you please to seat yourselves quietly," he said; "I speak to you now about to-morrow. As you all know—Mister Penrod Schofield, I am not sticking up in a tree outside that window! If you do me the fafer to examine I am here, insides of the room. Now then! Piano, pl—no, I do not wish the piano! As you all know, this is the last lesson of the season until next October. To-morrow is our special afternoon; beginning three o'clock, we dance the cotillon. But this afternoon comes the test of mannerss. You must see if each know how to make a little formal call like a grown-up people in good societies. You have had good, perfect instruction; let us see if we know how to perform like societies ladies and gentlemen twenty-six years of age.

"Now, when you're dismissed each lady will go to her home and prepare to receive a call. The gentlemen will allow the ladies time to reach their houses and to prepare to receive callers; then each gentleman will call upon a lady and beg the pleasure to engage her for a partner in the cotillon tomorrow. You all know the correct, proper form for these calls, because didn't I work teaching you last lesson till I thought I would drop dead? Yes! Now each gentleman, if he reach a lady's house behind some-other gentleman, then he must go somewhere else to a lady's house, and keep calling until he secures a partner; so, as there are the same number of both, everybody shall have a partner.

"Now please all remember that if in case—Mister Penrod Schofield, when you make your call on a lady I beg you to please remember that gentlemen in good societies do not scratch the back in societies as you appear to attempt; so please allow the hands to rest carelessly in the lap. Now please all remember that if in case—Mister Penrod Schofield, if you please! Gentlemen in societies do not scratch the back by causing frictions between it and the back of your chair, either! Nobody else is itching here! I do not itch! I cannot talk if you must itch! In the name of Heaven, why must you always itch? What was I saying? Where—ah! the cotillon—yes! For the cotillon it is important nobody shall fail to be here to-morrow; but if any one should be so very ill he cannot possible come he must write a very polite note of regrets in the form of good societies to his engaged partner to excuse himself—and he must give the reason.

"I do not think anybody is going to be that sick to-morrow—no; and I will find out and report to parents if anybody would try it and not be. But it is important for the cotillon that we have an even number of so many couples, and if it should happen that someone comes and her partner has sent her a polite note that he has genuine reasons why he cannot come, the note must be handed at once to me, so that I arrange some other partner. Is all understood? Yes. The gentlemen will remember now to allow the ladies plenty of time to reach their houses and prepare to receive calls. Ladies and gentlemen, I thank you for your polite attention."

It was nine blocks to the house of Marjorie Jones; but Penrod did it in less than seven minutes from a flying start—such was his haste to lay himself and his hand for the cotillon at the feet of one who had so recently spoken unamiably of him in public. He had not yet learned that the only safe male rebuke to a scornful female is to stay away from her—especially if that is what she desires. However, he did not wish to rebuke her; simply and ardently he wished to dance the cotillon with her. Resentment was swallowed up in hope.

The fact that Miss Jones' feeling for him bore a striking resemblance to that of Simon Legree for Uncle Tom, deterred him not at all. Naturally, he was not wholly unconscious that when he should lay his hand for the cotillon at her feet it would be her inward desire to step on it; but he believed that if he were first in the field Marjorie would have to accept. These things are governed by law.

It was his fond intention to reach her house even in advance of herself, and with grave misgiving he beheld a large automobile at rest before the sainted gate. Forthwith, a sinking feeling became a portent inside him as little Maurice Levy emerged from the front door of the house.

" 'Lo, Penrod!" said Maurice airily.

"What you doin' in there?" inquired Penrod.

"In where?"

"In Marjorie's."

"Well, what shouldn't I be doin' in Marjorie's?" Mr. Levy returned indignantly. "I was inviting her for my partner in the cotillon—what you s'pose?"

"You haven't got any right to!" Penrod protested hotly. "You can't do it yet."

"I did do it yet!" said Maurice.

"You can't!" insisted Penrod. "You got to allow them time first. He said the ladies had to be allowed time to prepare."

"Well, ain't she had time to prepare?"

"When?" Penrod demanded, stepping close to his rival threateningly. "I'd like to know when——"

"When?" echoed the other with shrill triumph. "When? Why, in mamma's sixty-horse powder limousine automobile, what Marjorie came home with me in! I guess that's when!"

An impulse in the direction of violence became visible upon the countenance of Penrod.

"I expect you need some wiping down," he began dangerously. "I'll give you sumpthing to remem——"

"Oh, you will!" Maurice cried with astonishing truculence, contorting himself into what he may have considered a posture of defense. "Let's see you try it, you—you itcher!"

For the moment, defiance from such a source was dumfounding. Then, luckily, Penrod recollected something and glanced at the automobile.

Perceiving therein not only the alert chauffeur but the magnificent outlines of Mrs. Levy, his enemy's mother, he manœuvred his lifted hand so that it seemed he had but meant to scratch his ear.

"Well, I guess I better be goin'," he said casually. "See you t'-morrow!"

Maurice mounted to the lap of luxury, and Penrod strolled away with an assumption of careless ease which was put to a severe strain when, from the rear window of the car, a sudden protuberance in the nature of a small, dark, curly head shrieked scornfully:

"Go on—you big stiff!"

The cotillon loomed dismally before Penrod now; but it was his duty to secure a partner and he set about it with a dreary heart. The delay occasioned by his fruitless attempt on Marjorie and the altercation with his enemy at her gate had allowed other ladies ample time to prepare for callers—and to receive them. Sadly he went from house to house, finding that he had been preceded in one after the other. Altogether his hand for the cotillon was declined eleven times that afternoon on the legitimate ground of previous engagement. This, with Marjorie, scored off all except five of the seventeen possible partners; and four of the five were also sealed away from him, as he learned in chance encounters with other boys upon the street.

One lady alone remained; he bowed to the inevitable and entered this lorn damsel's gate at twilight with an air of great discouragement. The lorn damsel was Miss Rennsdale, aged eight.

We are apt to forget that there are actually times of life when too much youth is a handicap. Miss Rennsdale was beautiful; she danced like a première; she had every charm but age. On that account alone had she been allowed so much time to prepare to receive callers that it was only by the most manful efforts she could keep her lip from trembling.

A decorous maid conducted the long-belated applicant to her where she sat upon a sofa beside a nursery governess. The decorous maid announced him composedly as he made his entrance.

"Mr. Penrod Schofield!"

Miss Rennsdale suddenly burst into loud sobs.

"Oh!" she wailed. "I just knew it would be him!"

The decorous maid's composure vanished at once—likewise her decorum. She clapped her hand over her mouth and fled, uttering sounds. The governess, however, set herself to comfort her heartbroken charge, and presently succeeded in restoring Miss Rennsdale to a semblance of that poise with which a lady receives callers and accepts invitation to dance cotillons. But she continued to sob at intervals.

Feeling himself at perhaps a disadvantage, Penrod made offer of his hand for the morrow with a little embarrassment. Following the form prescribed by Professor Bartet, he advanced several paces toward the stricken lady and bowed formally.

"I hope," he said by rote, "you're well, and your parents also in good health. May I have the pleasure of dancing the cotillon as your partner t'-morrow afternoon?"

The wet eyes of Miss Rennsdale searched his countenance without pleasure, and a shudder wrung her small shoulders; but the governess whispered to her instructively, and she made a great effort.

"I thu-thank you fu-for your polite invu-invu-invutation; and I ac——" Thus far she progressed when emotion overcame her again. She beat frantically upon the sofa with fists and heels. "Oh, I *did* want it to be Georgie Bassett!"

"No, no, no!" said the governess, and whispered urgently, whereupon Miss Rennsdale was able to complete her acceptance.

"And I ac-accept wu-with pu-pleasure!" she moaned, and immediately, uttering a loud yell, flung herself face downward upon the sofa, clutching her governess convulsively.

Somewhat disconcerted, Penrod bowed again.

"I thank you for your polite acceptance," he murmured hurriedly; "and I trust—I trust—I forget. Oh, yes—I trust we shall have a most enjoyable occasion. Pray present my compliments to your parents; and I must now wish you a very good afternoon."

Concluding these courtly demonstrations with another bow he withdrew in fair order, though thrown into partial confusion in the hall by a final wail from his crushed hostess:

"Oh! Why couldn't it be anybody but *him!*"

CHAPTER XIII

THE SMALLPOX MEDICINE

Next morning Penrod woke in profound depression of spirit, the cotillon ominous before him. He pictured Marjorie Jones and Maurice, graceful and light-hearted, flitting by him fairylike, loosing silvery laughter upon him as he engaged in the struggle to keep step with a partner about four years and two feet his junior. It was hard enough for Penrod to keep step with a girl of his size.

The foreboding vision remained with him, increasing in vividness, throughout the forenoon. He found himself unable to fix his mind upon anything else, and, having bent his gloomy footsteps toward the sawdust-box, after breakfast, presently descended therefrom, abandoning Harold Ramorez where he had left him the preceding Saturday. Then, as he sat communing silently with wistful Duke, in the storeroom, coquettish fortune looked his way.

It was the habit of Penrod's mother not to throw away anything whatsoever until years of storage conclusively proved there would never be a use for it; but a recent house-cleaning had ejected upon the back porch a great quantity of bottles and other paraphernalia of medicine, left over from illnesses in the family during a period of several years. This débris Della, the cook, had collected in a large market basket, adding to it some bottles of flavouring extracts that had proved unpopular in the household; also, old catsup bottles; a jar or two of preserves gone bad; various rejected dental liquids—and other things. And she carried the basket out to the storeroom in the stable.

Penrod was at first unaware of what lay before him. Chin on palms, he sat upon the iron rim of a former aquarium and stared morbidly through the

open door at the checkered departing back of Della. It was another who saw
treasure in the basket she had left.

Mr. Samuel Williams, aged eleven, and congenial to Penrod in years, sex,
and disposition, appeared in the doorway, shaking into foam a black liquid
within a pint bottle, stoppered by a thumb.

"Yay, Penrod!" the visitor gave greeting.

"Yay," said Penrod with slight enthusiasm. "What you got?"

"Lickrish water."

"Drinkin's!" demanded Penrod promptly. This is equivalent to the cry of
"Biters" when an apple is shown, and establishes unquestionable title.

"Down to there!" stipulated Sam, removing his thumb to affix it firmly
as a mark upon the side of the bottle—a check upon gormandizing that remained carefully in place while Penrod drank. This rite concluded, the visitor's eye fell upon the basket deposited by Della. He emitted tokens of
pleasure.

"Looky! Looky! Looky there! That ain't any good pile o' stuff—oh, no!"

"What for?"

"Drug store!" shouted Sam. "We'll be partners——"

"Or else," Penrod suggested, "I'll run the drug store and you be a
customer——"

"No! Partners!" insisted Sam with such conviction that his host yielded;
and within ten minutes the drug store was doing a heavy business with imaginary patrons. Improvising counters with boards and boxes, and setting
forth a very druggish-looking stock from the basket, each of the partners
found occupation to his taste—Penrod as salesman and Sam as prescription
clerk.

"Here you are, madam!" said Penrod briskly, offering a vial of Sam's mixing
to an invisible matron. "This will cure your husband in a few minutes.
Here's the camphor, mister. Call again! Fifty cents' worth of pills? Yes,
madam. There you are! Hurry up with that dose for the nigger lady, Bill!"

"I'll 'tend to it soon's I get time, Jim," replied the prescription clerk. "I'm
busy fixin' the smallpox medicine for the sick policeman downtown."

Penrod stopped sales to watch this operation. Sam had found an empty
pint bottle and, with the pursed lips and measuring eye of a great chemist,
was engaged in filling it from other bottles. First, he poured into it some of
the syrup from the condemned preserves; and a quantity of extinct hair oil;
next the remaining contents of a dozen small vials cryptically labelled with
physicians' prescriptions; then some remnants of catsup and essence of beef
and what was left in several bottles of mouthwash; after that a quantity of
rejected flavouring extract—topping off by shaking into the mouth of the bottle various powders from small pink papers, relics of Mr. Schofield's influenza
of the preceding winter.

Sam examined the combination with concern, appearing unsatisfied. "We
got to make that smallpox medicine good and strong!" he remarked; and, his

artistic sense growing more powerful than his appetite, he poured about a quarter of the licorice water into the smallpox medicine.

"What you doin'?" protested Penrod. "What you want to waste that lickrish water for? We ought to keep it to drink when we're tired."

"I guess I got a right to use my own lickrish water any way I want to," replied the prescription clerk. "I tell you, you can't get smallpox medicine too strong. Look at her now!" He held the bottle up admiringly. "She's as black as lickrish. I bet you she's strong all right!"

"I wonder how she tastes?" said Penrod thoughtfully.

"Don't smell so awful much," observed Sam, sniffing the bottle—"a good deal, though!"

"I wonder if it'd make us sick to drink it?" said Penrod.

Sam looked at the bottle thoughtfully; then his eye, wandering, fell upon Duke, placidly curled up near the door, and lighted with the advent of an idea new to him, but old, old in the world—older than Egypt!

"Let's give Duke some!" he cried.

That was the spark. They acted immediately; and a minute later Duke, released from custody with a competent potion of the smallpox medicine inside him, settled conclusively their doubts concerning its effect. The patient animal, accustomed to expect the worst at all times, walked out of the door, shaking his head with an air of considerable annoyance, opening and closing his mouth with singular energy—and so repeatedly that they began to count the number of times he did it. Sam thought it was thirty-nine times, but Penrod had counted forty-one before other and more striking symptoms appeared.

All things come from Mother Earth and must return—Duke restored much at this time. Afterward, he ate heartily of grass; and then, over his shoulder, he bent upon his master one inscrutable look and departed feebly to the front yard.

The two boys had watched the process with warm interest. "I told you she was strong!" said Mr. Williams proudly.

"Yes, sir—she is!" Penrod was generous enough to admit. "I expect she's strong enough——" He paused in thought, and added: "We haven't got a horse any more."

"I bet you she'd fix him if you had!" said Sam. And it may be that this was no idle boast.

The pharmaceutical game was not resumed; the experiment upon Duke had made the drug store commonplace and stimulated the appetite for stronger meat. Lounging in the doorway, the near-vivisectionists sipped licorice water alternately and conversed.

"I bet some of our smallpox medicine would fix ole P'fessor Bartet all right!" quoth Penrod. "I wish he'd come along and ask us for some."

"We could tell him it was lickrish water," added Sam, liking the idea. "The two bottles look almost the same."

"Then we wouldn't have to go to his ole cotillon this afternoon," Penrod sighed. "There wouldn't be any!"

"Who's your partner, Pen?"

"Who's yours?"

"Who's yours? I just asl you."

"Oh, she's all right!" And Penrod smiled boastfully.

"I bet you wanted to dance with Marjorie!" said his friend.

"Me? I wouldn't dance with that girl if she begged me to! I wouldn't dance with her to save her from drowning! I wouldn't da——"

"Oh, no—you wouldn't!" interrupted Mr. Williams skeptically.

Penrod changed his tone and became persuasive.

"Looky here, Sam," he said confidentially. "I've got a mighty nice partner, but my mother don't like her mother; and so I've been thinking I better not dance with her. I'll tell you what I'll do; I've got a mighty good sling in the house, and I'll give it to you if you'll change partners."

"You want to change and you don't even know who mine is!" said Sam, and he made the simple though precocious deduction: "Yours must be a lala! Well, I invited Mabel Rorebeck, and she wouldn't let me change if I wanted to. Mabel Rorebeck'd rather dance with me," he continued serenely, "than anybody; and she said she was awful afraid you'd ast her. But I ain't goin' to dance with Mabel after all, because this morning she sent me a note about her uncle died last night—and P'fessor Bartet'll have to find me a partner after I get there. Anyway I bet you haven't got any sling—and I bet your partner's Baby Rennsdale!"

"What if she is?" said Penrod. "She's good enough for *me!*" This speech held not so much modesty in solution as intended praise of the lady. Taken literally, however, it was an understatement of the facts and wholly insincere.

"Yay!" jeered Mr. Williams, upon whom his friend's hypocrisy was quite wasted. "How can your mother not like her mother? Baby Rennsdale hasn't got any mother! You and her'll be a sight!"

That was Penrod's own conviction; and with this corroboration of it he grew so spiritless that he could offer no retort. He slid to a despondent sitting posture upon the door sill and gazed wretchedly upon the ground, while his companion went to replenish the licorice water at the hydrant—enfeebling the potency of the liquor no doubt, but making up for that in quantity.

"Your mother goin' with you to the cotillon?" asked Sam when he returned.

"No. She's goin' to meet me there. She's goin' somewhere first."

"So's mine," said Sam. "I'll come by for you."

"All right."

"I better go before long. Noon whistles been blowin'."

"All right," Penrod repeated dully.

Sam turned to go, but paused. A new straw hat was peregrinating along the fence near the two boys. This hat belonged to someone passing upon the sidewalk of the cross-street; and the someone was Maurice Levy. Even as they stared, he halted and regarded them over the fence with two small, dark eyes.

Fate had brought about this moment and this confrontation.

CHAPTER XIV

MAURICE LEVY'S CONSTITUTION

" 'Lo, Sam!" said Maurice cautiously. "What you doin'?"

Penrod at that instant had a singular experience—an intellectual shock like a flash of fire in the brain. Sitting in darkness, a great light flooded him with wild brilliance. He gasped!

"What you doin'?" repeated Mr. Levy.

Penrod sprang to his feet, seized the licorice bottle, shook it with stoppering thumb, and took a long drink with histrionic unction.

"What you doin'?" asked Maurice for the third time, Sam Williams not having decided upon a reply.

It was Penrod who answered.

"Drinkin' lickrish water," he said simply, and wiped his mouth with such delicious enjoyment that Sam's jaded thirst was instantly stimulated. He took the bottle eagerly from Penrod.

"A-a-h!" exclaimed Penrod, smacking his lips. "That was a good un!"

The eyes above the fence glistened.

"Ask him if he don't want some," Penrod whispered urgently. "Quit drinkin' it! It's no good any more. Ask him!"

"What for?" demanded the practical Sam.

"Go on and ask him!" whispered Penrod fiercely.

"Say, M'rice!" Sam called, waving the bottle. "Want some?"

"Bring it here!" Mr. Levy requested.

"Come on over and get some," returned Sam, being prompted.

"I can't. Penrod Schofield's after me."

"No, I'm not," said Penrod reassuringly. "I won't touch you, M'rice. I made up with you yesterday afternoon—don't you remember? You're all right with me, M'rice."

Maurice looked undecided. But Penrod had the delectable bottle again, and tilting it above his lips, affected to let the cool liquid purl enrichingly into him, while with his right hand he stroked his middle façade ineffably. Maurice's mouth watered.

"Here!" cried Sam, stirred again by the superb manifestations of his friend. "Gimme that!"

Penrod brought the bottle down, surprisingly full after so much gusto,

but withheld it from Sam; and the two scuffled for its possession. Nothing in the world could have so worked upon the desire of the yearning observer beyond the fence.

"Honest, Penrod—you ain't goin' to touch me if I come in your yard?" he called. "Honest?"

"Cross my heart!" answered Penrod, holding the bottle away from Sam. "And we'll let you drink all you want."

Maurice hastily climbed the fence, and while he was thus occupied Mr. Samuel Williams received a great enlightenment. With startling rapidity. Penrod, standing just outside the storeroom door, extended his arm within the room, deposited the licorice water upon the counter of the drug store, seized in its stead the bottle of smallpox medicine, and extended it cordially toward the advancing Maurice.

Genius is like that—great, simple, broad strokes!

Dazzled, Mr. Samuel Williams leaned against the wall. He had the sensations of one who comes suddenly into the presence of a chef-d'œuvre. Perhaps the first coherent thought was that almost universal one on such huge occasions: "Why couldn't I have done that!"

Sam might have been even more dazzled had he guessed that he figured not altogether as a spectator in the sweeping and magnificent conception of the new Talleyrand. Sam had no partner for the cotillon. If Maurice was to be absent from that festivity—as it began to seem he might be—Penrod needed a male friend to take care of Miss Rennsdale; and he believed he saw his way to compel Mr. Williams to be that male friend. For this he relied largely upon the prospective conduct of Miss Rennsdale when he should get the matter before her—he was inclined to believe she would favour the exchange. As for Talleyrand Penrod himself, he was going to dance that cotillon with Marjorie Jones!

"You can have all you can drink at one pull, M'rice," said Penrod kindly.

"You said I could have all I want!" protested Maurice, reaching for the bottle.

"No, I didn't," returned Penrod quickly, holding it away from the eager hand.

"He did, too! Didn't he, Sam?"

Sam could not reply; his eyes, fixed upon the bottle, protruded strangely.

"You heard him—didn't you, Sam?"

"Well, if I did say it I didn't mean it!" said Penrod hastily, quoting from one of the authorities. "Looky here, M'rice," he continued, assuming a more placative and reasoning tone, "that wouldn't be fair to us. I guess we want some of our own lickrish water, don't we? The bottle ain't much over two-thirds full anyway. What I meant was, you can have all you can drink at one pull."

"How do you mean?"

"Why, this way: you can gulp all you want, so long as you keep swallering;

but you can't take the bottle out of your mouth and commence again. Soon's you quit swallering it's Sam's turn."

"No; you can have next, Penrod," said Sam.

"Well, anyway, I mean M'rice has to give the bottle up the minute he stops swallering."

Craft appeared upon the face of Maurice, like a poster pasted on a wall.

"I can drink so long I don't stop swallering?"

"Yes; that's it."

"All right!" he cried. "Gimme the bottle!"

And Penrod placed it in his hand.

"You promise to let me drink until I quit swallering?" Maurice insisted.

"Yes!" said both boys together.

With that, Maurice placed the bottle to his lips and began to drink. Penrod and Sam leaned forward in breathless excitement. They had feared Maurice might smell the contents of the bottle; but that danger was past—this was the crucial moment. Their fondest hope was that he would make his first swallow a voracious one—it was impossible to imagine a second. They expected one big, gulping swallow and then an explosion, with fountain effects.

Little they knew the mettle of their man! Maurice swallowed once; he swallowed twice—and thrice—and he continued to swallow! No Adam's apple was sculptured on that juvenile throat, but the internal progress of the liquid was not a whit the less visible. His eyes gleamed with cunning and malicious triumph, sidewise, at the stunned conspirators; he was fulfilling the conditions of the draught, not once breaking the thread of that marvellous swallowing.

His audience stood petrified. Already Maurice had swallowed more than they had given Duke—and still the liquor receded in the uplifted bottle! And now the clear glass gleamed above the dark contents full half the vessel's length—and Maurice went on drinking! Slowly the clear glass increased in its dimensions—slowly the dark diminished.

Sam Williams made a horrified movement to check him—but Maurice protested passionately with his disengaged arm, and made vehement vocal noises remindful of the contract; whereupon Sam desisted and watched the continuing performance in a state of grisly fascination.

Maurice drank it all! He drained the last drop and threw the bottle in the air, uttering loud ejaculations of triumph and satisfaction.

"Hah!" he cried, blowing out his cheeks, inflating his chest, squaring his shoulders, patting his stomach, and wiping his mouth contentedly. "Hah! Aha! Waha! Wafwah! But that was good!"

The two boys stood looking at him in stupor.

"Well, I gotta say this," said Maurice graciously: "You stuck to your bargain all right and treated me fair."

Stricken with a sudden horrible suspicion, Penrod entered the storeroom in one stride and lifted the bottle of licorice water to his nose—then to his lips.

It was weak, but good; he had made no mistake. And Maurice had really drained—to the dregs—the bottle of old hair tonics, dead catsups, syrups of undesirable preserves, condemned extracts of vanilla and lemon, decayed chocolate, ex-essence of beef, mixed dental preparations, aromatic spirits of ammonia, spirits of nitre, alcohol, arnica, quinine, ipecac, sal volatile, nux vomica and licorice water—with traces of arsenic, belladonna and strychnine.

Penrod put the licorice water out of sight and turned to face the others. Maurice was seating himself on a box just outside the door and had taken a package of cigarettes from his pocket.

"Nobody can see me from here, can they?" he said, striking a match. "You fellers smoke?"

"No," said Sam, staring at him haggardly.

"No," said Penrod in a whisper.

Maurice lit his cigarette and puffed showily.

"Well, sir," he remarked, "you fellers are certainly square—I gotta say that much. Honest, Penrod, I thought you was after me! I did think so," he added sunnily; "but now I guess you like me, or else you wouldn't of stuck to it about lettin' me drink it all if I kept on swallering."

He chatted on with complete geniality, smoking his cigarette in content. And as he ran from one topic to another his hearers stared at him in a kind of torpor. Never once did they exchange a glance with each other; their eyes were frozen to Maurice. The cheerful conversationalist made it evident that he was not without gratitude.

"Well," he said as he finished his cigarette and rose to go, "you fellers have treated me nice—and some day you come over to my yard; I'd like to run with you fellers. You're the kind of fellers I like."

Penrod's jaw fell; Sam's mouth had been open all the time. Neither spoke.

"I gotta go," observed Maurice, consulting a handsome watch. "Gotta get dressed for the cotillon right after lunch. Come on, Sam. Don't you have to go, too?"

Sam nodded dazedly.

"Well, good-bye, Penrod," said Maurice cordially. "I'm glad you like me all right. Come on, Sam."

Penrod leaned against the doorpost and with fixed and glazing eyes watched the departure of his two visitors. Maurice was talking volubly, with much gesticulation, as they went; but Sam walked mechanically and in silence, staring at his brisk companion and keeping at a little distance from him.

They passed from sight, Maurice still conversing gayly—and Penrod slowly betook himself into the house, his head bowed upon his chest.

Some three hours later, Mr. Samuel Williams, waxen clean and in sweet raiment, made his reappearance in Penrod's yard, yodelling a code-signal to

summon forth his friend. He yodelled loud, long, and frequently, finally se-
curing a faint response from the upper air.

"Where are you?" shouted Mr. Williams, his roving glance searching am-
bient heights. Another low-spirited yodel reaching his ear, he perceived the
head and shoulders of his friend projecting above the roofridge of the stable.
The rest of Penrod's body was concealed from view, reposing upon the opposite slant of the gable and precariously secured by the crooking of his elbows
over the ridge.

"Yay! What you doin' up there?"

"Nothin'."

"You better be careful!" Sam called. "You'll slide off and fall down in the
alley if you don't look out. I come pert' near it last time we was up there.
Come on down! Ain't you goin' to the cotillon?"

Penrod made no reply. Sam came nearer.

"Say," he called up in a guarded voice, "I went to our telephone a while
ago and ast him how he was feelin', and he said he felt fine!"

"So did I," said Penrod. "He told me he felt bully!"

Sam thrust his hands in his pockets and brooded. The opening of the
kitchen door caused a diversion. It was Della.

"Mister Penrod," she bellowed forthwith, "come ahn down fr'm up there!
Y'r mamma's at the dancin' class waitin' fer ye, an' she's telephoned me
they're goin' to begin—an' what's the matter with ye? Come ahn down fr'm
up there!"

"Come on!" urged Sam. "We'll be late. There go Maurice and Marjorie
now."

A glittering car spun by, disclosing briefly a genre picture of Marjorie Jones
in pink, supporting a monstrous sheaf of American Beauty roses. Maurice,
sitting shining and joyous beside her, saw both boys and waved them a hearty
greeting as the car turned the corner.

Penrod uttered some muffled words and then waved both arms—either in
response or as an expression of his condition of mind; it may have been a
gesture of despair. How much intention there was in this act—obviously so
rash, considering the position he occupied—it is impossible to say. Undeniably there must remain a suspicion of deliberate purpose.

Della screamed and Sam shouted. Penrod had disappeared from view.

The delayed dance was about to begin a most uneven cotillon under the
direction of its slightly frenzied instructor, when Samuel Williams arrived.

Mrs. Schofield hurriedly left the ballroom; while Miss Rennsdale, flushing
with sudden happiness, curtsied profoundly to Professor Bartet and obtained
his attention.

"I have told you fifty times," he informed her passionately ere she spoke,
"I cannot make no such changes. If your partner comes you have to dance
with him. You are going to drive me crazy, sure! What is it? What now?
What you want?"

The damsel curtsied again and handed him the following communication, addressed to herself:

"Dear madam Please excuse me from dancing the cotilon with you this afternoon as I have fell off the barn

"Sincerly yours
"PENROD SCHOFIELD."

CHAPTER XV

THE TWO FAMILIES

Penrod entered the schoolroom, Monday morning, picturesquely leaning upon a man's cane shortened to support a cripple approaching the age of twelve. He arrived about twenty minutes late, limping deeply, his brave young mouth drawn with pain, and the sensation he created must have been a solace to him; the only possible criticism of this entrance being that it was just a shade too heroic. Perhaps for that reason it failed to stagger Miss Spence, a woman so saturated with suspicion that she penalized Penrod for tardiness as promptly and as coldly as if he had been a mere, ordinary, unmutilated boy. Nor would she entertain any discussion of the justice of her ruling. It seemed, almost, that she feared to argue with him.

However, the distinction of cane and limp remained to him, consolations which he protracted far into the week—until Thursday evening, in fact, when Mr. Schofield, observing from a window his son's pursuit of Duke round and round the backyard, confiscated the cane, with the promise that it should not remain idle if he saw Penrod limping again. Thus, succeeding a depressing Friday, another Saturday brought the necessity for new inventions.

It was a scented morning in apple-blossom time. At about ten of the clock Penrod emerged hastily from the kitchen door. His pockets bulged abnormally; so did his cheeks, and he swallowed with difficulty. A threatening mop, wielded by a cooklike arm in a checkered sleeve, followed him through the doorway, and he was preceded by a small, hurried, wistful dog with a warm doughnut in his mouth. The kitchen door slammed petulantly, enclosing the sore voice of Della, whereupon Penrod and Duke seated themselves upon the pleasant sward and immediately consumed the spoils of their raid.

From the cross-street which formed the side boundary of the Schofields' ample yard came a jingle of harness and the cadenced clatter of a pair of trotting horses, and Penrod, looking up, beheld the passing of a fat acquaintance, torpid amid the conservative splendours of a rather old-fashioned victoria. This was Roderick Magsworth Bitts, Junior, a fellow sufferer at the

Friday Afternoon Dancing Class, but otherwise not often a companion: a home-sheltered lad, tutored privately and preserved against the coarsening influences of rude comradeship and miscellaneous information. Heavily over-grown in all physical dimensions, virtuous, and placid, this cloistered mutton was wholly uninteresting to Penrod Schofield. Nevertheless, Roderick Magsworth Bitts, Junior, was a personage on account of the importance of the Magsworth Bitts family; and it was Penrod's destiny to increase Roderick's celebrity far, far beyond its present aristocratic limitations.

The Magsworth Bittses were important because they were impressive; there was no other reason. And they were impressive because they believed themselves important. The adults of the family were impregnably formal; they dressed with reticent elegance, and wore the same nose and the same expression—an expression which indicated that they knew something exquisite and sacred which other people could never know. Other people, in their presence, were apt to feel mysteriously ignoble and to become secretly uneasy about ancestors, gloves, and pronunciation. The Magsworth Bitts manner was withholding and reserved, though sometimes gracious, granting small smiles as great favours and giving off a chilling kind of preciousness. Natu-rally, when any citizen of the community did anything unconventional or improper, or made a mistake, or had a relative who went wrong, that citizen's first and worst fear was that the Magsworth Bittses would hear of it. In fact, this painful family had for years terrorized the community, though the com-munity had never realized that it was terrorized, and invariably spoke of the family as the "most charming circle in town." By common consent, Mrs. Roderick Magsworth Bitts officiated as the supreme model as well as critic-in-chief of morals and deportment for all the unlucky people prosperous enough to be elevated to her acquaintance.

Magsworth was the important part of the name. Mrs. Roderick Magsworth Bitts was a Magsworth born, herself, and the Magsworth crest decorated not only Mrs. Magsworth Bitts' note-paper but was on the china, on the table linen, on the chimney-pieces, on the opaque glass of the front door, on the victoria, and on the harness, though omitted from the garden-hose and the lawn-mower.

Naturally, no sensible person dreamed of connecting that illustrious crest with the unfortunate and notorious Rena Magsworth whose name had grown week by week into larger and larger type upon the front pages of newspapers, owing to the gradually increasing public and official belief that she had poisoned a family of eight. However, the statement that no sensible person could have connected the Magsworth Bitts family with the arsenical Rena takes no account of Penrod Schofield.

Penrod never missed a murder, a hanging or an electrocution in the news-papers; he knew almost as much about Rena Magsworth as her jurymen did, though they sat in a court-room two hundred miles away, and he had it in mind—so frank he was—to ask Roderick Magsworth Bitts, Junior, if the mur-deress happened to be a relative.

The present encounter, being merely one of apathetic greeting, did not afford the opportunity. Penrod took off his cap, and Roderick, seated between his mother and one of his grown-up sisters, nodded sluggishly, but neither Mrs. Magsworth Bitts nor her daughter acknowledged the salutation of the boy in the yard. They disapproved of him as a person of little consequence, and that little, bad. Snubbed, Penrod thoughtfully restored his cap to his head. A boy can be cut as effectually as a man, and this one was chilled to a low temperature. He wondered if they despised him because they had seen a last fragment of doughnut in his hand; then he thought that perhaps it was Duke who had disgraced him. Duke was certainly no fashionable looking dog.

The resilient spirits of youth, however, presently revived, and discovering a spider upon one knee and a beetle simultaneously upon the other, Penrod forgot Mrs. Roderick Magsworth Bitts in the course of some experiments infringing upon the domain of Doctor Carrel. Penrod's efforts—with the aid of a pin—to effect a transference of living organism were unsuccessful; but he convinced himself forever that a spider cannot walk with a beetle's legs. Della then enhanced zoölogical interest by depositing upon the back porch a large rat-trap from the cellar, the prison of four live rats awaiting execution.

Penrod at once took possession, retiring to the empty stable, where he installed the rats in a small wooden box with a sheet of broken window-glass—held down by a brickbat—over the top. Thus the symptoms of their agitation, when the box was shaken or hammered upon, could be studied at leisure. Altogether this Saturday was starting splendidly.

After a time, the student's attention was withdrawn from his specimens by a peculiar smell, which, being followed up by a system of selective sniffing, proved to be an emanation leaking into the stable from the alley. He opened the back door.

Across the alley was a cottage which a thrifty neighbour had built on the rear line of his lot and rented to negroes; and the fact that a negro family was now in process of "moving in" was manifested by the presence of a thin mule and a ramshackle wagon, the latter laden with the semblance of a stove and a few other unpretentious household articles.

A very small darky boy stood near the mule. In his hand was a rusty chain, and at the end of the chain the delighted Penrod perceived the source of the special smell he was tracing—a large raccoon. Duke, who had shown not the slightest interest in the rats, set up a frantic barking and simulated a ravening assault upon the strange animal. It was only a bit of acting, however, for Duke was an old dog, had suffered much, and desired no unnecessary sorrow, wherefore he confined his demonstrations to alarums and excursions, and presently sat down at a distance and expressed himself by intermittent threatenings in a quavering falsetto.

"What's that 'coon's name?" asked Penrod, intending no discourtesy.

"Aim gommo mame," said the small darky.

"What?"

"Aim gommo mame."

"*What?*"

The small darky looked annoyed.

"Aim *gommo* mame, I hell you," he said impatiently.

Penrod conceived that insult was intended.

"What's the matter of you?" he demanded advancing. "You get fresh with *me*, and I'll——"

"Hyuh, white boy!" A coloured youth of Penrod's own age appeared in the doorway of the cottage. "You let 'at brothuh mine alone. He ain' do nothin' to you."

"Well, why can't he answer?"

"He can't. He can't talk no better'n what he *was* talkin'. He tongue-tie'."

"Oh," said Penrod, mollified. Then, obeying an impulse so universally aroused in the human breast under like circumstances that it has become a quip, he turned to the afflicted one.

"Talk some more," he begged eagerly.

"I hoe you ackoom aim gommo mame," was the prompt response, in which a slight ostentation was manifest. Unmistakable tokens of vanity had appeared upon the small, swart countenance.

"What's he mean?" asked Penrod, enchanted.

"He say he tole you 'at 'coon ain' got no name."

"What's *your* name?"

"I'm name Herman."

"What's his name?" Penrod pointed to the tongue-tied boy.

"Verman."

"What!"

"Verman. Was three us boys in ow fam'ly. Ol'est one name Sherman. 'N'en come me; I'm Herman. 'N'en come him; he Verman. Sherman dead. Verman, he de littles' one."

"You goin' to live here?"

"Umhuh. Done move in f'm way outen on a fahm."

He pointed to the north with his right hand, and Penrod's eyes opened wide as they followed the gesture. Herman had no forefinger on that hand.

"Look there!" exclaimed Penrod. "You haven't got any finger!"

"*I* mum map," said Verman, with egregious pride.

"*He* done 'at," interpreted Herman, chuckling. "Yessuh; done chop 'er spang off, long 'go. He's a playin' wif a ax an' I lay my finguh on de do'-sill an' I say, 'Verman, chop 'er off!' So Verman he chop 'er right spang off up to de roots! Yessuh."

"What *for?*"

"Jes' fo' nothin'."

"He hoe me hoo," remarked Verman.

"Yessuh, I tole him to," said Herman, "an' he chop 'er off, an' ey ain't airy oth' one evuh grown on wheres de ole one use to grow. Nosuh!"

"But what'd you tell him to do it for?"

"Nothin'. I jes' said it 'at way—an' he jes' chop 'er off!"

Both brothers looked pleased and proud. Penrod's profound interest was flatteringly visible, a tribute to their unusualness.

"Hem bow goy," suggested Verman eagerly.

"Aw ri'," said Herman. "Ow sistuh Queenie, she a growed-up woman; she got a goituh."

"Got a what?"

"Goituh. Swellin' on her neck—grea' big swellin'. She heppin' mammy move in now. You look in de front-room winduh wheres she sweepin'; you kin see it on her."

Penrod looked in the window and was rewarded by a fine view of Queenie's goitre. He had never before seen one, and only the lure of further conversation on the part of Verman brought him from the window.

"Verman say tell you 'bout pappy," explained Herman. "Mammy an' Queenie move in town an' go git de house all fix up befo' pappy git out."

"Out of where?"

"Jail. Pappy cut a man, an' de police done kep' him in jail evuh sense Chris'mus-time; but dey goin' tuhn him loose ag'in nex' week."

"What'd he cut the other man with?"

"Wif a pitchfawk."

Penrod began to feel that a lifetime spent with this fascinating family was all too short. The brothers, glowing with amiability, were as enraptured as he. For the first time in their lives they moved in the rich glamour of sensationalism. Herman was prodigal of gesture with his right hand; and Verman, chuckling with delight, talked fluently, though somewhat consciously. They cheerfully agreed to keep the raccoon—already beginning to be mentioned as "our 'coon" by Penrod—in Mr. Schofield's empty stable, and, when the animal had been chained to the wall near the box of rats and supplied with a pan of fair water, they assented to their new friend's suggestion (inspired by a fine sense of the artistic harmonies) that the heretofore nameless pet be christened Sherman, in honour of their deceased relative.

At this juncture was heard from the front yard the sound of that yodelling which is the peculiar accomplishment of those whose voices have not "changed." Penrod yodelled a response; and Mr. Samuel Williams appeared, a large bundle under his arm.

"Yay, Penrod!" was his greeting, casual enough from without; but, having entered, he stopped short and emitted a prodigious whistle. "*Ya-a-ay!*" he then shouted. "Look at the 'coon!"

"I guess you better say, 'Look at the 'coon!'" Penrod returned proudly. "They's a good deal more'n him to look at, too. Talk some, Verman." Verman complied.

Sam was warmly interested. "What'd you say his name was?" he asked.

"Verman."

"How d'you spell it?"

"V-e-r-m-a-n," replied Penrod, having previously received this information from Herman.

"Oh!" said Sam.

"Point to sumpthing, Herman," Penrod commanded, and Sam's excitement, when Herman pointed was sufficient to the occasion.

Penrod, the discoverer, continued his exploitation of the manifold wonders of the Sherman, Herman, and Verman collection. With the air of a proprietor he escorted Sam into the alley for a good look at Queenie (who seemed not to care for her increasing celebrity) and proceeded to the dramatic climax—the recital of the episode of the pitchfork and its consequences.

The cumulative effect was enormous, and could have but one possible result. The normal boy is always at least one half Barnum.

"Let's get up a SHOW!"

Penrod and Sam both claimed to have said it first, a question left unsettled in the ecstasies of hurried preparation. The bundle under Sam's arm, brought with no definite purpose, proved to have been an inspiration. It consisted of broad sheets of light yellow wrapping-paper, discarded by Sam's mother in her spring house-cleaning. There were half-filled cans and buckets of paint in the storeroom adjoining the carriage-house, and presently the side wall of the stable flamed information upon the passer-by from a great and spreading poster.

"Publicity," primal requisite of all theatrical and amphitheatrical enterprise thus provided, subsequent arrangements proceeded with a fury of energy which transformed the empty hay-loft. True, it is impossible to say just what the hay-loft was transformed into, but history warrantably clings to the statement that it was transformed. Duke and Sherman were secured to the rear wall at a considerable distance from each other, after an exhibition of reluctance on the part of Duke, during which he displayed a nervous energy and agility almost miraculous in so small and middle-aged a dog. Benches were improvised for spectators; the rats were brought up; finally the rafters, corn-crib, and hay-chute were ornamented with flags and strips of bunting from Sam Williams' attic, Sam returning from the excursion wearing an old silk hat, and accompanied (on account of a rope) by a fine dachshund encountered on the highway. In the matter of personal decoration paint was generously used: an interpretation of the spiral, inclining to whites and greens, becoming brilliantly effective upon the dark facial backgrounds of Herman and Verman; while the countenances of Sam and Penrod were each supplied with the black moustache and imperial, lacking which, no professional showman can be esteemed conscientious.

It was regretfully decided, in council, that no attempt be made to add Queenie to the list of exhibits, her brothers warmly declining to act as ambassadors in that cause. They were certain Queenie would not like the idea, they said, and Herman picturesquely described her activity on occasions when she had been annoyed by too much attention to her appearance. However, Penrod's disappointment was alleviated by an inspiration which came to him in a moment of pondering upon the dachshund, and the entire party went forth to add an enriching line to the poster.

They found a group of seven, including two adults, already gathered in the street to read and admire this work.

SCHoFiELD & WiLLiAMS
BiG SHOW
ADMiSSioN 1 CENT oR 20 PiNS
MUSUEM oF CURioSiTES
Now GoiNG oN
SHERMAN HERMAN & VERMAN
THiER FATHERS iN JAiL STABED A
MAN WiTH A
PiTCHFORK
SHERMAN THE WiLD ANIMAL
CAPTURED iN AFRiCA
HERMAN THE ONE FiNGERED TATOOD
WILD MAN VERMAN THE SAVAGE TATOOD
WILD BoY TALKS ONLY iN HiS NAiTiVE
LANGUAGS. Do NoT FAIL TO SEE DUKE
THE INDiAN DOG ALSO THE MiCHiGAN
TRAiNED RATS

A heated argument took place between Sam and Penrod, the point at issue being settled, finally, by the drawing of straws; whereupon Penrod, with pardonable self-importance—in the presence of an audience now increased to nine—slowly painted the words inspired by the dachshund:

IMPoRTENT Do NoT MISS THE SoUTH AMERiCAN DoG PART ALLIGATOR.

CHAPTER XVI

THE NEW STAR

Sam, Penrod, Herman, and Verman withdrew in considerable state from non-paying view, and, repairing to the hay-loft, declared the exhibition open to the public. Oral proclamation was made by Sam, and then the loitering multitude was enticed by the seductive strains of a band; the two partners performing upon combs and paper, Herman and Verman upon tin pans with sticks.

The effect was immediate. Visitors appeared upon the stairway and sought admission. Herman and Verman took position among the exhibits, near the wall; Sam stood at the entrance, officiating as barker and ticket-seller; while Penrod, with debonair suavity, acted as curator, master of ceremonies, and lecturer. He greeted the first to enter with a courtly bow. They consisted of Miss Rennsdale and her nursery governess, and they paid spot cash for their admission.

"Walk in, lay-deeze, walk right in—pray do not obstruck the passageway," said Penrod, in a remarkable voice. "Pray be seated; there is room for each and all."

Miss Rennsdale and governess were followed by Mr. Georgie Bassett and baby sister (which proves the perfection of Georgie's character) and six or seven other neighbourhood children—a most satisfactory audience, although, subsequent to Miss Rennsdale and governess, admission was wholly by pin.

"Gen-til-mun and lay-deeze," shouted Penrod, "I will first call your at-tain-shon to our genuine South American dog, part alligator!" He pointed to the dachshund, and added, in his ordinary tone, "That's him." Straightway re-assuming the character of showman, he bellowed: "Next, you see Duke, the genuine, full-blooded Indian dog from the far Western Plains and Rocky Mountains. Next, the trained Michigan rats, captured way up there, and trained to jump and run all around the box at the—at the—at the slightest pre-text!" He paused, partly to take breath and partly to enjoy his own surprised discovery that this phrase was in his vocabulary.

"At the slightest pre-text!" he repeated, and continued, suiting the action to the word: "I will now hammer upon the box and each and all may see these genuine full-blooded Michigan rats perform at the slightest pre-text! There! (That's all they do now, but I and Sam are goin' to train 'em lots more before this afternoon.) Gen-til-mun and lay-deeze, I will kindly now call your at-tain-shon to Sherman, the wild animal from Africa, costing the lives of the wild trapper and many of his companions. Next, let me kindly interodoos Herman and Verman. Their father got mad and stuck his pitch-fork right inside of another man, exactly as promised upon the advertise-ments outside the big tent, and got put in jail. Look at them well, gen-til-mun and lay-deeze, there is no extra charge, and re-mem-bur you are each and all now looking at two wild, tattooed men which the father of is in jail. Point, Herman. Each and all will have a chance to see. Point to sumpthing else, Herman. This is the only genuine one-fingered tattooed wild man. Last on the programme, gen-til-mun and lay-deeze, we have Verman, the savage tattooed wild boy, that can't speak only his native foreign languages. Talk some, Verman."

Verman obliged and made an instantaneous hit. He was encored raptur-ously, again and again; and, thrilling with the unique pleasure of being appreciated and misunderstood at the same time, would have talked all day but too gladly. Sam Williams, however, with a true showman's foresight, whispered to Penrod, who rang down on the monologue.

"*Gen*-til-mun and *lay*-deeze, this closes our pufformance. Pray pass out quietly and with as little jostling as possible. As soon as you are all out there's goin' to be a new pufformance, and each and all are welcome at the same and simple price of admission. Pray pass out quietly and with as little jostling as possible. *Re-mem-bur* the price is only one cent, the tenth part of a dime, or twenty pins, no bent ones taken. Pray pass out quietly and with as little jostling as possible. The Schofield and Williams Military Band will play before each pufformance, and each and all are welcome for the same and simple price of admission. Pray pass out quietly and with as little jostling as possible."

Forthwith, the Schofield and Williams Military Band began a second overture, in which something vaguely like a tune was at times distinguishable; and all of the first audience returned, most of them having occupied the interval in hasty excursions for more pins; Miss Rennsdale and governess, however, again paying coin of the Republic and receiving deference and the best seats accordingly. And when a third performance found all of the same inveterate patrons once more crowding the auditorium, and seven recruits added, the pleasurable excitement of the partners in their venture will be understood by any one who has seen a metropolitan manager strolling about the foyer of his theatre some evening during the earlier stages of an assured "phenomenal run."

From the first, there was no question which feature of the entertainment was the attraction extraordinary: Verman—Verman, the savage tattooed wild boy, speaking only his native foreign languages—Verman was a triumph! Beaming, wreathed in smiles, melodious, incredibly fluent, he had but to open his lips and a dead hush fell upon the audience. Breathless, they leaned forward, hanging upon his every semi-syllable, and, when Penrod checked the flow, burst into thunders of applause, which Verman received with happy laughter.

Alas! he delayed not o'er long to display all the egregiousness of a new star; but for a time there was no caprice of his too eccentric to be forgiven. During Penrod's lecture upon the other curios, the tattooed wild boy continually stamped his foot, grinned, and gesticulated, tapping his tiny chest, and pointing to himself as it were to say: "Wait for Me! I am the Big Show." So soon they learn; so soon they learn! And (again alas!) this spoiled darling of public favour, like many another, was fated to know, in good time, the fickleness of that favour.

But during all the morning performances he was the idol of his audience and looked it! The climax of his popularity came during the fifth overture of the Schofield and Williams Military Band, when the music was quite drowned in the agitated clamours of Miss Rennsdale, who was endeavouring to ascend the stairs in spite of the physical dissuasion of her governess.

"I *won't* go home to lunch!" screamed Miss Rennsdale, her voice accompanied by a sound of ripping. "I *will* hear the tattooed wild boy talk some more! It's lovely—I *will* hear him talk! I *will*! I *will*! I want to listen to Verman—I *want* to—I WANT to——"

Wailing, she was borne away—of her sex not the first to be fascinated by obscurity, nor the last to champion its eloquence.

Verman was almost unendurable after this, but, like many, many other managers, Schofield and Williams restrained their choler, and even laughed fulsomely when their principal attraction essayed the rôle of a comedian in private, and capered and squawked in sheer, fatuous vanity.

The first performance of the afternoon rivalled the successes of the morning, and although Miss Rennsdale was detained at home, thus drying up the single source of cash income developed before lunch, Maurice Levy appeared, escorting Marjorie Jones, and paid coin for two admissions, dropping the money into Sam's hand with a careless—nay, a contemptuous—gesture. At sight of Marjorie, Penrod Schofield flushed under his new moustache (repainted since noon) and lectured as he had never lectured before. A new grace invested his every gesture; a new sonorousness rang in his voice; a simple and manly pomposity marked his very walk as he passed from curio to curio. And when he fearlessly handled the box of rats and hammered upon it with cool *insouciance*, he beheld—for the first time in his life—a purl of admiration eddying in Marjorie's lovely eye, a certain softening of that eye. And then Verman spake—and Penrod was forgotten. Marjorie's eye rested upon him no more.

A heavily equipped chauffeur ascended the stairway, bearing the message that Mrs. Levy awaited her son and his lady. Thereupon, having devoured the last sound permitted (by the managers) to issue from Verman, Mr. Levy and Miss Jones departed to a real matinée at a real theatre, the limpid eyes of Marjorie looking back softly over her shoulder—but only at the tattooed wild boy. Nearly always it is woman who puts the irony into life.

After this, perhaps because of sated curiosity, perhaps on account of a pin famine, the attendance began to languish. Only four responded to the next call of the band; the four dwindled to three; finally the entertainment was given for one *blasé* auditor, and Schofield and Williams looked depressed. Then followed an interval when the band played in vain.

About three o'clock Schofield and Williams were gloomily discussing various unpromising devices for startling the public into a renewal of interest, when another patron unexpectedly appeared and paid a cent for his admission. News of the Big Show and Museum of Curiosities had at last penetrated the far, cold spaces of interstellar niceness, for this new patron consisted of no less than Roderick Magsworth Bitts, Junior, escaped in a white "sailor suit" from the Manor during a period of severe maternal and tutorial preoccupation.

He seated himself without parley, and the pufformance was offered for his entertainment with admirable conscientiousness. True to the Lady Clara caste and training, Roderick's pale, fat face expressed nothing except an impervious superiority and, as he sat, cold and unimpressed upon the front bench, like a large, white lump, it must be said that he made a discouraging audience "to play to." He was not, however, unresponsive—far from it. He offered comment very chilling to the warm grandiloquence of the orator.

"That's my uncle Ethelbert's dachshund," he remarked, at the beginning of the lecture. "You better take him back if you don't want to get arrested." And when Penrod, rather uneasily ignoring the interruption, proceeded to the exploitation of the genuine, full-blooded Indian dog, Duke, "Why don't you try to give that old dog away?" asked Roderick. "You couldn't sell him."

"My papa would buy me a lots better 'coon than that," was the information volunteered a little later, "only I wouldn't want the nasty old thing."

Herman of the missing finger obtained no greater indulgence. "Pooh!" said Roderick. "We have two fox-terriers in our stables that took prizes at the kennel show, and their tails were *bit* off. There's a man that always bites fox-terriers' tails off."

"Oh, my gosh, what a lie!" exclaimed Sam Williams ignorantly. "Go on with the show whether he likes it or not, Penrod. He's paid his money."

Verman, confident in his own singular powers, chuckled openly at the failure of the other attractions to charm the frosty visitor, and, when his turn came, poured forth a torrent of conversation which was straightway damned.

"Rotten," said Mr. Bitts languidly. "Anybody could talk like that. *I* could do it if I wanted to."

Verman paused suddenly.

"*Yes*, you could!" exclaimed Penrod, stung. "Let's hear you do it, then."

"Yessir!" the other partner shouted. "Let's just hear you *do* it!"

"I said I could if I wanted to," responded Roderick. "I didn't say I *would*."

"Yay! Knows he can't!" sneered Sam.

"I can, too, if I try."

"Well, let's hear you try!"

So challenged, the visitor did try, but, in the absence of an impartial jury, his effort was considered so pronounced a failure that he was howled down, derided, and mocked with great clamours.

"Anyway," said Roderick, when things had quieted down, "if I couldn't get up a better show than this I'd sell out and leave town."

Not having enough presence of mind to inquire what he would sell out, his adversaries replied with mere formless yells of scorn.

"I could get up a better show than this with my left hand," Roderick asserted.

"Well, what would you have in your ole show?" asked Penrod, condescending to language.

"That's all right, what I'd *have*. I'd have enough!"

"You couldn't get Herman and Verman in *your* ole show."

"No, and I wouldn't want 'em, either!"

"Well, what *would* you have?" insisted Penrod derisively. "You'd have to have *sumpthing*—you couldn't be a show yourself!"

"How do *you* know?" This was but meandering while waiting for ideas, and evoked another yell.

"You think you could be a show all by yourself?" demanded Penrod.

"How do *you* know I couldn't?"

Two white boys and two black boys shrieked their scorn of the boaster.

"I could, too!" Roderick raised his voice to a sudden howl, obtaining a hearing.

"Well, why don't you tell us how?"

"Well, I know *how*, all right," said Roderick. "If anybody asks you, you can just tell him I know *how*, all right."

"Why, you can't *do* anything," Sam began argumentatively. "You talk about being a show all by yourself; what could you try to do? Show us sumpthing you can do."

"I didn't say I was going to *do* anything," returned the badgered one, still evading.

"Well, then, how'd you *be* a show?" Penrod demanded. "*We* got a show here, even if Herman didn't point or Verman didn't talk. Their father stabbed a man with a pitchfork, I guess, didn't he?"

"How do *I* know?"

"Well, I guess he's in jail, ain't he?"

"Well, what if their father is in jail? I didn't say he wasn't, did I?"

"Well, *your* father ain't in jail, is he?"

"Well, I never said he was, did I?"

"Well, then," continued Penrod, "how could you be a——" He stopped abruptly, staring at Roderick, the birth of an idea plainly visible in his altered expression. He had suddenly remembered his intention to ask Roderick Magsworth Bitts, Junior, about Rena Magsworth, and this recollection collided in his mind with the irritation produced by Roderick's claiming some mysterious attainment which would warrant his setting up as a show in his single person. Penrod's whole manner changed instantly.

"Roddy," he asked, almost overwhelmed by a prescience of something vast and magnificent, "Roddy, are you any relation of Rena Magsworth?"

Roderick had never heard of Rena Magsworth, although a concentration of the sentence yesterday pronounced upon her had burned, black and horrific, upon the face of every newspaper in the country. He was not allowed to read the journals of the day and his family's indignation over the sacrilegious coincidence of the name had not been expressed in his presence. But he saw that it was an awesome name to Penrod Schofield and Samuel Williams. Even Herman and Verman, though lacking many educational advantages on account of a long residence in the country, were informed on the subject of Rena Magsworth through hearsay, and they joined in the portentous silence.

"Roddy," repeated Penrod, "honest, is Rena Magsworth some relation of yours?"

There is no obsession more dangerous to its victims than a conviction—especially an inherited one—of superiority: this world is so full of Missourians.

And from his earliest years Roderick Magsworth Bitts, Junior, had been trained to believe in the importance of the Magsworth family. At every meal he absorbed a sense of Magsworth greatness, and yet, in his infrequent meetings with persons of his own age and sex, he was treated as negligible. Now, dimly, he perceived that there was a Magsworth claim of some sort which was impressive, even to boys. Magsworth blood was the essential of all true distinction in the world, he knew. Consequently, having been driven into a *cul-de-sac*, as a result of flagrant and unfounded boasting, he was ready to take advantage of what appeared to be a triumphal way out.

"Roddy," said Penrod again, with solemnity, "is Rena Magsworth some relation of yours?"

"*Is* she, Roddy?" asked Sam, almost hoarsely.

"She's my aunt!" shouted Roddy.

Silence followed. Sam and Penrod, spellbound, gazed upon Roderick Magsworth Bitts, Junior. So did Herman and Verman. Roddy's staggering lie had changed the face of things utterly. No one questioned it; no one realized that it was much too good to be true.

"Roddy," said Penrod, in a voice tremulous with hope, "Roddy, will you join our show?"

Roddy joined.

Even he could see that the offer implied his being starred as the paramount attraction of a new order of things. It was obvious that he had swelled out suddenly, in the estimation of the other boys, to that importance which he had been taught to believe his native gift and natural right. The sensation was pleasant. He had often been treated with effusion by grown-up callers and by acquaintances of his mothers and sisters; he had heard ladies speak of him as "charming" and "that delightful child," and little girls had sometimes shown him deference, but until this moment no boy had ever allowed him, for one moment, to presume even to equality. Now, in a trice, he was not only admitted to comradeship, but patently valued as something rare and sacred to be acclaimed and pedestalled. In fact, the very first thing that Schofield and Williams did was to find a box for him to stand upon.

The misgivings roused in Roderick's bosom by the subsequent activities of the firm were not bothersome enough to make him forego his prominence as Exhibit A. He was not a "quick-minded" boy, and it was long (and much happened) before he thoroughly comprehended the causes of his new celebrity. He had a shadowy feeling that if the affair came to be heard of at home it might not be liked, but, intoxicated by the glamour and bustle which surround a public character, he made no protest. On the contrary, he entered whole-heartedly into the preparations for the new show. Assuming, with Sam's assistance, a blue moustache and "sideburns," he helped in the painting of a new poster, which, supplanting the old one on the wall of the stable facing the cross-street, screamed bloody murder at the passers in that rather populous thoroughfare.

THE NEW STAR
SCHoFiELD & WiLLiAMS
NEW BIG SHoW
RoDERiCK MAGSWoRTH BiTTS JR
ONLY LiViNG NEPHEW
oF
RENA MAGSWORTH
THE FAMOS
MUDERE$S GoiNG To BE HUNG
NEXT JULY KiLED EiGHT PEOPLE
PUT ARSiNECK iN THiER MiLK ALSO
SHERMAN HERMAN AND VERMAN
THE MiCHiGAN RATS DOG PART
ALLiGATOR DUKE THE GENUiNE
InDiAN DoG ADMiSSioN 1 CENT oR
20 PiNS SAME AS BEFORE Do NoT
MiSS THiS CHANSE TO SEE RoD-
ERiCK
ONLY LiViNG NEPHEW oF RENA
MAGSWORTH THE GREAT FAMOS
MUDERESS
GoiNG To BE
HUNG

CHAPTER XVII

RETIRING FROM THE SHOW BUSINESS

Megaphones were constructed out of heavy wrapping-paper, and Penrod, Sam, and Herman set out in different directions, delivering vocally the inflammatory proclamation of the poster to a large section of the residential quarter, and leaving Roderick Magsworth Bitts, Junior, with Verman in the loft, shielded from all deadhead eyes. Upon the return of the heralds, the Schofield and Williams Military Band played deafeningly, and an awakened public once more thronged to fill the coffers of the firm.

Prosperity smiled again. The very first audience after the acquisition of Roderick was larger than the largest of the morning. Master Bitts—the only exhibit placed upon a box—was a supercurio. All eyes fastened upon him and remained, hungrily feasting, throughout Penrod's luminous oration.

But the glory of one light must ever be the dimming of another. We dwell in a vale of seesaws—and cobwebs spin fastest upon laurel. Verman, the tattooed wild boy, speaking only in his native foreign languages, Verman the gay, Verman the caperer, capered no more; he chuckled no more, he beckoned no more, nor tapped his chest, nor wreathed his idolatrous face in smiles. Gone, all gone, were his little artifices for attracting the general attention to himself; gone was every engaging mannerism which had endeared him to the mercurial public. He squatted against the wall and glowered at the new sensation. It was the old story—the old, old story of too much temperament: Verman was suffering from artistic jealousy.

The second audience contained a cash-paying adult, a spectacled young man whose poignant attention was very flattering. He remained after the lecture, and put a few questions to Roddy, which were answered rather confusedly upon promptings from Penrod. The young man went away without having stated the object of his interrogations, but it became quite plain, later in the day. This same object caused the spectacled young man to make several brief but stimulating calls directly after leaving the Schofield and Williams Big Show, and the consequences thereof loitered not by the wayside.

The Big Show was at high tide. Not only was the auditorium filled and throbbing; there was an indubitable line—by no means wholly juvenile—waiting for admission to the next pufformance. A group stood in the street examining the poster earnestly as it glowed in the long, slanting rays of the westward sun, and people in automobiles and other vehicles had halted wheel in the street to read the message so piquantly given to the world. These were the conditions when a crested victoria arrived at a gallop, and a large, chastely magnificent and highly flushed woman descended, and progressed across the yard with an air of violence.

At sight of her, the adults of the waiting line hastily disappeared, and most of the pausing vehicles moved instantly on their way. She was followed by a stricken man in livery.

The stairs to the auditorium were narrow and steep; Mrs. Roderick Magsworth Bitts was of a stout favour; and the voice of Penrod was audible during the ascent.

"Re-mem-bur, gentilmun and lay-deeze, each and all are now gazing upon Roderick Magsworth Bitts, Junior, the only living nephew of the great Rena Magsworth. She stuck ars'nic in the milk of eight separate and distinck people to put in their coffee and each and all of 'em died. The great ars'nic murderess, Rena Magsworth, gentilmun and lay-deeze, and Roddy's her only living nephew. She's a relation of all the Bitts family, but he's her one and only living nephew. Re-mem-bur! Next July she's goin' to be hung, and, each and all, you now see before you——"

Penrod paused abruptly, seeing something before himself—the august and awful presence which filled the entryway. And his words (it should be related) froze upon his lips.

Before herself, Mrs. Roderick Magsworth Bitts saw her son—her scion—wearing a moustache and sideburns of blue, and perched upon a box flanked by Sherman and Verman, the Michigan rats, the Indian dog Duke, Herman, and the dog part alligator.

Roddy, also, saw something before himself. It needed no prophet to read the countenance of the dread apparition in the entryway. His mouth opened —remained open—then filled to capacity with a calamitous sound of grief not unmingled with apprehension.

Penrod's reason staggered under the crisis. For a horrible moment he saw Mrs. Roderick Magsworth Bitts approaching like some fatal mountain in avalanche. She seemed to grow larger and redder; lightnings played about her head; he had a vague consciousness of the audience spraying out in flight, of the squealings, tramplings and dispersals of a stricken field. The mountain was close upon him——

He stood by the open mouth of the hay-chute which went through the floor to the manger below. Penrod also went through the floor. He propelled himself into the chute and shot down, but not quite to the manger, for Mr. Samuel Williams had thoughtfully stepped into the chute a moment in advance of his partner. Penrod lit upon Sam.

Catastrophic noises resounded in the loft; volcanoes seemed to romp upon the stairway.

There ensued a period when only a shrill keening marked the passing of Roderick as he was borne to the tumbril. Then all was silence.

. . . Sunset, striking through a western window, rouged the walls of the Schofields' library, where gathered a joint family council and court martial of four—Mrs. Schofield, Mr. Schofield, and Mr. and Mrs. Williams, parents of Samuel of that ilk. Mr. Williams read aloud a conspicuous passage from the last edition of the evening paper:

"Prominent people here believed close relations of woman sentenced to hang. Angry denial by Mrs. R. Magsworth Bitts. Relationship admitted by younger member of family. His statement confirmed by boy-friends——"

"Don't!" said Mrs. Williams, addressing her husband vehemently. "We've all read it a dozen times. We've got plenty of trouble on our hands without hearing *that* again!"

Singularly enough, Mrs. Williams did not look troubled; she looked as if she were trying to look troubled. Mrs. Schofield wore a similar expression. So did Mr. Schofield. So did Mr. Williams.

"What did she say when she called *you* up?" Mrs. Schofield inquired breathlessly of Mrs. Williams.

"She could hardly speak at first, and then when she did talk, she talked so fast I couldn't understand most of it, and——"

"It was just the same when she tried to talk to me," said Mrs. Schofield, nodding.

"I never did hear any one in such a state before," continued Mrs. Williams. "So furious——"

"Quite justly, of course," said Mrs. Schofield.

"Of course. And she said Penrod and Sam had enticed Roderick away from home—usually he's not allowed to go outside the yard except with his tutor or a servant—and had told him to say the horrible creature was his aunt——"

"How in the world do you suppose Sam and Penrod ever thought of such a thing as *that!*" exclaimed Mrs. Schofield. "It must have been made up just for their 'show.' Della says there were just *streams* going in and out all day. Of course it wouldn't have happened, but this was the day Margaret and I spend every month in the country with Aunt Sarah, and I didn't *dream*——"

"She said one thing I thought rather tactless," interrupted Mrs. Williams. "Of course we must allow for her being dreadfully excited and wrought up, but I do think it wasn't quite delicate in her, and she's usually the very soul of delicacy. She said that Roderick had *never* been allowed to associate with —common boys——"

"Meaning Sam and Penrod," said Mrs. Schofield. "Yes, she said that to me, too."

"She said that the most awful thing about it," Mrs. Williams went on, "was that, though she's going to prosecute the newspapers, many people would always believe the story, and——"

"Yes, I imagine they will," said Mrs. Schofield musingly. "Of course you and I and everybody who really knows the Bitts and Magsworth families understand the perfect absurdity of it; but I suppose there are ever so many who'll believe it, no matter what the Bittses and Magsworths say."

"Hundreds and hundreds!" said Mrs. Williams. "I'm afraid it will be a great come-down for them."

"I'm afraid so," said Mrs. Schofield gently. "A very great one—yes, a very, very great one."

"Well," observed Mrs. Williams, after a thoughtful pause, "there's only one thing to be done, and I suppose it had better be done right away."

She glanced toward the two gentlemen.

"Certainly," Mr. Schofield agreed. "But where *are* they?"

"Have you looked in the stable?" asked his wife.

"I searched it. They've probably started for the far West."

"Did you look in the sawdust-box?"

"No, I didn't."

"Then that's where they are."

Thus, in the early twilight, the now historic stable was approached by two fathers charged to do the only thing to be done. They entered the storeroom.

"Penrod!" said Mr. Schofield.

"Sam!" said Mr. Williams.

Nothing disturbed the twilight hush.

But by means of a ladder, brought from the carriage-house, Mr. Schofield mounted to the top of the sawdust-box. He looked within, and discerned the dim outlines of three quiet figures, the third being that of a small dog.

The two boys rose, upon command, descended the ladder after Mr. Schofield, bringing Duke with them, and stood before the authors of their being,
who bent upon them sinister and threatening brows. With hanging heads
and despondent countenances, each still ornamented with a moustache and
an imperial, Penrod and Sam awaited sentence.

This is a boy's lot: anything he does, anything whatever, may afterward
turn out to have been a crime—he never knows.

And punishment and clemency are alike inexplicable.

Mr. Williams took his son by the ear.

"You march home!" he commanded.

Sam marched, not looking back, and his father followed the small figure
implacably.

"You goin' to whip me?" quavered Penrod, alone with Justice.

"Wash your face at that hydrant," said his father sternly.

About fifteen minutes later, Penrod, hurriedly entering the corner drug
store, two blocks distant, was astonished to perceive a familiar form at the
soda counter.

"Yay, Penrod," said Sam Williams. "Want some sody? Come on. He
didn't lick me. He didn't do anything to me at all. He gave me a quarter."

"So'd mine," said Penrod.

CHAPTER XVIII

MUSIC

Boyhood is the longest time in life—for a boy. The last term of the school-
year is made of decades, not of weeks, and living through them is like waiting
for the millennium. But they do pass, somehow, and at last there came a day
when Penrod was one of a group that capered out from the gravelled yard of
"Ward School, Nomber Seventh," carolling a leave-taking of the institution,
of their instructress, and not even forgetting Mr. Capps, the janitor.

> "Good-bye, teacher! Good-bye, school!
> Good-bye, Cappsie, dern ole fool!"

Penrod sang the loudest. For every boy, there is an age when he "finds
his voice." Penrod's had not "changed," but he had found it. Inevitably that
thing had come upon his family and the neighbours; and his father, a somewhat dyspeptic man, quoted frequently the expressive words of the "Lady of
Shalott," but there were others whose sufferings were as poignant.

Vacation-time warmed the young of the world to pleasant languor; and a morning came that was like a brightly coloured picture in a child's fairy story. Miss Margaret Schofield, reclining in a hammock upon the front porch, was beautiful in the eyes of a newly made senior, well favoured and in fair raiment, beside her. A guitar rested lightly upon his knee, and he was trying to play—a matter of some difficulty, as the floor of the porch also seemed inclined to be musical. From directly under his feet came a voice of song, shrill, loud, incredibly piercing and incredibly flat, dwelling upon each syllable with incomprehensible reluctance to leave it.

> "I have lands and earthly pow-wur.
> I'd give all for a now-wur,
> Whi-ilst setting at *my-y-y* dear old mother's knee-ee,
> So-o-o rem-mem-bur whilst you're young——"

Miss Schofield stamped heartily upon the musical floor.

"It's Penrod," she explained. "The lattice at the end of the porch is loose, and he crawls under and comes out all bugs. He's been having a dreadful singing fit lately—running away to picture shows and vaudeville, I suppose."

Mr. Robert Williams looked upon her yearningly. He touched a thrilling chord on his guitar and leaned nearer. "But you said you *have* missed me," he began. "I——"

The voice of Penrod drowned all other sounds.

> "So-o-o rem-mem-bur, whi-i-ilst you're young,
> That the day-a-ys to you will come,
> When you're o-o-old and only in the way,
> Do not scoff at them *bee*-cause——"

"*Penrod!*" Miss Schofield stamped again.

"You *did* say you'd missed me," said Mr. Robert Williams, seizing hurriedly upon the silence. "Didn't you say——"

A livelier tune rose upward.

> "Oh, you talk about your fascinating beauties,
> Of your dem-*o*-zells, your belles,
> But the littil dame I met, while in the city,
> She's par excellaws the queen of all the swells.
> She's sweeter far——"

Margaret rose and jumped up and down repeatedly in a well-calculated area, whereupon the voice of Penrod cried chokedly, "*Quit* that!" and there were subterranean coughings and sneezings.

"You want to choke a person to death?" he inquired severely, appearing at the end of the porch, a cobweb upon his brow. And, continuing, he put

into practice a newly acquired phrase, "You better learn to be more con-
siderick of other people's comfort."

Slowly and grievedly he withdrew, passed to the sunny side of the house,
reclined in the warm grass beside his wistful Duke, and presently sang again.

> "She's sweeter far than the flower I named her after,
>   And the memery of her smile it haunts me YET!
> When in after years the moon is soffly beamun'
>   And at eve I smell the smell of mignonette
>   I will re-CALL that——"

"Pen-*rod!*"

Mr. Schofield appeared at an open window upstairs, a book in his hand.
"Stop it!" he commanded. "Can't I stay home with a headache *one* morning from the office without having to listen to—I never *did* hear such squawking!" He retired from the window, having too impulsively called upon his
Maker. Penrod, shocked and injured, entered the house, but presently his
voice was again audible as far as the front porch. He was holding converse
with his mother, somewhere in the interior.

"Well, what of it? Sam Williams told me his mother said if Bob ever did
think of getting married to Margaret, his mother said she'd like to know
what in the name o' goodness they expect to——"

Bang! Margaret thought it better to close the front door.

The next minute Penrod opened it. "I suppose you want the whole family
to get a sunstroke," he said reprovingly. "Keepin' every breath of air out o'
the house on a day like this!"

And he sat down implacably in the doorway.

The serious poetry of all languages has omitted the little brother; and yet
he is one of the great trials of love—the immemorial burden of courtship.
Tragedy should have found place for him, but he has been left to the haphazard vignettist of Grub Street. He is the grave and real menace of lovers;
his head is sacred and terrible, his power illimitable. There is one way—only
one—to deal with him; but Robert Williams, having a brother of Penrod's
age, understood that way.

Robert had one dollar in the world. He gave it to Penrod immediately.

Enslaved forever, the new Rockefeller rose and went forth upon the highway, an overflowing heart bursting the floodgates of song.

> "In her eyes the light of love was soffly gleamun',
>   So sweetlay,
>   So neatlay.
> On the banks the moon's soff light was brightly
>   streamun',
>   Words of love I then spoke *to* her.
>   She was purest of the *pew*-er:

'Littil sweetheart, do not sigh,
Do not weep and do not cry.
I will build a littil cottige just for yew-*ew*-ᴇᴡ and I.'"

In fairness, it must be called to mind that boys older than Penrod have these wellings of pent melody; a wife can never tell when she is to undergo a musical morning, and even the golden wedding brings her no security, a man of ninety is liable to bust-loose in song, any time.

Invalids murmured pitifully as Penrod came within hearing; and people trying to think cursed the day that they were born, when he went shrilling by. His hands in his pockets, his shining face uplifted to the sky of June, he passed down the street, singing his way into the heart's deepest hatred of all who heard him.

"One evuning I was sturow-ling
Midst the city of the *Dead*,
I viewed where all a-round me
Their *peace*-full graves was ꜱᴘʀᴇᴀᴅ.
But that which touched me mostlay——"

He had reached his journey's end, a junk-dealer's shop wherein lay the long-desired treasure of his soul—an accordion which might have possessed a high quality of interest for an antiquarian, being unquestionably a ruin, beautiful in decay, and quite beyond the sacrilegious reach of the restorer. But it was still able to disgorge sounds—loud, strange, compelling sounds, which could be heard for a remarkable distance in all directions; and it had one rich calf-like tone that had gone to Penrod's heart. He obtained the instrument for twenty-two cents, a price long since agreed upon with the junk-dealer, who falsely claimed a loss of profit, Shylock that he was! He had found the wreck in an alley.

With this purchase suspended from his shoulder by a faded green cord, Penrod set out in a somewhat homeward direction, but not by the route he had just travelled, though his motive for the change was not humanitarian. It was his desire to display himself thus troubadouring to the gaze of Marjorie Jones. Heralding his advance by continuous experiments in the music of the future, he pranced upon his blithesome way, the faithful Duke at his heels. (It was easier for Duke than it would have been for a younger dog, because, with advancing age, he had begun to grow a little deaf.)

Turning the corner nearest to the glamoured mansion of the Joneses, the boy jongleur came suddenly face to face with Marjorie, and, in the delicious surprise of the encounter, ceased to play, his hands, in agitation, falling from the instrument.

Bareheaded, the sunshine glorious upon her amber curls, Marjorie was strolling hand-in-hand with her baby brother, Mitchell, four years old. She wore pink that day—unforgettable pink, with a broad, black patent-leather belt, shimmering reflections dancing upon its surface. How beautiful she was! How sacred the sweet little baby brother, whose privilege it was to cling to that small hand, delicately powdered with freckles.

"Hello, Marjorie," said Penrod, affecting carelessness.

"Hello!" said Marjorie, with unexpected cordiality. She bent over her baby brother with motherly affectations. "Say 'howdy' to the gentymuns, Mitchy-Mitch," she urged sweetly, turning him to face Penrod.

"*Won't!*" said Mitchy-Mitch, and, to emphasize his refusal, kicked the gentymuns upon the shin.

Penrod's feelings underwent instant change, and in the sole occupation of disliking Mitchy-Mitch, he wasted precious seconds which might have been better employed in philosophic consideration of the startling example, just afforded, of how a given law operates throughout the universe in precisely the same manner perpetually. Mr. Robert Williams would have understood this, easily.

"Oh, oh!" Marjorie cried, and put Mitchy-Mitch behind her with too much sweetness. "Maurice Levy's gone to Atlantic City with his mamma," she remarked conversationally, as if the kicking incident were quite closed.

"That's nothin'," returned Penrod, keeping his eye uneasily upon Mitchy-Mitch. "I know plenty people been better places than that—Chicago and everywhere."

There was unconscious ingratitude in his low rating of Atlantic City, for it was largely to the attractions of that resort he owed Miss Jones' present attitude of friendliness. Of course, too, she was curious about the accordion. It would be dastardly to hint that she had noticed a paper bag which bulged the pocket of Penrod's coat, and yet this bag was undeniably conspicuous—"and children are very like grown people sometimes!"

Penrod brought forth the bag, purchased on the way at a drug store, and till this moment *unopened*, which expresses in a word the depth of his sentiment for Marjorie. It contained an abundant fifteen-cents' worth of lemon-drops, jaw-breakers, licorice sticks, cinnamon-drops, and shopworn chocolate-creams.

"Take all you want," he said, with off-hand generosity.

"Why, Penrod Schofield," exclaimed the wholly thawed damsel, "you nice boy!"

"Oh, that's nothin'," he returned airily. "I got a good deal of money, nowadays."

"Where from?"

"Oh—just around." With a cautious gesture he offered a jaw-breaker to Mitchy-Mitch, who snatched it indignantly and set about its absorption without delay.

"Can you play on that?" asked Marjorie, with some difficulty, her cheeks being rather too hilly for conversation.

"Want to hear me?"

She nodded, her eyes sweet with anticipation.

This was what he had come for. He threw back his head, lifted his eyes dreamily, as he had seen real musicians lift theirs, and distended the accordion preparing to produce the wonderful calf-like noise which was the instrument's great charm. But the distention evoked a long wail which was at once drowned in another one.

"Ow! Owowaoh! Wowohah! Waow*wow!*" shrieked Mitchy-Mitch and the accordion together.

Mitchy-Mitch, to emphasize his disapproval of the accordion, opening his mouth still wider, lost therefrom the jaw-breaker, which rolled in the dust. Weeping, he stooped to retrieve it, and Marjorie, to prevent him, hastily set her foot upon it. Penrod offered another jaw-breaker; but Mitchy-Mitch struck it from his hand, desiring the former, which had convinced him of its sweetness.

Marjorie moved inadvertently; whereupon Mitchy-Mitch pounced upon the remains of his jaw-breaker and restored them, with accretions, to his mouth. His sister, uttering a cry of horror, sprang to the rescue, assisted by Penrod, whom she prevailed upon to hold Mitchy-Mitch's mouth open while she excavated. This operation being completed, and Penrod's right thumb severely bitten, Mitchy-Mitch closed his eyes tightly, stamped, squealed, bellowed, wrung his hands, and then, unexpectedly, kicked Penrod again.

Penrod put a hand in his pocket and drew forth a copper two-cent piece, large, round, and fairly bright.

He gave it to Mitchy-Mitch.

Mitchy-Mitch immediately stopped crying and gazed upon his benefactor with the eyes of a dog.

This world!

Thereafter did Penrod—with complete approval from Mitchy-Mitch—play the accordion for his lady to his heart's content, and hers. Never had he so won upon her; never had she let him feel so close to her before. They strolled up and down upon the sidewalk, eating, one thought between them, and soon she had learned to play the accordion almost as well as he. So passed a happy hour, which the Good King René of Anjou would have envied them, while Mitchy-Mitch made friends with Duke, romped about his sister and her swain, and clung to the hand of the latter, at intervals, with fondest affection and trust.

The noon whistles failed to disturb this little Arcady; only the sound of Mrs. Jones' voice—for the third time summoning Marjorie and Mitchy-Mitch to lunch—sent Penrod on his way.

"I could come back this afternoon, I guess," he said, in parting.

"I'm not goin' to be here. I'm goin' to Baby Rennsdale's party."

Penrod looked blank, as she intended he should. Having thus satisfied herself, she added:

"There aren't goin' to be any boys there."

He was instantly radiant again.

"Marjorie——"

"Hum?"

"Do you wish I was goin' to be there?"

She looked shy, and turned away her head.

"*Marjorie Jones!*" (This was a voice from home.) "*How many more times shall I have to call you?*"

Marjorie moved away, her face still hidden from Penrod.

"Do you?" he urged.

At the gate, she turned quickly toward him, and said over her shoulder, all in a breath: "Yes! Come again to-morrow morning and I'll be on the corner. Bring your 'cordion!"

And she ran into the house, Mitchy-Mitch waving a loving hand to the boy on the sidewalk until the front door closed.

CHAPTER XIX

THE INNER BOY

Penrod went home in splendour, pretending that he and Duke were a long procession; and he made enough noise to render the auricular part of the illusion perfect. His own family were already at the lunch-table when he arrived, and the parade halted only at the door of the dining-room.

"Oh *Something!*" shouted Mr. Schofield, clasping his bilious brow with both hands. "Stop that noise! Isn't it awful enough for you to *sing?* Sit *down!* Not with that thing on! Take that green rope off your shoulder! Now take that thing out of the dining-room and throw it in the ash-can! Where did you get it?"

"Where did I get what, papa?" asked Penrod meekly, depositing the accordion in the hall just outside the dining-room door.

"That da—that third-hand concertina."

"It's a 'cordion," said Penrod, taking his place at the table, and noticing that both Margaret and Mr. Robert Williams (who happened to be a guest) were growing red.

"I don't care what you call it," said Mr. Schofield irritably. "I want to know where you got it."

Penrod's eyes met Margaret's: hers had a strained expression. She very slightly shook her head. Penrod sent Mr. Williams a grateful look, and might have been startled if he could have seen himself in a mirror at that moment; for he regarded Mitchy-Mitch with concealed but vigorous aversion, and the resemblance would have horrified him.

"A man gave it to me," he answered gently, and was rewarded by the visibly regained ease of his patron's manner, while Margaret leaned back in her chair and looked at her brother with real devotion.

"I should think he'd have been glad to," said Mr. Schofield. "Who was he?"

"Sir?" In spite of the candy which he had consumed in company with Marjorie and Mitchy-Mitch, Penrod had begun to eat lobster croquettes earnestly.

"Who *was* he?"

"Who do you mean, papa?"

"The man that gave you that ghastly Thing!"

"Yessir. A man gave it to me."

"I say, Who *was* he?" shouted Mr. Schofield.

"Well, I was just walking along, and the man came up to me—it was right down in front of Colgate's, where most of the paint's rubbed off the fence——"

"Penrod!" The father used his most dangerous tone.

"Sir?"

"Who was the man that gave you the concertina?"

"I don't know. I was walking along——"

"You never saw him before?"

"No, sir. I was just walk——"

"That will do," said Mr. Schofield, rising. "I suppose every family has its secret enemies and this was one of ours. I must ask to be excused!"

With that, he went out crossly, stopping in the hall a moment before passing beyond hearing. And, after lunch, Penrod sought in vain for his accordion; he even searched the library where his father sat reading, though, upon inquiry, Penrod explained that he was looking for a misplaced school-book. He thought he ought to study a little every day, he said, even during vacation-time. Much pleased, Mr. Schofield rose and joined the search, finding the missing work on mathematics with singular ease—which cost him precisely the price of the book the following September.

Penrod departed to study in the backyard. There, after a cautious survey of the neighbourhood, he managed to dislodge the iron cover of the cistern, and dropped the arithmetic within. A fine splash rewarded his listening ear. Thus assured that when he looked for that book again no one would find it for him, he replaced the cover, and betook himself pensively to the highway, discouraging Duke from following by repeated volleys of stones, some imaginary and others all too real.

Distant strains of brazen horns and the throbbing of drums were borne to him upon the kind breeze, reminding him that the world was made for joy, and that the Barzee and Potter Dog and Pony Show was exhibiting in a banlieue not far away. So, thither he bent his steps—the plentiful funds in his pocket burning hot holes all the way. He had paid twenty-two cents for the accordion, and fifteen for candy; he had bought the mercenary heart of Mitchy-Mitch for two: it certainly follows that there remained to him of his dollar, sixty-one cents—a fair fortune, and most unusual.

Arrived upon the populous and festive scene of the Dog and Pony Show, he first turned his attention to the brightly decorated booths which surrounded the tent. The cries of the peanut vendors, of the popcorn men, of the toy-balloon sellers, the stirring music of the band, playing before the performance to attract a crowd, the shouting of excited children and the barking of the dogs within the tent, all sounded exhilaratingly in Penrod's ears and set his blood a-tingle. Nevertheless, he did not squander his money or fling it to the winds in one grand splurge. Instead, he began cautiously with the purchase of an extraordinarily large pickle, which he obtained from an aged negress for his odd cent, too obvious a bargain to be missed. At an adjacent stand he bought a glass of raspberry lemonade (so alleged) and sipped it as he ate the pickle. He left nothing of either.

Next, he entered a small restaurant-tent and for a modest nickel was supplied with a fork and a box of sardines, previously opened, it is true, but more than half full. He consumed the sardines utterly, but left the tin box and the fork, after which he indulged in an inexpensive half-pint of lukewarm cider, at one of the open booths. Mug in hand, a gentle glow radiating toward his surface from various centres of activity deep inside him, he paused for breath —and the cool, sweet cadences of the watermelon man fell delectably upon his ear:

"Ice-cole *water*-melon; ice-cole water-*melon*; the biggest slice of *ice*-cole, ripe, red, *ice*-cole, rich an' rare; the biggest slice of ice-cole watermelon ever cut by the hand of man! *Buy* our *ice*-cole watermelon?"

Penrod, having drained the last drop of cider, complied with the watermelon man's luscious entreaty, and received a round slice of the fruit, magnificent in circumference and something over an inch in thickness. Leaving only the really dangerous part of the rind behind him, he wandered away from the vicinity of the watermelon man and supplied himself with a bag of peanuts, which, with the expenditure of a dime for admission, left a quarter still warm in his pocket. However, he managed to "break" the coin at a stand inside the tent, where a large, oblong paper box of popcorn was handed him, with twenty cents change. The box was too large to go into his pocket, but, having seated himself among some wistful Polack children, he placed it in his lap and devoured the contents at leisure during the performance. The popcorn was heavily larded with partially boiled molasses, and Penrod sandwiched mouthfuls of peanuts with gobs of this mass until the peanuts were all gone. After that, he ate with less avidity; a sense almost of satiety beginning to manifest itself to him, and it was not until the close of the performance that he disposed of the last morsel.

He descended a little heavily to the outflowing crowd in the arena, and bought a caterwauling toy balloon, but showed no great enthusiasm in manipulating it. Near the exit, as he came out, was a hot-waffle stand which he had overlooked, and a sense of duty obliged him to consume the three waffles, thickly powdered with sugar, which the waffle man cooked for him upon command.

They left a hottish taste in his mouth; they had not been quite up to his anticipation, indeed, and it was with a sense of relief that he turned to the "hokey-pokey" cart which stood close at hand, laden with square slabs of "Neapolitan ice-cream" wrapped in paper. He thought the ice-cream would be cooling, but somehow it fell short of the desired effect, and left a peculiar savour in his throat.

He walked away, too languid to blow his balloon, and passed a fresh-taffy booth with strange indifference. A bare-armed man was manipulating the taffy over a hook, pulling a great white mass to the desired stage of "candying," but Penrod did not pause to watch the operation; in fact, he averted his eyes (which were slightly glazed) in passing. He did not analyze his motives: simply, he was conscious that he preferred not to look at the mass of taffy.

For some reason, he put a considerable distance between himself and the taffy-stand, but before long halted in the presence of a red-faced man who flourished a long fork over a small cooking apparatus and shouted jovially: "Winnies! *Here's* your hot winnies! Hot winny-*wurst!* Food for the over-worked brain, nourishing for the weak stummick, entertaining for the tired business man! *Here's* your hot winnies, three for a nickel, a half-a-dime, the twentieth-pot-of-a-dollah!"

This, above all nectar and ambrosia, was the favourite dish of Penrod Scho-field. Nothing inside him now craved it—on the contrary! But memory is the great hypnotist; his mind argued against his inwards that opportunity knocked at his door: "winny-worst" was rigidly forbidden by the home au-thorities. Besides, there was a last nickel in his pocket; and nature protested against its survival. Also, the red-faced man had himself proclaimed his wares nourishing for the weak stummick.

Penrod placed the nickel in the red hand of the red-faced man.

He ate two of the three greasy, cigarlike shapes cordially pressed upon him in return. The first bite convinced him that he had made a mistake; these winnies seemed of a very inferior flavour, almost unpleasant, in fact. But he felt obliged to conceal his poor opinion of them, for fear of offending the red-faced man. He ate without haste or eagerness—so slowly, indeed, that he began to think the red-faced man might dislike him, as a deterrent of trade. Perhaps Penrod's mind was not working well, for he failed to remember that no law compelled him to remain under the eye of the red-faced man, but the virulent repulsion excited by his attempt to take a bite of the third sausage inspired him with at least an excuse for postponement.

"Mighty good," he murmured feebly, placing the sausage in the pocket of his jacket with a shaking hand. "Guess I'll save this one to eat at home, after —after dinner."

He moved sluggishly away, wishing he had not thought of dinner. A side-show, undiscovered until now, failed to arouse his interest, not even exciting a wish that he had known of its existence when he had money. For a time he stared without comprehension at a huge canvas poster depicting the chief attraction; the weather-worn colours conveying no meaning to his torpid eye.

Then, little by little, the poster became more vivid to his consciousness. There was a greenish-tinted person in the tent, it seemed, who thrived upon a reptilian diet.

Suddenly, Penrod decided that it was time to go home.

CHAPTER XX

BROTHERS OF ANGELS

"Indeed, doctor," said Mrs. Schofield, with agitation and profound conviction, just after eight o'clock that evening, "I shall *always* believe in mustard plasters—mustard plasters and hot-water bags. If it hadn't been for them I don't believe he'd have *lived* till you got here—I do *not!*"

"Margaret," called Mr. Schofield from the open door of a bedroom, "Margaret, where did you put that aromatic ammonia? Where's Margaret?"

But he had to find the aromatic spirits of ammonia himself, for Margaret was not in the house. She stood in the shadow beneath a maple tree near the street corner, a guitar-case in her hand; and she scanned with anxiety a briskly approaching figure. The arc light, swinging above, revealed this figure as that of him she awaited. He was passing toward the gate without seeing her, when she arrested him with a fateful whisper.

"*Bob!*"

Mr. Robert Williams swung about hastily. "Why, Margaret!"

"Here, take your guitar," she whispered hurriedly. "I was afraid if father happened to find it he'd break it all to pieces!"

"What for?" asked the startled Robert.

"Because I'm sure he knows it's yours."

"But what——"

"Oh, Bob," she moaned, "I was waiting here to tell you. I was so afraid you'd try to come in——"

"*Try!*" exclaimed the unfortunate young man, quite dumfounded. "*Try* to come——"

"Yes, before I warned you. I've been waiting here to tell you, Bob, you mustn't come near the house—if I were you I'd stay away from even this neighbourhood—far away! For a while I don't think it would be actually *safe* for——"

"Margaret, will you please——"

"It's all on account of that dollar you gave Penrod this morning," she wailed. "First, he bought that horrible concertina that made papa so furious——"

"But Penrod didn't tell that I——"

"Oh, wait!" she cried lamentably. "Listen! He didn't tell at lunch, but he got home about dinnertime in the most—well! I've seen pale people before, but nothing like Penrod. Nobody could *imagine* it—not unless they'd seen him! And he looked so *strange,* and kept making such unnatural faces, and at first all he would say was that he'd eaten a little piece of apple and thought it must have some microbes on it. But he got sicker and sicker, and we put him to bed—and then we all thought he was going to die—and, of *course,* no little piece of apple would have—well, and he kept getting worse—and then he said he'd had a dollar. He said he'd spent it for the concertina, and watermelon, and chocolate-creams, and licorice sticks, and lemon-drops, and peanuts, and jaw-breakers, and sardines, and raspberry lemonade, and pickles, and popcorn, and ice-cream, and cider, and sausage—there was sausage in his pocket, and mamma says his jacket is ruined—and cinnamon drops—and waffles—and he ate four or five lobster croquettes at lunch—and papa said, 'Who gave you that dollar?' Only he didn't say 'who'—he said something horrible, Bob! And Penrod thought he was going to die, and he said *you* gave it to him, and oh! it was just pitiful to hear the poor child, Bob, because he thought he was dying, you see, and he blamed you for the whole thing. He said if you'd only let him alone and not given it to him, he'd have grown up to be a good man—and now he couldn't! I never heard anything so heartrending—he was so weak he could hardly whisper, but he kept trying to talk, telling us over and over it was all your fault."

In the darkness Mr. Williams' facial expression could not be seen, but his voice sounded hopeful.

"Is he—is he still in a great deal of pain?"

"They say the crisis is past," said Margaret, "but the doctor's still up there. He said it was the acutest case of indigestion he had ever treated in the whole course of his professional practice."

"Of course I didn't know what he'd do with the dollar," said Robert.

She did not reply.

He began plaintively, "Margaret, you don't——"

"I've never seen papa and mamma so upset about anything," she said, rather primly.

"You mean they're upset about *me?*"

"We are *all* very much upset," returned Margaret, more starch in her tone as she remembered not only Penrod's sufferings but a duty she had vowed herself to perform.

"Margaret! *You* don't——"

"Robert," she said firmly and, also, with a rhetorical complexity which breeds a suspicion of pre-rehearsal—"Robert, for the present I can only look at it in one way: when you gave that money to Penrod you put into the hands of an unthinking little child a weapon which might be, and, indeed was, the means of his undoing. Boys are not respon——"

"But you saw me give him the dollar, and you didn't——"

"Robert!" she checked him with increasing severity. "I am only a woman and not accustomed to thinking everything out on the spur of the moment; but I cannot change my mind. Not now, at least."

"And you think I'd better not come in to-night?"

"To-night!" she gasped. "Not for *weeks!* Papa would——"

"But Margaret," he urged plaintively, "how can you blame me for——"

"I have not used the word 'blame,'" she interrupted. "But I must insist that for your carelessness to—to wreak such havoc—cannot fail to—to lessen my confidence in your powers of judgment. I cannot change my convictions in this matter—not to-night—and I cannot remain here another instant. The poor child may need me. Robert, good-night."

With chill dignity she withdrew, entered the house, and returned to the sick-room, leaving the young man in outer darkness to brood upon his crime—and upon Penrod.

That sincere invalid became convalescent upon the third day; and a week elapsed, then, before he found an opportunity to leave the house unaccompanied—save by Duke. But at last he set forth and approached the Jones neighbourhood in high spirits, pleasantly conscious of his pallor, hollow cheeks, and other perquisites of illness provocative of interest.

One thought troubled him a little because it gave him a sense of inferiority to a rival. He believed, against his will, that Maurice Levy could have successfully eaten chocolate-creams, licorice sticks, lemon-drops, jaw-breakers, peanuts, waffles, lobster croquettes, sardines, cinnamon-drops, watermelon, pickles, popcorn, ice-cream and sausage with raspberry lemonade and cider. Penrod had admitted to himself that Maurice could do it and afterward attend to business, or pleasure, without the slightest discomfort; and this was probably no more than a fair estimate of one of the great constitutions of all time. As a digester, Maurice Levy would have disappointed a Borgia.

Fortunately, Maurice was still at Atlantic City—and now the convalescent's heart leaped. In the distance he saw Marjorie coming—in pink again, with a ravishing little parasol over her head. And alone! No Mitchy-Mitch was to mar this meeting.

Penrod increased the feebleness of his steps, now and then leaning upon the fence as if for support.

"How do you do, Marjorie?" he said, in his best sick-room voice, as she came near.

To his pained amazement, she proceeded on her way, her nose at a celebrated elevation—an icy nose.

She cut him dead.

He threw his invalid's airs to the winds, and hastened after her.

"Marjorie," he pleaded, "what's the matter? Are you mad? Honest, that day you said to come back next morning, and you'd be on the corner, I was sick. Honest, I was *awful* sick, Marjorie! I had to have the doctor——"

"*Doctor!*" She whirled upon him, her lovely eyes blazing. "I guess *we've* had to have the doctor enough at *our* house, thanks to *you*, Mister Penrod

Schofield. Papa says you haven't got *near* sense enough to come in out of the rain, after what you did to poor little Mitchy-Mitch——"

"What?"

"Yes, and he's sick in bed *yet!*" Marjorie went on, with unabated fury. "And papa says if he ever catches you in this part of town——"

"*What'd* I do to Mitchy-Mitch?" gasped Penrod.

"You know well enough what you did to Mitchy-Mitch!" she cried. "You gave him that great, big, nasty two-cent piece!"

"Well, what of it?"

"Mitchy-Mitch swallowed it!"

"What!"

"And papa says if he ever just lays eyes on you, once, in this neighbourhood——"

But Penrod had started for home.

In his embittered heart there was increasing a critical disapproval of the Creator's methods. When He made pretty girls, thought Penrod, why couldn't He have left out their little brothers!

CHAPTER XXI

RUPE COLLINS

For several days after this, Penrod thought of growing up to be a monk, and engaged in good works so far as to carry some kittens (that otherwise would have been drowned) and a pair of Margaret's outworn dancing-slippers to a poor, ungrateful old man sojourning in a shed up the alley. And although Mr. Robert Williams, after a very short interval, began to leave his guitar on the front porch again, exactly as if he thought nothing had happened, Penrod, with his younger vision of a father's mood, remained coldly distant from the Jones neighbourhood. With his own family his manner was gentle, proud and sad, but not for long enough to frighten them. The change came with mystifying abruptness at the end of the week.

It was Duke who brought it about.

Duke could chase a much bigger dog out of the Schofields' yard and far down the street. This might be thought to indicate unusual valour on the part of Duke and cowardice on that of the bigger dogs whom he undoubtedly put to rout. On the contrary, all such flights were founded in mere superstition, for dogs are even more superstitious than boys and coloured people; and the most firmly established of all dog superstitions is that any dog—be he the smallest and feeblest in the world—can whip any trespasser whatsoever.

A rat-terrier believes that on his home grounds he can whip an elephant.

It follows, of course, that a big dog, away from his own home, will run from a little dog in the little dog's neighbourhood. Otherwise, the big dog must face a charge of inconsistency, and dogs are as consistent as they are superstitious. A dog believes in war, but he is convinced that there are times when it is moral to run; and the thoughtful physiognomist, seeing a big dog fleeing out of a little dog's yard, must observe that the expression of the big dog's face is more conscientious than alarmed: it is the expression of a person performing a duty to himself.

Penrod understood these matters perfectly; he knew that the gaunt brown hound Duke chased up the alley had fled only out of deference to a custom, yet Penrod could not refrain from bragging of Duke to the hound's owner, a fat-faced stranger of twelve or thirteen, who had wandered into the neighbourhood.

"You better keep that ole yellow dog o' yours back," said Penrod ominously, as he climbed the fence. "You better catch him and hold him till I get mine inside the yard again. Duke's chewed up some pretty bad bulldogs around here."

The fat-faced boy gave Penrod a fishy stare. "You'd oughta learn him not to do that," he said. "It'll make him sick."

"What will?"

The stranger laughed raspingly and gazed up the alley, where the hound, having come to a halt, now coolly sat down, and, with an expression of roguish benevolence, patronizingly watched the tempered fury of Duke, whose assaults and barkings were becoming perfunctory.

"What'll make Duke sick?" Penrod demanded.

"Eatin' dead bulldogs people leave around here."

This was not improvisation but formula, adapted from other occasions to the present encounter; nevertheless, it was new to Penrod, and he was so taken with it that resentment lost itself in admiration. Hastily committing the gem to memory for use upon a dog-owning friend, he inquired in a sociable tone:

"What's your dog's name?"

"Dan. You better call your ole pup, 'cause Dan eats *live* dogs."

Dan's actions poorly supported his master's assertion, for, upon Duke's ceasing to bark, Dan rose and showed the most courteous interest in making the little, old dog's acquaintance. Dan had a great deal of manner, and it became plain that Duke was impressed favourably in spite of former prejudice, so that presently the two trotted amicably back to their masters and sat down with the harmonious but indifferent air of having known each other intimately for years.

They were received without comment, though both boys looked at them reflectively for a time. It was Penrod who spoke first.

"What number you go to?" (In an "oral lesson in English," Penrod had been instructed to put this question in another form: "May I ask which of our public schools you attend?")

"Me? What number do I go to?" said the stranger, contemptuously. "I don't go to *no* number in vacation!"

"I mean when it ain't."

"Third," returned the fat-faced boy. "I got 'em *all* scared in *that* school."

"What of?" innocently asked Penrod, to whom "the Third"—in a distant part of town—was undiscovered country.

"What of? I guess you'd soon see what of, if you ever was in that school about one day. You'd be lucky if you got out alive!"

"Are the teachers mean?"

The other boy frowned with bitter scorn. "Teachers! Teachers don't order *me* around, I can tell you! They're mighty careful how they try to run over Rupe Collins."

"Who's Rupe Collins?"

"Who is he?" echoed the fat-faced boy incredulously. "Say, ain't you got *any* sense?"

"What?"

"Say, wouldn't you be just as happy if you had *some* sense?"

"Ye-es." Penrod's answer, like the look he lifted to the impressive stranger, was meek and placative. "Rupe Collins is the principal at your school, I guess."

The other yelled with jeering laughter, and mocked Penrod's manner and voice. " 'Rupe Collins is the principal at your school, I guess!' " He laughed harshly again, then suddenly showed truculence. "Say, 'bo, whyn't you learn enough to go in the house when it rains? What's the matter of you, anyhow?"

"Well," urged Penrod timidly, "nobody ever *told* me who Rupe Collins is: I got a *right* to think he's the principal, haven't I?"

The fat-faced boy shook his head disgustedly. "Honest, you make me sick!"

Penrod's expression became one of despair. "Well, who *is* he?" he cried.

" 'Who *is* he?' " mocked the other, with a scorn that withered. " 'Who *is* he?' ME!"

"Oh!" Penrod was humiliated but relieved: he felt that he had proved himself criminally ignorant, yet a peril seemed to have passed. "Rupe Collins is *your* name, then, I guess. I kind of thought it was, all the time."

The fat-faced boy still appeared embittered, burlesquing this speech in a hateful falsetto. " 'Rupe Collins is *your* name, then, I guess!' Oh, you 'kind of thought it was, all the time,' did you?" Suddenly concentrating his brow into a histrionic scowl he thrust his face within an inch of Penrod's. "Yes, sonny, Rupe Collins is my name, and you better look out what you say when he's around or you'll get in big trouble! *You understand that, 'bo?*"

Penrod was cowed but fascinated: he felt that there was something dangerous and dashing about this newcomer.

"Yes," he said, feebly, drawing back. "My name's Penrod Schofield."

"Then I reckon your father and mother ain't got good sense," said Mr. Collins promptly, this also being formula.

"Why?"

" 'Cause if they had they'd of give you a good name!" And the agreeable youth instantly rewarded himself for the wit with another yell of rasping laughter, after which he pointed suddenly at Penrod's right hand.

"Where'd you get that wart on your finger?" he demanded severely.

"Which finger?" asked the mystified Penrod, extending his hand.

"The middle one."

"Where?"

"There!" exclaimed Rupe Collins, seizing and vigorously twisting the wart-less finger naïvely offered for his inspection.

"Quit!" shouted Penrod in agony. "*Quee*-yut!"

"Say your prayers!" commanded Rupe, and continued to twist the luckless finger until Penrod writhed to his knees.

"*Ow!*" The victim, released, looked grievously upon the still painful finger.

At this Rupe's scornful expression altered to one of contrition. "Well, I declare!" he exclaimed remorsefully. "I didn't s'pose it would hurt. Turn about's fair play; so now you do that to me."

He extended the middle finger of his left hand and Penrod promptly seized it, but did not twist it, for he was instantly swung round with his back to his amiable new acquaintance: Rupe's right hand operated upon the back of Penrod's slender neck; Rupe's knee tortured the small of Penrod's back.

"*Ow!*" Penrod bent far forward involuntarily and went to his knees again.

"Lick dirt," commanded Rupe, forcing the captive's face to the sidewalk; and the suffering Penrod completed this ceremony.

Mr. Collins evinced satisfaction by means of his horse laugh. "You'd last jest about one day up at the Third!" he said. "You'd come runnin' home, yellin' '*Mom-muh, mom*-muh,' before recess was over!"

"No, I wouldn't," Penrod protested rather weakly, dusting his knees.

"You would, too!"

"No, I w——"

"Looky here," said the fat-faced boy, darkly, "what you mean, counterdicking me?"

He advanced a step and Penrod hastily qualified his contradiction.

"I mean, I don't *think* I would. I——"

"You better look out!" Rupe moved closer, and unexpectedly grasped the back of Penrod's neck again. "Say, 'I *would* run home yellin' "*Mom-muh!*" ' "

"Ow! I *would* run home yellin' 'Mom-muh.' "

"There!" said Rupe, giving the helpless nape a final squeeze. "That's the way we do up at the Third."

Penrod rubbed his neck and asked meekly:

"Can you do that to any boy up at the Third?"

"See here now," said Rupe, in the tone of one goaded beyond all endurance, "*you* say if I can! You better say it quick, or——"

"I knew you could," Penrod interposed hastily, with the pathetic semblance of a laugh. "I only said that in fun."

"In 'fun'!" repeated Rupe stormily. "You better look out how you——"

"Well, I *said* I wasn't in earnest!" Penrod retreated a few steps. "I knew you could, all the time. I expect *I* could do it to some of the boys up at the Third, myself. Couldn't I?"

"No, you couldn't."

"Well, there must be *some* boy up there that I could——"

"No, they ain't! You better——"

"I expect not, then," said Penrod, quickly.

"You *better* 'expect not.' Didn't I tell you once you'd never get back alive if you ever tried to come up around the Third? You want me to *show* you how we do up there, 'bo?"

He began a slow and deadly advance, whereupon Penrod timidly offered a diversion:

"Say, Rupe, I got a box of rats in our stable under a glass cover, so you can watch 'em jump around when you hammer on the box. Come on and look at 'em."

"All right," said the fat-faced boy, slightly mollified. "We'll let Dan kill 'em."

"No, *sir!* I'm goin' to keep 'em. They're kind of pets; I've had 'em all summer—I got names for 'em, and——"

"Looky here, 'bo. Did you hear me say we'll let Dan kill 'em?"

"Yes, but I won't——"

"*What* won't you?" Rupe became sinister immediately. "It seems to me you're gettin' pretty fresh around here."

"Well, I don't want——"

Mr. Collins once more brought into play the dreadful eye-to-eye scowl as practised "up at the Third," and, sometimes, also by young leading men upon the stage. Frowning appallingly, and thrusting forward his underlip, he placed his nose almost in contact with the nose of Penrod, whose eyes naturally became crossed.

"Dan kills the rats. See?" hissed the fat-faced boy, maintaining the horrible juxtaposition.

"Well, all right," said Penrod, swallowing. "*I* don't want 'em much." And when the pose had been relaxed, he stared at his new friend for a moment, almost with reverence. Then he brightened.

"Come on, Rupe!" he cried enthusiastically, as he climbed the fence. "We'll give our dogs a little live meat—'bo!"

CHAPTER XXII

THE IMITATOR

At the dinner-table, that evening, Penrod surprised his family by remarking, in a voice they had never heard him attempt—a law-giving voice of intentional gruffness:

"Any man that's makin' a hunderd dollars a month is makin' good money."

"What?" asked Mr. Schofield, staring, for the previous conversation had concerned the illness of an infant relative in Council Bluffs.

"Any man that's makin' a hunderd dollars a month is makin' good money."

"What *is* he talking about!" Margaret appealed to the invisible.

"Well," said Penrod, frowning, "that's what foremen at the ladder works get."

"How in the world do you know?" asked his mother.

"Well, I *know* it! A hunderd dollars a month is good money, I tell you!"

"Well, what of it?" said the father, impatiently.

"Nothin'. I only said it was good money."

Mr. Schofield shook his head, dismissing the subject; and here he made a mistake: he should have followed up his son's singular contribution to the conversation. That would have revealed the fact that there was a certain Rupe Collins whose father was a foreman at the ladder works. All clues are important when a boy makes his first remark in a new key.

" 'Good money'?" repeated Margaret, curiously. "What is 'good' money?"

Penrod turned upon her a stern glance. "Say, wouldn't you be just as happy if you had *some* sense?"

"Penrod!" shouted his father. But Penrod's mother gazed with dismay at her son: he had never before spoken like that to his sister.

Mrs. Schofield might have been more dismayed than she was, if she had realized that it was the beginning of an epoch. After dinner, Penrod was slightly scalded in the back as the result of telling Della, the cook, that there was a wart on the middle finger of her right hand. Della thus proving poor material for his new manner to work upon, he approached Duke, in the backyard, and, bending double, seized the lowly animal by the forepaws.

"I let you know my name's Penrod Schofield," hissed the boy. He protruded his underlip ferociously, scowled, and thrust forward his head until his nose touched the dog's. "And you better look out when Penrod Schofield's around, or you'll get in big trouble! *You understan' that, 'bo?*"

The next day, and the next, the increasing change in Penrod puzzled and distressed his family, who had no idea of its source. How might they guess that hero-worship takes such forms? They were vaguely conscious that a rather shabby boy, not of the neighbourhood, came to "play" with Penrod several times; but they failed to connect this circumstance with the peculiar behaviour of the son of the house, whose ideals (his father remarked) seemed to have suddenly become identical with those of Gyp the Blood.

Meanwhile, for Penrod himself, "life had taken on new meaning, new richness." He had become a fighting man—in conversation at least. "Do you want to know how I do when they try to slip up on me from behind?" he asked Della. And he enacted for her unappreciative eye a scene of fistic manœuvres wherein he held an imaginary antagonist helpless in a net of stratagems.

Frequently, when he was alone, he would outwit and pummel this same enemy, and, after a cunning feint, land a dolorous stroke full upon a face of air. "There! I guess you'll know better next time. That's the way we do up at the Third!"

Sometimes, in solitary pantomime, he encountered more than one opponent at a time, for numbers were apt to come upon him treacherously, especially at a little after his rising hour, when he might be caught at a disadvantage—perhaps standing on one leg to encase the other in his knickerbockers. Like lightning, he would hurl the trapping garment from him, and, ducking and pivoting, deal great sweeping blows among the circle of sneaking devils. (That was how he broke the clock in his bedroom.) And while these battles were occupying his attention, it was a waste of voice to call him to breakfast, though if his mother, losing patience, came to his room, she would find him seated on the bed pulling at a stocking. "Well, ain't I coming fast as I *can*?"

At the table and about the house generally he was bumptious, loud with fatuous misinformation, and assumed a domineering tone, which neither satire nor reproof seemed able to reduce; but it was among his own intimates that his new superiority was most outrageous. He twisted the fingers and squeezed the necks of all the boys of the neighbourhood, meeting their indignation with a hoarse and rasping laugh he had acquired after short practice in the stable, where he jeered and taunted the lawn-mower, the garden-scythe and the wheelbarrow quite out of countenance.

Likewise he bragged to the other boys by the hour, Rupe Collins being the chief subject of encomium—next to Penrod himself. "That's the way we do up at the Third," became staple explanation of violence, for Penrod, like Tartarin, was plastic in the hands of his own imagination, and at times convinced himself that he really was one of those dark and murderous spirits exclusively of whom "the Third" was composed—according to Rupe Collins.

Then, when Penrod had exhausted himself repeating to nausea accounts of the prowess of himself and his great friend, he would turn to two other subjects for vainglory. These were his father and Duke.

Mothers must accept the fact that between babyhood and manhood their sons do not boast of them. The boy, with boys, is a Choctaw; and either the influence or the protection of women is shameful. "Your mother won't let you," is an insult. But, "My father won't let me," is a dignified explanation and cannot be hooted. A boy is ruined among his fellows if he talks much of his mother or sisters; and he must recognize it as his duty to offer at least the appearance of persecution to all things ranked as female, such as cats and every species of fowl. But he must champion his father and his dog, ånd, ever ready to pit either against any challenger, must picture both as ravening for battle and absolutely unconquerable.

Penrod, of course, had always talked by the code, but, under the new stimulus, Duke was represented virtually as a cross between Bob, Son of Battle, and a South American vampire; and this in spite of the fact that Duke himself often sat close by, a living lie, with the hope of peace in his heart. As for Penrod's father, that gladiator was painted as of sentiments and dimensions suitable to a superdemon composed of equal parts of Goliath, Jack Johnson and the Emperor Nero.

Even Penrod's walk was affected; he adopted a gait which was a kind of taunting swagger; and, when he passed other children on the street, he practised the habit of feinting a blow; then, as the victim dodged, he rasped the triumphant horse laugh which he gradually mastered to horrible perfection. He did this to Marjorie Jones—ay! this was their next meeting, and such is Eros, young! What was even worse, in Marjorie's opinion, he went on his way without explanation, and left her standing on the corner talking about it, long after he was out of hearing.

Within five days from his first encounter with Rupe Collins, Penrod had become unbearable. He even almost alienated Sam Williams, who for a time submitted to finger twisting and neck squeezing and the new style of conversation, but finally declared that Penrod made him "sick." He made the statement with fervour, one sultry afternoon, in Mr. Schofield's stable, in the presence of Herman and Verman.

"You better look out, 'bo," said Penrod, threateningly. "I'll show you a little how we do up at the Third."

"Up at the Third!" Sam repeated with scorn. "You haven't ever been up there."

"I haven't?" cried Penrod. "I *haven't?*"

"No, you haven't!"

"Looky here!" Penrod, darkly argumentative, prepared to perform the eye-to-eye business. "When haven't I been up there?"

"You haven't *never* been up there!" In spite of Penrod's closely approaching nose Sam maintained his ground, and appealed for confirmation. "Has he, Herman?"

"I don' reckon so," said Herman, laughing.

"*What!*" Penrod transferred his nose to the immediate vicinity of Herman's nose. "You don't reckon so, 'bo, don't you? You better look out how you reckon around here! *You understan' that, 'bo?*"

Herman bore the eye-to-eye very well; indeed, it seemed to please him, for he continued to laugh while Verman chuckled delightedly. The brothers had been in the country picking berries for a week, and it happened that this was their first experience of the new manifestation of Penrod.

"*Haven't* I been up at the Third?" the sinister Penrod demanded.

"I don' reckon so. How come you asl *me*?"

"Didn't you just hear me *say* I been up there?"

"Well," said Herman mischievously, "hearin' ain't believin'!"

Penrod clutched him by the back of the neck, but Herman, laughing loudly, ducked and released himself at once, retreating to the wall.

"You take that back!" Penrod shouted, striking out wildly.

"Don' git mad," begged the small darky, while a number of blows falling upon his warding arms failed to abate his amusement, and a sound one upon the cheek only made him laugh the more unrestrainedly. He behaved exactly as if Penrod were tickling him, and his brother, Verman, rolled with joy in a wheelbarrow. Penrod pummelled till he was tired, and produced no greater effect.

"There!" he panted, desisting finally. "Now I reckon you know whether I been up there or not!"

Herman rubbed his smitten cheek. "Pow!" he exclaimed. "Pow-ee! You cert'ny did lan' me good one *nat* time! Oo-ee! she *hurt*!"

"You'll get hurt worse'n that," Penrod assured him, "if you stay around here much. Rupe Collins is comin' this afternoon, he said. We're goin' to make some policemen's billies out of the rake handle."

"You go' spoil new rake you' pa bought?"

"What do *we* care? I and Rupe got to have billies, haven't we?"

"How you make 'em?"

"Melt lead and pour in a hole we're goin' to make in the end of 'em. Then we're goin' to carry 'em in our pockets, and if anybody says anything to us— *oh*, oh! look out! They won't get a crack on the head—*oh*, no!"

"When's Rupe Collins coming?" Sam Williams inquired rather uneasily. He had heard a great deal too much of this personage, but as yet the pleasure of actual acquaintance had been denied him.

"He's liable to be here any time," answered Penrod. "You better look out. You'll be lucky if you get home alive, if you stay till *he* comes."

"I ain't afraid of him," Sam returned, conventionally.

"You are, too!" (There was some truth in the retort.) "There ain't any boy in this part of town but me that wouldn't be afraid of him. You'd be afraid to talk to him. You wouldn't get a word out of your mouth before old Rupie'd have you where you'd wished you never come around *him*, lettin' on like you was so much! *You* wouldn't run home yellin' 'Mom-muh' or nothin'! *Oh*, no!"

"Who Rupe Collins?" asked Herman.

" 'Who Rupe Collins?' " Penrod mocked, and used his rasping laugh, but, instead of showing fright, Herman appeared to think he was meant to laugh, too; and so he did, echoed by Verman. "You just hang around here a little

while longer," Penrod added, grimly, "and you'll find out who Rupe Collins
is, and I pity *you* when you do!"

"What he go' do?"

"You'll see; that's all! You just wait and——"

At this moment a brown hound ran into the stable through the alley door,
wagged a greeting to Penrod, and fraternized with Duke. The fat-faced boy
appeared upon the threshold and gazed coldly about the little company in
the carriage-house, whereupon the coloured brethren, ceasing from merriment, were instantly impassive, and Sam Williams moved a little nearer the
door leading into the yard.

Obviously, Sam regarded the newcomer as a redoubtable if not ominous
figure. He was a head taller than either Sam or Penrod; head and shoulders
taller than Herman, who was short for his age; and Verman could hardly be
used for purposes of comparison at all, being a mere squat brown spot, not
yet quite nine years on this planet. And to Sam's mind, the aspect of Mr.
Collins realized Penrod's portentous foreshadowings. Upon the fat face there
was an expression of truculent intolerance which had been cultivated by
careful habit to such perfection that Sam's heart sank at sight of it. A somewhat enfeebled twin to this expression had of late often decorated the visage
of Penrod, and appeared upon that ingenuous surface now, as he advanced
to welcome the eminent visitor.

The host swaggered toward the door with a great deal of shoulder movement, carelessly feinting a slap at Verman in passing, and creating by various
means the atmosphere of a man who has contemptuously amused himself
with underlings while awaiting an equal.

"Hello, 'bo!" Penrod said in the deepest voice possible to him.

"Who you callin' 'bo?" was the ungracious response, accompanied by immediate action of a similar nature. Rupe held Penrod's head in the crook of
an elbow and massaged his temples with a hard-pressing knuckle.

"I was only in fun, Rupie," pleaded the sufferer, and then, being set free,
"Come here, Sam," he said.

"What for?"

Penrod laughed pityingly. "Pshaw, I ain't goin' to hurt you. Come on."
Sam, maintaining his position near the other door, Penrod went to him and
caught him round the neck.

"Watch me, Rupie!" Penrod called, and performed upon Sam the knuckle
operation which he had himself just undergone, Sam submitting mechanically, his eyes fixed with increasing uneasiness upon Rupe Collins. Sam had
a premonition that something even more painful than Penrod's knuckle was
going to be inflicted upon him.

"*That* don' hurt," said Penrod, pushing him away.

"Yes, it does, too!" Sam rubbed his temple.

"Puh! It didn't hurt me, did it, Rupie? Come on in, Rupe: show this
baby where he's got a wart on his finger."

"*You* showed me that trick," Sam objected. "You already did that to me.

You tried it twice this afternoon and I don't know how many times before, only you weren't strong enough after the first time. Anyway, I know what it is, and I don't——"

"Come on, Rupe," said Penrod. "Make the baby lick dirt."

At this bidding, Rupe approached, while Sam, still protesting, moved to the threshold of the outer door; but Penrod seized him by the shoulders and swung him indoors with a shout.

"Little baby wants to run home to its Mom-muh! Here he is, Rupie."

Thereupon was Penrod's treachery to an old comrade properly rewarded, for as the two struggled, Rupe caught each by the back of the neck, simul-.taneously, and, with creditable impartiality, forced both boys to their knees.

"Lick dirt!" he commanded, forcing them still forward, until their faces were close to the stable floor.

At this moment he received a real surprise. With a loud whack something struck the back of his head, and, turning, he beheld Verman in the act of lifting a piece of lath to strike again.

"Em moys ome!" said Verman, the Giant Killer.

"He tongue-tie'," Herman explained. "He say, let 'em boys alone."

Rupe addressed his host briefly:

"Chase them nigs out o' here!"

"Don' call me nig," said Herman. "I mine my own biznuss. You let 'em boys alone."

Rupe strode across the still prostrate Sam, stepped upon Penrod, and, equipping his countenance with the terrifying scowl and protruded jaw, lowered his head to the level of Herman's.

"Nig, you'll be lucky if you leave here alive!" And he leaned forward till his nose was within less than an inch of Herman's nose.

It could be felt that something awful was about to happen, and Penrod, as he rose from the floor, suffered an unexpected twinge of apprehension and remorse: he hoped that Rupe wouldn't *really* hurt Herman. A sudden dislike of Rupe and Rupe's ways rose within him, as he looked at the big boy overwhelming the little darky with that ferocious scowl. Penrod, all at once, felt sorry about something indefinable; and, with equal vagueness, he felt foolish. "Come on, Rupe," he suggested, feebly, "let Herman go, and let's us make our billies out of the rake handle."

The rake handle, however, was not available, if Rupe had inclined to favour the suggestion. Verman had discarded his lath for the rake, which he was at this moment lifting in the air.

"You ole black nigger," the fat-faced boy said venomously to Herman, "I'm agoin' to——"

But he had allowed his nose to remain too long near Herman's. Penrod's familiar nose had been as close with only a ticklish spinal effect upon the not very remote descendant of Congo man-eaters. The result produced by the glare of Rupe's unfamiliar eyes, and by the dreadfully suggestive proximity of Rupe's unfamiliar nose, was altogether different. Herman's and Verman's Bangala great-grandfathers never considered people of their own jungle neighbourhood proper material for a meal, but they looked upon strangers —especially truculent strangers—as distinctly edible.

Penrod and Sam heard Rupe suddenly squawk and bellow; saw him writhe and twist and fling out his arms like flails, though without removing his face from its juxtaposition; indeed, for a moment, the two heads seemed even closer.

Then they separated—and battle was on!

CHAPTER XXIII

COLOURED TROOPS IN ACTION

How neat and pure is the task of the chronicler who has the tale to tell of a "good rousing fight" between boys or men who fight in the "good old English way," according to a model set for fights in books long before Tom Brown went to Rugby. There are seconds and rounds and rules of fair-play, and always there is great good feeling in the end—though sometimes, to vary the model, "the Butcher" defeats the hero—and the chronicler who stencils this fine old pattern on his page is certain of applause as the stirrer of "red blood." There is no surer recipe.

But when Herman and Verman set to 't the record must be no more than a few fragments left by the expurgator. It has been perhaps sufficiently suggested that the altercation in Mr. Schofield's stable opened with mayhem in respect to the aggressor's nose. Expressing vocally his indignation and the extremity of his pained surprise, Mr. Collins stepped backward, holding his left hand over his nose, and striking at Herman with his right. Then Verman hit him with the rake.

Verman struck from behind. He struck as hard as he could. And he struck with the tines down. For, in his simple, direct African way he wished to kill his enemy, and he wished to kill him as soon as possible. That was his single, earnest purpose.

On this account, Rupe Collins was peculiarly unfortunate. He was plucky and he enjoyed conflict, but neither his ambitions nor his anticipations had ever included murder. He had not learned that an habitually aggressive person runs the danger of colliding with beings in one of those lower stages of evolution wherein theories about "hitting below the belt" have not yet made their appearance.

The rake glanced from the back of Rupe's head to his shoulder, but it felled him. Both darkies jumped full upon him instantly, and the three rolled and twisted upon the stable floor, unloosing upon the air sincere maledictions closely connected with complaints of cruel and unusual treatment; while certain expressions of feeling presently emanating from Herman and Verman indicated that Rupe Collins, in this extremity, was proving himself not too slavishly addicted to fighting by rule. Dan and Duke, mistaking all for mirth, barked gayly.

From the panting, pounding, yelling heap issued words and phrases hitherto quite unknown to Penrod and Sam; also, a hoarse repetition in the voice of Rupe concerning his ear left it not to be doubted that additional mayhem was taking place. Appalled, the two spectators retreated to the doorway nearest the yard, where they stood dumbly watching the cataclysm.

The struggle increased in primitive simplicity: time and again the howling Rupe got to his knees only to go down again as the earnest brothers, in their own way, assisted him to a more reclining position. Primal forces operated here, and the two blanched, slightly higher products of evolution, Sam and Penrod, no more thought of interfering than they would have thought of interfering with an earthquake.

At last, out of the ruck rose Verman, disfigured and maniacal. With a wild eye he looked about him for his trusty rake; but Penrod, in horror, had long since thrown the rake out into the yard. Naturally, it had not seemed necessary to remove the lawn-mower.

The frantic eye of Verman fell upon the lawn-mower, and instantly he leaped to its handle. Shrilling a wordless war-cry, he charged, propelling the whirling, deafening knives straight upon the prone legs of Rupe Collins. The lawn-mower was sincerely intended to pass longitudinally over the body of Mr. Collins from heel to head; and it was the time for a death-song. Black Valkyrie hovered in the shrieking air.

"Cut his gizzud out!" shrieked Herman, urging on the whirling knives.

They touched and lacerated the shin of Rupe, as, with the supreme agony of effort a creature in mortal peril puts forth before succumbing, he tore himself free of Herman and got upon his feet.

Herman was up as quickly. He leaped to the wall and seized the garden-scythe that hung there.

"I'm go' to cut you' gizzud out," he announced definitely, "an' eat it!"

Rupe Collins had never run from anybody (except his father) in his life; he was not a coward; but the present situation was very, very unusual. He was already in a badly dismantled condition, and yet Herman and Verman seemed discontented with their work: Verman was swinging the grass-cutter about for a new charge, apparently still wishing to mow him, and Herman had made a quite plausible statement about what he intended to do with the scythe.

Rupe paused but for an extremely condensed survey of the horrible advance of the brothers, and then, uttering a blood-curdled scream of fear, ran out of the stable and up the alley at a speed he had never before attained, so that even Dan had hard work to keep within barking distance. And a 'cross-shoulder glance, at the corner, revealing Verman and Herman in pursuit, the latter waving his scythe overhead, Mr. Collins slackened not his gait, but, rather, out of great anguish, increased it; the while a rapidly developing purpose became firm in his mind—and ever after so remained—not only to refrain from visiting that neighbourhood again, but never by any chance to come within a mile of it.

From the alley door, Penrod and Sam watched the flight, and were without words. When the pursuit rounded the corner, the two looked wanly at each other, but neither spoke until the return of the brothers from the chase.

Herman and Verman came back, laughing and chuckling.

"Hiyi!" cackled Herman to Verman, as they came, "See 'at ole boy run!"

"Who-ee!" Verman shouted in ecstasy.

"Nev' did see boy run so fas'!" Herman continued, tossing the scythe into the wheelbarrow. "I bet he home in bed by viss time!"

Verman roared with delight, appearing to be wholly unconscious that the lids of his right eye were swollen shut and that his attire, not too finical before the struggle, now entitled him to unquestioned rank as a *sansculotte*. Herman was a similar ruin, and gave as little heed to his condition.

Penrod looked dazedly from Herman to Verman and back again. So did Sam Williams.

"Herman," said Penrod, in a weak voice, "you wouldn't *honest* of cut his gizzard out, would you?"

"Who? Me? I don' know. He mighty mean ole boy!" Herman shook his head gravely, and then, observing that Verman was again convulsed with unctuous merriment, joined laughter with his brother. "Sho'! I guess I uz dess *talkin'* whens I said 'at! Reckon he thought I meant it, f'm de way he tuck an' run. Hiyi! Reckon he thought ole Herman bad man! No, suh! I uz dess talkin', 'cause I nev' would cut *nobody*! I ain' tryin' git in no jail—*no*, suh!"

Penrod looked at the scythe: he looked at Herman. He looked at the lawnmower, and he looked at Verman. Then he looked out in the yard at the rake. So did Sam Williams.

"Come on, Verman," said Herman. "We ain' got 'at stove-wood f' supper yit."

Giggling reminiscently, the brothers disappeared, leaving silence behind them in the carriage-house. Penrod and Sam retired slowly into the shadowy interior, each glancing, now and then, with a preoccupied air, at the open, empty doorway where the late afternoon sunshine was growing ruddy. At intervals one or the other scraped the floor reflectively with the side of his shoe. Finally, still without either having made any effort at conversation, they went out into the yard and stood, continuing their silence.

"Well," said Sam, at last, "I guess it's time I better be gettin' home. So long, Penrod!"

"So long, Sam," said Penrod, feebly.

With a solemn gaze he watched his friend out of sight. Then he went slowly into the house, and after an interval occupied in a unique manner, appeared in the library, holding a pair of brilliantly gleaming shoes in his hand.

Mr. Schofield, reading the evening paper, glanced frowningly over it at his offspring.

"Look, papa," said Penrod. "I found your shoes where you'd taken 'em off in your room, to put on your slippers, and they were all dusty. So I took 'em out on the back porch and gave 'em a good blacking. They shine up fine, don't they?"

"Well, I'll be d-dud-dummed!" said the startled Mr. Schofield.

Penrod was zigzagging back to normal.

CHAPTER XXIV

"LITTLE GENTLEMAN"

The midsummer sun was stinging hot outside the little barber-shop next to the corner drug store and Penrod, undergoing a toilette preliminary to his very slowly approaching twelfth birthday, was adhesive enough to retain upon his face much hair as it fell from the shears. There is a mystery here: the tonsorial processes are not unagreeable to manhood; in truth, they are soothing; but the hairs detached from a boy's head get into his eyes, his ears, his nose, his mouth, and down his neck, and he does everywhere itch excruciatingly. Wherefore he blinks, winks, weeps, twitches, condenses his countenance, and squirms; and perchance the barber's scissors clip more than intended—belike an outlying flange of ear.

"Um—muh—ow!" said Penrod, this thing having happened.

"D' I touch y' up a little?" inquired the barber, smiling falsely.

"Ooh—uh!" The boy in the chair offered inarticulate protest, as the wound was rubbed with alum.

"That don't hurt!" said the barber. "You will get it, though, if you don't sit stiller," he continued, nipping in the bud any attempt on the part of his patient to think that he already had "it."

"Pfuff!" said Penrod, meaning no disrespect, but endeavouring to dislodge a temporary moustache from his lip.

"You ought to see how still that little Georgie Bassett sits," the barber went on, reprovingly. "I hear everybody says he's the best boy in town."

"Pfuff! Phirr!" There was a touch of intentional contempt in this.

"I haven't heard nobody around the neighbourhood makin' no such remarks," added the barber, "about nobody of the name of Penrod Schofield."

"Well," said Penrod, clearing his mouth after a struggle, "who wants 'em to? Ouch!"

"I hear they call Georgie Bassett the 'little gentleman,'" ventured the barber, provocatively, meeting with instant success.

"They better not call *me* that," returned Penrod truculently. "I'd like to hear anybody try. Just once, that's all! I bet they'd never try it ag—— *Ouch!*"

"Why? What'd you do to 'em?"

"It's all right what I'd *do!* I bet they wouldn't want to call me that again long as they lived!"

"What'd you do if it was a little girl? You wouldn't hit her, would you?"

"Well, I'd—— Ouch!"

"You wouldn't hit a little girl, would you?" the barber persisted, gathering into his powerful fingers a mop of hair from the top of Penrod's head and pulling that suffering head into an unnatural position. "Doesn't the Bible say it ain't never right to hit the weak sex?"

"Ow! *Say,* look *out!*"

"So you'd go and punch a pore, weak, little girl, would you?" said the barber, reprovingly.

"Well, who said I'd hit her?" demanded the chivalrous Penrod. "I bet I'd *fix* her though, all right. She'd see!"

"You wouldn't call her names, would you?"

"No, I wouldn't! What hurt is it to call anybody names?"

"Is that *so!*" exclaimed the barber. "Then you was intending what I heard you hollering at Fisher's grocery delivery wagon driver fer a favour, the other day when I was goin' by your house, was you? I reckon I better tell him, because he says to me after*werds* if he ever lays eyes on you when you ain't in your own yard, he's goin' to do a whole lot o' things you ain't goin' to like! Yessir, that's what he says to *me!*"

"He better catch me first, I guess, before he talks so much."

"Well," resumed the barber, "that ain't sayin' what you'd do if a young lady ever walked up and called you a little gentleman. *I* want to hear what you'd do to her. I guess I know, though—come to think of it."

"What?" demanded Penrod.

"You'd sick that pore ole dog of yours on her cat, if she had one, I expect," guessed the barber derisively.

"No, I would not!"

"Well, what *would* you do?"

"I'd do enough. Don't worry about that!"

"Well, suppose it was a boy, then: what'd you do if a boy come up to you and says, 'Hello, little gentleman'?"

"He'd be lucky," said Penrod, with a sinister frown, "if he got home alive."

"Suppose it was a boy twice your size?"

"Just let him try," said Penrod ominously. "You just let him try. He'd never see daylight again; that's all!"

The barber dug ten active fingers into the helpless scalp before him and did his best to displace it, while the anguished Penrod, becoming instantly a seething crucible of emotion, misdirected his natural resentment into maddened brooding upon what he would do to a boy "twice his size" who should dare to call him "little gentleman." The barber shook him as his father had never shaken him; the barber buffeted him, rocked him frantically to and fro; the barber seemed to be trying to wring his neck; and Penrod saw himself in staggering zigzag pictures, destroying large, screaming, fragmentary boys who had insulted him.

The torture stopped suddenly; and clenched, weeping eyes began to see again, while the barber applied cooling lotions which made Penrod smell like a coloured housemaid's ideal.

"Now what," asked the barber, combing the reeking locks gently, "what would it make you so mad fer, to have somebody call you a little gentleman? It's a kind of compliment, as it were, you might say. What would you want to hit anybody fer *that* fer?"

To the mind of Penrod, this question was without meaning or reasonableness. It was within neither his power nor his desire to analyze the process by which the phrase had become offensive to him, and was now rapidly assuming the proportions of an outrage. He knew only that his gorge rose at the thought of it.

"You just let 'em try it!" he said threateningly, as he slid down from the chair. And as he went out of the door, after further conversation on the same subject, he called back those warning words once more: "Just let 'em try it! Just once—that's all I ask 'em to. They'll find out what they *get!*"

The barber chuckled. Then a fly lit on the barber's nose and he slapped at it, and the slap missed the fly but did not miss the nose. The barber was irritated. At this moment his birdlike eye gleamed a gleam as it fell upon customers approaching: the prettiest little girl in the world, leading by the hand her baby brother, Mitchy-Mitch, coming to have Mitchy-Mitch's hair clipped, against the heat.

It was a hot day and idle, with little to feed the mind—and the barber was a mischievous man with an irritated nose. He did his worst.

Meanwhile, the brooding Penrod pursued his homeward way; no great distance, but long enough for several one-sided conflicts with malign insulters made of thin air. "You better *not* call me that!" he muttered. "You just try it, and you'll get what other people got when *they* tried it. You better not ack fresh with *me!* Oh, you *will*, will you?" He delivered a vicious kick full upon the shins of an iron fence-post, which suffered little, though Penrod instantly regretted his indiscretion. "Oof!" he grunted, hopping; and went on after bestowing a look of awful hostility upon the fence-post. "I guess you'll know better next time," he said, in parting, to this antagonist. "You just let me catch you around here again and I'll——" His voice sank to inarticulate but ominous murmurings. He was in a dangerous mood.

Nearing home, however, his belligerent spirit was diverted to happier interests by the discovery that some workmen had left a caldron of tar in the cross-street, close by his father's stable. He tested it, but found it inedible. Also, as a substitute for professional chewing-gum it was unsatisfactory, being insufficiently boiled down and too thin, though of a pleasant, lukewarm temperature. But it had an excess of one quality—it was sticky. It was the stickiest tar Penrod had ever used for any purposes whatsoever, and nothing upon which he wiped his hands served to rid them of it; neither his polka-dotted shirt waist nor his knickerbockers; neither the fence, nor even Duke, who came unthinkingly wagging out to greet him, and retired wiser.

Nevertheless, tar is tar. Much can be done with it, no matter what its condition; so Penrod lingered by the caldron, though from a neighbouring yard could be heard the voices of comrades, including that of Sam Williams. On the ground about the caldron were scattered chips and sticks and bits of wood to the number of a great multitude. Penrod mixed quantities of this refuse into the tar, and interested himself in seeing how much of it he could keep moving in slow swirls upon the ebon surface.

Other surprises were arranged for the absent workmen. The caldron was almost full, and the surface of the tar near the rim. Penrod endeavoured to ascertain how many pebbles and brickbats, dropped in, would cause an over-flow. Labouring heartily to this end, he had almost accomplished it, when he received the suggestion for an experiment on a much larger scale. Embedded at the corner of a grass-plot across the street was a whitewashed stone, the size of a small watermelon and serving no purpose whatever save the ques-tionable one of decoration. It was easily pried up with a stick; though getting it to the caldron tested the full strength of the ardent labourer. Instructed to perform such a task, he would have sincerely maintained its impossibility; but now, as it was unbidden, and promised rather destructive results, he set about it with unconquerable energy, feeling certain that he would be re-warded with a mighty splash. Perspiring, grunting vehemently, his back ach-ing and all muscles strained, he progressed in short stages until the big stone lay at the base of the caldron. He rested a moment, panting, then lifted the stone, and was bending his shoulders for the heave that would lift it over the rim, when a sweet, taunting voice, close behind him, startled him cruelly.

"How do you do, *little gentleman!*"

Penrod squawked, dropped the stone, and shouted, "Shut up, you dern fool!" purely from instinct, even before his about-face made him aware who had so spitefully addressed him.

It was Marjorie Jones. Always dainty, and prettily dressed, she was in speckless and starchy white to-day, and a refreshing picture she made, with the new-shorn and powerfully scented Mitchy-Mitch clinging to her hand. They had stolen up behind the toiler, and now stood laughing together in sweet merriment. Since the passing of Penrod's Rupe Collins period he had experienced some severe qualms at the recollection of his last meeting with Marjorie and his Apache behaviour; in truth, his heart instantly became as wax at sight of her, and he would have offered her fair speech; but, alas! in Marjorie's wonderful eyes there shone a consciousness of new powers for his undoing, and she denied him opportunity.

"Oh, *oh!*" she cried, mocking his pained outcry. "What a way for a *little gentleman* to talk! Little gentlemen don't say wicked——"

"Marjorie!" Penrod, enraged and dismayed, felt himself stung beyond all endurance. Insult from her was bitterer to endure than from any other. "Don't you call me that again!"

"Why not, *little gentleman?*"

He stamped his foot. "You better stop!"

Marjorie sent into his furious face her lovely, spiteful laughter.

"Little gentleman, little gentleman, little gentleman!" she said deliberately. "How's the little gentleman, this afternoon? Hello, little gentleman!"

Penrod, quite beside himself, danced eccentrically. "Dry up!" he howled. "Dry up, dry up, dry up, dry *up!*"

Mitchy-Mitch shouted with delight and applied a finger to the side of the caldron—a finger immediately snatched away and wiped upon a handkerchief by his fastidious sister.

"'Ittle gellamun!" said Mitchy-Mitch.

"You better look out!" Penrod whirled upon this small offender with grim satisfaction. Here was at least something male that could without dishonour be held responsible. "You say that again, and I'll give you the worst——"

"You will *not!*" snapped Marjorie, instantly vitriolic. "He'll say just whatever he wants to, and he'll say it just as *much* as he wants to. Say it again, Mitchy-Mitch!"

"'Ittle gellamun!" said Mitchy-Mitch promptly.

"Ow-*yah!*" Penrod's tone-production was becoming affected by his mental condition. "You say that again, and I'll——"

"Go on, Mitchy-Mitch," cried Marjorie. "He can't do a thing. He don't *dare!* Say it some more, Mitchy-Mitch—say it a whole lot!"

Mitchy-Mitch, his small, fat face shining with confidence in his immunity, complied.

"'Ittle gellamun!" he squeaked malevolently. "'Ittle gellamun! 'Ittle gellamun! 'Ittle gellamun!"

The desperate Penrod bent over the whitewashed rock, lifted it, and then —outdoing Porthos, John Ridd, and Ursus in one miraculous burst of strength —heaved it into the air.

Marjorie screamed.

But it was too late. The big stone descended into the precise midst of the caldron and Penrod got his mighty splash. It was far, far beyond his expectations.

Spontaneously there were grand and awful effects—volcanic spectacles of nightmare and eruption. A black sheet of eccentric shape rose out of the caldron and descended upon the three children, who had no time to evade it.

After it fell, Mitchy-Mitch, who stood nearest the caldron, was the thickest, though there was enough for all. Br'er Rabbit would have fled from any of them.

CHAPTER XXV

TAR

When Marjorie and Mitchy-Mitch got their breath, they used it vocally; and seldom have more penetrating sounds issued from human throats. Coincidentally, Marjorie, quite baresark, laid hands upon the largest stick within reach and fell upon Penrod with blind fury. He had the presence of mind to flee, and they went round and round the caldron, while Mitchy-Mitch feebly endeavoured to follow—his appearance, in this pursuit, being pathetically like that of a bug fished out of an ink-well, alive but discouraged.

Attracted by the riot, Samuel Williams made his appearance, vaulting a fence, and was immediately followed by Maurice Levy and Georgie Bassett. They stared incredulously at the extraordinary spectacle before them.

"Little GEN-TIL-MUN!" shrieked Marjorie, with a wild stroke that landed full upon Penrod's tarry cap.

"*Oooch!*" bleated Penrod.

"It's Penrod!" shouted Sam Williams, recognizing him by the voice. For an instant he had been in some doubt.

"Penrod Schofield!" exclaimed Georgie Bassett. "*What* does this mean?" That was Georgie's style, and had helped to win him his title.

Marjorie leaned, panting, upon her stick. "I cu-called—uh—him—oh!" she sobbed—"I called him a lul-little—oh—gentleman! And oh—lul-look!—oh! lul-look at my du-dress! Lul-look at Mu-mitchy– oh—Mitch—oh!"

Unexpectedly, she smote again—with results—and then, seizing the indistinguishable hand of Mitchy-Mitch, she ran wailing homeward down the street.

" 'Little gentleman'?" said Georgie Bassett, with some evidences of disturbed complacency. "Why, that's what they call *me!*"

"Yes, and you *are* one, too!" shouted the maddened Penrod. "But you better not let anybody call *me* that! I've stood enough around here for one day, and you can't run over *me*, Georgie Bassett. Just you put that in your gizzard and smoke it!"

"Anybody has a perfect right," said Georgie, with dignity, "to call a person a little gentleman. There's lots of names nobody ought to call, but this one's a *nice*——"

"You better look out!"

Unavenged bruises were distributed all over Penrod, both upon his body and upon his spirit. Driven by subtle forces, he had dipped his hands in catastrophe and disaster: it was not for a Georgie Bassett to beard him. Penrod was about to run amuck.

"I haven't called you a little gentleman, yet," said Georgie. "I only said it. Anybody's got a right to *say* it."

"Not around *me!* You just try it again and——"

"I shall say it," returned Georgie, "all I please. Anybody in this town has a right to *say* 'little gentleman'——"

Bellowing insanely, Penrod plunged his right hand into the caldron, rushed upon Georgie and made awful work of his hair and features.

Alas, it was but the beginning! Sam Williams and Maurice Levy screamed with delight, and, simultaneously infected, danced about the struggling pair, shouting frantically:

"Little gentleman! Little gentleman! Sick him, Georgie! Sick him, little gentleman! Little gentleman! Little gentleman!"

The infuriated outlaw turned upon them with blows and more tar, which gave Georgie Bassett his opportunity and later seriously impaired the purity of his fame. Feeling himself hopelessly tarred, he dipped both hands repeatedly into the caldron and applied his gatherings to Penrod. It was bringing coals to Newcastle, but it helped to assuage the just wrath of Georgie.

The four boys gave a fine imitation of the Laocoön group complicated by an extra figure—frantic splutterings and chokings, strange cries and stranger words issued from this tangle; hands dipped lavishly into the inexhaustible reservoir of tar, with more and more picturesque results. The caldron had been elevated upon bricks and was not perfectly balanced; and under a heavy impact of the struggling group it lurched and went partly over, pouring forth a Stygian tide which formed a deep pool in the gutter.

It was the fate of Master Roderick Bitts, that exclusive and immaculate person, to make his appearance upon the chaotic scene at this juncture. All in the cool of a white "sailor suit," he turned aside from the path of duty—which led straight to the house of a maiden aunt—and paused to hop with joy upon the sidewalk. A repeated epithet continuously half panted, half squawked, somewhere in the nest of gladiators, caught his ear, and he took it up excitedly, not knowing why.

"Little gentleman!" shouted Roderick, jumping up and down in childish glee. "Little gentleman! Little gentleman! Lit——"

A frightful figure tore itself free from the group, encircled this innocent bystander with a black arm, and hurled him headlong. Full length and flat on his face went Roderick into the Stygian pool. The frightful figure was Penrod. Instantly, the pack flung themselves upon him again, and, carrying them with him, he went over upon Roderick, who from that instant was as active a belligerent as any there.

Thus began the Great Tar Fight, the origin of which proved, afterward, so difficult for parents to trace, owing to the opposing accounts of the combatants. Marjorie said Penrod began it; Penrod said Mitchy-Mitch began it; Sam Williams said Georgie Bassett began it; Georgie and Maurice Levy said Penrod began it; Roderick Bitts, who had not recognized his first assailant, said Sam Williams began it.

Nobody thought of accusing the barber. But the barber did not begin it; it was the fly on the barber's nose that began it—though, of course, something else began the fly. Somehow, we never manage to hang the real offender.

The end came only with the arrival of Penrod's mother, who had been having a painful conversation by telephone with Mrs. Jones, the mother of Marjorie, and came forth to seek an errant son. It is a mystery how she was able to pick out her own, for by the time she got there his voice was too hoarse to be recognizable.

Mr. Schofield's version of things was that Penrod was insane. "He's a stark, raving lunatic!" declared the father, descending to the library from a before-dinner interview with the outlaw, that evening. "I'd send him to military school, but I don't believe they'd take him. Do you know *why* he says all that awfulness happened?"

"When Margaret and I were trying to scrub him," responded Mrs. Schofield wearily, "he said 'everybody' had been calling him names."

"'Names!'" snorted her husband. "'Little gentleman!' *That's* the vile epithet they called him! And because of it he wrecks the peace of six homes!"

"*Sh!* Yes; he told us about it," said Mrs. Schofield, moaning. "He told us several hundred times, I should guess, though I didn't count. He's got it fixed in his head, and we couldn't get it out. All we could do was to put him in the closet. He'd have gone out again after those boys if we hadn't. I don't know *what* to make of him!"

"He's a mystery to *me!*" said her husband. "And he refuses to explain why he objects to being called 'little gentleman.' Says he'd do the same thing —and worse—if anybody dared to call him that again. He said if the President of the United States called him that he'd try to whip him. How long did you have him locked up in the closet?"

"*Sh!*" said Mrs. Schofield warningly. "About two hours; but I don't think it softened his spirit at all, because when I took him to the barber's to get his hair clipped again, on account of the tar in it, Sammy Williams and Maurice Levy were there for the same reason, and they just *whispered* 'little gentleman,' so low you could hardly hear them—and Penrod began fighting with them right before me, and it was really all the barber and I could do to drag him away from them. The barber was very kind about it, but Penrod——"

"I tell you he's a lunatic!" Mr. Schofield would have said the same thing of a Frenchman infuriated by the epithet "camel." The philosophy of insult needs expounding.

"*Sh!*" said Mrs. Schofield. "It does seem a kind of frenzy."

"Why on earth should any sane person mind being called——"

"*Sh!*" said Mrs. Schofield. "It's beyond *me!*"

"What are you *sh*-ing me for?" demanded Mr. Schofield explosively.

"*Sh!*" said Mrs. Schofield. "It's Mr. Kinosling, the new rector of Saint Joseph's."

"Where?"

"*Sh!* On the front porch with Margaret; he's going to stay for dinner. I do hope——"

"Bachelor, isn't he?"

"Yes."

"*Our* old minister was speaking of him the other day," said Mr. Schofield, "and he didn't seem so terribly impressed."

"*Sh!* Yes; about thirty, and of course *so* superior to most of Margaret's friends—boys home from college. She thinks she likes young Robert Williams, I know—but he laughs so much! Of course there isn't any comparison. Mr. Kinosling talks so intellectually; it's a good thing for Margaret to hear that kind of thing, for a change—and, of course, he's very spiritual. He seems very much interested in her." She paused to muse. "I think Margaret likes him; he's so different, too. It's the third time he's dropped in this week, and I——"

"Well," said Mr. Schofield grimly, "if you and Margaret want him to come again, you'd better not let him see Penrod."

"But he's asked to see him; he seems interested in meeting all the family. And Penrod nearly always behaves fairly well at table." She paused, and then put to her husband a question referring to his interview with Penrod upstairs. "Did you—did you—do it?"

"No," he answered gloomily. "No, I didn't, but——" He was interrupted by a violent crash of china and metal in the kitchen, a shriek from Della, and the outrageous voice of Penrod. The well-informed Della, ill-inspired to set up for a wit, had ventured to address the scion of the house roguishly as "little gentleman," and Penrod, by means of the rapid elevation of his right foot, had removed from her supporting hands a laden tray. Both parents started for the kitchen, Mr. Schofield completing his interrupted sentence on the way.

"But I will, now!"

The rite thus promised was hastily but accurately performed in that apartment most distant from the front porch; and, twenty minutes later, Penrod descended to dinner. The Rev. Mr. Kinosling had asked for the pleasure of meeting him, and it had been decided that the only course possible was to cover up the scandal for the present, and to offer an undisturbed and smiling family surface to the gaze of the visitor.

Scorched but not bowed, the smouldering Penrod was led forward for the social formulæ simultaneously with the somewhat bleak departure of Robert Williams, who took his guitar with him, this time, and went in forlorn unconsciousness of the powerful forces already set in secret motion to be his allies.

The punishment just undergone had but made the haughty and unyielding soul of Penrod more stalwart in revolt; he was unconquered. Every time the one intolerable insult had been offered him, his resentment had become the hotter, his vengeance the more instant and furious. And, still burning with outrage, but upheld by the conviction of right, he was determined to continue to the last drop of his blood the defense of his honour, whenever it

should be assailed, no matter how mighty or august the powers that attacked
it. In all ways, he was a very sore boy.

During the brief ceremony of presentation, his usually inscrutable countenance wore an expression interpreted by his father as one of insane ob-
stinacy, while Mrs. Schofield found it an incentive to inward prayer. The fine
graciousness of Mr. Kinosling, however, was unimpaired by the glare of virulent suspicion given him by this little brother: Mr. Kinosling mistook it for a
natural curiosity concerning one who might possibly become, in time, a
member of the family. He patted Penrod upon the head, which was, for
many reasons, in no condition to be patted with any pleasure to the patter.
Penrod felt himself in the presence of a new enemy.

"How do you do, my little lad," said Mr. Kinosling. "I trust we shall become fast friends."

To the ear of this little lad, it seemed he said, "A trost we shall bick-home
fawst frainds." Mr. Kinosling's pronunciation was, in fact, slightly precious;
and the little lad, simply mistaking it for some cryptic form of mockery of
himself, assumed a manner and expression which argued so ill for the proposed friendship that Mrs. Schofield hastily interposed the suggestion of
dinner, and the small procession went in to the dining-room.

"It has been a delicious day," said Mr. Kinosling, presently; "warm but
balmy." With a benevolent smile he addressed Penrod, who sat opposite him.
"I suppose, little gentleman, you have been indulging in the usual outdoor
sports of vacation?"

Penrod laid down his fork and glared, open-mouthed at Mr. Kinosling.

"You'll have another slice of breast of the chicken?" Mr. Schofield inquired, loudly and quickly.

"A lovely day!" exclaimed Margaret, with equal promptitude and emphasis. "Lovely, oh, lovely! Lovely!"

"Beautiful, beautiful, beautiful!" said Mrs. Schofield, and after a glance at
Penrod which confirmed her impression that he intended to say something,
she continued, "Yes, beautiful, beautiful, beautiful, beautiful, beautiful,
beautiful!"

Penrod closed his mouth and sank back in his chair—and his relatives took
breath.

Mr. Kinosling looked pleased. This responsive family, with its ready enthusiasm, made the kind of audience he liked. He passed a delicate white
hand gracefully over his tall, pale forehead, and smiled indulgently.

"Youth relaxes in summer," he said. "Boyhood is the age of relaxation; one
is playful, light, free, unfettered. One runs and leaps and enjoys one's
self with one's companions. It is good for the little lads to play with their
friends; they jostle, push, and wrestle, and simulate little, happy struggles
with one another in harmless conflict. The young muscles are toughening. It
is good. Boyish chivalry develops, enlarges, expands. The young learn quickly,
intuitively, spontaneously. They perceive the obligations of *noblesse oblige*.
They begin to comprehend the necessity of caste and its requirements. They

learn what birth means—ah,—that is, they learn what it means to be well born. They learn courtesy in their games; they learn politeness, consideration for one another in their pastimes, amusements, lighter occupations. I make it my pleasure to join them often, for I sympathize with them in all their wholesome joys as well as in their little bothers and perplexities. I understand them, you see; and let me tell you it is no easy matter to understand the little lads and lassies." He sent to each listener his beaming glance, and, permitting it to come to rest upon Penrod, inquired:

"And what do you say to that, little gentleman?"

Mr. Schofield uttered a stentorian cough. "More? You'd better have some more chicken! More! Do!"

"More chicken!" urged Margaret simultaneously. "Do please! Please! More! Do! More!"

"Beautiful, beautiful," began Mrs. Schofield. "Beautiful, beautiful, beautiful, beautiful——"

It is not known in what light Mr. Kinosling viewed the expression of Penrod's face. Perhaps he mistook it for awe; perhaps he received no impression at all of its extraordinary quality. He was a rather self-engrossed young man, just then engaged in a double occupation, for he not only talked, but supplied from his own consciousness a critical though favourable auditor as well, which of course kept him quite busy. Besides, it is oftener than is expected the case that extremely peculiar expressions upon the countenances of boys are entirely overlooked, and suggest nothing to the minds of people staring straight at them. Certainly Penrod's expression—which, to the perception of his family, was perfectly horrible—caused not the faintest perturbation in the breast of Mr. Kinosling.

Mr. Kinosling waived the chicken, and continued to talk. "Yes, I think I may claim to understand boys," he said, smiling thoughtfully. "One has been a boy one's self. Ah, it is not all playtime! I hope our young scholar here does not overwork himself at his Latin, at his classics, as I did, so that at the age of eight years I was compelled to wear glasses. He must be careful not to strain the little eyes at his scholar's tasks, not to let the little shoulders grow round over his scholar's desk. Youth is golden; we should keep it golden, bright, glistening. Youth should frolic, should be sprightly; it should play its cricket, its tennis, its hand-ball. It should run and leap; it should laugh, should sing madrigals and glees, carol with the lark, ring out in chanties, folk-songs, ballads, roundelays——"

He talked on. At any instant Mr. Schofield held himself ready to cough vehemently and shout, "More chicken," to drown out Penrod in case the fatal words again fell from those eloquent lips; and Mrs. Schofield and Margaret kept themselves prepared at all times to assist him. So passed a threatening meal, which Mrs. Schofield hurried, by every means with decency, to its conclusion. She felt that somehow they would all be safer out in the dark of the front porch, and led the way thither as soon as possible.

"No cigar, I thank you." Mr. Kinosling, establishing himself in a wicker chair beside Margaret, waved away her father's proffer. "I do not smoke. I have never tasted tobacco in any form." Mrs. Schofield was confirmed in her opinion that this would be an ideal son-in-law. Mr. Schofield was not so sure.

"No," said Mr. Kinosling. "No tobacco for me. No cigar, no pipe, no cigarette, no cheroot. For me, a book—a volume of poems, perhaps. Verses, rhymes, lines metrical and cadenced—those are my dissipation. Tennyson by preference: 'Maud,' or 'Idylls of the King'—poetry of the sound Victorian days; there is none later. Or Longfellow will rest me in a tired hour. Yes; for me, a book, a volume in the hand, held lightly between the fingers."

Mr. Kinosling looked pleasantly at his fingers as he spoke, waving his hand in a curving gesture which brought it into the light of a window faintly illumined from the interior of the house. Then he passed those graceful fingers over his hair, and turned toward Penrod, who was perched upon the railing in a dark corner.

"The evening is touched with a slight coolness," said Mr. Kinosling. "Perhaps I may request the little gentleman——"

"B'gr-r-*ruff!*" coughed Mr. Schofield. "You'd better change your mind about a cigar."

"No, I thank you. I was about to request the lit——"

"*Do* try one," Margaret urged. "I'm sure papa's are nice ones. Do try——"

"No, I thank you. I remarked a slight coolness in the air, and my hat is in the hallway. I was about to request——"

"I'll get it for you," said Penrod suddenly.

"If you will be so good," said Mr. Kinosling. "It is a black bowler hat, little gentleman, and placed upon a table in the hall."

"I know where it is." Penrod entered the door, and a feeling of relief, mutually experienced, carried from one to another of his three relatives their interchanged congratulations that he had recovered his sanity.

"'The day is done, and the darkness,'" began Mr. Kinosling—and recited that poem entire. He followed it with "The Children's Hour," and after a pause, at the close, to allow his listeners time for a little reflection upon his rendition, he passed his hand again over his head, and called, in the direction of the doorway:

"I believe I will take my hat now, little gentleman."

"Here it is," said Penrod, unexpectedly climbing over the porch railing, in the other direction. His mother and father and Margaret had supposed him to be standing in the hallway out of deference, and because he thought it tactful not to interrupt the recitations. All of them remembered, later, that this supposed thoughtfulness on his part struck them as unnatural.

"Very good, little gentleman!" said Mr. Kinosling, and being somewhat chilled, placed the hat firmly upon his head, pulling it down as far as it would go. It had a pleasant warmth, which he noticed at once. The next instant, he noticed something else, a peculiar sensation of the scalp—a sensation which he was quite unable to define. He lifted his hand to take the hat

off, and entered upon a strange experience: his hat seemed to have decided
to remain where it was.

"Do you like Tennyson as much as Longfellow, Mr. Kinosling?" inquired
Margaret.

"I—ah—I cannot say," he returned absently. "I—ah—each has his own—ugh!
flavour and savour, each his—ah—ah——"

Struck by a strangeness in his tone, she peered at him curiously through
the dusk. His outlines were indistinct, but she made out that his arms were
uplifted in a singular gesture. He seemed to be wrenching at his head.

"Is—is anything the matter?" she asked anxiously. "Mr. Kinosling, are you
ill?"

"Not at—ugh!—all," he replied, in the same odd tone. "I—ah—I believe—
ugh!"

He dropped his hands from his hat, and rose. His manner was slightly
agitated. "I fear I may have taken a trifling—ah—cold. I should—ah—perhaps
be—ah—better at home. I will—ah—say good-night."

At the steps, he instinctively lifted his hand to remove his hat, but did not
do so, and, saying "Good-night," again in a frigid voice, departed with visible
stiffness from that house, to return no more.

"Well, of all——!" cried Mrs. Schofield, astounded. "What was the matter?
He just went—like that!" She made a flurried gesture. "In heaven's name,
Margaret, what *did* you say to him?"

"*I!*" exclaimed Margaret indignantly. "Nothing! He just *went!*"

"Why, he didn't even take off his hat when he said good-night!" said Mrs.
Schofield.

Margaret, who had crossed to the doorway, caught the ghost of a whisper
behind her, where stood Penrod.

"*You bet he didn't!*"

He knew not that he was overheard.

A frightful suspicion flashed through Margaret's mind—a suspicion that
Mr. Kinosling's hat would have to be either boiled off or shaved off. With
growing horror she recalled Penrod's long absence when he went to bring the
hat.

"Penrod," she cried, "let me see your hands!"

She had toiled at those hands herself late that afternoon, nearly scalding
her own, but at last achieving a lily purity.

"Let me see your hands!"

She seized them.

Again they were tarred!

CHAPTER XXVI

Perhaps middle-aged people might discern Nature's real intentions in the matter of pain if they would examine a boy's punishments and sorrows, for he prolongs neither beyond their actual duration. With a boy, trouble must be of Homeric dimensions to last overnight. To him, every next day is really a new day. Thus, Penrod woke, next morning, with neither the unspared rod, nor Mr. Kinosling in his mind. Tar, itself, so far as his consideration of it went, might have been an undiscovered substance. His mood was cheerful and mercantile; some process having worked mysteriously within him, during the night, to the result that his first waking thought was of profits connected with the sale of old iron—or perhaps a ragman had passed the house, just before he woke.

By ten o'clock he had formed a partnership with the indeed amiable Sam, and the firm of Schofield and Williams plunged headlong into commerce. Heavy dealings in rags, paper, old iron and lead gave the firm a balance of twenty-two cents on the evening of the third day; but a venture in glassware, following, proved disappointing on account of the skepticism of all the druggists in that part of town, even after seven laborious hours had been spent in cleansing a wheelbarrow-load of old medicine bottles with hydrant water and ashes. Likewise, the partners were disheartened by their failure to dispose of a crop of "greens," although they had uprooted specimens of that decorative and unappreciated flower, the dandelion, with such persistence and energy that the Schofields' and Williams' lawns looked curiously haggard for the rest of that summer.

The fit passed: business languished; became extinct. The dog-days had set in.

One August afternoon was so hot that even boys sought indoor shade. In the dimness of the vacant carriage-house of the stable, lounged Masters Penrod Schofield, Samuel Williams, Maurice Levy, Georgie Bassett, and Herman. They sat still and talked. It is a hot day, in rare truth, when boys devote themselves principally to conversation, and this day was that hot.

Their elders should beware such days. Peril hovers near when the fierceness of weather forces inaction and boys in groups are quiet. The more closely volcanoes, Western rivers, nitroglycerin, and boys are pent, the deadlier is their action at the point of outbreak. Thus, parents and guardians should look for outrages of the most singular violence and of the most peculiar nature during the confining weather of February and August.

The thing which befell upon this broiling afternoon began to brew and stew peacefully enough. All was innocence and languor; no one could have foretold the eruption.

They were upon their great theme: "When I get to be a man!" Being human, though boys, they considered their present estate too commonplace to be dwelt upon. So, when the old men gather, they say: "When I was a boy!" It really is the land of nowadays that we never discover.

"When I'm a man," said Sam Williams, "I'm goin' to hire me a couple of coloured waiters to swing me in a hammock and keep pourin' ice-water on me all day out o' those waterin'-cans they sprinkle flowers from. I'll hire you for one of 'em, Herman."

"No; you ain' goin' to," said Herman promptly. "You ain' no flowuh. But nev' min' nat, anyway. Ain' nobody goin' haih me whens I'm a man. Goin' be my own boss. I'm go' be a rai'road man!"

"You mean like a superintendent, or sumpthing like that, and sell tickets?" asked Penrod.

"Sup'in—nev' min' nat! Sell ticket? No suh! Go' be a *po*'tuh! My uncle a po'tuh right now. Solid gole buttons—oh, oh!"

"Generals get a lot more buttons than porters," said Penrod. "Generals——"

"Po'tuhs make the bes' livin'," Herman interrupted. "My uncle spen' mo' money 'n any white man 'n'is town."

"Well, I rather be a general," said Penrod, "or a senator, or sumpthing like that."

"Senators live in Warshington," Maurice Levy contributed the information. "I been there. Warshington ain't so much; Niag'ra Falls is a hunderd times as good as Warshington. So's 'Tlantic City, I was there, too. I been everywhere there is. I——"

"Well, anyway," said Sam Williams, raising his voice in order to obtain the floor, "anyway, I'm goin' to lay in a hammock all day, and have ice-water sprinkled on top o' me, and I'm goin' to lay there all night, too, and the next day. I'm goin' to lay there a couple o' years, maybe."

"I bet you don't!" exclaimed Maurice. "What'd you do in winter?"

"What?"

"What you goin' to do when it's winter, out in a hammock with water sprinkled on top o' you all day? I bet you——"

"I'd stay right there," Sam declared, with strong conviction, blinking as he looked out through the open doors at the dazzling lawn and trees, trembling in the heat. "They couldn't sprinkle too much for *me!*"

"It'd make icicles all over you, and——"

"I wish it would," said Sam. "I'd eat 'em up."

"And it'd snow on you——"

"Yay! I'd swaller it as fast as it'd come down. I wish I had a *barrel* o' snow right now. I wish this whole barn was full of it. I wish they wasn't anything in the whole world except just good ole snow."

Penrod and Herman rose and went out to the hydrant, where they drank long and ardently. Sam was still talking about snow when they returned.

"No, I wouldn't just roll in it. I'd stick it all round inside my clo'es, and fill my hat. No, I'd freeze a big pile of it all hard, and I'd roll her out flat and then I'd carry her down to some ole tailor's and have him make me a *suit* out of her, and——"

"Can't you keep still about your ole snow?" demanded Penrod petulantly. "Makes me so thirsty I can't keep still, and I've drunk so much now I bet I bust. That ole hydrant water's mighty near hot anyway."

"I'm goin' to have a big store, when I grow up," volunteered Maurice.

"Candy store?" asked Penrod.

"No, sir! I'll have candy in it, but not to eat, so much. It's goin' to be a deportment store: ladies' clothes, gentlemen's clothes, neckties, china goods, leather goods, nice lines in woollings and lace goods——"

"Yay! I wouldn't give a five-for-a-cent marble for your whole store," said Sam. "Would you, Penrod?"

"Not for ten of 'em; not for a million of 'em! I'm goin' to have——"

"Wait!" clamoured Maurice. "You'd be foolish, because they'd be a toy deportment in my store where they'd be a hunderd marbles! So, how much would you think your five-for-a-cent marble counts for? And when I'm keepin' my store I'm goin' to get married."

"Yay!" shrieked Sam derisively. "*Married!* Listen!" Penrod and Herman joined in the howl of contempt.

"Certumly I'll get married," asserted Maurice stoutly. "I'll get married to Marjorie Jones. She likes me awful good, and I'm her beau."

"What makes you think so?" inquired Penrod in a cryptic voice.

"Because she's my beau, too," came the prompt answer. "I'm her beau because she's my beau; I guess that's plenty reason! I'll get married to her as soon as I get my store running nice."

Penrod looked upon him darkly, but, for the moment, held his peace.

"Married!" jeered Sam Williams. "Married to Marjorie Jones! You're the only boy I ever heard say he was going to get married. I wouldn't get married for—why, I wouldn't for—for——" Unable to think of any inducement the mere mention of which would not be ridiculously incommensurate, he proceeded: "I wouldn't do it! What you want to get married for? What do married people do, except just come home tired, and worry around and kind of scold? You better not do it, M'rice; you'll be mighty sorry."

"Everybody gets married," stated Maurice, holding his ground. "They gotta."

"I'll bet *I* don't!" Sam returned hotly. "They better catch me before they tell *me* I have to. Anyway, I bet nobody has to get married unless they want to."

"They do, too," insisted Maurice. "They *gotta!*"

"Who told you?"

"Look at what my own papa told me!" cried Maurice, heated with argument. "Didn't he tell me your papa had to marry your mamma, or else he never'd got to handle a cent of her money? Certumly, people gotta marry. Everybody. You don't know anybody over twenty years old that isn't married—except maybe teachers."

"Look at policemen!" shouted Sam triumphantly. "You don't s'pose anybody can make policemen get married, I reckon, do you?"

"Well, policemen, maybe," Maurice was forced to admit. "Policemen and teachers don't, but everybody else gotta."

"Well, I'll be a policeman," said Sam. "*Then* I guess they won't come around tellin' me I have to get married. What you goin' to be, Penrod?"

"Chief police," said the laconic Penrod.

"What you?" Sam inquired of quiet Georgie Bassett.

"I am going to be," said Georgie, consciously, "a minister."

This announcement created a sensation so profound that it was followed by silence. Herman was the first to speak.

"You mean preachuh?" he asked incredulously. "You go' *preach?*"

"Yes," answered Georgie, looking like Saint Cecilia at the organ.

Herman was impressed. "You know all 'at preachuh talk?"

"I'm going to learn it," said Georgie simply.

"How loud kin you holler?" asked Herman doubtfully.

"He can't holler at all," Penrod interposed with scorn. "He hollers like a girl. He's the poorest hollerer in town!"

Herman shook his head. Evidently he thought Georgie's chance of being ordained very slender. Nevertheless, a final question put to the candidate by the coloured expert seemed to admit one ray of hope.

"How good kin you clim a pole?"

"He can't climb one at all," Penrod answered for Georgie. "Over at Sam's turning-pole you ought to see him try to——"

"Preachers don't have to climb poles," Georgie said with dignity.

"*Good* ones do," declared Herman. "Bes' one ev' *I* hear, he clim up an' down same as a circus man. One n'em big 'vivals outen whens we livin' on a fahm, preachuh clim big pole right in a middle o' the church, what was to hol' roof up. He clim way high up, an' holler: 'Goin' to heavum, goin' to heavum, goin' to heavum *now*. Hallelujah, praise my Lawd!' An' he slide down little, an' holler: 'Devil's got a hol' o' my coat-tails; devil tryin' to drag me down! Sinnuhs, take wawnun! Devil got a hol' o' my coat-tails; I'm a-goin' to hell, oh Lawd!' Nex', he clim up little mo', an' yell an' holler: 'Done shuck ole devil loose; goin' straight to heavum agin! Goin' to heavum, goin' to heavum, my Lawd!' Nex', he slide down some mo' an' holler, 'Leggo my coat-tails, ole devil! Goin' to hell agin, sinnuhs! Goin' straight to hell, my Lawd!' An' he clim an' he slide, an' he slide, an' he clim, an' all time holler: 'Now 'm a-goin' to heavum; now 'm a-goin' to hell! Goin' to heavum, heavum, heavum, my Lawd!' Las' he slide all a-way down, jes' a-squallin' an' a-kickin' an' a-rarin' up an' squealin', 'Goin' to hell. Goin' to hell! Ole Satum got my soul! Goin' to hell! Goin' to hell! Goin' to hell, hell, hell!'"

Herman possessed that extraordinary facility for vivid acting which is the great native gift of his race, and he enchained his listeners. They sat fascinated and spellbound.

"Herman, tell that again!" said Penrod, breathlessly.

Herman, nothing loath, accepted the encore and repeated the Miltonic episode, expanding it somewhat, and dwelling with a fine art upon those portions of the narrative which he perceived to be most exciting to his audience. Plainly, they thrilled less to Paradise gained than to its losing, and the dreadful climax of the descent into the Pit was the greatest treat of all.

The effect was immense and instant. Penrod sprang to his feet.

"Georgie Bassett couldn't do that to save his life," he declared. "I'm goin' to be a preacher! *I'd* be all right for one, wouldn't I, Herman?"

"So am I!" Sam Williams echoed loudly. "I guess I can do it if *you* can. I'd be better'n Penrod, wouldn't I, Herman?"

"I am, too!" Maurice shouted. "I got a stronger voice than anybody here, and I'd like to know what——"

The three clamoured together indistinguishably, each asserting his qualifications for the ministry according to Herman's theory, which had been accepted by these sudden converts without question.

"Listen to *me!*" Maurice bellowed, proving his claim to at least the voice by drowning the others. "Maybe I can't climb a pole so good, but who can holler louder'n this? Listen to *me-e-e!*"

"Shut up!" cried Penrod, irritated. "Go to heaven; go to hell!"

"Oo-o-oh!" exclaimed Georgie Bassett, profoundly shocked.

Sam and Maurice, awed by Penrod's daring, ceased from turmoil, staring wide-eyed.

"You cursed and swore!" said Georgie.

"I did not!" cried Penrod, hotly. "That isn't swearing."

"You said, 'Go to a big H'!" said Georgie.

"I did not! I said, 'Go to heaven,' before I said a big H. That isn't swearing, is it, Herman? It's almost what the preacher said, ain't it, Herman? It ain't swearing now, any more—not if you put 'go to heaven' with it, is it, Herman? You can say it all you want to, long as you say 'go to heaven' first, *can't* you, Herman? Anybody can say it if the preacher says it, can't they, Herman? I guess I know when I ain't swearing, don't I, Herman?"

Judge Herman ruled for the defendant, and Penrod was considered to have carried his point. With fine consistency, the conclave established that it was proper for the general public to "say it," provided "go to heaven" should in all cases precede it. This prefix was pronounced a perfect disinfectant, removing all odour of impiety or insult; and, with the exception of Georgie Bassett (who maintained that the minister's words were "going" and "gone," not "go"), all the boys proceeded to exercise their new privilege so lavishly that they tired of it.

But there was no diminution of evangelical ardour; again were heard the clamours of dispute as to which was the best qualified for the ministry, each of the claimants appealing passionately to Herman, who, pleased but confused, appeared to be incapable of arriving at a decision.

During a pause, Georgie Bassett asserted his prior rights. "Who said it first, I'd like to know?" he demanded. "I was going to be a minister from long back of to-day, I guess. And I guess I said I was going to be a minister right to-day before any of you said anything at all. *Didn't* I, Herman? *You* heard me, didn't you, Herman? That's the very thing started you talking about it, wasn't it, Herman?"

"You' right," said Herman. "You the firs' one to say it."

Penrod, Sam, and Maurice immediately lost faith in Herman. They turned from him and fell hotly upon Georgie.

"What if you did say it first?" Penrod shouted. "You couldn't *be* a minister if you were a hunderd years old!"

"I bet his mother wouldn't let him be one," said Sam. "She never lets him do anything."

"She would, too," retorted Georgie. "Ever since I was little, she——"

"He's too sissy to be a preacher!" cried Maurice. "Listen at his squeaky voice!"

"I'm going to be a better minister," shouted Georgie, "than all three of you put together. I could do it with my left hand!"

The three laughed bitingly in chorus. They jeered, derided, scoffed, and raised an uproar which would have had its effect upon much stronger nerves than Georgie's. For a time he contained his rising choler and chanted monotonously, over and over: "*I could! I could, too! I could! I could, too!*" But their tumult wore upon him, and he decided to avail himself of the recent decision whereby a big H was rendered innocuous and unprofane. Having used the expression once, he found it comforting, and substituted it for: "I could! I could, too!"

But it relieved him only temporarily. His tormentors were unaffected by it and increased their howlings, until at last Georgie lost his head altogether. Badgered beyond bearing, his eyes shining with a wild light, he broke through the besieging trio, hurling little Maurice from his path with a frantic hand. "I'll show you!" he cried, in this sudden frenzy. "You give me a chance, and I'll prove it right *now!*"

"That's talkin' business!" shouted Penrod. "Everybody keep still a minute. Everybody!"

He took command of the situation at once, displaying a fine capacity for organization and system. It needed only a few minutes to set order in the place of confusion and to determine, with the full concurrence of all parties, the conditions under which Georgie Bassett was to defend his claim by undergoing what may be perhaps intelligibly defined as the Herman test. Georgie declared he could do it easily. He was in a state of great excitement and in no condition to think calmly or, probably, he would not have made the attempt at all. Certainly he was overconfident.

CHAPTER XXVII

CONCLUSION OF THE QUIET AFTERNOON

It was during the discussion of the details of this enterprise that Georgie's mother, a short distance down the street, received a few female callers, who came by appointment to drink a glass of iced tea with her, and to meet the Rev. Mr. Kinosling. Mr. Kinosling was proving almost formidably interesting to the women and girls of his own and other flocks. What favour of his fellow clergymen a slight precociousness of manner and pronunciation cost him was more than balanced by the visible ecstasies of ladies. They blossomed at his touch.

He had just entered Mrs. Bassett's front door, when the son of the house, followed by an intent and earnest company of four, opened the alley gate and came into the yard. The unconscious Mrs. Bassett was about to have her first experience of a fatal coincidence. It was her first, because she was the mother of a boy so well behaved that he had become a proverb of transcendency. Fatal coincidences were plentiful in the Schofield and Williams families, and would have been familiar to Mrs. Bassett had Georgie been permitted greater intimacy with Penrod and Sam.

Mr. Kinosling sipped his iced tea and looked about him approvingly. Seven ladies leaned forward, for it was to be seen that he meant to speak.

"This cool room is a relief," he said, waving a graceful hand in a neatly limited gesture, which everybody's eyes followed, his own included. "It is a relief and a retreat. The windows open, the blinds closed—that is as it should be. It is a retreat, a fastness, a bastion against the heat's assault. For me, a quiet room—a quiet room and a book, a volume in the hand, held lightly between the fingers. A volume of poems, lines metrical and cadenced; something by a sound Victorian. We have no later poets."

"Swinburne?" suggested Miss Beam, an eager spinster. "Swinburne, Mr. Kinosling? Ah, *Swinburne!*"

"Not Swinburne," said Mr. Kinosling chastely. "No."

That concluded all the remarks about Swinburne.

Miss Beam retired in confusion behind another lady; and somehow there became diffused an impression that Miss Beam was erotic.

"I do not observe your manly little son," Mr. Kinosling addressed his hostess.

"He's out playing in the yard," Mrs. Bassett returned. "I heard his voice just now, I think."

"Everywhere I hear wonderful report of him," said Mr. Kinosling. "I may say that I understand boys, and I feel that he is a rare, a fine, a pure, a lofty spirit. I say spirit, for spirit is the word I hear spoken of him."

A chorus of enthusiastic approbation affirmed the accuracy of this proclamation, and Mrs. Bassett flushed with pleasure. Georgie's spiritual perfection was demonstrated by instances of it, related by the visitors; his piety was cited, and wonderful things he had said were quoted.

"Not all boys are pure, of fine spirit, of high mind," said Mr. Kinosling, and continued with true feeling: "You have a neighbour, dear Mrs. Bassett, whose household I indeed really feel it quite impossible to visit until such time when better, firmer, stronger handed, more determined discipline shall prevail. I find Mr. and Mrs. Schofield and their daughter charming——"

Three or four ladies said "Oh!" and spoke a name simultaneously. It was as if they had said, "Oh, the bubonic plague!"

"Oh! Penrod Schofield!"

"Georgie does not play with him," said Mrs. Bassett quickly—"that is, he avoids him as much as he can without hurting Penrod's feelings. Georgie is very sensitive to giving pain. I suppose a mother should not tell these things, and I know people who talk about their own children are dreadful bores, but it was only last Thursday night that Georgie looked up in my face so sweetly, after he had said his prayers and his little cheeks flushed, as he said: "Mamma, I think it would be right for me to go more with Penrod. I think it would make him a better boy."

A sibilance went about the room. "Sweet! How sweet! The sweet little soul! Ah, *sweet!*"

"And that very afternoon," continued Mrs. Bassett, "he had come home in a dreadful state. Penrod had thrown tar all over him."

"Your son has a forgiving spirit!" said Mr. Kinosling with vehemence. "A too forgiving spirit, perhaps." He set down his glass. "No more, I thank you. No more cake, I thank you. Was it not Cardinal Newman who said——"

He was interrupted by the sounds of an altercation just outside the closed blinds of the window nearest him.

"Let him pick his tree!" It was the voice of Samuel Williams. "Didn't we come over here to give him one of his own trees? Give him a fair show, can't you?"

"The little lads!" Mr. Kinosling smiled. "They have their games, their outdoor sports, their pastimes. The young muscles are toughening. The sun will not harm them. They grow; they expand; they learn. They learn fair play, honour, courtesy, from one another, as pebbles grow round in the brook. They learn more from themselves than from us. They take shape, form, outline. Let them."

"Mr. Kinosling!" Another spinster—undeterred by what had happened to Miss Beam—leaned far forward, her face shining and ardent. "Mr. Kinosling, there's a question I *do* wish to ask you."

"My dear Miss Cosslit," Mr. Kinosling responded, again waving his hand and watching it, "I am entirely at your disposal."

"Was Joan of Arc," she asked fervently, "inspired by spirits?"

He smiled indulgently. "Yes—and no," he said. "One must give both answers. One must give the answer, yes; one must give the answer, no."

"Oh, thank you!" said Miss Cosslit, blushing. "She's one of my great enthusiasms, you know."

"And I have a question, too," urged Mrs. Lora Rewbush, after a moment's hasty concentration. "I've never been able to settle it for myself, but now——"

"Yes?" said Mr. Kinosling encouragingly.

"Is—ah—is—oh, yes: Is Sanskrit a more difficult language than Spanish, Mr. Kinosling?"

"It depends upon the student," replied the oracle smiling. "One must not look for linguists everywhere. In my own especial case—if one may cite one's self as an example—I found no great, no insurmountable difficulty in mastering, in conquering either."

"And may I ask one?" ventured Mrs. Bassett. "Do you think it is right to wear egrets?"

"There are marks of quality, of caste, of social distinction," Mr. Kinosling began, "which must be permitted, allowed, though perhaps regulated. Social distinction, one observes, almost invariably implies spiritual distinction as well. Distinction of circumstances is accompanied by mental distinction. Distinction is hereditary; it descends from father to son, and if there is one thing more true than 'Like father, like son,' it is—" he bowed gallantly to Mrs. Bassett—"it is, 'Like mother, like son.' What these good ladies have said this afternoon of your——"

This was the fatal instant. There smote upon all ears the voice of Georgie, painfully shrill and penetrating—fraught with protest and protracted strain. His plain words consisted of the newly sanctioned and disinfected curse with a big H.

With an ejaculation of horror, Mrs. Bassett sprang to the window and threw open the blinds.

Georgie's back was disclosed to the view of the tea-party. He was endeavouring to ascend a maple tree about twelve feet from the window. Embracing the trunk with arms and legs, he had managed to squirm to a point above the heads of Penrod and Herman, who stood close by, watching him earnestly —Penrod being obviously in charge of the performance. Across the yard were Sam Williams and Maurice Levy, acting as a jury on the question of voice-power, and it was to a complaint of theirs that Georgie had just replied.

"That's right, Georgie," said Penrod encouragingly. "They can, too, hear you. Let her go!"

"Going to heaven!" shrieked Georgie, squirming up another inch. "Going to heaven, heaven, heaven!"

His mother's frenzied attempts to attract his attention failed utterly. Georgie was using the full power of his lungs, deafening his own ears to all other sounds. Mrs. Bassett called in vain; while the tea-party stood petrified in a cluster about the window.

"Going to heaven!" Georgie bellowed. "Going to heaven! Going to heaven, my Lord! Going to heaven, heaven, heaven!"

He tried to climb higher, but began to slip downward, his exertions causing damage to his apparel. A button flew into the air, and his knickerbockers and his waistband severed relations.

"Devil's got my coat-tails, sinners! Old devil's got my coat-tails!" he announced appropriately. Then he began to slide. He relaxed his clasp of the tree and slid to the ground.

"Going to hell!" shrieked Georgie, reaching a high pitch of enthusiasm in this great climax. "Going to hell! Going to hell! I'm gone to hell, hell, hell!"

With a loud scream, Mrs. Bassett threw herself out of the window, alighting by some miracle upon her feet with ankles unsprained.

Mr. Kinosling, feeling that his presence as spiritual adviser was demanded in the yard, followed with greater dignity through the front door. At the corner of the house a small departing figure collided with him violently. It was Penrod, tactfully withdrawing from what promised to be a family scene of unusual painfulness.

Mr. Kinosling seized him by the shoulders and, giving way to emotion, shook him viciously.

"You horrible boy!" exclaimed Mr. Kinosling. "You ruffianly creature! Do you know what's going to happen to you when you grow up? Do you realize what you're going to *be!*"

With flashing eyes, the indignant boy made known his unshaken purpose. He shouted the reply:

"A minister!"

CHAPTER XXVIII

TWELVE

This busy globe which spawns us is as incapable of flattery and as intent upon its own affair, whatever that is, as a gyroscope; it keeps steadily whirling along its lawful track, and, thus far seeming to hold a right of way, spins doggedly on, with no perceptible diminution of speed to mark the most gigantic human events—it did not pause to pant and recuperate even when what seemed to Penrod its principal purpose was accomplished, and an enormous shadow, vanishing westward over its surface, marked the dawn of his twelfth birthday.

To be twelve is an attainment worth the struggle. A boy, just twelve, is like a Frenchman just elected to the Academy.

Distinction and honour wait upon him. Younger boys show deference to a person of twelve: his experience is guaranteed, his judgment, therefore, mellow; consequently, his influence is profound. Eleven is not quite satisfactory: it is only an approach. Eleven has the disadvantage of six, of nineteen, of forty-four, and of sixty-nine. But, like twelve, seven is an honourable age, and the ambition to attain it is laudable. People look forward to being seven. Similarly, twenty is worthy, and so, arbitrarily, is twenty-one; forty-five has great solidity; seventy is most commendable and each year thereafter an increasing honour. Thirteen is embarrassed by the beginnings of a new colthood; the child becomes a youth. But twelve is the very top of boyhood.

Dressing, that morning, Penrod felt that the world was changed from the world of yesterday. For one thing, he seemed to own more of it; this day was *his* day. And it was a day worth owning; the midsummer sunshine, pouring gold through his window, came from a cool sky, and a breeze moved pleasantly in his hair as he leaned from the sill to watch the tribe of clattering blackbirds take wing, following their leader from the trees in the yard to the day's work in the open country. The blackbirds were his, as the sunshine and the breeze were his, for they all belonged to the day which was his birthday and therefore most surely his. Pride suffused him: he was twelve!

His father and his mother and Margaret seemed to understand the difference between to-day and yesterday. They were at the table when he descended, and they gave him a greeting which of itself marked the milestone. Habitually, his entrance into a room where his elders sat brought a cloud of apprehension: they were prone to look up in pathetic expectancy, as if their thought was, "What new awfulness is he going to start *now?*" But this morning they laughed; his mother rose and kissed him twelve times, so did Margaret; and his father shouted, "Well, well! How's the *man?*"

Then his mother gave him a Bible and "The Vicar of Wakefield"; Margaret gave him a pair of silver-mounted hair brushes; and his father gave him a "Pocket Atlas" and a small compass.

"And now, Penrod," said his mother, after breakfast, "I'm going to take you out in the country to pay your birthday respects to Aunt Sarah Crim."

Aunt Sarah Crim, Penrod's great-aunt, was his oldest living relative. She was ninety, and when Mrs. Schofield and Penrod alighted from a carriage at her gate they found her digging with a spade in the garden.

"I'm glad you brought him," she said, desisting from labour. "Jinny's baking a cake I'm going to send for his birthday party. Bring him in the house. I've got something for him."

She led the way to her "sitting-room," which had a pleasant smell, unlike any other smell, and, opening the drawer of a shining old what-not, took therefrom a boy's "sling-shot," made of a forked stick, two strips of rubber and a bit of leather.

"This isn't for you," she said, placing it in Penrod's eager hand. "No. It would break all to pieces the first time you tried to shoot it, because it is thirty-five years old. I want to send it back to your father. I think it's time. You give it to him from me, and tell him I say I believe I can trust him with it now. I took it away from him thirty-five years ago, one day after he'd killed my best hen with it, accidentally, and broken a glass pitcher on the back porch with it—accidentally. He doesn't look like a person who's ever done things of that sort, and I suppose he's forgotten it so well that he believes he never *did*, but if you give it to him from me I think he'll remember. You look like him, Penrod. He was anything but a handsome boy."

After this final bit of reminiscence—probably designed to be repeated to Mr. Schofield—she disappeared in the direction of the kitchen, and returned with a pitcher of lemonade and a blue china dish sweetly freighted with flat ginger cookies of a composition that was her own secret. Then, having set this collation before her guests, she presented Penrod with a superb, intricate, and very modern machine of destructive capacities almost limitless. She called it a pocket-knife.

"I suppose you'll do something horrible with it," she said, composedly. "I hear you do that with everything, anyhow, so you might as well do it with this, and have more fun out of it. They tell me you're the Worst Boy in Town."

"Oh, Aunt Sarah!" Mrs. Schofield lifted a protesting hand.

"Nonsense!" said Mrs. Crim.

"But on his birthday!"

"That's the time to say it. Penrod, aren't you the Worst Boy in Town?"

Penrod, gazing fondly upon his knife and eating cookies rapidly, answered as a matter of course, and absently, "Yes'm."

"Certainly!" said Mrs. Crim. "Once you accept a thing about yourself as established and settled, it's all right. Nobody minds. Boys are just like people, really."

"No, no!" Mrs. Schofield cried, involuntarily.

"Yes, they are," returned Aunt Sarah. "Only they're not quite so awful, because they haven't learned to cover themselves all over with little pretences. When Penrod grows up he'll be just the same as he is now, except that whenever he does what he wants to do he'll tell himself and other people a little story about it to make his reason for doing it seem nice and pretty and noble."

"No, I won't!" said Penrod suddenly.

"There's one cookie left," observed Aunt Sarah. "Are you going to eat it?"

"Well," said her great-nephew, thoughtfully, "I guess I better."

"Why?" asked the old lady. "Why do you guess you'd 'better'?"

"Well," said Penrod, with a full mouth, "it might get all dried up if nobody took it, and get thrown out and wasted."

"You're beginning finely," Mrs. Crim remarked. "A year ago you'd have taken the cookie without the same sense of thrift."

"Ma'am?"

"Nothing. I see that you're twelve years old, that's all. There are more cookies, Penrod." She went away, returning with a fresh supply and the observation, "Of course, you'll be sick before the day's over; you might as well get a good start."

Mrs. Schofield looked thoughtful. "Aunt Sarah," she ventured, "don't you really think we improve as we get older?"

"Meaning," said the old lady, "that Penrod hasn't much chance to escape the penitentiary if he doesn't? Well, we do learn to restrain ourselves in some things; and there are people who really want someone else to take the last cookie, though they aren't very common. But it's all right, the world seems to be getting on." She gazed whimsically upon her great-nephew and added, "Of course, when you watch a boy and think about him, it doesn't seem to be getting on very fast."

Penrod moved uneasily in his chair; he was conscious that he was her topic but unable to make out whether or not her observations were complimentary; he inclined to think they were not. Mrs. Crim settled the question for him.

"I suppose Penrod is regarded as the neighbourhood curse?"

"Oh, no," cried Mrs. Schofield. "He——"

"I dare say the neighbours are right," continued the old lady placidly. "He's had to repeat the history of the race and go through all the stages from the primordial to barbarism. You don't expect boys to be civilized, do you?"

"Well, I——"

"You might as well expect eggs to crow. No; you've got to take boys as they are, and learn to know them as they are."

"Naturally, Aunt Sarah," said Mrs. Schofield, "I *know* Penrod."

Aunt Sarah laughed heartily. "Do you think his father knows him, too?"

"Of course, men are different," Mrs. Schofield returned, apologetically. "But a mother knows——"

"Penrod," said Aunt Sarah, solemnly, "does your father understand you?"

"Ma'am?"

"About as much as he'd understand Sitting Bull!" she laughed. "And I'll tell you what your mother thinks you are, Penrod. Her real belief is that you're a novice in a convent."

"Ma'am?"

"Aunt Sarah!"

"I know she thinks that, because whenever you don't behave like a novice she's disappointed in you. And your father really believes that you're a decorous, well-trained young business man, and whenever you don't live up to that standard you get on his nerves and he thinks you need a walloping. I'm sure a day very seldom passes without their both saying they don't know what on earth to do with you. Does whipping do you any good, Penrod?"

"Ma'am?"

"Go on and finish the lemonade; there's about a glassful left. Oh, take it, take it; and don't say why! Of *course* you're a little pig."

Penrod laughed gratefully, his eyes fixed upon her over the rim of his up-tilted glass.

"Fill yourself up uncomfortably," said the old lady. "You're twelve years old, and you ought to be happy—if you aren't anything else. It's taken over nineteen hundred years of Christianity and some hundreds of thousands of years of other things to produce you, and there you sit!"

"Ma'am?"

"It'll be your turn to struggle and muss things up for the betterment of posterity, soon enough," said Aunt Sarah Crim. "Drink your lemonade!"

CHAPTER XXIX

FANCHON

"Aunt Sarah's a funny old lady," Penrod observed, on the way back to the town. "What's she want me to give papa this old sling for? Last thing she said was to be sure not to forget to give it to him. *He* don't want it; and she said, herself, it ain't any good. She's older than you or papa, isn't she?"

"About fifty years older," answered Mrs. Schofield, turning upon him a stare of perplexity. "Don't cut into the leather with your new knife, dear; the livery man might ask us to pay if—— No. I wouldn't scrape the paint off, either—nor whittle your shoe with it. *Couldn't* you put it up until we get home?"

"We goin' straight home?"

"No. We're going to stop at Mrs. Gelbraith's and ask a strange little girl to come to your party, this afternoon."

"Who?"

"Her name is Fanchon. She's Mrs. Gelbraith's little niece."

"What makes her so queer?"

"I didn't say she's queer."

"You said——"

"No; I mean that she is a stranger. She lives in New York and has come to visit here."

"What's she live in New York for?"

"Because her parents live there. You must be very nice to her, Penrod; she has been very carefully brought up. Besides, she doesn't know the children here, and you must help to keep her from feeling lonely at your party."

"Yes'm."

When they reached Mrs. Gelbraith's, Penrod sat patiently humped upon a gilt chair during the lengthy exchange of greetings between his mother and and Mrs. Gelbraith. That is one of the things a boy must learn to bear:

when his mother meets a compeer there is always a long and dreary wait for him, while the two appear to be using strange symbols of speech, talking for the greater part, it seems to him, simultaneously, and employing a wholly incomprehensible system of emphasis at other times not in vogue. Penrod twisted his legs, his cap and his nose.

"Here she is!" Mrs. Gelbraith cried, unexpectedly, and a dark-haired, demure person entered the room wearing a look of gracious social expectancy. In years she was eleven, in manner about sixty-five, and evidently had lived much at court. She performed a curtsey in acknowledgment of Mrs. Schofield's greeting, and bestowed her hand upon Penrod, who had entertained no hope of such an honour, showed his surprise that it should come to him, and was plainly unable to decide what to do about it.

"Fanchon, dear," said Mrs. Gelbraith, "take Penrod out in the yard for a while, and play."

"Let go the little girl's hand, Penrod," Mrs. Schofield laughed, as the children turned toward the door.

Penrod hastily dropped the small hand, and exclaiming, with simple honesty, "Why, I don't want it!" followed Fanchon out into the sunshiny yard, where they came to a halt and surveyed each other.

Penrod stared awkwardly at Fanchon, no other occupation suggesting itself to him, while Fanchon, with the utmost coolness, made a very thorough visual examination of Penrod, favouring him with an estimating scrutiny which lasted until he literally wiggled. Finally, she spoke.

"Where do you buy your ties?" she asked.

"What?"

"Where do you buy your neckties? Papa gets his at Skoone's. You ought to get yours there. I'm sure the one you're wearing isn't from Skoone's."

"Skoone's?" Penrod repeated. "Skoone's?"

"On Fifth Avenue," said Fanchon. "It's a very smart shop, the men say."

"Men?" echoed Penrod, in a hazy whisper. "Men?"

"Where do your people go in summer?" inquired the lady. "We go to Long Shore, but so many middle-class people have begun coming there, mamma thinks of leaving. The middle classes are simply awful, don't you think?"

"What?"

"They're so boorjaw. You speak French, of course?"

"Me?"

"We ran over to Paris last year. It's lovely, don't you think? Don't you love the Rue de la Paix?"

Penrod wandered in a labyrinth. This girl seemed to be talking, but her words were dumfounding, and of course there was no way for him to know that he was really listening to her mother. It was his first meeting with one of those grown-up little girls, wonderful product of the winter apartment and summer hotel; and Fanchon, an only child, was a star of the brand. He began to feel resentful.

"I suppose," she went on, "I'll find everything here fearfully Western. Some nice people called yesterday, though. Do you know the Magsworth Bittses? Auntie says they're charming. Will Roddy be at your party?"

"I guess he will," returned Penrod, finding this intelligible. "The mutt!"

"Really!" Fanchon exclaimed airily. "Aren't you great pals with him?"

"What's 'pals'?"

"Good heavens! Don't you know what it means to say you're 'great pals' with any one? You *are* an odd child!"

It was too much.

"Oh, Bugs!" said Penrod.

This bit of ruffianism had a curious effect. Fanchon looked upon him with sudden favour.

"I like you, Penrod!" she said, in an odd way, and, whatever else there may have been in her manner, there certainly was no shyness.

"Oh, Bugs!" This repetition may have lacked gallantry, but it was uttered in no very decided tone. Penrod was shaken.

"Yes, I do!" She stepped closer to him, smiling. "Your hair is ever so pretty."

Sailors' parrots swear like mariners, they say; and gay mothers ought to realize that all children are imitative, for, as the precocious Fanchon leaned toward Penrod, the manner in which she looked into his eyes might have made a thoughtful observer wonder where she had learned her pretty ways.

Penrod was even more confused than he had been by her previous mysteries: but his confusion was of a distinctly pleasant and alluring nature: he wanted more of it. Looking intentionally into another person's eyes is an act unknown to childhood; and Penrod's discovery that it could be done was sensational. He had never thought of looking into the eyes of Marjorie Jones.

Despite all anguish, contumely, tar, and Maurice Levy, he still secretly thought of Marjorie, with pathetic constancy, as his "beau"—though that is not how he would have spelled it. Marjorie was beautiful; her curls were long and the colour of amber; her nose was straight and her freckles were honest; she was much prettier than this accomplished visitor. But beauty is not all.

"I do!" breathed Fanchon, softly.

She seemed to him a fairy creature from some rosier world than this. So humble is the human heart, it glorifies and makes glamorous almost any poor thing that says to it: "I like you!"

Penrod was enslaved. He swallowed, coughed, scratched the back of his neck, and said, disjointedly:

"Well—I don't care—if you want to. I just as soon."

"We'll dance together," said Fanchon, "at your party."

"I guess so. I just as soon."

"Don't you want to, Penrod?"

"Well, I'm willing to."

"No. Say you *want* to!"

"Well——"

He used his toe as a gimlet, boring into the ground, his wide open eyes staring with intense vacancy at a button on his sleeve. His mother appeared upon the porch in departure, calling farewells over her shoulder to Mrs. Gelbraith, who stood in the doorway.

"Say it!" whispered Fanchon.

"Well, I just as *soon*."

She seemed satisfied.

CHAPTER XXX

THE BIRTHDAY PARTY

A dancing floor had been laid upon a platform in the yard, when Mrs. Schofield and her son arrived at their own abode; and a white and scarlet striped canopy was in process of erection overhead, to shelter the dancers from the sun. Workmen were busy everywhere under the direction of Margaret, and the smitten heart of Penrod began to beat rapidly. All this was for him; he was Twelve!

After lunch, he underwent an elaborate toilette and murmured not. For the first time in his life he knew the wish to be sand-papered, waxed, and polished to the highest possible degree. And when the operation was over, he stood before the mirror in new bloom, feeling encouraged to hope that his resemblance to his father was not so strong as Aunt Sarah seemed to think.

The white gloves upon his hands had a pleasant smell, he found; and, as he came down the stairs, he had great content in the twinkling of his new dancing slippers. He stepped twice on each step, the better to enjoy their effect and at the same time he deeply inhaled the odour of the gloves. In spite of everything, Penrod had his social capacities. Already it is to be perceived that there were in him the makings of a cotillon leader.

Then came from the yard a sound of tuning instruments, squeak of fiddle, croon of 'cello, a falling triangle ringing and tinkling to the floor; and he turned pale.

Chosen guests began to arrive, while Penrod, suffering from stage-fright and perspiration, stood beside his mother, in the "drawing-room," to receive them. He greeted unfamiliar acquaintances and intimate fellow-criminals with the same frigidity, murmuring: "'M glad to see y'," to all alike, largely increasing the embarrassment which always prevails at the beginning of children's festivities. His unnatural pomp and circumstance had so thoroughly upset him, in truth, that Marjorie Jones received a distinct shock, now to be related. Doctor Thrope, the kind old clergyman who had baptized Penrod, came in for a moment to congratulate the boy, and had just moved away when it was Marjorie's turn, in the line of children, to speak to Penrod. She gave him what she considered a forgiving look, and, because of the occasion, addressed him in a perfectly courteous manner.

"I wish you many happy returns of the day, Penrod."

"Thank you, sir!" he returned, following Dr. Thrope with a glassy stare in which there was absolutely no recognition of Marjorie. Then he greeted Maurice Levy, who was next to Marjorie: " 'M glad to see y'!"

Dumfounded, Marjorie turned aside, and stood near, observing Penrod with gravity. It was the first great surprise of her life. Customarily, she had seemed to place his character somewhere between that of the professional rioter and that of the orangoutang; nevertheless, her manner at times just hinted a consciousness that this Caliban was her property. Wherefore, she stared at him incredulously as his head bobbed up and down, in the dancing-school bow, greeting his guests. Then she heard an adult voice, near her, exclaim:

"What an exquisite child!"

Marjorie glanced up—a little consciously, though she was used to it—naturally curious to ascertain who was speaking of her. It was Sam Williams' mother addressing Mrs. Bassett, both being present to help Mrs. Schofield make the festivities festive.

"Exquisite!"

Here was a second heavy surprise for Marjorie: they were not looking at her. They were looking with beaming approval at a girl she had never seen; a dark and modish stranger of singularly composed and yet modest aspect. Her downcast eyes, becoming in one thus entering a crowded room, were all that produced the effect of modesty, counteracting something about her which might have seemed too assured. She was very slender, very dainty, and her apparel was disheartening to the other girls; it was of a knowing picturesqueness wholly unfamiliar to them. There was a delicate trace of powder upon the lobe of Fanchon's left ear, and the outlines of her eyelids, if very closely scrutinized, would have revealed successful experimentation with a burnt match.

Marjorie's lovely eyes dilated: she learned the meaning of hatred at first sight. Observing the stranger with instinctive suspicion, all at once she seemed, to herself, awkward. Poor Marjorie underwent that experience which hearty, healthy, little girls and big girls undergo at one time or another—from heels to head she felt herself, somehow, too *thick*.

Fanchon leaned close to Penrod and whispered in his ear:

"Don't you forget!"

Penrod blushed.

Marjorie saw the blush. Her lovely eyes opened even wider, and in them there began to grow a light. It was the light of indignation;—at least, people whose eyes glow with that light always call it indignation.

Roderick Magsworth Bitts, Junior, approached Fanchon, when she had made her curtsey to Mrs. Schofield. Fanchon whispered in Roderick's ear also.

"Your hair *is* pretty, Roddy! Don't forget what you said yesterday!"

Roderick likewise blushed.

Maurice Levy, captivated by the newcomer's appearance, pressed close to Roderick.

"Give us an intaduction, Roddy?"

Roddy being either reluctant or unable to perform the rite, Fanchon took matters into her own hands, and was presently favourably impressed with Maurice, receiving the information that his tie had been brought to him by his papa from Skoone's, whereupon she privately informed him that she liked wavy hair, and arranged to dance with him. Fanchon also thought sandy hair attractive, Sam Williams discovered, a few minutes later, and so catholic was her taste that a ring of boys quite encircled her before the musicians in the yard struck up their thrilling march, and Mrs. Schofield brought Penrod to escort the lady from out-of-town to the dancing pavilion.

Headed by this pair, the children sought partners and paraded solemnly out of the front door and round a corner of the house. There they found the gay marquee; the small orchestra seated on the lawn at one side of it, and a punch bowl of lemonade inviting attention, under a tree. Decorously the small couples stepped upon the platform, one after another, and began to dance.

"It's not much like a children's party in our day," Mrs. Williams said to Penrod's mother. "We'd have been playing 'Quaker-meeting,' 'Clap-in, Clap-out,' or 'Going to Jerusalem,' I suppose."

"Yes, or 'Post-office' and 'Drop-the-handkerchief,'" said Mrs. Schofield. "Things change so quickly. Imagine asking little Fanchon Gelbraith to play 'London Bridge'! Penrod seems to be having a difficult time with her, poor boy; he wasn't a shining light in the dancing class."

However, Penrod's difficulty was not precisely of the kind his mother supposed. Fanchon was showing him a new step, which she taught her next partner in turn, continuing instructions during the dancing. The children crowded the floor, and in the kaleidoscopic jumble of bobbing heads and intermingling figures her extremely different style of motion was unobserved by the older people, who looked on, nodding time benevolently.

Fanchon fascinated girls as well as boys. Many of the former eagerly sought her acquaintance and thronged about her between the dances, when, accepting the deference due a cosmopolitan and an oracle of the mode, she gave demonstrations of the new step to succeeding groups, professing astonishment to find it unknown: it had been "all the go," she explained, at the Long Shore Casino for fully two seasons. She pronounced "slow" a "Fancy Dance" executed during an intermission by Baby Rennsdale and Georgie Bassett, giving it as her opinion that Miss Rennsdale and Mr. Bassett were "dead ones"; and she expressed surprise that the punch bowl contained lemonade and not champagne.

The dancing continued, the new step gaining instantly in popularity, fresh couples adventuring with every number. The word "step" is somewhat misleading, nothing done with the feet being vital to the evolutions introduced by Fanchon. Fanchon's dance came from the Orient by a roundabout way; pausing in Spain, taking on a Gallic frankness in gallantry at the Bal Bullier in Paris, combining with a relative from the South Seas encountered in San Francisco, flavouring itself with a carefree negroid abandon in New Orleans, and, accumulating, too, something inexpressible from Mexico and South America, it kept, throughout its travels, to the underworld, or to circles where nature is extremely frank and rank, until at last it reached the dives of New York, when it immediately broke out in what is called civilized society. Thereafter it spread, in variously modified forms—some of them disinfected—to watering-places, and thence, carried by hundreds of older male and female Fanchons, over the country, being eagerly adopted everywhere and made wholly pure and respectable by the supreme moral axiom that anything is all right if enough people do it. Everybody was doing it.

Not quite everybody. It was perhaps some test of this dance that earth could furnish no more grotesque sight than that of children doing it.

Earth, assisted by Fanchon, was furnishing this sight at Penrod's party. By the time ice-cream and cake arrived, about half the guests had either been initiated into the mysteries by Fanchon or were learning by imitation, and the education of the other half was resumed with the dancing, when the attendant ladies, unconscious of what was happening, withdrew into the house for tea.

"That orchestra's a dead one," Fanchon remarked to Penrod. "We ought to liven them up a little!"

She approached the musicians.

"Don't you know," she asked the leader, "the Slingo Sligo Slide?"

The leader giggled, nodded, rapped with his bow upon his violin; and Penrod, following Fanchon back upon the dancing floor, blindly brushed with his elbow a solitary little figure standing aloof on the lawn at the edge of the platform.

It was Marjorie.

In no mood to approve of anything introduced by Fanchon, she had scornfully refused, from the first, to dance the new "step," and, because of its bonfire popularity, found herself neglected in a society where she had reigned as beauty and belle. Faithless Penrod, dazed by the sweeping Fanchon, had utterly forgotten the amber curls; he had not once asked Marjorie to dance. All afternoon the light of indignation had been growing brighter in her eyes, though Maurice Levy's defection to the lady from New York had not fanned this flame. From the moment Fanchon had whispered familiarly in Penrod's ear, and Penrod had blushed, Marjorie had been occupied exclusively with resentment against that guilty pair. It seemed to her that Penrod had no right to allow a strange girl to whisper in his ear; that his blushing, when the strange girl did it, was atrocious; and that the strange girl, herself, ought to be arrested.

Forgotten by the merrymakers, Marjorie stood alone upon the lawn, clenching her small fists, watching the new dance at its high tide, and hating it with a hatred that made every inch of her tremble. And, perhaps because jealousy is a great awakener of the virtues, she had a perception of something in it worse than lack of dignity—something vaguely but outrageously reprehensible. Finally, when Penrod brushed by her, touched her with his elbow, and did not even see her, Marjorie's state of mind (not unmingled with emotion!) became dangerous. In fact, a trained nurse, chancing to observe her at this juncture, would probably have advised that she be taken home and put to bed. Marjorie was on the verge of hysterics.

She saw Fanchon and Penrod assume the double embrace required by the dance; the "Slingo Sligo Slide" burst from the orchestra like the lunatic shriek of a gin-maddened nigger; and all the little couples began to bob and dip and sway.

Marjorie made a scene. She sprang upon the platform and stamped her foot.

"Penrod Schofield!" she shouted. "You BEHAVE yourself!"

The remarkable girl took Penrod by the ear. By his ear she swung him away from Fanchon and faced him toward the lawn.

"You march straight out of here!" she commanded.

Penrod marched.

He was stunned; obeyed automatically, without question, and had very little realization of what was happening to him. Altogether, and without reason, he was in precisely the condition of an elderly spouse detected in flagrant misbehaviour. Marjorie, similarly, was in precisely the condition of the party who detects such misbehaviour. It may be added that she had acted with a promptness, a decision and a disregard of social consequences all to be commended to the attention of ladies in like predicament.

"You ought to be ashamed of yourself!" she raged, when they reached the lawn. "Aren't you ashamed of yourself?"

"What for?" he inquired, helplessly.

"You be quiet!"

"But what'd I do, Marjorie? I haven't done anything to you," he pleaded. "I haven't even seen you, all aftern——"

"You be quiet!" she cried, tears filling her eyes. "Keep still! You ugly boy! Shut *up!*"

She slapped him.

He should have understood from this how much she cared for him. But he rubbed his cheek and declared ruefully:

"I'll never speak to you again!"

"You will, too!" she sobbed, passionately.

"I will not!"

He turned to leave her, but paused.

His mother, his sister Margaret, and their grown-up friends had finished their tea and were approaching from the house. Other parents and guardians were with them, coming for their children; and there were carriages and automobiles waiting in the street. But the "Slingo Slide" went on, regardless.

The group of grown-up people hesitated and came to a halt, gazing at the pavilion.

"What are they doing?" gasped Mrs. Williams, blushing deeply. "What is it? What *is* it?"

"*What is it?*" Mrs. Gelbraith echoed in a frightened whisper. "*What*——"

"They're Tangoing!" cried Margaret Schofield. "Or Bunny Hugging or Grizzly Bearing, or——"

"They're only Turkey Trotting," said Robert Williams.

With fearful outcries the mothers, aunts, and sisters rushed upon the pavilion.

"Of course it was dreadful," said Mrs. Schofield, an hour later, rendering her lord an account of the day, "but it was every bit the fault of that one extraordinary child. And of all the quiet, demure little things—that is, I mean, when she first came. We all spoke of how exquisite she seemed—so well trained, so finished! Eleven years old! I never saw anything like her in my life!"

"I suppose it's the New Child," her husband grunted.

"And to think of her saying there ought to have been champagne in the lemonade!"

"Probably she'd forgotten to bring her pocket flask," he suggested musingly.

"But aren't you proud of Penrod?" cried Penrod's mother. "It was just as I told you: he was standing clear outside the pavilion——"

"I never thought to see the day! And Penrod was the only boy not doing it, the only one to refuse? *All* the others were——"

"Every one!" she returned triumphantly. "Even Georgie Bassett!"

"Well," said Mr. Schofield, patting her on the shoulder. "I guess we can hold up our heads at last."

CHAPTER XXXI

OVER THE FENCE

Penrod was out in the yard, staring at the empty marquee. The sun was on the horizon line, so far behind the back fence, and a western window of the house blazed in gold unbearable to the eye: his day was nearly over. He sighed, and took from the inside pocket of his new jacket the "sling-shot" Aunt Sarah Crim had given him that morning.

He snapped the rubbers absently. They held fast; and his next impulse was entirely irresistible. He found a shapely stone, fitted it to the leather, and drew back the ancient catapult for a shot. A sparrow hopped upon a branch between him and the house, and he aimed at the sparrow, but the reflection from the dazzling window struck in his eyes as he loosed the leather.

He missed the sparrow, but not the window. There was a loud crash, and to his horror he caught a glimpse of his father, stricken in mid-shaving, ducking a shower of broken glass, glittering razor flourishing wildly. Words crashed with the glass, stentorian words, fragmentary but colossal.

Penrod stood petrified, a broken sling in his hand. He could hear his parent's booming descent of the back stairs, instant and furious; and then, red-hot above white lather, Mr. Schofield burst out of the kitchen door and hurtled forth upon his son.

"What do you mean?" he demanded, shaking Penrod by the shoulder. "Ten minutes ago, for the very first time in our lives, your mother and I were saying we were proud of you, and here you go and throw a rock at me through the window when I'm shaving for dinner!"

"I didn't!" Penrod quavered. "I was shooting at a sparrow, and the sun got in my eyes, and the sling broke——"

"What sling?"

"This'n."

"Where'd you get that devilish thing? Don't you know I've forbidden you a thousand times——"

"It ain't mine," said Penrod. "It's yours."

"What?"

"Yes, sir," said the boy meekly. "Aunt Sarah Crim gave it to me this morning and told me to give it back to you. She said she took it away from you thirty-five years ago. You killed her hen, she said. She told me some more to tell you, but I've forgotten."

"Oh!" said Mr. Schofield.

He took the broken sling in his hand, looked at it long and thoughtfully—and he looked longer, and quite as thoughtfully, at Penrod. Then he turned away, and walked toward the house.

"I'm sorry, papa," said Penrod.

Mr. Schofield coughed, and, as he reached the door, called back, but without turning his head.

"Never mind, little boy. A broken window isn't much harm."

When he had gone in, Penrod wandered down the yard to the back fence, climbed upon it, and sat in reverie there.

A slight figure appeared, likewise upon a fence beyond two neighbouring yards.

"Yay, Penrod!" called comrade Sam Williams.

"Yay!" returned Penrod, mechanically.

"I caught Billy Blue Hill!" shouted Sam, describing retribution in a manner perfectly clear to his friend. "You were mighty lucky to get out of it."

"I know that!"

"You wouldn't of, if it hadn't been for Marjorie."

"Well, don't I know that?" Penrod shouted, with heat.

"Well, so long!" called Sam, dropping from his fence; and the friendly voice came then, more faintly, "Many happy returns of the day, Penrod!"

And now, a plaintive little whine sounded from below Penrod's feet, and, looking down, he saw that Duke, his wistful, old, scraggly dog sat in the grass, gazing seekingly up at him.

The last shaft of sunshine of that day fell graciously and like a blessing upon the boy sitting on the fence. Years afterward, a quiet sunset would recall to him sometimes the gentle evening of his twelfth birthday, and bring him the picture of his boy self, sitting in rosy light upon the fence, gazing pensively down upon his wistful, scraggly, little old dog, Duke. But something else, surpassing, he would remember of that hour, for, in the side street, close by, a pink skirt flickered from behind a shade tree to the shelter of the fence, there was a gleam of amber curls, and Penrod started, as something like a tiny white wing fluttered by his head, and there came to his ears the sound of a light laugh and of light footsteps departing, the laughter tremulous, the footsteps fleet.

In the grass, between Duke's forepaws, there lay a white note, folded in the shape of a cocked hat, and the sun sent forth a final amazing glory as Penrod opened it and read:

"Your my Bow."

Little Florence

By the end of October, with the dispersal of foliage that has served all summer long as a screen for whatever small privacy may exist between American neighbours, we begin to perceive the rise of our autumn high tides of gossip. At this season of the year, in our towns of moderate size and ambition, where apartment houses have not yet condensed and at the same time sequestered the population, one may look over back yard beyond back yard, both up and down the street; especially if one takes the trouble to sit for an hour or so daily, upon the top of a high fence at about the middle of a block.

Of course an adult who followed such a course would be thought peculiar, no doubt he would be subject to inimical comment; but boys are considered so inexplicable that they have gathered for themselves many privileges denied their parents and elders, and a boy can do such a thing as this to his full content, without anybody's thinking about it at all. So it was that Herbert Illingsworth Atwater, Jr., sat for a considerable time upon such a fence, after school hours, every afternoon of the last week in October; and only one person particularly observed him or was stimulated to any mental activity by his procedure. Even at that, this person was affected only because she was Herbert's relative, of an age sympathetic to his and of a sex antipathetic.

In spite of the fact that Herbert, thus seriously disporting himself on his father's back fence, attracted only an audience of one (and she hostile at a rather distant window), his behaviour might well have been thought piquant by anybody. After climbing to the top of the fence he would produce from interior pockets a small memorandum-book and a pencil. His expression was gravely alert, his manner more than businesslike; yet nobody could have failed to comprehend that he was enjoying himself, especially when his attitude became tenser, as it frequently did. Then he would rise, balancing himself at adroit ease, his feet one before the other on the inner rail, below the top of the boards, and with eyes dramatically shielded beneath a scoutish palm, he would gaze sternly in the direction of some object or movement that had attracted his attention; and then, having satisfied himself of something or other, he would sit and decisively enter a note in his memorandum-book.

He was not always alone; sometimes he was joined by a friend, male, and, though shorter than Herbert, about as old; and this companion was inspired, it seemed, by motives precisely similar to those from which sprang Herbert's own actions. Like Herbert he would sit upon the top of the high fence; like Herbert he would rise at intervals, for the better study of something this side the horizon; then, also like Herbert, he would sit again and write firmly in a little note-book. And seldom in the history of the world have any such sessions been invested by the participants with so intentional an appearance of importance.

That was what most irritated their lone observer at the somewhat distant upstairs back window. The important importance of Herbert and his friend was so extreme as to be all too plainly visible across four intervening broad back yards; in fact, there was sometimes reason to suspect that the two performers were aware of their audience and even of her goaded condition; and that they deliberately increased the outrageousness of their importance on her account. And upon the Saturday of that week, when the note-book writers were upon the fence the greater part of the afternoon, Florence's fascinated indignation became vocal.

"Vile Things!" she said.

Her mother, sewing beside another window of the room, looked up inquiringly.

"What are, Florence?"

"Cousin Herbert and that nasty little Henry Rooter."

"Are you watching them again?" her mother asked.

"Yes, I am," said Florence; and added tartly, "Not because I care to, but merely to amuse myself at their expense."

Mrs. Atwater murmured, "Couldn't you find some other way to amuse yourself, Florence?"

"I don't call this amusement," the inconsistent girl responded, not without chagrin. "Think I'd spend all my days starin' at Herbert Illingsworth Atwater, Junior, and that nasty little Henry Rooter, and call it *amusement?*"

"Then why do you do it?"

"Why do I do *what*, mamma?" Florence inquired, as in despair of Mrs. Atwater's ever learning to put things clearly.

"Why do you 'spend all your days' watching them? You don't seem able to keep away from the window, and it appears to make you irritable. I should think if they wouldn't let you play with them you'd be too proud——"

"Oh, good heavens, mamma!"

"Don't use such expressions, Florence, please."

"Well," said Florence, "I got to use *some* expression when you accuse me of wantin' to 'play' with those two vile things! My goodness mercy, mamma, I don't want to 'play' with 'em! I'm more than four years old, I guess;

though you don't ever seem willing to give me credit for it. I don't haf to 'play' all the time, mamma: and anyway, Herbert and that nasty little Henry Rooter aren't playing, either."

"Aren't they?" Mrs. Atwater inquired. "I thought the other day you said you wanted them to let you play with them at being a newspaper reporter or editor or something like that, and they were rude and told you to go away. Wasn't that it?"

Florence sighed. "No, mamma, it cert'nly wasn't."

"They weren't rude to you?"

"Yes, they cert'nly were!"

"Well, then——"

"Mamma, *can't* you understand?" Florence turned from the window to beseech Mrs. Atwater's concentration upon the matter. "It isn't *'playing'*! I didn't want to 'play' being a reporter; *they* ain't 'playing'——"

"*Aren't* playing, Florence."

"Yes'm. They're not. Herbert's got a real printing-press; Uncle Joseph gave it to him. It's a *real* one, mamma, can't you understand?"

"I'll try," said Mrs. Atwater. "You mustn't get so excited about it, Florence."

"I'm not!" Florence returned vehemently. "I guess it'd take more than those two vile things and their old printing-press to get *me* excited! *I* don't care what they do; it's far less than nothing to me! All *I* wish is they'd fall off the fence and break their vile ole necks!"

With this manifestation of impersonal calmness, she turned again to the window; but her mother protested. "Do quit watching those foolish boys; you mustn't let them upset you so by their playing."

Florence moaned. "They don't 'upset' me, mamma! They have no effects on me by the slightest degree! And I *told* you, mamma, they're not 'playing'."

"Then what are they doing?"

"Well, they're having a newspaper. They got the printing-press and an office in Herbert's stable, and everything. They got somebody to give 'em some ole banisters and a railing from a house that was torn down somewheres, and then they got it stuck up in the stable loft, so it runs across with a kind of a gate in the middle of these banisters, and on one side is the printing-press and a desk from that nasty little Henry Rooter's mother's attic; and a table and some chairs, and a map on the wall; and that's their newspaper office. They go out and look for what's the news, and write it down in lead pencil; and then they go up to their office and write it in ink; and then they print it for their newspaper."

"But what do they do on the fence?"

"That's where they go to watch what the news is," Florence explained morosely. "They think they're so grand, sittin' up there, pokin' around! They go other places, too; and they ask people. That's all they said *I* could be!" Here the lady's bitterness became strongly intensified. "They said maybe I could be one o' the ones they asked if I knew anything, sometimes, if they happened to think of it! I just respectf'ly told 'em I'd decline to wipe my oldest shoes on 'em to save their lives!"

Mrs. Atwater sighed. "You mustn't use such expressions, Florence."

"I don't see why not," the daughter promptly objected. "They're a lot more refined than the expressions they used on me!"

"Then I'm very glad you didn't play with them."

But at this, Florence once more gave way to filial despair. "Mamma, you just *can't* see through anything! I've said anyhow fifty times they ain't—aren't—playing! They're getting up a *real* newspaper, and have people *buy* it and everything. They been all over this part of town and got every aunt and uncle they have besides their own fathers and mothers, and some people in the neighbourhood, and Kitty Silver and two or three other coloured people besides. They're going to charge twenty-five cents a year, collect-in-advance because they want the money first; and even papa gave 'em a quarter last night; he told me so."

"How often do they intend to publish their paper, Florence?" Mrs. Atwater inquired absently, having resumed her sewing.

"Every week; and they're goin' to have the first one a week from to-day."

"What do they call it?"

"The North End Daily Oriole. It's the silliest name *I* ever heard for a newspaper; and I told 'em so. I told 'em what *I* thought of it, I guess!"

"Was that the reason?" Mrs. Atwater asked.

"Was it what reason, mamma?"

"Was it the reason they wouldn't let you be a reporter with them?"

"Poot!" Florence exclaimed airily. "*I* didn't want anything to do with their ole paper. But anyway I didn't make fun o' their callin' it 'The North End Daily Oriole' till after they said I couldn't be in it. *Then* I did, you bet!"

"Florence, don't say——"

"Mamma, I got to say somep'n! Well, I told 'em I wouldn't be in their ole paper if they begged me on their bented knees; and I said if they begged me a thousand years I wouldn't be in any paper with such a crazy name and I wouldn't tell 'em any news if I knew the President of the United States had the scarlet fever! I just politely informed 'em they could say what they liked, if they was dying *I* declined so much as wipe the oldest shoes I got on 'em!"

"But why *wouldn't* they let you be on the paper?" her mother insisted.

Upon this Florence became analytical. "Just so's they could act so important." And she added, as a consequence, "They ought to be arrested!"

Mrs. Atwater murmured absently, but forbore to press her inquiry; and Florence was silent, in a brooding mood. The journalists upon the fence had disappeared from view, during her conversation with her mother; and presently she sighed, and quietly left the room. She went to her own apartment, where, at a small and rather battered little white desk, after a period of earnest reverie, she took up a pen, wet the point in purple ink, and without great effort or any critical delayings, produced a poem.

It was in a sense an original poem, though like the greater number of all literary projections, it was so strongly inspirational that the source of its inspiration might easily become manifest to a cold-blooded reader. Nevertheless, to the poetess herself, as she explained later in good faith, the words just seemed to *come* to her;—doubtless with either genius or some form of miracle implied; for sources of inspiration are seldom recognized by inspired writers themselves. She had not long ago been party to a musical Sunday afternoon at her Great-Uncle Joseph's house, where Mr. Clairdyce sang some of his songs again and again, and her poem may have begun to coagulate within her then.

THE ORGANEST

BY FLORENCE ATWATER

The organest was seated at his organ in a church,
In some beautiful woods of maple and birch,
He was very weary while he played upon the keys,
But he was a great organest and always played with ease,
    When the soul is weary,
    And the wind is dreary,
I would like to be an organest seated all day at the organ,
Whether my name might be Fairchild or Morgan,
    I would play music like a vast amen,
    The way it sounds in a church of men.

Florence read her poem seven or eight times, the deepening pleasure of her expression being evidence that repetition failed to denature this work, but on the contrary, enhanced an appreciative surprise at its singular merit. Finally she folded the sheet of paper with a delicate carefulness unusual to her, and placed it in her skirt pocket; then she went downstairs and out into the back yard. Her next action was straightforward and anything but prudish; she climbed the high wooden fences, one after the other, until she came to a pause at the top of that whereon the two journalists had lately made themselves so odiously impressive.

Before her, if she had but taken note of them, were a lesson in history and the markings of a profound transition in human evolution. Beside the old frame stable was a little brick garage, obviously put to the daily use intended by its designer. Quite as obviously the stable was obsolete; anybody would have known from its outside that there was no horse within it. There, visible, was the end of the pastoral age.

All this was lost upon Florence. She sat upon the fence, her gaze unfavourably though wistfully fixed upon a sign of no special æsthetic merit above the stable door.

THE NORTH END DAILY ORIOLE
ATWATER & ROOTER OWNERS &
PROPREITORS SUBSCRIBE NOW 25 CENTS

The inconsistency of the word "daily" did not trouble Florence; moreover, she had found no fault with "Oriole" until the Owners & Propreitors had explained to her in the plainest terms known to their vocabularies that she was excluded from the enterprise. Then, indeed, she had been reciprocally explicit in regard not only to them and certain personal characteristics of theirs, which she pointed out as fundamental, but in regard to any newspaper which should deliberately call itself an "Oriole." The partners remained superior in manner, though unable to conceal a natural resentment; they had adopted "Oriole" not out of a sentiment for the city of Baltimore, nor, indeed, on account of any ornithologic interest of theirs, but as a relic left over from an abandoned club or secret society, which they had previously contemplated forming, its members to be called "The Orioles" for no reason whatever. The two friends had talked of this plan at many meetings throughout the summer, and when Mr. Joseph Atwater made his great-nephew the unexpected present of a printing-press, and a newspaper consequently took the place of the club, Herbert and Henry still entertained an affection for their former scheme and decided to perpetuate the name. They were the more sensitive to attack upon it by an ignorant outsider and girl like Florence, and her chance of ingratiating herself with them, if that could be now her intention, was not a promising one.

She descended from the fence with pronounced inelegance, and, approaching the old double doors of the "carriage-house," which were open, paused to listen. Sounds from above assured her that the editors were editing—or at least that they could be found at their place of business. Therefore, she ascended the cobwebby stairway, emerged from it into the former hay loft, and thus made her appearance in the printing-room of *The North End Daily Oriole*.

Herbert, frowning with the burden of composition, sat at a table beyond the official railing, and his partner was engaged at the press, earnestly setting type. This latter person (whom Florence so seldom named otherwise than as "that nasty little Henry Rooter") was of a pure, smooth, fair-haired appearance, and strangely clean for his age and occupation. His profile was of a symmetry he had not yet himself begun to appreciate; his dress was scrupulous and modish; and though he was short, nothing outward about him confirmed the more sinister of Florence's two adjectives. Nevertheless, her poor opinion of him was plain in her expression as she made her present intrusion upon his working hours. He seemed to reciprocate.

"Listen! Didn't I and Herbert tell you to keep out o' here?" he said. "Look at her, Herbert! She's back again!"

"You get out o' here, Florence," said Herbert, abandoning his task with a look of pain. "How often we got to tell you we don't want you around here when we're in our office like this?"

"For heaven's sake!" Henry Rooter thought fit to add. "Can't you quit runnin' up and down our office stairs once in a while, long enough for us to get our newspaper work done? Can't you give us a little *peace?*"

The pinkiness of Florence's altering complexion was justified; she had not been within a thousand miles of their old office for four days. With some heat she stated this to be the fact, adding, "And I only came then because I knew somebody ought to see that this stable isn't ruined. It's my own uncle and aunt's stable, I guess, isn't it? Answer me that, if you'll kindly please to do so!"

"It's my father and mother's stable," Herbert asserted. "Haven't I got a right to say who's allowed in my own father and mother's stable?"

"You have not," the prompt Florence replied. "It's my own uncle and aunt's stable, and I got as much right here as anybody."

"You have not!" Henry Rooter protested hotly. "This isn't either your ole aunt and uncle's stable."

"It *isn't?*"

"No, it is not! This isn't anybody's stable. It's my and Herbert's News-paper Building, and I guess you haven't got the face to stand there and claim you got a right to go in a Newspaper Building and say you got a right there when everybody tells you to stay outside of it, I guess!"

"Oh, haven't I?"

"No, you 'haven't—I'!" Mr. Rooter maintained bitterly. "You just walk downtown and go in any Newspaper Buildings down there and tell 'em you got a right to stay there all day long when they tell you to get out o' there! Just try it! That's all I ask!"

Florence uttered a cry of derision. "And pray, whoever told you I was bound to do everything you ask me to, Mister Henry Rooter?" And she con-cluded by reverting to that hostile impulse, so ancient, which, in despair of touching an antagonist effectively, reflects upon his ancestors. "If you got anything you want to ask, you go ask your grandmother!"

"Here!" Herbert sprang to his feet. "You try and behave like a lady!"

"Who'll make me?" she inquired.

"You got to behave like a lady as long as you're in our Newspaper Building, anyway," Herbert said ominously. "If you expect to come up here after you been told five dozen times to keep out——"

"For heaven's sakes!" his partner interposed. "When we goin' to get our newspaper *work* done? She's *your* cousin; I should think you could get her out!"

"Well, I'm goin' to, ain't I?" Herbert protested plaintively. "I expect to get her out, don't I?"

"Oh, do you?" Miss Atwater inquired, with severe mockery. "Pray, how would you expect to accomplish it, pray?"

Herbert looked desperate, but was unable to form a reply consistent with a few new rules of etiquette and gallantry that he had begun to observe during the past year or so. "Now, see here, Florence," he said. "You're old enough to know when people tell you to keep out of a place, why, it means they want you to stay away from there."

Florence remained cold to this reasoning. "Oh, poot!" she said.

"Now, look here!" her cousin remonstrated, and went on with his argument. "We got our newspaper work to do, and you ought to have sense enough to know newspaper work like this newspaper work we got on *our* hands here isn't—well, it ain't any child's play."

His partner appeared to approve of the expression, for he nodded severely and then used it himself. "No, you *bet* it isn't any child's play!" he said.

"No, sir," Herbert continued. "This newspaper work we got on our hands here isn't any child's play."

"No, sir," Henry Rooter again agreed. "Newspaper work like this isn't any child's play at *all!*"

"It isn't any child's play, Florence," said Herbert. "It ain't any child's play at all, Florence. If it was just child's play or something like that, why, it wouldn't matter so much your always pokin' up here, and——"

"Well," his partner interrupted judicially;—"we wouldn't want her around, even if it *was* child's play."

"No, we wouldn't; that's so," Herbert agreed. "We wouldn't want you around, anyhow, Florence." Here his tone became more plaintive. "So, for mercy's sakes can't you go on home and give us a little rest? What you want, anyhow?"

"Well, I guess it's about time you was askin' me that," she said, not unreasonably. "If you'd asked me that in the first place, instead of actin' like you'd never been taught anything, and was only fit to associate with hoodlums, perhaps my time is of *some* value, myself!"

Here the lack of rhetorical cohesion was largely counteracted by the strong expressiveness of her tone and manner, which made clear her position as a person of worth, dealing with the lowest of her inferiors. She went on, not pausing:

"I thought being as I was related to you, and all the family and everybody else is goin' to haf to read your ole newspaper, anyway it'd be a good thing if what was printed in it wasn't *all* a disgrace to the family, because the name of our family's got mixed up with this newspaper;—so here!"

Thus speaking, she took the poem from her pocket and with dignity held it forth to her cousin.

"What's that?" Herbert inquired, not moving a hand. He was but an amateur, yet already enough of an editor to be suspicious.

"It's a poem," Florence said. "I don't know whether I exackly ought to have it in your ole newspaper or not, but on account of the family's sake I guess I better. Here, take it."

Herbert at once withdrew a few steps, placing his hands behind him. "Listen here," he said;—"you think we got time to read a lot o' nothin' in your ole hand-writin' that nobody can read anyhow, and then go and toil and moil to print it on our printin'-press? I guess we got work enough printin' what we write for our newspaper our own selves! My goodness, Florence, I *told* you this isn't any child's play!"

For the moment, Florence appeared to be somewhat baffled. "Well," she said. "Well, you better put this poem in your ole newspaper if you want to have anyhow one thing in it that won't make everybody sick that reads it."

"I won't do it!" Herbert said decisively.

"What you take us for?" his partner added.

"All right, then," Florence responded. "I'll go and tell Uncle Joseph and he'll take this printing-press back."

"He will not take it back. I already did tell him how you kept pokin' around, tryin' to *run* everything, and how we just worried our lives out tryin' to keep you away. He said he bet it was a hard job; that's what Uncle Joseph said! So go on, tell him anything you want to. You don't get your ole poem in *our* newspaper!"

"Not if she lived to be two hunderd years old!" Henry Rooter added. Then he had an afterthought. "Not unless she pays for it."

"How do you mean?" Herbert asked, puzzled by this codicil.

Now Henry's brow had become corrugated with no little professional impressiveness. "You know what we were talkin' about this morning?" he said. "How the right way to run our newspaper, we ought to have some advertisements in it and everything? Well, we want money, don't we? We could put this poem in our newspaper like an advertisement;—that is, if Florence has got any money, we could."

Herbert frowned. "If her ole poem isn't too long I guess we could. Here, let's see it, Florence." And, taking the sheet of paper in his hand, he studied the dimensions of the poem, without paining himself to read it. "Well, I guess, maybe we can do it," he said. "How much ought we to charge her?"

This question sent Henry Rooter into a state of calculation, while Florence observed him with veiled anxiety; but after a time he looked up, his brow showing continued strain. "Do you keep a bank, Florence—for nickels and dimes and maybe quarters, you know?" he inquired.

It was her cousin who impulsively replied for her. "No, she don't," he said.

"Not since I was about seven years old!" And Florence added sharply, though with dignity: "Do you still make mud pies in your back yard, pray?"

"Now, see here!" Henry objected. "Try and be a lady anyway for a few minutes, can't you? I got to figure out how much we got to charge you for your ole poem, don't I?"

"Well, then," Florence returned, "you better ask *me* somep'n about that, hadn't you?"

"Well," said Henry Rooter, "have you got any money at home?"

"No, I haven't."

"Have you got any money with you?"

"Yes, I have."

"How much is it?"

"I won't tell you."

Henry frowned. "I guess we ought to make her pay about two dollars and a half," he said, turning to his partner.

Herbert became deferential; it seemed to him that he had formed a business association with a genius, and for a moment he was dazzled; then he remembered Florence's financial capacities, always well known to him, and he looked depressed. Florence, herself, looked indignant.

"Two dollars and a half!" she cried. "Why, I could buy this whole place for two dollars and a half, printing-press, railing, and all—yes, and you thrown in, Mister Henry Rooter!"

"See here, Florence," Henry said earnestly. "Haven't you got two dollars and a half?"

"Of course she hasn't!" his partner assured him. "She never had two dollars and a half in her life!"

"Well, then," said Henry gloomily, "what we goin' to do about it? How much *you* think we ought to charge her?"

Herbert's expression became noncommittal. "Just let me think a minute," he said, and with his hand to his brow he stepped behind the unsuspicious Florence.

"I got to think," he murmured; then with the straightforwardness of his age, he suddenly seized his damsel cousin from the rear and held her in a tight but far from affectionate embrace, pinioning her arms. She shrieked, "Murder!" and "Let me go!" and "Help! Hay-yulp!"

"Look in her pocket," Herbert shouted. "She keeps her money in her skirt pocket when she's got any. It's on the left side of her. Don't let her kick you! Look out!"

"I got it!" said the dexterous Henry, retreating and exhibiting coins. "It's one dime and two nickels—twenty cents. Has she got any more pockets?"

"No, I haven't!" Florence fiercely informed him, as Herbert released her. "And I guess you better hand that money back if you don't want to be arrested for stealing!"

But Henry was unmoved. "Twenty cents," he said calculatingly. "Well, all right; it isn't much, but you can have your poem in our newspaper for twenty cents, Florence. If you don't want to pay that much, why, take your ole twenty cents and go on away."

"Yes," said Herbert. "That's as cheap as we'll do it, Florence. Take it or leave it."

"Take it or leave it," Henry Rooter agreed. "That's the way to talk to her; take it or leave it, Florence. If you don't take it you got to leave it."

Florence was indignant, but she decided to take it. "All right," she said coldly. "I wouldn't pay another cent if I died for it."

"Well, you haven't got another cent, so that's all right," Mr. Rooter remarked; and he honourably extended an open palm toward his partner. "Here, Herbert; you can have the dime, or the two nickels, whichever you rather. It makes no difference to me; I'd as soon have one as the other."

Herbert took the two nickels, and turned to Florence. "See here, Florence," he said, in a tone of strong complaint. "This business is all done and paid for now. What you want to hang around here any *more* for?"

"Yes, Florence," his partner faithfully seconded him, at once. "We haven't got any more time to waste around here to-day, and so what you want to stand around in the way and everything for? You ought to know yourself we don't want you."

"I'm not in the way," said Florence hotly. "Whose way am I in?"

"Well, anyhow, if you don't go," Herbert informed her, "we'll carry you downstairs and lock you out."

"I'd just like to see you!" she returned, her eyes flashing. "Just you dare to lay a finger on me again!" And she added, "Anyway, if you did, those ole doors haven't got any lock on 'em: I'll come right back in and walk right straight up the stairs again!"

Herbert advanced toward her. "Now you pay attention to me," he said. "You've paid for your ole poem, and we got to have some peace around here. I'm goin' straight over to your mother and ask her to come and get you."

Florence gave up. "What difference would *that* make, Mister Taddle-tale?" she inquired mockingly. "I wouldn't be here when she came, would I? I'll thank you to notice there's some value to my time, myself; and I'll just politely ask you to excuse me, pray!"

With a proud air she crushingly departed, returning to her own home far from dissatisfied with what she had accomplished. Moreover, she began to expand with the realization of a new importance; and she was gratified with the effect upon her parents, at dinner that evening, when she informed them that she had written a poem, which was to be published in the prospective first number of *The North End Daily Oriole*.

"Written a *poem?*" said her father. "Well, I declare! Why, that's remarkable, Florence!"

"I'm glad the boys were nice about it," said her mother. "I should have feared they couldn't appreciate it, after being so cross to you about letting you have anything to do with the printing-press. They must have thought it was a very good poem."

"Where is the poem, Florence?" Mr. Atwater asked. "Let's read it and see what our little girl can do when she really tries."

Unfortunately Florence had not a copy, and when she informed her father of this fact, he professed himself greatly disappointed as well as eager for the first appearance of *The Oriole*, that he might felicitate himself upon the evidence of his daughter's heretofore unsuspected talent. Florence was herself anxious for the newspaper's début, and she made her anxiety so clear to Atwater & Rooter, Owners & Propreitors, every afternoon after school, during the following week, that by Thursday further argument and repartee on their part were felt to be indeed futile; and in order to have a little peace around there, they carried her downstairs. At least, they defined their action as "carrying," and, having deposited her in the yard, they were obliged to stand guard at the doors, which they closed and contrived to hold against her until her strength was worn out for that day.

Florence consoled herself. During the week she dropped in on all the members of "the family"—her grandfather, uncles and aunts and cousins, her great-aunts and great-uncles—and in each instance, after no protracted formal preliminaries, lightly remarked that she wrote poetry now; her first to appear in the forthcoming *Oriole*. And when Great-Aunt Carrie said, "Why, Florence, you're wonderful! I couldn't write a poem to save my life. I never *could* see how they do it," Florence laughed, made a deprecatory little side motion with her head, and responded, "Why, Aunt Carrie, that's nothing! It just kind of comes to you."

This also served as her explanation when some of her school friends expressed their admiration, after being told the news in confidence; though to one of the teachers she said, smiling ruefully, as in remembrance of midnight oil, "It *does* take work, of course!"

When opportunity offered, upon the street, she joined people she knew (or even rather distant acquaintances) to walk with them a little way and lead the conversation to the subject of poetry, including her own contribution to that art. Altogether, if Florence was not in a fair way to become a poetic celebrity it was not her own fault but entirely that of *The North End Daily Oriole*, which was to make its appearance on Saturday, but failed to do so on account of too much enthusiasm on the part of Atwater & Rooter in manipulating the printing-press. It broke, had to be repaired; and Florence, her nerves upset by the accident, demanded her money back. This was impossible, and the postponement proved to be but an episode; moreover, it gave her time to let more people know of the treat that was coming.

Among these was Noble Dill. Until the Friday following her disappointment she had found no opportunity to acquaint her Very Ideal with the news; and but for an encounter partly due to chance, he might not have heard of it. A sentimental enrichment of colour in her cheeks was the result of her catching sight of him, as she was on the point of opening and entering her own front door, that afternoon, on her return from school. He was passing the house, walking somewhat dreamily.

Florence stepped into the sheltering vestibule, peeping round it with earnest eyes to watch him as he went by; obviously he had taken no note of her. Satisfied of this, she waited until he was at a little distance, then ran lightly down to the gate, hurried after him and joined him.

"Why, Mr. Dill!" she exclaimed, in her mother's most polished manner. "How supprising to see you! I presume as we both happen to be walking the same direction we might just's well keep together."

"Surprising to see me?" Noble said vaguely. "I haven't been away anywhere in particular, Florence." Then, at a thought, he brightened. "I'm glad to see you, Florence. Do you know if any of your family or relatives have heard when your Aunt Julia is coming home?"

"Aunt Julia? She's out of town," said Florence. "She's visiting different people she used to know when she was away at school."

"Yes, I know," Mr. Dill returned. "But she's been gone six weeks."

"Oh, I don't believe it's that long," Florence said casually; then with more earnestness: "Mr. Dill, I was goin' to ask you somep'n—it's kind of a funny question for *me* to ask, but——"

"Yes, she has," Noble interrupted, not aware that his remark was an interruption. "Oh, yes, she has!" he said. "It was six weeks day-before-yesterday afternoon. I saw your father downtown this morning, and he said he didn't know that any of the family had heard just when she was coming home. I thought maybe some of your relatives had a letter from her by this afternoon's mail, perhaps."

"I guess not," said Florence. "Mr. Dill, there was a question I thought I'd ask you. It's kind of a funny question for *me*——"

"Are you *sure* nobody's heard from your Aunt Julia to-day?" Noble insisted.

"I guess they haven't. Mr. Dill, I was goin' to ask you——"

"It's strange," he murmured, "I don't see how people can enjoy visits that long. I should think they'd get anxious about what might happen at home."

"Oh, grandpa's all right; he says he kind of likes to have the house nice and quiet to himself; and anyway Aunt Julia enjoys visiting," Florence assured him. "Aunt Fanny saw a newspaper from one the places where Aunt Julia's visiting her school room-mate. It had her picture in it and called her 'the famous Northern Beauty'; it was down South somewhere. Well, Mr. Dill, I was just sayin' I believe I'd ask you——"

But a sectional rancour seemed all at once to affect the young man. "Oh, yes. I heard about that," he said. "Your Aunt Fanny lent my mother the newspaper. Those people in *that* part of the country—well——" He paused, remembering that it was only Florence he addressed; and he withheld from utterance his opinion that the Civil War ought to be fought all over again. "Your father said your grandfather hadn't heard from her for several days, and even then she hadn't said when she was coming home."

"No, I expect she didn't," said Florence. "Mr. Dill, I was goin' to ask you somep'n—it's kind of a queer kind of question for *me* to ask, I guess——" She paused. However, he did not interrupt her, seeming preoccupied with gloom; whereupon Florence permitted herself a deprecatory laugh, and continued, "It might be you'd answer yes, or it might be you'd answer no; but anyway I was goin' to ask you—it's kind of a funny question for *me* to ask, I expect—but do you like poetry?"

"What?"

"Well, as things have turned out lately I guess it's kind of a funny question, Mr. Dill, but do you like poetry?"

Noble's expression took on a coldness; for the word brought to his mind a thought of Newland Sanders. "Do I like poetry?" said Noble. "No, I don't."

Florence was momentarily discouraged; but at her age people usually possess an invaluable faculty, which they lose later in life; and it is a pity that they do lose it. At thirteen—especially the earlier months of thirteen—they are still able to set aside and dismiss from their minds almost any facts, no matter how audibly those facts have asked for recognition. Children superbly allow themselves to become deaf, so to speak, to undesirable circumstances; most frequently, of course, to undesirable circumstances in the way of parental direction; so that fathers, mothers, nurses, or governesses, not comprehending that this mental deafness is for the time being entirely genuine, are liable to hoarseness both of throat and temper. Thirteen is an age when the fading of this gift or talent, one of the most beautiful of childhood, begins to impair its helpfulness under the mistaken stress of discipline; but Florence retained something of it. In a moment or two Noble Dill's disaffection toward poetry was altogether as if it did not exist.

She coughed, inclined her head a little to one side, in her mother's manner of politeness to callers, and, repeating her deprecatory laugh, remarked: "Well, of course it's kind of a funny question for *me* to ask, of course."

"What is, Florence?" Noble inquired absently.

"Well—what I was saying was that 'course it's sort of queer *me* askin' if you liked poetry, of course, on account of my *writing* poetry the way I do now."

She looked up at him with a bright readiness to respond modestly to whatever exclamation his wonder should dictate; but Noble's attention had straggled again.

"Has she written your mother lately?" he asked.

Florence's expression denoted a mental condition slightly disturbed. "No," she said. "It's goin' to be printed in *The North End Daily Oriole*."

"What?"

"My poem. It's about a vast amen—anyhow, that's proba'ly the best thing in it, I guess—and they're goin' to have it out to-morrow, or else they'll have to settle with *me*; that's one thing certain! I'll bring one over to your house and leave it at the door for you, Mr. Dill."

Noble had but a confused notion of what she thus generously promised. However, he said, "Thank you," and nodded vaguely.

"Of course, I don't know as it's so awful good," Florence admitted insincerely. "The family all seem to think it's something pretty much; but I don't know if it is or not. *Really*, I don't!"

"No," said Noble, still confused. "I suppose not."

"I'm half way through another one I think myself'll be a good deal better. I'm not goin' as fast with it as I did with the other one, and I expect it'll be quite a ways ahead of this one." She again employed the deprecatory little laugh. "I don't know how I do it, myself. The family all think it's sort of funny I don't know how I do it, myself; but that's the way it is. They all say if they could do it they're sure they'd know how they did it; but I guess they're wrong. I presume if you can do it, why, it just *comes* to you. Don't you presume that's the way it is, Mr. Dill?"

"I—guess so." They had reached his gate, and he stopped. "You're sure none of your family have heard anything to-day?" he asked anxiously.

"From Aunt Julia? I don't think they have."

He sighed, and opened the gate. "Well, good evening, Florence."

"Good evening." Her eyes followed him wistfully as he passed within the enclosure; then she turned and walked quickly toward her own home; but at the corner of the next fence she called back over her shoulder, "I'll leave it with your mother for you, if you're not home when I bring it."

"What?" he shouted, from his front door.

"I'll leave it with your *mother*."

"Leave what?"

"The *poem!*"

"Oh!" said Noble. "Thanks!"

But when his mother handed him a copy of the first issue of *The North End Daily Oriole*, the next day, when he came home to lunch, he read it without edification; there was nothing about Julia in it.

THE NORTH END DAILY ORIOLE

Atwater & Rooter Owners & Propreitors

SUBSCRIBE NOW 25 Cents Per Year

Subscriptions shloud be brought to the East etrance of Atwater & Rooter Newspaper Building every afternoon 4.30 to 6. 25 cents.

NEWS OF THE CITY

The Candidates for mayor at the election are Mr P. N. Gordon and John T Milo. The contest is very great between these candidates.

Holcombs chickens get in MR. Joseph Atwater's yard a god deal lately. He says chickens are out of place in a city of this size.

Minnie the cook of Mr. F. L. Smith's residisence goes downtown every Thrusday afts about three her regular day for it.

A new ditch is being dug accross the MR. Henry D. Vance backyrad. ;Tis about dug but nobody is working there now. Patty Fairchild received the highest mark in declamation of the 7A at Sumner School last Friday.

Balf's grorcey wagon ran over a cat of the Mr. Rayfort family. Geo. the driver of the wagom stated he had not but was willing to take it away and burg it somewheres Geo. stated regret and claimed nothing but an accident which could not be helped and not his team that did the damage.

MissColfield teacher of the 7A atSumner School was reproted on the sink list. We hope she will soon be well.

There were several deaths in the city this week.

Mr. Fairchild father of Patty Fairchild was on the sick list several days and did not go to his office but is out now.

Been Kriso the cHauffeur of the Mr. R. G. Atwater family washes their car on Monday. In using the hose he turned water over the fence accidently and hit Lonnie the washWOman in back of MRS. Bruffs who called him some low names. Ben told her if he had have been a man he wrould strike her but soon the distrubance was at an end. There is a good deal more of other news which will be printed in our next NO.

Advertisements & Poems
20 Cents Each Up.

———

JOSEPH K. ATWATER & CO.
127 South Iowa St,
Steam Pumps.

———

THE Organstep
BY Florence Atwater

The Organstep was seated at his organ in a
In some beautifil words of vagle and brir
But he was a gReat organstep and always
When the soil is weary
And the mind is drearq
I would play music like a vast amen
The way it sounds in a church of new
Subscribe NOW 25 cents Adv & Poetry
20 cents up. Atwater & Rooter News
Paper Building 25 cents per YEAR

Such was the first issue, complete, of *The North End Daily Oriole*. What had happened to the poem was due partly to Atwater & Rooter's natural lack of experience in a new and exacting trade; partly to their enviable unconsciousness of any necessity for proof-reading; and somewhat to their haste in getting through the final and least interesting stage of their undertaking; for of course so far as the printers were concerned, the poem was mere hack work anti-climax.

And as they later declared, under fire, anybody that could make out more than three words in five of Florence's ole hand-writing was welcome to do it. Besides, what did it matter if a little bit was left out at the end of one or two of the lines? They couldn't be expected to run the lines out over their margin, could they? And they never knew anything crazier than makin' all this fuss, because: Well, what if some of it wasn't printed just exactly right, who in the world was goin' to notice it, and what was the difference of just a few words different in that ole poem, anyhow?

For by the time these explanations (so to call them) took place, Florence was indeed makin' a fuss. Her emotion, at first, had been happily stimulated at sight of "BY Florence Atwater." A singular tenderness had risen in her—a tremulous sense as of something almost sacred coming at last into its own; and she hurried to distribute, gratis, among relatives and friends, several copies of the *Oriole*, paying for them, too (though not without injurious argument), at the rate of two cents a copy. But upon returning to her own home, she became calm enough (for a moment or so) to look over the poem with attention to details. She returned hastily to the Newspaper Building, but would have been wiser to remain away, since all subscribers had received their copies by the time she got there; and under the circumstances little reparation was practicable.

She ended her oration—or professed to end it—by declaring that she would never have another poem in their ole vile newspaper as long as she lived.

"You're right about that!" Henry Rooter agreed heartily. "We wouldn't *let* another one in it. Not for fifty dollars! Just look at all the trouble we took, moiling and toiling, to get your ole poem printed as nice as we could, so it wouldn't ruin our newspaper, and then you come over here and go on like this, and all this and that, why, I wouldn't go through it again for a *hunderd* dollars! We're makin' good money anyhow, with our newspaper, Florence Atwater. You needn't think we depend on *you* for our living!"

"That's so," his partner declared. "We knew you wouldn't be satisfied, anyway, Florence. Didn't we, Henry?"

"I should say we did!"

"Yes, sir!" said Herbert. "Right when we were havin' the worst time tryin' to print it and make out some o' the words, I said right then we were just throwing away our time. I said, 'What's the use? That ole girl's bound to raise Cain anyhow, so what's the use wastin' a whole lot of our good time and brains like this, just to suit *her*? Whatever we do, she's certain to come over and insult us.' Isn't that what I said, Henry?"

"Yes, it is; and I said then you were right, and you *are* right!"

"Cert'nly I am," said Herbert. "Didn't I tell you she'd be just the way some the family say she is? A good many of 'em say she'd find fault with the undertaker at her own funeral. That's just exactly what I said!"

"Oh, you did?" Florence burlesqued a polite interest. "How *virry* considerate of you! Then, perhaps you'll try to be a gentleman enough for one simple moment to allow me to tell you my last remarks on this subject. I've said enough——"

"Oh, *have* you?" Herbert interrupted with violent sarcasm. "Oh, no! Say not so! Florence, say not so!"

At this, Henry Rooter loudly shouted with applausive hilarity; whereupon Herbert, rather surprised at his own effectiveness, naturally repeated his waggery.

"Say not so, Florence! Say not so! Say not so!"

"I'll tell you one thing!" his lady cousin cried, thoroughly infuriated. "I wish to make just one last simple remark that I would care to soil myself with in *your* respects, Mister Herbert Illingsworth Atwater and Mister Henry Rooter!"

"Oh, say not so, Florence!" they both entreated. "Say not so! Say not so!"

"I'll just simply state the simple truth," Florence announced. "In the first

place, you're goin' to live to see the day when you'll come and beg me on
your bented knees to have me put poems or anything I want to in your ole
newspaper, but I'll just *laugh* at you! '*Indeed?*' I'll say! 'So you come beggin'
around *me*, do you? Ha, ha!' I'll say! 'I guess it's a little too late for that!
Why, I wouldn't —'"

"Oh, say not so, Florence! Say not so!"

"'*Me* to allow you to have one of my poems?' I'll say, 'Much less than
that!' I'll say, 'because even if I was wearing the oldest shoes I got in the
world I wouldn't take the trouble to—'"

Her conclusion was drowned out. "Oh, *Florence*, say not so! Say not so,
Florence! Say not so!"

The hateful entreaty still murmured in her resentful ears, that night, as
she fell asleep; and she passed into the beginnings of a dream with her lips
slightly dimpling the surface of her pillow in belated repartee. And upon
waking, though it was Sunday, her first words, half slumbrous in the silence
of the morning, were, "Vile Things!" Her faculties became more alert during
the preparation of a toilet that was to serve not only for breakfast, but with
the addition of gloves, a hat, and a blue-velvet coat, for Church and Sunday-
school as well; and she planned a hundred vengeances. That is to say, her
mind did not occupy itself with plots possible to make real; but rather it
dabbled among those fragmentary visions that love to overlap and displace
one another upon the changeful retina of the mind's eye.

In all of these pictures, wherein prevailingly she seemed to be some sort
of deathly powerful Queen of Poetry, the postures assumed by the figures
of Messrs. Atwater and Rooter (both in an extremity of rags) were miserably
suppliant. So she soothed herself a little—but not long. Herbert, in the next
pew, in church, and Henry in the next beyond that, were perfect composi-
tions in smugness. They were cold, contented, aristocratic; and had an imperturbable understanding between themselves (even then perceptible to the
sensitive Florence) that she was a nuisance now capably disposed of by their
beautiful discovery of "Say not so!" Florence's feelings were unbecoming to
the place and occasion.

But at four o'clock, that afternoon, she was assuaged into a milder condition by the arrival, according to an agreement made in Sunday-school, of
the popular Miss Patty Fairchild.

Patty was thirteen and a half; an exquisite person with gold-dusted hair,
eyes of singing blue, and an alluring air of sweet self-consciousness. Henry
Rooter and Herbert Illingsworth Atwater, Jr., out gathering news, saw her
entering Florence's gate, and immediately forgot that they were reporters.
They became silent, gradually moving toward the house of their newspaper's
sole poetess.

Florence and Patty occupied themselves indoors for half an hour; then went out in the yard to study a mole's tunnel that had interested Florence recently. They followed it across the lawn at the south side of the house, discussing the habits of moles and other matters of zoology; and finally lost the track near the fence, which was here the "side fence" and higher than their heads. Patty looked through a knot-hole to see if the tunnel was visible in the next yard, but, without reporting upon her observations, she turned, as if carelessly, and leaned back against the fence, covering the knot-hole.

"Florence," she said, in a tone softer than she had been using heretofore; —"Florence, do you know what I think?"

"No. Could you see any more tracks over there?"

"Florence," said Patty;—"I was just going to tell you something, only maybe I better not."

"Why not?" Florence inquired. "Go on and tell me."

"No," said Patty gently. "You might think it was silly."

"No, I won't."

"Yes, you *might.*"

"I promise I won't."

"Well, then—oh, Florence I'm *sure* you'll think it's silly!"

"I *promised* I wouldn't."

"Well—I don't think I better say it."

"Go on," Florence urged. "Patty, you *got* to."

"Well, then, if I got to," said Patty. "What I was going to say, Florence: Don't you think your cousin Herbert and Henry Rooter have got the nicest eyes of any boy in town?"

"*Who?*" Florence was astounded.

"I do," Patty said in her charming voice. "I think Herbert and Henry've got the nicest eyes of any boy in town."

"You do?" Florence cried incredulously.

"Yes, I really do, Florence. I think Herbert Atwater and Henry Rooter have got the nicest eyes of any boy in town."

"Well, I never heard anything like *this* before!" Florence declared.

"But *don't* you think they've got the nicest eyes of any boy in town?" Patty insisted, appealingly.

"I think," said Florence, "their eyes are just horrable!"

"What?"

"*Herbert's* eyes," continued Florence, ardently, "are the very worst lookin' ole squinty eyes I ever saw, and that nasty little Henry *Rooter's* eyes——"

But Patty had suddenly become fidgety; she hurried away from the fence. "Come over here, Florence," she said. "Let's go over to the other side of the yard and talk."

It was time for her to take some such action. Messrs. Atwater and Rooter, seated quietly together upon a box on the other side of the fence (though with their backs to the knot-hole), were beginning to show signs of inward disturbance. Already flushed with the unexpected ineffabilities overheard, their complexions had grown even pinker upon Florence's open-hearted expressions of opinion. Slowly they turned their heads to look at the fence, upon the other side of which stood the maligner of their eyes. Not that they cared what *that* ole girl thought—but she oughtn't to be allowed to go around talking like this and perhaps prejudicing everybody that had a kind word to say for them.

"Come on over here, Florence," called Patty huskily, from the other side of the yard. "Let's talk over here."

Florence was puzzled, but consented. "What you want to talk over here for?" she asked as she came near her friend.

"Oh, I don't know," said Patty. "Let's go out in the front yard."

She led the way round the house, and a moment later uttered a cry of surprise as the firm of Atwater & Rooter, passing along the pavement, hesitated at the gate. Their celebrated eyes showed doubt for a moment, then a brazenness: Herbert and Henry decided to come in.

"Isn't this the funniest thing?" cried Patty. "After what I just said awhile ago—*you* know, Florence. Don't you dare to tell 'em!"

"I cert'nly won't!" her hostess promised, and, turning inhospitably to the two callers, "What on earth you want around here?" she inquired.

Herbert chivalrously took upon himself the duty of response. "Look here; this is my own aunt and uncle's yard, isn't it? I guess if I want to come in it I got a perfect right to."

"I should say so," his partner said warmly.

"Why, of course!" the cordial Patty agreed. "We can play some nice Sunday games, or something. Let's sit on the porch steps and think what to do."

"*I* just as soon," said Henry Rooter. "*I* got nothin' p'ticular to do."

"I haven't either," said Herbert.

Thereupon, Patty sat between them on the steps.

"This is *per-feckly* grand!" she cried. "Come on, Florence, aren't you going to sit down with all the rest of us?"

"Well, pray kindly excuse *me!*" said Miss Atwater; and she added that she would neither sit on the same steps with Herbert Atwater and Henry Rooter, nor, even if they entreated her with accompanying genuflections, would she have anything else whatever to do with them. She concluded with a reference to the oldest pair of shoes she might ever come to possess; and withdrew to the railing of the veranda at a point farthest from the steps; and, seated there, swinging one foot rhythmically, she sang hymns in a tone at once plaintive and inimical.

It was not lost upon her, however, that her withdrawal had little effect upon her guests. They chattered gaily, and Patty devised, or remembered, harmless little games that could be played by a few people as well as by many; and the three participants were so congenial and noisy and made so merry, that before long Florence was unable to avoid the impression that whether she liked it or not she was giving quite a party.

At times the noted eyes of Atwater & Rooter were gentled o'er with the soft cast of enchantment, especially when Patty felt called upon to reprove the two with little coquetries of slaps and pushes. Noted for her sprightliness, she was never sprightlier; her pretty laughter tooted continuously, and the gentlemen accompanied it with doting sounds so repulsive to Florence that without being actively conscious of what she did, she embodied the phrase, "perfeckly sickening," in the hymn she was crooning, and repeated it over and over to the air of "Rock of Ages."

"Now I tell you what let's play," the versatile Patty proposed, after exhausting the pleasures of "Geography," "Ghosts" and other tests of intellect. "Let's play 'Truth.' We'll each take a piece o' paper and a pencil, and then each of us asks the other one some question, and we haf to write down the answer and sign your name and fold it up so nobody can see it except the one that asked the question, and we haf to keep it a secret and never tell as long as we live."

"All right," said Henry Rooter. "I'll be the one to ask you a question, Patty."

"No," Herbert said promptly. "I ought to be the one to ask Patty."

"Why ought you?" Henry demanded. "Why ought you?"

"Listen!" Patty cried, "I know the way we'll do. I'll ask each of you a question—we haf to whisper it—and each one of you'll ask me one, and then we'll write it. That'll be simply grand!" She clapped her hands; then checked herself. "Oh, I guess we can't either. We haven't got any paper and pencils unless——" Here she seemed to recall her hostess. "Oh, Florrie, dear! Run in the house and get us some paper and pencils."

Florence gave no sign other than to increase the volume of her voice as she sang: "Perf'ly sick'ning, clef' for me, let me *perf'ly sick-kin-ning!*"

"We got plenty," said Herbert; whereupon he and Henry produced pencils and their professional note-books, and supplied their fair friend and themselves with material for "Truth." "Come on, Patty, whisper me whatever you want to."

"No; I ought to have her whisper *me,* first," Henry Rooter objected. "I'll write the answer to *any* question; I don't care what it's about."

"Well, it's got to be the *truth,* you know," Patty warned them. "We all haf to write down just exackly the truth on our word of honour and sign our name. Promise?"

They promised earnestly.

"All right," said Patty. "Now I'll whisper Henry a question first, and then you can whisper yours to me first, Herbert."

This seemed to fill all needs happily, and the whispering and writing began, and continued with a coziness little to the taste of the piously singing Florence. She altered all previous opinions of her friend Patty, and when the latter finally closed the session on the steps, and announced that she must go home, the hostess declined to accompany her into the house to help her find where she had left her hat and wrap.

"I haven't the *least* idea where I took 'em off!" Patty declared in the airiest manner. "If you won't come with me, Florrie, s'pose you just call in the front door and tell your mother to get 'em for me."

"Oh, they're *somewhere* in there," Florence said coldly, not ceasing to swing her foot, and not turning her head. "You can find 'em by yourself, I presume, or if you can't I'll have our maid throw 'em out in the yard or somep'n to-morrow."

"Well, *thank* you!" Miss Fairchild rejoined, as she entered the house.

The two boys stood waiting, having in mind to go with Patty as far as her own gate. "That's a *pretty* way to speak to company!" Herbert addressed his cousin with heavily marked severity. "Next time you do anything like that I'll march straight in the house and inform your mother of the fact."

Florence still swung her foot and looked dreamily away. She sang, to the air of "Rock of Ages":

"Henry Rooter, Herbert, too—they make me sick, they make me sick, that's what they do."

However, they were only too well prepared with their annihilating response.

"Oh, say not so! Florence, say not so! *Florence!* Say not so!"

They even sent this same odious refrain back to her from the street, as they departed with their lovely companion; and, so tenuous is feminine loyalty sometimes, under these stresses, Miss Fairchild mingled her sweet, tantalizing young soprano with their changing and cackling falsetto.

"Say not so, Florence! Oh, say not so! Say not so!"

They went satirically down the street, their chumminess with one another bountifully increased by their common derision of the outsider on the porch; and even at a distance they still contrived to make themselves intolerable; looking back over their shoulders, at intervals, with say-not-so expressions on their faces. Even when these faces were far enough away to be but yellowish oval planes, their say-not-so expressions were still bitingly eloquent.

Now a northern breeze chilled the air, as the hateful three became indistinguishable in the haze of autumn dusk, whereupon Florence stopped swinging her foot, left the railing, and went morosely into the house. And here it was her fortune to make two discoveries vital to her present career; the first arising out of a conversation between her father and mother in the library, where a gossipy fire of soft coal encouraged this proper Sunday afternoon entertainment for man and wife.

"Sit down and rest, Florence," said her mother. "I'm afraid you play too hard when Patty and the boys are here. Do sit down quietly and rest yourself a little while." And as Florence obeyed, Mrs. Atwater turned to her husband, resuming: "Well, that's what *I* said. I told Aunt Carrie I thought the same way about it that *you* did. Of course nobody *ever* knows what Julia's going to do next, and nobody needs to be surprised at anything she does do.

Ever since she came home from school, about four-fifths of all the young men in town have been wild about her—and so's every old bachelor, for the matter of that!"

"Yes," Mr. Atwater added. "And every old widower, too."

His wife warmly accepted the amendment. "And every old widower, too," she said, nodding. "Rather! And of course Julia's just done exactly as she pleased about everything, and naturally she's going to do as she pleases about *this*."

"Well, of course it's her own affair, Mollie," Mr. Atwater said mildly. "She couldn't be expected to consult the whole Atwater family connection before she——"

"Oh, no," she agreed. "I don't say she could. Still, it *is* rather upsetting, coming so suddenly like this, when not one of the family has ever seen him —never even heard his very name before."

"Well, that part of it isn't especially strange, Mollie. He was born and brought up in a town three hundred miles from here. I don't see just how we *could* have heard his name unless he visited here or got into the papers in some way."

Mrs. Atwater seemed unwilling to yield a mysterious point. She rocked decorously in her rocking-chair, shook her head, and after setting her lips rigidly, opened them to insist that she could never change her mind: Julia had acted very abruptly. "Why couldn't she have let her poor father know at least a *few* days before she did?"

Mr. Atwater sighed. "Why, she explains in her letter that she only knew it, herself, an hour before she wrote."

"Her poor father!" his wife repeated commiseratingly.

"Why, Mollie, I don't see how father's especially to be pitied."

"Don't you?" said Mrs. Atwater. "That old man, to have to live in that big house all alone, except a few negro servants?"

"Why, no! About half the houses in the neighbourhood, up and down the street, are fully occupied by close relatives of his: I doubt if he'll be really as lonely as he'd like to be. And he's often said he'd give a great deal if Julia had been a plain, unpopular girl. I'm strongly of the opinion, myself, that he'll be pleased about this. Of course it may upset him a little at first."

"Yes; I think it will!" Mrs. Atwater shook her head forebodingly. "And he isn't the only one it's going to upset."

"No, he isn't," her husband admitted seriously. "That's always been the trouble with Julia; she never could bear to seem disappointing; and so, of course, I suppose every one of 'em has a special idea that he's really about the top of the list with her."

"Every last one of 'em is positive of it," said Mrs. Atwater. "That was Julia's way with 'em!"

"Yes, Julia's always been much too kind-hearted for other people's good." Thus Mr. Atwater summed up Julia; and he was her brother. Additionally, since he was the older, he had known her since her birth.

"If you ask *me*," said his wife, "I'll really be surprised if it all goes through without a suicide."

"Oh, not quite suicide, perhaps," Mr. Atwater protested. "I'm glad it's a fairly dry town though."

She failed to fathom his simple meaning. "Why?"

"Well, some of 'em might feel *that* desperate at least," he explained. "Prohibition's a safeguard for the disappointed in love."

This phrase and a previous one stirred Florence, who had been sitting quietly, according to request, and "resting", but not resting her curiosity. "*Who's* disappointed in love, papa?" she inquired with an explosive eagerness that slightly startled her preoccupied parents. "What *is* all this about Aunt Julia, and grandpa goin' to live alone, and people committing suicide and prohibition and everything? What *is* all this, mamma?"

"Nothing, Florence."

"Nothing! That's what you always say about the very most inter'sting things that happen in the whole family! What *is* all this, papa?"

"It's nothing that would be interesting to little girls, Florence. Merely some family matters."

"My goodness!" Florence exclaimed. "I'm not a 'little girl' any more, papa! You're *always* forgetting my age! And if it's a family matter I belong to the family, I guess, about as much as anybody else, don't I? Grandpa himself isn't any *more* one of the family than I am, I don't care *how* old he is!"

This was undeniable, and her father laughed. "It's really nothing you'd care about one way or the other," he said.

"Well, I'd care about it if it's a secret," Florence insisted. "If it's a secret I'd want to know it, whatever it's about."

"Oh, it isn't a secret, particularly, I suppose. At least, it's not to be made public for a time; it's only to be known in the family."

"Well, didn't I just *prove* I'm as much one o' the family as——"

"Never mind," her father said soothingly. "I don't suppose there's any harm in your knowing it—if you won't go telling everybody. Your Aunt Julia has just written us that she's engaged."

Mrs. Atwater uttered an exclamation, but she was too late to check him. "I'm afraid you oughtn't to have told Florence. She *isn't* just the most discreet——"

"Pshaw!" he laughed. "She certainly is 'one of the family', however, and Julia wrote that all of the family might be told. You'll not speak of it outside the family, will you, Florence?"

But Florence was not yet able to speak of it, even inside the family; so surprising, sometimes, are parents' theories of what will not interest their children. She sat staring, her mouth open, and in the uncertain illumination of the room these symptoms of her emotional condition went unobserved.

"I say, you won't speak of Julia's engagement outside the family, will you, Florence?"

"Papa!" she gasped. "Did Aunt Julia write she was *engaged?*"

"Yes."

"To get *married?*"

"It would seem so."

"To *who?*"

"'To whom,' Florence," her mother suggested primly.

"Mamma!" the daughter cried. "Who's Aunt Julia engaged to get married to? Noble Dill?"

"Good gracious, *no!*" Mrs. Atwater exclaimed. "What an absurd idea! It's to a young man in the place she's visiting—a stranger to all of us. Julia only met him a few weeks ago." Here she forgot Florence, and turned again to her husband, wearing her former expression of experienced foreboding. "It's just as I said. It's exactly like Julia to do such a reckless thing!"

"But as we don't know anything at all about the young man," he remonstrated, "how do you know it's reckless?"

"How do you know he's young?" Mrs. Atwater retorted crisply. "All in the world she said about him was that he's a lawyer. He may be a widower, for all we know, or divorced, with seven or eight children."

"Oh, no, Mollie!"

"Why, he *might!*" she insisted. "For all we know, he may be a widower for the third or fourth *time,* or divorced, with any *number* of children! If such a person proposed to Julia, you know yourself she'd hate to be disappointing!"

Her husband laughed. "I don't think she'd go so far as to actually accept 'such a person' and write home to announce her engagement to the family. I suppose most of her swains here have been in the habit of proposing to her just as frequently as she was unable to prevent them from going that far; and while I don't think she's been as discouraging with them as she might have been, she's never really accepted any of 'em. She's never been engaged before."

"No," Mrs. Atwater admitted. "Not to this extent! She's never quite announced it to the family before, that is."

"Yes; I'd hate to have Julia's job when she comes back!" Julia's brother admitted ruefully.

"What job?"

"Breaking it to her admirers."

"Oh, *she* isn't going to do that!"

"She'll have to, now," he said. "She'll either have to write the news to 'em, or else tell 'em, face to face, when she comes home."

"She won't do either."

"Why, how could she get out of it?"

His wife smiled pityingly. "She hasn't set a time for coming home, has she? Don't you know enough of Julia's ways to see she'll never in the world stand up to the music? She writes that all the family can be told, because she knows the news will leak out, here and there, in confidence, little by little, so by the time she gets home they'll all have been through their first spasms, and after that she hopes they'll just send her some forgiving flowers and greet her with manly hand-clasps—and get ready to usher at the wedding!"

"Well," said Mr. Atwater, "I'm afraid you're right. It does seem rather like Julia to stay away till the first of the worst is over. I'm really sorry for some of 'em. I suppose it *will* get whispered about, and they'll hear it; and there are some of the poor things that might take it pretty hard."

" 'Take it pretty hard!' " his wife echoed loudly. "There's *one* of 'em, at least, who'll just merely lose his reason!"

"Which one?"

"Noble Dill."

At this, the slender form of Florence underwent a spasmodic seizure in her chair, but as the fit was short and also noiseless, it passed without being noticed.

"Yes," said Mr. Atwater thoughtfully. "I suppose he will."

"He certainly will!" Mrs. Atwater declared. "Noble's mother told me last week that he'd got so he was just as liable to drop a fountain-pen in his coffee as a lump of sugar; and when any one speaks to him he either doesn't know it, or else jumps. When he says anything, himself, she says they can scarcely ever make out what he's talking about. He was trying enough before Julia went away; but since she's been gone Mrs. Dill says he's like nothing in her experience. She says he doesn't inherit it; Mr. Dill wasn't anything like this about her."

Mr. Atwater smiled faintly. "Mrs. Dill wasn't anything like Julia."

"No," said his wife. "She was quite a sensible girl. I'd hate to be in her place now, though, when she tells Noble about *this*."

"How can Mrs. Dill tell him, since she doesn't know it herself?"

"Well—perhaps she ought to know it, so that she *could* tell him. *Some-body* ought to tell him, and it ought to be done with the greatest tact. It ought to be broken to him with the most delicate care and sympathy, or the consequences——"

"Nobody could foretell the consequences," her husband interrupted:—"no matter how tactfully it's broken to Noble."

"No," she said, "I suppose that's true. I think the poor thing's likely to lose his reason unless it *is* done tactfully, though."

"Do you think we really ought to tell Mrs. Dill, Mollie? I mean, seriously: Do you?"

For some moments she considered his question, then replied, "No. It's possible we'd be following a Christian course in doing it; but still we're rather bound not to speak of it outside the family, and when it does get outside the family I think we'd better not be the ones responsible—especially since it might easily be traced to us. I think it's usually better to keep out of things when there's any doubt."

"Yes," he said, meditating. "I never knew any harm to come of people's sticking to their own affairs."

But as he and his wife became silent for a time, musing in the firelight, their daughter's special convictions were far from coinciding with theirs, although she, likewise, was silent—a singularity they should have observed. So far were they from a true comprehension of her, they were unaware that she had more than a casual, young-cousinly interest in Julia Atwater's engagement and in those possible consequences to Noble Dill just sketched with some intentional exaggeration. They did not even notice her expression when Mr. Atwater snapped on the light, in order to read; and she went quietly out of the library and up the stairs to her own room.

On the floor, near her bed, where Patty Fairchild had left her coat and hat, Florence made another discovery. Two small, folded slips of paper lay there, dropped by Miss Fairchild when she put on her coat in the darkening room. They were the replies to Patty's whispered questions in the game on the steps—the pledged Truth, written by Henry Rooter and Herbert Atwater on their sacred words and honours. The infatuated pair had either overestimated Patty's caution, or else each had thought she would so prize his little missive that she would treasure it in a tender safety, perhaps pinned upon her blouse (at the first opportunity) over her heart. It is positively safe to say that neither of the two veracities would ever have been set upon paper had Herbert and Henry any foreshadowing that Patty might be careless; and the partners would have been seized with the utmost horror could they have conceived the possibility of their trustful messages ever falling into the hands of the relentless creature who now, without an instant's honourable hesitation, unfolded and read them.

"*Yes if I got to tell the truth I know I have got pretty eyes,*" Herbert had unfortunately written. "*I am glad you think so too Patty because your eyes are too Herbert Illingsworth Atwater, Jr.*"

And Mr. Henry Rooter had likewise ruined himself in a coincidental manner:

"*Well Patty my eyes are pretty but suppose I would like to trade with yours because you have beautiful eyes also, sure as my name is Henry Rooter.*"

Florence stood close to the pink-shaded electric drop-light over her small white dressing-table, reading again and again these pathetically honest little confidences. Her eyelids were withdrawn to an unprecedented retirement, so remarkably she stared; while her mouth seemed to prepare itself for the attempted reception of a bulk beyond its capacity. And these plastic tokens, so immoderate as to be ordinarily the consequence of nothing short of horror, were overlaid by others, subtler and more gleaming, which wrought the true significance of the contortion—a joy that was dumfounding.

Her thoughts were first of Fortune's kindness in selecting her for a favour so miraculously dovetailing into the precise need of her life; then she considered Henry and Herbert, each at this hour probably brushing his hair in preparation for the Sunday evening meal, and both touchingly unconscious of the calamity now befalling them; but what eventually engrossed her mind was a thought about Wallie Torbin.

This Master Torbin, fourteen years of age, was in all the town the boy most dreaded by his fellow-boys, and also by girls, including many of both sexes who knew him only by sight—and hearing. He had no physical endowment or attainment worth mention; but boys who could "whip him with one hand" became sycophants in his presence; the terror he inspired was moral. He had a special over-development of a faculty exercised clumsily enough by most human beings, especially in their youth; in other words, he had a genius—not, however, a genius having to do with anything generally recognized as art or science. True, if he had been a violinist prodigy or mathematical prodigy, he would have had some respect from his fellows—about equal to that he might have received if he were gifted with some pleasant deformity, such as six toes on a foot—but he would never have enjoyed such deadly prestige as had actually come to be his. In brief, then, Wallie Torbin had a genius for mockery.

Almost from his babyhood he had been a child of one purpose: to increase by burlesques the sufferings of unfortunate friends. If one of them wept, Wallie incessantly pursued him, yelping in horrid mimicry; if one were chastised he could not appear out-of-doors for days except to encounter Wallie and a complete rehearsal of the recent agony. "Quit, Papa! *Pah*-puh, quee-yet! I'll *never* do it again, Pah-puh! Oh, *lemme* alone, Pah-*puh!*"

As he grew older, his insatiate curiosity enabled him to expose unnumbered weaknesses, indiscretions, and social misfortunes on the part of acquaintances and schoolmates; and to every exposure his noise and energy gave a hideous publicity: the more his victim sought privacy the more persistently he was followed by Wallie, vociferous and attended by hilarious spectators. But above all other things, what most stimulated the demoniac boy to prodigies of satire was a tender episode or any symptom connected with the dawn of love. Florence herself had suffered at intervals throughout her eleventh summer because Wallie discovered that Georgie Beck had sent her a valentine; and the humourist's many, many squealings of that valentine's affectionate quatrain finally left her unable to decide which she hated the more, Wallie or Georgie. That was the worst of Wallie: he never "let up"; and in Florence's circle there was no more sobering threat than, "I'll tell Wallie Torbin!" As for Henry Rooter and Herbert Illingsworth Atwater, Jr., they would as soon have had a Head-hunter on their trail as Wallie Torbin in the possession of anything that could incriminate them in an implication of love—or an acknowledgment (in their own handwriting!) of their own beauty.

The fabric of civilized life is interwoven with blackmail: even some of the noblest people do favours for other people who are depended upon not to tell somebody something that the noblest people have done. Blackmail is born into us all, and our nurses teach us more blackmail by threatening to tell our parents if we won't do this and that—and our parents threaten to tell the doctor—and so we learn! Blackmail is part of the daily life of a child. Displeased, his first resort to get his way with other children is a threat to "tell," but by-and-by his experience discovers the mutual benefit of honour among blackmailers. Therefore, at eight it is no longer the ticket to threaten to tell the teacher; and, a little later, threatening to tell any adult at all is considered something of a breakdown in morals. Notoriously, the code is more liable to infraction by people of the physically weaker sex, for the very reason, of course, that their inferiority of muscle so frequently compels such a sin, if they are to have their way. But for Florence there was now no such temptation. Looking to the demolition of Atwater & Rooter, an exposure before adults of the results of "Truth" would have been an effect of the sickliest pallor compared to what might be accomplished by a careful use of the catastrophic Wallie Torbin.

On Sunday evening it was her privileged custom to go to the house of fat old Great-Uncle Joseph and remain until nine o'clock, in chatty companionship with Uncle Joseph and Aunt Carrie, his wife, and a few other relatives (including Herbert) who were in the habit of dropping in there, on Sunday evenings. In summer, lemonade and cake were frequently provided; in the autumn, one still found cake, and perhaps a pitcher of clear new cider: apples were a certainty.

This evening was glorious: there were apples and cider and cake, with walnuts, perfectly cracked, and a large open-hearted box of candy; for Uncle Joseph and Aunt Carrie had foreseen the coming of several more Atwaters than usual, to talk over the new affairs of their beautiful relative, Julia. Seldom have any relative's new affairs been more thoroughly talked over than were Julia's that evening; though all the time by means of symbols, since it was thought wiser that Herbert and Florence should not yet be told of Julia's engagement; and Florence's parents were not present to confess their indiscretion. Julia was referred to as "the traveller"; other makeshifts were employed with the most knowing caution, and all the while Florence merely ate inscrutably. The more sincere Herbert was placid; the foods absorbing his attention.

"Well, all I say is, the traveller better enjoy herself on her travels," said Aunt Fanny, finally, as the subject appeared to be wearing toward exhaustion. "She certainly is in for it when the voyaging is over and she arrives in the port she sailed from, and has to show her papers. I agree with the rest of you: she'll have a great deal to answer for, and most of all about the shortest one. My own opinion is that the shortest one is going to burst like a balloon."

"The shortest one," as the demure Florence had understood from the first, was none other than her Very Ideal. Now she looked up from the stool where she sat with her back against a pilaster of the mantelpiece. "Uncle Joseph," she said;—"I was just thinking. What is a person's reason?"

The fat gentleman, rosy with firelight and cider, finished his fifth glass before responding. "Well, there *are* persons I never could find any reason for at all. 'A person's reason'? What do you mean, 'a person's reason,' Florence?"

"I mean: like when somebody says, 'They'll lose their reason,'" she explained. "Has everybody got a reason, and if they have, what is it, and how do they lose it, and what would they do then?"

"Oh! I see!" he said. "You needn't worry. I suppose since you heard it you've been hunting all over yourself for your reason and looking to see if there was one hanging out of anybody else, somewhere. No; it's something you can't see, ordinarily, Florence. Losing your reason is just another way of saying, 'going crazy'!"

"Oh!" she murmured, and appeared to be disturbed.

At this, Herbert thought proper to offer a witticism for the pleasure of the company.

"*You* know, Florence," he said, "it only means acting like *you* most always do." He applauded himself with a burst of changing laughter ranging from a bullfrog croak to a collapsing soprano; then he added: "Espeshually when you come around my and Henry's Newspaper Building! You cert'nly 'lose your reason' every time you come around *that* ole place!"

"Well, course I haf to act like the people that's already there," Florence retorted, not sharply, but in a musing tone that should have warned him. It was not her wont to use a quiet voice for repartee. Thinking her humble, he laughed the more raucously.

"Oh, Florence!" he besought her. "Say not so! Say not so!"

"Children, children!" Uncle Joseph remonstrated.

Herbert changed his tone; he became seriously plaintive. "Well, she does act that way, Uncle Joseph! When she comes around there you'd think we were runnin' a lunatic asylum, the way she takes on. She hollers and bellers and squalls and squawks. The least little teeny thing she don't like about the way we run our paper, she comes flappin' over there and goes to screechin' around you could hear her out at the Poor House Farm!"

"Now, now, Herbert," his Aunt Fanny interposed. "Poor little Florence isn't saying anything impolite to you—not right now, at any rate. Why don't you be a little sweet to her just for once?"

Her unfortunate expression revolted all the manliness in Herbert's bosom. "Be a little *sweet* to her?" he echoed with poignant incredulity, and then in candour made plain how poorly Aunt Fanny inspired him. "I just exackly as soon be a little sweet to an alligator," he said.

"Oh, oh!" said Aunt Carrie.

"I would!" Herbert insisted. "Or a mosquito I'd rather, to *either* of 'em, 'cause anyway they don't make so much noise. Why, you just ought to *hear* her," he went on, growing more and more severe. "You ought to just come around our Newspaper Building any afternoon you please, after school, when Henry and I are tryin' to do our work in anyway *some* peace. Why, she just squawks and squalls and squ——"

"It must be terrible," Uncle Joseph interrupted. "What do you do all that for, Florence, every afternoon?"

"Just for exercise," she answered dreamily; and her placidity the more exasperated her journalist cousin.

"She does it because she thinks *she* ought to be runnin' our own newspaper, my and Henry's; that's why she does it! She thinks she knows more about how to run newspapers than anybody alive; but there's one thing she's goin' to find out; and that is, she don't get anything *more* to do with my and Henry's newspaper. We wouldn't have another single one of her ole poems in it, no matter how much she offered to pay us! Uncle Joseph, I think you ought to *tell* her she's got no business around my and Henry's Newspaper Building."

"But, Herbert," Aunt Fanny suggested;—"you might let Florence have a little share in it of some sort. Then everything would be all right."

"It would?" he said. "It *woo*-wud? Oh, my goodness, Aunt Fanny, I guess you'd like to see our newspaper just utterly ruined! Why, we wouldn't let that girl have any more to do with it than we would some horse!"

"Oh, oh!" both Aunt Fanny and Aunt Carrie exclaimed, shocked.

"We wouldn't," Herbert insisted. "A horse would know any amount more how to run a newspaper than she does. Soon as we got our printing-press, we said right then that we made up our minds Florence Atwater wasn't ever goin' to have a single thing to do with our newspaper. If you let her have anything to do with anything she wants to run the whole thing. But she might just as well learn to stay away from our Newspaper Building, because after we got her out yesterday we fixed a way so's she'll never get in *there* again!"

Florence looked at him demurely. "Are you sure, Herbert?" she inquired.

"Just you try it!" he advised her, and he laughed tauntingly. "Just come around to-morrow and try it; that's all I ask!"

"I cert'nly intend to," she responded with dignity. "I may have a slight supprise for you."

"Oh, *Florence*, say not so! Say not so, Florence! Say not so!"

At this, she looked full upon him, and already she had something in the nature of a surprise for him; for so powerful was the still balefulness of her glance that he was slightly startled. "I might say not so," she said. "I might, if I was speaking of what pretty eyes you say yourself you know you have, Herbert."

It staggered him. "What—what do you mean?"

"Oh, nothin'," she replied airily.

Herbert began to be mistrustful of the solid earth: somewhere there was a fearful threat to his equipoise. "What you talkin' about?" he said with an effort to speak scornfully; but his sensitive voice almost failed him.

"Oh, nothin'," said Florence. "Just about what pretty eyes you know you have, and Patty's being pretty, too, and so you're glad she thinks yours are pretty, the way *you* do—and everything!"

Herbert visibly gulped. He believed that Patty had betrayed him; had betrayed the sworn confidence of "Truth!"

"That's all I was talkin' about," Florence added. "Just about how you knew you had such pretty eyes. Say not so, Herbert! Say not so!"

"Look here!" he said. "When'd you see Patty again between this afternoon and when you came over here?"

"What makes you think I saw her?"

"Did you telephone her?"

"What makes you think so?"

Once more Herbert gulped. "Well, I guess you're ready to believe anything anybody tells you," he said, with palsied bravado. "You don't believe everything Patty Fairchild says, do you?"

"Why, Herbert! Doesn't she always tell the *truth?*"

"Her? Why, half the time," poor Herbert babbled, "you can't tell whether she's just makin' up what she says or not. If you've gone and believed everything that ole girl told you, you haven't got even what little sense I used to think you had!" So base we are under strain, sometimes—so base when our good name is threatened with the truth of us! "I wouldn't believe anything she said," he added, in a sickish voice, "if she told me fifty times and crossed her heart!"

"Wouldn't you if she said you *wrote down* how pretty you knew your eyes were, Herbert? Wouldn't you if it was on paper in your own handwriting?"

"What's this about Herbert having 'pretty eyes'?" Uncle Joe inquired, again bringing general attention to the young cousins; and Herbert shuddered. This fat uncle had an unpleasant reputation as a joker.

The nephew desperately fell back upon the hopeless device of attempting to drown out his opponent's voice as she began to reply. He became vociferous with scornful laughter, badly cracked. "Florence got mad!" he shouted, mingling the purported information with hoots and cacklings. "She got mad because I and Henry played some games with Patty and wouldn't let her play! She's tryin' to make up stories on us to get even. She made it up! It's all made up! She——"

"No, no," Mr. Atwater interrupted. "Let Florence tell us. Florence, what was it about Herbert's knowing he had 'pretty eyes'?"

Herbert attempted to continue the drowning out. He bawled. "She made it *up!* It's somep'n she made up her*self!* She——"

"Herbert," said Uncle Joseph;—"if you don't keep quiet, I'll take back the printing-press."

Herbert substituted a gulp for the continuation of his noise.

"Now, Florence," said Uncle Joseph, "tell us what you were saying about how Herbert knows he has such 'pretty eyes'."

Then it seemed to Herbert that a miracle befell. Florence looked up, smiling modestly. "Oh, it wasn't anything, Uncle Joseph," she said. "I was just trying to tease Herbert any way I could think of."

"Oh, was that all?" A hopeful light faded out of Uncle Joseph's large and inexpressive face. "I thought perhaps you'd detected him in some indiscretion."

Florence laughed, "I was just teasin' him. It wasn't anything, Uncle Joseph."

Hereupon, Herbert resumed a confused breathing. Dazed, he remained uneasy, profoundly so: and gratitude was no part of his emotion. He well understood that in conflicts such as these Florence was never susceptible to impulses of compassion; in fact, if there was warfare between them, experience had taught him to be wariest when she seemed kindest. He moved away from her, and went into another room where his condition was one of increasing mental discomfort, though he looked over the pictures in his greatuncle's copy of "Paradise Lost." These illustrations, by M. Gustave Doré, failed to aid in reassuring his troubled mind.

When Florence left the house, he impulsively accompanied her, maintaining a nervous silence as they walked the short distance between Uncle Joseph's front gate and her own. There, however, he spoke.

"Look here! You don't haf to go and believe everything that ole girl told you, do you?"

"No," said Florence heartily. "I don't haf to."

"Well, look here," he urged, helpless but to repeat. "You don't haf to believe whatever it was she went and told you, do you?"

"What was it you think she told me, Herbert?"

"All that guff—you know. Well, whatever it was you *said* she told you."

"I didn't," said Florence. "I didn't say she told me anything at all."

"Well, she did, didn't she?"

"Why, no," Florence replied, lightly. "She didn't say anything to *me*. Only I'm glad to have your *opinion* of her, how she's such a story-teller and all—if I ever want to tell her, and everything!"

But Herbert had greater alarms than this, and the greater obscured the lesser. "Look here," he said, "if she didn't tell you, how'd you know it then?"

"How'd I know what?"

"That—that big story about my ever writin' I knew I had"—he gulped again—"pretty eyes."

"Oh, about *that!*" Florence said, and swung the gate shut between them. "Well, I guess it's too late to tell you to-night, Herbert; but maybe if you and that nasty little Henry Rooter do every single thing I tell you to, and do it just *exackly* like I tell you from this time on, why maybe—I only say 'maybe' —well, maybe I'll tell you some day when I feel like it."

She ran up the path and up the veranda steps, but paused before opening the front door, and called back to the waiting Herbert:

"The only person I'd ever *think* of tellin' about it before I tell you would be a boy I know." She coughed, and added as by an afterthought, "He'd just love to know all about it; I know he would. So, when I tell anybody about it I'll only tell just you and this other boy."

"What other boy?" Herbert demanded.

And her reply, trilling through the darkness, left him demoralized with horror.

"Wallie Torbin!"

The next afternoon, about four o'clock, Herbert stood gloomily at the main entrance of Atwater & Rooter's Newspaper Building awaiting his partner. The other entrances were not only nailed fast but massively barricaded; and this one (consisting of the ancient carriage-house doors, opening upon a driveway through the yard) had recently been made effective for exclusion. A long and heavy plank leaned against the wall, near by, ready to be set in hook-shaped iron supports fastened to the inner sides of the doors; and when the doors were closed, with this great plank in place, a person inside the building might seem entitled to count upon the enjoyment of privacy, except in case of earthquake, tornado, or fire. In fact, the size of the plank and the substantial quality of the iron fastenings could be looked upon, from a certain viewpoint, as a real compliment to the energy and persistence of Florence Atwater.

Herbert had been in no complimentary frame of mind, however, when he devised the obstructions, nor was he now in such a frame of mind. He was pessimistic in regard to his future, and also embarrassed in anticipation of some explanations it would be necessary to make to his partner. He strongly hoped that Henry's regular after-school appearance at the Newspaper Building would precede Florence's, because these explanations required both deliberation and tact, and he was convinced that it would be almost impossible to make them at all if Florence got there first.

He understood that he was unfortunately within her power; and he saw that it would be dangerous to place in operation for her exclusion from the Building this new mechanism contrived with such hopeful care, and at a cost of two dollars and twenty-five cents taken from the *Oriole's* treasury. What he wished Henry to believe was that for some good reason, which Herbert had not yet been able to invent, it would be better to show Florence a little politeness. He had a desperate hope that he might find some diplomatic way to prevail on Henry to be as subservient to Florence as she had seemed to demand, and he was determined to touch any extremity of unveracity, rather than permit the details of his answer in "Truth" to come to his partner's knowledge. Henry Rooter was not Wallie Torbin; but in possession of material such as this he could easily make himself intolerable.

Therefore, it was in a flurried state of mind that Herbert waited; and when his friend appeared, over the fence, his perturbation was not decreased. He even failed to notice the unusual gravity of Henry's manner.

"Hello, Henry! I thought I wouldn't start in working till you got here. I didn't want to haf to come all the way downstairs again to open the door and hi'st our good ole plank up again."

"I see," said Henry, glancing nervously at their good ole plank. "Well, I guess Florence'll never get in *this* good ole door—that is, she won't if we don't let her, or something."

This final clause would have astonished Herbert if he had been less pre-occupied with his troubles. "You bet she won't!" he said mechanically. "She couldn't ever get in here again—if the *family* didn't go intafering around and give me the dickens and everything, because they think—they *say* they do, anyhow—they say they think—they think——"

He paused, disguising a little choke as a cough of scorn for the family's thinking.

"What did you say your family think?" Henry asked absently.

"Well, they say we ought to let her have a share in our newspaper." Again he paused, afraid to continue lest his hypocrisy appear so bare-faced as to invite suspicion. "Well, maybe we *ought*," he said finally, his eyes guiltily upon his toe, which slowly scuffed the ground. "I don't say we ought, and I don't say we oughtn't."

He expected at the least a sharp protest from his partner, who, on the contrary, surprised him. "Well, that's the way *I* look at it," Henry said. "I don't say we ought and I don't say we oughtn't."

And he, likewise, stared at the toe of a shoe that scuffed the ground. Herbert felt a little better; this particular subdivision of his difficulties seemed to be working out with unexpected ease.

"I don't say we will and I don't say we won't," Henry added. "That's the way I look at it. My father and mother are always talkin' to me: how I got to be polite and everything, and I guess maybe it's time I began to pay some 'tention to what they say. You don't have your father and mother for always, you know, Herbert."

Herbert's mood at once chimed with this unprecedented filial melancholy. "No, you don't, Henry. That's what I often think about, myself. No, sir, a fellow doesn't have his father and mother to advise him our whole life, and you ought to do a good deal what they say while they're still alive."

"That's what I say," Henry agreed gloomily; and then, without any alteration of his tone, or of the dejected thoughtfulness of his attitude, he changed the subject in a way that painfully startled his companion. "Have you seen Wallie Torbin to-day, Herbert?"

"What!"

"Have you seen Wallie Torbin to-day?"

Herbert swallowed. "Why, what makes—what makes you ask me that, Henry?" he said.

"Oh, nothin'." Henry still kept his eyes upon his gloomily scuffing toe. "I just wondered, because I didn't happen to see him in school this afternoon when I happened to look in the door of the Eight-A when it was open. I didn't want to know on account of anything particular. I just happened to say that about him because I didn't have anything else to think about just then, so I just happened to think about him, the way you do when you haven't got anything much on your mind and might get to thinkin' about you can't tell what. That's all the way it was; I just happened to kind of wonder if he was around anywhere maybe."

Henry's tone was obviously, even elaborately, sincere; and Herbert was reassured. "Well, I didn't see him," he responded. "Maybe he's sick."

"No, he isn't," his friend said. "Florence said she saw him chasin' his dog down the street about noon."

At this Herbert's uneasiness was uncomfortably renewed. "*Florence* did? Where'd you see Florence?"

Mr. Rooter swallowed. "A little while ago," he said, and again swallowed. "On the way home from school."

"Look—look here!" Herbert was flurried to the point of panic. "Henry— did Florence—did she go and tell you—did she tell you——?"

"*I* didn't hardly notice what she was talkin' about," Henry said doggedly. "She didn't have anything to say that *I'd* ever care two cents about. She came up behind me and walked along with me a ways, but I got too many things on my mind to hardly pay the least attention to anything *she* ever talks about. She's a girl what I think about her the less people pay any 'tention to what she says the better off they are."

"That's the way with me, Henry," his partner assured him earnestly. "I never pay any notice to what *she* says. The way I figure it out about *her*, Henry, everybody'd be a good deal better off if nobody ever paid the least notice to anything she says. I never even notice what she says, myself."

"I don't either," said Henry. "All *I* think about is what my father and mother say, because I'm not goin' to have their advice all the rest o' my life, after they're dead. If they want me to be polite, why, I'll do it and that's all there is about it."

"It's the same way with me, Henry. If she comes flappin' around here blattin' and blubbin' how she's goin' to have somep'n to do with our newspaper, why, the only reason *I'd* ever let her would be because my *family* say I ought to show more politeness to her than up to now. I wouldn't do it on any other account, Henry."

"Neither would I. That's just the same way *I* look at it, Herbert. If I ever begin to treat her any better, she's got my father and mother to thank, not me. That's the only reason *I'd* be willing to say we better leave the plank down and let her in, if she comes around here like she's liable to."

"Well," said Herbert. "*I'm* willing. I don't want to get in trouble with the family."

And they mounted the stairs to their editorial, reportorial, and printing rooms; and began to work in a manner not only preoccupied but apprehensive. At intervals they would give each other a furtive glance, and then seem to reflect upon their fathers' and mothers' wishes and the troublous state of the times. Florence did not keep them waiting long, however.

She might have been easier to bear had her manner of arrival been less assured. She romped up the stairs, came skipping across the old floor, swinging her hat by a ribbon, flung open the gate in the sacred railing, and, flouncing into the principal chair, immodestly placed her feet on the table in front of that chair. Additionally, such was her lively humour, she affected to light and smoke the stub of a lead pencil. "Well, men," she said heartily, "I don't want to see any loafin' around here, men. I expect I'll have a pretty good newspaper this week; yes, sir, a pretty good newspaper, and I guess you men got to jump around a good deal to do everything I think of, or else maybe I guess I'll have to turn you off. I don't want to haf to do that, men."

The blackmailed partners made no reply, on account of an inability that was perfect for the moment. They stared at her helplessly, though not kindly; for in their expressions the conflict between desire and policy was almost staringly vivid. And such was their preoccupation, each with the bitterness of his own case, that neither wondered at the other's strange complaisance.

Florence made it clear to them that henceforth she was the editor of *The North End Daily Oriole*. (She said she had decided not to change the name.) She informed them that they were to be her printers; she did not care to get all inky and nasty herself, she said. She would, however, do all the writing for her newspaper, and had with her a new poem. Also, she would furnish all the news and it would be printed just as she wrote it, and printed *nicely*, too, or else—— She left the sentence unfinished.

Thus did this cool hand take possession of an established industry, and in much the same fashion did she continue to manage it. There were unsuppressible protests; there was covert anguish; there was even a strike—but it was a short one. When the printers remained away from their late Newspaper Building, on Wednesday afternoon, Florence had an interview with Herbert after dinner at his own door. He explained coldly that Henry and he had grown tired of the printing-press and had decided to put in all their spare time building a theatre in Henry's attic; but Florence gave him to understand that the theatre could not be; she preferred the *Oriole*.

Henry and Herbert had both stopped "speaking" to Patty Fairchild, for each believed her treacherous to himself; but Florence now informed Herbert that far from depending on mere hearsay, she had in her own possession the confession of his knowledge that he had ocular beauty; that she had discovered the paper where Patty had lost it; and that it was now in a secure place, and in an envelope, upon the outside of which was already written, "For Wallie Torbin. Kindness of Florence A."

Herbert surrendered.

So did Henry Rooter, a little later that evening, after a telephoned conversation with the slave-driver.

Therefore, the two miserable printers were back in their places the next afternoon. They told each other that the theatre they had planned wasn't so much after all; and anyhow your father and mother didn't last all your life, and it was better to do what they wanted, and be polite while they were alive.

And on Saturday the new *Oriole*, now in every jot and item the inspired organ of feminism, made its undeniably sensational appearance.

A copy, neatly folded, was placed in the hand of Noble Dill, as he set forth for his place of business, after lunching at home with his mother. Florence was the person who placed it there; she came hurriedly from somewhere in the neighbourhood, out of what yard or alley he did not notice, and slipped the little oblong sheet into his lax fingers.

"There!" she said breathlessly. "There's a good deal about you in it this week, Mr. Dill, and I guess—I guess——"

"What, Florence?"

"I guess maybe you'll——" She looked up at him shyly; then, with no more to say, turned and ran back in the direction whence she had come. Noble walked on, not at once examining her little gift, but carrying it absently in fingers still lax at the end of a dangling arm. There was no life in him for anything. Julia was away.

Away! And yet the dazzling creature looked at him from sky, from earth, from air; looked at him with the most poignant kindness, yet always shook her head! She had answered his first letter by a kind little note, his second by a kinder and littler one, and his third, fourth, fifth, and sixth by no note at all; but by the kindest message (through one of her aunts) that she was thinking about him a great deal. And even this was three weeks ago. Since then from Julia—nothing at all!

But yesterday something a little stimulating had happened. On the street, downtown, he had come face to face, momentarily, with Julia's father; and for the first time in Noble's life Mr. Atwater nodded to him pleasantly. Noble went on his way, elated. Was there not something almost fatherly in this strange greeting?

An event so singular might be interpreted in the happiest way: What had Julia written her father, to change him so toward Noble? And Noble was still dreamily interpreting as he walked down the street with *The North End Daily Oriole* idle in an idle hand.

He found a use for that hand presently, and, having sighed, lifted it to press it upon his brow, but did not complete the gesture. As his hand came within the scope of his gaze, levelled on the unfathomable distance, he observed that the fingers held a sheet of printed paper; and he remembered Florence. Instead of pressing his brow he unfolded the journal she had thrust upon him. As he began to read, his eye was lustreless, his gait slack and dreary; but soon his whole demeanour changed, it cannot be said for the better.

THE NORTH END DAILY ORIOLE

Atwater & Co., Owners & Propietors
Subscribe NOW 25 cents Per. Year. Sub-

scriptions should be brought to the East
Main Entrance of Atwater & Co., News-
               paper Building every afternoon
               430 to VI 25 Cents

POEMS

My Soul by Florence Atwater

When my heart is dreary
Then my soul is weary
As a bird with a broken wing
Who never again will sing
Like the sound of a vast amen
That comes from a church of men.

When my soul is dreary
It could never be cheery
But I think of my ideal
And everything seems real
Like the sound of the bright church bells peal.

Poems by Florence Atwater will be in
the paper each and every Sat.

Advertisements 45c. each Up

Joseph K. Atwater Co.
127 South Iowa St.
Steam Pumps

The News of the City

————

Miss Florence Atwater of tHis City
received a mark of 94 in History Examination
at the concusion of the school Term last June.

Blue hair ribbons are in style again.

Miss Patty Fairchild of this City has not
been doing as well in Declamation lately
as formerly.

MR. Noble Dill of this City is seldom
seen on the streets of the City without
smoking a cigarette.

Miss Julia Atwater of this City is out
of the City.

The MR. Rayfort family of this City
have been presentde with the present
of a new Cat by Geo. the man employeD by
Balf & CO. This cat is perfectly
baeutiful and still quit young.

Miss Julia Atwater of this City is visiting
friends in the Soth. The family have had

many letters from her that are read by each
and all of the famild.

Mr. Noble Dill of this City is in business
with his Father.

There was quite a wind storm Thursday doing
damage to shade trees in many parts of our
beautiful City.

From Letters to the family Miss Julia
Atwater of this City is enjoying her visit
in the south a greadeal.

Miss Patty Fairchild of the 7 A of this
City, will probably not pass in ARithmetiC—
unless great improvement takes place before
Examination.

Miss Julia Atwater of this City wrote a
letter to the family stating while visiting
in the SOuth she has made an engagement
to be married to MR. Crum of that City.
The family do not know who this MR. Crum
is but It is said he is a widower though
he has been diVorced with a great many
children.

The new ditch of the MR. Henry D. Vance,
backyard of this City is about through
now as little remain to be done and it is
thought the beighborhood will son look
better. Subscribe NOW 25c. Per Year Adv.
45c. up. Atwater & Co. Newspaper Building
25 Cents Per Years.

It may be assumed that the last of the news items was wasted upon Noble
Dill and that he never knew of the neighbourhood improvement believed
to be imminent as a result of the final touches to the ditch of the Mr. Henry
D. Vance back yard.

Throughout that afternoon adult members of the Atwater family connection
made futile efforts to secure all the copies of the week's edition of *The North
End Daily Oriole*. It could not be done.

It was a trying time for "the family." Great-Aunt Carrie said that she
had the "worst afternoon of any of 'em," because young Newland Sanders
came to her house at two and did not leave until five; all the time counting
over, one by one, the hours he'd spent with Julia since she was seventeen
and turned out, unfortunately, to be a Beauty. Newland had not restrained
himself, Aunt Carrie said, and long before he left she wished Julia had never

been born—and as for Herbert Illingsworth Atwater, Junior, the only thing to do with him was to send him to some strict Military School.

Florence's father telephoned to her mother from downtown at three, and said that Mr. George Plum and the ardent vocalist, Clairdyce, had just left his office. They had not called in company, however, but coincidentally; and each had a copy of *The North End Daily Oriole*, already somewhat worn with folding and unfolding. Mr. Clairdyce's condition was one of desperate calm, Florence's father said, but Mr. Plum's agitation left him rather unpresentable for the street, though he had finally gone forth with his hair just as he had rumpled it, and with his hat in his hand. They wished the truth, they said: Was it true or was it not true? Mr. Atwater had told them that he feared Julia was indeed engaged, though he knew nothing of her fiancé's previous marriage or marriages, or of the number of his children. They had responded that they cared nothing about that. This man Crum's record was a matter of indifference to them, they said. All they wanted to know was whether Julia was engaged or not—and she was!

"The odd thing to *me*," Mr. Atwater continued to his wife, "is where on earth Herbert could have got his story about this Crum's being a widower, and divorced, and with all those children. Do you know if Julia's written any of the family about these things and they haven't told the rest of us?"

"No," said Mrs. Atwater. "I'm sure she hasn't. Every letter she's written to any of us has passed all through the family, and I know I've seen every one of 'em. She's never said anything about him at all, except that he was a lawyer. I'm sure *I* can't imagine where Herbert got his awful information; I never thought he was the kind of boy to just make up such things out of whole cloth."

Florence, sitting quietly in a chair near by, with a copy of "Sesame and Lilies" in her lap, listened to her mother's side of this conversation with an expression of impersonal interest; and if she could have realized how completely her parents had forgotten (naturally enough) the details of their first rambling discussion of Julia's engagement, she might really have felt as little alarm as she showed.

"Well," said Mr. Atwater, "I'm glad *our* branch of the family isn't responsible. That's a comfort, anyhow, especially as people are reading copies of Herbert's dreadful paper all up and down the town, my clerk says. He tells me that over at the Unity Trust Company, where young Murdock Hawes is cashier, they only got hold of one copy, but typewrote it and multigraphed it, and some of 'em have already learned it by heart to recite to poor young Hawes. He's the one who sent Julia the three five-pound boxes of chocolates from New York all at the same time, you remember."

"Yes," Mrs. Atwater sighed. "Poor thing!"

"Florence is out among the family, I suppose?" he inquired.

"No; she's right here. She's just started to read Ruskin this afternoon. She says she's going to begin and read all of him straight through. That's very nice, don't you think?"

He seemed to muse before replying.

"I think that's very nice, at her age especially," Mrs. Atwater urged. "Don't you?"

"Ye-es! Oh, yes! At least I suppose so. Ah—you don't think—of course she hasn't had anything at all to do with this?"

"Well, I don't *see* how she could. You know Aunt Fanny told us how Herbert declared before them all, only last Sunday night, that Florence should never have one thing to do with his printing-press, and said they wouldn't even let her come near it."

"Yes, that's a fact. I'm glad Herbert made it so clear that she can't be implicated. I suppose the family are all pretty well down on Uncle Joseph?"

"Uncle Joseph is being greatly blamed," said Mrs. Atwater primly. "He really ought to have known better than to put such an instrument as a printing-press into the hands of an irresponsible boy of that age. Of course it simply encouraged him to print all kinds of things. We none of us think Uncle Joseph ever dreamed that Herbert would publish anything exactly like *this*, and of course Uncle Joseph says himself he never dreamed such a thing; he's said so time and time and time again, all afternoon. But of course he's greatly blamed."

"I suppose there've been quite a good many of 'em over there blaming him?" her husband inquired.

"Yes—until he telephoned to a garage and hired a car and went for a drive. He said he had plenty of money with him and didn't know when he'd be back."

"Serves him right," said Mr. Atwater. "Does anybody know where Herbert is?"

"Not yet!"

"Well——" and he returned to a former theme. "I *am* glad we aren't implicated. Florence is right there with you, you say?"

"Yes," Mrs. Atwater replied. "She's right here, reading. You aren't worried about her, are you?" she added.

"Oh, no; I'm sure it's all right. I only thought——"

"Only thought what?"

"Well, it *did* strike me as curious," said Mr. Atwater; "especially after Aunt Fanny's telling us how Herbert declared Florence could never have a single thing to do with his paper again——"

"Well, what?"

"Well, here's her poem right at the top of it, and a *very* friendly item about her history mark of last June. It doesn't seem like Herbert to be so complimentary to Florence, all of a sudden. Just struck me as rather curious; that's all."

"Why, yes," said Mrs. Atwater, "it does seem a little odd, when you think of it."

"Have you *asked* Florence if she had anything to do with getting out this week's *Oriole*?"

"Why, no; it never occurred to me, especially after what Aunt Fanny told us," said Mrs. Atwater. "I'll ask her now."

But she was obliged to postpone putting the intended question. "Sesame and Lilies" lay sweetly upon the seat of the chair that Florence had occupied; but Florence herself had gone somewhere else.

She had gone for a long, long ramble; and pedestrians who encountered her, and happened to notice her expression, were interested; and as they went on their way several of them interrupted the course of their meditations to say to themselves that she was the most thoughtful looking young girl they had ever seen. There was a touch of wistfulness about her, too; as of one whose benevolence must renounce all hope of comprehension and reward.

Now, among those who observed her unusual expression was a gentleman of great dimensions disposed in a closed automobile that went labouring among mudholes in an unpaved outskirt of the town. He rapped upon the glass before him, to get the driver's attention, and a moment later the car drew up beside Florence, as she stood in a deep reverie at the intersection of two roads.

Uncle Joseph opened the door and took his cigar from his mouth. "Get in, Florence," he said. "I'll take you for a ride." She started violently; whereupon he restored the cigar to his mouth, puffed upon it, breathing heavily the while as was his wont, and added, "I'n not going home. I'm out for a nice long ride. Get in."

"I was takin' a walk," she said dubiously. "I haf to take a whole lot of exercise, and I ought to walk and walk and walk. I guess I ought to keep on walkin'."

"Get in," he said. "I'm out riding. I don't know *when* I'll get home!"

Florence stepped in, Uncle Joseph closed the door, and the car slowly bumped onward.

"You know where Herbert is?" Uncle Joseph inquired.

"No," said Florence, in a gentle voice.

"I do," he said. "Herbert and your friend Henry Rooter came to our house with one of the last copies of the *Oriole* they were distributing to subscribers; and after I read it I kind of foresaw that the feller responsible for their owning a printing-press was going to be in some sort of family trouble or other. I had quite a talk with 'em and they hinted they hadn't had much to do with this number of the paper, except the mechanical end of it; but they wouldn't come out right full with what they meant. They seemed to have some good reason for protecting a third party, and said quite a good deal about their fathers and mothers being but mortal and so on; so Henry and Herbert thought they oughtn't to expose this third party—whoever she may happen to be. Well, I thought they better not stay too long, because I was compromised enough already, without being seen in their company; and I gave 'em something to help 'em out with at the movies. You can stay at movies an awful long time, and if you've got money enough to go to several of 'em, why, you're fixed for pretty near as long as you please. A body ought to be able to live a couple o' months at the movies for nine or ten dollars, I should think."

He was silent for a time, then asked, "I don't suppose your papa and mamma will be worrying about you, will they, Florence?"

"Oh, no!" she said quickly. "Not in the least! There was nothin' at all for me to do at our house this afternoon."

"That's good," he said, "because before we go back I was thinking some of driving around by way of Texas."

Florence looked at him trustfully and said nothing. It seemed to her that he suspected something; she was not sure; but his conversation was a little peculiar, though not in the least sinister. Indeed she was able to make out that he had more the air of an accomplice than of a prosecutor or a detective. Nevertheless, she was convinced that far, far the best course for her to pursue, during the next few days, would be one of steadfast reserve. And such a course was congenial to her mood, which was subdued, not to say apprehensive; though she was sure her recent conduct, if viewed sympathetically, would be found at least Christian. The trouble was that probably it would not be viewed sympathetically. No one would understand how carefully and tactfully she had prepared the items of the *Oriole* to lead suavely up to the news of Aunt Julia's engagement and break it to Noble Dill in a manner that would save his reason.

Therefore, on account of this probable lack of comprehension on the part of the family and public, it seemed to her that the only wise and good course to follow would be to claim nothing for herself, but to allow Herbert and Henry to remain undisturbed in full credit for publishing the *Oriole*. This involved a disappointment, it is true; nevertheless, she decided to bear it.

She had looked forward to surprising "the family" delightfully. As they fluttered in exclamation about her, she had expected to say, "Oh, the *poem* isn't so much, I guess—I wrote it quite a few days ago and I'm writing a couple new ones now—but I did take quite a lot o' time and trouble with the rest of the paper, because I had to write every single word of it, or else let Henry and Herbert try to, and 'course they'd just of ruined it. Oh, it isn't so much to talk about, I guess; it just sort of *comes* to me to do things that way."

Thirteen attempts to exercise a great philanthropy, and every grown person in sight, with the possible exception of Great-Uncle Joseph, goes into wholly unanticipated fits of horror. Cause and effect have no honest relation: Fate operates without justice or even rational sequence; life and the universe appear to be governed, not in order and with system, but by Chance, becoming sinister at any moment without reason.

And while Florence, thus a pessimist, sat beside fat Uncle Joseph during their long, long drive, relatives of hers were indeed going into fits; at least, so Florence would have described their gestures and incoherences of comment. Moreover, after the movies, straight into such a fitful scene did the luckless Herbert walk when urged homeward by thoughts of food, at about six that evening. Henry Rooter had strongly advised him against entering the house. "You better not," he said earnestly. "*Honest,* you better not, Herbert!"

"Well, we got apple dumplings for dinner," Herbert said, his tone showing the strain of mental uncertainty. "Eliza told me this morning we were goin' to have 'em. I kind of hate to go in, but I guess I better, Henry."

"*You* won't see any apple dumplings," Henry predicted.

"Well, I believe I better try it, Henry."

"You better come home with me. My father and mother'll be perfectly willing to have you."

"I know that," said Herbert. "But I guess I better go in and try it, anyhow, Henry. I didn't have anything to do with what's in the *Oriole.* It's every last word ole Florence's doing. I haven't got any more right to be picked on for that than a child."

"Yes," Henry admitted. "But if you go and tell 'em so, I bet she'd get even with you some way that would probably get *me* in trouble, too, before we get through with the job. *I* wouldn't tell 'em if I was you, Herbert!"

"Well, I wasn't intending to," Herbert responded gloomily; and the thought of each, unknown to the other, was the same, consisting of a symbolic likeness of Wallie Torbin at his worst. "I *ought* to tell on Florence; by rights I ought," said Herbert; "but I've decided I won't. There's no tellin' what she wouldn't do. Not that she could do anything to *me,* particyourly——"

"Nor me, either," his friend interposed hurriedly. "I don't worry about anything like that! Still, if I was you I wouldn't tell. She's only a girl, we got to remember."

"Yes," said Herbert. "That's the way *I* look at it, Henry; and the way I look at it is just simply this: long as she *is* a girl, why, simply let her go. You can't tell what she'd do, and so what's the use to go and tell on a girl?"

"That's the way *I* look at it," Henry agreed. "What's the use? If I was in your place, I'd act just the same way you do."

"Well," said Herbert, "I guess I better go on in the house, Henry. It's a good while after dark."

"You're makin' a big mistake!" Henry Rooter called after him. "*You* won't see any apple dumplings, I bet a hunderd dollars! You better come on home with me."

Herbert no more than half opened his front door before he perceived that his friend's advice had been excellent. So clearly Herbert perceived this, that he impulsively decided not to open the door any farther, but on the contrary to close it and retire; and he would have done so, had his mother not reached forth and detained him. She was, in fact, just inside that door, standing in the hall with one of his great-aunts, one of his aunts, two aunts-by-marriage, and an elderly unmarried cousin, who were all just on the point of leaving. However, they changed their minds and decided to remain, now that Herbert was among them.

The captive's father joined them, a few minutes later, but it had already become clear to Herbert that *The North End Daily Oriole* was in one sense a thing of the past, though in another sense this former owner and proprietor was certain that he would never hear the last of it. However, on account of the life of blackmail and slavery now led by the members of the old régime, the *Oriole's* extinction was far less painful to Herbert than his father supposed; and the latter wasted a great deal of severity, insisting that the printing-press should be returned that very night to Uncle Joseph. Herbert's heartiest retrospective wish was that the ole printing-press had been returned to Uncle Joseph long ago.

"If you can find him to give it to!" Aunt Harriet suggested. "Nobody *knows* where he goes when he gets the way he did this afternoon when we were discussing it with him! I only hope he'll be back to-night!"

"He can't stay away forever," Aunt Fanny remarked. "That garage is charging him five dollars an hour for the automobile he's in, and surely even Joseph will decide there's a limit to wildness *some* time!"

"I don't care when he comes back," Herbert's father declared grimly. "Whenever he does he's got to take that printing-press back—and Herbert will be let out of the house long enough to carry it over. His mother or I will go with him."

Herbert bore much more than this. He had seated himself on the third step of the stairway, and maintained as much dogged silence as he could. Once, however, they got a yelp of anguish out of him. It was when Cousin Virginia said: "Oh, Herbert, Herbert! How could you make up that terrible falsehood about Mr. Crum? And, *think* of it; right on the same page with your Cousin Florence's pure little poem!"

Herbert uttered sounds incoherent but loud, and expressive of a supreme physical revulsion. The shocked audience readily understood that he liked neither Cousin Virginia's chiding nor Cousin Florence's pure little poem.

"Shame!" said his father.

Herbert controlled himself. It could be seen that his spirit was broken, when Aunt Fanny mourned, shaking her head at him, smiling ruefully:

"Oh, if boys could only be girls!"

Herbert just looked at her.

"The worst thing," said his father;—"that is, if there's any part of it that's worse than another—the worst thing about it all is this rumour about Noble Dill."

"What about that poor thing?" Aunt Harriet asked. "We haven't heard."

"Why, I walked up from downtown with old man Dill," said Mr. Atwater, "and the Dill family all are very much worried. It seems that Noble started downtown after lunch, as usual, and pretty soon he came back to the house and he had a copy of this awful paper that little Florence had given him, and——"

"*Who* gave it to him?" Aunt Fanny asked. "*Who?*"

"Little Florence."

"Why, that's curious," Cousin Virginia murmured. "I must telephone and ask her mother about that."

The brooding Herbert looked up, and there was a gleam in his dogged eye; but he said nothing.

"Go on," Aunt Harriet urged. "What did Noble do?"

"Why, his mother said he just went up to his room and changed his shoes and necktie——"

"I thought so," Aunt Fanny whispered. "Crazy!"

"And then," Mr. Atwater continued, "he left the house and she supposed he'd gone down to the office; but she was uneasy, and telephoned his father. Noble hadn't come. He didn't come all afternoon, and he didn't go back to the house; and they telephoned around to every place he *could* go that they know of, and they couldn't find him or hear anything about him at all—not anywhere." Mr. Atwater coughed, and paused.

"But what," Aunt Harriet cried;—"*what* do they think's become of him?"

"Old man Dill said they were all pretty anxious," said Mr. Atwater. "They're afraid Noble has—they're afraid he's disappeared."

Aunt Fanny screamed.

Then, in perfect accord, they all turned to look at Herbert, who rose and would have retired upstairs had he been permitted.

As that perturbing evening wore on, word gradually reached the most outlying members of the Atwater family connection that Noble Dill was missing. Ordinarily, this bit of news would have caused them no severe anxiety. Noble's person and intellect were so commonplace—"insignificant" was the term usually preferred in his own circle—that he was considered to be as nearly negligible as it is charitable to consider a fellow-being. True, there was one thing that set him apart; he was found worthy of a superlative when he fell in love with Julia; and of course this distinction caused him to become better known and more talked about than he had been in his earlier youth.

However, the eccentricities of a person in such an extremity of love are seldom valued except as comedy, and even then with no warmth of heart for the comedian, but rather with an incredulous disdain; so it is safe to say that under other circumstances, Noble might have been missing, indeed, and few of the Atwaters would have missed him. But as matters stood they worried a great deal about him, fearing that a rash act on his part might reflect notoriety upon themselves on account of their beautiful relative—and *The North End Daily Oriole*. And when nine o'clock came and Mrs. Dill reported to Herbert's father, over the telephone, that nothing had yet been heard of her son, the pressure of those who were blaming the *Oriole* more than they blamed Julia became so wearing that Herbert decided he would rather spend the remaining days of his life running away from Wallie Torbin than put in any more of such a dog's evening as he *was* putting in. Thus he defined it.

He made a confession; that is to say, it was a proclamation. He proclaimed his innocence. He began history with a description of events distinctly subsequent to Sunday pastimes with Patty Fairchild, and explained how he and Henry had felt that their parents would not always be with them, and as their parents wished them to be polite, they had resolved to be polite to Florence. Proceeding, he related in detail her whole journalistic exploit.

Of the matter in hand he told the perfect and absolute truth—and was immediately refuted, confuted, and demonstrated to be a false witness by Aunt Fanny, Aunt Carrie, and Cousin Virginia, who had all heard him vehemently declare, no longer ago than the preceding Sunday evening, that he and his partner had taken secure measures to prevent Florence from ever again setting foot within the Newspaper Building. In addition, he was quite showered with definitions; and these, though so various, all sought to phrase but the one subject: his conduct in seeking to drag Florence into the mire, when she was absent and could not defend herself. Poor Florence would answer later in the evening, he was told severely; and though her cause was thus championed against the slander, it is true that some of her defenders felt stirrings of curiosity in regard to Florence. In fact, there was getting to be something almost like a cloud upon her reputation. There were several things for her to explain;—among them, her taking it upon herself to see that Noble received a copy of the *Oriole*, and also her sudden departure from home and rather odd protraction of absence therefrom. It was not thought she was in good company. Uncle Joseph had telephoned from a suburb that they were dining at a farmhouse and would thence descend to the general region of the movies.

"*Nobody* knows what that man'll do, when he decides to!" Aunt Carrie said nervously. "Letting the poor child stay up so late! She ought to be in bed this minute, even if it is Saturday night! Or else she ought to be here to listen to her own bad little cousin trying to put his terrible responsibility on her shoulders."

One item of this description of himself the badgered Herbert could not bear in silence, although he had just declared that since the truth was so ill-respected among his persecutors he would open his mouth no more until the day of his death. He passed over "bad," but furiously stated his height in feet, inches, and fractions of inches.

Aunt Fanny shook her head in mourning. "That may be, Herbert," she said gently. "But you must try to realize it can't bring poor young Mr. Dill back to his family."

Again Herbert just looked at her. He had no indifference more profound than that upon which her strained conception of the relation between cause and effect seemed to touch;—from his point of view, to be missing should be the lightest of calamities. It is true that he was concerned with the restoration of Noble Dill to the rest of the Dills so far as such an event might affect his own incomparable misfortunes, but not otherwise. He regarded Noble and Noble's disappearance merely as unfair damage to himself, and he continued to look at this sorrowing great-aunt of his until his thoughts made his strange gaze appear to her so hardened that she shook her head and looked away.

"Poor young Mr. Dill!" she said. "If someone could only have been with him and kept talking to him until he got used to the idea a little!"

Cousin Virginia nodded comprehendingly. "Yes, it might have tided him over," she said. "He wasn't handsome, nor impressive, of course, nor anything like that, but he always spoke so nicely to people on the street. I'm sure he never harmed even a kitten, poor soul!"

"I'm sure he never did," Herbert's mother agreed gently. "Not even a kitten. I do wonder where he is now."

But Aunt Fanny uttered a little cry of protest. "I'm afraid we may hear!" she said. "Any moment!"

Love at Seventeen

William Sylvanus Baxter paused for a moment of thought in front of the drug-store at the corner of Washington Street and Central Avenue. He had an internal question to settle before he entered the store: he wished to allow the young man at the soda-fountain no excuse for saying, "Well, make up your mind what it's goin' to be, can't you?" Rudeness of this kind, especially in the presence of girls and women, was hard to bear, and though William Sylvanus Baxter had borne it upon occasion, he had reached an age when he found it intolerable. Therefore, to avoid offering opportunity for anything of the kind, he decided upon chocolate and strawberry, mixed, before approaching the fountain. Once there, however, and a large glass of these flavors and diluted ice-cream proving merely provocative, he said, languidly—an affectation, for he could have disposed of half a dozen with gusto: "Well, now I'm here, I might as well go one more. Fill 'er up again. Same."

Emerging to the street, penniless, he bent a fascinated and dramatic gaze upon his reflection in the drug-store window, and then, as he turned his back upon the alluring image, his expression altered to one of lofty and uncondescending amusement. That was his glance at the passing public. From the heights, he seemed to bestow upon the world a mysterious derision—for William Sylvanus Baxter was seventeen long years of age, and had learned to present the appearance of one who possesses inside information about life and knows all strangers and most acquaintances to be of inferior caste, costume, and intelligence.

He lingered upon the corner awhile, not pressed for time. Indeed, he found many hours of these summer months heavy upon his hands, for he had no important occupation, unless some intermittent dalliance with a work on geometry (anticipatory of the distant autumn) might be thought important, which is doubtful, since he usually went to sleep on the shady side porch at his home, with the book in his hand. So, having nothing to call him elsewhere, he lounged before the drug-store in the early afternoon sunshine, watching the passing to and fro of the lower orders and bourgeoisie of the middle-sized midland city which claimed him (so to speak) for a native son.

Apparently quite unembarrassed by his presence, they went about their business, and the only people who looked at him with any attention were pedestrians of color. It is true that when the gaze of these fell upon him it was instantly arrested, for no colored person could have passed him without a little pang of pleasure and of longing. Indeed, the tropical violence of William Sylvanus Baxter's tie and the strange brilliancy of his hat might have made it positively unsafe for him to walk at night through the negro quarter of the town. And though no man could have sworn to the color of that hat, whether it was blue or green, yet its color was a saner thing than its shape, which was blurred, tortured, and raffish; it might have been the miniature model of a volcano that had blown off its cone and misbehaved disastrously on its lower slopes as well. He had the air of wearing it as a matter of course and with careless ease, but that was only an air—it was the apple of his eye.

For the rest, his costume was neutral, subordinate, and even a little neglected in the matter of a detail or two: one pointed flap of his soft collar was held down by a button, but the other showed a frayed thread where the button once had been; his low patent-leather shoes were of a luster not solicitously cherished, and there could be no doubt that he needed to get his hair cut, while something might have been done, too, about the individualized hirsute prophecies which had made independent appearances, here and there, upon his chin. He examined these from time to time by the sense of touch, passing his hand across his face and allowing his finger-tips a slight tapping motion wherever they detected a prophecy.

Thus he fell into a pleasant musing and seemed to forget the crowded street.

He was roused by the bluff greeting of an acquaintance not dissimilar to himself in age, manner, and apparel.

"H'lo, Silly Bill!" said this person, halting beside William Sylvanus Baxter. "What's the news?"

William showed no enthusiasm; on the contrary, a frown of annoyance appeared upon his brow. The nickname "Silly Bill"—long ago compounded by merry child-comrades from "William" and "Sylvanus"—was not to his taste, especially in public, where he preferred to be addressed simply and manfully as "Baxter." Any direct expression of resentment, however, was difficult, since it was plain that Johnnie Watson intended no offense whatever and but spoke out of custom.

"Don't know any," William replied, coldly.

"Dull times, ain't it?" said Mr. Watson, a little depressed by his friend's manner. "I heard May Parcher was comin' back to town yesterday, though."

"Well, let her!" returned William, still severe.

"They said she was goin' to bring a girl to visit her," Johnnie began in a confidential tone. "They said she was a reg'lar ringdinger and—"

"Well, what if she is?" the discouraging Mr. Baxter interrupted. "Makes little difference to *me*, I guess!"

"Oh no, it don't. *You* don't take any interest in girls! *Oh* no!"

"No, I do not!" was the emphatic and heartless retort. "I never saw one in my life I'd care whether she lived or died!"

"Honest?" asked Johnnie, struck by the conviction with which this speech was uttered. "Honest, is that so?"

"Yes, 'honest'!" William replied, sharply. "They could *all* die, *I* wouldn't notice!"

Johnnie Watson was profoundly impressed. "Why, *I* didn't know you felt that way about 'em, Silly Bill. I always thought you were kind of—"

"Well, I do feel that way about 'em!" said William Sylvanus Baxter, and, outraged by the repetition of the offensive nickname, he began to move away. "You can tell 'em so for me, if you want to!" he added over his shoulder. And he walked haughtily up the street, leaving Mr. Watson to ponder upon this case of misogyny, never until that moment suspected.

It was beyond the power of his mind to grasp the fact that William Sylvanus Baxter's cruel words about "girls" had been uttered because William was annoyed at being called "Silly Bill" in a public place, and had not known how to object otherwise than by showing contempt for any topic of conversation proposed by the offender. This latter, being of a disposition to accept statements as facts, was warmly interested, instead of being hurt, and decided that here was something worth talking about, especially with representatives of the class so sweepingly excluded from the sympathies of Silly Bill.

William, meanwhile, made his way toward the "residence section" of the town, and presently—with the passage of time—found himself eased of his annoyance. He walked in his own manner, using his shoulders to emphasize an effect of carelessness which he wished to produce upon observers. For his consciousness of observers was abnormal, since he had it whether any one was looking at him or not, and it reached a crucial stage whenever he perceived persons of his own age, but of opposite sex, approaching.

A person of this description was encountered upon the sidewalk within a hundred yards of his own home, and William Sylvanus Baxter saw her while yet she was afar off. The quiet and shady thoroughfare was empty of all human life, at the time, save for those two; and she was upon the same side of the street that he was; thus it became inevitable that they should meet, face to face, for the first time in their lives. He had perceived, even in the distance, that she was unknown to him, a stranger, because he knew all the girls in this part of the town who dressed as famously in the mode as that! And then, as the distance between them lessened, he saw that she was ravishingly pretty; far, far prettier, indeed, than any girl he knew. At least it seemed so, for it is, unfortunately, much easier for strangers to be beautiful. Aside from this advantage of mystery, the approaching vision was piquant and graceful enough to have reminded a much older boy of a spotless white kitten, for, in spite of a charmingly managed demureness, there was precisely that kind of playfulness somewhere expressed about her. Just now it was most definite in the look she bent upon the light and fluffy burden which she carried nestled in the inner curve of her right arm: a tiny dog with hair like cotton and a pink ribbon round his neck—an animal sated with indulgence and idiotically unaware of his privilege. He was half asleep!

William did not see the dog, for it is the plain, anatomical truth-that when he saw how pretty the girl was, his heart—his physical heart—began to do things the like of which, experienced by an elderly person, would have brought the doctor in haste. In addition, his complexion altered—he broke out in fiery patches. He suffered from breathlessness and from pressure on the diaphragm.

Afterward, he could not have named the color of the little parasol she carried in her left hand, and yet, as it drew nearer and nearer, a rosy haze suffused the neighborhood, and the whole world began to turn an exquisite pink. Beneath this gentle glow, with eyes downcast in thought, she apparently took no note of William, even when she and William had come within a few yards of each other. Yet he knew that she would look up and that their eyes must meet—a thing for which he endeavored to prepare himself by a strange weaving motion of his neck against the friction of his collar—for thus, instinctively, he strove to obtain greater ease and some decent appearance of manly indifference. He felt that his efforts were a failure; that his agitation was ruinous and must be perceptible at a distance of miles, not feet. And then, in the instant of panic that befell, when her dark-lashed eyelids slowly lifted, he had a flash of inspiration.

He opened his mouth somewhat, and as her eyes met his, full and startlingly, he placed three fingers across the orifice, and also offered a slight vocal proof that she had surprised him in the midst of a yawn.

"Oh, hum!" he said.

For the fraction of a second, the deep blue spark in her eyes glowed brighter—gentle arrows of turquoise shot him through and through—and then her glance withdrew from the ineffable collision. Her small, white-shod feet continued to bear her onward, away from him, while his own dimmed shoes peregrinated in the opposite direction—William necessarily, yet with excruciating reluctance, accompanying them. But just at the moment when he and the lovely creature were side by side, and her head turned from him, she spoke—that is, she murmured, but he caught the words.

"You Flopit, wake up!" she said, in the tone of a mother talking baby-talk. "So indifferink!"

William's feet and his breath halted spasmodically. For an instant he thought she had spoken to him, and then for the first time he perceived the fluffy head of the dog bobbing languidly over her arm, with the motion of her walking; and he comprehended that Flopit, and not William Sylvanus Baxter, was the gentleman addressed. But—but had she *meant* him?

His breath returning, though not yet operating in its usual manner, he stood gazing after her, while the glamorous parasol passed down the shady street, catching splashes of sunshine through the branches of the maple-trees; and the cottony head of the tiny dog continued to be visible, bobbing rhythmically over a filmy sleeve. Had she meant that William was indifferent? Was it William that she really addressed?

He took two steps to follow her, but a suffocating shyness stopped him abruptly and, in a horror lest she should glance round and detect him in the act, he turned and strode fiercely to the gate of his own home before he dared to look again. And when he did look, affecting great casualness in the action, she was gone, evidently having turned the corner. Yet the street did not seem quite empty; there was still something warm and fragrant about it, and a rosy glamor lingered in the air. William rested an elbow upon the gate-post, and with his chin reposing in his hand gazed long in the direction in which the unknown had vanished. And his soul was tremulous, for she had done her work but too well.

" 'Indifferink'!" he murmured, thrilling at his own exceedingly indifferent imitation of her voice. "Indifferink!" that was just what he would have her think—that he was a cold, indifferent man. It was what he wished all girls to think. And "sarcastic"! He had been envious one day when May Parcher said that Joe Bullitt was "awfully sarcastic." William had spent the ensuing hour in an object-lesson intended to make Miss Parcher see that William Sylvanus Baxter was twice as sarcastic as Joe Bullitt ever thought of being, but this great effort had been unsuccessful, because William failed to understand that Miss Parcher had only been sending a sort of message to Mr. Bullitt. It was a device not unique among her sex; her hope was that William would repeat her remark in such a manner that Joe Bullitt would hear it and call to inquire what she meant.

" 'So indifferink'!" murmured William, leaning dreamily upon the gate-post. "Indifferink!" He tried to get the exact cooing quality of the unknown's voice. "Indifferink!" And, repeating the honeyed word, so entrancingly distorted, he fell into a kind of stupor; vague, beautiful pictures rising before him, the one least blurred being of himself, on horseback, sweeping between Flopit and a racing automobile. And then, having restored the little animal to its mistress, William sat carelessly in the saddle (he had the Guardsman's seat) while the perfectly trained steed wheeled about, forelegs in the air, preparing to go. "But shall I not see you again, to thank you more properly?" she cried, pleading. "Some other day—perhaps," he answered.

And left her in a cloud of dust.

"Oh, Will—ee!"

Thus a shrill voice, to his ears hideously different from that other, interrupted and dispersed his visions. Little Jane, his ten-year-old sister, stood upon the front porch, the door open behind her, and in her hand she held a large slab of bread-and-butter covered with apple sauce and powdered sugar. Evidence that she had sampled this compound was upon her cheeks, and to her brother she was a repulsive sight.

"Will—ee!" she shrilled. "Look! *Good!*" And to emphasize the adjective she indelicately patted the region of her body in which she believed her stomach to be located. "There's a slice for you on the dining-room table," she informed him, joyously.

Outraged, he entered the house without a word to her, and, proceeding to the dining-room, laid hands upon the slice she had mentioned, but declined to eat it in Jane's company. He was in an exalted mood, and though in no condition of mind or body would he refuse food of almost any kind, Jane was an intrusion he could not suffer at this time.

He carried the refection to his own room and, locking the door, sat down to eat, while, even as he ate, the spell that was upon him deepened in intensity.

"Oh, eyes!" he whispered, softly, in that cool privacy and shelter from the world. "Oh, eyes of blue!"

The mirror of a dressing-table sent him the reflection of his own eyes, which also were blue; and he gazed upon them and upon the rest of his image the while he ate his bread-and-butter and apple sauce and sugar. Thus, watching himself eat, he continued to stare dreamily at the mirror until the bread-and-butter and apple sauce and sugar had disappeared, whereupon he rose and approached the dressing-table to study himself at greater advantage.

He assumed as repulsive an expression as he could command, at the same time making the kingly gesture of one who repels unwelcome attentions; and it is beyond doubt that he was thus acting a little scene of indifference. Other symbolic dramas followed, though an invisible observer might have been puzzled for a key to some of them. One, however, would have proved easily intelligible: his expression having altered to a look of pity and contrition, he turned from the mirror, and, walking slowly to a chair across the room, used his right hand in a peculiar manner, seeming to stroke the air at a point about ten inches above the back of the chair. "There, there, little girl," he said in a low, gentle voice. "I didn't know you cared!"

Then, with a rather abrupt dismissal of this theme, he returned to the mirror and, after a questioning scrutiny, nodded solemnly, forming with his lips the words, "The real thing—the real thing at last!" He meant that, after many imitations had imposed upon him, Love—the real thing—had come to him in the end. And as he turned away he murmured, "And even her name —unknown!"

This evidently was a thought that continued to occupy him, for he walked up and down the room, frowning; but suddenly his brow cleared and his eye lit with purpose. Seating himself at a small writing-table by the window, he proceeded to express his personality—though with considerable labor—in something which he did not doubt to be a poem.

Three-quarters of an hour having sufficed for its completion, including "rewriting and polish," he solemnly signed it, and then read it several times in a state of hushed astonishment. He had never dreamed that he could do anything like this:

MILADY

I do not know her name
Though it would be the same
Where roses bloom at twilight
And the lark takes his flight
It would be the same anywhere
Where music sounds in air
I was never introduced to the lady
So I could not call her Lass or Sadie
So I will call her Milady
By the sands of the sea
She always will be
Just Milady to me.
WILLIAM SYLVANUS BAXTER, Esq., July 14

It is impossible to say how many times he might have read the poem over, always with increasing amazement at his new-found powers, had he not been interrupted by the odious voice of Jane.

"Will—ee!"

To William, in his high and lonely mood, this piercing summons brought an actual shudder, and the very thought of Jane (with tokens of apple sauce and sugar still upon her cheek, probably) seemed a kind of sacrilege. He fiercely swore his favorite oath, acquired from the hero of a work of fiction he admired, "Ye gods!" and concealed his poem in the drawer of the writing-table, for Jane's footsteps were approaching his door.

"Will—ee! Mamma wants you." She tried the handle of the door.

"G'way!" he said.

"Will—ee!" Jane hammered upon the door with her fist. "Will—ee!"

"What you want?" he shouted.

Jane explained, certain pauses indicating that her attention was partially diverted to another slice of bread-and-butter and apple sauce and sugar. "Will—ee, mamma wants you—wants you to go help Genesis bring some wash-tubs home—and a tin clo'es-boiler—from the second-hand man's store."

"What!"

Jane repeated the outrageous message, adding, "She wants you to hurry—and I got some more bread-and-butter and apple sauce and sugar for comin' to tell you."

William left no doubt in Jane's mind about his attitude in reference to the whole matter. His refusal was direct and infuriated, but, in the midst of a multitude of plain statements which he was making, there was a decisive tapping upon the door at a point higher than Jane could reach, and his mother's voice interrupted:

"Hush, Willie! Open the door, please."

He obeyed furiously, and Mrs. Baxter walked in with a deprecating air, while Jane followed, so profoundly interested that, until almost the close of the interview, she held her bread-and-butter and apple sauce and sugar at a sort of way-station on its journey to her mouth.

"That's a nice thing to ask me to do!" stormed the unfortunate William. "Ye gods! Do you think Joe Bullitt's mother would dare to—"

"Wait, dearie!" Mrs. Baxter begged, pacifically. "I just want to explain—"

" 'Explain'! Ye gods!"

"Now, now, just a minute, Willie!" she said. "What I wanted to explain was why it's necessary for you to go with Genesis for the—"

"Never!" he shouted. "Never! You expect me to walk through the public streets with that awful-lookin' old nigger—"

"Genesis isn't old," she managed to interpolate. "He—"

But her frantic son disregarded her. "Second-hand wash-tubs!" he vociferated. "And tin clothes-boilers! *That's* what you want your *son* to carry through the public streets in broad daylight! Ye gods!"

"Well, there isn't anybody else," she said. "Please don't rave so, Willie, and say 'Ye gods' so much; it really isn't nice. I'm sure nobody'll notice you—"

" 'Nobody'!" His voice cracked in anguish. "Oh no! Nobody except the whole town! *Why*, when there's anything disgusting has to be done in this family—why do *I* always have to be the one? Why can't Genesis bring the second-hand wash-tubs without *me*? Why can't the second-hand store deliver 'em? Why can't—"

"That's what I want to tell you," she interposed, hurriedly, and as the youth lifted his arms on high in a gesture of ultimate despair, and then threw himself miserably into a chair, she obtained the floor. "The second-hand store doesn't deliver things," she said. "I bought them at an auction, and it's going out of business, and they have to be taken away before half past four this afternoon. Genesis can't bring them in the wheelbarrow, because, he says, the wheel is broken, and he says he can't possibly carry two tubs and a wash-boiler himself; and he can't make two trips because it's a mile and a half, and I don't like to ask him, anyway; and it would take too long, because he has to get back and finish cutting the grass before your papa gets home this evening. Papa said he *had* to! Now, I don't like to ask you, but it really isn't much. You and Genesis can just slip up there and—"

"Slip!" moaned William. " 'Just *slip* up there'! Ye gods!"

"Genesis is waiting on the back porch," she said. "Really it isn't worth your making all this fuss about."

"Oh no!" he returned, with plaintive satire. "It's nothing! Nothing at all!"

"Why, *I* shouldn't mind it," she said, briskly, "if I had the time. In fact, I'll have to, if you won't."

"Ye gods!" He clasped his head in his hands, crushed, for he knew that the curse was upon him and he must go. "Ye gods!"

And then, as he stamped to the door, his tragic eye fell upon Jane, and he emitted a final cry of pain:

"Can't you *ever* wash your face?" he shouted.

Genesis and his dog were waiting just outside the kitchen door, and of all the world these two creatures were probably the last in whose company William Sylvanus Baxter desired to make a public appearance. Genesis was an out-of-doors man and seldom made much of a toilet; his overalls in particular betraying at important points a lack of the anxiety he should have felt, since only Genesis himself, instead of a supplementary fabric, was directly underneath them. And the aged, grayish, sleeveless and neckless garment which sheltered him from waist to collar-bone could not have been mistaken for a jersey, even though what there was of it was dimly of a jerseyesque character. Upon the feet of Genesis were things which careful study would have revealed to be patent-leather dancing-pumps, long dead and several times buried; and upon his head, pressing down his markedly criminal ears, was a once-derby hat of a brown not far from Genesis's own color, though decidedly without his gloss. A large ring of strange metal, with the stone missing, adorned a finger of his right hand, and from a corner of his mouth projected an unlighted and spreading cigar stub which had the appearance of belonging to its present owner merely by right of salvage.

And Genesis's dog, scratching himself at his master's feet, was the true complement of Genesis, for although he was a youngish dog, and had not long been the property of Genesis, he was a dog that would have been recognized anywhere in the world as a colored person's dog. He was not a special breed of dog—though there was something rather houndlike about him—he was just a dog. His expression was grateful but anxious, and he was unusually bald upon the bosom, but otherwise whitish and brownish, with a gaunt, haunting face and no power to look anybody in the eye.

He rose apprehensively as the fuming William came out of the kitchen, but he was prepared to follow his master faithfully, and when William and Genesis reached the street the dog was discovered at their heels, whereupon William came to a decisive halt.

"Send that dog back," he said, resolutely. "I'm not going through the streets with a dog like that, anyhow!"

Genesis chuckled. "He ain' goin' back," he said. "'Ain' nobody kin make 'at dog go back. I 'ain' had him mo'n two weeks, but I don' b'lieve Pres'dent United States kin make 'at dog go back! I show you." And, wheeling suddenly, he made ferocious gestures, shouting, "G'on back, dog!"

The dog turned, ran back a few paces, halted, and then began to follow again, whereupon Genesis pretended to hurl stones at him; but the animal only repeated his manœuver—and he repeated it once more when William aided Genesis by using actual missiles, which were dodged with almost careless adeptness.

"I'll show him!" said William, hotly. "I'll show him he can't follow *me!*" He charged upon the dog, shouting fiercely, and this seemed to do the work, for the hunted animal, abandoning his partial flights, turned a tucked-under tail, ran all the way back to the alley, and disappeared from sight. "There!" said William. "I guess that'll show him!"

"I ain' bettin' on it!" said Genesis, as they went on. "He nev' did stop foll'in' me yet. I reckon he the foll'indest dog in the worl'! Name Clem."

"Well, he can't follow *me!*" said the surging William, in whose mind's eye lingered the vision of an exquisite doglet, with pink-ribboned throat and a cottony head bobbing gently over a filmy sleeve. "He doesn't come within a mile of *me*, no matter what his name is!"

"Name Clem fer short," said Genesis, amiably. "I trade in a mandoline fer him what had her neck kind o' busted off on one side. I couldn' play her nohow, an' I found her, anyways. Yessuh, I trade in 'at mandoline fer him 'cause always did like to have me a good dog—but I d'in' have me no name fer him; an' this here Blooie Bowers, what I trade in the mandoline to, he say *he* d'in' have no name fer him. Say nev' did know if *was* a name fer him 'tall. So I'z spen' the evenin' at 'at lady's house, Fanny, what used to be cook fer Miz Johnson, nex' do' you' maw's; an' I ast Fanny what am I go'n' a do about it, an' Fanny say, 'Call him Clematis,' she say. ''At's a nice name!' she say. 'Clematis.' So 'at's name I name him, Clematis. Call him Clem fer short, but Clematis his real name. He'll come, whichever one you call him, Clem or Clematis. Make no diff'ence to him, long's he git his vittles. Clem or Clematis, *he* ain' carin'!"

William's ear was deaf to this account of the naming of Clematis; he walked haughtily, but as rapidly as possible, trying to keep a little in advance of his talkative companion, who had never received the training as a servitor which should have taught him his proper distance from the Young Master. William's suffering eyes were fixed upon remoteness; and his lips moved, now and then, like a martyr's, pronouncing inaudibly a sacred word. "Milady! Oh, Milady!"

Thus they had covered some three blocks of their journey—the too-democratic Genesis chatting companionably and William burning with mortification—when the former broke into loud laughter.

"What I tell you?" he cried, pointing ahead. "Look ayonnuh! No, suh, Pres'dent United States hisse'f ain' go tell 'at dog stay home!"

And there, at the corner before them, waited Clematis, roguishly lying in a mud-puddle in the gutter. He had run through alleys parallel to their course—and in the face of such demoniac cunning the wretched William despaired of evading his society. Indeed, there was nothing to do but to give up, and so the trio proceeded, with William unable to decide which contaminated him more, Genesis or the loyal Clematis. To his way of thinking, he was part of a dreadful pageant, and he winced pitiably whenever the eye of a respectable passer-by fell upon him. Everybody seemed to stare—nay, to leer! And he felt that the whole world would know his shame by nightfall.

Nobody, he reflected, seeing him in such company, could believe that he belonged to "one of the oldest and best families in town." Nobody would understand that he was not walking with Genesis for the pleasure of his companionship—until they got the tubs and the wash-boiler, when his social condition must be thought even more degraded. And nobody, he was shudderingly positive, could see that Clematis was not his dog. Clematis kept himself humbly a little in the rear, but how was any observer to know that he belonged to Genesis and not to William?

And how frightful that *this* should befall him on such a day, the very day that his soul had been split asunder by the turquoise shafts of Milady's eyes and he had learned to know the Real Thing at last!

"Milady! Oh, Milady!"

For in the elder teens adolescence may be completed, but not by experience, and these years know their own tragedies. It is the time of life when one finds it unendurable not to seem perfect in all outward matters: in worldly position, in the equipments of wealth, in family, and in the grace, elegance, and dignity of all appearances in public. And yet the youth is continually betrayed by the child still intermittently insistent within him, and by the child which undiplomatic people too often assume him to be. Thus with William's attire: he could ill have borne any suggestion that it was not of the mode, but taking care of it was a different matter. Also, when it came to his appetite, he could and would eat anything at any time, but something younger than his years led him—often in semi-secrecy—to candy-stores and soda-water fountains and ice-cream parlors; he still relished green apples and knew cravings for other dangerous inedibles. But these survivals were far from painful to him; what injured his sensibilities was the disposition on the part of people—especially his parents, and frequently his aunts and uncles —to regard him as a little boy. Briefly, the deference his soul demanded in its own right, not from strangers only, but from his family, was about that which is supposed to be shown a Grand Duke visiting his Estates. Therefore William suffered often.

But the full ignominy of the task his own mother had set him this afternoon was not realized until he and Genesis set forth upon the return journey from the second-hand shop, bearing the two wash-tubs, a clothes-wringer (which Mrs. Baxter had forgotten to mention), and the tin boiler— and followed by the lowly Clematis.

There was something really pageant-like about the little excursion now, and the glittering clothes-boiler, borne on high, sent flashing lights far down the street. The wash-tubs were old-fashioned, of wood; they refused to fit one within the other; so William, with his right hand, and Genesis, with his left, carried one of the tubs between them; Genesis carried the heavy wringer with his right hand, and he had fastened the other tub upon his back by means of a bit of rope which passed over his shoulder; thus the tin boiler, being a lighter burden, fell to William.

The cover would not stay in place, but continually fell off when he essayed to carry the boiler by one of its handles, and he made shift to manage the accursed thing in various ways—the only one proving physically endurable being, unfortunately, the most grotesque. He was forced to carry the cover in his left hand and to place his head partially within the boiler itself, and to support it—tilted obliquely to rest upon his shoulders—as a kind of monstrous tin cowl or helmet. This had the advantage of somewhat concealing his face, though when he leaned his head back, in order to obtain clearer vision of what was before him, the boiler slid off and fell to the pavement with a noise that nearly caused a runaway, and brought the hot-cheeked William much derisory attention from a passing street-car. However, he presently caught the knack of keeping it in position, and it fell no more.

Seen from the rear, William was unrecognizable—but interesting. He appeared to be a walking clothes-boiler, armed with a shield and connected, by means of a wash-tub, with a negro of informal ideas concerning dress. In fact, the group was whimsical, and three young people who turned in behind it, out of a cross-street, indulged immediately in fits of inadequately suppressed laughter, though neither Miss May Parcher nor Mr. Johnnie Watson even remotely suspected that the legs beneath the clothes-boiler belonged to an acquaintance. And as for the third of this little party, Miss Parcher's visitor, those peregrinating legs suggested nothing familiar to her.

"Oh, see the fun-ee laundrymans!" she cried, addressing a cottony doglet's head that bobbed gently up and down over her supporting arm. "Sweetest Flopit must see, too! Flopit, look at the fun-ee laundrymans!"

"'Sh!" murmured Miss Parcher, choking. "He might hear you."

He might, indeed, since they were not five yards behind him and the dulcet voice was clear and free. Within the shadowy interior of the clothes-boiler were features stricken with sudden, utter horror. "*Flopit!*"

The attention of Genesis was attracted by a convulsive tugging of the tub which he supported in common with William; it seemed passionately to urge greater speed. A hissing issued from the boiler, and Genesis caught the words, huskily whispered:

"Walk faster! You got to walk faster."

The tub between them tugged forward with a pathos of appeal wasted upon the easy-going Genesis.

"I got plenty time cut 'at grass befo' you' pa gits home," he said, reassuringly. "Thishere rope what I got my extry tub slung to is 'mos' wo' plum thew my hide."

Having uttered this protest, he continued to ambulate at the same pace, though somewhat assisted by the forward pull of the connecting tub, an easance of burden which he found pleasant; and no supplementary message came from the clothes-boiler, for the reason that it was incapable of further speech. And so the two groups maintained for a time their relative positions, about fifteen feet apart.

The amusement of the second group having abated through satiety, the minds of its components turned to other topics. "Now Flopit must have his darlin' 'ickle run," said Flopit's mistress, setting the doglet upon the ground. "That's why sweetest Flopit and I and all of us came for a walk, instead of sitting on the nice, cool porchkins. *See* the sweetie toddle! Isn't he adorable, May? *Isn't* he adorable, Mr. Watson?"

Mr. Watson put a useless sin upon his soul, since all he needed to say was a mere "Yes." He fluently avowed himself to have become insane over the beauty of Flopit.

Flopit, placed upon the ground, looked like something that had dropped from a Christmas tree, and he automatically made use of fuzzy legs, somewhat longer than a caterpillar's, to patter after his mistress. He was neither enterprising nor inquisitive; he kept close to the rim of her skirt, which was as high as he could see, and he wished to be taken up and carried again. He was in a half-stupor; it was his desire to remain in that condition, and his propulsion was almost wholly subconscious, though surprisingly rapid, considering his dimensions.

"My goo'ness!" exclaimed Genesis, glancing back over his shoulder. " 'At li'l' thing ack like he think he go'n a *git* somewheres!" And then, in answer to a frantic pull upon the tub, "Look like you mighty strong t'day," he said. "I cain' go no fastuh!" He glanced back again, chuckling. " 'At li'l' bird do well not mix up nothin' 'ith ole man Clematis!"

Clematis, it happened, was just coming into view, having been detained round the corner by his curiosity concerning a set of Louis XVI furniture which some house-movers were unpacking upon the sidewalk. A curl of excelsior, in fact, had attached itself to his nether lip, and he was pausing to remove it—when his roving eye fell upon Flopit. Clematis immediately decided to let the excelsior remain where it was, lest he miss something really important.

He approached with glowing eagerness at a gallop.

Then, having almost reached his goal, he checked himself with surprising abruptness and walked obliquely beside Flopit, but upon a parallel course, his manner agitated and his brow furrowed with perplexity. Flopit was about the size of Clematis's head, and although Clematis was certain that Flopit was something alive, he could not decide what.

Flopit paid not the slightest attention to Clematis. The self-importance of dogs, like that of the minds of men, is in directly inverse ratio to their size; and if the self-importance of Flopit could have been taken out of him and given to an elephant, that elephant would have been insufferable.

Flopit continued to pay no attention to Clematis.

All at once, a roguish and irresponsible mood seized upon Clematis; he

laid his nose upon the ground, deliberating a bit of gaiety, and then, with a little rush, set a large, rude paw upon the sensitive face of Flopit and capsized him. Flopit uttered a bitter complaint in an asthmatic voice.

"Oh, nassy dray bid Horror!" cried his mistress, turning quickly at this sound and waving a pink parasol at Clematis. "Shoo! *Dirty* dog! Go 'way!" And she was able somehow to connect him with the wash-tub and boiler, for she added, "Nassy laundrymans to have bad doggies!"

Mr. Watson rushed upon Clematis with angry bellowings and imaginary missiles. "You disgusting brute!" he roared. "How *dare* you?"

Apparently much alarmed, Clematis lowered his ears, tucked his tail underneath him, and fled to the rear, not halting once or looking back until he disappeared round the corner whence he had come. "There!" said Mr. Watson. "I guess *he* won't bother us again very soon!"

It must be admitted that Milady was one of those people who do not mind being overheard, no matter what they say. "Lucky for us," she said, "we had a nice dray bid *mans* to protect us, wasn't it, Flopit?" And she thought it necessary to repeat something she had already made sufficiently emphatic. "Nassy laundrymans!"

"I expect I gave that big mongrel the fright of his life," said Mr. Watson, with complacency. "He'll probably run a mile!"

The shoulders of Genesis shook as he was towed along by the convulsive tub. He knew from previous evidence that Clematis possessed both a high quality and a large quantity of persistence, and it was his hilarious opinion that the dog had not gone far. As a matter of fact, the head of Clematis was at this moment cautiously extended from behind the fence-post at the corner whither he had fled. Viewing with growing assurance the scene before him, he permitted himself to emerge wholly, and sat down, with his head tilted to one side in thought. Almost at the next corner the clothes-boiler with legs, and the wash-tubs, and Genesis were marching on; and just behind them went three figures not so familiar to Clematis, and connected in his mind with a vague, mild apprehension. But all backs were safely toward him, and behind them pattered that small live thing which had so profoundly interested him.

He rose and came on apace, silently.

When he reached the side of Flopit, some eight or nine seconds later, Clematis found himself even more fascinated and perplexed than during their former interview, though again Flopit seemed utterly to disregard him. Clematis was not at all sure that Flopit *was* a dog, but he felt that it was his business to find out. Heaven knows, so far, Clematis had not a particle of animosity in his heart, but he considered it his duty to himself—in case Flopit turned out not to be a dog—to learn just what he was. The thing might be edible.

Therefore, again pacing obliquely beside Flopit (while the human beings ahead went on, unconscious of the approaching climax behind them) Clematis sought to detect, by senses keener than sight, some evidence of Flopit's standing in the zoological kingdom; and, sniffing at the top of Flopit's head —though Clematis was uncertain about its indeed being a head—he found himself baffled and mentally much disturbed.

Flopit did not smell like a dog; he smelled of violets.

Clematis frowned and sneezed as the infinitesimal particles of sachet powder settled in the lining of his nose. He became serious, and was conscious of a growing feeling of dislike; he began to be upset over the whole matter. But his conscience compelled him to persist in his attempt to solve the mystery; and also he remembered that one should be courteous, no matter what some other thing chooses to be. Hence he sought to place his nose in contact with Flopit's, for he had perceived on the front of the mysterious stranger a buttony something which might possibly be a nose.

Flopit evaded the contact. He felt that he had endured about enough from this Apache, and that it was nearly time to destroy him. Having no experience of battle, save with bedroom slippers and lace handkerchiefs, Flopit had little doubt of his powers as a warrior. Betrayed by his majestic self-importance, he had not the remotest idea that he was small. Usually he saw the world from a window, or from the seat of an automobile, or over his mistress's arm. He looked down on all dogs, thought them ruffianly, despised them; and it is the miraculous truth that not only was he unaware that he was small, but he did not even know that he was a dog, himself. He did not think about himself in that way.

From these various ignorances of his sprang his astonishing, his incredible, valor. Clematis, with head lowered close to Flopit's, perceived something peering at him from beneath the tangled curtain of cottony, violet-scented stuff which seemed to be the upper part of Flopit's face. It was Flopit's eye, a red-rimmed eye and sore—and so demoniacally malignant that Clematis, indescribably startled, would have withdrawn his own countenance at once— but it was too late. With a fearful oath Flopit sprang upward and annexed himself to the under lip of the horrified Clematis.

Horror gave place to indignation instantly; and as Miss Parcher and her guest turned, screaming, Clematis's self-command went all to pieces.

Miss Parcher became faint and leaned against the hedge along which they had been passing, but her visitor continued to scream, while Mr. Watson endeavored to kick Clematis without ruining Flopit—a difficult matter.

Flopit was baresark from the first, and the mystery is where he learned the dog-cursing that he did. In spite of the David-and-Goliath difference in size it would be less than justice to deny that a very fair dog-fight took place. It was so animated, in truth, that the one expert in such matters who was present found himself warmly interested. Genesis relieved himself of the burden of the wash-tub upon his back, dropped the handle of that other in which he had a half-interest, and watched the combat; his mouth, like his eyes, wide open in simple pleasure.

He was not destined to enjoy the spectacle to the uttermost; a furious young person struck him a frantic, though harmless, blow with a pink parasol.

"You stop them!" she screamed. "You make that horrible dog stop, or I'll have you arrested!"

Genesis rushed forward.

"You *Clem!*" he shouted.

And instantly Clematis was but a whitish and brownish streak along the hedge. He ran like a dog in a moving picture when they speed the film, and he shot from sight, once more, round the corner, while Flopit, still cursing, was seized and squeezed in his mistress's embrace.

But she was not satisfied. "Where's that laundryman with the tin thing on his head?" she demanded. "He ought to be arrested for having such a dog. It's *his* dog, isn't it? Where is he?"

Genesis turned and looked round about the horizon, mystified. William Sylvanus Baxter and the clothes-boiler had disappeared from sight.

"If he owns that dog," asserted the still furious owner of Flopit, "I *will* have him arrested. Where is he? Where is that laundryman?"

"Why, he," Genesis began slowly, "*he* ain' no laundrym—" He came to an uncertain pause. If she chose to assume, with quick feminine intuition, that the dog was William's and that William was a laundryman, it was not Genesis's place to enlighten her. " 'Tic'larly," he reflected, "since she talk so free about gittin' people 'rested!" He became aware that William had squirmed through the hedge and now lay prostrate on the other side of it, but this, likewise, was something within neither his duty nor his inclination to reveal.

"Thishere laundryman," said Genesis, resuming—"thishere laundryman what own the dog, I reckon he mus' hopped on 'at street-car what went by."

"Well, he *ought* to be arrested!" she said, and, pressing her cheek to Flopit's, she changed her tone. "Izzum's ickle heart a-beatin' so floppity! Um's own mumsy make ums all right, um's p'eshus Flopit!"

Then with the consoling Miss Parcher's arm about her, and Mr. Watson even more dazzled with love than when he had first met her, some three hours past, she made her way between the tubs, and passed on down the street. Not till the three (and Flopit) were out of sight did William come forth from the hedge.

"Hi yah!" exclaimed Genesis. " 'At lady go'n a'rest ev'y man what own a dog, 'f she had her way!"

But William spoke no word.

In silence, then, they resumed their burdens and their journey. Clematis was waiting for them at the corner ahead.

Little Marie from Kansas City

On a warm and bright Saturday morning in May, Master Orvard Stone, a large-headed, partly toothless little boy not yet eight years old, was being dressed in his best by Corbena, the indulgent colored woman more usually familiar to his sight against a background of kitchen. The fact that Corbena was dressing him emphasized in his mind the brilliant unusualness of the day, the wedding anniversary of his grandfather and grandmother, though Orvard, naturally, felt no interest whatever in his grandparents' part in the celebration and was preoccupied with imaginings about himself and also with a few predominant physical sensations. Sometimes while he was being dressed, one of his legs desired to make twisting movements, impulses he encouraged; sometimes an arm or shoulder moved with a like urgency for self-expression, and at other times he itched here or there, and consequently scratched himself, to the detriment of Corbena.

She spoke to him with warmth, loudly, yet not unreasonably. "Listen me! You the squirmishest li'l boy in the Uniten States, Orvie Stone! How many times I ben told you stand still? Tooken me half an hour to git them li'l white shorties and white socks and shirtwaist and one them li'l shiny leather shoes on you, and how'm I ever goin' git that other shoe and necktie and li'l blue jacket on you in time you can start to you' grammaw and grampaw's big party wif you' papa and mamma? You take and cut out all this twis'in' and slidin' and scratchin' and half settin' down 'en stretchin' up, and wiggle-footin' and turtle-headin'! Listen me! I rather undertaking put socks and pants on seven squirrels right fresh out the wildwood!"

Orvard's father, in white trousers, brown shoes, a soft-collared shirt, and with his hair wet, appeared in the open doorway. "Orvie!" he said sternly. "If you don't stand still and let Corbena get you ready in time, your mother and I won't take you to the anniversary at all, and then you'll miss meeting your dear little Cousin Marie that you've never seen and's come all the way from Kansas City with her papa and mamma for your grandfather's and grandmother's wedding anniversary. If you're not ready you'll have to spend the whole day here with Corbena, because the party begins this morning and

509

won't be over until this evening. All your nice little cousins will be having a jolly day in Grandpa's big yard; but you'll have to stay here in the house all alone with Corbena. What do you suppose your mamma and I will have to say when all the uncles and aunts and cousins ask where *our* little boy is? We'll have to tell them he wouldn't stand still long enough to be dressed, so we had to leave him at home! That would be very mortifying to your mother and me. You don't want to mortify your mamma and papa, do you?"

Orvie made no reply. Instead, he put the knuckle of his right thumb into the unobstructed front section of his mouth and looked with apparent earnestness at a high-colored wall-paper bird he hated because of its oppressive repetitions.

"Answer me!" his father said, with increasing severity. "Do you want to mortify your mamma and papa? Orvie, take that thumb out of your mouth and answer me! Do you wish your mamma and papa to have to feel mortified about their little boy?"

Orvie didn't care a continental whether or not his mamma and papa would have to feel mortified about their little boy. He was so indifferent upon the point, indeed, that his father's voice was principally an ineloquent sound in the ears. Moreover, Mr. Stone's threat to feel mortified lost weight because of a vacancy in the son's vocabulary, the word "mortified" as yet having no place therein, no matter how often heard. In addition, Orvie could not have accepted calamity as possible to his parents, because they were grown people, all-powerful and therefore impervious. He continued to look at the oppressive bird and somewhat to enjoy the presence of the knuckle of his thumb in his mouth.

"Take that thumb out of your mouth!" his father said again. "If you're not ready in time, you don't go with us, and that's all there is to it. My goodness!" Then he disappeared from the doorway, but could still be heard speaking. "I can't do a thing with him, Clara—not a thing! My goodness!"

Orvie was glad his father had gone away from the doorway and thus had stopped looking at him. What his father said only bored him; but Orvie felt actively uncomfortable if people looked at him. He couldn't bear to look at them when they were looking at him, and when he thought they were going to look at him he always hurriedly did whatever he could to avoid being aware of their observation.

He didn't so much mind children's looking at him, if he knew them well, because they seldom looked at him for more than an instant at a time; but grown people kept their eyes fixed on him intolerably, and it made his insides feel queer.

"You heard whut you' papa say!" Corbena warned him. "How I goin' git you' li'l shoe on you, lessen you unscrunch you' foot? Listen me! Turn 'em toes up straight. Keep foot scrunch' and you ain't goin' to no grampaw-grammaw weddin' party!"

From the next room, voices were audible in discussion of Orvard; he heard them uninterestedly. "Talk about stubbornness!" his father said. "I can't even get him to take that eternal thumb out of his mouth! It's a perfectly horrible habit at his age. At his age he ought to know better. I declare it's disgusting!"

"It's his shyness," Orvie's mother said. "It's his terrible shyness, Frank."

"Shyness! It's time he got over it. Other children don't behave that way at his age."

"I know they don't," Mrs. Stone admitted. "I believe Orvie's the shyest child I ever knew, Frank. Miss Peters spoke of it to me again the other day —about its effect on him at school. She says she thinks he's almost as bright as any child she has and probably often knows the answers to questions; but in the schoolroom he's simply too shy to speak. In spite of everything she does, she can hardly get him to open his mouth, and when he does he usually just mutters something and keeps turned half away from her. Here at home, if he happens to be in the room when callers come in, or even some of the neighbors that he knows well, why, if I make him stay, he positively goes and stands behind the door or gets under a table or behind the sofa or even under a chair. Really, it's embarrassing; but I've simply given up. I've said everything on earth to him that I could; but you absolutely can't reason it out of him."

"No; I've tried that enough, myself, goodness knows!"

Mrs. Stone's voice became more plaintive. "Well, after all, you can't punish a child simply for being abnormally shy. I suppose I'll have the same kind of time with him at your father's to-day that I usually do when I take him to any kind of a party. If it's indoors and he can find a staircase, he's usually under it, and if it's outdoors you have to look for him in the bushes! Maybe he'll behave a little better to-day, though, because the children will all be his relatives."

"He'd better!" Mr. Stone said darkly. "I don't intend to be mortified about him, especially before George and Emma who've never seen him. Their little girl, Marie, is a perfectly wonderful, lovely little child, and when I went out to Father's last night to see George and Emma they said she'd been the pet of everybody all the way on the train; you could tell they were just bursting with pride over her, and when you see her, Clara, you won't wonder why. Really, she's a little darling!"

"Well, of course, little girls are different," Mrs. Stone said. "I don't think they're so apt to suffer from shyness as boys are."

" 'Suffer'!" Mr. Stone repeated with a vehement grimness. "Never mind! If I find Orvie hiding around in the bushes in Father's yard to-day, with his thumb in his mouth, I'll take measures to get some of this idiotic shyness out of him. My goodness!"

In the next room, little Orvard took his thumb out of his mouth, looked at it affably and put it back again.

Thus to overhear his parents discussing him was no novelty to Orvard; frequently he was in the same room with them when they talked about him to each other, and he was often present when either or both of them talked about him to other people. He was used to it, even hardened to it; in particular, he was impenetrably encased in indifference when the subject was, as it seemed perpetually to be, his shyness. He didn't know what his shyness was, though he understood it to be somehow connected with his inward disturbances when people looked at him, and he knew, in a bored way, that his parents were determined to annoy him about it. What he deduced from the conversation of his father and mother, as they completed their dressing, was that when he and they arrived at his grandfather's, it would be wiser to keep out of the shrubbery.

Therefore, a little later, when young Mr. and Mrs. Stone and their son had driven out to old Mr. and Mrs. Stone's place at the end of Walnut Street, Orvie quitted his parents as inconspicuously and hurriedly as possible as soon as they entered the gate; then, avoiding the lilac and mock orange and hydrangea bushes, he immediately went behind a tree.

It was a large, old, gray beech tree, and the thickness and solidity of its intervention between himself and the public gave him a feeling of comfort. Moreover, it stood near the remoter border of the broad, old-fashioned, shady yard and at a reassuring distance from the big brick house. Orvie supposed the grown people would presently all go into the house, and he hoped that this incarceration would cause his parents to forget him, as it sometimes did; but the continuing sound of adult voices numerously engaging in laughter and lively talk disappointed him, and justifiably he began to fear that this all-day party was going to be outdoors.

Placing the knuckle of his thumb in its customary niche, he leaned back against the beech tree, and, wobbling here and there with different parts of his person, and at times scratching a shoulder blade against an imperfection of the bark that soothed him through his jacket, shirtwaist and slight inner garment, he remained for half an hour in his chosen arboreal but really fragile seclusion. Then the approach of gay voices alarmed him, and he foresaw the possible necessity of a dash to another tree; but, before risking so sharp a peril of exposure, he decided to study the danger with one eye.

This eye, therefore, together with a corner of his forehead and some adjacent brown hair, was projected from the sheltering circumference of the beech tree and qualmishly surveyed the jovial and rather noisy scene beyond. Uncles, aunts, great-uncles, great-aunts, cousins of all degrees and ages, were everywhere upon the lawn, chatting, laughing, moving, shifting, breaking up merry groups only to form merrier others. In the shade of the tall walnut tree near the house, Orvie's grandfather and grandmother sat in two easy-chairs on a ceremonial rug, and here most of the great-uncles and great-aunts and elderly cousins seemed to cluster. Little danger threatened from that quarter; but there was another unpleasantly different group, a group in motion not thirty feet from the beech tree, and, perceiving the direction of this movement, the surveying eye had a tendency to protrude. The group consisted of Orvie's mother and an astounding little girl about eight years old, and nine or ten more customary little girls and boys, Orvie's first and second and even third cousins.

In the one flashing instant of perception before he swiftly withdrew the reconnoitering eye, Orvie was startled by the astounding little girl's appearance as a concentration of heavenly pinkness and goldness. A seemingly ancient memory quivered dimly within him, and he realized that her name beautifully was Marie; but at the same time, because of his shyness, she horrified him.

"Now, children," he heard his mother saying loudly, "all spread out and look for little Orvie. He must come and meet his darling little Cousin Marie and his dear Uncle George and Aunt Emma that he's never seen. We'll make a little game of it; we'll look in all the bushes and behind all the trees."

But Mrs. Stone had no more than uttered the frightful word "trees" when there rose upon the air a gloating screech from young throats. Orvie risked his all upon a dash for another tree, and lost.

"There he goes!" screamed his hateful little cousins Bennie, Freddie, Paulie, Ernie, Malvern, Sadie, Josie, Henrietta, Pauline and Babe. "*I'll* get him!" every one of these shrieked cruelly, already in pursuit; but it was Orvie's mother who got him.

As she reached him he put his body upon the ground, hunched up, with his face turned dumbly away. Stooping, she took him under his arms, so not to disarrange his broad white collar and other neck gear, and lifted him. Orvie shut his eyes and imparted such laxity to his legs as would make it impossible to set him properly upon his feet, and he continued this simple defense until his mother said to him privately, "*Shame on you!*" in a whisper the fierceness of which he dared not disregard. His legs resumed their powers; he opened one eye as a compromise and found himself confronting not only a cluster of contemporary cousins but, so closely that she stood almost touching him, the startling pinkness and goldness—in a word, that mystic ineffability—already recognized by him as composing the being of his new little cousin, Marie.

His mother's voice came from above him, speaking dreadfully, commanding him to do the unthinkable. "Shame on you, Orvie! This is your dear little Cousin Marie all the way from Kansas City, and you must come and meet her papa and mamma, your dear Uncle George and Aunt Emma. First, kiss dear little Marie and then we'll go see dear Uncle George and Aunt Emma. Orvie, kiss your precious little cousin!"

Thus, in a tone of false good-fellowship, his terrifying mother asked of him the impossible. Uttering faint sounds of horror, Orvie sought to depart through her skirt; but it proved impenetrable, and Mrs. Stone used compulsion. "Nonsense!" she said, and, placing her right hand behind his head and her left hand behind little Marie's head, appallingly pushed Orvie's face against the face of little Marie.

Orvie's open mouth had the sensation of encountering with a rubbing motion several noses and cheeks and some hair. His own nose, flattened, was dazed with a momentary suffocation, yet smelled fabric, soap and hair. When the stupefying contact was concluded, he had, in fact, a hair in his mouth, which worked feebly to eject it.

"There!" his mother said. "That's nice. Now we'll go and see dear Uncle George and Aunt Emma."

She seized him irresistibly by his right wrist and dragged him across the grass. Orvie would have sat down, like a pup resisting a leash; in fact, attempting this mode of opposition, he made a rapid series of squatting motions, but was jerked along too swiftly to complete the purpose of any of them. Mrs. Stone thus energetically hauled him to the group about his grandfather and grandmother, where, not relaxing her hold upon him, she placed him before two tall grown-up people, complete strangers to him, and said, "This is our little Orvie. Kiss your dear Uncle George and Aunt Emma, Orvie."

Still powerfully constrained by the wrist, Orvie felt with repugnance a moist part of his Aunt Emma's face against his cheek, and then his Uncle George's smoky mustache repulsively tickling his nose.

"Pfoo!" Orvie said indistinctly, in protest; but stood helpless, still trying to work a golden hair out of his mouth.

"That's nice," his mother said, and released him among all his little cousins; for they had closely attended upon his heels. "Don't let him run away again, children," she added benignly, as she turned away. "Don't let him hide behind any more trees or anywhere."

The grown people, again concerned with their own affairs, immediately seemed remote. Orvie found himself spiritually alone, a solitary, serious figure surrounded by malignantly humorous kinsfolk of his own age. His little Cousin Bennie kicked him from behind and his little Cousin Malvern, a copyist, did the same.

"That'll teach you!" little Bennie said.

"So'll that!" said Malvern.

Then little Bennie and Malvern and Freddie and Paulie and Ernie and Sadie and Josie and Henrietta and Pauline and Babe, hideously thrusting forward their faces at him, screeched goadingly in his ears, "Yi, yi, yi, yi, yi, Orvie! Yi, yi, yi, yi, yi!"

In the midst of them, Orvie again found himself confronting the exquisite pink-and-gold child, Marie. The others continued their taunting clamor; but Marie stood silent, dreamily looking at Orvie's perturbed mouth. She affected him strangely. Sunshine flashed from her hair; her pink dress had hypnotic white polka dots all over it, and she put a pink forefinger upon her pink chin in a mysterious way that made him tremble. Suddenly, for the first time in his life, he was in love. In his eyes Marie became a wavering, rosily gilded glamor; he still had her hair in his mouth, and, staring at her, continued to alter the shape of his face in the effort to get rid of it.

The alterations interested Marie. Hemmed in by yipping cousins, who pressed upon them and sometimes kicked little Orvie or poked his sides with fists or stiffened fingers, the two stood looking at each other's chins. The dramatic tenderness that is part of love seemed to emanate from one to the other and to vibrate between them; and thus for a few moments, amid all the yi-yi-ing, these two found each other.

Then the spell was broken. There were adult calls for little Marie, and Aunt Emma pushed through the vociferating circle and took the lovely child by the hand.

"Hush, children," Aunt Emma said. "Hush! Your little Cousin Marie is going to recite a poem your dear Aunt Fanny's written for the wedding anniversary. In our city, where we live, your little Cousin Marie is quite celebrated for the way she recites and sings and dances, and you must all be very quiet now while she declaims this poem to dear Grandpa and Grandma. Come, Marie darling."

Aunt Emma took Marie away from Orvard; he stood where he was and watched the golden hair and white-dotted pink dress as they receded. All the grown people, and children, too, now formed a large circle about the two chairs where sat the beaming grandfather and grandmother, and, in the center of the circle, facing the chairs, the bright figure of little Marie was alone, but nowise disturbed by this conspicuousness. She smiled with a charming complacency, curtsied, and, in a voice as clear and sweet as silver bells, recited.

> "Dear Grandpa and Grandma, on this sapphire day,
> We children weave garlands and round your knees play.
> Through silvered bright years of loving accord
> With good deeds and kindness your mem'ries are stored.

> "Your sons and your daughters,
> Your grandchildren all,
> Your nephews and nieces,
> Your sisters and brothers
> Who survive, and still others
> Bring chaplets of rosem'ry
> To hang in your hall.

> "Hail! Hail! The cry rings out sweet
> From old and from young and the most petite,
> Like your little Marie, and by that I mean me,
> For I came all the way from dear Kansas City
> To bring you my love and recite you this ditty!"

She curtsied again, to a response of vehement hand-clapping and outcries of delighted appreciation. Her grandparents laughed and glowed upon her with pleasure; aunts, uncles and other adult relatives beamed upon her, exclaiming, "Exquisite child!" "Like a lovely little fairy in a glade!" "Perfectly enchanting!" "What talent!" "Really, she's as good as anything on the professional stage!" "They ought to take her straight to Hollywood!"

Little Marie ran modestly to her mother; but, as the applause continued insistently, she came forward again, curtsied again and recited again. Her triumph was so emphatic, indeed, that she recited four times. She recited "Little Orphant Annie", two passages from "Hiawatha", and "Winken, Blinken and Nod". Then, as the applause was still exuberant, her happy and blushing mother announced that instead of reciting any more just now, little Marie would sing "Don't Cry, Little Girl, Don't Cry".

Little Marie sang "Don't Cry, Little Girl, Don't Cry" with so great an effect of pathos that several aunts and uncles sniffled flatteringly, her grandfather touched his eyes, and, when the song was finished, the applause was greater than ever. Her Uncle Henry, the fattest uncle present, lifted her upon his shoulder, and she sat there, kissing her little hands sweetly in acknowledgment of huzzas and waving handkerchiefs.

Then Uncle Henry set her down and she returned to the group of her contemporaries, who, in their own way, made evident their admiration of her. Little Cousin Josie took one of her hands and held it; little Pauline held the other, and little Sadie, standing behind Marie, poked among the golden curls with a forefinger.

Little Bennie cried, "Look, M'ree! Want to see me jump?" and so did little Malvern.

Little Ernie said, "No, look at me, M'ree! Look how I jump!" and all of them, except one, made much of her.

The older people glanced down caressingly upon these manifestations, murmuring, "Sweet!" and it became clear that little Marie was the heroine and bright jewel of Grandpa-and-Grandma's wedding anniversary.

In this loving, happy, big family she was the adored of all adorers—with one exception. Master Orvard Stone stood at a little distance behind his child cousins; he had, of course, his thumb in his mouth, but he was slowly twisting both feet and one hip, and a curious new mood had begun to dominate his being. A change was taking place within Orvard; his feelings toward little Marie had altered and already he no longer loved her.

Her exhibitions of talent had touched, roused and even stung something deep, deep inside of him—something at first inarticulate; but it was now in agitation, boiling toward expression. He began to be conscious of dislike— dislike for little Marie—and so profound and swift was the alteration of him that although he was unnoticed and at liberty, he did not even sidle toward a tree or a bush; he no longer had any desire to hide himself.

On the contrary, all at once, he wished to display himself. He was seized by an importunate desire to do something sparkling and magnificent that would make everybody look at him and clap their hands as loudly for him as they had for little Marie; and then, imagining this accomplished, he had a slight, bitter pleasure in picturing himself as maltreating little Marie, possibly kicking her and yelling, "Yi, yi!" spitefully in her face. For now he hated little Marie like poison and wished to make everybody look not at her but at himself continuously.

He said nothing, did nothing; but all the while, within him, his new mood became more turbulent, pressing for action. A piano sounded the Washington Post March indoors; he permitted himself to be lined up with the other children behind Grandpa and Grandma, and marched into the house to receive sustenance. Little Marie sat at Grandpa-and-Grandma's table, between them, throughout the merry luncheon; Orvie, in another room with the other children, could see her through an open doorway, and every time he looked at her he muttered, "Haw poot!" to himself.

After lunch, everybody marched outdoors again, Grandpa and Grandma returned to their chairs on the rug and kept little Marie with them. Then, presently, neighbors and friends began to come in with congratulations. A little later there was an agreeable flutter and commotion, as the Governor of the State and his wife arrived.

Orvie saw Aunt Emma take little Marie into the house mysteriously; then a wooden door was brought forth from the cellar and laid upon the grass before Grandpa and Grandma and the Governor and the Governor's wife, while a large circle was formed by all the guests about this nucleus. Cousin Frank and Cousin Rupert, grown-up men who had come from college for the celebration, stood near the door on the grass and began to play banjos. Aunt Emma returned with little Marie, and this hated child now wore little silver slippers, little silver trunks, a little silver brassière, and, upon her golden curls, a silver cap with a silver feather.

At the sight, Orvie could not restrain himself. He said, "Haw poot! Haw poot! *Haw* poot!" audibly, and was reproved by an adult voice near by. "Shame! Hush! Be quiet! Darling little Marie's going to do a tap dance for Grandpa and Grandma and the Governor."

Little Marie stepped upon the door and did the tap dance to an accompaniment of banjos and irrepressible bursts of applause, loudest when she made the clattering of her little silver shoes upon the door noisiest and most rapid. The sight of the intensely vibrant little silver figure and the sound of the applause were almost intolerable for Orvie. He looked about him upon the ground, naïvely considering the possibility of throwing some sort of missile at little Marie; but instinct rather than experience warned him that such a course would be inadvisable. He could no longer restrain himself, however, when, as an encore to the tap dance, little Marie gave utterance to a Blues croon, with the banjos plunking haltingly to assist her. The large circle of grown people and children listened in a rapturous hush, intent upon the infantile silver voice that wailed above the plunkings, "She done a-stole my man away!"

Orvie withdrew to a point sheltered from observation, a corner beyond a bay window of the house and invisible from the circle. There he lifted up his voice with all his might, squawking and bawling as loudly as he could, "Haw poot! Yay, yay, yay, yay, yay! Yi, yi, yi, yi! Lo, lo, lo, lo! Boo, boo, haw poot! Hoy, hoy, loy, loy! Yay——"

His fat Uncle Henry detached himself from the circle and came seeking the desecrator, calling out, "Stop that! Who's doing that? Who's making that disgusting noise?" He caught sight of Orvie and approached him overwhelmingly. "Stop that instantly, Orvie! Shame on you! I thought you were always such a nice quiet little boy. 'S matter with you? Don't you know little Marie's singing? What do you mean, making that uproar? Stop that! Shame on you!"

Orvie wished to say "Haw poot!" as scornful repartee; but Uncle Henry's fat face was too malevolently contorted. Alarmed, Orvie went hurriedly in silence round the corner of the house, where he was out of sight of everybody. Here, after waiting some moments, while the silver crooning still complained, "She done a-stole my man away!" he again lifted up his voice to its utmost.

"Baw! Baw! Baw! Yi, yi, yi! Hoo, hoo, hoo! Haw! Yi! Boo! Ack, yack, kack! Ya-a-a-a-y!"

Then, before anyone could come to admonish him, he moodily passed through the open front doorway of the house and ascended the stairs to the second floor.

He had no conscious motive for going upstairs. That is to say, he ascended without knowing why he did so; but his action had a cause that he did not stop to analyze. One day his father had taken him to an "amusement park", and Orvie had seen a man climb to a tiny platform high, high in the air at the top of a spindly tower, poise there, waving to the multitude of upturned faces far, far below him, and then dive all the long way down into a little insignificant tank of water, out of which he instantly emerged, undamaged and triumphant, to receive salvo on salvo of applause.

Nothing had ever made a more decisive impression upon Orvie; hundreds and hundreds of times he had thought of the figure glittering high in the sky, with everybody looking up at it, and then sliding swiftly and gracefully down through the air to spurt through a little liquid and thence lightly out upon the ground, amazing the world. Often as he fell asleep in bed Orvie had fancied himself to be that wondrous diving man who was now vaguely and fragmentarily in the back of his mind as he ascended his grandfather's stairway. What moved Orvie up that stairway was a dumb urge to place himself upon a height where he would have to be looked up at. He could not recite, he could not sing, he could not tap dance, and, if he bellowed, grown people with murderous faces came harshly to stop him; but heights perhaps were open to him. Probably at the seat of his impulses was a dim contemplation of some sort of exhibition to be performed upon Grandpa-and-Grandma's roof.

When he reached the top of the stairs, however, he decided to look down upon the fête from the roof of Grandpa-and-Grandma's side verandah. Therefore he went through a room, climbed across the sill of an open window and stood upon this roof, which was a tin one, protected by a white balustrade with a rail as high as Orvie's chest. He went to the rail and gazed down upon the pleasant scene beneath him.

On the grass, almost straight below him, had been placed a table covered with white damask, and upon this were large round layer cakes and plates of many intricate kinds of little cakes, and even candies; furthermore, there were plates of sandwiches and baskets of fruit, and all these were the adjuncts of a great glass bowl wherein floated, in a garnet liquid, cubes of ice, slices of orange and lemon, various berries. Looking almost directly down upon this regalement from a position some fourteen feet above, Orvie was not permitted by his unprecedented emotional condition to feel the interest he would have felt had he been his average self. His glance lingered not even upon the candies, though as yet no one was near the refreshment table, and he could easily have retraced his steps, hurried quietly downstairs and outdoors for a safely unobserved free raid upon sweets of which he would otherwise obtain later no more than a watched little boy's so-called proper share. No, so radical was the disturbance within little Orvie that he did not then give one thought to the delectable table. His whole being concentrated upon what was taking place beyond, on the lawn.

The company still stood in a great circle—a quiet one now, for little Marie's Blues crooning was finished. She sat upon Grandpa's knee, while the Governor, standing alone at a little distance before Grandpa and Grandma, was talking noisily and moving one of his arms in a peculiar way, often pushing his hand out toward Grandpa and Grandma as if he wanted everybody to notice it. Nobody else was saying anything; all eyes were upon the Governor, the baldness of whose head, odiously visible from above, produced in Orvie's nervous system the same sensation of annoyance that had been the first symptom of his dislike for little Marie.

All at once the Governor began to talk tremulously; he made slow motions with both arms, eliciting strong hand-clapping from the circle, and little Orvie's annoyance with him, developing swiftly, became a kind of hatred. Little Orvie hated little Marie by far and far the more; but he hated the Governor, too.

Looking down poisonously, Orvie saw that little Marie, on Grandpa's knee, was chewing gum self-contentedly and conceitedly swinging a tap-dancing silver foot to and fro, so perfectly at ease and accustomed she was to seats of honor. Near by stood little Orvie's mother, listening to the Governor, but at times glancing at little Marie and smiling tenderly.

Orvie called down to his mother loudly, "Mamma! Mamma, look at me up here! Look at *me*, Mamma! Look! Watch me, Mamma!" With that, he began to run up and down the roof, within the railing, stamping his feet on the tin as hard as he could and shouting, "Look, Mamma! Look at *me* up here, Mamma! Mamma! Watch me, Mamma!"

People, looking up angrily, shouted, "Stop that noise!" and "Be quiet!" The Governor stood silent and waited while little Orvie's father came beneath the verandah and called up huskily, but in a tone of almost incredible viciousness, "Hush! Stop that! Orvie, how dare you? What on earth's got into you? Do you want everybody to think you're an idiot? When the Governor's making a speech to Grandpa and Grandma—shame on you! Come down from there this instant! This instant!"

Orvie retired a few steps toward the wall of the house, where he was out of view. Mr. Stone, red, returned to his place in the circle; the Governor resumed his speech and finished it to emotional applause. When Orvie morosely returned to the railing and looked down again, the circle was once more quiet—and little Marie in her slight silver bedeckings was out in the center again, reciting again.

Orvie removed his thumb, let his mouth remain open, and, though not aware that he was doing anything difficult, swallowed consecutively without closing his lips.

Little Marie received another ovation from untiring relatives. The Governor kissed her, and once more the sickening fat Uncle Henry lifted her to his fat shoulder and bore her aloft, where she rode, kissing her little hands. The Governor gave Grandma his arm and they led the way to the refreshment table just below Orvie. Uncle Henry began to gallop and prance as he moved in that direction with little Marie joyously riding him.

The upper surface of the rail of the balcony was flat and about three inches wide. Carried beyond himself by hatred and unbearably stinging ambition, little Orvie climbed upon this rail and somewhat totteringly stood erect. No one observed him immediately; even in the minds of his parents he had again become so inconsequent a factor in the pleasures of the day that his presence on the roof of the verandah had been forgotten. Almost straight below him, Grandma was filling the first goblet of harmlessly garnet punch for the Governor, and undoubtedly the large glass punch bowl suggested something or became a symbol in the imagination of little Orvie.

Neither he nor anyone else understood this matter afterward; but, at the moment when he contrived to poise himself erect upon the rail, the punch bowl seemed to him rather like a tank of liquid far, far beneath a glittering figure upon a tiny platform high in the air.

"Look at *me*, Mamma!" little Orvie bawled startlingly, standing upon the rail. "Look, Mamma! Look at *me*, everybody! Hay, everybody! Look, Grandpa and Grandma! Look at *me*, everybody! Yi-i-i-i-i! Hurrah for me!"

With that, and with all upturned eyes indeed looking at him, but no opened mouth yet able to become vocal, he squatted himself somewhat, to enhance his spring, and jumped forth from the rail magnificently into the airy void.

A falling body descends a fraction over sixteen feet in the first second of its fall; consequently, a person has no time for reflection during a drop of something less than sixteen feet, and of course the circumstances prevent a reconsideration of the project—nevertheless, there is a period of poignant emotion, however brief. Little Orvie's feeling was not regret precisely but an intensified sensation of the kind an impulsive person sometimes has when he feels that he has perhaps overstepped or gone a shade too far.

The conclusion of his descent was complex. The impact was first, in a partially sitting position, upon the punch bowl. He caromed, upsetting the bowl, the table and his grandmother; but not the Governor, whose clothes, however, became mainly garnet. Little Orvie's grandmother sustained a bent rib, a thorough wetness, discolorations and an unsettling nervous shock. Little Orvie himself suffered no injury whatever, except the ruin of his clothes and being locked up in his grandfather's bathroom, unclad, for about two hours before being taken home, put to bed and exhorted tragically and tediously.

In fact, he became so bored with the passionate question, "What if you'd killed your dear Grandma dead?" that he finally went to sleep while it was being put to him.

The Magnificent Ambersons

CHAPTER I

Major Amberson had "made a fortune" in 1873, when other people were losing fortunes, and the magnificence of the Ambersons began then. Magnificence, like the size of a fortune, is always comparative, as even Magnificent Lorenzo may now perceive, if he has happened to haunt New York in 1916; and the Ambersons were magnificent in their day and place. Their splendour lasted throughout all the years that saw their Midland town spread and darken into a city, but reached its topmost during the period when every prosperous family with children kept a Newfoundland dog.

In that town, in those days, all the women who wore silk or velvet knew all the other women who wore silk or velvet, and when there was a new purchase of sealskin, sick people were got to windows to see it go by. Trotters were out, in the winter afternoons, racing light sleighs on National Avenue and Tennessee Street; everybody recognized both the trotters and the drivers; and again knew them as well on summer evenings, when slim buggies whizzed by in renewals of the snow-time rivalry. For that matter, everybody knew everybody else's family horse-and-carriage, could identify such a silhouette half a mile down the street, and thereby was sure who was going to market, or to a reception, or coming home from office or store to noon dinner or evening supper.

During the earlier years of this period, elegance of personal appearance was believed to rest more upon the texture of garments than upon their shaping. A silk dress needed no remodelling when it was a year or so old; it remained distinguished by merely remaining silk. Old men and governors wore broadcloth; "full dress" was broadcloth with "doeskin" trousers; and there were seen men of all ages to whom a hat meant only that rigid, tall silk thing known to impudence as a "stove-pipe." In town and country these men would wear no other hat, and, without self-consciousness, they went rowing in such hats.

Shifting fashions of shape replaced aristocracy of texture: dressmakers, shoemakers, hatmakers, and tailors, increasing in cunning and in power, found means to make new clothes old. The long contagion of the "Derby" hat arrived: one season the crown of this hat would be a bucket; the next it would be a spoon. Every house still kept its bootjack, but high-topped boots gave way to shoes and "congress gaiters"; and these were played through fashions that shaped them now with toes like box-ends and now with toes like the prows of racing shells.

Trousers with a crease were considered plebeian; the crease proved that the garment had lain upon a shelf, and hence was "ready-made"; these betraying trousers were called "hand-me-downs," in allusion to the shelf. In the early 'eighties, while bangs and bustles were having their way with women, that variation of dandy known as the "dude" was invented: he wore trousers as tight as stockings, dagger-pointed shoes, a spoon "Derby," a single-breasted coat called a "Chesterfield," with short flaring skirts, a torturing cylindrical collar, laundered to a polish and three inches high, while his other neckgear might be a heavy, puffed cravat or a tiny bow fit for a doll's braids. With evening dress he wore a tan overcoat so short that his black coat-tails hung visible, five inches below the overcoat; but after a season or two he lengthened his overcoat till it touched his heels, and he passed out of his tight trousers into trousers like great bags. Then, presently, he was seen no more, though the word that had been coined for him remained in the vocabularies of the impertinent.

It was a hairier day than this. Beards were to the wearers' fancy, and things as strange as the Kaiserliche boar-tusk moustache were commonplace. "Side-burns" found nourishment upon childlike profiles; great Dundreary whiskers blew like tippets over young shoulders; moustaches were trained as lambrequins over forgotten mouths; and it was possible for a Senator of the United States to wear a mist of white whisker upon his throat only, not a newspaper in the land finding the ornament distinguished enough to warrant a lampoon. Surely no more is needed to prove that so short a time ago we were living in another age!

. . . At the beginning of the Ambersons' great period most of the houses of the Midland town were of a pleasant architecture. They lacked style, but also lacked pretentiousness, and whatever does not pretend at all has style enough. They stood in commodious yards, well shaded by left-over forest trees, elm and walnut and beech, with here and there a line of tall sycamores where the land had been made by filling bayous from the creek. The house of a "prominent resident," facing Military Square, or National Avenue, or Tennessee Street, was built of brick upon a stone foundation, or of wood upon a brick foundation. Usually it had a "front porch" and a "back porch"; often a "side porch," too. There was a "front hall"; there was a "side hall"; and sometimes a "back hall." From the "front hall" opened three rooms, the "parlour," the "sitting room," and the "library"; and the library could show warrant to its title—for some reason these people bought books. Commonly, the family sat more in the library than in the "sitting room," while callers, when they came formally, were kept to the "parlour," a place of formidable polish and discomfort. The upholstery of the library furniture was a little shabby; but the hostile chairs and sofa of the "parlour" always looked new. For all the wear and tear they got they should have lasted a thousand years.

Upstairs were the bedrooms; "mother-and-father's room" the largest; a smaller room for one or two sons, another for one or two daughters; each of these rooms containing a double bed, a "washstand," a "bureau," a wardrobe, a little table, a rocking-chair, and often a chair or two that had been slightly damaged downstairs, but not enough to justify either the expense of repair or decisive abandonment in the attic. And there was always a "spare-room," for visitors (where the sewing-machine usually was kept), and during the 'seventies there developed an appreciation of the necessity for a bathroom. Therefore the architects placed bathrooms in the new houses, and the older houses tore out a cupboard or two, set up a boiler beside the kitchen stove, and sought a new godliness, each with its own bathroom. The great American plumber joke, that many-branched evergreen, was planted at this time.

At the rear of the house, upstairs, was a bleak little chamber, called "the girl's room," and in the stable there was another bedroom, adjoining the hayloft, and called "the hired man's room." House and stable cost seven or eight thousand dollars to build, and people with that much money to invest in such comforts were classified as the Rich. They paid the inhabitant of "the girl's room" two dollars a week, and, in the latter part of this period, two dollars and a half, and finally three dollars a week. She was Irish, ordinarily, or German, or it might be Scandinavian, but never native to the land unless she happened to be a person of colour. The man or youth who lived in the stable had like wages, and sometimes he, too, was lately a steerage voyager, but much oftener he was coloured.

After sunrise, on pleasant mornings, the alleys behind the stables were gay; laughter and shouting went up and down their dusty lengths, with a lively accompaniment of curry-combs knocking against back fences and stable walls, for the darkies loved to curry their horses in the alley. Darkies always prefer to gossip in shouts instead of whispers; and they feel that profanity, unless it be vociferous, is almost worthless. Horrible phrases were caught by early rising children and carried to older people for definition, sometimes at inopportune moments; while less investigative children would often merely repeat the phrases in some subsequent flurry of agitation, and yet bring about consequences so emphatic as to be recalled with ease in middle life.

. . . They have passed, those darky hired-men of the Midland town; and the introspective horses they curried and brushed and whacked and amiably cursed—those good old horses switch their tails at flies no more. For all their seeming permanence they might as well have been buffaloes—or the buffalo laprobes that grew bald in patches and used to slide from the careless drivers' knees and hang unconcerned, half way to the ground. The stables have been transformed into other likenesses, or swept away, like the woodsheds where were kept the stove-wood and kindling that the "girl" and the "hired-man" always quarrelled over: who should fetch it. Horse and stable and woodshed, and the whole tribe of the "hired-man," all are gone. They went quickly, yet so silently that we whom they served have not yet really noticed that they are vanished.

So with other vanishings. There were the little bunty street-cars on the long, single track that went its troubled way among the cobblestones. At the rear door of the car there was no platform, but a step where passengers clung in wet clumps when the weather was bad and the car crowded. The patrons —if not too absent-minded—put their fares into a slot; and no conductor paced the heaving floor, but the driver would rap remindingly with his elbow upon the glass of the door to his little open platform if the nickels and the passengers did not appear to coincide in number. A lone mule drew the car, and sometimes drew it off the track, when the passengers would get out and push it on again. They really owed it courtesies like this, for the car was genially accommodating: a lady could whistle to it from an upstairs window, and the car would halt at once and wait for her while she shut the window, put on her hat and cloak, went downstairs, found an umbrella, told the "girl" what to have for dinner, and came forth from the house.

The previous passengers made little objection to such gallantry on the part of the car: they were wont to expect as much for themselves on like occasion. In good weather the mule pulled the car a mile in a little less than twenty minutes, unless the stops were too long; but when the trolley-car came, doing its mile in five minutes and better, it would wait for nobody. Nor could its passengers have endured such a thing, because the faster they were carried the less time they had to spare! In the days before deathly contrivances hustled them through their lives, and when they had no telephones —another ancient vacancy profoundly responsible for leisure—they had time for everything: time to think, to talk, time to read, time to wait for a lady!

They even had time to dance "square dances," quadrilles, and "lancers"; they also danced the "racquette," and schottisches and polkas, and such whims as the "Portland Fancy." They pushed back the sliding doors between the "parlour" and the "sitting room," tacked down crash over the carpets, hired a few palms in green tubs, stationed three or four Italian musicians under the stairway in the "front hall"—and had great nights!

But these people were gayest on New Year's Day; they made it a true festival—something no longer known. The women gathered to "assist" the hostesses who kept "Open House"; and the carefree men, dandified and perfumed, went about in sleighs, or in carriages and ponderous "hacks," going from Open House to Open House, leaving fantastic cards in fancy baskets as they entered each doorway, and emerging a little later, more carefree than ever, if the punch had been to their liking. It always was, and, as the afternoon wore on, pedestrians saw great gesturing and waving of skin-tight lemon gloves, while ruinous fragments of song were dropped behind as the carriages rolled up and down the streets.

"Keeping Open House" was a merry custom; it has gone, like the all-day picnic in the woods, and like that prettiest of all vanished customs, the serenade. When a lively girl visited the town she did not long go unserenaded, though a visitor was not indeed needed to excuse a serenade. Of a summer night, young men would bring an orchestra under a pretty girl's window—or, it might be, her father's, or that of an ailing maiden aunt—and flute, harp, fiddle, 'cello, cornet, and bass viol would presently release to the dulcet stars such melodies as sing through "You'll Remember Me," "I Dreamt That I Dwelt in Marble Halls," "Silver Threads Among the Gold," "Kathleen Mavourneen," or "The Soldier's Farewell."

They had other music to offer, too, for these were the happy days of "Olivette" and "The Mascotte" and "The Chimes of Normandy" and "Giroflé-Girofla" and "Fra Diavola." Better than that, these were the days of "Pinafore" and "The Pirates of Penzance" and of "Patience." This last was needed in the Midland town, as elsewhere, for the "æsthetic movement" had reached thus far from London, and terrible things were being done to honest old furniture. Maidens sawed what-nots in two, and gilded the remains. They took the rockers from rocking-chairs and gilded the inadequate legs; they gilded the easels that supported the crayon portraits of their deceased uncles. In the new spirit of art they sold old clocks for new, and threw wax flowers and wax fruit, and the protecting glass domes, out upon the trashheap. They filled vases with peacock feathers, or cat-tails, or sumach, or sunflowers, and set the vases upon mantelpieces and marble-topped tables. They embroidered daisies (which they called "marguerites") and sunflowers and sumach and cat-tails and owls and peacock feathers upon plush screens and upon heavy cushions, then strewed these cushions upon floors where fathers fell over them in the dark. In the teeth of sinful oratory, the daughters went on embroidering: they embroidered daisies and sunflowers and sumach and cat-tails and owls and peacock feathers upon "throws" which they had the courage to drape upon horsehair sofas; they painted owls and daisies and sunflowers and sumach and cat-tails and peacock feathers upon tambourines. They hung Chinese umbrellas of paper to the chandeliers; they nailed paper fans to the walls. They "studied" painting on china, these girls; they sang Tosti's new songs; they sometimes still practised the old, genteel habit of lady-fainting, and were most charming of all when they drove forth, three or four in a basket phaeton, on a spring morning.

Croquet and the mildest archery ever known were the sports of people still young and active enough for so much exertion; middle-age played euchre. There was a theatre, next door to the Amberson Hotel, and when Edwin Booth came for a night, everybody who could afford to buy a ticket was there, and all the "hacks" in town were hired. "The Black Crook" also filled the theatre, but the audience then was almost entirely of men who looked uneasy as they left for home when the final curtain fell upon the shocking girls dressed as fairies. But the theatre did not often do so well; the people of the town were still too thrifty.

They were thrifty because they were the sons or grandsons of the "early settlers," who had opened the wilderness and had reached it from the East and the South with wagons and axes and guns, but with no money at all. The pioneers were thrifty or they would have perished: they had to store away food for the winter, or goods to trade for food, and they often feared they had not stored enough—they left traces of that fear in their sons and grandsons. In the minds of most of these, indeed, their thrift was next to their religion: to save, even for the sake of saving, was their earliest lesson and discipline. No matter how prosperous they were, they could not spend money either upon "art," or upon mere luxury and entertainment, without a sense of sin.

Against so homespun a background the magnificence of the Ambersons was as conspicuous as a brass band at a funeral. Major Amberson bought two hundred acres of land at the end of National Avenue; and through this tract he built broad streets and cross-streets; paved them with cedar block, and curbed them with stone. He set up fountains, here and there, where the streets intersected, and at symmetrical intervals placed cast-iron statues, painted white, with their titles clear upon the pedestals: Minerva, Mercury, Hercules, Venus, Gladiator, Emperor Augustus, Fisher Boy, Stag-hound, Mastiff, Greyhound, Fawn, Antelope, Wounded Doe, and Wounded Lion. Most of the forest trees had been left to flourish still, and, at some distance, or by moonlight, the place was in truth beautiful; but the ardent citizen, loving to see his city grow, wanted neither distance nor moonlight. He had not seen Versailles, but, standing before the Fountain of Neptune in Amberson Addition, at bright noon, and quoting the favourite comparison of the local newspapers, he declared Versailles outdone. All this Art showed a profit from the start, for the lots sold well and there was something like a rush to build in the new Addition. Its main thoroughfare, an oblique continuation of National Avenue, was called Amberson Boulevard, and here, at the juncture of the new Boulevard and the Avenue, Major Amberson reserved four acres for himself, and built his new house—the Amberson Mansion, of course.

This house was the pride of the town. Faced with stone as far back as the dining-room windows, it was a house of arches and turrets and girdling stone porches: it had the first porte-cochère seen in that town. There was a central "front hall" with a great black walnut stairway, and open to a green glass skylight called the "dome," three stories above the ground floor. A ballroom occupied most of the third story; and at one end of it was a carved walnut gallery for the musicians. Citizens told strangers that the cost of all this black walnut and wood-carving was sixty thousand dollars. "Sixty thousand dollars for the wood-work *alone!* Yes, sir, and hardwood floors all over the house! Turkish rugs and no carpets at all, except a Brussels carpet in the front parlour—I hear they call it the 'reception-room.' Hot and cold water upstairs and down, and stationary washstands in every last bedroom in the place! Their sideboard's built right into the house and goes all the way across one end of the dining room. It isn't walnut, it's solid mahogany! Not veneer-

ing—solid mahogany! Well, sir, I presume the President of the United States would be tickled to swap the White House for the new Amberson Mansion, if the Major'd give him the chance—but by the Almighty Dollar, you bet your sweet life the Major wouldn't!"

The visitor to the town was certain to receive further enlightenment, for there was one form of entertainment never omitted: he was always patriotically taken for "a little drive around our city," even if his host had to hire a hack, and the climax of the display was the Amberson Mansion. "Look at that greenhouse they've put up there in the side yard," the escort would continue. "And look at that brick stable! Most folks would think that stable plenty big enough and good enough to live in; it's got running water and four rooms upstairs for two hired men and one of 'em's family to live in. They keep one hired man loafin' in the house, and they got a married hired man out in the stable, and his wife does the washing. They got box-stalls for four horses, and they keep a coupay, and some new kinds of fancy rigs you never saw the beat of! 'Carts' they call two of 'em—'way up in the air they are—too high for me! I guess they got every new kind of fancy rig in there that's been invented. And harness—well, everybody in town can tell when Ambersons are out driving after dark, by the jingle. This town never did see so much style as Ambersons are putting on, these days; and I guess it's going to be expensive, because a lot of other folks'll try to keep up with 'em. The Major's wife and the daughter's been to Europe, and my wife tells me since they got back they make tea there every afternoon about five o'clock, and drink it. Seems to me it would go against a person's stomach, just before supper like that, and anyway tea isn't fit for much—not unless you're sick or something. My wife says Ambersons don't make lettuce salad the way other people do; they don't chop it up with sugar and vinegar at all. They pour olive oil on it with their vinegar, and they have it separate—not along with the rest of the meal. And they *eat* these olives, too: green things they are, something like a hard plum, but a friend of mine told me they tasted a good deal like a bad hickory-nut. My wife says she's going to buy some; you got to eat nine and then you get to like 'em, she says. Well, I wouldn't eat nine bad hickory-nuts to get to like *them*, and I'm going to let these olives alone. Kind of a woman's dish, anyway, I suspect, but most everybody'll be makin' a stagger to worm through nine of 'em, now Ambersons brought 'em to town. Yes, sir, the rest'll eat 'em, whether they get sick or not! Looks to me like some people in this city'd be willing to go crazy if they thought that would help 'em to be as high-toned as Ambersons. Old Aleck Minafer —he's about the closest old codger we got—he come in my office the other day, and he pretty near had a stroke tellin' me about his daughter Fanny. Seems Miss Isabel Amberson's got some kind of a dog—they call it a Saint Bernard—and Fanny was bound to have one, too. Well, old Aleck told her he didn't like dogs except rat-terriers, because a rat-terrier cleans up the mice, but she kept on at him, and finally he said all right she could have one. Then, by George! she says Ambersons *bought* their dog, and you can't get one without paying for it: they cost from fifty to a hundred dollars up! Old Aleck wanted to know if I ever heard of anybody buyin' a dog before, because, of course, even a Newfoundland or a setter you can usually get somebody to give you one. He says he saw some sense in payin' a nigger a dime, or even a quarter, to *drown* a dog for you, but to pay out fifty dollars and maybe more—well, sir, he like to choked himself to death, right there in my office! Of course everybody realizes that Major Amberson is a fine business man, but what with throwin' money around for dogs, and every which and what, some think all this style's bound to break him up, if his family don't quit!"

One citizen, having thus discoursed to a visitor, came to a thoughtful pause, and then added, "Does seem pretty much like squandering, yet when you see that dog out walking with this Miss Isabel, he seems worth the money."

"What's she look like?"

"Well, sir," said the citizen, "she's not more than just about eighteen or maybe nineteen years old, and I don't know as I know just how to put it—but she's kind of a *delightful* lookin' young lady!"

CHAPTER II

Another citizen said an eloquent thing about Miss Isabel Amberson's looks. This was Mrs. Henry Franklin Foster, the foremost literary authority and intellectual leader of the community—for both the daily newspapers thus described Mrs. Foster when she founded the Women's Tennyson Club; and her word upon art, letters, and the drama was accepted more as law than as opinion. Naturally, when "Hazel Kirke" finally reached the town, after its long triumph in larger places, many people waited to hear what Mrs. Henry Franklin Foster thought of it before they felt warranted in expressing any estimate of the play. In fact, some of them waited in the lobby of the theatre, as they came out, and formed an inquiring group about her.

"I didn't see the play," she informed them.

"What! Why, we saw you, right in the middle of the fourth row!"

"Yes," she said, smiling, "but I was sitting just behind Isabel Amberson. I couldn't look at anything except her wavy brown hair and the wonderful back of her neck."

The ineligible young men of the town (they were all ineligible) were unable to content themselves with the view that had so charmed Mrs. Henry Franklin Foster: they spent their time struggling to keep Miss Amberson's face turned toward them. She turned it most often, observers said, toward two: one excelling in the general struggle by his sparkle, and the other by that winning if not winsome old trait, persistence. The sparkling gentleman "led germans" with her, and sent sonnets to her with his bouquets—sonnets lacking neither music nor wit. He was generous, poor, well-dressed, and his amazing persuasiveness was one reason why he was always in debt. No one doubted that he would be able to persuade Isabel, but he unfortunately joined too merry a party one night, and, during a moonlight serenade upon the lawn before the Amberson Mansion, was easily identified from the windows as the person who stepped through the bass viol and had to be assisted to a waiting carriage. One of Miss Amberson's brothers was among the serenaders, and, when the party had dispersed, remained propped against the front door in a state of helpless liveliness; the Major going down in a dressing-gown and slippers to bring him in, and scolding mildly, while imperfectly concealing strong impulses to laughter. Miss Amberson also laughed at this brother, the next day, but for the suitor it was a different matter: she refused to see him when he called to apologize. "You seem to care a great deal about bass viols!" he wrote her. "I promise never to break another." She made no response to the note, unless it was an answer, two weeks later, when her engagement was announced. She took the persistent one, Wilbur Minafer, no breaker of bass viols or of hearts, no serenader at all.

A few people, who always foresaw everything, claimed that they were not surprised, because though Wilbur Minafer "might not be an Apollo, as it were," he was "a steady young business man, and a good church-goer," and Isabel Amberson was "pretty sensible—for such a showy girl." But the engagement astounded the young people, and most of their fathers and mothers, too; and as a topic it supplanted literature at the next meeting of the "Women's Tennyson Club."

"Wilbur *Minafer!*" a member cried, her inflection seeming to imply that Wilbur's crime was explained by his surname. "Wilbur *Minafer!* It's the queerest thing I ever heard! To think of her taking Wilbur Minafer, just because a man *any* woman would like a thousand times better was a little wild one night at a serenade!"

"No," said Mrs. Henry Franklin Foster. "It isn't that. It isn't even because she's afraid he'd be a dissipated husband and she wants to be safe. It isn't because she's religious or hates wildness; it isn't even because she hates wildness in *him.*"

"Well, but look how she's thrown him over for it."

"No, that wasn't her reason," said the wise Mrs. Henry Franklin Foster. "If men only knew it—and it's a good thing they don't—a woman doesn't really care much about whether a man's wild or not, if it doesn't affect herself, and Isabel Amberson doesn't care a thing!"

"Mrs. *Foster!*"

"No, she doesn't. What she minds is his making a clown of himself in her front yard! It made her think he didn't care much about *her.* She's probably mistaken, but that's what she thinks, and it's too late for her to think anything else now, because she's going to be married right away—the invitations will be out next week. It'll be a big Amberson-style thing, raw oysters floating in scooped-out blocks of ice and a band from out-of-town—champagne, showy presents; a colossal present from the Major. Then Wilbur will take Isabel on the carefulest little wedding trip he can manage, and she'll be a good wife to him, but they'll have the worst spoiled lot of children this town will ever see."

"How on earth do you make *that* out, Mrs. Foster?"

"She couldn't love Wilbur, could she?" Mrs. Foster demanded, with no challengers. "Well, it will all go to her children, and she'll ruin 'em!"

The prophetess proved to be mistaken in a single detail merely: except for that her foresight was accurate. The wedding was of Ambersonian magnificence, even to the floating oysters; and the Major's colossal present was a set of architect's designs for a house almost as elaborate and impressive as the Mansion, the house to be built in Amberson Addition by the Major. The orchestra was certainly not that local one which had suffered the loss of a bass viol; the musicians came, according to the prophecy and next morning's paper, from afar; and at midnight the bride was still being toasted in champagne, though she had departed upon her wedding journey at ten. Four days later the pair had returned to town, which promptness seemed fairly to demonstrate that Wilbur had indeed taken Isabel upon the carefulest little trip he could manage. According to every report, she was from the start "a good wife to him," but here in a final detail the prophecy proved inaccurate. Wilbur and Isabel did not have children; they had only one.

"Only one," Mrs. Henry Franklin Foster admitted. "But I'd like to know if he isn't spoiled enough for a whole carload!"

Again she found none to challenge her.

At the age of nine, George Amberson Minafer, the Major's one grandchild, was a princely terror, dreaded not only in Amberson Addition but in many other quarters through which he galloped on his white pony. "By golly, I guess you think you own this town!" an embittered labourer complained, one day, as Georgie rode the pony straight through a pile of sand the man was sieving. "I will when I grow up," the undisturbed child replied. "I guess my grandpa owns it now, you bet!" And the baffled workman, having no means to controvert what seemed a mere exaggeration of the facts, could only mutter "Oh, pull down your vest!"

"Don't haf to! Doctor says it ain't healthy!" the boy returned promptly. "But I tell you what I'll do: I'll pull down my vest if you'll wipe off your chin!"

This was stock and stencil: the accustomed argot of street badinage of the period; and in such matters Georgie was an expert. He had no vest to pull down; the incongruous fact was that a fringed sash girdled the juncture of his velvet blouse and breeches, for the Fauntleroy period had set in, and Georgie's mother had so poor an eye for appropriate things, where Georgie was concerned, that she dressed him according to the doctrine of that school in boy decoration. Not only did he wear a silk sash, and silk stockings, and a broad lace collar, with his little black velvet suit: he had long brown curls, and often came home with burrs in them.

Except upon the surface (which was not his own work, but his mother's) Georgie bore no vivid resemblance to the fabulous little Cedric. The storied boy's famous "Lean on *me*, grandfather," would have been difficult to imagine upon the lips of Georgie. A month after his ninth birthday anniversary, when the Major gave him his pony, he had already become acquainted with the toughest boys in various distant parts of the town, and had convinced them that the toughness of a rich little boy with long curls might be considered in many respects superior to their own. He fought them, learning how to go baresark at a certain point in a fight, bursting into tears of anger, reaching for rocks, uttering wailed threats of murder and attempting to fulfil them. Fights often led to intimacies, and he acquired the art of saying things more exciting than "Don't haf to!" and "Doctor says it ain't healthy!" Thus, on a summer afternoon, a strange boy, sitting bored upon the gate-post of the Reverend Malloch Smith, beheld George Amberson Minafer rapidly approaching on his white pony, and was impelled by bitterness to shout: "Shoot the ole jackass! Look at the girly curls! Say, bub, where'd you steal your mother's ole sash!"

"Your sister stole it for me!" Georgie instantly replied, checking the pony. "She stole it off our clo'es-line an' gave it to me."

"You go get your hair cut!" said the stranger hotly. "Yah! I haven't got any sister!"

"I know you haven't at home," Georgie responded. "I mean the one that's in jail."

"I dare you to get down off that pony!"

Georgie jumped to the ground, and the other boy descended from the Reverend Mr. Smith's gate-post—but he descended inside the gate. "I dare you outside that gate," said Georgie.

"Yah! I dare you half way here. I dare you——"

But these were luckless challenges, for Georgie immediately vaulted the fence—and four minutes later Mrs. Malloch Smith, hearing strange noises, looked forth from a window; then screamed, and dashed for the pastor's study. Mr. Malloch Smith, that grim-bearded Methodist, came to the front yard and found his visiting nephew being rapidly prepared by Master Minafer to serve as a principal figure in a pageant of massacre. It was with great physical difficulty that Mr. Smith managed to give his nephew a chance to escape into the house, for Georgie was hard and quick, and, in such matters, remarkably intense; but the minister, after a grotesque tussle, got him separated from his opponent, and shook him.

"You stop that, you!" Georgie cried fiercely; and wrenched himself away. "I guess you don't know who I am!"

"Yes, I do know!" the angered Mr. Smith retorted. "I know who you are, and you're a disgrace to your mother! Your mother ought to be ashamed of herself to allow——"

"Shut up about my mother bein' ashamed of herself!"

Mr. Smith, exasperated, was unable to close the dialogue with dignity. "She ought to be ashamed," he repeated. "A woman that lets a bad boy like you——"

But Georgie had reached his pony and mounted. Before setting off at his accustomed gallop, he paused to interrupt the Reverend Malloch Smith again. "You pull down your vest, you ole Billygoat, you!" he shouted, distinctly. "Pull down your vest, wipe off your chin—an' go to hell!"

Such precocity is less unusual, even in children of the Rich, than most grown people imagine. However, it was a new experience for the Reverend Malloch Smith, and left him in a state of excitement. He at once wrote a note to Georgie's mother, describing the crime according to his nephew's testimony; and the note reached Mrs. Minafer before Georgie did. When he got home she read it to him sorrowfully.

DEAR MADAM:

Your son has caused a painful distress in my household. He made an unprovoked attack upon a little nephew of mine who is visiting in my household, insulted him by calling him vicious names and falsehoods, stating that ladies of his family were in jail. He then tried to make his pony kick him, and when the child, who is only eleven years old, while your son is much older and stronger, endeavoured to avoid his indignities and withdraw quietly, he pursued him into the enclosure of my property and brutally assaulted him. When I appeared upon this scene he deliberately called insulting words to me, concluding with profanity, such as "go to hell," which was heard not only by myself but by my wife and the lady who lives next door. I trust such a state of undisciplined behaviour may be remedied for the sake of the reputation for propriety, if nothing higher, of the family to which this unruly child belongs.

Georgie had muttered various interruptions, and as she concluded the reading he said:

"He's an ole liar!"

"Georgie, you mustn't say 'liar.' Isn't this letter the truth?"

"Well," said Georgie, "how old am I?"

"Ten."

"Well, look how he says I'm older than a boy eleven years old."

"That's true," said Isabel. "He does. But isn't some of it true, Georgie?"

Georgie felt himself to be in a difficulty here, and he was silent.

"Georgie, did you say what he says you did?"

"Which one?"

"Did you tell him to—to—— Did you say, 'Go to hell?' "

Georgie looked worried for a moment longer; then he brightened. "Listen here, mamma; grandpa wouldn't wipe his shoe on that ole story-teller, would he?"

"Georgie, you mustn't——"

"I mean: none of the Ambersons wouldn't have anything to do with him, would they? He doesn't even know *you*, does he, mamma?"

"That hasn't anything to do with it."

"Yes, it has! I mean: none of the Amberson family go to see him, and they never have him come in their house; they wouldn't ask him to, and they prob'ly wouldn't even let him."

"That isn't what we're talking about."

"I bet," said Georgie emphatically, "I bet if he wanted to see any of 'em, he'd haf to go around to the side door!"

"No, dear, they——"

"Yes, they would, mamma! So what does it matter if I did say somep'm' to him he didn't like? That kind o' people, I don't see why you can't say anything you want to, to 'em!"

"No, Georgie. And you haven't answered me whether you said that dreadful thing he says you did."

"Well——" said Georgie. "Anyway, he said somep'm' to me that made me mad." And upon this point he offered no further details; he would not explain to his mother what had made him "mad" was Mr. Smith's hasty condemnation of herself: "Your mother ought to be ashamed," and, "A woman that lets a bad boy like you——" Georgie did not even consider excusing himself by quoting these insolences.

Isabel stroked his head. "They were terrible words for you to use, dear. From his letter he doesn't seem a very tactful person, but——"

"He's just riffraff," said Georgie.

"You mustn't say so," his mother gently agreed. "Where did you learn those bad words he speaks of? Where did you hear any one use them?"

"Well, I've heard 'em serreval places. I guess Uncle George Amberson was the *first* I ever heard say 'em. Uncle George Amberson said 'em to papa once. Papa didn't like it, but Uncle George was just laughin' at papa, an' then he said 'em while he was laughin'."

"That was wrong of him," she said, but almost instinctively he detected the lack of conviction in her tone. It was Isabel's great failing that whatever an Amberson did seemed right to her, especially if the Amberson was either her brother George, or her son George. She knew that she should be more severe with the latter now, but severity with him was beyond her power; and the Reverend Malloch Smith had succeeded only in rousing her resentment against himself. Georgie's symmetrical face—altogether an Amberson face—had looked never more beautiful to her. It always looked unusually beautiful when she tried to be severe with him. "You must promise me," she said feebly, "never to use those bad words again."

"I promise not to," he said promptly—and he whispered an immediate codicil under his breath: "Unless I get mad at somebody!" This satisfied a code according to which, in his own sincere belief, he never told lies.

"That's a good boy," she said, and he ran out to the yard, his punishment over. Some admiring friends were gathered there; they had heard of his adventure, knew of the note, and were waiting to see what was going to "happen" to him. They hoped for an account of things, and also that he would allow them to "take turns" riding his pony to the end of the alley and back.

They were really his henchmen: Georgie was a lord among boys. In fact, he was a personage among certain sorts of grown people, and was often fawned upon; the alley negroes delighted in him, chuckled over him, flattered him slavishly. For that matter, he often heard well-dressed people speaking of him admiringly: a group of ladies once gathered about him on the pavement where he was spinning a top. "I *know* this is Georgie!" one exclaimed, and turned to the others with the impressiveness of a showman. "Major Amberson's only grandchild!" The others said, "It *is?*" and made clicking sounds with their mouths; two of them loudly whispering, "So handsome!"

Georgie, annoyed because they kept standing upon the circle he had chalked for his top, looked at them coldly and offered a suggestion:

"Oh, go hire a hall!"

As an Amberson, he was already a public character, and the story of his adventure in the Reverend Malloch Smith's front yard became a town topic. Many people glanced at him with great distaste, thereafter, when they chanced to encounter him, which meant nothing to Georgie, because he innocently believed most grown people to be necessarily cross-looking as a normal phenomenon resulting from the adult state; and he failed to comprehend that the distasteful glances had any personal bearing upon himself. If he had perceived such a bearing, he would have been affected only so far, probably, as to mutter, "Riffraff!" Possibly he would have shouted it; and, certainly, most people believed a story that went round the town just after Mrs. Amberson's funeral, when Georgie was eleven. Georgie was reported to have differed with the undertaker about the seating of the family; his indignant voice had become audible: "Well, who *is* the most important person at my own grandmother's funeral?" And later he had projected his head from the window of the foremost mourners' carriage, as the undertaker happened to pass.

"*Riffraff!*"

There were people—grown people they were—who expressed themselves longingly: they *did* hope to live to see the day, they said, when that boy would get his come-uppance! (They used that honest word, so much better than "deserts," and not until many years later to be more clumsily rendered as "what is coming to him.") *Something* was bound to take him down, some day, and they only wanted to *be* there! But Georgie heard nothing of this, and the yearners for his taking down went unsatisfied, while their yearning grew the greater as the happy day of fulfilment was longer and longer postponed. His grandeur was not diminished by the Malloch Smith story; the rather it was increased, and among other children (especially among little girls) there was added to the prestige of his gilded position that diabolical glamour which must inevitably attend a boy who has told a minister to go to hell.

CHAPTER III

Until he reached the age of twelve, Georgie's education was a domestic process; tutors came to the house; and those citizens who yearned for his taking down often said: "Just wait till he has to go to public school; *then* he'll get it!" But at twelve Georgie was sent to a private school in the town, and there came from this small and dependent institution no report, or even rumour, of Georgie's getting anything that he was thought to deserve; therefore the yearning still persisted, though growing gaunt with feeding upon itself. For, although Georgie's pomposities and impudence in the little school were often almost unbearable, the teachers were fascinated by him. They did not like him—he was too arrogant for that—but he kept them in such a state of emotion that they thought more about him than they did about all of the other ten pupils. The emotion he kept them in was usually one resulting from injured self-respect, but sometimes it was dazzled admiration. So far as their conscientious observation went, he "studied" his lessons sparingly; but sometimes, in class, he flashed an admirable answer, with a comprehension not often shown by the pupils they taught; and he passed his examinations easily. In all, without discernible effort, he acquired at this school some rudiments of a liberal education and learned nothing whatever about himself.

The yearners were still yearning when Georgie, at sixteen, was sent away to a great "Prep School." "Now," they said brightly, "he'll get it! He'll find himself among boys just as important in their home towns as he is, and they'll knock the stuffing out of him when he puts on his airs with them! Oh, but that *would* be worth something to see!" They were mistaken, it appeared, for when Georgie returned, a few months later, he still seemed to have the same stuffing. He had been deported by the authorities, the offense being stated as "insolence and profanity"; in fact, he had given the principal of the school instructions almost identical with those formerly objected to by the Reverend Malloch Smith.

But he had not got his come-uppance, and those who counted upon it were embittered by his appearance upon the down-town streets driving a dog-cart at a criminal speed, making pedestrians retreat from the crossings, and behaving generally as if he "owned the earth." A disgusted hardware dealer of middle age, one of those who hungered for Georgie's downfall, was thus driven back upon the sidewalk to avoid being run over, and so far forgot himself as to make use of the pet street insult of the year: "Got 'ny *sense!* See here, bub, does your mother know you're out?"

Georgie, without even seeming to look at him, flicked the long lash of his whip dexterously, and a little spurt of dust came from the hardware man's trousers, not far below the waist. He was not made of hardware: he raved, looking for a missile; then, finding none, commanded himself sufficiently to shout after the rapid dog-cart: "Turn down your pants, you would-be dude! Raining in dear ole Lunnon! Git off the earth!"

Georgie gave him no encouragement to think that he was heard. The dog-cart turned the next corner, causing indignation there, likewise, and, having proceeded some distance farther, halted in front of the "Amberson Block" —an old-fashioned four-story brick warren of lawyers' offices, insurance and real-estate offices, with a "drygoods store" occupying the ground floor. Georgie tied his lathered trotter to a telegraph pole, and stood for a moment looking at the building critically: it seemed shabby, and he thought his grandfather ought to replace it with a fourteen-story skyscraper, or even a higher one, such as he had lately seen in New York—when he stopped there for a few days of recreation and rest on his way home from the bereaved school. About the entryway to the stairs were various tin signs, announcing the occupation and location of upper-floor tenants, and Georgie decided to take some of these with him if he should ever go to college. However, he did not stop to collect them at this time, but climbed the worn stairs—there was no elevator —to the fourth floor, went down a dark corridor, and rapped three times upon a door. It was a mysterious door, its upper half, of opaque glass, bearing no sign to state the business or profession of the occupants within; but over-head, upon the lintel, four letters had been smearingly inscribed, partly with purple ink and partly with a soft lead pencil, "F.O.T.A." and upon the plaster wall, above the lintel, there was a drawing dear to male adolescence: a skull and crossbones.

Three raps, similar to Georgie's, sounded from within the room. Georgie then rapped four times; the rapper within the room rapped twice, and Georgie rapped seven times. This ended precautionary measures; and a well-dressed boy of sixteen opened the door; whereupon Georgie entered quickly, and the door was closed behind him. Seven boys of congenial age were seated in a semicircular row of damaged office chairs, facing a platform whereon stood a solemn, red-haired young personage with a table before him. At one end of the room there was a battered sideboard, and upon it were some empty beer bottles, a tobacco can about two-thirds full, with a web of mold over the surface of the tobacco, a dusty cabinet photograph (not inscribed) of Miss Lillian Russell, several withered old pickles, a caseknife, and a half-petrified section of icing-cake on a sooty plate. At the other end of the room were two rickety card-tables and a stand of bookshelves where were displayed under dust four or five small volumes of M. Guy de Maupassant's stories, "Robinson Crusoe," "Sappho," "Mr. Barnes of New York," a work by Giovanni Boccaccio, a Bible, "The Arabian Nights' Entertainment," "Studies of the Human Form Divine," "The Little Minister," and a clutter of monthly magazines and illustrated weeklies of about that crispness one finds in such articles upon a doctor's ante-room table. Upon the wall, above the sideboard, was an old framed lithograph of Miss Della Fox in "Wang"; over the book-shelves there was another lithograph purporting to represent Mr. John L. Sullivan in a boxing costume, and beside it a halftone reproduction of "A Reading From Homer." The final decoration consisted of damaged papier-mâché—a round shield with two battle-axes and two cross-hilted swords, upon the wall over the little platform where stood the red-haired presiding officer. He addressed Georgie in a serious voice:

"Welcome, Friend of the Ace."

"Welcome, Friend of the Ace," Georgie responded, and all of the other boys repeated the words, "Welcome, Friend of the Ace."

"Take your seat in the secret semicircle," said the presiding officer. "We will now proceed to——"

But Georgie was disposed to be informal. He interrupted, turning to the boy who had admitted him: "Look here, Charlie Johnson, what's Fred Kinney doing in the president's chair? That's my place, isn't it? What you men been up to here, anyhow? Didn't you all agree I was to be president just the same, even if I was away at school?"

"Well——" said Charlie Johnson uneasily. "Listen! I didn't have much to do with it. Some of the other members thought that long as you weren't in town or anything, and Fred gave the sideboard, why——"

Mr. Kinney, presiding, held in his hand, in lieu of a gavel, and considered much more impressive, a Civil War relic known as a "horse-pistol." He rapped loudly for order. "All Friends of the Ace will take their seats!" he said sharply. "I'm president of the F.O.T.A. now, George Minafer, and don't you forget it! You and Charlie Johnson sit down, because I was elected perfectly fair, and we're goin' to hold a meeting here."

"Oh, you are, are you?" said George skeptically.

Charlie Johnson thought to mollify him. "Well, didn't we call this meeting just especially because you told us to? You said yourself we ought to have a kind of celebration because you've got back to town, George, and that's what we're here for now, and everything. What do you care about being president? All it amounts to is just calling the roll and——"

The president *de facto* hammered the table. "This meeting will now proceed to——"

"No, it won't," said George, and he advanced to the desk, laughing contemptuously. "Get off that platform."

"This meeting will come to order!" Mr. Kinney commanded fiercely.

"You put down that gavel," said George. "Whose is it, I'd like to know? It belongs to my grandfather, and you quit hammering it that way or you'll break it, and I'll have to knock your head off."

"This meeting will come to order! I was legally elected here, and I'm not going to be bulldozed!"

"All right," said Georgie. "You're president. Now we'll hold another election."

"We will not!" Fred Kinney shouted. "We'll have our reg'lar meeting, and then we'll play euchre a nickel a corner, what we're here for. This meeting will now come to ord——"

Georgie addressed the members. "I'd like to know who got up this thing in the first place," he said. "Who's the founder of the F.O.T.A., if you please? Who got this room rent free? Who got the janitor to let us have most of this furniture? You suppose you could keep this clubroom a minute if I told my grandfather I didn't want it for a literary club any more? I'd like to say a word on how you members been acting, too! When I went away I said I didn't care if you had a *vice*-president or something while I was gone, but here I hardly turned my back and you had to go and elect Fred Kinney president! Well, if that's what you want, you can have it. I was going to have a little celebration down here some night pretty soon, and bring some port wine, like we drink at school in our crowd there, and I *was* going to get my grandfather to give the club an extra room across the hall, and prob'ly I could get my Uncle George to give us his old billiard table, because he's got a new one, and the club could put it in the other room. Well, you got a new president now!" Here Georgie moved toward the door and his tone became plaintive, though undeniably there was disdain beneath his sorrow. "I guess all I better do is—resign!"

And he opened the door, apparently intending to withdraw.

"All in favour of having a new election," Charlie Johnson shouted hastily, "say, 'Aye'!"

"Aye" was said by everyone present except Mr. Kinney, who began a hot protest, but it was immediately smothered.

"All in favour of me being president instead of Fred Kinney," shouted Georgie, "say 'Aye.' The 'Ayes' have it!"

"I resign," said the red-headed boy, gulping as he descended from the platform. "I resign from the club!"

Hot-eyed, he found his hat and departed, jeers echoing after him as he plunged down the corridor. Georgie stepped upon the platform, and took up the emblem of office.

"Ole red-head Fred'll be around next week," said the new chairman. "He'll be around boot-lickin' to get us to take him back in again, but I guess we don't want him: that fellow always was a trouble-maker. We will now proceed with our meeting. Well, fellows, I suppose you want to hear from your president. I don't know that I have much to say, as I have already seen most of you a few times since I got back. I had a good time at the old school, back East, but had a little trouble with the faculty and came on home. My family stood by me as well as I could ask, and I expect to stay right here in the old town until whenever I decide to enter college. Now, I don't suppose there's any more business before the meeting. I guess we might as well play cards. Anybody that's game for a little quarter-limit poker or any limit they say, why I'd like to have 'em sit at the president's card-table."

When the diversions of the Friends of the Ace were concluded for that afternoon, Georgie invited his chief supporter, Mr. Charlie Johnson, to drive home with him to dinner, and as they jingled up National Avenue in the dog-cart, Charlie asked:

"What sort of men did you run up against at that school, George?"

"Best crowd there: finest set of men I ever met."

"How'd you get in with 'em?"

Georgie laughed. "I let them get in with *me*, Charlie," he said in a tone of gentle explanation. "It's vulgar to do any other way. Did I tell you the nickname they gave me—'King'? That was what they called me at that school, 'King Minafer.'"

"How'd they happen to do that?" his friend asked innocently.

"Oh, different things," George answered lightly. "Of course, any of 'em that came from anywhere out in this part the country knew about the family and all that, and so I suppose it was a good deal on account of—oh, on account of the family and the way I do things, most likely."

CHAPTER IV

When Mr. George Amberson Minafer came home for the holidays at Christmastide, in his sophomore year, probably no great change had taken place inside him, but his exterior was visibly altered. Nothing about him encouraged any hope that he had received his come-uppance; on the contrary, the yearners for that stroke of justice must yearn even more itchingly: the gilded youth's manner had become polite, but his politeness was of a kind which democratic people found hard to bear. In a word, M. le Duc had returned from the gay life of the capital to show himself for a week among the loyal peasants belonging to the old château, and their quaint habits and costumes afforded him a mild amusement.

Cards were out for a ball in his honour, and this pageant of the tenantry was held in the ballroom of the Amberson Mansion the night after his arrival. It was, as Mrs. Henry Franklin Foster said of Isabel's wedding, "a big Amberson-style thing," though that wise Mrs. Henry Franklin Foster had long ago gone the way of all wisdom, having stepped out of the Midland town, unquestionably into heaven—a long step, but not beyond her powers. She had successors, but no successor; the town having grown too large to confess that it was intellectually led and literarily authorized by one person; and some of these successors were not invited to the ball, for dimensions were now so metropolitan that intellectual leaders and literary authorities loomed in outlying regions unfamiliar to the Ambersons. However, all "old citizens" recognizable as gentry received cards, and of course so did their dancing descendants.

The orchestra and the caterer were brought from away, in the Amberson manner, though this was really a gesture—perhaps one more of habit than of ostentation—for servitors of gaiety as proficient as these importations were nowadays to be found in the town. Even flowers and plants and roped vines were brought from afar—not, however, until the stock of the local florists proved insufficient to obliterate the interior structure of the big house, in the Amberson way. It was the last of the great, long-remembered dances that "everybody talked about"—there were getting to be so many people in town that no later than the next year there were too many for "everybody" to hear of even such a ball as the Ambersons'.

George, white-gloved, with a gardenia in his buttonhole, stood with his mother and the Major, embowered in the big red and gold drawing room downstairs, to "receive" the guests; and, standing thus together, the trio offered a picturesque example of good looks persistent through three generations. The Major, his daughter, and his grandson were of a type all Amberson: tall, straight, and regular, with dark eyes, short noses, good chins; and the grandfather's expression, no less than the grandson's, was one of faintly amused condescension. There was a difference, however. The grandson's unlined young face had nothing to offer except this condescension; the grandfather's had other things to say. It was a handsome, worldly old face, conscious of its importance, but persuasive rather than arrogant, and not without tokens of sufferings withstood. The Major's short white hair was parted in the middle, like his grandson's, and in all he stood as briskly equipped to the fashion as exquisite young George.

Isabel, standing between her father and her son, caused a vague amazement in the mind of the latter. Her age, just under forty, was for George a thought of something as remote as the moons of Jupiter: he could not possibly have conceived such an age ever coming to be his own: five years was the limit of his thinking in time. Five years ago he had been a child not yet fourteen; and those five years were an abyss. Five years hence he would be almost twenty-four; what the girls he knew called "one of the older men." He could imagine himself at twenty-four, but beyond that, his powers staggered and refused the task. He saw little essential difference between thirty-eight and eighty-eight, and his mother was to him not a woman but wholly a mother. He had no perception of her other than as an adjunct to himself, his mother; nor could he imagine her thinking or doing anything—falling in love, walking with a friend, or reading a book—as a woman, and not as his mother. The woman, Isabel, was a stranger to her son; as completely a stranger as if he had never in his life seen her or heard her voice. And it was to-night, while he stood with her, "receiving," that he caught a disquieting glimpse of this stranger whom he thus fleetingly encountered for the first time.

Youth cannot imagine romance apart from youth. That is why the rôles of the heroes and heroines of plays are given by the managers to the most youthful actors they can find among the competent. Both middle-aged people and young people enjoy a play about young lovers; but only middle-aged people will tolerate a play about middle-aged lovers; young people will not come to see such a play, because, for them, middle-aged lovers are a joke— not a very funny one. Therefore, to bring both the middle-aged people and the young people into his house, the manager makes his romance as young as he can. Youth will indeed be served, and its profound instinct is to be not only scornfully amused but vaguely angered by middle-age romance. So, standing beside his mother, George was disturbed by a sudden impression, coming upon him out of nowhere, so far as he could detect, that her eyes were brilliant, that she was graceful and youthful—in a word, that she was romantically lovely.

He had one of those curious moments that seem to have neither a cause nor any connection with actual things. While it lasted, he was disquieted not by thoughts—for he had no definite thoughts—but by a slight emotion like that caused in a dream by the presence of something invisible, soundless, and yet fantastic. There was nothing different or new about his mother, except her new black and silver dress: she was standing there beside him, bending her head a little in her greetings, smiling the same smile she had worn for the half-hour that people had been passing the "receiving" group. Her face was flushed, but the room was warm; and shaking hands with so many people easily accounted for the pretty glow that was upon her. At any time she could have "passed" for twenty-five or twenty-six—a man of fifty would have honestly guessed her to be about thirty but possibly two or three years younger—and though extraordinary in this, she had been extraordinary in it for years. There was nothing in either her looks or her manner to explain George's uncomfortable feeling; and yet it increased, becoming suddenly a vague resentment, as if she had done something unmotherly to him.

The fantastic moment passed; and even while it lasted, he was doing his duty, greeting two pretty girls with whom he had grown up, as people say, and warmly assuring them that he remembered them very well—an assurance which might have surprised them "in anybody but Georgie Minafer!" It seemed unnecessary, since he had spent many hours with them no longer ago than the preceding August. They had with them their parents and an uncle from out of town; and George negligently gave the parents the same assurance he had given the daughters, but murmured another form of greeting to the out-of-town uncle, whom he had never seen before. This person George absently took note of as a "queer-looking duck." Undergraduates had not yet adopted "bird." It was a period previous to that in which a sophomore would have thought of the Sharon girls' uncle as a "queer-looking bird," or, perhaps a "funny-face bird." In George's time, every human male was to be defined, at pleasure, as a "duck"; but "duck" was not spoken with admiring affection, as in its former feminine use to signify a "dear"—on the contrary, "duck" implied the speaker's personal detachment and humorous superiority. An indifferent amusement was what George felt when his mother, with a gentle emphasis, interrupted his interchange of courtesies with the nieces to present him to the queer-looking duck, their uncle. This emphasis of Isabel's, though slight, enabled George to perceive that she considered the queer-looking duck a person of some importance; but it was far from enabling him to understand why. The duck parted his thick and longish black hair on the side; his tie was a forgetful looking thing, and his coat, though it fitted a good enough middle-aged figure, no product of this year, or of last year either. One of his eyebrows was noticeably higher than the other; and there were whimsical lines between them, which gave him an apprehensive expression; but his apprehensions were evidently more humorous than profound, for his prevailing look was that of a genial man of affairs, not much afraid of anything whatever. Nevertheless, observing only his unfashionable hair, his eyebrows, his preoccupied tie and his old coat, the olympic George set him down as a queer-looking duck, and having thus completed his portrait, took no interest in him.

The Sharon girls passed on, taking the queer-looking duck with them, and George became pink with mortification as his mother called his attention to a white-bearded guest waiting to shake his hand. This was George's great-uncle, old John Minafer: it was old John's boast that in spite of his connection by marriage with the Ambersons, he never had worn and never would wear a swaller-tail coat. Members of his family had exerted their influence uselessly —at eighty-nine conservative people seldom form radical new habits, and old John wore his "Sunday suit" of black broadcloth to the Amberson ball. The coat was square, with skirts to the knees; old John called it a "Prince Albert" and was well enough pleased with it, but his great-nephew considered it the next thing to an insult. George's purpose had been to ignore the man, but he had to take his hand for a moment; whereupon old John began to tell George that he was looking well, though there had been a time, during his fourth month, when he was so puny that nobody thought he would live. The great-nephew, in a fury of blushes, dropped old John's hand with some vigour, and seized that of the next person in the line. "'Member you v'ry well 'ndeed!" he said fiercely.

The large room had filled, and so had the broad hall and the rooms on the other side of the hall, where there were tables for whist. The imported orchestra waited in the ballroom on the third floor, but a local harp, 'cello, violin, and flute were playing airs from "The Fencing Master" in the hall, and people were shouting over the music. Old John Minafer's voice was louder and more penetrating than any other, because he had been troubled with deafness for twenty-five years, heard his own voice but faintly, and liked to hear it. "Smell o' flowers like this always puts me in mind o' funerals," he kept telling his niece, Fanny Minafer, who was with him; and he seemed to get a great deal of satisfaction out of this reminder. His tremulous yet strident voice cut through the voluminous sound that filled the room, and he was heard everywhere: "Always got to think o' funerals when I smell so many flowers!" And, as the pressure of people forced Fanny and himself against the white marble mantelpiece, he pursued this train of cheery thought, shouting, "Right here's where the Major's wife was laid out at *her* funeral. They had her in a good light from that big bow window." He paused to chuckle mournfully. "I s'pose that's where they'll put the Major when *his* time comes."

Presently George's mortification was increased to hear this sawmill droning harshly from the midst of the thickening crowd: "Ain't the dancin' broke out yet, Fanny? Hoopla! Le's push through and go see the young women-folks crack their heels! Start the circus! Hoopse-daisy!" Miss Fanny Minafer, in charge of the lively veteran, was almost as distressed as her nephew George, but she did her duty and managed to get old John through the press and out to the broad stairway, which numbers of young people were now ascending to the ballroom. And here the sawmill voice still rose over all others: "Solid black walnut every inch of it, balustrades and all. Sixty thousand dollars' worth o' carved woodwork in the house! Like water! Spent money like water! Always did! Still do! Like water! God knows where it all comes from!"

He continued the ascent, barking and coughing among the gleaming young heads, white shoulders, jewels, and chiffon, like an old dog slowly swimming up the rapids of a sparkling river; while down below, in the drawing room, George began to recover from the degradation into which this relic of early settler days had dragged him. What restored him completely was a dark-eyed little beauty of nineteen, very knowing in lustrous blue and jet; at sight of this dashing advent in the line of guests before him, George was fully an Amberson again.

"Remember you very well *indeed!*" he said, his graciousness more earnest than any he had heretofore displayed. Isabel heard him and laughed.

"But you don't, George!" she said. "You don't remember her yet, though of course you *will!* Miss Morgan is from out of town, and I'm afraid this is the first time you've ever seen her. You might take her up to the dancing; I think you've pretty well done your duty here."

"Be d'lighted," George responded formally, and offered his arm, not with a flourish, certainly, but with an impressiveness inspired partly by the appearance of the person to whom he offered it, partly by his being the hero of this tête, and partly by his youthfulness—for when manners are new they are apt to be elaborate. The little beauty entrusted her gloved fingers to his coat-sleeve, and they moved away together.

Their progress was necessarily slow, and to George's mind it did not lack stateliness. How could it? Musicians, hired especially for him, were sitting in a grove of palms in the hall and now tenderly playing "Oh, Promise Me" for his pleasuring; dozens and scores of flowers had been brought to life and tended to this hour that they might sweeten the air for him while they died; and the evanescent power that music and floral scents hold over youth stirred his appreciation of strange, beautiful qualities within his own bosom: he seemed to himself to be mysteriously angelic, and about to do something dramatic which would overwhelm the beautiful young stranger upon his arm.

Elderly people and middle-aged people moved away to let him pass with his honoured fair beside him. Worthy middle-class creatures, they seemed, leading dull lives but appreciative of better things when they saw them—and George's bosom was fleetingly touched with a pitying kindness. And since the primordial day when caste or heritage first set one person, in his own esteem, above his fellow-beings, it is to be doubted if anybody ever felt more

illustrious, or more negligently grand, than George Amberson Minafer felt at this party.

As he conducted Miss Morgan through the hall, toward the stairway, they passed the open double doors of a card room, where some squadrons of older people were preparing for action, and, leaning gracefully upon the mantelpiece of this room, a tall man, handsome, high-mannered, and sparklingly point-device, held laughing converse with that queer-looking duck, the Sharon girls' uncle. The tall gentleman waved a gracious salutation to George, and Miss Morgan's curiosity was stirred. "Who is that?"

"I didn't catch his name when my mother presented him to me," said George. "You mean the queer-looking duck."

"I mean the aristocratic duck."

"That's my Uncle George. Honourable George Amberson. I thought everybody knew him."

"He looks as though everybody ought to know him," she said. "It seems to run in your family."

If she had any sly intention, it skipped over George harmlessly. "Well, of course, I suppose most everybody does," he admitted—"out in this part of the country especially. Besides, Uncle George is in Congress; the family like to have someone there."

"Why?"

"Well, it's sort of a good thing in one way. For instance, my Uncle Sydney Amberson and his wife, Aunt Amelia, they haven't got much of anything to do with themselves—get bored to death around here, of course. Well, probably Uncle George'll have Uncle Sydney appointed minister or ambassador, or something like that, to Russia or Italy or somewhere, and that'll make it pleasant when any of the rest of the family go travelling, or things like that. I expect to do a good deal of travelling myself when I get out of college."

On the stairway he pointed out this prospective ambassadorial couple, Sydney and Amelia. They were coming down, fronting the ascending tide, and as conspicuous over it as a king and queen in a play. Moreover, as the clear-eyed Miss Morgan remarked, the very least they looked was ambassadorial. Sydney was an Amberson exaggerated, more pompous than gracious; too portly, flushed, starched to a shine, his stately jowl furnished with an Edward the Seventh beard. Amelia, likewise full-bodied, showed glittering blond hair exuberantly dressed; a pink, fat face cold under a white-hot tiara; a solid, cold bosom under a white-hot necklace; great, cold, gloved arms, and the rest of her beautifully upholstered. Amelia was an Amberson born, herself, Sydney's second-cousin: they had no children, and Sydney was without a business or a profession; thus both found a great deal of time to think about the appropriateness of their becoming Excellencies. And as George ascended the broad stairway, they were precisely the aunt and uncle he was most pleased to point out, to a girl from out of town, as his appurtenances in the way of relatives. At sight of them the grandeur of the Amberson family was instantly conspicuous as a permanent thing: it was impossible to doubt that the Ambersons were entrenched, in their nobility and riches, behind polished and glittering barriers which were as solid as they were brilliant, and would last.

CHAPTER V

The hero of the fête, with the dark-eyed little beauty upon his arm, reached the top of the second flight of stairs; and here, beyond a spacious landing, where two proud-like darkies tended a crystalline punch bowl, four wide archways in a rose-vine lattice framed gliding silhouettes of waltzers, already smoothly at it to the castanets of "*La Paloma.*" Old John Minafer, evidently surfeited, was in the act of leaving these delights. "D'want 'ny more o' that!" he barked. "Just slidin' around! Call that dancin'? Rather see a jig any day in the world! They ain't very modest, some of 'em. I don't mind *that*, though. Not me!"

Miss Fanny Minafer was no longer in charge of him: he emerged from the ballroom escorted by a middle-aged man of commonplace appearance. The escort had a dry, lined face upon which, not ornamentally but as a matter of course, there grew a business man's short moustache; and his thin neck showed an Adam's apple, but not conspicuously, for there was nothing conspicuous about him. Baldish, dim, quiet, he was an unnoticeable part of this festival, and although there were a dozen or more middle-aged men present, not casually to be distinguished from him in general aspect, he was probably the last person in the big house at whom a stranger would have glanced twice. It did not enter George's mind to mention to Miss Morgan that this was his father, or to say anything whatever about him.

Mr. Minafer shook his son's hand unobtrusively in passing.

"I'll take Uncle John home," he said, in a low voice. "Then I guess I'll go on home myself—I'm not a great hand at parties, you know. Good-night, George."

George murmured a friendly enough good-night without pausing. Ordinarily he was not ashamed of the Minafers; he seldom thought about them at all, for he belonged, as most American children do, to the mother's family— but he was anxious not to linger with Miss Morgan in the vicinity of old John, whom he felt to be a disgrace.

He pushed brusquely through the fringe of calculating youths who were gathered in the arches, watching for chances to dance only with girls who would soon be taken off their hands, and led his stranger lady out upon the floor. They caught the time instantly, and were away in the waltz.

George danced well, and Miss Morgan seemed to float as part of the music, the very dove itself of "*La Paloma.*" They said nothing as they danced; her eyes were cast down all the while—the prettiest gesture for a dancer—and there was left in the universe, for each of them, only their companionship in this waltz; while the faces of the other dancers, swimming by, denoted not people but merely blurs of colour. George became conscious of strange feelings within him: an exaltation of soul, tender, but indefinite, and seemingly located in the upper part of his diaphragm.

The stopping of the music came upon him like the waking to an alarm clock; for instantly six or seven of the calculating persons about the entryways bore down upon Miss Morgan to secure dances. George had to do with one already established as a belle, it seemed.

"Give me the next and the one after that," he said hurriedly, recovering some presence of mind, just as the nearest applicant reached them. "And give me every third one the rest of the evening."

She laughed. "Are you asking?"

"What do you mean, 'asking'?"

"It sounded as though you were just telling me to give you all those dances."

"Well, I want 'em!" George insisted.

"What about all the other girls it's your duty to dance with?"

"They'll have to go without," he said heartlessly; and then, with surprising vehemence: "Here! I want to know: Are you going to give me those—"

"Good gracious!" she laughed. "Yes!"

The applicants flocked round her, urging contracts for what remained, but they did not dislodge George from her side, though he made it evident that they succeeded in annoying him; and presently he extricated her from an accumulating siege—she must have connived in the extrication—and bore her off to sit beside him upon the stairway that led to the musicians' gallery, where they were sufficiently retired, yet had a view of the room.

"How'd all those ducks get to know you so quick?" George inquired, with little enthusiasm.

"Oh, I've been here a week."

"Looks as if you'd been pretty busy!" he said. "Most of those ducks, I don't know what my mother wanted to invite 'em here for."

"Don't you like them?"

"Oh, I used to see something of a few of 'em. I was president of a club we had here, and some of 'em belonged to it, but I don't care much for that sort of thing any more. I really don't see why my mother invited 'em."

"Perhaps it was on account of their parents," Miss Morgan suggested mildly. "Maybe she didn't want to offend their fathers and mothers."

"Oh, hardly! I don't think my mother need worry much about offending anybody in this old town."

"It must be wonderful," said Miss Morgan. "It must be wonderful, Mr. Amberson—Mr. Minafer, I mean."

"What must be wonderful?"

"To be so important as that!"

"*That* isn't 'important,'" George assured her. "Anybody that really is anybody ought to be able to do about as they like in their own town, I should think!"

She looked at him critically from under her shading lashes—but her eyes grew gentler almost at once. In truth, they became more appreciative than critical. George's imperious good looks were altogether manly, yet approached actual beauty as closely as a boy's good looks should dare; and dance-music and flowers have some effect upon nineteen-year-old girls as well as upon eighteen-year-old boys. Miss Morgan turned her eyes slowly from George, and pressed her face among the lilies-of-the-valley and violets of the pretty bouquet she carried, while, from the gallery above, the music of the next dance carolled out merrily in a new two-step. The musicians made the melody gay for the Christmastime with chimes of sleighbells, and the entrance to the shadowed stairway framed the passing flushed and lively dancers, but neither George nor Miss Morgan suggested moving to join the dance.

The stairway was draughty: the steps were narrow and uncomfortable; no older person would have remained in such a place. Moreover, these two young people were strangers to each other; neither had said anything in which the other had discovered the slightest intrinsic interest; there had not arisen between them the beginnings of congeniality, or even of friendliness—but stairways near ballrooms have more to answer for than have moonlit lakes and mountain sunsets. Some day the laws of glamour must be discovered, because they are so important that the world would be wiser now if Sir Isaac Newton had been hit on the head, not by an apple, but by a young lady.

Age, confused by its own long accumulation of follies, is everlastingly inquiring, "What does *she* see in *him?*" as if young love came about through thinking—or through conduct. Age wants to know: "What on earth can they *talk* about?" as if talking had anything to do with April rains! At seventy, one gets up in the morning, finds the air sweet under a bright sun, feels lively; thinks, "I am hearty, to-day," and plans to go for a drive. At eighteen, one goes to a dance, sits with a stranger on a stairway, feels peculiar, thinks nothing, and becomes incapable of any plan whatever. Miss Morgan and George stayed where they were.

They had agreed to this in silence and without knowing it; certainly without exchanging glances of intelligence—they had exchanged no glances at all. Both sat staring vaguely out into the ballroom, and, for a time, they did not speak. Over their heads the music reached a climax of vivacity: drums, cymbals, triangle, and sleighbells, beating, clashing, tinkling. Here and there were to be seen couples so carried away that, ceasing to move at the decorous, even glide, considered most knowing, they pranced and whirled through the throng, from wall to wall, galloping bounteously in abandon. George suffered a shock of vague surprise when he perceived that his aunt, Fanny Minafer, was the lady-half of one of these wild couples.

Fanny Minafer, who rouged a little, was like fruit which in some climates dries with the bloom on. Her features had remained prettily childlike; so had her figure, and there were times when strangers, seeing her across the street, took her to be about twenty; there were other times when at the same distance they took her to be about sixty, instead of forty, as she was. She had old days and young days; old hours and young hours; old minutes and young minutes; for the change might be that quick. An alteration in her expression, or a difference in the altitude of her head, would cause astonishing indentations to appear—and behold, Fanny was an old lady! But she had been never more childlike than she was to-night as she flew over the floor in the capable arms of the queer-looking duck; for this person was her partner.

The queer-looking duck had been a real dancer in his day, it appeared; and evidently his day was not yet over. In spite of the headlong, gay rapidity with which he bore Miss Fanny about the big room, he danced authoritatively, avoiding without effort the lightest collision with other couples, maintaining sufficient grace throughout his wildest moments, and all the while laughing and talking with his partner. What was most remarkable to George, and a little irritating, this stranger in the Amberson Mansion had no vestige of the air of deference proper to a stranger in such a place: he seemed thoroughly at home. He seemed offensively so, indeed, when, passing the entrance to the gallery stairway, he disengaged his hand from Miss Fanny's for an instant, and not pausing in the dance, waved a laughing salutation more than cordial, then capered lightly out of sight.

George gazed stonily at this manifestation, responding neither by word nor sign. "How's that for a bit of freshness?" he murmured.

"What was?" Miss Morgan asked.

"That queer-looking duck waving his hand at me like that. Except he's the Sharon girls' uncle I don't know him from Adam."

"You don't need to," she said. "He wasn't waving his hand to you: he meant me."

"Oh, he did?" George was not mollified by the explanation. "Everybody seems to mean you! You certainly do seem to've been pretty busy this week you've been here!"

She pressed her bouquet to her face again, and laughed into it, not displeased. She made no other comment, and for another period neither spoke. Meanwhile the music stopped; loud applause insisted upon its renewal; an encore was danced; there was an interlude of voices; and the changing of partners began.

"Well," said George finally, "I must say you don't seem to be much of a prattler. They say it's a great way to get a reputation for being wise, never saying much. Don't you ever talk *any?*"

"When people can understand," she answered.

He had been looking moodily out at the ballroom but he turned to her quickly, at this, saw that her eyes were sunny and content, over the top of her bouquet; and he consented to smile.

"Girls are usually pretty fresh!" he said. "They ought to go to a man's college about a year: they'd get taught a few things about freshness! What you got to do after two o'clock to-morrow afternoon?"

"A whole lot of things. Every minute filled up."

"All right," said George. "The snow's fine for sleighing: I'll come for you in a cutter at ten minutes after two."

"I can't possibly go."

"If you don't," he said, "I'm going to sit in the cutter in front of the gate, wherever you're visiting, all afternoon, and if you try to go out with anybody else he's got to whip me before he gets you." And as she laughed—though she blushed a little, too—he continued, seriously: "If you think I'm not in earnest you're at liberty to make quite a big experiment!"

She laughed again. "I don't think I've often had so large a compliment as that," she said, "especially on such short notice—and yet, I don't think I'll go with you."

"You be ready at ten minutes after two."

"No, I won't."

"Yes, you will!"

"Yes," she said, "I will!" And her partner for the next dance arrived, breathless with searching.

"Don't forget I've got the third from now," George called after her.

"I won't."

"And every third one after that."

"I know!" she called, over her partner's shoulder, and her voice was amused—but meek.

When "the third from now" came, George presented himself before her without any greeting, like a brother, or a mannerless old friend. Neither did she greet him, but moved away with him, concluding, as she went, an exchange of badinage with the preceding partner: she had been talkative enough with him, it appeared. In fact, both George and Miss Morgan talked much more to every one else that evening, than to each other; and they said nothing at all at this time. Both looked preoccupied, as they began to dance, and preserved a gravity of expression to the end of the number. And when "the third one after that" came, they did not dance, but went back to the gallery stairway, seeming to have reached an understanding without any verbal consultation, that this suburb was again the place for them.

"Well," said George, coolly, when they were seated, "what did you say your name was?"

"Morgan."

"Funny name!"

"Everybody else's name always is."

"I didn't mean it was really funny," George explained. "That's just one of my crowd's bits of horsing at college. We always say 'funny name' no matter what it is. I guess we're pretty fresh sometimes; but I knew your name was Morgan because my mother said so downstairs. I meant: what's the rest of it?"

"Lucy."

He was silent.

"Is 'Lucy' a funny name, too?" she inquired.

"No. Lucy's very much all right!" he said, and he went so far as to smile. Even his Aunt Fanny admitted that when George smiled "in a certain way" he was charming.

"Thanks about letting my name be Lucy," she said.

"How old are you?" George asked.

"I don't really know, myself."

"What do you mean: you don't really know yourself?"

"I mean I only know what they tell me. I believe them, of course, but believing isn't really knowing. You believe some certain day is your birthday—at least, I suppose you do—but you don't really know it is because you can't remember."

"Look here!" said George. "Do you always talk like this?"

Miss Lucy Morgan laughed forgivingly, put her young head on one side, like a bird, and responded cheerfully: "I'm willing to learn wisdom. What are you studying in school?"

"College!"

"At the university! Yes. What are you studying there?"

George laughed. "Lot o' useless guff!"

"Then why don't you study some useful guff?"

"What do you mean: 'useful'?"

"Something you'd use later, in your business or profession?"

George waved his hand impatiently. "I don't expect to go into any 'business or profession.' "

"No?"

"Certainly not!" George was emphatic, being sincerely annoyed by a suggestion which showed how utterly she failed to comprehend the kind of person he was.

"Why not?" she asked mildly.

"Just look at 'em!" he said, almost with bitterness, and he made a gesture presumably intended to indicate the business and professional men now dancing within range of vision. "That's a fine career for a man, isn't it! Lawyers, bankers, politicians! What do they get out of life, I'd like to know! What do they ever know about *real* things? Where do they ever *get*?"

He was so earnest that she was surprised and impressed. Evidently he had deep-seated ambitions, for he seemed to speak with actual emotion of these despised things which were so far beneath his planning for the future. She had a vague, momentary vision of Pitt, at twenty-one, prime minister of England; and she spoke, involuntarily in a lowered voice, with deference:

"What do you want to be?" she asked.

George answered promptly.

"A yachtsman," he said.

CHAPTER VI

Having thus, in a word, revealed his ambition for a career above courts, marts, and polling booths, George breathed more deeply than usual, and, turning his face from the lovely companion whom he had just made his confidante, gazed out at the dancers with an expression in which there was both sternness and a contempt for the squalid lives of the unyachted Midlanders before him. However, among them, he marked his mother; and his sombre grandeur relaxed momentarily; a more genial light came into his eyes.

Isabel was dancing with the queer-looking duck; and it was to be noted that the lively gentleman's gait was more sedate than it had been with Miss Fanny Minafer, but not less dexterous and authoritative. He was talking to Isabel as gaily as he had talked to Miss Fanny, though with less laughter, and Isabel listened and answered eagerly: her colour was high and her eyes had a look of delight. She saw George and the beautiful Lucy on the stairway, and nodded to them. George waved his hand vaguely: he had a momentary return of that inexplicable uneasiness and resentment which had troubled him downstairs.

"How lovely your mother is!" Lucy said.

"I think she is," he agreed gently.

"She's the gracefulest woman in that ballroom. She dances like a girl of sixteen."

"Most girls of sixteen," said George, "are bum dancers. Anyhow, I wouldn't dance with one unless I had to."

"Well, you'd better dance with your mother! I never saw anybody lovelier. How wonderfully they dance together!"

"Who?"

"Your mother and—and the queer-looking duck," said Lucy. "I'm going to dance with him pretty soon."

"I don't care—so long as you don't give him one of the numbers that belong to me."

"I'll try to remember," she said, and thoughtfully lifted to her face the bouquet of violets and lilies, a gesture which George noted without approval.

"Look here! Who sent you those flowers you keep makin' such a fuss over?"

"He did."

"Who's 'he'?"

"The queer-looking duck."

George feared no such rival; he laughed loudly. "I s'pose he's some old widower!" he said, the object thus described seeming ignominious enough to a person of eighteen, without additional characterization. "Some old widower!"

Lucy became serious at once. "Yes, he is a widower," she said. "I ought to have told you before; he's my father."

George stopped laughing abruptly. "Well, that's a horse on me. If I'd known he was your father, of course I wouldn't have made fun of him. I'm sorry."

"Nobody could make fun of him," she said quietly.

"Why couldn't they?"

"It wouldn't make him funny: it would only make themselves silly."

Upon this, George had a gleam of intelligence. "Well, I'm not going to make myself silly any more, then; I don't want to take chances like that with *you*. But I thought he was the Sharon girls' uncle. He came with them——"

"Yes," she said, "I'm always late to everything: I wouldn't let them wait for me. We're visiting the Sharons."

"About time I knew that! You forget my being so fresh about your father, will you? Of course he's a distinguished looking man, in a way."

Lucy was still serious. "'In a way?'" she repeated. "You mean, not in your way, don't you?"

George was perplexed. "How do you mean: not in my way?"

"People pretty often say 'in a way' and 'rather distinguished looking,' or 'rather' so-and-so, or 'rather' anything, to show that *they're* superior, don't they? In New York last month I overheard a climber sort of woman speaking of me as 'little Miss Morgan,' but she didn't mean my height; she meant that she was important. Her husband spoke of a friend of mine as 'little Mr. Pembroke' and 'little Mr. Pembroke' is six-feet-three. This husband and wife were really so terribly unimportant that the only way they knew to pretend to be important was calling people 'little' Miss or Mister so-and-so. It's a kind of snob slang, I think. Of course people don't always say 'rather' or 'in a way' to be superior."

"I should say not! I use both of 'em a great deal myself," said George. "One thing I don't see though: What's the use of a man being six-feet-three? Men that size can't handle themselves as well as a man about five-feet-eleven and a half can. Those long, gangling men, they're nearly always too kind of wormy to be any good in athletics, and they're so awkward they keep falling over chairs or——"

"Mr. Pembroke is in the army," said Lucy primly. "He's extraordinarily graceful."

"In the army? Oh, I suppose he's some old friend of your father's."

"They got on very well," she said, "after I introduced them."

George was a straightforward soul, at least. "See here!" he said. "Are you engaged to anybody?"

"No."

Not wholly mollified, he shrugged his shoulders. "You seem to know a good many people! Do you live in New York?"

"No. We don't live anywhere."

"What you mean: you don't live anywhere?"

"We've lived all over," she answered. "Papa used to live here in this town, but that was before I was born."

"What do you keep moving around so for? Is he a promoter?"

"No. He's an inventor."

"What's he invented?"

"Just lately," said Lucy, "he's been working on a new kind of horseless carriage."

"Well, I'm sorry for him," George said, in no unkindly spirit. "Those things are never going to amount to anything. People aren't going to spend their lives lying on their backs in the road and letting grease drip in their faces. Horseless carriages are pretty much a failure, and your father better not waste his time on 'em."

"Papa'd be so grateful," she returned, "if he could have your advice."

Instantly George's face became flushed. "I don't know that I've done anything to be insulted for!" he said. "I don't see that what I said was particularly fresh."

"No, indeed!"

"Then what do you——"

She laughed gaily. "I don't! And I don't mind your being such a lofty person at all. I think it's ever so interesting—but papa's a great man!"

"Is he?" George decided to be good-natured. "Well, let us hope so. I hope so, I'm sure."

Looking at him keenly, she saw that the magnificent youth was incredibly sincere in this bit of graciousness. He spoke as a tolerant, elderly statesman might speak of a promising young politician; and with her eyes still upon him, Lucy shook her head in gentle wonder. "I'm just beginning to understand," she said.

"Understand what?"

"What it means to be a real Amberson in this town. Papa told me something about it before we came, but I see he didn't say half enough!"

George superbly took this all for tribute. "Did your father say he knew the family before he left here?"

"Yes. I believe he was particularly a friend of your Uncle George; and he didn't say so, but I imagine he must have known your mother very well, too. He wasn't an inventor then; he was a young lawyer. The town was smaller in those days, and I believe he was quite well known."

"I dare say. I've no doubt the family are all very glad to see him back, especially if they used to have him at the house a good deal, as he told you."

"I don't think he meant to boast of it," she said. "He spoke of it quite calmly."

George stared at her for a moment in perplexity, then perceiving that her intention was satirical, "Girls really ought to go to a man's college," he said—"just a month or two, anyhow. It'd take some of the freshness out of 'em!"

"I can't believe it," she retorted, as her partner for the next dance arrived.

"It would only make them a little politer on the surface—they'd be really just as awful as ever, after you got to know them a few minutes."

"What do you mean: 'after you got to know them a——'"

She was departing to the dance. "Janie and Mary Sharon told me all about what sort of a *little* boy you were," she said, over her shoulder. "You must think it out!"

She took wing away on the breeze of the waltz, and George, having stared gloomily after her for a few moments, postponed filling an engagement, and strolled round the fluctuating outskirts of the dance to where his uncle, George Amberson, stood smilingly watching, under one of the rose-vine arches at the entrance to the room.

"Hello, young namesake," said the uncle. "Why lingers the laggard heel of the dancer? Haven't you got a partner?"

"She's sitting around waiting for me somewhere," said George. "See here: Who is this fellow Morgan that Aunt Fanny Minafer was dancing with a while ago?"

Amberson laughed. "He's a man with a pretty daughter, Georgie. Meseemed you've been spending the evening noticing something of that sort—or do I err?"

"Never mind! What sort is he?"

"I think we'll have to give him a character, Georgie. He's an old friend; used to practise law here—perhaps he had more debts than cases, but he paid 'em all up before he left town. Your question is purely mercenary, I take it: you want to know his true worth before proceeding further with the daughter. I cannot inform you, though I notice signs of considerable prosperity in that becoming dress of hers. However, you never can tell. It is an age when every sacrifice is made for the young, and how your own poor mother managed to provide those genuine pearl studs for you out of her allowance from father, I can't——"

"Oh, dry up!" said the nephew. "I understand this Morgan——"

"Mr. Eugene Morgan," his uncle suggested. "Politeness requires that the young should——"

"I guess the 'young' didn't know much about politeness in your day," George interrupted. "I understand that Mr. Eugene Morgan used to be a great friend of the family."

"Oh, the Minafers?" the uncle inquired, with apparent innocence. "No, I seem to recall that he and your father were not——"

"I mean the Ambersons," George said impatiently. "I understand he was a good deal around the house here."

"What is your objection to that, George?"

"What do you mean: my objection?"

"You seemed to speak with a certain crossness."

"Well," said George, "I meant he seems to feel awfully at home here. The way he was dancing with Aunt Fanny——"

Amberson laughed. "I'm afraid your Aunt Fanny's heart was stirred by ancient recollections, Georgie."

"You mean she used to be silly about him?"

"She wasn't considered singular," said the uncle. "He was—he was popular. Could you bear a question?"

"What do you mean: could I bear——"

"I only wanted to ask: Do you take this same passionate interest in the parents of every girl you dance with? Perhaps it's a new fashion we old bachelors ought to take up. Is it the thing this year to——"

"Oh, go on!" said George, moving away. "I only wanted to know——" He left the sentence unfinished, and crossed the room to where a girl sat waiting for his nobility to find time to fulfil his contract with her for this dance.

"Pardon f' keep' wait," he muttered, as she rose brightly to meet him; and she seemed pleased that he came at all—but George was used to girls' looking radiant when he danced with them, and she had little effect upon him. He danced with her perfunctorily, thinking the while of Mr. Eugene Morgan and his daughter. Strangely enough, his thoughts dwelt more upon the father than the daughter, though George could not possibly have given a reason —even to himself—for this disturbing preponderance.

By a coincidence, though not an odd one, the thoughts and conversation of Mr. Eugene Morgan at this very time were concerned with George Amberson Minafer, rather casually, it is true. Mr. Morgan had retired to a room set apart for smoking, on the second floor, and had found a grizzled gentleman lounging in solitary possession.

"Gene Morgan!" this person exclaimed, rising with great heartiness. "I'd heard you were in town—I don't believe you know me!"

"Yes, I do, Fred Kinney!" Mr. Morgan returned with equal friendliness. "Your real face—the one I used to know—it's just underneath the one you're masquerading in to-night. You ought to have changed it more if you wanted a disguise."

"Twenty years!" said Mr. Kinney. "It makes some difference in faces, but more in behaviour!"

"It does so!" his friend agreed with explosive emphasis. "My own behaviour began to be different about that long ago—quite suddenly."

"I remember," said Mr. Kinney sympathetically. "Well, life's odd enough as we look back."

"Probably it's going to be odder still—if we could look forward."

"Probably."

They sat and smoked.

"However," Mr. Morgan remarked presently, "I still dance like an Indian. Don't you?"

"No. I leave that to my boy Fred. He does the dancing for the family."

"I suppose he's upstairs hard at it?"

"No, he's not here." Mr. Kinney glanced toward the open door and lowered his voice. "He wouldn't come. It seems that a couple of years or so ago he had a row with young Georgie Minafer. Fred was president of a literary club they had, and he said this young Georgie got himself elected instead, in an overbearing sort of way. Fred's red-headed, you know—I suppose you remember his mother? You were at the wedding——"

"I remember the wedding," said Mr. Morgan. "And I remember your bachelor dinner—most of it, that is."

"Well, my boy Fred's as red-headed now," Mr. Kinney went on, "as his mother was then, and he's very bitter about his row with Georgie Minafer. He says he'd rather burn his foot off than set it inside any Amberson house or any place else where young Georgie is. Fact is, the boy seemed to have so much feeling over it I had my doubts about coming myself, but my wife said it was all nonsense; we mustn't humour Fred in a grudge over such a little thing, and while she despised that Georgie Minafer, herself, as much as any one else did, she wasn't going to miss a big Amberson show just on account of a boys' rumpus, and so on and so on; and so we came."

"Do people dislike young Minafer generally?"

"I don't know about 'generally.' I guess he gets plenty of toadying; but there's certainly a lot of people that are glad to express their opinions about him."

"What's the matter with him?"

"Too much Amberson, I suppose, for one thing. And for another, his mother just fell down and worshipped him from the day he was born. That's what beats me! I don't have to tell you what Isabel Amberson is, Eugene Morgan. She's got a touch of the Amberson high stuff about her, but you can't get anybody that ever knew her to deny that she's just about the finest woman in the world."

"No," said Eugene Morgan. "You can't get anybody to deny that."

"Then I can't see how she doesn't see the truth about that boy. He thinks he's a little tin god on wheels—and honestly, it makes some people weak and sick just to think about him! Yet that high-spirited, intelligent woman, Isabel Amberson, actually sits and worships him! You can hear it in her voice when she speaks to him or speaks of him. You can see it in her eyes when she looks at him. My Lord! What *does* she see when she looks at him?"

Morgan's odd expression of genial apprehension deepened whimsically, though it denoted no actual apprehension whatever, and cleared away from his face altogether when he smiled; he became surprisingly winning and persuasive when he smiled. He smiled now, after a moment, at this question of his old friend. "She sees something that we don't see," he said.

"What does she see?"

"An angel."

Kinney laughed aloud. "Well, if she sees an angel when she looks at Georgie Minafer, she's a funnier woman than I thought she was!"

"Perhaps she is," said Morgan. "But that's what she sees."

"My Lord! It's easy to see you've only known him an hour or so. In that time have you looked at Georgie and seen an angel?"

"No. All I saw was a remarkably good-looking fool-boy with the pride of

Satan and a set of nice new drawing-room manners that he probably couldn't use more than half an hour at a time without busting."

"Then what——"

"Mothers are right," said Morgan. "Do you think this young George is the same sort of creature when he's with his mother that he is when he's bull-dozing your boy Fred? Mothers see the angel in us because the angel is there. If it's shown to the mother, the son has got an angel to show, hasn't he? When a son cuts somebody's throat the mother only sees it's possible for a misguided angel to act like a devil—and she's entirely right about that!"

Kinney laughed, and put his hand on his friend's shoulder. "I remember what a fellow you always were to argue," he said. "You mean Georgie Minafer is as much of an angel as any murderer is, and that Georgie's mother is always right."

"I'm afraid she always has been," Morgan said lightly.

The friendly hand remained upon his shoulder. "She was wrong once, old fellow. At least, so it seemed to me."

"No," said Morgan, a little awkwardly. "No——"

Kinney relieved the slight embarrassment that had come upon both of them: he laughed again. "Wait till you know young Georgie a little better," he said. "Something tells me you're going to change your mind about his having an angel to show, if you see anything of him!"

"You mean beauty's in the eye of the beholder, and the angel is all in the eye of the mother. If you were a painter, Fred, you'd paint mothers with angels' eyes holding imps in their laps. Me, I'll stick to the Old Masters and the cherubs."

Mr. Kinney looked at him musingly. "Somebody's eyes must have been pretty angelic," he said, "if they've been persuading you that Georgie Minafer is a cherub!"

"They are," said Morgan heartily. "They're more angelic than ever." And as a new flourish of music sounded overhead he threw away his cigarette, and jumped up briskly. "Good-bye, I've got this dance with her."

"With whom?"

"With Isabel!"

The grizzled Mr. Kinney affected to rub his eyes. "It startles me, your jumping up like that to go and dance with Isabel Amberson! Twenty years seem to have passed—but have they? Tell me, have you danced with poor old Fanny, too, this evening?"

"Twice!"

"My Lord!" Kinney groaned, half in earnest. "Old times starting all over again! My Lord!"

"Old times?" Morgan laughed gaily from the doorway. "Not a bit! There aren't any old times. When times are gone they're not old, they're dead! There aren't any times but new times!"

And he vanished in such a manner that he seemed already to have begun dancing.

CHAPTER VII

The appearance of Miss Lucy Morgan the next day, as she sat in George's fast cutter, proved so charming that her escort was stricken to soft words instantly, and failed to control a poetic impulse. Her rich little hat was trimmed with black fur; her hair was almost as dark as the fur; a great boa of black fur was about her shoulders; her hands were vanished into a black muff; and George's laprobe was black. "You look like—" he said. "Your face looks like—it looks like a snowflake on a lump of coal. I mean a—a snowflake that would be a rose-leaf, too!"

"Perhaps you'd better look at the reins," she returned. "We almost upset just then."

George declined to heed this advice. "Because there's too much pink in your cheeks for a snowflake," he continued. "What's that fairy story about snow-white and rose-red——"

"We're going pretty fast, Mr. Minafer!"

"Well, you see, I'm only here for two weeks."

"I mean the sleigh!" she explained. "We're not the only people on the street, you know."

"Oh, *they'll* keep out of the way."

"That's very patrician chariotcering, but it seems to me a horse like this needs guidance. I'm sure he's going almost twenty miles an hour."

"That's nothing," said George; but he consented to look forward again. "He can trot under three minutes, all right." He laughed. "I suppose your father thinks he can build a horseless carriage to go that fast!"

"They go that fast already, sometimes."

"Yes," said George; "they do—for about a hundred feet! Then they give a yell and burn up."

Evidently she decided not to defend her father's faith in horseless carriages, for she laughed, and said nothing. The cold air was polka-dotted with snowflakes, and trembled to the loud, continuous jingling of sleighbells. Boys and girls, all aglow and panting jets of vapour, darted at the passing sleighs to ride on the runners, or sought to rope their sleds to any vehicle whatever, but the fleetest no more than just touched the flying cutter, though a hundred soggy mittens grasped for it, then reeled and whirled till sometimes the wearers of those daring mittens plunged flat in the snow and lay a-sprawl, reflecting. For this was the holiday time, and all the boys and girls in town were out, most of them on National Avenue.

But there came panting and chugging up that flat thoroughfare a thing which some day was to spoil all their sleigh-time merriment—save for the rashest and most disobedient. It was vaguely like a topless surrey, but cumbrous with unwholesome excrescences fore and aft, while underneath were spinning leather belts and something that whirred and howled and seemed to stagger. The ride-stealers made no attempt to fasten their sleds to a contrivance so nonsensical and yet so fearsome. Instead, they gave over their sport and concentrated all their energies in their lungs, so that up and down the street the one cry shrilled increasingly: "Git a hoss! Git a hoss! Git a hoss! Mister, why don't you git a hoss?" But the mahout in charge, sitting solitary on the front seat, was unconcerned—he laughed, and now and then ducked a snowball without losing any of his good-nature. It was Mr. Eugene Morgan who exhibited so cheerful a countenance between the forward visor of a deer-stalker cap and the collar of a fuzzy gray ulster. "Git a hoss!" the children shrieked, and gruffer voices joined them. "Git a hoss! Git a hoss! Git a *hoss!*"

George Minafer was correct thus far: the twelve miles an hour of such a machine would never overtake George's trotter. The cutter was already scurrying between the stone pillars at the entrance to Amberson Addition.

"That's my grandfather's," said George, nodding toward the Amberson Mansion.

"I ought to know that!" Lucy exclaimed. "We stayed there late enough last night: papa and I were almost the last to go. He and your mother and Miss Fanny Minafer got the musicians to play another waltz when everybody else had gone downstairs and the fiddles were being put away in their cases. Papa danced part of it with Miss Minafer and the rest with your mother. Miss Minafer's your aunt, isn't she?"

"Yes; she lives with us. I tease her a good deal."

"What about?"

"Oh, anything handy—whatever's easy to tease an old maid about."

"Doesn't she mind?"

"She usually has sort of a grouch on me," laughed George. "Nothing much. That's our house just beyond grandfather's." He waved a sealskin gauntlet to indicate the house Major Amberson had built for Isabel as a wedding gift. "It's almost the same as grandfather's, only not as large and hasn't got a regular ballroom. We gave the dance, last night, at grandfather's on account of the ballroom, and because I'm the only grandchild, you know. Of course, some day that'll be my house, though I expect my mother will most likely go on living where she does now, with father and Aunt Fanny. I suppose I'll probably build a country house, too—somewhere East, I guess." He stopped speaking, and frowned as they passed a closed carriage and pair. The body of this comfortable vehicle sagged slightly to one side; the paint was old and seamed with hundreds of minute cracks like little rivers on a black map; the coachman, a fat and elderly darky, seemed to drowse upon the box; but the open window afforded the occupants of the cutter a glimpse of a tired, fine old face, a silk hat, a pearl tie, and an astrachan collar, evidently out to take the air.

"There's your grandfather now," said Lucy. "Isn't it?"

George's frown was not relaxed. "Yes, it is; and he ought to give that rat-trap away and sell those old horses. They're a disgrace, all shaggy—not even clipped. I suppose he doesn't notice it—people get awful funny when they get old; they seem to lose their self-respect, sort of."

"He seemed a real Brummell to me," she said.

"Oh, he keeps up about what he *wears*, well enough, but—well, look at that!" He pointed to a statue of Minerva, one of the cast-iron sculptures Major Amberson had set up in opening the Addition years before. Minerva was intact, but a blackish streak descended unpleasantly from her forehead to the point of her straight nose, and a few other streaks were sketched in a repellent dinge upon the folds of her drapery.

"That must be from soot," said Lucy. "There are so many houses around here."

"Anyhow, somebody ought to see that these statues are kept clean. My grandfather owns a good many of these houses, I guess, for renting. Of course, he sold most of the lots—there aren't any vacant ones, and there used to be heaps of 'em when I was a boy. Another thing I don't think he ought to allow: a good many of these people bought big lots and they built houses on 'em; then the price of the land kept getting higher, and they'd sell part of their yards and let the people that bought it build houses on it to live in, till they haven't hardly any of 'em got big, open yards any more, and it's getting all too much built up. The way it used to be, it was like a gentleman's country estate, and that's the way my grandfather ought to keep it. He lets these people take too many liberties: they do anything they want to."

"But how could he stop them?" Lucy asked, surely with reason. "If he sold them the land, it's theirs, isn't it?"

George remained serene in the face of this apparently difficult question. "He ought to have all the trades-people boycott the families that sell part of their yards that way. All he'd have to do would be to tell the trades-people they wouldn't get any more orders from the family if they didn't do it."

"From 'the family'? What family?"

"Our family," said George, unperturbed. "The Ambersons."

"I see!" she murmured, and evidently she did see something that he did not, for, as she lifted her muff to her face, he asked:

"What are you laughing at now?"

"Why?"

"You always seem to have some little secret of your own to get happy over!"

"'Always!'" she exclaimed. "What a big word, when we only met last night!"

"That's another case of it," he said, with obvious sincerity. "One of the reasons I don't like you—much!—is you've got that way of seeming quietly superior to everybody else."

"I!" she cried. "I have?"

"Oh, you think you keep it sort of confidential to yourself, but it's plain enough! I don't believe in that kind of thing."

"You don't?"

"No," said George emphatically. "Not with *me!* I think the world's like this: there's a few people that their birth and position, and so on, puts them at the top, and they ought to treat each other entirely as equals." His voice betrayed a little emotion as he added, "I wouldn't speak like this to everybody."

"You mean you're confiding your deepest creed—or code, whatever it is—to me?"

"Go on, make fun of it, then!" George said bitterly. "You do think you're terribly clever! It makes me tired!"

"Well, as you don't like my seeming 'quietly superior,' after this I'll be noisily superior," she returned cheerfully. "We aim to please!"

"I had a notion before I came for you to-day that we were going to quarrel," he said.

"No, we won't; it takes two!" She laughed and waved her muff toward a new house, not quite completed, standing in a field upon their right. They had passed beyond Amberson Addition, and were leaving the northern fringes of the town for the open country. "Isn't that a beautiful house!" she exclaimed. "Papa and I call it our Beautiful House."

George was not pleased. "Does it belong to you?"

"Of course not! Papa brought me out here the other day, driving in his machine, and we both loved it. It's so spacious and dignified and plain."

"Yes, it's plain enough!" George grunted.

"Yet it's lovely; the gray-green roof and shutters give just enough colour, with the trees, for the long white walls. It seems to me the finest house I've seen in this part of the country."

George was outraged by an enthusiasm so ignorant—not ten minutes ago they had passed the Amberson Mansion. "Is that a sample of your taste in architecture?" he asked.

"Yes. Why?"

"Because it strikes me you better go somewhere and study the subject a little!"

Lucy looked puzzled. "What makes you have so much feeling about it? Have I offended you?"

"'Offended' nothing!" George returned brusquely. "Girls usually think they know it all as soon as they've learned to dance and dress and flirt a little. They never know anything about things like architecture, for instance. That house is about as bum a house as any house I ever saw!"

"Why?"

"'Why?'" George repeated. "Did you ask me 'why?'"

"Yes."

"Well, for one thing—" he paused—"for one thing—well, just look at it! I shouldn't think you'd have to do any more than look at it if you'd ever given any attention to architecture."

"What is the matter with its architecture, Mr. Minafer?"

"Well, it's this way," said George. "It's like this. Well, for instance, that house—well, it was built like a town house." He spoke of it in the past tense, because they had now left it far behind them—a human habit of curious significance. "It was like a house meant for a street in the city. What kind of a house was that for people of any taste to build out here in the country?"

"But papa says it's built that way on purpose. There are a lot of other houses being built in this direction, and papa says the city's coming out this way; and in a year or two that house will be right in town."

"It was a bum house, anyhow," said George crossly. "I don't even know the people that are building it. They say a lot of riffraff come to town every year nowadays and there's other riffraff that have always lived here, and have made a little money, and act as if they owned the place. Uncle Sydney was talking about it yesterday: he says he and some of his friends are organizing a country club, and already some of these riffraff are worming into it—people he never heard of at all! Anyhow, I guess it's pretty clear you don't know a great deal about architecture."

She demonstrated the completeness of her amiability by laughing. "I'll know something about the North Pole before long," she said, "if we keep going much farther in this direction!"

At this he was remorseful. "All right, we'll turn and drive south awhile till you get warmed up again. I expect we have been going against the wind about long enough. Indeed, I'm sorry!"

He said, "Indeed, I'm sorry," in a nice way, and looked very strikingly handsome when he said it, she thought. No doubt it is true that there is more rejoicing in heaven over one sinner repented than over all the saints who consistently remain holy, and the rare, sudden gentlenesses of arrogant people have infinitely more effect than the continual gentleness of gentle people. Arrogance turned gentle melts the heart; and Lucy gave her companion a little sidelong, sunny nod of acknowledgment. George was dazzled by the quick glow of her eyes, and found himself at a loss for something to say.

Having turned about, he kept his horse to a walk, and at this gait the sleighbells tinkled but intermittently. Gleaming wanly through the whitish vapour that kept rising from the trotter's body and flanks, they were like tiny fog-bells, and made the only sounds in a great winter silence. The white road ran between lonesome rail fences; and frozen barnyards beyond the fences showed sometimes a harrow left to rust, with its iron seat half filled with stiffened snow, and sometimes an old dead buggy, its wheels forever set, it seemed, in the solid ice of deep ruts. Chickens scratched the metallic earth with an air of protest, and a masterless ragged colt looked up in sudden horror at the mild tinkle of the passing bells, then blew fierce clouds of steam at the sleigh. The snow no longer fell, and far ahead, in a grayish cloud that lay upon the land, was the town.

Lucy looked at this distant thickening reflection. "When we get this far out we can see there must be quite a little smoke hanging over the town," she said. "I suppose that's because it's growing. As it grows bigger it seems to get ashamed of itself, so it makes this cloud and hides in it. Papa says it used to be a bit nicer when he lived here: he always speaks of it differently—he always has a gentle look, a particular tone of voice, I've noticed. He must have been very fond of it. It must have been a lovely place: everybody must have been so jolly. From the way he talks, you'd think life here then was just one long midsummer serenade. He declares it was always sunshiny, that the air wasn't like the air anywhere else—that, as he remembers it, there always seemed to be gold-dust in the air. I doubt it! I think it doesn't seem to be duller air to him now just on account of having a little soot in it sometimes, but probably because he was twenty years younger then. It seems to me the gold-dust he thinks was here is just his being young that he remembers. I think it was just youth. It *is* pretty pleasant to be young, isn't it?" She laughed absently, then appeared to become wistful. "I wonder if we really do enjoy it as much as we'll look back and think we did! I don't suppose so. Anyhow, for my part I feel as if I must be missing something about it, somehow, because I don't ever seem to be thinking about what's happening at the present moment; I'm always looking forward to something —thinking about things that will happen when I'm older."

"You're a funny girl," George said gently. "But your voice sounds pretty nice when you think and talk along together like that!"

The horse shook himself all over, and the impatient sleighbells made his wish audible. Accordingly, George tightened the reins, and the cutter was off again at a three-minute trot, no despicable rate of speed. It was not long before they were again passing Lucy's Beautiful House, and here George thought fit to put an appendix to his remark. "You're a funny girl, and you know a lot—but I don't believe you know much about architecture!"

Coming toward them, black against the snowy road, was a strange silhouette. It approached moderately and without visible means of progression, so the matter seemed from a distance; but as the cutter shortened the distance, the silhouette was revealed to be Mr. Morgan's horseless carriage, conveying four people atop: Mr. Morgan with George's mother beside him, and, in the rear seat, Miss Fanny Minafer and the Honourable George Amberson. All four seemed to be in the liveliest humour, like high-spirited people upon a new adventure; and Isabel waved her handkerchief dashingly as the cutter flashed by them.

"For the Lord's sake!" George gasped.

"Your mother's a dear," said Lucy. "And she does wear the most bewitching *things!* She looked like a Russian princess, though I doubt if they're that handsome."

George said nothing; he drove on till they had crossed Amberson Addition and reached the stone pillars at the head of National Avenue. There he turned.

"Let's go back and take another look at that old sewing-machine," he said. "It certainly is the weirdest, craziest——"

He left the sentence unfinished, and presently they were again in sight of the old sewing-machine. George shouted mockingly.

Alas! three figures stood in the road, and a pair of legs, with the toes turned up, indicated that a fourth figure lay upon its back in the snow, beneath a horseless carriage that had decided to need a horse.

George became vociferous with laughter, and coming up at his trotter's best gait, snow spraying from runners and every hoof, swerved to the side of the road and shot by, shouting, "Git a hoss! Git a hoss! Git a hoss!"

Three hundred yards away he turned and came back, racing; leaning out as he passed, to wave jeeringly at the group about the disabled machine: "Git a hoss! Git a hoss! Git a——"

The trotter had broken into a gallop, and Lucy cried a warning: "Be careful!" she said. "Look where you're driving! There's a ditch on that side. *Look——*"

George turned too late; the cutter's right runner went into the ditch and snapped off; the little sleigh upset, and, after dragging its occupants some fifteen yards, left them lying together in a bank of snow. Then the vigorous young horse kicked himself free of all annoyances, and disappeared down the road, galloping cheerfully.

CHAPTER VIII

When George regained some measure of his presence of mind, Miss Lucy Morgan's cheek, snowy and cold, was pressing his nose slightly to one side; his right arm was firmly about her neck; and a monstrous amount of her fur boa seemed to mingle with an equally unplausible quantity of snow in his mouth. He was confused, but conscious of no objection to any of these juxtapositions. She was apparently uninjured, for she sat up, hatless, her hair down, and said mildly:

"Good heavens!"

Though her father had been under his machine when they passed, he was the first to reach them. He threw himself on his knees beside his daughter, but found her already laughing, and was reassured. "They're all right," he called to Isabel, who was running toward them, ahead of her brother and Fanny Minafer. "This snowbank's a feather bed—nothing the matter with them at all. Don't look so pale!"

"Georgie!" she gasped. "*Georgie!*"

Georgie was on his feet, snow all over him.

"Don't make a fuss, mother! Nothing's the matter. That darned silly horse——"

Sudden tears stood in Isabel's eyes. "To see you down underneath—dragging—oh!——" Then with shaking hands she began to brush the snow from him.

"Let me alone," he protested. "You'll ruin your gloves. You're getting snow all over you, and——"

"No, no!" she cried. "You'll catch cold; you mustn't catch cold!" And she continued to brush him.

Amberson had brought Lucy's hat; Miss Fanny acted as lady's-maid; and both victims of the accident were presently restored to about their usual appearance and condition of apparel. In fact, encouraged by the two older gentlemen, the entire party, with one exception, decided that the episode was after all a merry one, and began to laugh about it. But George was glummer than the December twilight now swiftly closing in.

"That darned horse!" he said.

"I wouldn't bother about Pendennis, Georgie," said his uncle. "You can send a man out for what's left of the cutter to-morrow, and Pendennis will gallop straight home to his stable: he'll be there a *long* while before we will, because all we've got to depend on to get us home is Gene Morgan's broken-down chafing-dish yonder."

They were approaching the machine as he spoke, and his friend, again underneath it, heard him. He emerged, smiling. "She'll go," he said.

"What!"

"All aboard!"

He offered his hand to Isabel. She was smiling but still pale, and her eyes, in spite of the smile, kept upon George in a shocked anxiety. Miss Fanny had already mounted to the rear seat, and George, after helping Lucy Morgan to climb up beside his aunt, was following. Isabel saw that his shoes were light things of patent leather, and that snow was clinging to them. She made a little rush toward him, and, as one of his feet rested on the iron step of the machine, in mounting, she began to clean the snow from his shoe with her almost aërial lace handkerchief. "You mustn't catch cold!" she cried.

"Stop that!" George shouted, and furiously withdrew his foot.

"Then stamp the snow off," she begged. "You mustn't ride with wet feet."

"They're not!" George roared, thoroughly outraged. "For heaven's sake get in! You're standing in the snow yourself. Get in!"

Isabel consented, turning to Morgan, whose habitual expression of apprehensiveness was somewhat accentuated. He climbed up after her, George Amberson having gone to the other side. "You're the same Isabel I used to know!" he said in a low voice. "You're a divinely ridiculous woman."

"Am I, Eugene?" she said, not displeased. " 'Divinely' and 'ridiculous' just counterbalance each other, don't they? Plus one and minus one equal nothing; so you mean I'm nothing in particular?"

THE MAGNIFICENT AMBERSONS

"No," he answered, tugging at a lever. "That doesn't seem to be precisely what I meant. There!" This exclamation referred to the subterranean machinery, for dismaying sounds came from beneath the floor, and the vehicle plunged, then rolled noisily forward.

"Behold!" George Amberson exclaimed. "She does move! It must be another accident."

" 'Accident?' " Morgan shouted over the din. "No! She breathes, she stirs; she seems to feel a thrill of life along her keel!" And he began to sing "The Star Spangled Banner."

Amberson joined him lustily, and sang on when Morgan stopped. The twilight sky cleared, discovering a round moon already risen; and the musical congressman hailed this bright presence with the complete text and melody of "The Danube River."

His nephew, behind, was gloomy. He had overheard his mother's conversation with the inventor: it seemed curious to him that this Morgan, of whom he had never heard until last night, should be using the name "Isabel" so easily; and George felt that it was not just the thing for his mother to call Morgan "Eugene"; the resentment of the previous night came upon George again. Meanwhile, his mother and Morgan continued their talk; but he could no longer hear what they said; the noise of the car and his uncle's songful mood prevented. He marked how animated Isabel seemed; it was not strange to see his mother so gay, but it was strange that a man not of the family should be the cause of her gaiety. And George sat frowning.

Fanny Minafer had begun to talk to Lucy. "Your father wanted to prove that his horseless carriage would run, even in the snow," she said. "It really does, too."

"Of course!"

"It's so interesting! He's been telling us how he's going to change it. He says he's going to have wheels all made of rubber and blown up with air. I don't understand what he means at all; I should think they'd explode—but Eugene seems to be very confident. He always was confident, though. It seems so like old times to hear him talk!"

She became thoughtful, and Lucy turned to George. "You tried to swing underneath me and break the fall for me when we went over," she said. "I knew you were doing that, and—it was nice of you."

"Wasn't any fall to speak of," he returned brusquely. "Couldn't have hurt either of us."

"Still it was friendly of you—and awfully quick, too. I'll not—I'll not forget it!"

Her voice had a sound of genuineness, very pleasant; and George began to forget his annoyance with her father. This annoyance of his had not been alleviated by the circumstance that neither of the seats of the old sewing-machine was designed for three people, but when his neighbour spoke thus gratefully, he no longer minded the crowding—in fact, it pleased him so much that he began to wish the old sewing-machine would go even slower. And she had spoken no word of blame for his letting that darned horse get the cutter into the ditch. George presently addressed her hurriedly, almost tremulously, speaking close to her ear:

"I forgot to tell you something: you're pretty nice! I thought so the first second I saw you last night. I'll come for you to-night and take you to the Assembly at the Amberson Hotel. You're going, aren't you?"

"Yes, but I'm going with papa and the Sharons, I'll see you there."

"Looks to me as if you were awfully conventional," George grumbled; and his disappointment was deeper than he was willing to let her see—though she probably did see. "Well, we'll dance the cotillion together, anyhow."

"I'm afraid not. I promised Mr. Kinney."

"What!" George's tone was shocked, as at incredible news. "Well, you could break *that* engagement, I guess, if you wanted to! Girls always can get out of things when they want to. Won't you?"

"I don't think so."

"Why not?"

"Because I promised him. Several days ago."

George gulped, and lowered his pride, "I don't—oh, look here! I only want to go to that thing to-night to get to see something of you; and if you don't dance the cotillion with me, how can I? I'll only be here two weeks, and the others have got all the rest of your visit to see you. *Won't* you do it, please?"

"I couldn't."

"See here!" said the stricken George. "If you're going to decline to dance that cotillion with me simply because you've promised a—a—a miserable red-headed outsider like Fred Kinney, why we might as well quit!"

"Quit what?"

"You know perfectly well what I mean," he said huskily.

"I don't."

"Well, you ought to!"

"But I don't at all!"

George, thoroughly hurt, and not a little embittered, expressed himself in a short outburst of laughter: "Well, I ought to have seen it!"

"Seen what?"

"That you might turn out to be a girl who'd like a fellow of the red-headed Kinney sort. I ought to have seen it from the first!"

Lucy bore her disgrace lightly. "Oh, dancing a cotillion with a person doesn't mean that you like him—but I don't see anything in particular the matter with Mr. Kinney. What is?"

"If you don't see anything the matter with him for yourself," George responded, icily, "I don't think pointing it out would help you. You probably wouldn't understand."

"You might try," she suggested. "Of course I'm a stranger here, and if people have done anything wrong or have something unpleasant about them, I wouldn't have any way of knowing it, just at first. If poor Mr. Kinney——"

"I prefer not to discuss it," said George curtly. "He's an enemy of mine."

"Why?"

"I prefer not to discuss it."

"Well, but——"

"I prefer not to discuss it!"

"Very well." She began to hum the air of the song which Mr. George Amberson was now discoursing, "O moon of my delight that knows no wane" —and there was no further conversation on the back seat.

They had entered Amberson Addition, and the moon of Mr. Amberson's delight was overlaid by a slender Gothic filagree; the branches that sprang from the shade trees lining the street. Through the windows of many of the houses rosy lights were flickering; and silver tinsel and evergreen wreaths and brilliant little glass globes of silver and wine colour could be seen, and glimpses were caught of Christmas trees, with people decking them by fire-light—reminders that this was Christmas Eve. The ride-stealers had disappeared from the highway, though now and then, over the gasping and howling of the horseless carriage, there came a shrill jeer from some young passer-by upon the sidewalk:

"Mister, fer heaven's sake go an' git a hoss! Git a hoss! *Git* a hoss!"

The contrivance stopped with a heart-shaking jerk before Isabel's house. The gentlemen jumped down, helping Isabel and Fanny to descend; there were friendly leavetakings—and one that was not precisely friendly.

"It's 'au revoir,' till to-night, isn't it?" Lucy asked, laughing.

"Good afternoon!" said George, and he did not wait, as his relatives did, to see the old sewing-machine start briskly down the street, toward the Sharons'; its lighter load consisting now of only Mr. Morgan and his daughter. George went into the house at once.

He found his father reading the evening paper in the library. "Where are your mother and your Aunt Fanny?" Mr. Minafer inquired, not looking up.

"They're coming," said his son; and, casting himself heavily into a chair, stared at the fire.

His prediction was verified a few moments later; the two ladies came in cheerfully, unfastening their fur cloaks. "It's all right, Georgie," said Isabel. "Your Uncle George called to us that Pendennis got home safely. Put your shoes close to the fire, dear, or else go and change them." She went to her husband and patted him lightly on the shoulder, an action which George watched with sombre moodiness. "You might dress before long," she suggested. "We're all going to the Assembly, after dinner, aren't we? Brother George said he'd go with us."

"Look here," said George abruptly. "How about this man Morgan and his old sewing-machine? Doesn't he want to get grandfather to put money into it? Isn't he trying to work Uncle George for that? Isn't that what he's up to?"

It was Miss Fanny who responded. "You little silly!" she cried, with sur-

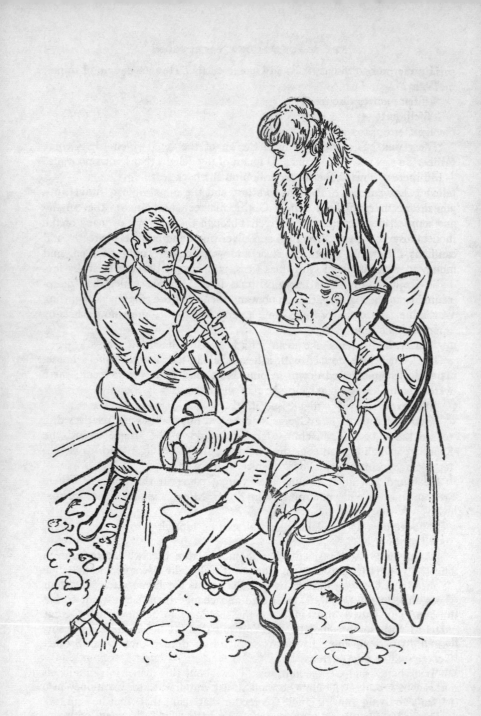

prising sharpness. "What on earth are you talking about? Eugene Morgan's perfectly able to finance his own inventions these days."

"I'll bet he borrows money of Uncle George," the nephew insisted.

Isabel looked at him in grave perplexity. "Why do you say such a thing, George?" she asked.

"He strikes me as that sort of man," he answered doggedly. "Isn't he, father?"

Minafer set down his paper for the moment. "He was a fairly wild young fellow twenty years ago," he said, glancing at his wife absently. "He was like you in one thing, Georgie; he spent too much money—only he didn't have any mother to get money out of a grandfather for him, so he was usually in debt. But I believe I've heard he's done fairly well of late years. No, I can't say I think he's a swindler, and I doubt if he needs anybody else's money to back his horseless carriage."

"Well, what's he brought the old thing here for, then? People that own elephants don't take their elephants around with 'em when they go visiting. What's he got it here for?"

"I'm sure I don't know," said Mr. Minafer, resuming his paper. "You might ask him."

Isabel laughed and patted her husband's shoulder again. "Aren't you going to dress? Aren't we all going to the dance?"

He groaned faintly. "Aren't your brother and Georgie escorts enough for you and Fanny?"

"Wouldn't you enjoy it at all?"

"You know I don't."

Isabel let her hand remain upon his shoulder a moment longer; she stood behind him, looking into the fire, and George, watching her broodingly, thought there was more colour in her face than the reflection of the flames accounted for. "Well, then," she said indulgently, "stay at home and be happy. We won't urge you if you'd really rather not."

"I really wouldn't," he said contentedly.

Half an hour later, George was passing through the upper hall, in a bathrobe stage of preparation for the evening's gaieties, when he encountered his Aunt Fanny. He stopped her. "Look here!" he said.

"What in the world is the matter with you?" she demanded, regarding him with little amiability. "You look as if you were rehearsing for a villain in a play. Do change your expression!"

His expression gave no sign of yielding to the request; on the contrary, its sombreness deepened. "I suppose you don't know why father doesn't want to go to-night," he said solemnly. "You're his only sister, and yet you don't know!"

"He never wants to go anywhere that I ever heard of," said Fanny. "What *is* the matter with you?"

"He doesn't want to go because he doesn't like this man Morgan."

"Good gracious!" Fanny cried impatiently. "Eugene Morgan isn't in your father's thoughts at all, one way or the other. Why should he be?"

George hesitated. "Well—it strikes me—— Look here, what makes you and —and everybody—so excited over him?"

"'Excited!'" she jeered. "Can't people be glad to see an old friend without silly children like you having to make a to-do about it? I've just been in your mother's room suggesting that she might give a little dinner for them——"

"For who?"

"For *whom*, Georgie! For Mr. Morgan and his daughter."

"Look here!" George said quickly. "Don't do that! Mother mustn't do that. It wouldn't look well."

"'Wouldn't look well!'" Fanny mocked him; and her suppressed vehemence betrayed a surprising acerbity. "See here, Georgie Minafer, I suggest that you just march straight on into your room and finish your dressing! Sometimes you say things that show you have a pretty mean little mind!"

George was so astounded by this outburst that his indignation was delayed by his curiosity. "Why, what upsets *you* in this way?" he inquired.

"I know what you mean," she said, her voice still lowered, but not decreasing in sharpness. "You're trying to insinuate that I'd get your mother to invite Eugene Morgan here on my account because he's a widower!"

"I *am*?" George gasped, nonplussed. "I'm trying to insinuate that you're setting your cap at him and getting mother to help you? Is that what you mean?"

Beyond a doubt that was what Miss Fanny meant. She gave him a white-hot look. "You attend to your own affairs!" she whispered fiercely, and swept away.

George, dumfounded, returned to his room for meditation.

He had lived for years in the same house with his Aunt Fanny, and it now appeared that during all those years he had been thus intimately associating with a total stranger. Never before had he met the passionate lady with whom he had just held a conversation in the hall. So she wanted to get married! And wanted George's mother to help her with this horseless-carriage widower!

"Well, I *will* be shot!" he muttered aloud. "I will—I certainly will be shot!" And he began to laugh. "Lord 'lmighty!"

But presently, at the thought of the horseless-carriage widower's daughter, his grimness returned, and he resolved upon a line of conduct for the evening. He would nod to her carelessly when he first saw her; and, after that, he would notice her no more: he would not dance with her; he would not favour her in the cotillion—he would not go near her!

. . . He descended to dinner upon the third urgent summons of a coloured butler, having spent two hours dressing—and rehearsing.

CHAPTER IX

The Honourable George Amberson was a congressman who led cotillions—
the sort of congressman an Amberson would be. He did it negligently, to-
night, yet with infallible dexterity, now and then glancing humorously at
the spectators, people of his own age. They were seated in a tropical grove
at one end of the room whither they had retired at the beginning of the
cotillion, which they surrendered entirely to the twenties and the late 'teens.
And here, grouped with that stately pair, Sydney and Amelia Amberson, sat
Isabel with Fanny, while Eugene Morgan appeared to bestow an amiable devotion impartially upon the three sisters-in-law. Fanny watched his face eagerly, laughing at everything he said; Amelia smiled blandly, but rather
because of graciousness than because of interest; while Isabel, looking out
at the dancers, rhythmically moved a great fan of blue ostrich feathers, listened to Eugene thoughtfully, yet all the while kept her shining eyes on
Georgie.

Georgie had carried out his rehearsed projects with precision. He had
given Miss Morgan a nod studied into perfection during his lengthy toilet
before dinner. "Oh, yes, I do seem to remember that curious little outsider!"
this nod seemed to say. Thereafter, all cognizance of her evaporated: the
curious little outsider was permitted no further existence worth the struggle.
Nevertheless, she flashed in the corner of his eye too often. He was aware of
her dancing demurely, and of her viciously flirtatious habit of never looking
up at her partner, but keeping her eyes concealed beneath downcast lashes;
and he had over-sufficient consciousness of her between the dances, though
it was not possible to see her at these times, even if he had cared to look
frankly in her direction—she was invisible in a thicket of young dresscoats.
The black thicket moved as she moved, and her location was hatefully apparent, even if he had not heard her voice laughing from the thicket. It was
annoying how her voice, though never loud, pursued him. No matter how
vociferous were other voices, all about, he seemed unable to prevent himself
from constantly recognizing hers. It had a quaver in it, not pathetic—rather
humorous than pathetic—a quality which annoyed him to the point of rage,
because it was so difficult to get away from. She seemed to be having a
"wonderful time!"

An unbearable soreness accumulated in his chest: his dislike of the girl and
her conduct increased until he thought of leaving this sickening Assembly
and going home to bed. *That* would show her! But just then he heard her
laughing, and decided that it wouldn't show her. So he remained.

When the young couples seated themselves in chairs against the walls,
round three sides of the room, for the cotillion, George joined a brazen-faced
group clustering about the doorway—youths with no partners, yet eligible to

be "called out" and favoured. He marked that his uncle placed the infernal Kinney and Miss Morgan, as the leading couple, in the first chairs at the head of the line upon the leader's right; and this disloyalty on the part of Uncle George was inexcusable, for in the family circle the nephew had often expressed his opinion of Fred Kinney. In his bitterness, George uttered a significant monosyllable.

The music flourished; whereupon Mr. Kinney, Miss Morgan, and six of their neighbours rose and waltzed knowingly. Mr. Amberson's whistle blew; then the eight young people went to the favour table and were given toys and trinkets wherewith to delight the new partners it was now their privilege to select. Around the walls, the seated non-participants in this ceremony looked rather conscious; some chattered, endeavouring not to appear expectant; some tried not to look wistful; and others were frankly solemn. It was a trying moment; and whoever secured a favour, this very first shot, might consider the portents happy for a successful evening.

Holding their twinkling gewgaws in their hands, those about to bestow honour came toward the seated lines, where expressions became feverish. Two of the approaching girls seemed to wander, not finding a predetermined object in sight; and these two were Janie Sharon, and her cousin, Lucy. At this, George Amberson Minafer, conceiving that he had little to anticipate from either, turned a proud back upon the room and affected to converse with his friend, Mr. Charlie Johnson.

The next moment a quick little figure intervened between the two. It was Lucy, gaily offering a silver sleighbell decked with white ribbon.

"I almost couldn't find you!" she cried.

George stared, took her hand, led her forth in silence, danced with her. She seemed content not to talk; but as the whistle blew, signalling that this episode was concluded, and he conducted her to her seat, she lifted the little bell toward him. "You haven't taken your favour. You're supposed to pin it on your coat," she said. "Don't you want it?"

"If you insist!" said George stiffly. And he bowed her into her chair; then turned and walked away, dropping the sleighbell haughtily into his trousers' pocket.

The figure proceeded to its conclusion, and George was given other sleighbells, which he easily consented to wear upon his lapel; but, as the next figure began, he strolled with a bored air to the tropical grove, where sat his elders, and seated himself beside his Uncle Sydney. His mother leaned across Miss Fanny, raising her voice over the music to speak to him.

"Georgie, nobody will be able to see you here. You'll not be favoured. You ought to be where you can dance."

"Don't care to," he returned. "Bore!"

"But you ought——" She stopped and laughed, waving her fan to direct his attention behind him. "Look! Over your shoulder!"

He turned, and discovered Miss Lucy Morgan in the act of offering him a purple toy balloon.

"I found you!" she laughed.

George was startled. "Well——" he said.

"Would you rather 'sit it out?'" Lucy asked quickly, as he did not move. "I don't care to dance if you——"

"No," he said, rising. "It would be better to dance." His tone was solemn, and solemnly he departed with her from the grove. Solemnly he danced with her.

Four times, with not the slightest encouragement, she brought him a favour: four times in succession. When the fourth came, "Look here!" said George huskily. "You going to keep this up all night? What do you mean by it?"

For an instant she seemed confused. "That's what cotillions are for, aren't they?" she murmured.

"What do you mean: what they're for?"

"So that a girl can dance with a person she wants to?"

George's huskiness increased. "Well, do you mean you—you want to dance with me all the time—all evening?"

"Well, this much of it—evidently!" she laughed.

"Is it because you thought I tried to keep you from getting hurt this afternoon when we upset?"

She shook her head.

"Was it because you want to even things up for making me angry—I mean, for hurting my feelings on the way home?"

With her eyes averted—for girls of nineteen can be as shy as boys, sometimes—she said, "Well—you only got angry because I couldn't dance the cotillion with you. I—I didn't feel terribly hurt with you for getting angry about *that!*"

"Was there any other reason? Did my telling you I liked you have anything to do with it?"

She looked up gently, and, as George met her eyes, something exquisitely touching, yet queerly delightful, gave him a catch in the throat. She looked instantly away, and, turning, ran out from the palm grove, where they stood, to the dancing-floor.

"Come on!" she cried. "Let's dance!"

He followed her.

"See here—I—I——" he stammered. "You mean—— Do you——"

"No, no!" she laughed. "Let's dance!"

He put his arm about her almost tremulously, and they began to waltz. It was a happy dance for both of them.

Christmas day is the children's, but the holidays are youth's dancing-time. The holidays belong to the early twenties and the 'teens, home from school and college. These years possess the holidays for a little while, then possess them only in smiling, wistful memories of holly and twinkling lights and dance-music, and charming faces all aglow. It is the liveliest time in life, the happiest of the irresponsible times in life. Mothers echo its happiness—nothing is like a mother who has a son home from college, except another mother with a son home from college. Bloom does actually come upon these mothers; it is a visible thing; and they run like girls, walk like athletes, laugh like sycophants. Yet they give up their sons to the daughters of other mothers, and find it proud rapture enough to be allowed to sit and watch.

Thus Isabel watched George and Lucy dancing, as together they danced away the holidays of that year into the past.

"They seem to get along better than they did at first, those two children," Fanny Minafer said, sitting beside her at the Sharons' dance, a week after the Assembly. "They seemed to be always having little quarrels of some sort, at first. At least George did: he seemed to be continually pecking at that lovely, dainty, little Lucy, and being cross with her over nothing."

" 'Pecking?' " Isabel laughed. "What a word to use about Georgie! I think I never knew a more angelically amiable disposition in my life!"

Miss Fanny echoed her sister-in-law's laugh, but it was a rueful echo, and not sweet. "He's amiable to you!" she said. "That's all the side of him you ever happen to see. And why wouldn't he be amiable to anybody that simply fell down and worshipped him every minute of her life? Most of us would!"

"Isn't he worth worshipping? Just look at him! Isn't he *charming* with Lucy! See how hard he ran to get it when she dropped her handkerchief back there."

"Oh, I'm not going to argue with you about George!" said Miss Fanny. "I'm fond enough of him, for that matter. He *can* be charming, and he's certainly stunning *looking*, if only——"

"Let the 'if only' go, dear," Isabel suggested good-naturedly. "Let's talk about that dinner you thought I should——"

"I?" Miss Fanny interrupted quickly. "Didn't you want to give it yourself?"

"Indeed, I did, my dear!" said Isabel heartily. "I only meant that unless you had proposed it, perhaps I wouldn't——"

But here Eugene came for her to dance, and she left the sentence uncompleted. Holiday dances can be happy for youth renewed as well as for youth in bud—and yet it was not with the air of a rival that Miss Fanny watched her brother's wife dancing with the widower. Miss Fanny's eyes narrowed a little, but only as if her mind engaged in a hopeful calculation. She looked pleased.

CHAPTER X

A few days after George's return to the university it became evident that not quite everybody had gazed with complete benevolence upon the various young collegians at their holiday sports. The Sunday edition of the principal morning paper even expressed some bitterness under the heading, "Gilded Youths of the Fin-de-Siècle"—this was considered the knowing phrase of the time, especially for Sunday supplements—and there is no doubt that from certain references in this bit of writing some people drew the conclusion that Mr. George Amberson Minafer had not yet got his come-uppance, a postponement still irritating. Undeniably, Fanny Minafer was one of the people who drew this conclusion, for she cut the article out and enclosed it in a letter to her nephew, having written on the border of the clipping, "I wonder whom it can mean!"

George read part of it:

We debate sometimes what is to be the future of this nation when we think that in a few years public affairs may be in the hands of the *fin-de-siècle* gilded youths we see about us during the Christmas holidays. Such foppery, such luxury, such insolence, was surely never practised by the scented, overbearing patricians of the Palatine, even in Rome's most decadent epoch. In all the wild orgy of wastefulness and luxury with which the nineteenth century reaches its close, the gilded youth has been surely the worst symptom. With his airs of young milord, his fast horses, his gold and silver cigarette-cases, his clothes from a New York tailor, his recklessness of money showered upon him by indulgent mothers or doting grandfathers, he respects nothing and nobody. He is blasé, if you please. Watch him at a social function, how condescendingly he deigns to select a partner for the popular waltz or two-step; how carelessly he shoulders older people out of his way, with what a blank stare he returns the salutation of some old acquaintance whom he may choose in his royal whim to forget! The unpleasant part of all this is that the young women he so condescendingly selects as partners for the dance greet him with seeming rapture, though in their hearts they must feel humiliated by his languid hauteur, and many older people beam upon him almost fawningly if he unbends so far as to throw them a careless, disdainful word!

One wonders what has come over the new generation. Of such as these the Republic was not made. Let us pray that the future of our country is not in the hands of these *fin-de-siècle* gilded youths, but rather in the calloused palms of young men yet unknown, labouring upon the farms of the land. When we compare the young manhood of Abraham Lincoln with the specimens we are now producing, we see too well that it bodes ill for the twentieth century——

George yawned, and tossed the clipping into his waste-basket, wondering why his aunt thought such dull nonsense worth the sending. As for her insinuation, pencilled upon the border, he supposed she meant to joke—a supposition which neither surprised him not altered his lifelong opinion of her wit.

He read her letter with more interest:

. . . The dinner your mother gave for the Morgans was a lovely affair. It was last Monday evening, just ten days after you left. It was peculiarly appropriate that your mother should give this dinner, because her brother George, your uncle, was Mr. Morgan's most intimate friend before he left here a number of years ago, and it was a pleasant occasion for the formal announcement of some news which you heard from Lucy Morgan before you returned to college. At least she told me she had told you the night before you left that her father had decided to return here to live. It was appropriate that your mother, herself an old friend, should assemble a representative selection of Mr. Morgan's old friends around him at such a time. He was in great spirits and most entertaining. As your time was so charmingly taken up during your visit home with a younger member of his family, you probably overlooked opportunities of hearing him talk, and do not know what an interesting man he can be.

He will soon begin to build his factory here for the manufacture of automobiles, which he says is a term he prefers to "horseless carriages." Your Uncle George told me he would like to invest in this factory, as George thinks there is a future for automobiles; perhaps not for general use, but as an interesting novelty, which people with sufficient means would like to own for their amusement and the sake of variety. However, he said Mr. Morgan laughingly declined his offer, as Mr. M. was fully able to finance this venture, though not starting in a very large way. Your uncle said other people are manufacturing automobiles in different parts of the country with success. Your father is not very well, though he is not actually ill, and the doctor tells him he ought not to be so much at his office, as the long years of application indoors with no exercise are beginning to affect him unfavourably, but I believe your father would die if he had to give up his work, which is all that has ever interested him outside of his family. I never could understand it. Mr. Morgan took your mother and me with Lucy to see Modjeska in "Twelfth Night" yesterday evening, and Lucy said she thought the Duke looked rather like you, only much more democratic in his manner. I suppose you will think I have written a great deal about the Morgans in this letter, but thought you would be interested because of your interest in a younger member of his family. Hoping that you are finding college still as attractive as ever,

> Affectionately,
> AUNT FANNY

George read one sentence in this letter several times. Then he dropped the missive in his waste-basket to join the clipping, and strolled down the corridor of his dormitory to borrow a copy of "Twelfth Night." Having secured one, he returned to his study and refreshed his memory of the play—but received no enlightenment that enabled him to comprehend Lucy's strange remark. However, he found himself impelled in the direction of correspondence, and presently wrote a letter—not a reply to his Aunt Fanny.

Dear Lucy:

No doubt you will be surprised at hearing from me so soon again, especially as this makes two in answer to the one received from you since getting back to the old place. I hear you have been making comments about me at the theatre, that some actor was more democratic in his manners than I am, which I do not understand. You know my theory of life because I explained it to you on our first drive together, when I told you I would not talk to everybody about things I feel like the way I spoke to you of my theory of life. I believe those who are able should have a true theory of life, and I developed my theory of life long, long ago.

Well, here I sit smoking my faithful briar pipe, indulging in the fragrance of my *tabac* as I look out on the campus from my many paned window, and things are different with me from the way they were way back in Freshman year. I can see now how boyish in many ways I was then. I believe what has changed me as much as anything was my visit home at the time I met you. So I sit here with my faithful briar and dream the old dreams over as it were, dreaming of the waltzes we waltzed together and of that last night before we parted, and you told me the good news you were going to live there, and I would find my friend waiting for me, when I get home next summer.

I will be glad my friend will be waiting for me. I am not capable of friendship except for the very few, and, looking back over my life, I remember there were times when I doubted if I could feel a great friendship for anybody—especially girls. I do not take a great interest in many people, as you know, for I find most of them shallow. Here in the old place I do not believe in being hail-fellow-well-met with every Tom, Dick, and Harry just because he happens to be a classmate, any more than I do at home, where I have always been careful who I was seen with, largely on account of the family, but also because my disposition ever since my boyhood has been to encourage real intimacy from but the few.

What are you reading now? I have finished both "Henry Esmond" and "The Virginians." I like Thackeray because he is not trashy, and because he writes principally of nice people. My theory of literature is an author who does not indulge in trashiness—writes about people you could introduce into your own home. I agree with my Uncle Sydney, as I once heard him say he did not care to read a book or go to a play about people he would not care to meet at his own dinner table. I believe we should live by certain standards and ideals, as you know from my telling you my theory of life.

Well, a letter is no place for deep discussions, so I will not go into the subject. From several letters from my mother, and one from Aunt Fanny, I hear you are seeing a good deal of the family since I left. I hope sometimes you think of the member who is absent. I got a silver frame for your photograph in New York, and I keep it on my desk. It is the only girl's photograph I ever took the trouble to have framed, though, as I told you frankly, I have had any number of other girls' photographs, yet all were only passing fancies, and oftentimes I have questioned in years past if I was capable of much friendship toward the feminine sex, which I usually found shallow until our own friendship began. When I look at your photograph, I say to myself, "At last, at last here is one that will not prove shallow."

My faithful briar has gone out. I will have to rise and fill it, then once more in the fragrance of My Lady Nicotine, I will sit and dream the old dreams over, and think, too, of the true friend at home awaiting my return in June for the summer vacation.

Friend, this is from your friend,

G. A. M.

George's anticipations were not disappointed. When he came home in June his friend was awaiting him; at least, she was so pleased to see him again that for a few minutes after their first encounter she was a little breathless, and a great deal glowing, and quiet withal. Their sentimental friendship continued, though sometimes he was irritated by her making it less sentimental than he did, and sometimes by what he called her "air of superiority." Her air was usually, in truth, that of a fond but amused older sister; and George did not believe such an attitude was warranted by her eight months of seniority.

Lucy and her father were living at the Amberson Hotel, while Morgan got his small machine-shops built in a western outskirt of the town; and George grumbled about the shabbiness and the old-fashioned look of the hotel, though it was "still the best in the place, of course." He remonstrated with his grandfather, declaring that the whole Amberson Estate would be getting "run-down and out-at-heel, if things weren't taken in hand pretty soon." He urged the general need of rebuilding, renovating, varnishing, and lawsuits.

But the Major, declining to hear him out, interrupted querulously, saying that he had enough to bother him without any advice from George; and retired to his library, going so far as to lock the door audibly.

"Second childhood!" George muttered, shaking his head; and he thought sadly that the Major had not long to live. However, this surmise depressed him for only a moment or so. Of course, people couldn't be expected to live forever, and it would be a good thing to have someone in charge of the Estate who wouldn't let it get to looking so rusty that riffraff dared to make fun of it. For George had lately undergone the annoyance of calling upon the Morgans, in the rather stuffy red velours and gilt parlour of their apartment at the hotel, one evening when Mr. Frederick Kinney also was a caller, and Mr. Kinney had not been tactful. In fact, though he adopted a humorous tone of voice, in expressing his sympathy for people who, through the city's poverty in hotels, were obliged to stay at the Amberson, Mr. Kinney's intention was interpreted by the other visitor as not at all humorous, but, on the contrary, personal and offensive.

George rose abruptly, his face the colour of wrath. "Good-night, Miss Morgan. Good-night, Mr. Morgan," he said. "I shall take pleasure in calling at some other time when a more courteous sort of people may be present."

"Look here!" the hot-headed Fred burst out. "Don't you try to make me out a boor, George Minafer! I wasn't hinting anything at you; I simply forgot all about your grandfather owning this old building. Don't you try to put *me* in the light of a boor! I won't——"

But George walked out in the very course of this vehement protest, and it was necessarily left unfinished.

Mr. Kinney remained only for a few moments after George's departure; and as the door closed upon him, the distressed Lucy turned to her father. She was plaintively surprised to find him in a condition of immoderate laughter.

"I didn't—I didn't think I could hold out!" he gasped, and, after choking until tears came to his eyes, felt blindly for the chair from which he had risen to wish Mr. Kinney an indistinct good-night. His hand found the arm of the chair; he collapsed feebly, and sat uttering incoherent sounds.

"Papa!"

"It brings things back so!" he managed to explain. "This very Fred Kinney's father and young George's father, Wilbur Minafer, used to do just such things when they were at that age—and, for that matter, so did George Amberson and I, and all the rest of us!" And, in spite of his exhaustion, he began to imitate: "'Don't you try to put *me* in the light of a boor!' 'I shall take pleasure in calling at some time when a more courteous sort of people——'" He was unable to go on.

There is a mirth for every age, and Lucy failed to comprehend her father's, but tolerated it a little ruefully.

"Papa, I think they were shocking. Weren't they *awful!*"

"Just—just boys!" he moaned, wiping his eyes.

But Lucy could not smile at all; she was beginning to look indignant. "I can forgive that poor Fred Kinney," she said. "He's just blundering—but George—oh, George behaved outrageously!"

"It's a difficult age," her father observed, his calmness somewhat restored. "Girls don't seem to have to pass through it quite as boys do, or their *savoir faire* is instinctive—or something!" And he gave away to a return of his convulsion.

She came and sat upon the arm of his chair. "Papa, *why* should George behave like that?"

"He's sensitive."

"Rather! But why is he? He does anything he likes to, without any regard for what people think. Then why should he mind so furiously when the least little thing reflects upon him, or on anything or anybody connected with him?"

Eugene patted her hand. "That's one of the greatest puzzles of human vanity, dear; and I don't pretend to know the answer. In all my life, the most arrogant people that I've known have been the most sensitive. The people who have done the most in contempt of other people's opinion, and who consider themselves the highest above it, have been the most furious if it went against them. Arrogant and domineering people can't stand the least, lightest, faintest breath of criticism. It just kills them."

"Papa, do you think George is *terribly* arrogant and domineering?"

"Oh, he's still only a boy," said Eugene consolingly. "There's plenty of fine stuff in him—can't help but be, because he's Isabel Amberson's son."

Lucy stroked his hair, which was still almost as dark as her own. "You liked her pretty well once, I guess, papa."

"I do still," he said quietly.

"She's lovely—lovely! Papa—" she paused, then continued—"I wonder sometimes——"

"What?"

"I wonder just how she happened to marry Mr. Minafer."

"Oh, Minafer's all right," said Eugene. "He's a quiet sort of man, but he's a good man and a kind man. He always was, and those things count."

"But in a way—well, I've heard people say there wasn't anything to him at all except business and saving money. Miss Fanny Minafer herself told me that everything George and his mother have of their own—that is, just to spend as they like—she says it has always come from Major Amberson."

"Thrift, Horatio!" said Eugene lightly. "Thrift's an inheritance, and a common enough one here. The people who settled the country *had* to save, so making and saving were taught as virtues, and the people, to the third generation, haven't found out that making and saving are only means to an end. Minafer doesn't believe in money being spent. He believes God made it to be invested and saved."

"But George isn't saving. He's reckless, and even if he is arrogant and conceited and bad-tempered, he's awfully generous."

"Oh, he's an Amberson," said her father. "The Ambersons aren't saving. They're too much the other way, most of them."

"I don't think I should have called George bad-tempered," Lucy said thoughtfully. "No. I don't think he is."

"Only when he's cross about something?" Morgan suggested, with a semblance of sympathetic gravity.

"Yes," she said brightly, not perceiving that his intention was humorous. "All the rest of the time he's really very amiable. Of course, he's much more a perfect *child*, the whole time, than he realizes! He certainly behaved awfully to-night." She jumped up, her indignation returning. "He did, indeed, and it won't do to encourage him in it. I think he'll find me pretty cool—for a week or so!"

Whereupon her father suffered a renewal of his attack of uproarious laughter.

CHAPTER XI

In the matter of coolness, George met Lucy upon her own predetermined ground; in fact, he was there first, and, at their next encounter, proved loftier and more formal than she did. Their estrangement lasted three weeks, and then disappeared without any preliminary treaty: it had worn itself out, and they forgot it.

At times, however, George found other disturbances to the friendship. Lucy was "too much the village belle," he complained; and took a satiric attitude toward his competitors, referring to them as her "local swains and bumpkins," sulking for an afternoon when she reminded him that he, too, was at least "local." She was a belle with older people as well; Isabel and Fanny were continually taking her driving, bringing her home with them to lunch or dinner, and making a hundred little engagements with her, and the Major had taken a great fancy to her, insisting upon her presence and her father's at the Amberson family dinner at the Mansion every Sunday evening. She knew how to flirt with old people, he said, as she sat next him at the table on one of these Sunday occasions; and he had always liked her father, even when Eugene was a "terror" long ago. "Oh, yes, he was!" the Major laughed, when she remonstrated. "He came up here with my son George and some others for a serenade one night, and Eugene stepped into a bass fiddle, and the poor musicians just gave up! I had a pretty half-hour getting my son George upstairs. I remember! It was the last time Eugene ever touched a drop—but he'd touched plenty before that, young lady, and he daren't deny it! Well, well; there's another thing that's changed: hardly anybody drinks nowadays. Perhaps it's just as well, but things used to be livelier. That serenade was just before Isabel was married—and don't you fret, Miss Lucy:

your father remembers it well enough!" The old gentleman burst into laughter, and shook his finger at Eugene across the table. "The fact is," the Major went on hilariously, "I believe if Eugene hadn't broken that bass fiddle and given himself away, Isabel would never have taken Wilbur! I shouldn't be surprised if that was about all the reason that Wilbur got her! What do you think, Wilbur?"

"I shouldn't be surprised," said Wilbur placidly. "If your notion is right, I'm glad Gene broke the fiddle. He was giving me a hard run!"

The Major always drank three glasses of champagne at his Sunday dinner, and he was finishing the third. "What do *you* say about it, Isabel? By Jove!" he cried, pounding the table. "She's blushing!"

Isabel did blush, but she laughed. "Who wouldn't blush!" she cried, and her sister-in-law came to her assistance.

"The important thing," said Fanny jovially, "is that Wilbur did get her, and not only got her, but kept her!"

Eugene was as pink as Isabel, but he laughed without any sign of embarrassment other than his heightened colour. "There's another important thing—that is, for me," he said. "It's the only thing that makes me forgive that bass viol for getting in my way."

"What is it?" the Major asked.

"Lucy," said Morgan gently.

Isabel gave him a quick glance, all warm approval, and there was a murmur of friendliness round the table.

George was not one of those who joined in this applause. He considered his grandfather's nonsense indelicate, even for second childhood, and he thought that the sooner the subject was dropped the better. However, he had only a slight recurrence of the resentment which had assailed him during the winter at every sign of his mother's interest in Morgan; though he was still ashamed of his aunt sometimes, when it seemed to him that Fanny was almost publicly throwing herself at the widower's head. Fanny and he had one or two arguments in which her fierceness again astonished and amused him.

"You drop your criticisms of your relatives," she bade him, hotly, one day, "and begin thinking a little about your own behaviour! You say people will 'talk' about my—about my merely being pleasant to an old friend! What do I care how they talk? I guess if people are talking about anybody in this family they're talking about the impertinent little snippet that hasn't any respect for anything, and doesn't even know enough to attend to his own affairs!"

"'Snippet,' Aunt Fanny!" George laughed. "How elegant! And '*little* snippet'—when I'm over five-feet-eleven?"

"I said it!" she snapped, departing. "I don't see how Lucy can stand you!"

"You'd make an amiable stepmother-in-law!" he called after her. "I'll be careful about proposing to Lucy!"

These were but roughish spots in a summer that glided by evenly and quickly enough, for the most part, and, at the end, seemed to fly. On the last night before George went back to be a Junior, his mother asked him confidently if it had not been a happy summer.

He hadn't thought about it, he answered. "Oh, I suppose so. Why?"

"I just thought it would be nice to hear you say so," she said, smiling. "I mean, it's pleasant for people of my age to know that people of your age realize that they're happy."

"People of your age!" he repeated. "You know you don't look precisely like an old woman, mother. Not precisely!"

"No," she said. "And I suppose I feel about as young as you do, inside, but it won't be many years before I must begin to *look* old. It does come!" She sighed, still smiling. "It's seemed to me that it must have been a happy summer for you—a real 'summer of roses and wine'—without the wine, perhaps. 'Gather ye roses while ye may'—or was it primroses? Time does really fly, or perhaps it's more like the sky—and smoke——"

George was puzzled. "What do you mean: time being like the sky and smoke?"

"I mean the things that we have and that we think are so solid—they're like smoke, and time is like the sky that the smoke disappears into. You know how a wreath of smoke goes up from a chimney, and seems all thick and black and busy against the sky, as if it were going to do such important things and last forever, and you see it getting thinner and thinner—and then, in such a little while, it isn't there at all; nothing is left but the sky, and the sky keeps on being just the same forever."

"It strikes me you're getting mixed up," said George cheerfully. "I don't see much resemblance between time and the sky, or between things and smoke-wreaths; but I do see one reason you like Lucy Morgan so much. She talks that same kind of wistful, moony way sometimes—I don't mean to say I mind it in either of you, because I rather like to listen to it, and you've got a very good voice, mother. It's nice to listen to, no matter how much smoke and sky, and so on, you talk. So's Lucy's, for that matter; and I see why you're congenial. She talks that way to her father, too; and he's right there with the same kind of guff. Well, it's all right with *me!*" He laughed, teasingly, and allowed her to retain his hand, which she had fondly seized. "I've got plenty to think about when people drool along!"

She pressed his hand to her cheek, and a tear made a tiny warm streak across one of his knuckles.

"For heaven's sake!" he said. "What's the matter? Isn't everything all right?"

"You're going away!"

"Well, I'm coming back, don't you suppose? Is *that* all that worries you?"

She cheered up, and smiled again, but shook her head. "I never can bear to see you go—that's the most of it. I'm a little bothered about your father, too."

"Why?"

"It seems to me he looks so badly. Everybody thinks so."

"What nonsense!" George laughed. "He's been looking that way all summer. He isn't much different from the way he's looked all his life, that I can see. What's the matter with him?"

"He never talks much about his business to me but I think he's been worrying about some investments he made last year. I think his worry has affected his health."

"What investments?" George demanded. "He hasn't gone into Mr. Morgan's automobile concern, has he?"

"No," Isabel smiled. "The 'automobile concern' is all Eugene's, and it's so small I understand it's taken hardly anything. No; your father has always prided himself on making only the most absolutely safe investments, but two or three years ago he and your Uncle George both put a great deal— pretty much everything they could get together, I think—into the stock of rolling-mills some friends of theirs owned, and I'm afraid the mills haven't been doing well."

"What of that? Father needn't worry. You and I could take care of him the rest of his life on what grandfather——"

"Of course," she agreed. "But your father's always lived so for his business and taken such pride in his sound investments; it's a passion with him. I——"

"Pshaw! *He* needn't worry! You tell him we'll look after him: we'll build him a little stone bank in the back yard, if he busts up, and he can go and put his pennies in it every morning. That'll keep him just as happy as he ever was!" He kissed her. "Good-night, I'm going to tell Lucy good-bye. Don't sit up for me."

She walked to the front gate with him, still holding his hand, and he told her again not to "sit up" for him.

"Yes, I will," she laughed. "You won't be very late."

"Well—it's my last night."

"But I know Lucy, and she knows I want to see you, too, your last night. You'll see: she'll send you home promptly at eleven!"

But she was mistaken: Lucy sent him home promptly at ten.

CHAPTER XII

Isabel's uneasiness about her husband's health—sometimes reflected in her letters to George during the winter that followed—had not been alleviated when the accredited Senior returned for his next summer vacation, and she confided to him in his room, soon after his arrival, that "something" the doctor had said to her lately had made her more uneasy than ever.

"Still worrying over his rolling-mills investments?" George asked, not seriously impressed.

"I'm afraid it's past that stage from what Dr. Rainey says. His worries only aggravate his condition now. Dr. Rainey says we ought to get him away."

"Well, let's do it, then."

"He won't go."

"He's a man awfully set in his ways; that's true," said George. "I don't think there's anything much the matter with him, though, and he looks just the same to me. Have you seen Lucy lately? How is she?"

"Hasn't she written you?"

"Oh, about once a month," he answered carelessly. "Never says much about herself. How's she look?"

"She looks—pretty!" said Isabel. "I suppose she wrote you they've moved?"

"Yes; I've got her address. She said they were building."

"They did. It's all finished, and they've been in it a month. Lucy is so capable; she keeps house exquisitely. It's small, but oh, such a pretty little house!"

"Well, that's fortunate," George said. "One thing I've always felt they didn't know a great deal about is architecture."

"Don't they?" asked Isabel, surprised. "Anyhow, their house is charming. It's way out beyond the end of Amberson Boulevard; it's quite near that big white house with a gray-green roof somebody built out there a year or so ago. There are any number of houses going up, out that way; and the trolley-line runs within a block of them now, on the next street, and the traction people are laying tracks more than three miles beyond. I suppose you'll be driving out to see Lucy to-morrow."

"I thought——" George hesitated. "I thought perhaps I'd go after dinner this evening."

At this, his mother laughed, not astonished. "It was only my feeble joke about 'to-morrow,' Georgie! I was pretty sure you couldn't wait that long. Did Lucy write you about the factory?"

"No. What factory?"

"The automobile shops. They had rather a dubious time at first, I'm afraid, and some of Eugene's experiments turned out badly, but this spring they've finished eight automobiles and sold them all, and they've got twelve more almost finished, and they're sold already! Eugene's so gay over it!"

"What do his old sewing-machines look like? Like that first one he had when they came here?"

"No, indeed! These have rubber tires blown up with air—pneumatic! And they aren't so high; they're very easy to get into, and the engine's in front— Eugene thinks that's a great improvement. They're very interesting to look at; behind the driver's seat there's a sort of box where four people can sit, with a step and a little door in the rear, and——"

"I know all about it," said George. "I've seen any number like that, East. You can see all you want of 'em, if you stand on Fifth Avenue half an hour, any afternoon. I've seen half-a-dozen go by almost at the same time—within a few minutes, anyhow; and of course electric hansoms are a common sight there any day. I hired one, myself, the last time I was there. How fast do Mr. Morgan's machines go?"

"Much *too* fast! It's very exhilarating—but rather frightening; and they do make a fearful uproar. He says, though, he thinks he sees a way to get around the noisiness in time."

"I don't mind the noise," said George. "Give me a horse, for mine, though, any day. I must get up a race with one of these things: Pendennis'll leave it one mile behind in a two-mile run. How's grandfather?"

"He looks well, but he complains sometimes of his heart: I suppose that's natural at his age—and it's an Amberson trouble." Having mentioned this, she looked anxious instantly. "Did *you* ever feel any weakness there, Georgie?"

"No!" he laughed.

"Are you *sure*, dear?"

"No!" And he laughed again. "Did you?"

"Oh, I think not—at least, the doctor told me he thought my heart was about all right. He said I needn't be alarmed."

"I should think not! Women do seem to be always talking about health: I suppose they haven't got enough else to think of!"

"That must be it," she said gaily. "We're an idle lot!"

George had taken off his coat. "I don't like to hint to a lady," he said, "but I do want to dress before dinner."

"Don't be long; I've got to do a lot of looking at you, dear!" She kissed him and ran away, singing.

But his Aunt Fanny was not so fond; and at the dinner-table there came a spark of liveliness into her eye when George patronizingly asked her what was the news in her own "particular line of sport."

"What do you mean, Georgie?" she asked quietly.

"Oh I mean: What's the news in the fast set generally? You been causing any divorces lately?"

"No," said Fanny, the spark in her eye getting brighter. "I haven't been causing anything."

"Well, what's the gossip? You usually hear pretty much everything that goes on around the nooks and crannies in this town, I hear. What's the last from the gossips' corner, auntie?"

Fanny dropped her eyes, and the spark was concealed, but a movement of her lower lip betokened a tendency to laugh, as she replied, "There hasn't been much gossip lately, except the report that Lucy Morgan and Fred Kinney are engaged—and that's quite old, by this time."

Undeniably, this bit of mischief was entirely successful, for there was a clatter upon George's plate. "What—what do you think you're talking about?" he gasped.

Miss Fanny looked up innocently. "About the report of Lucy Morgan's engagement to Fred Kinney."

George turned dumbly to his mother, and Isabel shook her head reassuringly. "People are always starting rumours," she said. "I haven't paid any attention to this one."

"But you—you've heard it?" he stammered.

"Oh, one hears all sorts of nonsense, dear. I haven't the slightest idea that it's true."

"Then you *have* heard it!"

"I wouldn't let it take my appetite," his father suggested dryly. "There are plenty of girls in the world!"

George turned pale.

"Eat your dinner, Georgie," his aunt said sweetly. "Food will do you good. I didn't say I knew this rumour was true. I only said I'd heard it."

"When? When did you hear it!"

"Oh, months ago!" And Fanny found any further postponement of laughter impossible.

"Fanny, you're a hard-hearted creature," Isabel said gently. "You *really* are. Don't pay any attention to her, George. Fred Kinney's only a clerk in his uncle's hardware place: he couldn't marry for ages—even if anybody would accept him!"

George breathed tumultuously. "I don't care anything about 'ages'! What's that got to do with it?" he said, his thoughts appearing to be somewhat disconnected. "'Ages,' don't mean anything! I only want to know—I want to know—— I want——" He stopped.

"What do you want?" his father asked crossly. "Why don't you say it? Don't make such a fuss."

"I'm not—not at all," George declared, pushing his chair back from the table.

"You must finish your dinner, dear," his mother urged. "Don't——"

"I have finished. I've eaten all I want. I don't want any more than I wanted. I don't want—I——" He rose, still incoherent. "I prefer—I want—— Please excuse me!"

He left the room, and a moment later the screens outside the open front door were heard to slam.

"Fanny! You shouldn't——"

"Isabel, don't reproach me. He did have plenty of dinner, and I only told the truth: everybody has been saying——"

"But there isn't any truth in it."

"We don't actually know there isn't," Miss Fanny insisted, giggling. "We've never *asked* Lucy."

"I wouldn't ask her anything so absurd!"

"George would," George's father remarked. "That's what he's gone to do."

Mr. Minafer was not mistaken: that was what his son had gone to do. Lucy and her father were just rising from their dinner table when the stirred youth arrived at the front door of the new house. It was a cottage, however, rather than a house; and Lucy had taken a free hand with the architect,

THE MAGNIFICENT AMBERSONS 593

achieving results in white and green, outside, and white and blue, inside to such effect of youth and daintiness that her father complained of "too much springtime!" The whole place, including his own bedroom, was a young damsel's boudoir, he said, so that nowhere could he smoke a cigar without feeling like a ruffian. However, he was smoking when George arrived, and he encouraged George to join him in the pastime, but the caller, whose air was both tense and preoccupied, declined with something like agitation.

"I never smoke—that is, I'm seldom—I mean, no thanks," he said. "I mean not at all. I'd rather not."

"Aren't you well, George?" Eugene asked, looking at him in perplexity. "Have you been overworking at college? You do look rather pa——"

"I don't work," said George. "I mean I don't work. I think, but I don't work. I only work at the end of the term. There isn't much to do."

Eugene's perplexity was little decreased, and a tinkle of the door-bell afforded him obvious relief. "It's my foreman," he said, looking at his watch. "I'll take him out in the yard to talk. This is no place for a foreman." And he departed, leaving the "living room" to Lucy and George. It was a pretty room, white panelled and blue curtained—and no place for a foreman, as Eugene said. There was a grand piano, and Lucy stood leaning back against it, looking intently at George, while her fingers, behind her, absently struck a chord or two. And her dress was the dress for that room, being of blue and white, too; and the high colour in her cheeks was far from interfering with the general harmony of things—George saw with dismay that she was prettier than ever, and naturally he missed the reassurance he might have felt had he been able to guess that Lucy, on her part, was finding him better looking than ever. For, however unusual the scope of George's pride, vanity of beauty was not included; he did not think about his looks.

"What's wrong, George?" she asked softly.

"What do you mean: 'What's wrong?' "

"You're awfully upset about something. Didn't you get through your examination all right?"

"Certainly I did. What makes you think anything's 'wrong' with me?"

"You do look pale, as papa said, and it seemed to me that the way you talked sounded—well, a little confused."

" 'Confused'! I said I didn't care to smoke. What in the world is confused about that?"

"Nothing. But——"

"See here!" George stepped close to her. "Are you glad to see me?"

"You needn't be so fierce about it!" Lucy protested, laughing at his dramatic intensity. "Of course I am! How long have I been looking forward to it?"

"I don't know," he said sharply, abating nothing of his fierceness. "How long have you?"

"Why—ever since you went away!"

"Is that true? Lucy, is that true?"

"You *are* funny!" she said. "Of course it's true. Do tell me what's the matter with you, George!"

"I will!" he exclaimed. "I was a boy when I saw you last. I see that now, though I didn't then. Well, I'm not a boy any longer. I'm a man, and a man has a right to demand a totally different treatment."

"Why has he?"

"What?"

"I don't seem to be able to understand you at all, George. Why shouldn't a boy be treated just as well as a man?"

George seemed to find himself at a loss. "Why shouldn't— Well, he shouldn't, because a man has a right to certain explanations."

"What explanations?"

"Whether he's been made a toy of!" George almost shouted. "*That's* what I want to know!"

Lucy shook her head despairingly. "You *are* the queerest person! You say you're a man now, but you talk more like a boy than ever. What *does* make you so excited?"

"'Excited'!" he stormed. "Do you dare to stand there and call me 'excited'? I tell you, I never have been more calm or calmer in my life! I don't know that a person needs to be called 'excited' because he demands explanations that are his simple due!"

"What in the world do you want me to explain?"

"Your conduct with Fred *Kinney!*" George shouted.

Lucy uttered a sudden cry of laughter; she was delighted. "It's been awful!" she said. "I don't know that I ever heard of worse misbehaviour! Papa and I have been twice to dinner with his family, and I've been three times to church with Fred—and once to the circus! I don't know when they'll be here to arrest me!"

"Stop that!" George commanded fiercely. "I want to know just one thing, and I mean to know it, too!"

"Whether I enjoyed the circus?"

"I want to know if you're engaged to him!"

"No!" she cried, and lifting her face close to his for the shortest instant possible, she gave him a look half merry, half defiant, but all fond. It was an adorable look.

"*Lucy!*" he said huskily.

But she turned quickly from him, and ran to the other end of the room. He followed awkwardly, stammering:

"Lucy, I want—I want to ask you. Will you—will you—will you be engaged to *me?*"

She stood at a window, seeming to look out into the summer darkness, her back to him.

"Will you, Lucy?"

"No," she murmured, just audibly.

"Why not?"

"I'm older than you."

"Eight months!"

"You're too young."

"Is that—" he said, gulping—"is that the only reason you won't?"

She did not answer.

As she stood, persistently staring out of the window, with her back to him, she did not see how humble his attitude had become; but his voice was low, and it shook so that she could have no doubt of his emotion. "Lucy, please forgive me for making such a row," he said, thus gently. "I've been—I've been terribly upset—terribly! You know how I feel about you, and always have felt about you. I've shown it in every single thing I've done since the first time I met you, and I know you know it. Don't you?"

Still she did not move or speak.

"Is the only reason you won't be engaged to me you think I'm too young, Lucy?"

"It's—it's reason enough," she said faintly.

At that he caught one of her hands, and she turned to him: there were tears in her eyes, tears which he did not understand at all.

"Lucy, you little dear!" he cried. "I *knew* you——"

"No, no!" she said, and she pushed him away, withdrawing her hand. "George, let's not talk of solemn things."

" 'Solemn things'! Like what?"

"Like—being engaged."

But George had become altogether jubilant, and he laughed triumphantly. "Good gracious, *that* isn't solemn!"

"It is, too!" she said, wiping her eyes. "It's too solemn for us."

"No, it isn't! I——"

"Let's sit down and be sensible, dear," she said. "You sit over there——"

"I will if you'll call me 'dear' again."

"No," she said. "I'll only call you that once again this summer—the night before you go away."

"That will have to do, then," he laughed, "so long as I know we're engaged."

"But we're not!" she protested. "And we never will be, if you don't promise not to speak of it again until—until I tell you to!"

"I won't promise that," said the happy George. "I'll only promise not to speak of it till the next time you call me 'dear'; and you've promised to call me that the night before I leave for my senior year."

"Oh, but I didn't!" she said earnestly, then hesitated. "Did I?"

"Didn't you?"

"I don't think I meant it," she murmured, her wet lashes flickering above troubled eyes.

"I know *one* thing about you," he said gaily, his triumph increasing. "You never went back on anything you said, yet, and I'm not afraid of this being the first time!"

"But we mustn't let——" she faltered; then went on tremulously, "George, we've got on so well together, we won't let this make a difference between us, will we?" And she joined in his laughter.

"It will all depend on what you tell me the night before I go away. You agree we're going to settle things then, don't you, Lucy?"

"I don't promise."

"Yes, you do! Don't you?"

"Well—"

CHAPTER XIII

That night George began a jubilant warfare upon his Aunt Fanny, opening the campaign upon his return home at about eleven o'clock. Fanny had retired, and was presumably asleep, but George, on the way to his own room, paused before her door, and serenaded her in a full baritone:

> "As I walk along the Boy de Balong
> With my independent air,
> The people all declare,
> 'He must be a millionaire!'
> *Oh*, you hear them sigh, and wish to die,
> And see them wink the other eye
> At the man that broke the bank at Monte Carlo!"

Isabel came from George's room, where she had been reading, waiting for him. "I'm afraid you'll disturb your father, dear. I wish you'd sing more, though—in the daytime! You have a splendid voice."

"Good-night, old lady!"

"I thought perhaps I—— Didn't you want me to come in with you and talk a little?"

"Not to-night. You go to bed. Good-night, old lady!"

He kissed her hilariously, entered his room with a skip, closed his door noisily; and then he could be heard tossing things about, loudly humming "The Man that Broke the Bank at Monte Carlo."

Smiling, his mother knelt outside his door to pray; then, with her "Amen," pressed her lips to the bronze door-knob; and went silently to her own apartment.

. . . After breakfasting in bed, George spent the next morning at his grandfather's and did not encounter his Aunt Fanny until lunch, when she seemed to be ready for him.

"Thank you so much for the serenade, George!" she said. "Your poor father tells me he'd just got to sleep for the first time in two nights, but after your kind attentions he lay awake the rest of last night."

"Perfecly true," Mr. Minafer said grimly.

"Of course, I didn't know, sir," George hastened to assure him. "I'm awfully sorry. But Aunt Fanny was so gloomy and excited before I went out, last evening, I thought she needed cheering up."

"I!" Fanny jeered. "I was gloomy? I was excited? You mean about that engagement?"

"Yes. Weren't you? I thought I heard you worrying over somebody's being engaged. Didn't I hear you say you'd heard Mr. Eugene Morgan was engaged to marry some pretty little seventeen-year-old girl?"

Fanny was stung, but she made a brave effort. "Did you ask Lucy?" she said, her voice almost refusing the teasing laugh she tried to make it utter. "Did you ask her when Fred Kinney and she——"

"Yes. That story wasn't true. But the other one——" Here he stared at Fanny, and then affected dismay. "Why, what's the matter with your face, Aunt Fanny? It seems agitated!"

" 'Agitated!' " Fanny said disdainfully, but her voice undeniably lacked steadiness. " 'Agitated!' "

"Oh, come!" Mr. Minafer interposed. "Let's have a little peace!"

"I'm willing," said George. "I don't want to see poor Aunt Fanny all stirred up over a rumour I just this minute invented myself. She's so excitable—about certain subjects—it's hard to control her." He turned to his mother. "What's the matter with grandfather?"

"Didn't you see him this morning?" Isabel asked.

"Yes. He was glad to see me, and all that, but he seemed pretty fidgety. Has he been having trouble with his heart again?"

"Not lately. No."

"Well, he's not himself. I tried to talk to him about the estate; it's disgraceful—it really is—the way things are looking. He wouldn't listen, and he seemed upset. What's he upset over?"

Isabel looked serious; however, it was her husband who suggested gloomily, "I suppose the Major's bothered about this Sydney and Amelia business, most likely."

"What Sydney and Amelia business?" George asked.

"Your mother can tell you, if she wants to," Minafer said. "It's not my side of the family, so I keep off."

"It's rather disagreeable for all of us, Georgie," Isabel began. "You see, your Uncle Sydney wanted a diplomatic position, and he thought brother George, being in Congress, could arrange it. George did get him the offer of a South American ministry, but Sydney wanted a European ambassadorship and he got quite indignant with poor George for thinking he'd take anything smaller—and he believes George didn't work hard enough for him. George had done his best, of course, and now he's out of Congress, and won't run again—so there's Sydney's idea of a big diplomatic position gone for good. Well, Sydney and your Aunt Amelia are terribly disappointed, and they say they've been thinking for years that this town isn't really fit to live in—'for a gentleman,' Sydney says—and it *is* getting rather big and dirty. So they've sold their house and decided to go abroad to live permanently; there's a villa near Florence they've often talked of buying. And they want father to let them have their share of the estate now, instead of waiting for him to leave it to them in his will."

"Well, I suppose that's fair enough," George said. "That is, in case he intended to leave them a certain amount in his will."

"Of course that's understood, Georgie. Father explained his will to us long ago; a third to them, and a third to brother George, and a third to us."

Her son made a simple calculation in his mind. Uncle George was a bachelor, and probably would never marry; Sydney and Amelia were childless. The Major's only grandchild appeared to remain the eventual heir of the entire property, no matter if the Major did turn over to Sydney a third of it now. And George had a fragmentary vision of himself, in mourning, arriving to take possession of a historic Florentine villa—he saw himself walking up a cypress-bordered path, with ancient carven stone balustrades in the distance, and servants in mourning livery greeting the new signore. "Well, I suppose it's grandfather's own affair. He can do it or not, just as he likes. I don't see why he'd mind much."

"He seemed rather confused and pained about it," Isabel said. "I think they oughtn't to urge it. George says that the estate won't stand taking out the third that Sydney wants, and that Sydney and Amelia are behaving like a couple of pigs." She laughed, continuing, "Of course *I* don't know whether they are or not: I never have understood any more about business myself than a little pig would! But I'm on George's side, whether he's right or wrong; I always was from the time we were children: and Sydney and Amelia are hurt with me about it, I'm afraid. They've stopped speaking to George entirely. Poor father! Family rows at his time of life."

George became thoughtful. If Sydney and Amelia were behaving like pigs, things might not be so simple as at first they seemed to be. Uncle Sydney and Aunt Amelia might live an *awful* long while, he thought; and besides, people didn't always leave their fortunes to relatives. Sydney might die first, leaving everything to his widow, and some curly-haired Italian adventurer might get round her, over there in Florence; she might be fool enough to marry again—or even adopt somebody!

He became more and more thoughtful, forgetting entirely a plan he had formed for the continued teasing of his Aunt Fanny; and, an hour after lunch, he strolled over to his grandfather's, intending to apply for further information, as a party rightfully interested.

He did not carry out this intention, however. Going into the big house by a side entrance, he was informed that the Major was upstairs in his bedroom, that his sons Sydney and George were both with him, and that a serious argument was in progress. "You kin stan' right in de middle dat big sta'y-way," said old Sam, the ancient negro, who was his informant, "an' you kin heah all you a-mind to wivout goin' on up no fudda. Mist' Sydney an' Mist' Jawge talkin' louduh'n I evuh heah nobody ca'y on in nish heah house! Quollin', honey, big quollin'!"

"All right," said George shortly. "You go on back to your own part of the house, and don't make any talk. Hear me?"

"Yessuh, yessuh," Sam chuckled, as he shuffled away. "Plenty talkin' wivout Sam! Yessuh!"

George went to the foot of the great stairway. He could hear angry voices overhead—those of his two uncles—and a plaintive murmur, as if the Major tried to keep the peace.

Such sounds were far from encouraging to callers, and George decided not to go upstairs until this interview was over. His decision was the result of no timidity, nor of a too sensitive delicacy. What he felt was, that if he interrupted the scene in his grandfather's room, just at this time, one of the three gentlemen engaging in it might speak to him in a peremptory manner (in the heat of the moment) and George saw no reason for exposing his dignity to such mischances. Therefore he turned from the stairway, and going quietly into the library, picked up a magazine—but he did not open it, for his attention was instantly arrested by his Aunt Amelia's voice, speaking in the next room. The door was open and George heard her distinctly.

"Isabel does? *Isabel!*" she exclaimed, her tone high and shrewish. "You needn't tell me anything about Isabel Minafer, I guess, my dear old Frank Bronson! I know her a little better than you do, don't you think?"

George heard the voice of Mr. Bronson replying—a voice familiar to him as that of his grandfather's attorney-in-chief and chief intimate as well. He was a contemporary of the Major's, being over seventy, and they had been through three years of the War in the same regiment. Amelia addressed him now, with an effect of angry mockery, as "my dear old Frank Bronson"; but that (without the mockery) was how the Amberson family almost always spoke of him: "dear old Frank Bronson." He was a hale, thin old man, six feet three inches tall, and without a stoop.

"I doubt your knowing Isabel," he said stiffly. "You speak of her as you do because she sides with her brother George, instead of with you and Sydney."

"*Poot!*" Aunt Amelia was evidently in a passion. "You know what's been going on over there, well enough, Frank Bronson!"

"I don't even know what you're talking about."

"Oh, you don't? You don't know that Isabel takes George's side simply because he's Eugene Morgan's best friend?"

"It seems to me you're talking pure nonsense," said Bronson sharply. "Not impure nonsense, I hope!"

Amelia became shrill. "I thought you were a man of the world: don't tell me you're blind! For nearly two years Isabel's been pretending to chaperone Fanny Minafer with Eugene, and all the time she's been dragging that poor fool Fanny around to chaperone *her* and Eugene! Under the circumstances, she knows people will get to thinking Fanny's a pretty slim kind of chaperone,

and Isabel wants to please George because she thinks there'll be less talk if she can keep her own brother around, seeming to approve. 'Talk!' She'd better look out! The whole town will be talking, the first thing she knows! She——"

Amelia stopped, and stared at the doorway in a panic, for her nephew stood there.

She kept her eyes upon his white face for a few strained moments, then, regaining her nerve, looked away and shrugged her shoulders.

"You weren't intended to hear what I've been saying, George," she said quietly. "But since you seem to——"

"Yes, I did."

"So!" She shrugged her shoulders again. "After all, I don't know but it's just as well, in the long run."

He walked up to where she sat. "You—you——" he said thickly. "It seems —it seems to me you're—you're pretty common!"

Amelia tried to give the impression of an unconcerned person laughing with complete indifference, but the sounds she produced were disjointed and uneasy. She fanned herself, looking out of the open window near her. "Of course, if you want to make more trouble in the family than we've already got, George, with your eavesdropping, you can go and repeat——"

Old Bronson had risen from his chair in great distress. "Your aunt was talking nonsense because she's piqued over a business matter, George," he said. "She doesn't mean what she said, and neither she nor any one else gives the slightest credit to such foolishness—no one in the world!"

George gulped, and wet lines shone suddenly along his lower eyelids. "They —they'd better not!" he said, then stalked out of the room, and out of the house. He stamped fiercely across the stone slabs of the front porch, descended the steps, and halted abruptly, blinking in the strong sunshine.

In front of his own gate, beyond the Major's broad lawn, his mother was just getting into her victoria, where sat already his Aunt Fanny and Lucy Morgan. It was a summer fashion-picture: the three ladies charmingly dressed, delicate parasols aloft; the lines of the victoria graceful as those of a violin; the trim pair of bays in glistening harness picked out with silver, and the serious black driver whom Isabel, being an Amberson, dared even in that town to put into a black livery coat, boots, white breeches, and cockaded hat. They jingled smartly away, and, seeing George standing on the Major's lawn, Lucy waved, and Isabel threw him a kiss.

But George shuddered, pretending not to see them, and stooped as if searching for something lost in the grass, protracting that posture until the victoria was out of hearing. And ten minutes later, George Amberson, somewhat in the semblance of an angry person plunging out of the Mansion, found a pale nephew waiting to accost him.

"I haven't time to talk, Georgie."

"Yes, you have. You'd better!"

"What's the matter, then?"

His namesake drew him away from the vicinity of the house. "I want to tell you something I just heard Aunt Amelia say, in there."

"I don't want to hear it," said Amberson. "I've been hearing entirely too much of what 'Aunt Amelia' says, lately."

"She says my mother's on your side about this division of the property because you're Eugene Morgan's best friend."

"What in the name of heaven has that got to do with your mother's being on my side?"

"She said——" George paused to swallow. "She said——" He faltered.

"You look sick," said his uncle, and laughed shortly. "If it's because of anything Amelia's been saying, I don't blame you! What else did she say?"

George swallowed again, as with nausea, but under his uncle's encouragement he was able to be explicit. "She said my mother wanted you to be friendly to her about Eugene Morgan. She said my mother had been using Aunt Fanny as a chaperone."

Amberson emitted a laugh of disgust. "It's wonderful what tommy-rot a woman in a state of spite can think of! I suppose you don't doubt that Amelia Amberson created this specimen of tommy-rot herself?"

"I know she did."

"Then what's the matter?"

"She said——" George faltered again. "She said—she implied people were —were talking about it."

"Of all the damn nonsense!" his uncle exclaimed.

George looked at him haggardly. "You're sure they're not?"

"Rubbish! Your mother's on my side about this division because she knows Sydney's a pig and always has been a pig, and so has his spiteful wife. I'm trying to keep them from getting the better of your mother as well as from getting the better of me, don't you suppose? Well, they're in a rage because Sydney always could do what he liked with father unless your mother interfered, and they know I got Isabel to ask him not to do what they wanted. They're keeping up the fight and they're sore—and Amelia's a woman who always says any damn thing that comes into her head! That's all there is to it."

"But she said," George persisted wretchedly; "she said there was *talk*. She said——"

"Look here, young fellow!" Amberson laughed good-naturedly. "There probably *is* some harmless talk about the way your Aunt Fanny goes after poor Eugene, and I've no doubt I've abetted it myself. People can't help being amused by a thing like that. Fanny was always languishing at him, twenty-odd years ago, before he left here. Well, we can't blame the poor thing if she's got her hopes up again, and I don't know that I blame her, myself, for using your mother the way she does."

"How do you mean?"

Amberson put his hand on George's shoulder. "You like to tease Fanny," he said, "but I wouldn't tease her about this, if I were you. Fanny hasn't got much in her life. You know, Georgie, just being an aunt isn't really the great career it may sometimes appear to you! In fact, I don't know of anything much that Fanny *has* got, except her feeling about Eugene. She's always had it—and what's funny to us is pretty much life-and-death to her, I suspect. Now, I'll not deny that Eugene Morgan is attracted to your mother. He is; and that's another case of 'always was'; but I know him, and he's a knight, George—a crazy one, perhaps, if you've read 'Don Quixote.' And I think your mother likes him better than she likes any man outside her own family, and that he interests her more than anybody else—and 'always has.' And that's all there is to it, except——"

"Except what?" George asked quickly, as he paused.

"Except that I suspect——" Amberson chuckled, and began over: "I'll tell you in confidence. I think Fanny's a fairly tricky customer, for such an innocent old girl! There isn't any real harm in her, but she's a great diplomatist—lots of cards up her lace sleeves, Georgie! By the way, did you ever notice how proud she is of her arms? Always flashing 'em at poor Eugene!" And he stopped to laugh again.

"I don't see anything confidential about that," George complained. "I thought——"

"Wait a minute! My idea is—don't forget it's a confidential one, but I'm devilish right about it, young Georgie!—it's this: Fanny uses your mother for a decoy duck. She does everything in the world she can to keep your mother's friendship with Eugene going, because she thinks that's what keeps Eugene about the place, so to speak. Fanny's always with your mother, you see; and whenever he sees Isabel he sees Fanny. Fanny thinks he'll get used to the idea of her being around, and some day her chance may come! You see, she's probably afraid—perhaps she even knows, poor thing!—that she wouldn't get to see much of Eugene if it weren't for Isabel's being such a friend of his. There! D'you see?"

"Well—I suppose so." George's brow was still dark, however. "If you're sure whatever talk there is, is about Aunt Fanny. If that's so——"

"Don't be an ass," his uncle advised him lightly, moving away. "I'm off for a week's fishing to forget that woman in there, and her pig of a husband." (His gesture toward the Mansion indicated Mr. and Mrs. Sydney Amberson.) "I recommend a like course to you, if you're silly enough to pay any attention to such rubbishings! Good-bye!"

. . . George was partially reassured, but still troubled: a word haunted him like the recollection of a nightmare. "*Talk!*"

He stood looking at the houses across the street from the Mansion; and though the sunshine was bright upon them, they seemed mysteriously threatening. He had always despised them, except the largest of them, which was the home of his henchman, Charlie Johnson. The Johnsons had originally owned a lot three hundred feet wide, but they had sold all of it except the meagre frontage before the house itself, and five houses were now crowded into the space where one used to squire it so spaciously. Up and down the street, the same transformation had taken place: every big, comfortable old brick house now had two or three smaller frame neighbours crowding up to it on each side, cheap-looking neighbours, most of them needing paint and not clean—and yet, though they were cheap looking, they had cost as much to build as the big brick houses, whose former ample yards they occupied. Only where George stood was there left a sward as of yore; the great, level, green lawn that served for both the Major's house and his daughter's. This serene domain—unbroken, except for the two gravelled carriage-drives—alone remained as it had been during the early glories of the Amberson Addition.

George stared at the ugly houses opposite, and hated them more than ever; but he shivered. Perhaps the riffraff living in those houses sat at the windows to watch their betters; perhaps they dared to gossip——

He uttered an exclamation, and walked rapidly toward his own front gate. The victoria had returned with Miss Fanny alone; she jumped out briskly and the victoria waited.

"Where's mother?" George asked sharply, as he met her.

"At Lucy's. I only came back to get some embroidery, because we found the sun too hot for driving. I'm in a hurry."

But, going into the house with her, he detained her when she would have hastened upstairs.

"I haven't time to talk now, Georgie; I'm going right back. I promised your mother——"

"You listen!" said George.

"What on earth——"

He repeated what Amelia had said. This time, however, he spoke coldly, and without the emotion he had exhibited during the recital to his uncle: Fanny was the one who showed agitation during this interview, for she grew fiery red, and her eyes dilated. "What on earth do you want to bring such trash to *me* for?" she demanded, breathing fast.

"I merely wished to know two things: whether it is your duty or mine to speak to father of what Aunt Amelia——"

Fanny stamped her foot. "You little fool!" she cried. "You *awful* little fool!"

"I decline——"

"Decline, my hat! Your father's a sick man, and you——"

"He doesn't seem so to me."

"Well, he does to me! And you want to go troubling him with an Amberson family row! It's just what that cat would *love* you to do!"

"Well, I——"

"Tell your father if you like! It will only make him a little sicker to think he's got a son silly enough to listen to such craziness!"

"Then you're *sure* there isn't any talk?"

Fanny disdained a reply in words. She made a hissing sound of utter contempt and snapped her fingers. Then she asked scornfully: "What's the other thing you wanted to know?"

George's pallor increased. "Whether it mightn't be better, under the circumstances," he said, "if this family were not so intimate with the Morgan family—at least for a time. It might be better——"

Fanny stared at him incredulously. "You mean you'd quit seeing Lucy?"

"I hadn't thought of that side of it, but if such a thing were necessary on account of talk about my mother, I—I——" He hesitated unhappily. "I suggested that if all of us—for a time—perhaps only for a time—it might be better if——"

"See here," she interrupted. "We'll settle this nonsense right now. If Eugene Morgan comes to this house, for instance, to see *me*, your mother can't get up and leave the place the minute he gets here, can she? What do you want her to do: insult him? Or perhaps you'd prefer she'd insult Lucy? That would do just as well. What is it you're up to, anyhow? Do you really love your Aunt Amelia so much that you want to please her? Or do you really hate your Aunt *Fanny* so much that you want to—that you want to——"

She choked and sought for her handkerchief; suddenly she began to cry.

"Oh, see here," George said. "I don't hate you, Aunt Fanny. That's silly. I don't——"

"You do! You *do!* You want to—you want to destroy the only thing—that I—that I ever——" And, unable to continue, she became inaudible in her handkerchief.

George felt remorseful, and his own troubles were lightened: all at once it became clear to him that he had been worrying about nothing. He perceived that his Aunt Amelia was indeed an old cat, and that to give her scandalous meanderings another thought would be the height of folly. By no means insusceptible to such pathos as that now exposed before him, he did not lack pity for Fanny, whose almost spoken confession was lamentable; and he was granted the vision to understand that his mother also pitied Fanny infinitely more than he did. This seemed to explain everything.

He patted the unhappy lady awkwardly upon her shoulder. "There, there!" he said. "I didn't mean anything. Of course the only thing to do about Aunt Amelia is to pay no attention to her. It's all right, Aunt Fanny. Don't cry. I feel a lot better now, myself. Come on; I'll drive back there with you. It's all over, and nothing's the matter. Can't you cheer up?"

Fanny cheered up; and presently the customarily hostile aunt and nephew were driving out Amberson Boulevard amiably together in the hot sunshine.

CHAPTER XIV

"*Almost*" was Lucy's last word on the last night of George's vacation—that vital evening which she had half consented to agree upon for "settling things" between them. "Almost engaged," she meant. And George, discontented with the "almost," but contented that she seemed glad to wear a sapphire locket with a tiny photograph of George Amberson Minafer inside it, found himself wonderful in a new world at the final instant of their parting. For, after declining to let him kiss her "good-bye," as if his desire for such a ceremony were the most preposterous absurdity in the world, she had leaned suddenly close to him and left upon his cheek the veriest feather from a fairy's wing.

She wrote him a month later:

No. It must keep on being almost.

Isn't almost pretty pleasant? You know well enough that I care for you. I did from the first minute I saw you, and I'm pretty sure you knew it—I'm afraid you did. I'm afraid you always knew it. I'm not conventional and cautious about being engaged, as you say I am, dear. (I always read over the "dears" in your letters a time or two, as you say you do in mine—only I read all of your letters a time or two!) But it's such a solemn thing it scares me. It means a good deal to a lot of people besides you and me, and that scares me, too. You write that I take your feeling for me "too lightly" and that I "take the whole affair too lightly." Isn't that odd! Because to myself I seem to take it as something so much more solemn than you do. I shouldn't be a bit surprised to find myself an old lady, some day, still thinking of you—while you'd be away and away with somebody else perhaps, and me forgotten ages ago! "Lucy Morgan," you'd say, "Lucy Morgan? Let me see: I seem to remember the name. Didn't I know some Lucy Morgan or other, once upon a time?" Then you'd shake your big white head and stroke your long white beard—you'd have such a distinguished long white beard! and you'd say, 'No. I don't seem to remember any Lucy Morgan; I wonder what made me think I did?' And poor me! I'd be deep in the ground, wondering if you'd heard about it and what you were saying! Good-bye for to-day. Don't work too hard—dear!

George immediately seized pen and paper, plaintively but vigorously requesting Lucy not to imagine him with a beard, distinguished or otherwise, even in the extremities of age. Then, after inscribing his protest in the matter of this visioned beard, he concluded his missive in a tone mollified to tenderness, and proceeded to read a letter from his mother which had reached him simultaneously with Lucy's. Isabel wrote from Asheville, where she had just arrived with her husband.

I think your father looks better already, darling, though we've been here only a few hours. It may be we've found just the place to build him up. The doctors said they hoped it would prove to be, and if it is, it would be worth the long struggle we had with him to get him to give up and come. Poor dear man, he was so blue, not about his health but about giving up the worries down at his office and forgetting them for a time—if he only will forget them! It took the pressure of the family and all his best friends, to get him to come—but father and brother George and Fanny and Eugene Morgan all kept at him so constantly that he just had to give in. I'm afraid that in my anxiety to get him to do what the doctors wanted him to, I wasn't able to back up brother George as I should in his difficulty with Sydney and Amelia. I'm so sorry! George is more upset than I've ever seen him—they've got what they wanted, and they're sailing before long, I hear, to live in Florence. Father said he couldn't stand the constant persuading—I'm afraid the word he used was "nagging." I can't understand people behaving like that. George says they may be Ambersons, but they're vulgar! I'm afraid I almost agree with him. At least, I think they were inconsiderate. But I don't see why I'm unburdening myself of all this to you, poor darling! We'll have forgotten all about it long before you come home for the holidays, and it should mean little or nothing to you, anyway. Forget that I've been so foolish!

Your father is waiting for me to take a walk with him—that's a splendid sign, because he hasn't felt he could walk much, at home, lately. I mustn't keep him waiting. Be careful to wear your mackintosh and rubbers in rainy weather, and, as soon as it begins to get colder, your ulster. Wish you could see your father now. Looks so much better! We plan to stay six weeks if the place agrees with him. It does really seem to already! He's just called in the door to say he's waiting. Don't smoke too much, darling boy.

Devotedly, your mother

ISABEL

But she did not keep her husband there for the six weeks she anticipated. She did not keep him anywhere that long. Three weeks after writing this letter, she telegraphed suddenly to George that they were leaving for home at once; and four days later, when he and a friend came whistling into his study, from lunch at the club, he found another telegram upon his desk.

He read it twice before he comprehended its import.

Papa left us at ten this morning, dearest.

MOTHER

The friend saw the change in his face. "Not bad news?"

George lifted utterly dumfounded eyes from the yellow paper.

"My father," he said weakly. "She says—she says he's *dead*. I've got to go home."

. . . His Uncle George and the Major met him at the station when he arrived—the first time the Major had ever come to meet his grandson. The old gentleman sat in his closed carriage (which still needed paint) at the entrance to the station, but he got out and advanced to grasp George's hand tremulously, when the latter appeared. "Poor fellow!" he said, and patted him repeatedly upon the shoulder. "Poor fellow! Poor Georgie!"

George had not yet come to a full realization of his loss: so far, his condition was merely dazed; and as the Major continued to pat him, murmuring "Poor fellow!" over and over, George was seized by an almost irresistible impulse to tell his grandfather that he was not a poodle. But he said

"Thanks," in a low voice, and got into the carriage, his two relatives following with deferential sympathy. He noticed that the Major's tremulousness did not disappear, as they drove up the street, and that he seemed much feebler than during the summer. Principally, however, George was concerned with his own emotion, or rather, with his lack of emotion; and the anxious sympathy of his grandfather and his uncle made him feel hypocritical. He was not grief-stricken; but he felt that he ought to be, and, with a secret shame, concealed his callousness beneath an affectation of solemnity.

But when he was taken into the room where lay what was left of Wilbur Minafer, George had no longer to pretend; his grief was sufficient. It needed only the sight of that forever inert semblance of the quiet man who had been always so quiet a part of his son's life—so quiet a part that George had seldom been consciously aware that his father was indeed a part of his life. As the figure lay there, its very quietness was what was most lifelike; and suddenly it struck George hard. And in that unexpected, racking grief of his son, Wilbur Minafer became more vividly George's father than he had ever been in life.

When George left the room, his arm was about his black-robed mother, his shoulders were still shaken with sobs. He leaned upon his mother; she gently comforted him; and presently he recovered his composure and became self-conscious enough to wonder if he had not been making an unmanly display of himself. "I'm all right again, mother," he said awkwardly. "Don't worry about me: you'd better go lie down, or something; you look pretty pale."

Isabel did look pretty pale, but not ghastly pale, as Fanny did. Fanny's grief was overwhelming; she stayed in her room, and George did not see her until the next day, a few minutes before the funeral, when her haggard face appalled him. But by this time he was quite himself again, and during the short service in the cemetery his thoughts even wandered so far as to permit him a feeling of regret not directly connected with his father. Beyond the open flower-walled grave was a mound where new grass grew; and here lay his great-uncle, old John Minafer, who had died the previous autumn; and beyond this were the graves of George's grandfather and grandmother Minafer, and of his grandfather Minafer's second wife, and her three sons, George's half-uncles, who had been drowned together in a canoe accident when George was a child—Fanny was the last of the family. Next beyond was the Amberson family lot, where lay the Major's wife and their sons Henry and Milton, uncles whom George dimly remembered; and beside them lay Isabel's older sister, his Aunt Estelle, who had died in her girlhood, long before George was born. The Minafer monument was a granite block, with the name chiselled upon its one polished side, and the Amberson monument was a white marble shaft, taller than any other in that neighbourhood. But farther on there was a newer section of the cemetery, an addition which had been thrown open to occupancy only a few years before, after dexterous modern treatment by a landscape specialist. There were some large new mausoleums here, and shafts taller than the Ambersons', as well as a number of monuments of some sculptural pretentiousness; and altogether the new section appeared to be a more fashionable and important quarter than that older one which contained the Amberson and Minafer lots. This was what caused George's regret, during the moment or two when his mind strayed from his father and the reading of the service.

. . . On the train, going back to college, ten days later, this regret (though it was as much an annoyance as a regret) recurred to his mind, and a feeling developed within him that the new quarter of the cemetery was in bad taste —not architecturally or sculpturally perhaps, but in presumption: it seemed to flaunt a kind of parvenu ignorance, as if it were actually pleased to be unaware that all the aristocratic and really important families were buried in the old section.

The annoyance gave way before a recollection of the sweet mournfulness of his mother's face, as she had said good-bye to him at the station, and of how lovely she looked in her mourning. He thought of Lucy, whom he had seen only twice, and he could not help feeling that in these quiet interviews he had appeared to her as tinged with heroism—she had shown, rather than said, how brave she thought him in his sorrow. But what came most vividly to George's mind, during these retrospections, was the despairing face of his Aunt Fanny. Again and again he thought of it; he could not avoid its haunting. And for days, after he got back to college, the stricken likeness of Fanny would appear before him unexpectedly, and without a cause that he could trace in his immediately previous thoughts. Her grief had been so silent, yet it had so amazed him.

George felt more and more compassion for this ancient antagonist of his, and he wrote to his mother about her:

I'm afraid poor Aunt Fanny might think now father's gone we won't want her to live with us any longer and because I always teased her so much she might think I'd be for turning her out. I don't know where on earth she'd go or what she could live on if we did do something like this, and of course we never would do such a thing, but I'm pretty sure she had something of the kind on her mind. She didn't say anything, but the way she looked is what makes me think so. Honestly, to me she looked just scared sick. You tell her there isn't any danger in the world of my treating her like that. Tell her everything is to go on just as it always has. Tell her to cheer up!

CHAPTER XV

Isabel did more for Fanny than telling her to cheer up. Everything that Fanny inherited from her father, old Aleck Minafer, had been invested in Wilbur's business; and Wilbur's business, after a period of illness corresponding in dates to the illness of Wilbur's body, had died just before Wilbur did. George Amberson and Fanny were both "wiped out to a miracle of precision," as Amberson said. They "owned not a penny and owed not a penny," he continued, explaining his phrase. "It's like the moment just before drowning: you're not under water and you're not out of it. All you know is that you're not dead yet."

He spoke philosophically, having his "prospects" from his father to fall back upon; but Fanny had neither "prospects" nor philosophy. However, a legal survey of Wilbur's estate revealed the fact that his life insurance was left clear of the wreck; and Isabel, with the cheerful consent of her son, promptly turned this salvage over to her sister-in-law. Invested, it would yield something better than nine hundred dollars a year, and thus she was assured of becoming neither a pauper nor a dependent, but proved to be, as Amberson said, adding his efforts to the cheering up of Fanny, "an heiress, after all, in spite of rolling mills and the devil." She was unable to smile, and he continued his humane gaieties. "See what a wonderfully desirable income nine hundred dollars is, Fanny: a bachelor, to be in your class, must have exactly forty-nine thousand one hundred a year. Then, you see, all you need to do, in order to have fifty thousand a year, is to be a little encouraging when some bachelor in your class begins to show by his haberdashery what he wants you to think about him!"

She looked at him wanly, murmured a desolate response—she had "sewing to do"—and left the room; while Amberson shook his head ruefully at his sister. "I've often thought that humour was not my forte," he sighed. "Lord! She doesn't 'cheer up' much!"

The collegian did not return to his home for the holidays. Instead, Isabel joined him, and they went South for the two weeks. She was proud of her stalwart, good-looking son at the hotel where they stayed, and it was meat and drink to her when she saw how people stared at him in the lobby and on the big verandas—indeed, her vanity in him was so dominant that she was unaware of their staring at her with more interest and an admiration friendlier than George evoked. Happy to have him to herself for this fortnight, she loved to walk with him, leaning upon his arm, to read with him, to watch the sea with him—perhaps most of all she liked to enter the big dining room with him.

Yet both of them felt constantly the difference between this Christmastime and other Christmastimes of theirs—in all, it was a sorrowful holiday. But when Isabel came East for George's commencement, in June, she brought Lucy with her—and things began to seem different, especially when George Amberson arrived with Lucy's father on Class Day. Eugene had been in New York, on business; Amberson easily persuaded him to this outing; and they made a cheerful party of it, with the new graduate of course the hero and centre of it all.

His uncle was a fellow alumnus. "Yonder was where I roomed when I was here," he said, pointing out one of the university buildings to Eugene. "I don't know whether George would let my admirers place a tablet to mark the spot, or not. He owns all these buildings now, you know."

"Didn't you, when you were here? Like uncle, like nephew."

"Don't tell George you think he's like me. Just at this time we should be careful of the young gentleman's feelings."

"Yes," said Eugene. "If we weren't he mightn't let us exist at all."

"I'm sure I didn't have it so badly at his age," Amberson said reflectively, as they strolled on through the commencement crowd. "For one thing, I had brothers and sisters, and my mother didn't just sit at my feet as George's does; and I wasn't an only grandchild, either. Father's always spoiled Georgie a lot more than he did any of his own children."

Eugene laughed. "You need only three things to explain all that's good and bad about Georgie."

"Three?"

"He's Isabel's only child. He's an Amberson. He's a boy."

"Well, Mister Bones, of these three things which are the good ones and which are the bad ones?"

"All of them," said Eugene.

It happened that just then they came in sight of the subject of their discourse. George was walking under the elms with Lucy, swinging a stick and pointing out to her various objects and localities which had attained historical value during the last four years. The two older men marked his gestures, careless and graceful; they observed his attitude, unconsciously noble, his easy proprietorship of the ground beneath ·his feet and round about, of the branches overhead, of the old buildings beyond, and of Lucy.

"I don't know," Eugene said, smiling whimsically. "I don't know. When I spoke of his being a human being—I don't know. Perhaps it's more like deity."

"I wonder if I *was* like that!" Amberson groaned. "You don't suppose every Amberson has had to go through it, do you?"

"Don't worry! At least half of it is a combination of youth, good looks, and college; and even the noblest Ambersons get over their nobility and come to be people in time. It takes more than time, though."

"I should say it *did* take more than time!" his friend agreed, shaking a rueful head.

Then they walked over to join the loveliest Amberson, whom neither time nor trouble seemed to have touched. She stood alone, thoughtful under the great trees, chaperoning George and Lucy at a distance; but, seeing the two friends approaching, she came to meet them.

"It's charming, isn't it!" she said, moving her black-gloved hand to indicate the summery dressed crowd strolling about them, or clustering in groups, each with its own hero. "They seem so eager and so confident, all these boys —it's touching. But of course youth doesn't know it's touching."

Amberson coughed. "No, it doesn't seem to take itself as pathetic, precisely! Eugene and I were just speaking of something like that. Do you know what I think whenever I see these smooth, triumphal young faces? I always think: 'Oh, how you're going to catch it'!"

"George!"

"Oh, yes," he said. "Life's most ingenious: it's got a special walloping for every mother's son of 'em!"

"Maybe," said Isabel, troubled—"maybe some of the mothers can take the walloping for them."

"Not one!" her brother assured her, with emphasis. "Not any more than she can take on her own face the lines that are bound to come on her son's. I suppose you know that all these young faces have got to get lines on 'em?"

"Maybe they won't," she said, smiling wistfully. "Maybe times will change, and nobody will have to wear lines."

"Times have changed like that for only one person that I know," Eugene said. And as Isabel looked inquiring, he laughed, and she saw that she was the "only one person." His implication was justified, moreover, and she knew it. She blushed charmingly.

"Which is it puts the lines on the faces?" Amberson asked. "Is it age or trouble? Of course we can't decide that wisdom does it—we must be polite to Isabel."

"I'll tell you what puts the lines there," Eugene said. "Age puts some, and trouble puts some, and work puts some, but the deepest are carved by lack of faith. The serenest brow is the one that believes the most."

"In what?" Isabel asked gently.

"In everything!"

She looked at him inquiringly, and he laughed as he had a moment before, when she looked at him that way. "Oh, yes, you do!" he said.

She continued to look at him inquiringly a moment or two longer, and there was an unconscious earnestness in her glance, something trustful as well as inquiring, as if she knew that whatever he meant it was all right. Then her eyes drooped thoughtfully, and she seemed to address some inquiries to herself. She looked up suddenly. "Why, I believe," she said, in a tone of surprise, "I believe I do!"

And at that both men laughed. "Isabel!" her brother exclaimed. "You're a foolish person! There are times when you look exactly fourteen years old!"

But this reminded her of her real affair in that part of the world. "Good gracious!" she said. "Where have the children got to? We must take Lucy pretty soon, so that George can go and sit with the Class. We must catch up with them."

She took her brother's arm, and the three moved on, looking about them in the crowd.

"Curious," Amberson remarked, as they did not immediately discover the young people they sought. "Even in such a concourse one would think we couldn't fail to see the proprietor."

"Several hundred proprietors to-day," Eugene suggested.

"No; they're only proprietors of the university," said George's uncle. "We're looking for the proprietor of the universe."

"There he is!" cried Isabel fondly, not minding this satire at all. "And doesn't he look it!"

Her escorts were still laughing at her when they joined the proprietor of the universe and his pretty friend, and though both Amberson and Eugene declined to explain the cause of their mirth, even upon Lucy's urgent request, the portents of the day were amiable, and the five made a happy party—that is to say, four of them made a happy audience for the fifth, and the mood of this fifth was gracious and cheerful.

George took no conspicuous part in either the academic or the social celebrations of his class; he seemed to regard both sets of exercises with a tolerant amusement, his own "crowd" "not going in much for either of those sorts of things," as he explained to Lucy. What his crowd had gone in for remained ambiguous; some negligent testimony indicating that, except for an astonishing reliability which they all seemed to have attained in matters relating to musical comedy, they had not gone in for anything. Certainly the question one of them put to Lucy, in response to investigations of hers, seemed to point that way: "Don't you think," he said, "really, don't you think that being things is rather better than doing things?"

He said "rahthuh bettuh" for "rather better," and seemed to do it deliberately, with perfect knowledge of what he was doing. Later, Lucy mocked him to George, and George refused to smile: he somewhat inclined to such pronunciations, himself. This inclination was one of the things that he had acquired in the four years.

What else he had acquired, it might have puzzled him to state, had anybody asked him and required a direct reply within a reasonable space of time. He had learned how to pass examinations by "cramming"; that is, in three or four days and nights he could get into his head enough of a selected fragment of some scientific or philosophical or literary or linguistic subject to reply plausibly to six questions out of ten. He could retain the information necessary for such a feat just long enough to give a successful performance; then it would evaporate utterly from his brain, and leave him undisturbed. George, like his "crowd," not only preferred "being things" to "doing things," but had contented himself with four years of "being things" as a preparation for going on "being things." And when Lucy rather shyly pressed him for his friend's probable definition of the "things" it seemed so superior and beautiful to be, George raised his eyebrows slightly, meaning that she should have understood without explanation; but he did explain: "Oh, family and all that —being a gentleman, I suppose."

Lucy gave the horizon a long look, but offered no comment.

CHAPTER XVI

"Aunt Fanny doesn't look much better," George said to his mother, a few minutes after their arrival, on the night they got home. He stood with a towel in her doorway, concluding some sketchy ablutions before going downstairs to a supper which Fanny was hastily preparing for them. Isabel had not telegraphed; Fanny was taken by surprise when they drove up in a station cab at eleven o'clock; and George instantly demanded "a little decent food." (Some criticisms of his had publicly disturbed the composure of the dining-car steward four hours previously.) "I never saw anybody take things so hard as she seems to," he observed, his voice muffled by the towel. "Doesn't she get over it at all? I thought she'd feel better when we turned over the insurance to her—gave it to her absolutely, without any strings to it. She looks about a thousand years old!"

"She looks quite girlish, sometimes, though," his mother said.

"Has she looked that way much since father——"

"Not so much," Isabel said thoughtfully. "But she will, as time goes on."

"Time'll have to hurry, then, it seems to me," George observed, returning to his own room.

When they went down to the dining room, he pronounced acceptable the salmon salad, cold beef, cheese, and cake which Fanny made ready for them without disturbing the servants. The journey had fatigued Isabel, she ate nothing, but sat to observe with tired pleasure the manifestations of her son's appetite, meanwhile giving her sister-in-law a brief summary of the events of commencement. But presently she kissed them both good-night—taking care to kiss George lightly upon the side of his head, so as not to disturb his eating—and left aunt and nephew alone together.

"It never was becoming to her to look pale," Fanny said absently, a few moments after Isabel's departure.

"Wha'd you say, Aunt Fanny?"

"Nothing. I suppose your mother's been being pretty gay? Going a lot?"

"How could she?" George asked cheerfully. "In mourning, of course all she could do was just sit around and look on. That's all Lucy could do either, for the matter of that."

"I suppose so," his aunt assented. "How did Lucy get home?"

George regarded her with astonishment. "Why, on the train with the rest of us, of course."

"I didn't mean that," Fanny explained. "I meant from the station Did you drive out to their house with her before you came here?"

"No. She drove home with her father, of course."

"Oh, I see. So Eugene came to the station to meet you."

"'To meet us?'" George echoed, renewing his attack upon the salmon salad. "How could he?"

"I don't know what you mean," Fanny said drearily, in the desolate voice that had become her habit. "I haven't seen him while your mother's been away."

"Naturally," said George. "He's been East himself."

At this Fanny's drooping eyelids opened wide.

"Did you *see* him?"

"Well, naturally, since he made the trip home with us!"

"He did?" she said sharply. "He's been with you all the time?"

"No; only on the train and the last three days before we left. Uncle George got him to come."

Fanny's eyelids drooped again, and she sat silent until George pushed back his chair and lit a cigarette, declaring his satisfaction with what she had provided. "You're a fine housekeeper," he said benevolently. "You know how to make things look dainty as well as taste the right way. I don't believe you'd stay single very long if some of the bachelors and widowers around town could just once see——"

She did not hear him. "It's a little odd," she said.

"What's odd?"

"Your mother's not mentioning that Mr. Morgan had been with you."

"Didn't think of it, I suppose," said George carelessly; and, his benevolent mood increasing, he conceived the idea that a little harmless rallying might serve to elevate his aunt's drooping spirits. "I'll tell you something, in confidence," he said solemnly.

She looked up, startled. "What?"

"Well, it struck me that Mr. Morgan was looking pretty absent-minded, most of the time; and he certainly is dressing better than he used to. Uncle George told me he heard that the automobile factory had been doing quite well—won a race, too! I shouldn't be a bit surprised if all the young fellow had been waiting for was to know he had an assured income before he proposed."

"What 'young fellow'?"

"This young fellow Morgan," laughed George. "Honestly, Aunt Fanny, I shouldn't be a bit surprised to have him request an interview with me any day, and declare that his intentions are honourable, and ask my permission to pay his addresses to you. What had I better tell him?"

Fanny burst into tears.

"Good heavens!" George cried. "I was only teasing. I didn't mean——"

"Let me alone," she said lifelessly; and, continuing to weep, rose and began to clear away the dishes.

"Please, Aunt Fanny——"

"Just let me alone."

George was distressed. "I didn't mean anything, Aunt Fanny! I didn't know you'd got so sensitive as all that."

"You'd better go up to bed," she said desolately, going on with her work and her weeping.

"Anyhow," he insisted, "do let these things wait. Let the servants 'tend to the table in the morning."

"No."

"But, why not?"

"Just let me alone."

"Oh, Lord!" George groaned, going to the door. There he turned. "See here, Aunt Fanny, there's not a bit of use your bothering about those dishes to-night. What's the use of a butler and three maids if—"

"Just let me alone."

He obeyed, and could still hear a pathetic sniffing from the dining room as he went up the stairs.

"By George!" he grunted, as he reached his own room; and his thought was that living with a person so sensitive to kindly raillery might prove lugubrious. He whistled, long and low, then went to the window and looked through the darkness to the great silhouette of his grandfather's house. Lights were burning over there, upstairs; probably his newly arrived uncle was engaged in talk with the Major.

George's glance lowered, resting casually upon the indistinct ground, and he beheld some vague shapes, unfamiliar to him. Formless heaps, they seemed; but, without much curiosity, he supposed that sewer connections or water pipes might be out of order, making necessary some excavations. He hoped the work would not take long; he hated to see that sweep of lawn made unsightly by trenches and lines of dirt, even temporarily. Not greatly disturbed, however, he pulled down the shade, yawned, and began to undress, leaving further investigation for the morning.

But in the morning he had forgotten all about it, and raised his shade, to let in the light, without even glancing toward the ground. Not until he had finished dressing did he look forth from his window, and then his glance was casual. The next instant his attitude became electric, and he gave utterance to a bellow of dismay. He ran from his room, plunged down the stairs, out of the front door, and, upon a nearer view of the destroyed lawn, began to release profanity upon the breezeless summer air, which remained unaffected. Between his mother's house and his grandfather's, excavations for the cellars of five new houses were in process, each within a few feet of its neighbour. Foundations of brick were being laid; everywhere were piles of brick and stacked lumber, and sand heaps and mortar beds.

It was Sunday, and so the workmen implicated in these defacings were denied what unquestionably they would have considered a treat; but as the fanatic orator continued the monologue, a gentleman in flannels emerged upward from one of the excavations, and regarded him contemplatively.

"Obtaining any relief, nephew?" he inquired with some interest. "You must have learned quite a number of those expressions in childhood—it's so long since I'd heard them I fancied they were obsolete."

"Who wouldn't swear?" George demanded hotly. "In the name of God, what does grandfather mean, doing such things?"

"My private opinion is," said Amberson gravely, "he desires to increase his income by building these houses to rent."

"Well, in the name of God, can't he increase his income any other way but this?"

"In the name of God, it would appear he couldn't."

"It's beastly! It's a damn degradation! It's a crime!"

"I don't know about its being a crime," said his uncle, stepping over some planks to join him. "It might be a mistake, though. Your mother said not to tell you until we got home, so as not to spoil commencement for you. She rather feared you'd be upset."

"'Upset'! Oh, my Lord, I should think I *would* be upset! He's in his second childhood. What did you let him *do* it for, in the name of——"

"Make it in the name of heaven this time, George; it's Sunday. Well, I thought, myself, it was a mistake."

"I should say so!"

"Yes," said Amberson. "I wanted him to put up an apartment building instead of these houses."

"An apartment building! *Here?*"

"Yes; that was my idea."

George struck his hands together despairingly. "An apartment house! Oh, my Lord!"

"Don't worry! Your grandfather wouldn't listen to me, but he'll wish he had, some day. He says that people aren't going to live in miserable little flats when they can get a whole house with some grass in front and plenty of back yard behind. He sticks it out that apartment houses will never do in a town of this type, and when I pointed out to him that a dozen or so of 'em already *are* doing, he claimed it was just the novelty, and that they'd all be empty as soon as people got used to 'em. So he's putting up these houses."

"Is he getting miserly in his old age?"

"Hardly! Look what he gave Sydney and Amelia!"

"I don't mean he's a miser, of course," said George. "Heaven knows he's liberal enough with mother and me; but why on earth didn't he *sell* something or other rather than do a thing like this?"

"As a matter of fact," Amberson returned coolly, "I believe he *has* sold something or other, from time to time."

"Well, in heaven's name," George cried, "what did he do it for?"

"To get money," his uncle mildly replied. "That's my deduction."

"I suppose you're joking—or trying to!"

"That's the best way to look at it," Amberson said amiably. "Take the whole thing as a joke—and in the meantime, if you haven't had your breakfast——"

"I haven't!"

"Then if I were you I'd go in and get some. And"—he paused, becoming serious—"and if I were you I wouldn't say anything to your grandfather about this."

"I don't think I could trust myself to speak to him about it," said George. "I want to treat him respectfully, because he *is* my grandfather, but I don't believe I could if I talked to him about such a thing as this!"

And with a gesture of despair, plainly signifying that all too soon after leaving bright college years behind him he had entered into the full tragedy of life, George turned bitterly upon his heel and went into the house for his breakfast.

His uncle, with his head whimsically upon one side, gazed after him not altogether unsympathetically, then descended again into the excavation whence he had lately emerged. Being a philosopher he was not surprised, that afternoon, in the course of a drive he took in the old carriage with the Major, when George was encountered upon the highway, flashing along in his runabout with Lucy beside him and Pendennis doing better than three minutes.

"He seems to have recovered," Amberson remarked: "Looks in the highest good spirits."

"I beg your pardon."

"Your grandson," Amberson explained. "He was inclined to melancholy this morning, but seemed jolly enough just now when they passed us."

"What was he melancholy about? Not getting remorseful about all the money he's spent at college, was he?" The Major chuckled feebly, but with sufficient grimness. "I wonder what he thinks I'm made of," he concluded querulously.

"Gold," his son suggested, adding gently, "And he's right about part of you, father."

"What part?"

"Your heart."

The Major laughed ruefully. "I suppose that may account for how heavy it feels, sometimes, nowadays. This town seems to be rolling right over that old heart you mentioned, George—rolling over it and burying it under! When I think of those devilish workmen digging up my lawn, yelling around my house——"

"Never mind, father. Don't think of it. When things are a nuisance it's a good idea not to keep remembering 'em."

"I *try* not to," the old gentleman murmured. "I try to keep remembering that I won't be remembering anything very long." And, somehow convinced that this thought was a mirthful one, he laughed loudly, and slapped his knee. "Not so very long now, my boy!" he chuckled, continuing to echo his own amusement. "Not so very long. Not so very long!"

CHAPTER XVII

Young George paid his respects to his grandfather the following morning, having been occupied with various affairs and engagements on Sunday until after the Major's bedtime; and topics concerned with building or excavations were not introduced into the conversation, which was a cheerful one until George lightly mentioned some new plans of his. He was a skillful driver, as the Major knew, and he spoke of his desire to extend his proficiency in this art: in fact, he entertained the ambition to drive a four-in-hand. However, as the Major said nothing, and merely sat still, looking surprised, George went on to say that he did not propose to "go in for coaching just at the start"; he thought it would be better to begin with a tandem. He was sure Pendennis could be trained to work as a leader; and all that one needed to buy at present, he said, would be "comparatively inexpensive—a new trap, and the harness, of course, and a good bay to match Pendennis." He did not care for a special groom; one of the stablemen would do.

At this point the Major decided to speak. "You say one of the stablemen would do?" he inquired, his widened eyes remaining fixed upon his grandson. "That's lucky, because one's all there is, just at present, George. Old fat Tom does it all. Didn't you notice, when you took Pendennis out, yesterday?"

"Oh, that will be all right, sir. My mother can lend me her man."

"Can she?" The old gentleman smiled faintly. "I wonder——" He paused.

"What, sir?"

"Whether you mightn't care to go to law-school somewhere perhaps. I'd be glad to set aside a sum that would see you through."

This senile divergence from the topic in hand surprised George painfully. "I have no interest whatever in the law," he said. "I don't care for it, and the idea of being a professional man has never appealed to me. None of the family has ever gone in for that sort of thing, to my knowledge, and I don't care to be the first. I was speaking of driving a tandem——"

"I know you were," the Major said quietly.

George looked hurt. "I beg your pardon. Of course if the idea doesn't appeal to you——" And he rose to go.

The Major ran a tremulous hand through his hair, sighing deeply. "I—I don't like to refuse you anything, Georgie," he said. "I don't know that I often have refused you whatever you wanted—in reason——"

"You've always been more than generous, sir," George interrupted quickly. "And if the idea of a tandem doesn't appeal to you, why—of course——" And he waved his hand, heroically dismissing the tandem.

The Major's distress became obvious. "Georgie, I'd like to, but—but I've an idea tandems are dangerous to drive, and your mother might be anxious. She—"

"No, sir; I think not. She felt it would be rather a good thing—help to keep me out in the open air. But if perhaps your finances—"

"Oh, it isn't that so much," the old gentleman said hurriedly. "I wasn't thinking of that altogether." He laughed uncomfortably. "I guess we could still afford a new horse or two, if need be—"

"I thought you said—"

The Major waved his hand airily. "Oh, a few retrenchments where things were useless: nothing gained by a raft of idle darkies in the stable—nor by a lot of extra land that might as well be put to work for us in rentals. And if you want this thing so very much—"

"It's not important enough to bother about, really, of course."

"Well, let's wait till autumn then," said the Major in a tone of relief. "We'll see about it in the autumn, if you're still in the mind for it then. That will be a great deal better. You remind me of it, along in September —or October. We'll see what can be done." He rubbed his hands cheerfully. "We'll see what can be done about it then, Georgie. We'll see."

And George, in reporting this conversation to his mother, was ruefully humorous. "In fact, the old boy cheered up so much," he told her, "you'd have thought he'd got a real load off his mind. He seemed to think he'd fixed *me* up perfectly, and that I was just as good as driving a tandem around his library right that minute! Of course I know he's anything but miserly; still I can't help thinking he must be salting a lot of money away. I know prices are higher than they used to be, but he doesn't spend within thousands of what he used to, and *we* certainly can't be spending more than we always have spent. Where does it all go to? Uncle George told me grandfather had sold some pieces of property, and it looks a little queer. If he's really 'property poor,' of course we ought to be more saving than we are, and help him out. *I* don't mind giving up a tandem if it seems a little too expensive just now. I'm perfectly willing to live quietly till he gets his bank balance where he wants it. But I have a faint suspicion, not that he's getting miserly—not that at all—but that old age has begun to make him timid about money. There's no doubt about it, he's getting a little queer: he can't keep his mind on a subject long. Right in the middle of talking about one thing he'll wander off to something else; and I shouldn't be surprised if he turned out to be a lot better off than any of us guess. It's entirely possible that whatever he's sold just went into government bonds, or even his safety deposit box. There was a friend of mine in college had an old uncle like that: made the whole family think he was poor as dirt—and then left seven millions. People get terribly queer as they get old, sometimes, and grandfather certainly doesn't act the way he used to. He seems to be a totally different man. For instance, he said he thought tandem driving might be dangerous—"

"Did he?" Isabel asked quickly. "Then I'm glad he doesn't want you to have one. I didn't dream—"

"But it's not. There isn't the slightest——"

Isabel had a bright idea. "Georgie! Instead of a tandem wouldn't it interest you to get one of Eugene's automobiles?"

"I don't think so. They're fast enough, of course. In fact, running one of those things is getting to be quite on the cards for sport, and people go all over the country in 'em. But they're dirty things, and they keep getting out of order, so that you're always lying down on your back in the mud, and——"

"Oh, no," she interrupted eagerly. "Haven't you noticed? You don't see nearly so many people doing that nowadays as you did two or three years ago, and, when you do, Eugene says it's apt to be one of the older patterns. The way they make them now, you can get at most of the machinery from the top. I do think you'd be interested, dear."

George remained indifferent. "Possibly—but I hardly think so. I know a lot of good people are really taking them up, but still——"

" 'But still' what?" she said as he paused.

"But still—well, I suppose I'm a little old-fashioned and fastidious, but I'm afraid being a sort of engine driver never will appeal to me, mother. It's exciting, and I'd like that part of it, but still it doesn't seem to me precisely the thing a gentleman ought to do. Too much overalls and monkey-wrenches and grease!"

"But Eugene says people are hiring mechanics to do all that sort of thing for them. They're beginning to have them just the way they have coachmen; and he says it's developing into quite a profession."

"I know that, mother, of course; but I've seen some of these mechanics, and they're not very satisfactory. For one thing, most of them only pretend to understand the machinery and they let people break down a hundred miles from nowhere, so that about all these fellows are good for is to hunt up a farmer and hire a horse to pull the automobile. And friends of mine at college that've had a good deal of experience tell me the mechanics who do understand the engines have no training at all as servants. They're awful! They say anything they like, and usually speak to members of the family as 'Say!' No, I believe I'd rather wait for September and a tandem, mother."

Nevertheless, George sometimes consented to sit in an automobile, while waiting for September, and he frequently went driving in one of Eugene's cars with Lucy and her father. He even allowed himself to be escorted with his mother and Fanny through the growing factory, which was now, as the foreman of the paint shop informed the visitors, "turning out a car and a quarter a day." George had seldom been more excessively bored, but his mother showed a lively interest in everything, wishing to have all the machinery explained to her. It was Lucy who did most of the explaining, while her father looked on and laughed at the mistakes she made, and Fanny remained in the background with George, exhibiting a bleakness that over-matched his boredom.

From the factory Eugene took them to lunch at a new restaurant, just opened in the town, a place which surprised Isabel with its metropolitan air, and, though George made fun of it to her, in a whisper, she offered everything the tribute of pleased exclamations; and her gaiety helped Eugene's to make the little occasion almost a festive one.

George's ennui disappeared in spite of himself, and he laughed to see his mother in such spirits. "I didn't know mineral waters could go to a person's head," he said. "Or perhaps it's this place. It might pay to have a new restaurant opened somewhere in town every time you get the blues."

Fanny turned to him with a wan smile. "Oh, *she* doesn't 'get the blues,' George!" Then she added, as if fearing her remark might be thought unpleasantly significant, "I never knew a person of a more even disposition. I wish I could be like that!" And though the tone of this afterthought was not so enthusiastic as she tried to make it, she succeeded in producing a fairly amiable effect.

"No," Isabel said, reverting to George's remark, and overlooking Fanny's. "What makes me laugh so much at nothing is Eugene's factory. Wouldn't anybody be delighted to see an old friend take an idea out of the air like that—an idea that most people laughed at him for—wouldn't any old friend of his be happy to see how he'd made his idea into such a splendid, humming thing as that factory—all shiny steel, clicking and buzzing away, and with all those workmen, such *muscled* looking men and yet so intelligent looking?"

"Hear! Hear!" George applauded. "We seem to have a lady orator among us. I hope the waiters won't mind."

Isabel laughed, not discouraged. "It's beautiful to see such a thing," she said. "It makes us all happy, dear old Eugene!"

And with a brave gesture she stretched out her hand to him across the small table. He took it quickly, giving her a look in which his laughter tried to remain, but vanished before a gratitude threatening to become emotional in spite of him. Isabel, however, turned instantly to Fanny. "Give him your hand, Fanny," she said gaily; and, as Fanny mechanically obeyed, "There!" Isabel cried. "If brother George were here, Eugene would have his three oldest and best friends congratulating him all at once. We know what brother George thinks about it, though. It's just beautiful, Eugene!"

Probably if her brother George had been with them at the little table, he would have made known what he thought about herself, for it must inevitably have struck him that she was in the midst of one of those "times" when she looked "exactly fourteen years old." Lucy served as a proxy for Amberson, perhaps, when she leaned toward George and whispered: "Did you *ever* see anything so lovely?"

"As what?" George inquired, not because he misunderstood, but because he wished to prolong the pleasant neighbourliness of whispering.

"As your mother! Think of her doing that! She's a darling! And papa"—here she imperfectly repressed a tendency to laugh—"papa looks as if he were either going to explode or utter loud sobs!"

Eugene commanded his features, however, and they resumed their customary apprehensiveness. "I used to write verse," he said—"if you remember——"

"Yes," Isabel interrupted gently. "I remember."

"I don't recall that I've written any for twenty years or so," he continued. "But I'm almost thinking I could do it again, to thank you for making a factory visit into such a kind celebration."

"Gracious!" Lucy whispered, giggling. "Aren't they sentimental!"

"People that age always are," George returned. "They get sentimental over anything at all. Factories or restaurants, it doesn't matter what!"

And both of them were seized with fits of laughter which they managed to cover under the general movement of departure, as Isabel had risen to go.

Outside, upon the crowded street, George helped Lucy into his runabout, and drove off, waving triumphantly, and laughing at Eugene who was struggling with the engine of his car, in the tonneau of which Isabel and Fanny had established themselves. "Looks like a hand-organ man grinding away for pennies," said George, as the runabout turned the corner and into National Avenue. "I'll still take a horse, any day."

He was not so cocksure, half an hour later, on an open road, when a siren whistle wailed behind him, and before the sound had died away, Eugene's car, coming from behind with what seemed fairly like one long leap, went by the runabout and dwindled almost instantaneously in perspective, with a lace handkerchief in a black-gloved hand fluttering sweet derision as it was swept onward into minuteness—a mere white speck—and then out of sight.

George was undoubtedly impressed. "Your father does know how to drive some," the dashing exhibition forced him to admit. "Of course Pendennis isn't as young as he was, and I don't care to push him too hard. I wouldn't mind handling one of those machines on the road like that, myself, if that was all there was to it—no cranking to do, or fooling with the engine. Well, I enjoyed part of that lunch quite a lot, Lucy."

"The salad?"

"No. Your whispering to me."

"Blarney!"

George made no response, but checked Pendennis to a walk. Whereupon Lucy protested quickly, "Oh, don't!"

"Why? Do you want him to trot his legs off?"

"No, but——"

" 'No, but'—what?"

She spoke with apparent gravity: "I know when you make him walk it's so you can give all your attention to—to proposing to me again!"

And as she turned a face of exaggerated colour to him, "By the Lord, but you're a little witch!" George cried.

"George, *do* let Pendennis trot again!"

"I won't!"

She clucked to the horse. "Get up, Pendennis! Trot! Go on! Commence!"

Pendennis paid no attention; she meant nothing to him, and George laughed at her fondly. "You *are* the prettiest thing in this world, Lucy!" he exclaimed. "When I see you in winter, in furs, with your cheeks red, I think you're prettiest then, but when I see you in summer, in a straw hat and a shirtwaist and a duck skirt and white gloves and those little silver buckled slippers, and your rose-coloured parasol, and your cheeks not red but with a kind of pinky glow about them, then I see I must have been wrong about the winter! When are you going to drop the 'almost' and say we're really engaged?"

"Oh, not for *years*! So there's the answer, and let's trot again."

But George was persistent; moreover, he had become serious during the last minute or two. "I want to know," he said. "I really mean it."

"Let's don't be serious, George," she begged him hopefully. "Let's talk of something pleasant."

He was a little offended. "Then it isn't pleasant for you to know that I want to marry you?"

At this she became as serious as he could have asked; she looked down, and her lip quivered like that of a child about to cry. Suddenly she put her hand upon one of his for just an instant, and then withdrew it.

"Lucy!" he said huskily. "Dear, what's the matter? You look as if you were going to cry. You always do that," he went on plaintively, "whenever I can get you to talk about marrying me."

"I know it," she murmured.

"Well, why do you?"

Her eyelids flickered, and then she looked up at him with a sad gravity, tears seeming just at the poise. "One reason's because I have a feeling that it's never going to be."

"Why?"

"It's just a feeling."

"You haven't any reason or——"

"It's just a feeling."

"Well, if that's all," George said, reassured, and laughing confidently, "I guess I won't be very much troubled!" But at once he became serious again, adopting the tone of argument. "Lucy, how is anything ever going to get a *chance* to come of it, so long as you keep sticking to 'almost'? Doesn't it strike you as unreasonable to have a 'feeling' that we'll never be married, when what principally stands between us is the fact that you won't be really engaged to me? That does seem pretty absurd! Don't you *care* enough about me to marry me?"

She looked down again, pathetically troubled. "Yes."

"Won't you always care that much about me?"

"I'm—yes—I'm afraid so, George. I never do change much about anything."

"Well, then, why in the world won't you drop the 'almost'?"

Her distress increased. "Everything is—everything——"

"What about 'everything'?"

"Everything is so—so unsettled."

And at that he uttered an exclamation of impatience. "If you aren't the queerest girl! *What* is 'unsettled'?"

"Well, for one thing," she said, able to smile at his vehemence, "you haven't settled on anything to do. At least, if you have you've never spoken of it."

As she spoke, she gave him the quickest possible side glance of hopeful scrutiny; then looked away, not happily. Surprise and displeasure were intentionally visible upon the countenance of her companion; and he permitted a significant period of silence to elapse before making any response. "Lucy," he said, finally, with cold dignity, "I should like to ask you a few questions."

"Yes?"

"The first is: Haven't you perfectly well understood that I don't mean to go into business or adopt a profession?"

"I wasn't quite sure," she said gently. "I really didn't know—quite."

"Then of course it's time I did tell you. I never have been able to see any occasion for a man's going into trade, or being a lawyer, or any of those things if his position and family were such that he didn't need to. You know, yourself, there are a lot of people in the East—in the South, too, for that matter—that don't think we've got any particular family or position or culture in this part of the country. I've met plenty of that kind of provincial snobs myself, and they're pretty galling. There were one or two men in my crowd at college, their families had lived on their income for three generations, and they never dreamed there was anybody in their class out here. I had to show them a thing or two, right at the start, and I guess they won't forget it! Well, I think it's time all their sort found out that three generations *can* mean just as much out here as anywhere else. That's the way I feel about it, and let me tell you I feel it pretty deeply!"

"But what *are* you going to do, George?" she cried.

George's earnestness surpassed hers; he had become flushed and his breathing was emotional. As he confessed, with simple genuineness, he did feel what he was saying "pretty deeply"; and in truth his state approached the tremulous. "I expect to live an honourable life," he said. "I expect to contribute my share to charities, and to take part in—in movements."

"What kind?"

"Whatever appeals to me," he said.

Lucy looked at him with grieved wonder. "But you really don't mean to have any regular business or profession at *all*?"

"I certainly do not!" George returned promptly and emphatically.

"I was afraid so," she said in a low voice.

George continued to breathe deeply throughout another protracted interval of silence. Then he said, "I should like to revert to the questions I was asking you, if you don't mind."

"No, George. I think we'd better——"

"Your father is a business man——"

"He's a mechanical genius," Lucy interrupted quickly. "Of course he's both. And he was a lawyer once—he's done all sorts of things."

"Very well. I merely wished to ask if it's his influence that makes you think I ought to 'do' something?"

Lucy frowned slightly. "Why, I suppose almost everything I think or say must be owing to his influence in one way or another. We haven't had anybody but each other for so many years, and we always think about alike, so of course——"

"I see!" And George's brow darkened with resentment. "So that's it, is it? It's your father's idea that I ought to go into business and that you oughtn't to be engaged to me until I do."

Lucy gave a start, her denial was so quick. "No! I've never once spoken to him about it. Never!"

George looked at her keenly, and he jumped to a conclusion not far from the truth. "But you know without talking to him that it's the way he does feel about it? I see."

She nodded gravely. "Yes."

George's brow grew darker still. "Do you think I'd be much of a man," he said, slowly, "if I let any other man dictate to me my own way of life?"

"George! Who's 'dictating' your——"

"It seems to me it amounts to that!" he returned.

"Oh, no! I only know how papa thinks about things. He's never, never spoken unkindly, or 'dictatingly' of you." She lifted her hand in protest, and her face was so touching in its distress that for the moment George forgot his anger. He seized that small, troubled hand.

"Lucy," he said huskily. "Don't you know that I love you?"

"Yes—I do."

"Don't you love me?"

"Yes—I do."

"Then what does it matter what your father thinks about my doing something or not doing anything? He has his way, and I have mine. I don't believe in the whole world scrubbing dishes and selling potatoes and trying law cases. Why, look at your father's best friend, my Uncle George Amberson—he's never done anything in his life, and——"

"Oh, yes, he has," she interrupted. "He was in politics."

"Well, I'm glad he's out," George said. "Politics is a dirty business for a gentleman, and Uncle George would tell you that himself. Lucy, let's not talk any more about it. Let me tell mother when I get home that we're engaged. Won't you, dear?"

She shook her head.

"Is it because——"

For a fleeting instant she touched to her cheek the hand that held hers. "No," she said, and gave him a sudden little look of renewed gaiety. "Let's let it stay 'almost'."

"Because your father——"

"Oh, because it's better!"

George's voice shook. "Isn't it your father?"

"It's his ideals I'm thinking of—yes."

George dropped her hand abruptly and anger narrowed his eyes. "I know what you mean," he said. "I dare say I don't care for your father's ideals any more than he does for mine!"

He tightened the reins, Pendennis quickening eagerly to the trot; and when George jumped out of the runabout before Lucy's gate, and assisted her to descend, the silence in which they parted was the same that had begun when Pendennis began to trot.

CHAPTER XVIII

That evening, after dinner, George sat with his mother and his Aunt Fanny upon the veranda. In former summers, when they sat outdoors in the evening, they had customarily used an open terrace at the side of the house, looking toward the Major's, but that more private retreat now afforded too blank and abrupt a view of the nearest of the new houses; so, without consultation, they had abandoned it for the Romanesque stone structure in front, an oppressive place.

Its oppression seemed congenial to George; he sat upon the copestone of the stone parapet, his back against a stone pilaster; his attitude not comfortable, but rigid, and his silence not comfortable, either, but heavy. However, to the eyes of his mother and his aunt, who occupied wicker chairs at a little distance, he was almost indistinguishable except for the stiff white shield of his evening frontage.

"It's so nice of you always to dress in the evening, Georgie," his mother said, her glance resting upon this surface. "Your Uncle George always used to, and so did father, for years; but they both stopped quite a long time ago. Unless there's some special occasion, it seems to me we don't see it done any more, except on the stage and in the magazines."

He made no response, and Isabel, after waiting a little while, as if she expected one, appeared to acquiesce in his mood for silence, and turned her head to gaze thoughtfully out at the street.

There, in the highway, the evening life of the Midland city had begun. A rising moon was bright upon the tops of the shade trees, where their branches met overhead, arching across the street, but only filtered splashings of moonlight reached the block pavement below; and through this darkness flashed the firefly lights of silent bicycles gliding by in pairs and trios—or sometimes a dozen at a time might come, and not so silent, striking their little bells; the riders' voices calling and laughing; while now and then a pair of invisible experts would pass, playing mandolin and guitar as if handle-bars were of no account in the world—their music would come swiftly, and then too swiftly die away. Surreys rumbled lightly by, with the plod-plod of honest old horses, and frequently there was the glitter of whizzing spokes from a runabout or a sporting buggy, and the sharp, decisive hoof-beats of a trotter. Then, like a cowboy shooting up a peaceful camp, a frantic devil would hurtle out of the distance, bellowing, exhaust racketing like a machine gun gone amuck—and at these horrid sounds the surreys and buggies would hug the curbstone, and the bicycles scatter to cover, cursing; while children rushed from the side-walks to drag pet dogs from the street. The thing would roar by, leaving a long wake of turbulence; then the indignant street would quiet down for a few minutes—till another came.

"There are a great many more than there used to be," Miss Fanny ob-served, in her lifeless voice, as the lull fell after one of these visitations. "Eugene is right about that; there seem to be at least three or four times as many as there were last summer, and you never hear the ragamuffins shout-ing 'Get a horse!' nowadays; but I think he may be mistaken about their go-ing on increasing after this. I don't believe we'll see so many next summer as we do now."

"Why?" asked Isabel.

"Because I've begun to agree with George about their being more a fad than anything else, and I think it must be the height of the fad just now. You know how roller-skating came in—everybody in the world seemed to be crowding to the rinks—and now only a few children use rollers for getting to school. Besides, people won't permit the automobiles to be used. Really, I think they'll make laws against them. You see how they spoil the bicycling and the driving; people just seem to hate them! They'll never stand it—never in the world! Of course I'd be sorry to see such a thing happen to Eugene, but I shouldn't be really surprised to see a law passed forbidding the sale of automobiles, just the way there is with concealed weapons."

"Fanny!" exclaimed her sister-in-law. "You're not in earnest?"

"I am, though!"

Isabel's sweet-toned laugh came out of the dusk where she sat. "Then you didn't mean it when you told Eugene you'd enjoyed the drive this after-noon?"

"I didn't say it so very enthusiastically, did I?"

"Perhaps not, but he certainly thought he'd pleased you."

"I don't think I gave him any right to think he'd pleased me," Fanny said slowly.

"Why not? Why shouldn't you, Fanny?"

Fanny did not reply at once, and when she did, her voice was almost in-audible, but much more reproachful than plaintive. "I hardly think I'd want any one to get the notion he'd pleased me just now. It hardly seems time, yet—to me."

Isabel made no response, and for a time the only sound upon the dark veranda was the creaking of the wicker rocking-chair in which Fanny sat—

a creaking which seemed to denote content and placidity on the part of the chair's occupant, though at this juncture a series of human shrieks could have been little more eloquent of emotional disturbance. However, the creaking gave its hearer one great advantage: it could be ignored.

"Have you given up smoking, George?" Isabel asked presently.

"No."

"I hoped perhaps you had, because you've not smoked since dinner. We shan't mind if you care to."

"No, thanks."

There was silence again, except for the creaking of the rocking-chair; then a low, clear whistle, singularly musical, was heard softly rendering an old air from "Fra Diavolo." The creaking stopped.

"Is that you, George?" Fanny asked abruptly.

"Is that me what?"

"Whistling 'On Yonder Rock Reclining'?"

"It's I," said Isabel.

"Oh," Fanny said dryly.

"Does it disturb you?"

"Not at all. I had an idea George was depressed about something, and merely wondered if he could be making such a cheerful sound." And Fanny resumed her creaking.

"Is she right, George?" his mother asked quickly, leaning forward in her chair to peer at him through the dusk. "You didn't eat a very hearty dinner, but I thought it was probably because of the warm weather. Are you troubled about anything?"

"No!" he said angrily.

"That's good. I thought we had such a nice day, didn't you?"

"I suppose so," he muttered, and, satisfied, she leaned back in her chair; but "Fra Diavolo" was not revived. After a time she rose, went to the steps, and stood for several minutes looking across the street. Then her laughter was faintly heard.

"Are you laughing about something?" Fanny inquired.

"Pardon?" Isabel did not turn, but continued her observation of what had interested her upon the opposite side of the street.

"I asked: Were you laughing at something?"

"Yes, I was!" And she laughed again. "It's that funny, fat old Mrs. Johnson. She has a habit of sitting at her bedroom window with a pair of opera-glasses."

"Really!"

"Really. You can see the window through the place that was left when we had the dead walnut tree cut down. She looks up and down the street, but mostly at father's and over here. Sometimes she forgets to put out the light in her room, and there she is, spying away for all the world to see!"

However, Fanny made no effort to observe this spectacle, but continued her creaking. "I've always thought her a very good woman," she said primly.

"So she is," Isabel agreed. "She's a good, friendly old thing, a little too intimate in her manner, sometimes, and if her poor old opera-glasses afford her the quiet happiness of knowing what sort of young man our new cook is walking out with, I'm the last to begrudge it to her! Don't you want to come and look at her, George?"

"What? I beg your pardon. I hadn't noticed what you were talking about."

"It's nothing," she laughed. "Only a funny old lady—and she's gone now. I'm going, too—at least, I'm going indoors to read. It's cooler in the house, but the heat's really not bad anywhere, since nightfall. Summer's dying. How quickly it goes, once it begins to die."

When she had gone into the house, Fanny stopped rocking, and, leaning forward, drew her black gauze wrap about her shoulders and shivered. "Isn't it queer," she said drearily, "how your mother can use such words?"

"What words are you talking about?" George asked.

"Words like 'die' and 'dying.' I don't see how she can bear to use them so soon after your poor father——" She shivered again.

"It's almost a year," George said absently, and he added: "It seems to me you're using them yourself."

"I? Never!"

"Yes, you did."

"When?"

"Just this minute."

"Oh!" said Fanny. "You mean when I repeated what *she* said? That's hardly the same thing, George."

He was not enough interested to argue the point. "I don't think you'll convince anybody that mother's unfeeling," he said indifferently.

"I'm not trying to convince anybody. I mean merely that in my opinion —well, perhaps it may be just as wise for me to keep my opinions to myself."

She paused expectantly, but her possible anticipation that George would urge her to discard wisdom and reveal her opinion was not fulfilled. His back was toward her, and he occupied himself with opinions of his own about other matters. Fanny may have felt some disappointment as she rose to withdraw.

However, at the last moment she halted with her hand upon the latch of the screen door.

"There's *one* thing I hope," she said. "I hope at least she won't leave off her full mourning on the *very* anniversary of Wilbur's death!"

The light door clanged behind her, and the sound annoyed her nephew. He had no idea why she thus used inoffensive wood and wire to dramatize her departure from the veranda, the impression remaining with him being that she was critical of his mother upon some point of funeral millinery. Throughout the desultory conversation he had been profoundly concerned with his own disturbing affairs, and now was preoccupied with a dialogue taking place (in his mind) between himself and Miss Lucy Morgan. As he beheld the vision, Lucy had just thrown herself at his feet. "George, you *must* forgive me!" she cried. "Papa was utterly wrong! I have told him so, and the truth is that I have come to rather dislike him as you do, and as you always have, in your heart of hearts. George, I understand you: thy people shall be my people and thy gods my gods. George, won't you take me back?"

"Lucy, are you *sure* you understand me?" And in the darkness George's bodily lips moved in unison with those which uttered the words in his imaginary rendering of this scene. An eavesdropper, concealed behind the column, could have heard the whispered word "sure," the emphasis put upon it in the vision was so poignant. "You say you understand me, but are you *sure?*"

Weeping, her head bowed almost to her waist, the ethereal Lucy made reply: "*Oh*, so sure! I will never listen to father's opinions again. I do not even care if I never see him again!"

"Then I pardon you," he said gently.

This softened mood lasted for several moments—until he realized that it had been brought about by processes strikingly lacking in substance. Abruptly he swung his feet down from the copestone to the floor of the veranda. "Pardon nothing!" No meek Lucy had thrown herself in remorse at his feet; and now he pictured her as she probably really was at this moment: sitting on the white steps of her own front porch in the moonlight, with red-headed Fred Kinney and silly Charlie Johnson and four or five others—all of them laughing, most likely, and some idiot playing the guitar!

George spoke aloud: "Riffraff!"

And because of an impish but all too natural reaction of the mind, he could see Lucy with much greater distinctness in this vision than in his former pleasing one. For a moment she was miraculously real before him, every line and colour of her. He saw the moonlight shimmering in the chiffon of her skirt, brightest on her crossed knee and the tip of her slipper; saw the blue curve of the characteristic shadow behind her, as she leaned back against the white step; saw the watery twinkling of sequins in the gauze wrap over her white shoulders as she moved, and the faint, symmetrical lights in her black hair—and not one alluring, exasperating twentieth-of-an-inch of her laughing profile was spared him as she seemed to turn to the infernal Kinney——

"Riffraff!" And George began furiously to pace the stone floor. "Riffraff!" By this hard term—a favourite with him since childhood's scornful hour—he meant to indicate, not Lucy, but the young gentlemen who, in his vision, surrounded her. "Riffraff!" he said again, aloud, and again:

"Riffraff!"

At that moment, as it happened, Lucy was playing chess with her father; and her heart, though not remorseful, was as heavy as George could have wished. But she did not let Eugene see that she was troubled, and he was pleased when he won three games of her. Usually she beat him.

CHAPTER XIX

George went driving the next afternoon alone, and, encountering Lucy and her father on the road, in one of Morgan's cars, lifted his hat, but nowise relaxed his formal countenance as they passed. Eugene waved a cordial hand quickly returned to the steering-wheel; but Lucy only nodded gravely and smiled no more than George did. Nor did she accompany Eugene to the Major's for dinner, the following Sunday evening, though both were bidden to attend that feast, which was already reduced in numbers and gaiety by the absence of George Amberson. Eugene explained to his host that Lucy had gone away to visit a school-friend.

The information, delivered in the library, just before old Sam's appearance to announce dinner, set Miss Minafer in quite a flutter. "Why, George!" she said, turning to her nephew. "How does it happen you didn't tell us?" And with both hands opening, as if to express her innocence of some conspiracy, she exclaimed to the others, "He's never said one word to us about Lucy's planning to go away!"

"Probably afraid to," the Major suggested. "Didn't know but he might break down and cry if he tried to speak of it!" He clapped his grandson on the shoulder, inquiring jocularly, "That it, Georgie?"

Georgie made no reply, but he was red enough to justify the Major's developing a chuckle into laughter; though Miss Fanny, observing her nephew keenly, got an impression that this fiery blush was in truth more fiery than tender. She caught a glint in his eye less like confusion than resentment, and saw a dilation of his nostrils which might have indicated not so much a sweet agitation as an inaudible snort. Fanny had never been lacking in curiosity, and, since her brother's death, this quality was more than ever alert. The fact that George had spent all the evenings of the past week at home had not been lost upon her, nor had she failed to ascertain, by diplomatic inquiries, that since the day of the visit to Eugene's shops George had gone driving alone.

At the dinner-table she continued to observe him, sidelong; and toward the conclusion of the meal she was not startled by an episode which brought discomfort to the others. After the arrival of coffee the Major was rallying Eugene upon some rival automobile shops lately built in a suburb, and already promising to flourish.

"I suppose they'll either drive you out of the business," said the old gentleman, "or else the two of you'll drive all the rest of us off the streets."

"If we do, we'll even things up by making the streets five or ten times as long as they are now," Eugene returned.

"How do you propose to do that?"

"It isn't the distance from the centre of a town that counts," said Eugene; "it's the time it takes to get there. This town's already spreading; bicycles and trolleys have been doing their share, but the automobile is going to carry city streets clear out to the county line."

The Major was skeptical. "Dream on, fair son!" he said. "It's lucky for us that you're only dreaming; because if people go to moving that far, real estate values in the old residence part of town are going to be stretched pretty thin."

"I'm afraid so," Eugene assented. "Unless you keep things so bright and clean that the old section will stay more attractive than the new ones."

"Not very likely! How are things going to be kept 'bright and clean' with soft coal and our kind of city government?"

"They aren't," Eugene replied quickly. "There's no hope of it, and already the boarding-house is marching up National Avenue. There are two in the next block below here, and there are a dozen in the half-mile below that. My relatives, the Sharons, have sold their house and are building in the country—at least, they call it 'the country.' It will be city in two or three years."

"Good gracious!" the Major exclaimed, affecting dismay. "So your little shops are going to ruin all your old friends, Eugene!"

"Unless my old friends take warning in time, or abolish smoke and get a new kind of city government. I should say the best chance is to take warning."

"Well, well!" the Major laughed. "You have enough faith in miracles, Eugene—granting that trolleys and bicycles and automobiles are miracles. So you think they're to change the face of the land, do you?"

"They're already doing it, Major; and it can't be stopped. Automobiles——"

At this point he was interrupted. George was the interrupter. He had said nothing since entering the dining room, but now he spoke in a loud and peremptory voice, using the tone of one in authority who checks idle prattle and settles a matter forever.

"Automobiles are a useless nuisance," he said.

There fell a moment's silence.

Isabel gazed incredulously at George, colour slowly heightening upon her cheeks and temples, while Fanny watched him with a quick eagerness, her eyes alert and bright. But Eugene seemed merely quizzical, as if not taking this brusquerie to himself. The Major was seriously disturbed.

"What did you say, George?" he asked, though George had spoken but too distinctly.

"I said all automobiles were a nuisance," George answered, repeating not only the words but the tone in which he had uttered them. And he added, "They'll never amount to anything but a nuisance. They had no business to be invented."

The Major frowned. "Of course you forget that Mr. Morgan makes them, and also did his share in inventing them. If you weren't so thoughtless he might think you rather offensive."

"That would be too bad," said George coolly. "I don't think I could survive it."

Again there was a silence, while the Major stared at his grandson, aghast. But Eugene began to laugh cheerfully.

"I'm not sure he's wrong about automobiles," he said. "With all their speed forward they may be a step backward in civilization—that is, in spiritual civilization. It may be that they will not add to the beauty of the world, nor to the life of men's souls. I am not sure. But automobiles have come, and they bring a greater change in our life than most of us suspect. They are here, and almost all outward things are going to be different because of what they bring. They are going to alter war, and they are going to alter peace. I think men's minds are going to be changed in subtle ways because of automobiles; just how, though, I could hardly guess. But you can't have the immense outward changes that they will cause without some inward ones, and it may be that George is right, and that the spiritual alteration will be bad for us. Perhaps, ten or twenty years from now, if we can see the inward change in men by that time, I shouldn't be able to defend the gasoline engine, but would have to agree with him that automobiles 'had no business to be invented.'" He laughed good-naturedly, and looking at his watch, apologized for having an engagement which made his departure necessary when he would so much prefer to linger. Then he shook hands with the Major, and bade Isabel, George, and Fanny a cheerful good-night—a collective farewell cordially addressed to all three of them together—and left them at the table.

Isabel turned wondering, hurt eyes upon her son. "George, dear!" she said. "What *did* you mean?"

"Just what I said," he returned, lighting one of the Major's cigars, and his manner was imperturbable enough to warrant the definition (sometimes merited by imperturbability) of stubbornness.

Isabel's hand, pale and slender, upon the tablecloth, touched one of the fine silver candlesticks aimlessly: the fingers were seen to tremble. "Oh, he was hurt!" she murmured.

"I don't see why he should be," George said. "I didn't say anything about *him*. He didn't seem to me to be hurt—seemed perfectly cheerful. What made you think he was hurt?"

"I know him!" was all of her reply, half whispered.

The Major stared hard at George from under his white eyebrows. "You didn't mean '*him*,' you say, George? I suppose if we had a clergyman as a guest here you'd expect him not to be offended, and to understand that your remarks were neither personal nor untactful, if you said the church was a nuisance and ought never to have been invented. By Jove, but you're a puzzle!"

"In what way, may I ask, sir?"

"We seem to have a new kind of young people these days," the old gentleman returned, shaking his head. "It's a new style of courting a pretty girl, certainly, for a young fellow to go deliberately out of his way to try and make an enemy of her father by attacking his business! By Jove! That's a new way to win a woman!"

George flushed angrily and seemed about to offer a retort, but held his breath for a moment; and then held his peace. It was Isabel who responded to the Major. "Oh, no!" she said. "Eugene would never be anybody's enemy —he couldn't!—and last of all Georgie's. I'm afraid he was hurt, but I don't fear his not having understood that George spoke without thinking of what he was saying—I mean, without realizing its bearing on Eugene."

Again George seemed upon the point of speech, and again controlled the impulse. He thrust his hands in his pockets, leaned back in his chair, and smoked, staring inflexibly at the ceiling.

"Well, well," said his grandfather, rising. "It wasn't a very successful little dinner!"

Thereupon he offered his arm to his daughter, who took it fondly, and they left the room, Isabel assuring him that all his little dinners were pleasant, and that this one was no exception.

George did not move, and Fanny, following the other two, came round the table, and paused close beside his chair; but George remained posed in his great imperturbability, cigar between teeth, eyes upon ceiling, and paid no attention to her. Fanny waited until the sound of Isabel's and the Major's voices became inaudible in the hall. Then she said quickly, and in a low voice so eager that it was unsteady:

"George, you've struck *just* the treatment to adopt: you're doing the right thing!"

She hurried out, scurrying after the others with a faint rustling of her black skirts, leaving George mystified but incurious. He did not understand why she should bestow her approbation upon him in the matter, and cared so little whether she did or not that he spared himself even the trouble of being puzzled about it.

In truth, however, he was neither so comfortable nor so imperturbable as he appeared. He felt some gratification: he had done a little to put the man in his place—that man whose influence upon his daughter was precisely the same thing as a contemptuous criticism of George Amberson Minafer, and of George Amberson Minafer's "ideals of life." Lucy's going away without a word was intended, he supposed, as a bit of punishment. Well, he wasn't the sort of man that people were allowed to punish: he could demonstrate that to them—since they started it!

It appeared to him as almost a kind of insolence, this abrupt departure— not even telephoning! Probably she wondered how he would take it; she even might have supposed he would show some betraying chagrin when he heard of it.

He had no idea that this was just what he had shown; and he was satisfied with his evening's performance. Nevertheless, he was not comfortable in his mind; though he could not have explained his inward perturbations, for he was convinced, without any confirmation from his Aunt Fanny, that he had done "just the right thing."

CHAPTER XX

Isabel came to George's door that night, and when she had kissed him good-night she remained in the open doorway with her hand upon his shoulder and her eyes thoughtfully lowered, so that her wish to say something more than good-night was evident. Not less obvious was her perplexity about the manner of saying it; and George, divining her thought, amiably made an opening for her.

"Well, old lady," he said indulgently, "you needn't look so worried. I won't be tactless with Morgan again. After this I'll just keep out of his way."

Isabel looked up, searching his face with the fond puzzlement which her eyes sometimes showed when they rested upon him; then she glanced down the hall toward Fanny's room, and, after another moment of hesitation, came quickly in, and closed the door.

"Dear," she said, "I wish you'd tell me something: Why don't you like Eugene?"

"Oh, I like him well enough," George returned, with a short laugh, as he sat down and began to unlace his shoes. "I like him well enough—in his place."

"No, dear," she said hurriedly. "I've had a feeling from the very first that you didn't really like him—that you really never liked him. Sometimes you've seemed to be friendly with him, and you'd laugh with him over something in a jolly, companionable way, and I'd think I was wrong, and that you really did like him, after all; but to-night I'm sure my other feeling was the right one: you don't like him. I can't understand it dear; I don't see what can be the matter."

"Nothing's the matter."

This easy declaration naturally failed to carry great weight, and Isabel went on, in her troubled voice, "It seems so queer, especially when you feel as you do about his daughter."

At this, George stopped unlacing his shoes abruptly, and sat up. "How do I feel about his daughter?" he demanded.

"Well, it's seemed—as if—as if——" Isabel began timidly. "It did seem—— At least, you haven't looked at any other girl, ever since they came here, and—and certainly you've seemed very much interested in her. Certainly you've been very great *friends?*"

"Well, what of that?"

"It's only that I'm like your grandfather: I can't see how you could be so much interested in a girl and—and not feel very pleasantly toward her father."

"Well, I'll tell you something," George said slowly; and a frown of concentration could be seen upon his brow, as from a profound effort at self-examination. "I haven't ever thought much on that particular point, but I admit there may be a little something in what you say. The truth is, I don't believe I've ever thought of the two together, exactly—at least, not until lately. I've always thought of Lucy just as Lucy, and of Morgan just as Morgan. I've always thought of her as a person herself, not as anybody's daughter. I don't see what's very extraordinary about that. You've probably got plenty of friends, for instance, that don't care much about your son——"

"No, indeed!" she protested quickly. "And if I knew anybody who felt like that, I wouldn't——"

"Never mind," he interrupted. "I'll try to explain a little more. If I have a friend, I don't see that it's incumbent upon me to like that friend's relatives. If I didn't like them, and pretended to, I'd be a hypocrite. If that friend likes me and wants to stay my friend he'll have to stand my not liking his relatives, or else he can quit. I decline to be a hypocrite about it; that's all. Now, suppose I have certain ideas or ideals which I have chosen for the regulation of my own conduct in life. Suppose some friend of mine has a relative with ideals directly the opposite of mine, and my friend believes more in the relative's ideals than in mine: Do you think I ought to give up my own just to please a person who's taken up ideals that I really despise?"

"No, dear; of course people can't give up their ideals; but I don't see what this has to do with dear little Lucy and——"

"I didn't say it had anything to do with them," he interrupted. "I was merely putting a case to show how a person would be justified in being a friend of one member of a family, and feeling anything but friendly toward another. I don't say, though, that I feel unfriendly to Mr. Morgan. I don't say that I feel friendly to him, and I don't say that I feel unfriendly; but if you really think that I was rude to him to-night——"

"Just thoughtless, dear. You didn't see that what you said to-night——"

"Well, I'll not say anything of that sort again where he can hear it. There, isn't that enough?"

This question, delivered with large indulgence, met with no response; for Isabel, still searching his face with her troubled and perplexed gaze, seemed not to have heard it. On that account, George repeated it, and rising, went to her and patted her reassuringly upon the shoulder. "There, old lady, you needn't fear my tactlessness will worry you again. I can't quite promise to like people I don't care about one way or another, but you can be sure I'll be careful, after this, not to let them see it. It's all right, and you'd better toddle along to bed, because I want to undress."

"But, George," she said earnestly, "you *would* like him, if you'd just let yourself. You say you don't dislike him. Why don't you like him? I can't understand at all. *What* is it that you don't——"

"There, there!" he said. "It's all right, and you toddle along."

"But, George——"

"Now, now! I really do want to get into bed. Good-night, old lady."

"Good-night, dear. But——"

"Let's not talk of it any more," he said. "It's all right, and nothing in the world to worry about. So good-night, old lady. I'll be polite enough to him, never fear—if we happen to be thrown together. So *good*-night!"

"But, George, dear——"

"I'm going to bed, old lady; so good-night."

Thus the interview closed perforce. She kissed him again before going slowly to her own room, her perplexity evidently not dispersed; but the subject was not renewed between them the next day or subsequently. Nor did Fanny make any allusion to the cryptic approbation she had bestowed upon her nephew after the Major's "not very successful little dinner"; though she annoyed George by looking at him oftener and longer than he cared to be looked at by an aunt. He could not glance her way, it seemed, without finding her red-rimmed eyes fixed upon him eagerly, with an alert and hopeful calculation in them which he declared would send a nervous man into fits. For thus, one day, he broke out, in protest:

"It would!" he repeated vehemently. "Given time it would—straight into fits! What do you find the matter with me? Is my tie *always* slipping up behind? Can't you look at something else? My Lord! We'd better buy a cat for you to stare at, Aunt Fanny! A cat could stand it, maybe. What in the name of goodness do you expect to *see*?"

But Fanny laughed good-naturedly, and was not offended. "It's more as if I expected *you* to see something, isn't it?" she said quietly, still laughing.

"Now, what do you mean by that?"

"Never mind!"

"All right, I don't. But for heaven's sake stare at somebody else awhile. Try it on the housemaid!"

"Well, well," Fanny said indulgently, and then chose to be more obscure in her meaning than ever, for she adopted a tone of deep sympathy for her final remark, as she left him: "I don't wonder you're nervous these days, poor boy!"

And George indignantly supposed that she referred to the ordeal of Lucy's continued absence. During this period he successfully avoided contact with Lucy's father, though Eugene came frequently to the house, and spent several evenings with Isabel and Fanny; and sometimes persuaded them and the Major to go for an afternoon's motoring. He did not, however, come again to the Major's Sunday evening dinner, even when George Amberson returned. Sunday evening was the time, he explained, for going over the week's work with his factory managers.

. . . When Lucy came home the autumn was far enough advanced to smell of burning leaves, and for the annual editorials, in the papers, on the purple haze, the golden branches, the ruddy fruit, and the pleasure of long tramps in the brown forest. George had not heard of her arrival, and he met her, on the afternoon following that event, at the Sharons', where he had gone in the secret hope that he might hear something about her. Janie Sharon had just begun to tell him that she heard Lucy was expected home soon, after having "a perfectly gorgeous time"—information which George received with no responsive enthusiasm—when Lucy came demurely in, a proper little autumn figure in green and brown.

Her cheeks were flushed, and her dark eyes were bright indeed; evidences, as George supposed, of the excitement incidental to the perfectly gorgeous time just concluded; though Janie and Mary Sharon both thought they were the effect of Lucy's having seen George's runabout in front of the house as she came in. George took on colour, himself, as he rose and nodded indifferently; and the hot suffusion to which he became subject extended its area to include his neck and ears. Nothing could have made him much more indignant than his consciousness of these symptoms of the icy indifference which it was his purpose not only to show but to feel.

She kissed her cousins, gave George her hand, said "How d'you do," and took a chair beside Janie with a composure which augmented George's indignation.

"How d'you do," he said. "I trust that ah—I trust—I do trust——"

He stopped, for it seemed to him that the word "trust" sounded idiotic. Then, to cover his awkwardness, he coughed, and even to his own rosy ears his cough was ostentatiously a false one. Whereupon, seeking to be plausible, he coughed again, and instantly hated himself: the sound he made was an atrocity. Meanwhile, Lucy sat silent, and the two Sharon girls leaned forward, staring at him with strained eyes, their lips tightly compressed; and both were but too easily diagnosed as subject to an agitation which threatened their self-control. He began again.

"I tr—I hope you have had a—a pleasant time. I tr—I hope you are well. I hope you are extremely—I hope extremely—extremely——" And again he stopped in the midst of his floundering, not knowing how to progress beyond "extremely," and unable to understand why the infernal word kept getting into his mouth.

"I beg your pardon?" Lucy said.

George was never more furious; he felt that he was "making a spectacle of himself"; and no young gentleman in the world was more loath than George Amberson Minafer to look a figure of fun. And while he stood there, undeniably such a figure, with Janie and Mary Sharon threatening to burst at any moment, if laughter were longer denied them, Lucy sat looking at him with her eyebrows delicately lifted in casual, polite inquiry. Her own complete composure was what most galled him.

"Nothing of the slightest importance!" he managed to say. "I was just leaving. *Good* afternoon!" And with long strides he reached the door, and hastened through the hall; but before he closed the front door he heard from

Janie and Mary Sharon the outburst of wild, irrepressible emotion which his performance had inspired.

He drove home in a tumultuous mood, and almost ran down two ladies who were engaged in absorbing conversation at a crossing. They were his Aunt Fanny and the stout Mrs. Johnson; a jerk of the reins at the last instant saved them by a few inches; but their conversation was so interesting that they were unaware of their danger, and did not notice the runabout, nor how close it came to them. George was so furious with himself and with the girl whose unexpected coming into a room could make him look such a fool, that it might have soothed him a little if he had actually run over the two absorbed ladies without injuring them beyond repair. At least, he said to himself that he wished he had; it might have taken his mind off of himself for a few minutes. For, in truth, to be ridiculous (and know it) was one of several things that George was unable to endure. He was savage.

He drove into the Major's stable too fast, the sagacious Pendennis saving himself from going through a partition by a swerve which splintered a shaft of the runabout and almost threw the driver to the floor. George swore, and then swore again at the fat old darkey, Tom, for giggling at his swearing.

"Hoopee!" said old Tom. "'Mus' been some white lady use Mist' Jawge mighty bad! White lady say, 'No, suh, I ain' go'n out ridin' 'ith Mist' Jawge no mo'!' Mist' Jawge drive in. 'Dam de dam worl'! Dam de dam hoss! Dam de dam nigga'! Dam de dam dam!' Hoopee!"

"That'll do!" George said sternly.

"Yessuh!"

George strode from the stable, crossed the Major's back yard, then passed behind the new houses, on his way home. These structures were now approaching completion, but still in a state of rawness hideous to George—though, for that matter, they were never to be anything except hideous to him. Behind them, stray planks, bricks, refuse of plaster and lath, shingles, straw, empty barrels, strips of twisted tin and broken tiles were strewn everywhere over the dried and pitted gray mud where once the suave lawn had lain like a green lake around those stately islands, the two Amberson houses. And George's state of mind was not improved by his present view of this repulsive area, nor by his sensations when he kicked an uptilted shingle only to discover that what uptilted it was a brickbat on the other side of it. After that, the whole world seemed to be one solid conspiracy of malevolence.

In this temper he emerged from behind the house nearest to his own, and, glancing toward the street, saw his mother standing with Eugene Morgan upon the cement path that led to the front gate. She was bareheaded, and Eugene held his hat and stick in his hand; evidently he had been calling upon her, and she had come from the house with him, continuing their conversation and delaying their parting.

They had paused in their slow walk from the front door to the gate, yet still stood side by side, their shoulders almost touching, as though neither Isabel nor Eugene quite realized that their feet had ceased to bear them forward; and they were not looking at each other, but at some indefinite point before them, as people do who consider together thoughtfully and in harmony. The conversation was evidently serious; his head was bent, and Isabel's lifted left hand rested against her cheek; but all the significances of their thoughtful attitude denoted companionableness and a shared understanding. Yet, a stranger, passing, would not have thought them married: somewhere about Eugene, not quite to be located, there was a romantic gravity; and Isabel, tall and graceful, with high colour and absorbed eyes, was visibly no wife walking down to the gate with her husband.

George stared at them. A hot dislike struck him at the sight of Eugene; and a vague revulsion, like a strange, unpleasant taste in his mouth, came over him as he looked at his mother: her manner was eloquent of so much thought about her companion and of such reliance upon him. And the picture the two thus made was a vivid one indeed, to George, whose angry eyes, for some reason, fixed themselves most intently upon Isabel's lifted hand, upon the white ruffle at her wrist, bordering the graceful black sleeve, and upon the little indentations in her cheek where the tips of her fingers rested. She should not have worn white at her wrist, or at the throat either, George felt; and then, strangely, his resentment concentrated upon those tiny indentations at the tips of her fingers—actual changes, however slight and fleeting, in his mother's face, made because of Mr. Eugene Morgan. For the moment, it seemed to George that Morgan might have claimed the ownership of a face that changed for him. It was as if he owned Isabel.

The two began to walk on toward the gate, where they stopped again, turning to face each other, and Isabel's glance, passing Eugene, fell upon George. Instantly she smiled and waved her hand to him; while Eugene turned and nodded; but George, standing as in some rigid trance, and staring straight at them, gave these signals of greeting no sign of recognition whatever. Upon this, Isabel called to him, waving her hand again.

"Georgie!" she called, laughing. "Wake up, dear! Georgie, hello!"

George turned away as if he had neither seen nor heard, and stalked into the house by the side door.

CHAPTER XXI

He went to his room, threw off his coat, waistcoat, collar, and tie, letting them lie where they chanced to fall, and then, having violently enveloped himself in a black velvet dressing-gown, continued this action by lying down with a vehemence that brought a wheeze of protest from his bed. His repose was only a momentary semblance, however, for it lasted no longer than the time it took him to groan "Riffraff!" between his teeth. Then he sat up, swung his feet to the floor, rose, and began to pace up and down the large room.

He had just been consciously rude to his mother for the first time in his life; for, with all his riding down of populace and riffraff, he had never before been either deliberately or impulsively disregardful of her. When he had hurt her it had been accidental; and his remorse for such an accident was always adequate compensation—and more—to Isabel. But now he had done a rough thing to her; and he did not repent; the rather he was the more irritated with her. And when he heard her presently go by his door with a light step, singing cheerfully to herself as she went to her room, he perceived that she had mistaken his intention altogether, or, indeed, had failed to perceive that he had any intention at all. Evidently she had concluded that he refused to speak to her and Morgan out of sheer absent-mindedness, supposing him so immersed in some preoccupation that he had not seen them or heard her calling to him. Therefore there was nothing of which to repent, even if he had been so minded; and probably Eugene himself was unaware that any disapproval had recently been expressed. George snorted. What sort of a dreamy loon did they take him to be?

There came a delicate, eager tapping at his door, not done with a knuckle but with the tip of a fingernail, which was instantly clarified to George's mind's eye as plainly as if he saw it: the long and polished white-mooned pink shield on the end of his Aunt Fanny's right forefinger. But George was in no mood for human communications, and even when things went well he had little pleasure in Fanny's society. Therefore it is not surprising that at the sound of her tapping, instead of bidding her enter, he immediately crossed the room with the intention of locking the door to keep her out.

Fanny was too eager, and, opening the door before he reached it, came quickly in, and closed it behind her. She was in a street dress and a black hat, with a black umbrella in her black-gloved hand—for Fanny's heavy mourning, at least, was nowhere tempered with a glimpse of white, though the anniversary of Wilbur's death had passed. An infinitesimal perspiration gleamed upon her pale skin; she breathed fast, as if she had run up the stairs; and excitement was sharp in her widened eyes. Her look was that of a person who had just seen something extraordinary or heard thrilling news.

"Now, what on earth do *you* want?" her chilling nephew demanded.

"George," she said hurriedly, "I saw what you did when you wouldn't speak to them. I was sitting with Mrs. Johnson at her front window, across the street, and I saw it all."

"Well, what of it?"

"You did right!" Fanny said with a vehemence not the less spirited because she suppressed her voice almost to a whisper. "You did exactly right! You're behaving splendidly about the whole thing, and I want to tell you I know your father would thank you if he could see what you're doing."

"My Lord!" George broke out at her. "You make me dizzy! For heaven's sake quit the mysterious detective business—at least do quit it around me! Go and try it on somebody else, if you like; but I don't want to hear it!"

She began to tremble, regarding him with a fixed gaze. "You don't care to hear then," she said huskily, "that I approve of what you're doing?"

"Certainly not! Since I haven't the faintest idea what you think I'm 'doing,' naturally I don't care whether you approve of it or not. All I'd like, if you please, is to be alone. I'm not giving a tea here, this afternoon, if you'll permit me to mention it!"

Fanny's gaze wavered; she began to blink; then suddenly she sank into a chair and wept silently, but with a terrible desolation.

"Oh, for the Lord's sake!" he moaned. "What in the world is wrong with you?"

"You're always picking on me," she quavered wretchedly, her voice indistinct with the wetness that bubbled into it from her tears. "You do—you always pick on me! You've always done it—always—ever since you were a little boy! Whenever anything goes wrong with you, you take it out on me! You do! You always——"

George flung to heaven a gesture of despair; it seemed to him the last straw that Fanny should have chosen this particular time to come and sob in his room over his mistreatment of her!

"Oh, my Lord!" he whispered; then, with a great effort, addressed her in a reasonable tone: "Look here, Aunt Fanny; I don't see what you're making all this fuss about. Of course I know I've teased you sometimes, but——"

"'Teased' me?" she wailed. "'Teased' me! Oh, it does seem too hard, sometimes—this mean old life of mine does seem too hard! I don't think I can stand it! Honestly, I don't think I can! I came in here just to show you I sympathized with you—just to say something pleasant to you, and you treat me as if I were—oh, no, you wouldn't treat a servant the way you treat me! You wouldn't treat anybody in the world like this except old Fanny! 'Old Fanny' you say. 'It's nobody but old Fanny, so I'll kick her—nobody will resent it. I'll kick her all I want to!' You do! That's how you think of me—I know it! And you're right: I haven't got anything in the world, since my brother died—nobody—nothing—nothing!"

"Oh my Lord!" George groaned.

Fanny spread out her small, soaked handkerchief, and shook it in the air to dry it a little, crying as damply and as wretchedly during this operation as before—a sight which gave George a curious shock to add to his other agitations, it seemed so strange. "I ought not to have come," she went on, "because I might have known it would only give you an excuse to pick on me again! I'm sorry enough I came, I can tell you! I didn't mean to speak of it again to you, at all; and I wouldn't have, but I saw how you treated them, and I guess I got excited about it, and couldn't help following the impulse —but I'll know better next time, I can tell you! I'll keep my mouth shut as I meant to, and as I would have, if I hadn't got excited and if I hadn't felt sorry for you. But what does it matter to anybody if I'm sorry for them? I'm only old Fanny!"

"Oh, good gracious! How *can* it matter to me who's sorry for me when I don't know what they're sorry about!"

"You're so proud," she quavered, "and so hard! I *tell* you I didn't mean to speak of it to you, and I never, never in the world would have *told* you about it, nor have made the faintest reference to it, if I hadn't seen that somebody else had told you, or you'd found out for yourself some way. I——"

In despair of her intelligence, and in some doubt of his own, George struck the palms of his hands together. "Somebody else had told me what? I'd found *what* out for myself?"

"How people are talking about your mother."

Except for the incidental teariness of her voice, her tone was casual, as though she mentioned a subject previously discussed and understood; for Fanny had no doubt that George had only pretended to be mystified because, in his pride, he would not in words admit that he knew what he knew.

"What did you say?" he asked incredulously.

"Of course I understood what you were doing," Fanny went on, drying her handkerchief again. "It puzzled other people when you began to be rude to Eugene, because they couldn't see how you could treat him as you did when you were so interested in Lucy. But I remembered how you came to me, that other time when there was so much talk about Isabel; and I knew you'd give Lucy up in a minute, if it came to a question of your mother's reputation, because you said then that——"

"Look here," George interrupted in a shaking voice. "Look here, I'd like——" He stopped, unable to go on, his agitation was so great. His chest heaved as from hard running, and his complexion, pallid at first, had become mottled; fiery splotches appearing at his temples and cheeks. "What do you mean by telling me—telling me there's talk about—about——" He gulped, and began again: "What do you mean by using such words as 'reputation'? What do you mean, speaking of a 'question' of my—my mother's reputation?"

Fanny looked up at him woefully over the handkerchief which she now applied to her reddened nose. "God knows I'm sorry for you, George," she murmured. "I wanted to say so, but it's only old Fanny, so whatever she says —even when it's sympathy—pick on her for it! Hammer her!" She sobbed. "Hammer her! It's only poor old lonely Fanny!"

"You look here!" George said harshly. "When I spoke to my Uncle George after that rotten thing I heard Aunt Amelia say about my mother, he said if there was any gossip it was about *you!* He said people might be laughing about the way you ran after Morgan, but that was all."

Fanny lifted her hands, clenched them, and struck them upon her knees. "Yes; it's always Fanny!" she sobbed. "Ridiculous old Fanny—always, always!"

"You listen!" George said. "After I'd talked to Uncle George I saw *you;* and you said I had a mean little mind for thinking there might be truth in what Aunt Amelia said about people talking. You denied it. And that wasn't the only time; you'd attacked me before then, because I intimated that

Morgan might be coming here too often. You made me believe that mother let him come entirely on your account, and *now* you say——"

"I think he did," Fanny interrupted desolately. "I think he did come as much to see me as anything—for a *while* it looked like it. Anyhow, he liked to dance with me. He danced with me as much as he danced with her, and he acted as if he came on my account at least as much as he did on hers. He *did* act a good deal that way—and if Wilbur hadn't died——"

"You told me there *wasn't* any talk."

"I didn't think there was much, then," Fanny protested. "I didn't know how much there was."

"What!"

"People don't come and tell such things to a person's family, you know. You don't suppose anybody was going to say to George Amberson that his sister was getting herself talked about, do you? Or that they were going to say much to *me?*"

"You told me," said George, fiercely, "that mother never saw him except when she was chaperoning you."

"They weren't much alone together, then," Fanny returned. "Hardly ever, before Wilbur died. But you don't suppose *that* stops people from talking, do you? Your father never went anywhere, and people saw Eugene with her everywhere she went—and though I was with them people just thought"— she choked—"they just thought I didn't count! 'Only old Fanny Minafer,' I suppose they'd say! Besides, everybody knew that he's been engaged to her——"

"What's that?" George cried.

"Everybody knows it. Don't you remember your grandfather speaking of it at the Sunday dinner one night?"

"He didn't say they were engaged or——"

"Well, they were! Everybody knows it; and she broke it off on account of that serenade when Eugene didn't know what he was doing. He drank when he was a young man, and she wouldn't stand it, but everybody in this town knows that Isabel has never really cared for any other man in her life! Poor Wilbur! He was the only soul alive that didn't know it!"

Nightmare had descended upon the unfortunate George; he leaned back against the foot-board of his bed, gazing wildly at his aunt. "I believe I'm going crazy," he said. "You mean when you told me there wasn't any talk, you told me a falsehood?"

"No!" Fanny gasped.

"You did!"

"I tell you I didn't know how much talk there *was*, and it wouldn't have amounted to much if Wilbur had lived." And Fanny completed this with a fatal admission: "I didn't want you to interfere."

George overlooked the admission; his mind was not now occupied with analysis. "What do you mean," he asked, "when you say that if father had lived, the talk wouldn't have amounted to anything?"

648 THE MAGNIFICENT AMBERSONS

"Things might have been—they might have been different."

"You mean Morgan might have married *you?*"

Fanny gulped. "No. Because I don't know that I'd have accepted him." She had ceased to weep, and now she sat up stiffly. "I certainly didn't care enough about him to marry him; I wouldn't have let myself care that much until he showed that he wished to marry me. I'm not that sort of person!" The poor lady paid her vanity this piteous little tribute. "What I mean is, if Wilbur hadn't died, people wouldn't have had it proved before their very *eyes* that what they'd been talking about was true!"

"You say—you say that people believe——" George shuddered, then forced himself to continue, in a sick voice: "They believe my mother is—is in love with that man?"

"Of course!"

"And because he comes here—and they see her with him driving—and all that—they think they were right when they said she was in—in love with him before—before my father died?"

She looked at him gravely with her eyes now dry between their reddened lids. "Why, George," she said, gently, "don't *you* know that's what they say? You *must* know that everybody in town thinks they're going to be married very soon."

George uttered an incoherent cry; and sections of him appeared to writhe. He was upon the verge of actual nausea.

"You know it!" Fanny cried, getting up. "You don't think I'd have spoken of it to you unless I was sure you knew it?" Her voice was wholly genuine, as it had been throughout the wretched interview: Fanny's sincerity was unquestionable. "George, *I* wouldn't have told you, if you didn't know. What other reason could you have for treating Eugene as you did, or for refusing to speak to them like that, a while ago in the yard? Somebody *must* have told you."

"Who told *you?*" he said.

"What?"

"Who told you there was talk? Where *is* this talk? Where does it come from? Who does it?"

"Why, I suppose pretty much everybody," she said. "I know it must be pretty general."

"Who said so?"

"What?"

George stepped close to her. "You say people don't speak to a person of gossip about that person's family. Well, how did you hear it, then? How did you get hold of it? Answer me!"

Fanny looked thoughtful. "Well, of course nobody not one's most intimate friends would speak to them about such things, and then only in the kindest, most considerate way."

"Who's spoken of it to you in any way at all?" George demanded.

"Why——" Fanny hesitated.

"You answer me!"

"I hardly think it would be fair to give names."

"Look here," said George. "One of your most intimate friends is that mother of Charlie Johnson's, for instance. Has *she* ever mentioned this to you? You say everybody is talking. Is she one?"

"Oh, she may have intimated——"

"I'm asking you: Has she ever spoken of it to you?"

"She's a very kind, discreet woman, George; but she may have intimated——"

George had a sudden intuition, as there flickered into his mind the picture of a street-crossing and two absorbed ladies almost run down by a fast horse. "You and she have been talking about it to-day!" he cried. "You were talking about it with her not two hours ago. Do you deny it?"

"I——"

"Do you deny it?"

"No!"

"All right," said George. "That's enough!"

She caught at his arm as he turned away. "What are you going to do, George?"

"I'll not talk about it, now," he said heavily. "I think you've done a good deal for one day, Aunt Fanny!"

And Fanny, seeing the passion in his face, began to be alarmed. She tried to retain possession of the black velvet sleeve which her fingers had clutched, and he suffered her to do so, but used this leverage to urge her to the door. "George, you know I'm sorry for you, whether you care or not," she whimpered. "I never in the world would have spoken of it, if I hadn't thought you knew all about it. *I* wouldn't have——"

But he had opened the door with his free hand. "Never mind!" he said, and she was obliged to pass out into the hall, the door closing quickly behind her.

CHAPTER XXII

George took off his dressing-gown and put on a collar and a tie, his fingers shaking so that the tie was not his usual success; then he picked up his coat and waistcoat, and left the room while still in process of donning them, fastening the buttons as he ran down the front stairs to the door. It was not until he reached the middle of the street that he realized that he had forgotten his hat; and he paused for an irresolute moment, during which his eye wandered, for no reason, to the Fountain of Neptune. This castiron replica of too elaborate sculpture stood at the next corner, where the Major had placed it when the Addition was laid out so long ago. The street corners had been shaped to conform with the great octagonal basin, which was no great inconvenience for horse-drawn vehicles, but a nuisance to speeding automobiles; and, even as George looked, one of the latter, coming too fast, saved itself only by a dangerous skid as it rounded the fountain. This skid was to George's liking, though he would have been more pleased to see the car go over, for he was wishing grief and destruction, just then, upon all the automobiles in the world.

His eyes rested a second or two longer upon the Fountain of Neptune, not an enlivening sight even in the shielding haze of autumn twilight. For more than a year no water had run in the fountain: the connections had been broken, and the Major was evasive about restorations, even when reminded by his grandson that a dry fountain is as gay as a dry fish. Soot streaks and a thousand pits gave Neptune the distinction, at least, of leprosy, which the mermaids associated with him had been consistent in catching; and his trident had been so deeply affected as to drop its prongs. Altogether, this heavy work of heavy art, smoked dry, hugely scabbed, cracked, and crumbling, was a dismal sight to the distracted eye of George Amberson Minafer, and its present condition of craziness may have added a mite to his own. His own was sufficient, with no additions, however, as he stood looking at the Johnsons' house and those houses on both sides of it—that row of riffraff dwellings he had thought so damnable, the day when he stood in his grandfather's yard, staring at them, after hearing what his Aunt Amelia said of the "talk" about his mother.

He decided that he needed no hat for the sort of call he intended to make, and went forward hurriedly. Mrs. Johnson was at home, the Irish girl who came to the door informed him, and he was left to await the lady, in a room like an elegant well—the Johnsons' "reception room": floor space, nothing to mention; walls, blue calcimined; ceiling, twelve feet from the floor; inside shutters and gray lace curtains; five gilt chairs, a brocaded sofa, soiled, and an inlaid walnut table, supporting two tall alabaster vases; a palm, with two leaves, dying in a corner.

Mrs. Johnson came in, breathing noticeably; and her round head, smoothly but economically decorated with the hair of an honest woman, seemed to be lingering far in the background of the Alpine bosom which took precedence of the rest of her everywhere; but when she was all in the room, it was to be seen that her breathing was the result of hospitable haste to greet the visitor, and her hand, not so dry as Neptune's Fountain, suggested that she had paused for only the briefest ablutions. George accepted this cold, damp lump mechanically.

"Mr. Amberson—I mean Mr. Minafer!" she exclaimed. "I'm really delighted: I understood you asked for me. Mr. Johnson's out of the city, but Charlie's downtown and I'm looking for him at any minute, now, and he'll be so pleased that you——"

"I didn't want to see Charlie," George said. "I want——"

"Do sit down," the hospitable lady urged him, seating herself upon the sofa. "Do sit down."

"No, I thank you. I wish——"

"Surely you're not going to run away again, when you've just come. Do sit down, Mr. Minafer. I hope you're all well at your house and at the dear old Major's, too. He's looking——"

"Mrs. Johnson," George said, in a strained loud voice which arrested her attention immediately, so that she was abruptly silent, leaving her surprised mouth open. She had already been concealing some astonishment at this un-exampled visit, however, and the condition of George's ordinarily smooth hair (for he had overlooked more than his hat) had not alleviated her perplexity. "Mrs. Johnson," he said, "I have come to ask you a few questions which I would like you to answer, if you please."

She became grave at once. "Certainly, Mr. Minafer. Anything I can——"

He interrupted sternly, yet his voice shook in spite of its sternness. "You were talking with my Aunt Fanny about my mother this afternoon."

At this Mrs. Johnson uttered an involuntary gasp, but she recovered herself. "Then I'm sure our conversation was a very pleasant one, if we were talking of your mother, because——"

Again he interrupted. "My aunt has told me what the conversation virtu-ally was, and I don't mean to waste any time, Mrs. Johnson. You were talking about a——" George's shoulders suddenly heaved uncontrollably; but he went fiercely on: "You were discussing a scandal that involved my mother's name."

"Mr. Minafer!"

"Isn't that the truth?"

"I don't feel called upon to answer, Mr. Minafer," she said with visible agitation. "I do not consider that you have any right——"

"My aunt told me you repeated this scandal to her."

"I don't think your aunt can have said that," Mrs. Johnson returned sharply. "I did not repeat a scandal of any kind to your aunt and I think you are mistaken in saying she told you I did. We may have discussed some matters that have been a topic of comment about town——"

"Yes!" George cried. "I think you may have! That's what I'm here about, and what I intend to——"

"Don't tell *me* what you intend, please," Mrs. Johnson interrupted crisply. "And I should prefer that you would not make your voice quite so loud in this house, which I happen to own. Your aunt may have told you—though I think it would have been very unwise in her if she did, and not very con-siderate of *me*—she may have told you that we discussed some such topic as I have mentioned, and possibly that would have been true. If I talked it over with her, you may be sure I spoke in the most charitable spirit, and without sharing in other people's disposition to put an evil interpretation on what *may* be nothing more than unfortunate appearances and——"

"My God!" said George. "I can't stand this!"

"You have the option of dropping the subject," Mrs. Johnson suggested tartly, and she added: "Or of leaving the house."

"I'll do that soon enough, but first I mean to know——"

"I am perfectly willing to tell you anything you wish if you will remember to ask it quietly. I'll also take the liberty of reminding you that I had a perfect right to discuss the subject with your aunt. Other people may be less considerate in not confining their discussion of it, as I have, to charitable views expressed only to a member of the family. Other people——"

"Other people!" the unhappy George repeated viciously. "That's what I want to know about—these other people!"

"I beg your pardon."

"I want to ask you about them. You say you know of other people who talk about this."

"I presume they do."

"How many?"

"What?"

"I want to know how many other people talk about it?"

"Dear, dear!" she protested. "How should I know that?"

"Haven't you heard anybody mention it?"

"I presume so."

"Well, how *many* have you heard?"

Mrs. Johnson was becoming more annoyed than apprehensive, and she showed it. "Really, this isn't a court-room," she said. "And I'm not a defendant in a libel-suit, either!"

The unfortunate young man lost what remained of his balance. "You may be!" he cried. "I intend to know just who's dared to say these things, if I have to force my way into every house in town, and I'm going to make them take every word of it back! I mean to know the name of every slanderer that's spoken of this matter to you and of every tattler you've passed it on to yourself. I mean to know——"

"You'll know *something* pretty quick!" she said, rising with difficulty; and her voice was thick with the sense of insult. "You'll know that you're out in the street. Please to leave my house!"

George stiffened sharply. Then he bowed, and strode out of the door.

Three minutes later, dishevelled and perspiring, but cold all over, he burst into his Uncle George's room at the Major's without knocking. Amberson was dressing.

"Good gracious, Georgie!" he exclaimed. "What's up?"

"I've just come from Mrs. Johnson's—across the street," George panted.

"You have your own tastes!" was Amberson's comment. "But curious as they are, you ought to do something better with your hair, and button your waistcoat to the right buttons—even for Mrs. Johnson! What were you doing over there?"

"She told me to leave the house," George said desperately. "I went there because Aunt Fanny told me the whole town was talking about my mother and that man Morgan—that they say my mother is going to marry him and that proves she was too fond of him before my father died—she said this Mrs. Johnson was one that talked about it, and I went to her to ask who were the others."

Amberson's jaw fell in dismay. "Don't tell me you did that!" he said, in a low voice; and then, seeing that it was true, "Oh, now you *have* done it!"

CHAPTER XXIII

"I've 'done it'?" George cried. "What do you mean: I've done it? And what have I done?"

Amberson had collapsed into an easy chair beside his dressing-table, the white evening tie he had been about to put on dangling from his hand, which had fallen limply on the arm of the chair. The tie dropped to the floor before he replied; and the hand that had held it was lifted to stroke his graying hair reflectively. "By Jove!" he muttered. "That *is* too bad!"

George folded his arms bitterly. "Will you kindly answer my question? What have I done that wasn't honourable and right? Do you think these riff-raff can go about bandying my mother's name——"

"They can now," said Amberson. "I don't know if they could before, but they certainly can now!"

"What do you mean by that?"

His uncle sighed profoundly, picked up his tie, and, preoccupied with despondency, twisted the strip of white lawn till it became unwearable. Meanwhile, he tried to enlighten his nephew. "Gossip is never fatal, Georgie," he said, "until it is denied. Gossip goes on about every human being alive and about all the dead that are alive enough to be remembered, and yet almost never does any harm until some defender makes a controversy. Gossip's a nasty thing, but it's sickly, and if people of good intentions will let it entirely alone, it will die, ninety-nine times out of a hundred."

"See here," George said: "I didn't come to listen to any generalizing dose of philosophy! I ask you——"

"You asked me what you've done, and I'm telling you." Amberson gave him a melancholy smile, continuing: "Suffer me to do it in my own way. Fanny says there's been talk about your mother, and that Mrs. Johnson does some of it. I don't know, because naturally nobody would come to me with such stuff or mention it before me; but it's presumably true—I suppose it is. I've seen Fanny with Mrs. Johnson quite a lot; and that old lady is a notorious gossip, and that's why she ordered you out of her house when you pinned her down that she'd been gossiping. I have a suspicion Mrs. Johnson has been quite a comfort to Fanny in their long talks; but she'll probably quit speaking to her over this, because Fanny told you. I suppose it's true that the 'whole town,' a lot of others, that is, do share in the gossip. In this town, naturally, anything about any Amberson has always been a stone dropped into the centre of a pond, and a lie would send the ripples as far as a truth would. I've been on a steamer when the story went all over the boat, the second day out, that the prettiest girl on board didn't have any ears; and you can take it as a rule that when a woman's past thirty-five the prettier her hair is, the more certain you are to meet somebody with reliable information that it's a wig. You can be sure that for many years there's been more gossip in this place about the Ambersons than about any other family. I dare say it isn't so much so now as it used to be, because the town got too big long ago, but it's the truth that the more prominent you are the more gossip there is about you, and the more people would like to pull you down. Well, they can't do it as long as you refuse to know what gossip there is about you. But the minute you notice it, it's got you! I'm not speaking of certain kinds of slander that sometimes people have got to take to the courts; I'm talking of the wretched buzzing the Mrs. Johnsons do—the thing you seem to have such a horror of—people 'talking'—the kind of thing that has assailed your mother. People who have repeated a slander either get ashamed or forget it, if they're let alone. Challenge them, and in self-defense they believe everything they've said: they'd rather believe you a sinner than believe themselves liars, naturally. Submit to gossip and you kill it; fight it and you make it strong. People will forget almost any slander except one that's been fought."

"Is that all?" George asked.

"I suppose so," his uncle murmured sadly.

"Well, then, may I ask what you'd have done, in my place?"

"I'm not sure, Georgie. When I was your age I was like you in many ways, especially in not being very cool-headed, so I can't say. Youth can't be trusted for much, except asserting itself and fighting and making love."

"Indeed!" George snorted. "May I ask what you think I *ought* to have done?"

"Nothing."

"'Nothing?'" George echoed, mocking bitterly. "I suppose you think I mean to let my mother's good name——"

"Your mother's good name!" Amberson cut him off impatiently. "Nobody has a good name in a bad mouth. Nobody has a good name in a silly mouth, either. Well, your mother's name was in some silly mouths, and all you've done was to go and have a scene with the worst old woman gossip in the town—a scene that's going to make her into a partisan against your mother, whereas she was a mere prattler before. Don't you suppose she'll be all over town with this to-morrow? To-morrow? Why, she'll have her telephone going to-night as long as any of her friends are up! People that never heard anything about this are going to hear it all now, with embellishments. And she'll see to it that everybody who's hinted anything about poor Isabel will know that you're on the warpath; and that will put them on the defensive and make them vicious. The story will grow as it spreads and——"

George unfolded his arms to strike his right fist into his left palm. "But do you suppose I'm going to tolerate such things?" he shouted. "What do you suppose I'll be doing?"

"Nothing helpful."

"Oh, you think so, do you?"

"You can do absolutely nothing," said Amberson. "Nothing of any use. The more you do the more harm you'll do."

"You'll see! I'm going to stop this thing if I have to force my way into every house on National Avenue and Amberson Boulevard!"

His uncle laughed rather sourly, but made no other comment.

"Well, what do you propose to do?" George demanded. "Do you propose to sit there——"

"Yes."

"—and let this riffraff bandy my mother's good name back and forth among them? Is that what you propose to do?"

"It's all I can do," Amberson returned. "It's all any of us can do now: just sit still and hope that the thing may die down in time, in spite of your stirring up that awful old woman."

George drew a long breath, then advanced and stood close before his uncle. "Didn't you understand me when I told you that people are saying my mother means to marry this man?"

"Yes, I understood you."

"You say that my going over there has made matters worse," George went on. "How about it if such a—such an unspeakable marriage did take place? Do you think that would make people believe they'd been wrong in saying —you know what they say."

"No," said Amberson deliberately; "I don't believe it would. There'd be more badness in the bad mouths and more silliness in the silly mouths, I dare say. But it wouldn't hurt Isabel and Eugene, if they never heard of it; and if they did hear of it, then they could take their choice between placating gossip or living for their own happiness. If they have decided to marry——"

George almost staggered. "Good God!" he gasped. "You speak of it calmly!"

Amberson looked up at him inquiringly. "Why shouldn't they marry if they want to?" he asked. "It's their own affair."

"Why shouldn't they?" George echoed. "Why shouldn't they?"

"Yes. Why shouldn't they? I don't see anything precisely monstrous about two people getting married when they're both free and care about each other. What's the matter with their marrying?"

"It would be monstrous!" George shouted. "Monstrous even if this horrible thing hadn't happened, but now in the face of this—oh, that you can sit there and even speak of it! Your own sister! O God! Oh——" He became incoherent, swinging away from Amberson and making for the door, wildly gesturing.

"For heaven's sake, don't be so theatrical!" said his uncle, and then, seeing that George was leaving the room: "Come back here. You mustn't speak to your mother of this!"

"Don't 'tend to," George said indistinctly; and he plunged out into the big dimly lit hall. He passed his grandfather's room on the way to the stairs; and the Major was visible within, his white head brightly illumined by a lamp, as he bent low over a ledger upon his roll-top desk. He did not look up, and his grandson strode by the door, not really conscious of the old figure stooping at its tremulous work with long additions and subtractions that refused to balance as they used to. George went home and got a hat and overcoat without seeing either his mother or Fanny. Then he left word that he would be out for dinner, and hurried away from the house.

He walked the dark streets of Amberson Addition for an hour, then went downtown and got coffee at a restaurant. After that he walked through the lighted parts of the town until ten o'clock, when he turned north and came back to the purlieus of the Addition. He strode through the length and breadth of it again, his hat pulled down over his forehead, his overcoat collar turned up behind. He walked fiercely, though his feet ached, but by and by he turned homeward, and, when he reached the Major's, went in and sat upon the steps of the huge stone veranda in front—an obscure figure in that lonely and repellent place. All lights were out at the Major's, and finally, after twelve, he saw his mother's window darken at home.

He waited half an hour longer, then crossed the front yards of the new houses and let himself noiselessly in the front door. The light in the hall had been left burning, and another in his own room, as he discovered when he got there. He locked the door quickly and without noise, but his fingers were still upon the key when there was a quick footfall in the hall outside.

"Georgie, dear?"

He went to the other end of the room before replying.

"Yes?"

"I'd been wondering where you were, dear."

"Had you?"

There was a pause; then she said timidly: "Wherever it was, I hope you had a pleasant evening."

After a silence, "Thank you," he said, without expression.

Another silence followed before she spoke again.

"You wouldn't care to be kissed good-night, I suppose?" And with a little flurry of placative laughter, she added: "At your age, of course!"

"I'm going to bed, now," he said. "Good-night."

Another silence seemed blanker than those which had preceded it, and finally her voice came—it was blank, too.

"Good-night."

. . . After he was in bed his thoughts became more tumultuous than ever; while among all the inchoate and fragmentary sketches of this dreadful day, now rising before him, the clearest was of his uncle collapsed in a big chair with a white tie dangling from his hand; and one conviction, following upon that picture, became definite in George's mind: that his Uncle George Amberson was a hopeless dreamer from whom no help need be expected, an amiable imbecile lacking in normal impulses, and wholly useless in a struggle which required honour to be defended by a man of action.

Then would return a vision of Mrs. Johnson's furious round head, set behind her great bosom like the sun far sunk on the horizon of a mountain plateau—and her crackling, asthmatic voice . . . "Without sharing in other people's disposition to put an evil interpretation on what *may* be nothing more than unfortunate appearances." . . . "Other people may be less considerate in not confining their discussion of it, as I have, to charitable views." . . . "You'll know *something* pretty quick! You'll know you're out in the street." . . . And then George would get up again—and again—and pace the floor in his bare feet.

That was what the tormented young man was doing when daylight came gauntly in at his window—pacing the floor, rubbing his head in his hands, and muttering:

"It can't be true: this can't be happening to *me!*"

CHAPTER XXIV

Breakfast was brought to him in his room, as usual; but he did not make his normal healthy raid upon the dainty tray: the food remained untouched, and he sustained himself upon coffee—four cups of it, which left nothing of value inside the glistening little percolator. During this process he heard his mother being summoned to the telephone in the hall, not far from his door, and then her voice responding: "Yes? Oh, it's you! . . . Indeed I should! . . . Of course. . . . Then I'll expect you about three . . . Yes. . . . Goodbye till then." A few minutes later he heard her speaking to someone beneath his window and, looking out, saw her directing the removal of plants from a small garden bed to the Major's conservatory for the winter. There was an air of briskness about her; as she turned away to go into the house, she laughed gaily with the Major's gardener over something he said, and this unconcerned cheerfulness of her was terrible to her son.

He went to his desk, and, searching the jumbled contents of a drawer, brought forth a large, unframed photograph of his father, upon which he gazed long and piteously, till at last hot tears stood in his eyes. It was strange how the inconsequent face of Wilbur seemed to increase in high significance during this belated interview between father and son; and how it seemed to take on a reproachful nobility—and yet, under the circumstances, nothing could have been more natural than that George, having paid but the slightest attention to his father in life, should begin to deify him, now that he was dead. "Poor, poor father!" the son whispered brokenly. "Poor man, I'm glad you didn't know!"

He wrapped the picture in a sheet of newspaper, put it under his arm, and, leaving the house hurriedly and stealthily, went downtown to the shop of a silversmith, where he spent sixty dollars on a resplendently festooned silver frame for the picture. Having lunched upon more coffee, he returned to the house at two o'clock, carrying the framed photograph with him, and placed it upon the centre-table in the library, the room most used by Isabel and Fanny and himself. Then he went to a front window of the long "reception room," and sat looking out through the lace curtains.

The house was quiet, though once or twice he heard his mother and Fanny moving about upstairs, and a ripple of song in the voice of Isabel—a fragment from the romantic ballad of Lord Bateman.

> "Lord Bateman was a noble lord,
>   A noble lord of high degree;
> And he sailed West and he sailed East,
>   Far countries for to see. . . ."

The words became indistinct; the air was hummed absently; the humming shifted to a whistle, then drifted out of hearing, and the place was still again.

George looked often at his watch, but his vigil did not last an hour. At ten minutes of three, peering through the curtain, he saw an automobile stop in front of the house and Eugene Morgan jump lightly down from it. The car was of a new pattern, low and long, with an ample seat in the tonneau, facing forward; and a professional driver sat at the wheel, a strange figure in leather, goggled out of all personality and seemingly part of the mechanism.

Eugene himself, as he came up the cement path to the house, was a figure of the new era which was in time to be so disastrous to stiff hats and skirted coats; and his appearance afforded a debonair contrast to that of the queer-looking duck capering at the Amberson Ball in an old dress coat, and next day chugging up National Avenue through the snow in his nightmare of a sewing-machine. Eugene, this afternoon, was richly in the new outdoor mode: his motoring coat was soft gray fur; his cap and gloves were of gray suede; and though Lucy's hand may have shown itself in the selection of these high garnitures, he wore them easily, even with a becoming hint of jauntiness. Some change might be seen in his face, too, for a successful man is seldom to be mistaken, especially if his temper be genial. Eugene had begun to look like a millionaire.

But above everything else, what was most evident about him, as he came up the path, was his confidence in the happiness promised by his present errand; the anticipation in his eyes could have been read by a stranger. His look at the door of Isabel's house was the look of a man who is quite certain that the next moment will reveal something ineffably charming, inexpressibly dear.

. . . When the bell rang, George waited at the entrance of the "reception room" until a housemaid came through the hall on her way to answer the summons.

"You needn't mind, Mary," he told her. "I'll see who it is and what they want. Probably it's only a pedlar."

"Thank you, sir, Mister George," said Mary; and returned to the rear of the house.

George went slowly to the front door, and halted, regarding the misty silhouette of the caller upon the ornamental frosted glass. After a minute of waiting, this silhouette changed outline so that an arm could be distinguished —an arm outstretched toward the bell, as if the gentleman outside doubted whether or not it had sounded, and were minded to try again. But before the gesture was completed George abruptly threw open the door, and stepped squarely upon the middle of the threshold.

A slight change shadowed the face of Eugene; his look of happy anticipation gave way to something formal and polite. "How do you do, George," he said. "Mrs. Minafer expects to go driving with me, I believe—if you'll be so kind as to send her word that I'm here."

George made not the slightest movement.

"No," he said.

Eugene was incredulous, even when his second glance revealed how hot of eye was the haggard young man before him. "I beg your pardon. I said——"

"I heard you," said George. "You said you had an engagement with my mother, and I told you, No!"

Eugene gave him a steady look, and then he asked quietly: "What is the —the difficulty?"

George kept his own voice quiet enough, but that did not mitigate the vibrant fury of it. "My mother will have no interest in knowing that you came for her to-day," he said. "Or any other day!"

Eugene continued to look at him with a scrutiny in which began to gleam a profound anger, none the less powerful because it was so quiet. "I am afraid I do not understand you."

"I doubt if I could make it much plainer," George said, raising his voice slightly, "but I'll try. You're not wanted in this house, Mr. Morgan, now or at any other time. Perhaps you'll understand—this!"

And with the last word he closed the door in Eugene's face.

Then, not moving away, he stood just inside the door, and noted that the misty silhouette remained upon the frosted glass for several moments, as if the forbidden gentleman debated in his mind what course to pursue. "Let him ring again!" George thought grimly. "Or try the side door—or the kitchen!"

But Eugene made no further attempt; the silhouette disappeared; footsteps could be heard withdrawing across the floor of the veranda; and George, returning to the window in the "reception room," was rewarded by the sight of an automobile manufacturer in baffled retreat, with all his wooing furs

and fineries mocking him. Eugene got into his car slowly, not looking back at the house which had just taught him such a lesson; and it was easily visible —even from a window seventy feet distant—that he was not the same light suitor who had jumped so gallantly from the car only a few minutes earlier. Observing the heaviness of his movements as he climbed into the tonneau, George indulged in a sickish throat rumble which bore a distant cousinship to mirth.

The car was quicker than its owner; it shot away as soon as he had sunk into his seat; and George, having watched its impetuous disappearance from his field of vision, ceased to haunt the window. He went to the library, and, seating himself beside the table whereon he had placed the photograph of his father, picked up a book, and pretended to be engaged in reading it.

Presently Isabel's buoyant step was heard descending the stairs, and her low, sweet whistling, renewing the air of "Lord Bateman." She came into the library, still whistling thoughtfully, a fur coat over her arm, ready to put on, and two veils round her small black hat, her right hand engaged in buttoning the glove upon her left; and, as the large room contained too many pieces of heavy furniture, and the inside shutters excluded most of the light of day, she did not at once perceive George's presence. Instead, she went to the bay window at the end of the room, which afforded a view of the street, and glanced out expectantly; then bent her attention upon her glove; after that, looked out toward the street again, ceased to whistle, and turned toward the interior of the room.

"Why, Georgie!"

She came, leaned over from behind him, and there was a faint, exquisite odour as from distant apple-blossoms as she kissed his cheek. "Dear, I waited lunch almost an hour for you, but you didn't come! Did you lunch out somewhere?"

"Yes." He did not look up from the book.

"Did you have plenty to eat?"

"Yes."

"Are you sure? Wouldn't you like to have Maggie get you something now in the dining room? Or they could bring it to you here, if you think it would be cosier. Shan't I——"

"No."

A tinkling bell was audible, and she moved to the doorway into the hall. "I'm going out driving, dear. I——" She interrupted herself to address the housemaid, who was passing through the hall: "I think it's Mr. Morgan, Mary. Tell him I'll be there at once."

"Yes, ma'am."

Mary returned. "'Twas a pedlar, ma'am."

"Another one?" Isabel said, surprised. "I thought you said it was a pedlar when the bell rang a little while ago."

"Mister George said it was, ma'am; he went to the door," Mary informed her, disappearing.

"There seem to be a great many of them," Isabel mused. "What did yours want to sell, George?"

"He didn't say."

"You must have cut him off short!" she laughed; and then, still standing in the doorway, she noticed the big silver frame upon the table beside him. "Gracious, Georgie!" she exclaimed. "You *have* been investing!" and as she came across the room for a closer view, "Is it—is it Lucy?" she asked half timidly, half archly. But the next instant she saw whose likeness was thus set forth in elegiac splendour—and she was silent, except for a long, just-audible "*Oh!*"

He neither looked up nor moved.

"That was nice of you, Georgie," she said, in a low voice presently. "I ought to have had it framed, myself, when I gave it to you."

He said nothing, and, standing beside him, she put her hand gently upon his shoulder, then as gently withdrew it, and went out of the room. But she did not go upstairs; he heard the faint rustle of her dress in the hall, and then the sound of her footsteps in the "reception room." After a time, silence succeeded even these slight tokens of her presence; whereupon George rose and went warily into the hall, taking care to make no noise, and he obtained an oblique view of her through the open double doors of the "reception room." She was sitting in the chair which he had occupied so long; and she was looking out of the window expectantly—a little troubled.

He went back to the library, waited an interminable half hour, then returned noiselessly to the same position in the hall, where he could see her. She was still sitting patiently by the window.

Waiting for that man, was she? Well, it might be quite a long wait! And the grim George silently ascended the stairs to his own room, and began to pace his suffering floor.

CHAPTER XXV

He left his door open, however, and when he heard the front door-bell ring, by and by, he went half way down the stairs and stood to listen. He was not much afraid that Morgan would return, but he wished to make sure.

Mary appeared in the hall below him, but, after a glance toward the front of the house, turned back, and withdrew. Evidently Isabel had gone to the door. Then a murmur was heard, and George Amberson's voice, quick and serious: "I want to talk to you, Isabel" . . . and another murmur; then Isabel and her brother passed the foot of the broad, dark stairway, but did not look up, and remained unconscious of the watchful presence above them. Isabel still carried her cloak upon her arm, but Amberson had taken her hand, and retained it; and as he led her silently into the library there was something

THE MAGNIFICENT AMBERSONS

about her attitude, and the pose of her slightly bent head, that was both startled and meek. Thus they quickly disappeared from George's sight, hand in hand; and Amberson at once closed the massive double doors of the library.

For a time all that George could hear was the indistinct sound of his uncle's voice: what he was saying could not be surmised, though the troubled brotherliness of his tone was evident. He seemed to be explaining something at considerable length, and there were moments when he paused, and George guessed that his mother was speaking, but her voice must have been very low, for it was entirely inaudible to him.

Suddenly he did hear her. Through the heavy doors her outcry came, clear and loud:

"Oh, *no!*"

It was a cry of protest, as if something her brother told her must be untrue, or, if it were true, the fact he stated must be undone; and it was a sound of sheer pain.

Another sound of pain, close to George, followed it; this was a vehement sniffling which broke out just above him, and, looking up, he saw Fanny Minafer on the landing, leaning over the banisters and applying her handkerchief to her eyes and nose.

"I can guess what *that* was about," she whispered huskily. "He's just told her what you did to Eugene!"

George gave her a dark look over his shoulder. "You go on back to your room!" he said; and he began to descend the stairs; but Fanny, guessing his purpose, rushed down and caught his arm, detaining him.

"You're not going in *there?*" she whispered huskily. "You don't——"

"Let go of me!"

But she clung to him savagely. "No, you don't, Georgie Minafer! You'll keep away from there! You will!"

"You let go of——"

"I won't! You come back here! You'll come upstairs and let them alone; that's what you'll do!" And with such passionate determination did she clutch and tug, never losing a grip of him somewhere, though George tried as much as he could, without hurting her, to wrench away—with such utter forgetfulness of her maiden dignity did she assault him, that she forced him, stumbling upward, to the landing.

"Of all the ridiculous——" he began furiously; but she spared one hand from its grasp of his sleeve and clapped it over his mouth.

"Hush up!" Never for an instant in this grotesque struggle did Fanny raise her voice above a husky whisper. "Hush up! It's indecent—like squabbling outside the door of an operating-room! Go on to the top of the stairs—go on!"

And when George had most unwillingly obeyed, she planted herself in his way, on the top step. "There!" she said. "The idea of your going in there now! I never heard of such a thing!" And with the sudden departure of the nervous vigour she had shown so amazingly, she began to cry again. "I was an *awful* fool! I thought you knew what was going on or I never, never would have done it. Do you suppose I *dreamed* you'd go making everything into such a tragedy? Do you?"

"I don't care what you dreamed," George muttered.

But Fanny went on, always taking care to keep her voice from getting too loud, in spite of her most grievous agitation. "Do you dream I thought you'd go making such a fool of yourself at Mrs. Johnson's? Oh, I saw her this morning! She wouldn't talk to me, but I met George Amberson on my way back, and he told me what you'd done over there! And do you dream I thought you'd do what you've done here this afternoon to Eugene? Oh, I knew that, too! I was looking out of the front bedroom window, and I saw him drive up, and then go away again, and I knew you'd been to the door. Of course he went to George Amberson about it, and that's why George is here. He's got to tell Isabel the whole thing now, and you wanted to go in there interfering —God knows what! You stay here and let her brother tell her; he's got some consideration for her!"

"I suppose you think I haven't!" George said, challenging her, and at that Fanny laughed witheringly.

"You! Considerate of anybody!"

"I'm considerate of her good name!" he said hotly. "It seems to me that's about the first thing to be considerate of, in being considerate of a person! And look here: it strikes me you're taking a pretty different tack from what you did yesterday afternoon!"

Fanny wrung her hands. "I did a terrible thing!" she lamented. "Now that it's done and too late, I know what it *was!* I didn't have sense enough just to let things go on. I didn't have any business to interfere, and I didn't *mean* to interfere—I only wanted to talk, and let out a little! I did think you already knew everything I told you. I did! And I'd rather have cut my hand off than stir you up to doing what you *have* done! I was just suffering so that I wanted to let out a little—I didn't mean any real harm. But now I *see* what's happened—oh, I was a fool! I hadn't any business interfering. Eugene never would have looked at me, anyhow, and, oh, why couldn't I have seen that before! He never came here a single time in his life except on her account, never! and I might have let them alone, because he wouldn't have looked at me even if he'd never seen Isabel. And they haven't done any harm: she made Wilbur happy, and she was a true wife to him as long as he lived. It wasn't a crime for her to care for Eugene all the time; she certainly never *told* him she did—and she gave me every chance in the world! She left us alone together every time she could—even since Wilbur died—but what was the use? And here I go, not doing myself a bit of good by it, and just"—Fanny wrung her hands again—"just ruining them!"

"I suppose you mean I'm doing that," George said bitterly.

"Yes, I do!" she sobbed, and drooped upon the stairway railing, exhausted.

"On the contrary, I mean to save my mother from a calamity."

Fanny looked at him wanly, in a tired despair; then she stepped by him and went slowly to her own door, where she paused and beckoned to him.

"What do you want?"

"Just come here a minute."

"What for?" he asked impatiently.

"I just wanted to say something to you."

"Well, for heaven's sake, say it! There's nobody to hear." Nevertheless, after a moment, as she beckoned him again, he went to her, profoundly annoyed. "Well, what is it?"

"George," she said in a low voice, "I think you ought to be told something. If I were you, I'd let my mother alone."

"Oh, my Lord!" he groaned. "I'm doing these things *for* her, not against her!"

A mildness had come upon Fanny, and she had controlled her weeping. She shook her head gently. "No, I'd let her alone if I were you. I don't think she's very well, George."

"She! I never saw a healthier person in my life."

"No. She doesn't let anybody know, but she goes to the doctor regularly."

"Women are always going to doctors regularly."

"No. He told her to."

George was not impressed. "It's nothing at all; she spoke of it to me years ago—some kind of family failing. She said grandfather had it, too; and look at him! Hasn't proved very serious with him! You act as if I'd done something wrong in sending that man about his business, and as if I were going to persecute my mother, instead of protecting her. By Jove, it's sickening! You told me how all the riffraff in town were busy with her name, and then the minute I lift my hand to protect her, you begin to attack me and——"

"*Sh!*" Fanny checked him, laying her hand on his arm. "Your uncle is going."

The library doors were heard opening, and a moment later there came the sound of the front door closing.

George moved toward the head of the stairs, then stood listening; but the house was silent.

Fanny made a slight noise with her lips to attract his attention, and, when he glanced toward her, shook her head at him urgently. "Let her alone," she whispered. "She's down there by herself. Don't go down. Let her alone."

She moved a few steps toward him and halted, her face pallid and awestruck, and then both stood listening for anything that might break the silence downstairs. No sound came to them; that poignant silence was continued throughout long, long minutes, while the two listeners stood there under its mysterious spell; and in its plaintive eloquence—speaking, as it did, of the figure alone in the big, dark library, where dead Wilbur's new silver frame gleamed in the dimness—there was something that checked even George.

Above the aunt and nephew, as they kept this strange vigil, there was a triple window of stained glass, to illumine the landing and upper reaches of the stairway. Figures in blue and amber garments posed gracefully in panels, conceived by some craftsman of the Eighties to represent Love and Purity

666   THE MAGNIFICENT AMBERSONS

and Beauty, and these figures, leaded to unalterable attitudes, were little more motionless than the two human beings upon whom fell the mottled faint light of the window. The colours were growing dull; evening was coming on.

Fanny Minafer broke the long silence with a sound from her throat, a stifled gasp; and with that great companion of hers, her handkerchief, retired softly to the loneliness of her own chamber. After she had gone George looked about him bleakly, then on tiptoe crossed the hall and went into his own room, which was filled with twilight. Still tiptoeing, though he could not have said why, he went across the room and sat down heavily in a chair facing the window. Outside there was nothing but the darkening air and the wall of the nearest of the new houses. He had not slept at all, the night before, and he had eaten nothing since the preceding day at lunch, but he felt neither drowsiness nor hunger. His set determination filled him, kept him but too wide awake, and his gaze at the grayness beyond the window was wide-eyed and bitter.

Darkness had closed in when there was a step in the room behind him. Then someone knelt beside the chair, two arms went round him with infinite compassion, a gentle head rested against his shoulder, and there came the faint scent as of apple-blossoms far away.

"You mustn't be troubled, darling," his mother whispered.

CHAPTER XXVI

George choked. For an instant he was on the point of breaking down, but he commanded himself, bravely dismissing the self-pity roused by her compassion. "How can I help but be?" he said.

"No, no." She soothed him. "You mustn't. You mustn't be troubled, no matter what happens."

"That's easy enough to say!" he protested; and he moved as if to rise.

"Just let's stay like this a little while, dear. Just a minute or two. I want to tell you: brother George has been here, and he told me everything about —about how unhappy you'd been—and how you went so gallantly to that old woman with the opera-glasses." Isabel gave a sad little laugh. "What a terrible old woman she is! What a really terrible thing a vulgar old woman can be!"

"Mother, I——" And again he moved to rise.

"Must you? It seemed to me such a comfortable way to talk. Well——" She yielded; he rose, helped her to her feet, and pressed the light into being.

As the room took life from the sudden lines of fire within the bulbs Isabel made a deprecatory gesture, and, with a faint laugh of apologetic protest, turned quickly away from George. What she meant was: "You mustn't see my face until I've made it nicer for you." Then she turned again to him,

her eyes downcast, but no sign of tears in them, and she contrived to show
him that there was the semblance of a smile upon her lips. She still wore her
hat, and in her unsteady fingers she held a white envelope, somewhat
crumpled.

"Now, mother——"

"Wait, dearest," she said; and though he stood stone cold, she lifted her
arms, put them round him again, and pressed her cheek lightly to his. "Oh,
you do look so troubled, poor dear! One thing you couldn't doubt, beloved
boy: you know I could never care for anything in the world as I care for you—
never, never!"

"Now, mother——"

She released him, and stepped back. "Just a moment more, dearest. I want
you to read this first. We can get at things better." She pressed into his
hand the envelope she had brought with her, and as he opened it, and began
to read the long enclosure, she walked slowly to the other end of the room;
then stood there, with her back to him, and her head drooping a little, until
he had finished.

The sheets of paper were covered with Eugene's handwriting.

George Amberson will bring you this, dear Isabel. He is waiting while I write. He
and I have talked things over, and before he gives this to you he will tell you what
has happened. Of course I'm rather confused, and haven't had time to think matters
out very definitely, and yet I believe I should have been better prepared for what took
place to-day—I ought to have known it was coming, because I have understood for
quite a long time that young George was getting to dislike me more and more. Somehow, I've never been able to get his friendship; he's always had a latent distrust of
me—or something like distrust—and perhaps that's made me sometimes a little
awkward and diffident with him. I think it may be he felt from the first that I cared
a great deal about you, and he naturally resented it. I think perhaps he felt this even
during all the time when I was so careful—at least I thought I was—not to show,
even to you, how immensely I did care. And he may have feared that you were thinking too much about me—even when you weren't and only liked me as an old friend.
It's perfectly comprehensible to me, also, that at his age one gets excited about
gossip. Dear Isabel, what I'm trying to get at, in my confused way, is that you and
I don't care about this nonsensical gossip, ourselves, at all. Yesterday I thought the
time had come when I could ask you to marry me, and you were dear enough to
tell me "sometime it might come to that." Well, you and I, left to ourselves, and
knowing what we have been and what we are, we'd pay as much attention to "talk"
as we would to any other kind of old cats' mewing! We'd not be very apt to let such
things keep us from the plenty of life we have left to us for making up to ourselves
for old unhappinesses and mistakes. But now we're faced with—not the slander and
not our own fear of it, because we haven't any, but someone else's fear of it—your
son's. And, oh, dearest woman in the world, I know what your son is to you, and it
frightens me! Let me explain a little: I don't think he'll change—at twenty-one or
twenty-two so many things appear solid and permanent and terrible which forty sees
are nothing but disappearing miasma. Forty can't tell twenty about this; that's the
pity of it! Twenty can find out only by getting to be forty. And so we come to this,
dear: Will you live your own life your way, or George's way? I'm going a little further,
because it would be fatal not to be wholly frank now. George will act toward you only
as your long worship of him, your sacrifices—all the unseen little ones every day since

he was born—will make him act. Dear, it breaks my heart for you, but what you have to oppose now is the history of your own selfless and perfect motherhood. I remember saying once that what you worshipped in your son was the angel you saw in him—and I still believe that is true of every mother. But in a mother's worship she may not see that the Will in her son should not always be offered incense along with the angel. I grow sick with fear for you—for both you and me—when I think how the Will against us two has grown strong through the love you have given the angel—and how long your own sweet Will has served that other. Are you strong enough, Isabel? Can you make the fight? I promise you that if you will take heart for it, you will find so quickly that it has all amounted to nothing. You shall have happiness, and, in a little while, only happiness. You need only to write me a line—I can't come to your house—and tell me where you will meet me. We will come back in a month, and the angel in your son will bring him to you; I promise it. What is good in him will grow so fine, once you have beaten the turbulent Will—but it must be beaten!

Your brother, that good friend, is waiting with such patience; I should not keep him longer—and I am saying too much for wisdom, I fear. But, oh, my dear, won't you be strong—such a little short strength it would need! Don't strike my life down twice, dear—this time I've not deserved it.

EUGENE

Concluding this missive, George tossed it abruptly from him so that one sheet fell upon his bed and the others upon the floor; and at the faint noise of their falling Isabel came, and, kneeling, began to gather them up.

"Did you read it, dear?"

George's face was pale no longer, but pink with fury. "Yes, I did."

"All of it?" she asked gently, as she rose.

"Certainly!"

She did not look at him, but kept her eyes downcast upon the letter in her hands, tremulously rearranging the sheets in order as she spoke—and though she smiled, her smile was as tremulous as her hands. Nervousness and an irresistible timidity possessed her. "I—I wanted to say, George," she faltered. "I felt that if—if some day it *should* happen—I mean, if you came to feel differently about it, and Eugene and I—that is if we found that it seemed the most sensible thing to do—I was afraid you might think it would be a little queer about—Lucy. I mean if—if she were your step-sister. Of course, she'd not be even legally related to you, and if you—if you cared for her——"

Thus far she got stumblingly with what she wanted to say, while George watched her with a gaze that grew harder and hotter; but here he cut her off. "I have already given up all idea of Lucy," he said. "Naturally, I couldn't have treated her father as I deliberately did treat him—I could hardly have done that and expected his daughter ever to speak to me again."

Isabel gave a quick cry of compassion, but he allowed her no opportunity to speak. "You needn't think I'm making any particular sacrifice," he said sharply, "though I would, quickly enough, if I thought it necessary in a matter of honour like this. I *was* interested in her, and I could even say I did care for her; but she proved pretty satisfactorily that she cared little enough about me! She went away right in the midst of a—of a difference of opinion we were having; she didn't even let me know she was going, and never wrote a line to me, and then came back telling everybody she'd had 'a perfectly gorgeous time!' That's quite enough for me. I'm not precisely the sort to arrange for that kind of thing to be done to me more than once! The truth is, we're not congenial and we'd found that much out, at least, before she left. We should never have been happy; she was 'superior' all the time, and critical of me—not very pleasant, that! I was disappointed in her, and I might as well say it. I don't think she has the very deepest nature in the world, and——"

But Isabel put her hand timidly on his arm. "Georgie, dear, this is only a quarrel: all young people have them before they get adjusted, and you mustn't let——"

"If you please!" he said emphatically, moving back from her. "This isn't that kind. It's all over, and I don't care to speak of it again. It's settled. Don't you understand?"

"But, dear——"

"No. I want to talk to you about this letter of her father's."

"Yes, dear, that's why——"

"It's simply the most offensive piece of writing that I've ever held in my hands!"

She stepped back from him, startled. "But, dear, I thought——"

"I can't understand your even showing me such a thing!" he cried. "How *did* you happen to bring it to me?"

"Your uncle thought I'd better. He thought it was the simplest thing to do, and he said that he'd suggested it to Eugene, and Eugene had agreed. They thought——"

"Yes!" George said bitterly. "I should like to hear what they thought!"

"They thought it would be the most straightforward thing."

George drew a long breath. "Well, what do *you* think, mother?"

"I thought it would be the simplest and most straightforward thing; I thought they were right."

"Very well! We'll agree it was simple and straightforward. Now, what do you think of that letter itself?"

She hesitated, looking away. "I—of course I don't agree with him in the way he speaks of you, dear—except about the angel! I don't agree with some of the things he implies. You've always been unselfish—nobody knows that better than your mother. When Fanny was left with nothing, you were so quick and generous to give up what really should have come to you, and——"

"And yet," George broke in, "you see what he implies about me. Don't you think, really, that this was a pretty insulting letter for that man to be asking you to hand your son?"

"Oh, no!" she cried. "You can see how fair he means to be, and he didn't ask for me to give it to you. It was brother George who——"

"Never mind that, now! You say he tries to be fair, and yet do you suppose it ever occurs to him that I'm doing my simple duty? That I'm doing what my *father* would do if he were alive? That I'm doing what my father would ask me to do if he could speak from his grave out yonder? Do you suppose it ever occurs to that man for one minute that I'm *protecting* my mother?" George raised his voice advancing upon the helpless lady fiercely; and she could only bend her head before him. "He talks about my 'Will'—how it must be beaten down; yes, and he asks my *mother* to do that little thing to please him! What for? *Why* does he want me 'beaten' by my mother? Because I'm trying to protect her name! He's got my mother's name bandied up and down the streets of this town till I can't *step* in those streets without wondering what every soul I meet is thinking of me and of my family, and now he wants you to marry him so that every gossip in town will say 'There! What did I tell you? I guess *that* proves it's true!' You can't get away from it; that's exactly what they'd say, and this man pretends he cares for you, and yet asks you to marry him and give them the *right* to say it. He says he and you don't care what they say, but I know better! He may not care— probably he's that kind—but you do. There never was an Amberson yet that would let the Amberson name go trailing in the dust like that! It's the proudest name in this town and it's going to stay the proudest; and I tell you that's the deepest thing in my nature—not that I'd expect Eugene Morgan to understand—the very deepest thing in my nature is to protect that name, and to fight for it to the last breath when danger threatens it, as it does now—through my mother!" He turned from her, striding up and down and tossing his arms about, in a tumult of gesture. "I can't believe it of you, that you'd *think* of such a sacrilege! That's what it would be—sacrilege! When he talks about your unselfishness toward me, he's right—you have been unselfish and you have been a perfect mother. But what about him? Is it unselfish of him to want you to throw away your good name just to please him? That's all he asks of you—and to quit being my mother! Do you think I can believe you *really* care for him? I don't! You are my mother and you're an Amberson—and I believe you're too proud! You're too proud to care for a man who could write such a letter as that!" He stopped, faced her, and spoke with more self-control: "Well, what are you going to do about it, mother?"

George was right about his mother's being proud. And even when she laughed with a negro gardener, or even those few times in her life when people saw her weep, Isabel had a proud look—something that was independent and graceful and strong. But she did not have it now: she leaned against the wall, beside his dressing-table, and seemed beset with humility and with weakness. Her head drooped.

"What answer are you going to make to such a letter?" George demanded, like a judge on the bench.

"I—I don't quite know, dear," she murmured.

"You don't?" he cried. "You——"

"Wait," she begged him. "I'm so—confused."

"I want to know what you're going to write him. Do you think if you did what he wants you to I could bear to stay another day in this town, mother? Do you think I could ever bear even to see you again if you married him? I'd want to, but you surely know I just—couldn't!"

She made a futile gesture, and seemed to breathe with difficulty. "I—I wasn't—quite sure," she faltered, "about—about it's being wise for us to be married—even before knowing how you feel about it. I wasn't even sure it was quite fair to—to Eugene. I have—I seem to have that family trouble—like father's—that I spoke to you about once." She managed a deprecatory little dry laugh. "Not that it amounts to much, but I wasn't at all sure that it would be fair to him. Marrying doesn't mean so much, after all—not at my age. It's enough to know that—that people think of you—and to see them. I thought we were all—oh, pretty happy the way things were, and I don't think it would mean giving up a great deal for him or me, either, if we just went on as we have been. I—I see him almost every day, and——"

"Mother!" George's voice was loud and stern. "Do you think you could go on seeing him after *this!*"

She had been talking helplessly enough before; her tone was little more broken now. "Not—not even—see him?"

"How could you?" George cried. "Mother, it seems to me that if he ever set foot in this house again—oh! I can't speak of it! *Could* you see him, knowing what talk it makes every time he turns into this street, and knowing what that means to me! Oh, I *don't* understand all this—I don't! If you'd told me, a year ago, that such things were going to happen, I'd have thought you were insane—and now I believe I am!"

Then, after a preliminary gesture of despair, as though he meant harm to the ceiling, he flung himself heavily, face downward, upon the bed. His anguish was none the less real for its vehemence; and the stricken lady came to him instantly and bent over him, once more enfolding him in her arms. She said nothing, but suddenly her tears fell upon his head; she saw them, and seemed to be startled.

"Oh, this won't do!" she said. "I've never let you see me cry before, except when your father died. I mustn't!"

And she ran from the room.

. . . A little while after she had gone, George rose and began solemnly to dress for dinner. At one stage of these conscientious proceedings he put on, temporarily, his long black velvet dressing-gown, and, happening to catch sight in his pier glass of the picturesque and mediæval figure thus presented, he paused to regard it; and something profoundly theatrical in his nature came to the surface.

His lips moved; he whispered, half-aloud, some famous fragments:

> "'Tis not alone my inky cloak, good mother,
> Nor customary suits of solemn black . . ."

For, in truth, the mirrored princely image, with hair dishevelled on the white brow, and the long tragic fall of black velvet from the shoulders, had brought about (in his thought, at least) some comparisons of his own times, so out of joint, with those of that other gentle prince and heir whose widowed mother was minded to marry again.

> "But I have that within which passeth show;
> These but the trappings and the suits of Woe."

Not less like Hamlet did he feel and look as he sat gauntly at the dinner table with Fanny to partake of a meal throughout which neither spoke. Isabel had sent word "not to wait" for her, an injunction it was as well they obeyed, for she did not come at all. But with the renewal of sustenance furnished to his system, some relaxation must have occurred within the high-strung George. Dinner was not quite finished when, without warning, sleep hit him hard. His burning eyes could no longer restrain the lids above them; his head sagged beyond control; and he got to his feet, and went lurching upstairs, yawning with exhaustion. From the door of his room, which he closed mechanically, with his eyes shut, he went blindly to his bed, fell upon it soddenly, and slept—with his face full upturned to the light.

. . . It was after midnight when he woke, and the room was dark. He had not dreamed, but he woke with the sense that somebody or something had been with him while he slept—somebody or something infinitely compassionate; somebody or something infinitely protective, that would let him come to no harm and to no grief.

He got up, and pressed the light on. Pinned to the cover of his dressing-table was a square envelope, with the words, "For you, dear," written in pencil upon it. But the message inside was in ink, a little smudged here and there.

I have been out to the mail-box, darling, with a letter I've written to Eugene, and he'll have it in the morning. It would be unfair not to let him know at once, and my decision could not change if I waited. It would always be the same. I think it is a little better for me to write to you, like this, instead of waiting till you wake up and then telling you, because I'm foolish and might cry again, and I took a vow once, long ago, that you should never see me cry. Not that I'll feel like crying when we talk things over to-morrow. I'll be "all right and fine" (as you say so often) by that time—don't fear. I think what makes me most ready to cry now is the thought of the terrible suffering in your poor face, and the unhappy knowledge that it is I, your mother, who put it there. It shall never come again! I love you better than anything and everything else on earth. God gave you to me—and oh! how thankful I have been every day of my life for that sacred gift—and nothing can ever come between me and God's gift. I cannot hurt you, and I cannot let you stay hurt as you have been—not another instant after you wake up, my darling boy! It is beyond my power. And Eugene was right—I know you couldn't change about this. Your suffering shows how deep-seated the feeling is within you. So I've written him just about what I think you would like me to—though I told him I would always be fond of him and always his best friend, and I hoped his dearest friend. He'll understand about not seeing him. He'll understand that, though I didn't say it in so many words. You mustn't trouble about that—he'll understand. Good-night, my darling, my beloved, my beloved! You mustn't be troubled. I think I shouldn't mind anything very much so long as I have you "all to myself"—as people say—to make up for your long years away from me at college. We'll talk of what's best to do in the morning, shan't we? And for all this pain you'll forgive your loving and devoted mother.

ISABEL

CHAPTER XXVII

Having finished some errands downtown, the next afternoon, George Amberson Minafer was walking up National Avenue on his homeward way when he saw in the distance, coming toward him, upon the same side of the street, the figure of a young lady—a figure just under the middle height, comely indeed, and to be mistaken for none other in the world—even at two hundred yards. To his sharp discomfiture his heart immediately forced upon him the consciousness of its acceleration; a sudden warmth about his neck made him aware that he had turned red, and then, departing, left him pale. For a panicky moment he thought of facing about in actual flight; he had little doubt that Lucy would meet him with no token of recognition, and all at once this probability struck him as unendurable. And if she did not speak, was it the proper part of chivalry to lift his hat and take the cut bareheaded? Or should the finer gentleman acquiesce in the lady's desire for no further acquaintance, and pass her with stony mien and eyes constrained forward? George was a young man badly flustered.

But the girl approaching him was unaware of his trepidation, being perhaps somewhat preoccupied with her own. She saw only that he was pale, and that his eyes were darkly circled. But here he was advantaged with her, for the finest touch to his good looks was given by this toning down; neither pallor nor dark circles detracting from them, but rather adding to them a melancholy favour of distinction. George had retained his mourning, a tribute completed down to the final details of black gloves and a polished ebony cane (which he would have been pained to name otherwise than as a "walking-stick") and in the aura of this sombre elegance his straight figure and drawn face were not without a tristful and appealing dignity.

In everything outward he was cause enough for a girl's cheek to flush, her heart to beat faster, and her eyes to warm with the soft light that came into Lucy's now, whether she would or no. If his spirit had been what his looks proclaimed it, she would have rejoiced to let the light glow forth which now shone in spite of her. For a long time, thinking of that spirit of his, and what she felt it should be, she had a persistent sense: "It must be there!" but she had determined to believe this folly no longer. Nevertheless, when she met him at the Sharons', she had been far less calm than she seemed.

People speaking casually of Lucy were apt to define her as "a little beauty," a definition short of the mark. She was "a little beauty," but an independent, masterful, self-reliant little American, of whom her father's earlier gipsyings and her own sturdiness had made a woman ever since she was fifteen. But though she was the mistress of her own ways and no slave to any lamp save that of her own conscience, she had a weakness: she had fallen in love with George Amberson Minafer at first sight, and no matter how she disciplined herself, she had never been able to climb out. The thing had happened to her; that was all. George had looked just the way she had always wanted someone to look—the riskiest of all the moonshine ambushes wherein tricky romance snares credulous young love. But what was fatal to Lucy was that this thing having happened to her, she could not change it. No matter what she discovered in George's nature she was unable to take away what she had given him; and though she could think differently about him, she could not feel differently about him, for she was one of those too faithful victims of glamour. When she managed to keep the picture of George away from her mind's eye, she did well enough; but when she let him become visible, she could not choose but love what she disdained. She was a little angel who had fallen in love with high-handed Lucifer; quite an experience, and not apt to be soon succeeded by any falling in love with a tamer party—and the unhappy truth was that George did make better men seem tame. But though she was a victim, she was a heroic one, anything but helpless.

As they drew nearer, George tried to prepare himself to meet her with some remnants of aplomb. He decided that he would keep on looking straight ahead, and lift his hand toward his hat at the very last moment when it would be possible for her to see him out of the corner of her eye: then when she thought it over later, she would not be sure whether he had saluted her or merely rubbed his forehead. And there was the added benefit that any third person who might chance to look from a window, or from a passing carriage, would not think that he was receiving a snub, because he did not intend to lift his hat, but, timing the gesture properly, would in fact actually rub his forehead. These were the hasty plans which occupied his thoughts until he was within about fifty feet of her—when he ceased to have either plans or thoughts. He had kept his eyes from looking full at her until then, and as he saw her, thus close at hand, and coming nearer, a regret that was dumfounding took possession of him. For the first time he had the sense of having lost something of overwhelming importance.

Lucy did not keep to the right, but came straight to meet him, smiling, and with her hand offered to him.

"Why—you——" he stammered, as he took it. "Haven't you——" What he meant to say was, "Haven't you heard?"

"Haven't I what?" she asked; and he saw that Eugene had not yet told her.

"Nothing!" he gasped. "May I—may I turn and walk with you a little way?"

"Yes, indeed!" she said cordially.

He would not have altered what had been done: he was satisfied with all that—satisfied that it was right, and that his own course was right. But he began to perceive a striking inaccuracy in some remarks he had made to his mother. Now when he had put matters in such shape that even by the relinquishment of his "ideals of life" he could not have Lucy, knew that he could never have her, and knew that when Eugene told her the history of yesterday he could not have a glance or word even friendly from her—now when he must in good truth "give up all idea of Lucy," he was amazed that he could have used such words as "no particular sacrifice," and believed them when he said them! She had looked never in his life so bewitchingly pretty as she did to-day; and as he walked beside her he was sure that she was the most exquisite thing in the world.

"Lucy," he said huskily, "I want to tell you something. Something that matters."

"I hope it's a lively something then," she said; and laughed. "Papa's been so glum to-day he's scarcely spoken to me. Your Uncle George Amberson came to see him an hour ago and they shut themselves up in the library, and your uncle looked as glum as papa. I'd be glad if you'll tell me a funny story, George."

"Well, it may seem one to you," he said bitterly. "Just to begin with: when you went away you didn't let me know; not even a word—not a line——"

Her manner persisted in being inconsequent. "Why, no," she said. "I just trotted off for some visits."

"Well, at least you might have——"

"Why, no," she said again briskly. "Don't you remember, George? We'd had a grand quarrel, and didn't speak to each other all the way home from a long, long drive! So, as we couldn't play together like good children, of course it was plain that we oughtn't to play at all."

" 'Play!' " he cried.

"Yes. What I mean is that we'd come to the point where it was time to quit playing—well, what we were playing."

"At being lovers, you mean, don't you?"

"Something like that," she said lightly. "For us two, playing at being lovers was just the same as playing at cross-purposes. I had all the purposes, and that gave you all the crossness: things weren't getting along at all. It was absurd!"

"Well, have it your own way," he said. "It needn't have been absurd."

"No, it couldn't help but be!" she informed him cheerfully. "The way I am and the way you are, it couldn't ever be anything else. So what was the use?"

"I don't know," he sighed, and his sigh was abysmal. "But what I wanted to tell you is this: when you went away, you didn't let me know and didn't care how or when I heard it, but I'm not like that with you. This time, I'm going away. That's what I wanted to tell you. I'm going away to-morrow night—indefinitely."

She nodded sunnily. "That's nice for you. I hope you'll have ever so jolly a time, George."

"I don't expect to have a particularly 'jolly time.' "

"Well, then," she laughed, "if I were you I don't think I'd go."

It seemed impossible to impress this distracting creature, to make her serious. "Lucy," he said desperately, "this is our last walk together."

"Evidently!" she said. "If you're going away to-morrow night."

"Lucy—this may be the last time I'll see you—ever—ever in my life."

At that she looked at him quickly, across her shoulder, but she smiled as brightly as before, and with the same cordial inconsequence: "Oh, I can hardly think that!" she said. "And of course I'd be awfully sorry to think it. You're not moving away, are you, to live?"

"No."

"And even if you were, of course you'd be coming back to visit your relatives every now and then."

"I don't know when I'm coming back. Mother and I are starting to-morrow night for a trip around the world."

At this she did look thoughtful. "Your mother is going with you?"

"Good heavens!" he groaned. "Lucy, doesn't it make any difference to you that I am going?"

At this her cordial smile instantly appeared again. "Yes, of course," she said. "I'm sure I'll miss you ever so much. Are you to be gone long?"

He stared at her wanly. "I told you indefinitely," he said. "We've made no plans—at all—for coming back."

"That does sound like a long trip!" she exclaimed admiringly. "Do you plan to be travelling all the time, or will you stay in some one place the greater part of it? I think it would be lovely to——"

"Lucy!"

He halted; and she stopped with him. They had come to a corner at the edge of the "business section" of the city, and people were everywhere about them, brushing against them, sometimes, in passing.

"I can't stand this," George said, in a low voice. "I'm just about ready to go in this drug-store here, and ask the clerk for something to keep me from dying in my tracks! It's quite a shock, you see, Lucy!"

"What is?"

"To find out certainly, at last, how deeply you've cared for me! To see how much difference this makes to you! By Jove, I *have* mattered to you!"

Her cordial smile was tempered now with good-nature. "George!" She laughed indulgently. "Surely you don't want me to do pathos on a down-town corner!"

"*You* wouldn't 'do pathos' anywhere!"

"Well—don't you think pathos is generally rather foozling?"

"I can't stand this any longer," he said. "I can't! Good-bye, Lucy!" He took her hand. "It's good-bye—I think it's good-bye for good, Lucy!"

"Good-bye! I do hope you'll have the most splendid trip." She gave his hand a cordial little grip, then released it lightly. "Give my love to your mother. Good-bye!"

He turned heavily away, and a moment later glanced back over his shoulder. She had not gone on, but stood watching him, that same casual, cordial smile on her face to the very last; and now, as he looked back, she emphasized her friendly unconcern by waving her small hand to him cheerily, though perhaps with the slightest hint of preoccupation, as if she had begun to think of the errand that brought her downtown.

In his mind, George had already explained her to his own poignant dissatisfaction—some blond pup, probably, whom she had met during that "perfectly gorgeous time!" And he strode savagely onward, not looking back again.

But Lucy remained where she was until he was out of sight. Then she went slowly into the drug-store which had struck George as a possible source of stimulant for himself.

"Please let me have a few drops of aromatic spirits of ammonia in a glass of water," she said, with the utmost composure.

"Yes, *ma'am!*" said the impressionable clerk, who had been looking at her through the display window as she stood on the corner.

But a moment later, as he turned from the shelves of glass jars against the wall, with the potion she had asked for in his hand, he uttered an exclamation: "For goshes' sake, Miss!" And, describing this adventure to his fellow-boarders, that evening, "Sagged pretty near to the counter, she was," he said. "'F I hadn't been a bright, quick, ready-for-anything young fella she'd 'a' flummixed plum! I was watchin' her out the window—talkin' to some young s'iety fella, and she was all right then. She was all right when she come in the store, too. Yes, sir; the prettiest girl that ever walked in our place and took one good look at me. I reckon it must be the truth what some you town wags say about my face!"

CHAPTER XXVIII

At that hour the heroine of the susceptible clerk's romance was engaged in brightening the rosy little coal fire under the white mantelpiece in her pretty white-and-blue boudoir. Four photographs all framed in decorous plain silver went to the anthracite's fierce destruction—frames and all—and three packets of letters and notes in a charming Florentine treasure-box of painted wood; nor was the box, any more than the silver frames, spared this rousing finish. Thrown heartily upon live coal, the fine wood sparkled forth in stars, then burst into an alarming blaze which scorched the white mantelpiece, but Lucy stood and looked on without moving.

It was not Eugene who told her what had happened at Isabel's door. When she got home, she found Fanny Minafer waiting for her—a secret excursion of Fanny's for the purpose, presumably, of "letting out" again; because that was what she did. She told Lucy everything (except her own lamentable part in the production of the recent miseries) and concluded with a tribute to George: "The worst of it is, he thinks he's been such a hero, and Isabel does, too, and that makes him more than twice as awful. It's been the same all his life: everything he did was noble and perfect. He had a domineering nature to begin with, and she let it go on, and fostered it till it absolutely ruled her. I never saw a plainer case of a person's fault making them pay for having it! She goes about, overseeing the packing and praising George and pretending to be perfectly cheerful about what he's making her do and about the dreadful things he's done. She pretends he did such a fine thing—so manly and protective—going to Mrs. Johnson. And so heroic—doing what his 'principles' made him—even though he knew what it would cost him with you! And all the while it's almost killing her—what he said to your father! She's always been lofty enough, so to speak, and had the greatest idea of the Ambersons being superior to the rest of the world, and all that, but rudeness, or anything like a 'scene,' or any bad manners—they always just made her sick! But she could never see what George's manners were—oh, it's been a terrible adulation! . . . It's going to be a task for me, living in that big house, all alone: you must come and see me—I mean after they've gone, of course. I'll go crazy if I don't see something of people. I'm sure you'll come as often as you can. I know you too well to think you'll be sensitive about coming there, or being reminded of George. Thank heaven you're too well-balanced," Miss Fanny concluded, with a profound fervour, "you're too well-balanced to let anything affect you deeply about that—that monkey!"

The four photographs and the painted Florentine box went to their cremation within the same hour that Miss Fanny spoke; and a little later Lucy called her father in, as he passed her door, and pointed to the blackened area on the underside of the mantelpiece, and to the burnt heap upon the coal, where some metallic shapes still retained outline. She flung her arms about his neck in passionate sympathy, telling him that she knew what had happened to him; and presently he began to comfort her and managed an embarrassed laugh.

"Well, well——" he said. "I was too old for such foolishness to be getting into my head, anyhow."

"No, no!" she sobbed. "And if you knew how I despise myself for—for ever having thought one instant about—oh, Miss Fanny called him the right name: that *monkey!* He is!"

"There, I think I agree with you," Eugene said grimly, and in his eyes there was a steady light of anger that was to last. "Yes, I think I agree with you about *that!*"

"There's only one thing to do with such a person," she said vehemently. "That's to put him out of our thoughts forever—*forever!*"

And yet, the next day, at six o'clock, which was the hour, Fanny had told her, when George and his mother were to leave upon their long journey, Lucy touched that scorched place on her mantel with her hand just as the little clock above it struck. Then, after this odd, unconscious gesture, she went to a window and stood between the curtains, looking out into the cold November dusk; and in spite of every reasoning and reasonable power within her, a pain of loneliness struck through her heart. The dim street below her window, the dark houses across the way, the vague air itself—all looked empty, and cold and (most of all) uninteresting. Something more sombre than November dusk took the colour from them and gave them that air of desertion.

The light of her fire, flickering up behind her, showed suddenly a flying group of tiny snowflakes nearing the window-pane; and for an instant she felt the sensation of being dragged through a snowdrift under a broken cutter, with a boy's arms about her—an arrogant, handsome, too-conquering boy, who nevertheless did his best to get hurt himself, keeping her from any possible harm.

She shook the picture out of her eyes indignantly, then came and sat before her fire, and looked long and long at the blackened mantelpiece. She did not have the mantelpiece repainted—and, since she did not, might as well have kept his photographs. One forgets what made the scar upon his hand but not what made the scar upon his wall.

She played no *marche funèbre* upon her piano, even though Chopin's romantic lamentation was then at the top of nine-tenths of the music-racks in the country, American youth having recently discovered the distinguished congeniality between itself and this deathless bit of deathly gloom. She did not even play "Robin Adair"; she played "Bedelia" and all the new cakewalks, for she was her father's housekeeper, and rightly looked upon the office as being the same as that of his heart-keeper. Therefore it was her affair to keep both house and heart in what state of cheerfulness might be contrived. She made him "go out" more than ever; made him take her to all the gaieties of that winter, declining to go herself unless he took her, and, though Eugene danced no more, and quoted Shakespeare to prove all light-foot caperings beneath the dignity of his age, she broke his resolution for him at the New Year's Eve "Assembly" and half coaxed, half dragged him forth upon the floor, and made him dance the New Year in with her.

. . . New faces appeared at the dances of the winter; new faces had been appearing everywhere, for that matter, and familiar ones were disappearing, merged in the increasing crowd, or gone forever and missed a little and not long; for the town was growing and changing as it never had grown and changed before.

It was heaving up in the middle incredibly; it was spreading incredibly; and as it heaved and spread, it befouled itself and darkened its sky. Its boundary was mere shapelessness on the run; a raw, new house would appear on a country road; four or five others would presently be built at intervals between it and the outskirts of the town; the country road would turn into an asphalt street with a brick-faced drug-store and a frame grocery at a corner; then bungalows and six-room cottages would swiftly speckle the open green spaces—and a farm had become a suburb, which would immediately shoot out other suburbs into the country, on one side, and, on the other, join itself solidly to the city. You drove between pleasant fields and woodland groves one spring day; and in the autumn, passing over the same ground, you were warned off the tracks by an interurban trolley-car's gonging, and beheld, beyond cement sidewalks just dry, new house-owners busy "moving in." Gasoline and electricity were performing the miracles Eugene had predicted.

But the great change was in the citizenry itself. What was left of the patriotic old-stock generation that had fought the Civil War, and subsequently controlled politics, had become venerable and was little heeded. The descendants of the pioneers and early settlers were merging into the new crowd, becoming part of it, little to be distinguished from it. What happened to Boston and to Broadway happened in degree to the Midland city; the old stock became less and less typical, and of the grown people who called the place home, less than a third had been born in it. There was a German quarter; there was a Jewish quarter; there was a negro quarter—square miles of it—called "Bucktown"; there were many Irish neighbourhoods; and there were large settlements of Italians, and of Hungarians, and of Rumanians, and of Servians and other Balkan peoples. But not the emigrants, themselves, were the almost dominant type on the streets downtown. That type was the emigrant's prosperous offspring: descendant of the emigrations of the Seventies and Eighties and Nineties, those great folk-journeyings in search not so directly of freedom and democracy as of more money for the same labour. A new Midlander—in fact, a new American—was beginning dimly to emerge.

A new spirit of citizenship had already sharply defined itself. It was idealistic, and its ideals were expressed in the new kind of young men in business downtown. They were optimists—optimists to the point of belligerence—their motto being "Boost! Don't Knock!" And they were hustlers, believing in hustling and in honesty because both paid. They loved their city and worked for it with a plutonic energy which was always ardently vocal. They were viciously governed, but they sometimes went so far as to struggle for better government on account of the helpful effect of good government on the price of real estate and "betterment" generally; the politicians could not go too far with them, and knew it. The idealists planned and strove and shouted that their city should become a better, better, and better city—and what they meant, when they used the word "better," was "more prosperous," and the core of their idealism was this: "The more prosperous my beloved city, the more prosperous beloved I!" They had one supreme theory: that the perfect beauty and happiness of cities and of human life was to be brought about by more factories; they had a mania for factories; there was nothing they would not do to cajole a factory away from another city; and they were never more piteously embittered than when another city cajoled one away from them.

What they meant by Prosperity was credit at the bank; but in exchange for this credit they got nothing that was not dirty, and, therefore, to a sane mind, valueless; since whatever was cleaned was dirty again before the cleaning was half done. For, as the town grew, it grew dirty with an incredible completeness. The idealists put up magnificent business buildings and boasted of them, but the buildings were begrimed before they were finished. They boasted of their libraries, of their monuments and statues; and poured soot on them. They boasted of their schools, but the schools were dirty, like the children within them. This was not the fault of the children or their mothers. It was the fault of the idealists, who said: "The more dirt, the more prosperity." They drew patriotic, optimistic breaths of the flying powdered filth of the streets, and took the foul and heavy smoke with gusto into the profundities of their lungs. "Boost! Don't knock!" they said. And every year or so they boomed a great Clean-Up Week, when everybody was supposed to get rid of the tin cans in his back yard.

They were happiest when the tearing down and building up were most riotous, and when new factory districts were thundering into life. In truth, the city came to be like the body of a great dirty man, skinned, to show his busy works, yet wearing a few barbaric ornaments; and such a figure carved, coloured, and discoloured, and set up in the market-place, would have done well enough as the god of the new people. Such a god they had indeed made in their own image, as all peoples make the god they truly serve; though of course certain of the idealists went to church on Sunday, and there knelt to Another, considered to be impractical in business. But while the Growing went on, this god of their market-place was their true god, their familiar and spirit-control. They did not know that they were his helplessly obedient slaves, nor could they ever hope to realize their serfdom (as the first step toward becoming free men) until they should make the strange and hard discovery that matter should serve man's spirit.

"Prosperity" meant good credit at the bank, black lungs, and housewives' Purgatory. The women fought the dirt all they could; but if they let the air into their houses they let in the dirt. It shortened their lives, and kept them from the happiness of ever seeing anything white. And thus, as the city grew, the time came when Lucy, after a hard struggle, had to give up her blue-and-white curtains and her white walls. Indoors, she put everything into dull gray and brown, and outside had the little house painted the dark green nearest to black. Then she knew, of course, that everything was as dirty as ever, but was a little less distressed because it no longer looked so dirty as it was.

These were bad times for Amberson Addition. This quarter, already old, lay within a mile of the centre of the town, but business moved in other directions; and the Addition's share of Prosperity was only the smoke and dirt, with the bank credit left out. The owners of the original big houses sold them, or rented them to boarding-house keepers, and the tenants of the multitude of small houses moved "farther out" (where the smoke was thinner) or into apartment houses, which were built by dozens now. Cheaper tenants took their places, and the rents were lower and lower, and the houses shabbier and shabbier—for all these shabby houses, burning soft coal, did their best to help in the destruction of their own value. They helped to make the quarter so dingy and the air so foul to breathe that no one would live there who had money enough to get "farther out" where there were glimpses of ungrayed sky and breaths of cleaner winds. And with the coming of the new speed, "farther out" was now as close to business as the Addition had been in the days of its prosperity. Distances had ceased to matter.

The five new houses, built so closely where had been the fine lawn of the Amberson Mansion, did not look new. When they were a year old they looked as old as they would ever look; and two of them were vacant, having never been rented, for the Major's mistake about apartment houses had been a disastrous one. "He guessed wrong," George Amberson said. "He guessed wrong at just the wrong time! Housekeeping in a house is harder than in an apartment; and where the smoke and dirt are as thick as they are in the Addition, women can't stand it. People were crazy for apartments—too bad he couldn't have seen it in time. Poor man! he digs away at his ledgers by his old gas drop-light lamp almost every night—he still refuses to let the Mansion be torn up for wiring, you know. But he had one painful satisfaction this spring: he got his taxes lowered!"

Amberson laughed ruefully, and Fanny Minafer asked how the Major could have managed such an economy. They were sitting upon the veranda at Isabel's one evening during the third summer of the absence of their nephew and his mother; and the conversation had turned toward Amberson finances. "I said it was a '*painful* satisfaction,' Fanny," he explained. "The property has gone down in value, and they assessed it lower than they did fifteen years ago."

"But farther out——"

"Oh, yes, 'farther out!' Prices are magnificent 'farther out,' and farther in, too! We just happen to be the wrong spot, that's all. Not that I don't think something could be done if father would let me have a hand; but he won't. He can't, I suppose I ought to say. He's 'always done his own figuring,' he says; and it's his lifelong habit to keep his affairs, and even his books, to himself, and just hand us out the money. Heaven knows he's done enough of that!"

He sighed; and both were silent, looking out at the long flares of the constantly passing automobile headlights, shifting in vast geometric demonstrations against the darkness. Now and then a bicycle wound its nervous way among these portents, or, at long intervals, a surrey or buggy plodded forlornly by.

"There seem to be so many ways of making money nowadays," Fanny said thoughtfully. "Every day I hear of a new fortune some person has got hold of, one way or another—nearly always it's somebody you never heard of. It doesn't seem all to be in just making motor cars; I hear there's a great deal in manufacturing these things that motor cars use—new inventions particularly. I met dear old Frank Bronson the other day, and he told me——"

"Oh, yes, even dear old Frank's got the fever," Amberson laughed. "He's as wild as any of them. He told me about this invention he's gone into, too. 'Millions in it!' Some new electric headlight better than anything yet—'every car in America can't *help* but have 'em,' and all that. He's putting half he's laid by into it, and the fact is, he almost talked me into getting father to 'finance me' enough for me to go into it. Poor father! he's financed me before! I suppose he would again if I had the heart to ask him; and this seems to be a good thing, though probably old Frank is a *little* too sanguine. At any rate, I've been thinking it over."

"So have I," Fanny admitted. "He seemed to be certain it would pay twenty-five per cent. the first year, and enormously more after that; and I'm only getting four on my little principal. People *are* making such enormous fortunes out of everything to do with motor cars, it does seem as if——" She paused. "Well, I told him I'd think it over seriously."

"We may turn out to be partners and millionaires then," Amberson laughed. "I thought I'd ask Eugene's advice."

"I wish you would," said Fanny. "He probably knows exactly how much profit there would be in this."

Eugene's advice was to "go slow": he thought electric lights for automobiles were "coming—*some* day," but probably not until certain difficulties could be overcome. Altogether, he was discouraging, but by this time his two friends "had the fever" as thoroughly as old Frank Bronson himself had it; for they had been with Bronson to see the light working beautifully in a machine shop. They were already enthusiastic, and after asking Eugene's opinion they argued with him, telling him how they had seen with their own eyes that the difficulties he mentioned *had* been overcome. "Perfectly!" Fanny cried. "And if it worked in the shop it's bound to work any place else, isn't it?"

He would not agree that it was "bound to"—yet, being pressed, was driven to admit that "it *might*," and, retiring from what was developing into an oratorical contest, repeated a warning about not "putting too much into it."

George Amberson also laid stress on this caution later, though the Major had "financed him" again, and he was "going in." "You must be careful to leave yourself a 'margin of safety,' Fanny," he said. "I'm confident that is a pretty conservative investment of its kind, and all the chances are with us, but you must be careful to leave yourself enough to fall back on, in case anything *should* go wrong."

Fanny deceived him. In the impossible event of "anything going wrong" she would have enough left to "live on," she declared, and laughed excitedly, for she was having the best time that had come to her since Wilbur's death.

Like so many women for whom money has always been provided without their understanding how, she was prepared to be a thorough and irresponsible plunger.

Amberson, in his wearier way, shared her excitement, and in the winter, when the exploiting company had been formed, and he brought Fanny her importantly engraved shares of stock, he reverted to his prediction of possibilities, made when they first spoke of the new light.

"We seem to be partners, all right," he laughed. "Now let's go ahead and be millionaires before Isabel and young George come home."

"When they come home!" she echoed sorrowfully—and it was a phrase which found an evasive echo in Isabel's letters. In these letters Isabel was always planning pleasant things that she and Fanny and the Major and George and "brother George" would do—when she and her son came home. "They'll find things pretty changed, I'm afraid," Fanny said. "If they ever do come home!"

Amberson went over, the next summer, and joined his sister and nephew in Paris, where they were living. "Isabel does want to come home," he told Fanny gravely, on the day of his return, in October. "She's wanted to for a long while—and she ought to come while she can stand the journey——" And he amplified this statement, leaving Fanny looking startled and solemn when Lucy came by to drive him out to dinner at the new house Eugene had just completed.

This was no white-and-blue cottage, but a great Georgian picture in brick, five miles north of Amberson Addition, with four acres of its own hedged land between it and its next neighbour; and Amberson laughed wistfully as they turned in between the stone and brick gate pillars, and rolled up the crushed stone driveway. "I wonder, Lucy, if history's going on forever repeating itself," he said. "I wonder if this town's going on building up things and rolling over them, as poor father once said it was rolling over his poor old heart. It looks like it: here's the Amberson Mansion again, only it's Georgian instead of nondescript Romanesque; but it's just the same Amberson Mansion that my father built long before you were born. The only difference is that it's your father who's built this one now. It's all the same, in the long run."

Lucy did not quite understand, but she laughed as a friend should, and, taking his arm, showed him through vasty rooms where ivory-panelled walls and trim window hangings were reflected dimly in dark, rugless floors, and the sparse furniture showed that Lucy had been "collecting" with a long purse. "By Jove!" he said. "You *have* been going it! Fanny tells me you had a great 'house-warming' dance, and you keep right on being the belle of the ball, not any softer-hearted than you used to be. Fred Kinney's father says you've refused Fred so often that he got engaged to Janie Sharon just to prove that someone would have him in spite of his hair. Well, the material world do move, and you've got the new kind of house it moves into nowadays—if it has the new price! And even the grand old expanses of plate glass we used to be so proud of at the other Amberson Mansion—they've gone, too, with the crowded heavy gold and red stuff. Curious! *We've* still got the plate glass windows, though all we can see out of 'em is the smoke and the old Johnson house, which is a counter-jumper's boarding-house now, while you've got a view, and you cut it all up into little panes. Well, you're pretty refreshingly out of the smoke up here."

"Yes, for a while," Lucy laughed. "Until it comes and we have to move out farther."

"No, you'll stay here," he assured her. "It will be somebody else who'll move out farther."

He continued to talk of the house after Eugene arrived, and gave them no account of his journey until they had retired from the dinner table to Eugene's library, a gray and shadowy room, where their coffee was brought. Then, equipped with a cigar, which seemed to occupy his attention, Amberson spoke in a casual tone of his sister and her son.

"I found Isabel as well as usual," he said, "only I'm afraid 'as usual' isn't particularly well. Sydney and Amelia had been up to Paris in the spring, but she hadn't seen them. Somebody told her they were there, it seems. They'd left Florence and were living in Rome; Amelia's become a Catholic and is said to give great sums to charity and to go about with the gentry in consequence, but Sydney's ailing and lives in a wheel-chair most of the time. It struck me Isabel ought to be doing the same thing."

He paused, bestowing minute care upon the removal of the little band from his cigar; and as he seemed to have concluded his narrative, Eugene spoke out of the shadow beyond a heavily shaded lamp: "What do you mean by that?" he asked quietly.

"Oh, she's cheerful enough," said Amberson, still not looking at either his young hostess or her father. "At least," he added, "she manages to seem so. I'm afraid she hasn't been really well for several years. She isn't stout you know—she hasn't changed in looks much—and she seems rather alarmingly short of breath for a slender person. Father's been that way for years, of course; but never nearly so much as Isabel is now. Of course she makes nothing of it, but it seemed rather serious to me when I noticed she had to stop and rest twice to get up the one short flight of stairs in their two-floor apartment. I told her I thought she ought to make George let her come home."

" 'Let her?' " Eugene repeated, in a low voice. "Does she want to?"

"She doesn't urge it. George seems to like the life there—in his grand, gloomy, and peculiar way; and of course she'll never change about being proud of him and all that—he's quite a swell. But in spite of anything she said, rather than because, I know she does indeed want to come. She'd like to be with father, of course; and I think she's—well, she intimated one day that she feared it might even happen that she wouldn't get to see him again. At the time I thought she referred to his age and feebleness, but on the boat, coming home, I remembered the little look of wistfulness, yet of resignation, with which she said it, and it struck me all at once that I'd been mistaken: I saw she was really thinking of her own state of health."

"I see," Eugene said, his voice even lower than it had been before. "And you say he won't 'let' her come home?"

Amberson laughed, but still continued to be interested in his cigar. "Oh, I don't think he uses force! He's very gentle with her. I doubt if the subject is mentioned between them, and yet—and yet, knowing my interesting nephew as you do, wouldn't you think that was about the way to put it?"

"Knowing him as I do—yes," said Eugene slowly. "Yes, I should think that was about the way to put it."

A murmur out of the shadows beyond him—a faint sound, musical and feminine, yet expressive of a notable intensity—seemed to indicate that Lucy was of the same opinion.

CHAPTER XXIX

"Let her" was correct; but the time came—and it came in the spring of the next year—when it was no longer a question of George's letting his mother come home. He had to bring her, and to bring her quickly if she was to see her father again; and Amberson had been right: her danger of never seeing him again lay not in the Major's feebleness of heart but in her own. As it was, George telegraphed his uncle to have a wheeled chair at the station, for the journey had been disastrous and to this hybrid vehicle, placed close to the car platform, her son carried her in his arms when she arrived. She was unable to speak, but patted her brother's and Fanny's hands and looked "very sweet," Fanny found the desperate courage to tell her. She was lifted from the chair into a carriage, and seemed a little stronger as they drove home; for once she took her hand from George's, and waved it feebly toward the carriage window.

"Changed," she whispered. "So changed."

"You mean the town," Amberson said. "You mean the old place is changed, don't you, dear?"

She smiled and moved her lips: "Yes."

"It'll change to a happier place, old dear," he said, "now that you're back in it, and going to get well again."

But she only looked at him wistfully, her eyes a little frightened.

When the carriage stopped, her son carried her into the house, and up the stairs to her own room, where a nurse was waiting; and he came out a moment later, as the doctor went in. At the end of the hall a stricken group was clustered: Amberson, and Fanny, and the Major. George, deathly pale and speechless, took his grandfather's hand, but the old gentleman did not seem to notice his action.

"When are they going to let me see my daughter?" he asked querulously.

"They told me to keep out of the way while they carried her in, because it might upset her. I wish they'd let me go in and speak to my daughter. I think she wants to see me."

He was right—presently the doctor came out and beckoned to him; and the Major shuffled forward, leaning on a shaking cane; his figure, after all its years of proud soldierliness, had grown stooping at last, and his untrimmed white hair straggled over the back of his collar. He looked old—old and divested of the world—as he crept toward his daughter's room. Her voice was stronger, for the waiting group heard a low cry of tenderness and welcome as the old man reached the open doorway. Then the door was closed.

Fanny touched her nephew's arm. "George, you must need something to eat—I know she'd want you to. I've had things ready: I knew she'd want me to. You'd better go down to the dining room: there's plenty on the table, waiting for you. She'd want you to eat something."

He turned a ghastly face to her, it was so panic-stricken. "I don't want anything to *eat!*" he said savagely. And he began to pace the floor, taking care not to go near Isabel's door, and that his footsteps were muffled by the long, thick hall rug. After a while he went to where Amberson, with folded arms and bowed head, had seated himself near the front window. "Uncle George," he said hoarsely. "I didn't——"

"Well?"

"Oh, my God, I didn't think this thing the matter with her could ever be serious! I——" He gasped. "When that doctor I had meet us at the boat——" He could not go on.

Amberson only nodded his head, and did not otherwise change his attitude.

. . . Isabel lived through the night. At eleven o'clock Fanny came timidly to George in his room. "Eugene is here," she whispered. "He's downstairs. He wants——" She gulped. "He wants to know if he can't *see* her. I didn't know what to say. I said I'd see. I didn't know—the doctor said——"

"The doctor said we 'must keep her peaceful,'" George said sharply. "Do you think that man's coming would be very soothing? My God! if it hadn't been for him this mightn't have happened: we could have gone on living here quietly, and—why, it would be like taking a stranger into her room! She hasn't even spoken of him more than twice in all the time we've been away. Doesn't he know how *sick* she is? You tell him the doctor said she had to be quiet and peaceful. That's what he did say, isn't it?"

Fanny acquiesced tearfully. "I'll tell him. I'll tell him the doctor said she was to be kept very quiet. I—I didn't know——" And she pottered out.

An hour later the nurse appeared in George's doorway; she came noiselessly, and his back was toward her; but he jumped as if he had been shot, and his jaw fell, he so feared what she was going to say.

"She wants to see you."

The terrified mouth shut with a click; and he nodded and followed her; but she remained outside his mother's room while he went in.

Isabel's eyes were closed, and she did not open them or move her head, but she smiled and edged her hand toward him as he sat on a stool beside the bed. He took that slender, cold hand, and put it to his cheek.

"Darling, did you—get something to eat?" She could only whisper, slowly and with difficulty. It was as if Isabel herself were far away, and only able to signal what she wanted to say.

"Yes, mothei."

"All you—needed?"

"Yes, mother."

She did not speak again for a time; then, "Are you sure you didn't—didn't catch cold—coming home?"

"I'm all right, mother."

"That's good. It's sweet—it's sweet——"

"What is, mother darling?"

"To feel—my hand on your cheek. I—I *can* feel it."

But this frightened him horribly—that she seemed so glad she could feel it, like a child proud of some miraculous seeming thing accomplished. It frightened him so that he could not speak, and he feared that she would know how he trembled; but she was unaware, and again was silent. Finally she spoke again:

"I wonder if—if Eugene and Lucy know that we've come—home."

"I'm sure they do."

"Has he—asked about me?"

"Yes, he was here."

"Has he—gone?"

"Yes, mother."

She sighed faintly. "I'd like——"

"What, mother?"

"I'd like to have—seen him." It was just audible, this little regretful murmur. Several minutes passed before there was another. "Just—just once," she whispered, and then was still.

She seemed to have fallen asleep, and George moved to go, but a faint pressure upon his fingers detained him, and he remained, with her hand still pressed against his cheek. After a while he made sure she was asleep, and moved again, to let the nurse come in, and this time there was no pressure of the fingers to keep him. She was not asleep, but, thinking that if he went he might get some rest, and be better prepared for what she knew was coming, she commanded those longing fingers of hers—and let him go.

He found the doctor standing with the nurse in the hall; and, telling them that his mother was drowsing now, George went back to his own room, where he was startled to find his grandfather lying on the bed, and his uncle leaning against the wall. They had gone home two hours before, and he did not know they had returned.

"The doctor thought we'd better come over," Amberson said, then was silent, and George, shaking violently, sat down on the edge of the bed. His shaking continued, and from time to time he wiped heavy sweat from his forehead.

The hours passed, and sometimes the old man upon the bed would snore a little, stop suddenly, and move as if to rise, but George Amberson would set a hand upon his shoulder, and murmur a reassuring word or two. Now and then, either uncle or nephew would tiptoe into the hall and look toward Isabel's room, then come tiptoeing back, the other watching him haggardly.

Once George gasped defiantly: "That doctor in New York said she *might* get better! Don't you know he did? Don't you know he said she might?"

Amberson made no answer.

Dawn had been murking through the smoky windows, growing stronger for half an hour, when both men started violently at a sound in the hall; and the Major sat upon the bed, unchecked. It was the voice of the nurse speaking to Fanny Minafer, and the next moment, Fanny appeared in the doorway, making contorted efforts to speak.

Amberson said weakly: "Does she want us—to come in?"

But Fanny found her voice, and uttered a long, loud cry. She threw her arms about George, and sobbed in an agony of loss and compassion:

"She loved you!" she wailed. "She loved you! She loved you! Oh, how she did love you!"

Isabel had just left them.

CHAPTER XXX

Major Amberson remained dry-eyed through the time that followed: he knew that this separation from his daughter would be short; that the separation which had preceded it was the long one. He worked at his ledgers no more under his old gas drop-light, but would sit all evening staring into the fire, in his bedroom, and not speaking unless someone asked him a question. He seemed almost unaware of what went on around him, and those who were with him thought him dazed by Isabel's death, guessing that he was lost in reminiscences and vague dreams. "Probably his mind is full of pictures of his youth, or the Civil War, and the days when he and mother were young married people and all of us children were jolly little things—and the city was a small town with one cobbled street and the others just dirt roads with board sidewalks." This was George Amberson's conjecture, and the others agreed; but they were mistaken. The Major was engaged in the profoundest thinking of his life. No business plans which had ever absorbed him could compare in momentousness with the plans that absorbed him now, for he had to plan how to enter the unknown country where he was not even sure of being recognized as an Amberson—not sure of anything, except that Isabel would help him if she could. His absorption produced the outward effect of reverie, but of course it was not. The Major was occupied with the first really important matter that had taken his attention since he came home invalided, after the Gettysburg campaign, and went into business; and he realized that everything which had worried him or delighted him during this lifetime between then and to-day—all his buying and building and trading and banking—that it all was trifling and waste beside what concerned him now.

He seldom went out of his room, and often left untouched the meals they brought to him there; and this neglect caused them to shake their heads mournfully, again mistaking for dazedness the profound concentration of his mind. Meanwhile, the life of the little bereft group still forlornly centring upon him began to pick up again, as life will, and to emerge from its own period of dazedness. It was not Isabel's father but her son who was really dazed.

A month after her death he walked abruptly into Fanny's room, one night, and found her at her desk, eagerly adding columns of figures with which she had covered several sheets of paper. This mathematical computation was concerned with her future income to be produced by the electric headlight, now just placed on the general market; but Fanny was ashamed to be discovered doing anything except mourning, and hastily pushed the sheets aside, even as she looked over her shoulder to greet her hollow-eyed visitor.

"George! You startled me."

"I beg your pardon for not knocking," he said huskily. "I didn't think."

She turned in her chair and looked at him solicitously. "Sit down, George, won't you?"

"No. I just wanted——"

"I could hear you walking up and down in your room," said Fanny. "You were doing it ever since dinner, and it seems to me you're at it almost every evening. I don't believe it's good for you—and I know it would worry your mother terribly if she——" Fanny hesitated.

"See here," George said, breathing fast, "I want to tell you once more that what I did was right. How could I have done anything else but what I did do?"

"About what, George?"

"About everything!" he exclaimed; and he became vehement. "I did the right thing, I tell you! In heaven's name, I'd like to know what else there was for anybody in my position to do! It would have been a dreadful thing for me to just let matters go on and not interfere—it would have been terrible! What else on earth was there *for* me to do? I *had* to stop that talk, didn't I? Could a son do less than I did? Didn't it *cost* me something to do it? Lucy and I'd had a quarrel, but that would have come round in time—and it meant the end forever when I turned her father back from our door. I knew what it meant, yet I went ahead and did it because I knew it had to be done if the talk was to be stopped. I took mother away for the same reason. I knew that would help to stop it. And she was happy over there—she was perfectly happy. I tell you, I think she had a happy life, and that's my only consolation. She didn't live to be old; she was still beautiful and young looking, and I feel she'd rather have gone before she got old. She'd had a good husband, and all the comfort and luxury that anybody could have—and how could it be called anything but a happy life? She was always cheerful, and when I think of her I can always see her laughing—I can always hear that pretty laugh of hers. When I can keep my mind off of the trip home, and that last night, I *always* think of her gay and laughing. So how on earth *could* she have had anything but a happy life? People that aren't happy don't look cheerful all the time, do they? They look unhappy if they *are* unhappy; that's how they look! See here"—he faced her challengingly—"do *you* deny that I did the right thing?"

"Oh, I don't pretend to judge," Fanny said soothingly, for his voice and gesture both partook of wildness. "I know you think you did, George."

" 'Think I did!' " he echoed violently. "My God in heaven!" And he began to walk up and down the floor. "What else *was* there to do? What *choice* did I have? Was there any other way of stopping the talk?" He stopped, close in front of her, gesticulating, his voice harsh and loud: "Don't you hear me? I'm asking you: Was there any other way on earth of protecting her from the talk?"

Miss Fanny looked away. "It died down before long, I think," she said nervously.

"*That* shows I was right, doesn't it?" he cried. "If I hadn't acted as I did, that slanderous old Johnson woman would have kept on with her slanders— she'd *still* be——"

"No," Fanny interrupted. "She's dead. She dropped dead with apoplexy one day about six weeks after you left. I didn't mention it in my letters because I didn't want—I thought——"

"Well, the *other* people would have kept on, then. *They'd* have——"

"I don't know," said Fanny, still averting her troubled eyes. "Things are so changed here, George. The other people you speak of—one hardly knows what's become of them. Of course not a great many were doing the talking, and they—well, some of them are dead, and some might as well be—you never see them any more—and the rest, whoever they were, are probably so mixed in with the crowds of new people that seem never even to have heard of *us*— and I'm sure we certainly never heard of *them*—and people seem to forget things so soon—they seem to forget anything. You can't imagine how things have changed here!"

George gulped painfully before he could speak. "You—you mean to sit there and tell me that if I'd just let things go on—— Oh!" He swung away, walking the floor again. "I tell you I did the only right thing! If you don't think so, why in the name of heaven can't you say what *else* I should have done? It's easy enough to criticize, but the person who criticizes a man ought at least to tell him what *else* he should have done! You think I was wrong!"

"I'm not saying so," she said.

"You did at the time!" he cried. "You said enough then, I think! Well, what have you to say now, if you're so sure I was wrong?"

"Nothing, George."

"It's only because you're afraid to!" he said, and he went on with a sudden bitter divination: "You're reproaching yourself with what *you* had to do with all that; and you're trying to make up for it by doing and saying what you think mother would want you to, and you think I couldn't stand it if I got to thinking I might have done differently. Oh, I know! That's exactly what's in your mind: you *do* think I was wrong! So does Uncle George. I challenged him about it the other day, and he answered just as you're answering—evaded, and tried to be gentle! I don't care to be handled with gloves! I tell you I was right, and I don't need any coddling by people that think I wasn't! And I suppose you believe I was wrong not to let Morgan see her that last night when he came here, and she—she was dying. If you do, why in the name of God did you come and ask *me*? *You* could have taken him in! She *did* want to see him. She——"

Miss Fanny looked startled. "You think——"

"She told me so!" And the tortured young man choked. "She said—'just once.' She said 'I'd like to have seen him—just once!' She meant—to tell him good-bye! *That's* what she meant! And you put this on me, too; you put this responsibility on me! But I tell you, and I told Uncle George, that the responsibility isn't *all* mine! If you were so sure I was wrong all the time—when I took her away, and when I turned Morgan out—if you were so sure, what did you let me do it for? You and Uncle George were grown people, both of you, weren't you? You were older than I, and if you were so sure you were *wiser* than I, why did you just stand around with your hands hanging down, and let me go ahead? You could have stopped it if it was wrong, couldn't you?"

Fanny shook her head. "No, George," she said slowly. "Nobody could have stopped you. You were too strong, and——"

"And what?" he demanded loudly.

"And she loved you—too well."

George stared at her hard, then his lower lip began to move convulsively, and he set his teeth upon it but could not check its frantic twitching.

He ran out of the room.

She sat still, listening. He had plunged into his mother's room, but no sound came to Fanny's ears after the sharp closing of the door; and presently she rose and stepped out into the hall—but could hear nothing. The heavy black walnut door of Isabel's room, as Fanny's troubled eyes remained fixed upon it, seemed to become darker and vaguer; the polished wood took the distant ceiling light, at the end of the hall, in dim reflections which became mysterious; and to Fanny's disturbed mind the single sharp point of light on the bronze door-knob was like a continuous sharp cry in the stillness of night. What interview was sealed away from human eye and ear within the lonely darkness on the other side of that door—in that darkness where Isabel's own special chairs were, and her own special books, and the two great walnut wardrobes filled with her dresses and wraps? What tragic argument might be there vainly striving to confute the gentle dead? "In God's name, what else could I have done?" For his mother's immutable silence was surely answering him as Isabel in life would never have answered him, and he was beginning to understand how eloquent the dead can be. They cannot stop their eloquence, no matter how they have loved the living: they cannot choose. And so, no matter in what agony George should cry out, "What else could I have done?" and to the end of his life no matter how often he made that wild appeal, Isabel was doomed to answer him with the wistful, faint murmur: "I'd like to have—seen him. Just—just once."

A cheerful darkey went by the house, loudly and tunelessly whistling some broken thoughts upon women, fried food and gin; then a group of high-school boys, returning homeward after important initiations, were heard skylarking along the sidewalk, rattling sticks on the fences, squawking hoarsely, and even attempting to sing in the shocking new voices of uncompleted adolescence. For no reason, and just as a poultry yard falls into causeless agitation, they stopped in front of the house, and for half an hour produced the effect of a noisy multitude in full riot.

To the woman standing upstairs in the hall, this was almost unbearable; and she felt that she would have to go down and call to them to stop; but she was too timid, and after a time went back to her room, and sat at her desk again. She left the door open, and frequently glanced out into the hall, but gradually became once more absorbed in the figures which represented her prospective income from her great plunge in electric lights for automobiles. She did not hear George return to his own room.

. . . A superstitious person might have thought it unfortunate that her partner in this speculative industry (as in Wilbur's disastrous rolling-mills) was that charming but too haphazardous man of the world, George Amberson. He was one of those optimists who believe that if you put money into a great many enterprises one of them is sure to turn out a fortune, and therefore, in order to find the lucky one, it is only necessary to go into a large enough number of them. Altogether gallant in spirit, and beautifully game under catastrophe, he had gone into a great many, and the unanimity of their "bad luck," as he called it, gave him one claim to be a distinguished person, if he had no other. In business he was ill fated with a consistency which made him, in that alone, a remarkable man; and he declared, with some earnestness, that there was no accounting for it except by the fact that there had been so much good luck in his family before he was born that something had to balance it.

"You ought to have thought of my record and stayed out," he told Fanny, one day the next spring, when the affairs of the headlight company had begun to look discouraging. "I feel the old familiar sinking that's attended all my previous efforts to prove myself a business genius. I think it must be something like the feeling an aeronaut has when his balloon bursts, and, looking down, he sees below him the old home farm where he used to live—I mean the feeling he'd have just before he flattened out in that same old clay barnyard. Things do look bleak, and I'm only glad you didn't go into this confounded thing to the extent I did."

Miss Fanny grew pink. "But it *must* go right!" she protested. "We saw with our own eyes how perfectly it worked in the shop. The light was so bright no one could face it, and so there *can't* be any reason for it not to work. It simply——"

"Oh, you're right about that," Amberson said. "It certainly was a perfect thing—in the shop! The only thing *we* didn't know was how fast an automobile had to go to keep the light going. It appears that this was a matter of some importance."

"Well, how fast *does* one have to——"

"To keep the light from going entirely out," he informed her with elaborate deliberation, "it is computed by those enthusiasts who have bought our product—and subsequently returned it to us and got their money back—they compute that a motor car must maintain a speed of twenty-five miles an hour, or else there won't be any light at all. To make the illumination bright enough to be noticed by an approaching automobile, they state the speed must be more than thirty miles an hour. At thirty-five, objects in the path of the light begin to become visible; at forty they are revealed distinctly; and at fifty and above we have a real headlight. Unfortunately many people don't care to drive that fast at all times after dusk, especially in the traffic, or where policemen are likely to become objectionable."

"But think of that test on the road when we——"

"That test was lovely," he admitted. "The inventor made us happy with his oratory, and you and Frank Bronson and I went whirling through the night at a speed that thrilled us. It was an intoxicating sensation: we were intoxicated by the lights, the lights and the music. We must never forget that drive, with the cool wind kissing our cheeks and the road lit up for miles ahead. We must never forget it—and we never shall. It cost——"

"But something's got to be done."

"It has, indeed! *My* something would seem to be leaving my watch at my uncle's. Luckily, you——"

The pink of Fanny's cheeks became deeper. "But isn't that man going to *do* anything to remedy it? Can't he try to——"

"He can try," said Amberson. "He *is* trying, in fact. I've sat in the shop watching him try for several beautiful afternoons, while outside the windows all Nature was fragrant with spring and smoke. He hums ragtime to himself as he tries, and I think his mind is wandering to something else less tedious —to some new invention in which he'd take more interest."

"But you mustn't let him," she cried. "You must *make* him keep on trying!"

"Oh, yes. He understands that's what I sit there for. I'll keep sitting!"

However, in spite of the time he spent sitting in the shop, worrying the inventor of the fractious light, Amberson found opportunity to worry himself about another matter of business. This was the settlement of Isabel's estate.

"It's curious about the deed to her house," he said to his nephew. "You're absolutely sure it wasn't among her papers?"

"Mother didn't have any papers," George told him. "None at all. All she ever had to do with business was to deposit the cheques grandfather gave her and then write her own cheques against them."

"The deed to the house was never recorded," Amberson said thoughtfully. "I've been over to the courthouse to see. I asked father if he never gave her one, and he didn't seem able to understand me at first. Then he finally said he thought he must have given her a deed long ago; but he wasn't sure. I rather think he never did. I think it would be just as well to get him to execute one now in your favour. I'll speak to him about it."

George sighed. "I don't think I'd bother him about it: the house is mine, and you and I understand that it is. That's enough for me, and there isn't likely to be much trouble between you and me when we come to settling poor grandfather's estate. I've just been with him, and I think it would only confuse him for you to speak to him about it again. I notice he seems distressed if anybody tries to get his attention—he's a long way off, somewhere, and he likes to stay that way. I think—I think mother wouldn't want us to bother him about it; I'm sure she'd tell us to let him alone. He looks so white and queer."

Amberson shook his head. "Not much whiter and queerer than you do, young fellow! You'd better begin to get some air and exercise and quit hanging about in the house all day. I won't bother him any more than I can help; but I'll have the deed made out ready for his signature."

"I wouldn't bother him at all. I don't see——"

"You might see," said his uncle uneasily. "The estate is just about as involved and mixed-up as an estate can well get, to the best of my knowledge; and I haven't helped it any by what he let me have for this infernal headlight scheme which has finally gone trolloping forever to where the woodbine twineth. Leaves me flat, and poor old Frank Bronson just half flat, and Fanny —well, thank heaven! I kept her from going in so deep that it would leave *her* flat. It's rough on her as it is, I suspect. You ought to have that deed."

"No. Don't bother him."

"I'll bother him as little as possible. I'll wait till some day when he seems to brighten up a little."

But Amberson waited too long. The Major had already taken eleven months since his daughter's death to think important things out. He had got as far with them as he could, and there was nothing to detain him longer in the world. One evening his grandson sat with him—the Major seemed to like best to have young George with him, so far as they were able to guess his preferences—and the old gentleman made a queer gesture: he slapped his knee as if he had made a sudden discovery, or else remembered that he had forgotten something.

George looked at him with an air of inquiry, but said nothing. He had grown to be almost as silent as his grandfather. However, the Major spoke without being questioned.

"It must be in the sun," he said. "There wasn't anything here but the sun in the first place, and the earth came out of the sun, and we came out of the earth. So, whatever we are, we must have been in the sun. We go back to the earth we came out of, so the earth will go back to the sun that it came out of. And time means nothing—nothing at all—so in a little while we'll all be back in the sun together. I wish——"

He moved his hand uncertainly as if reaching for something, and George jumped up. "Did you want anything, grandfather?"

"What?"

"Would you like a glass of water?"

"No—no. No; I don't want anything." The reaching hand dropped back upon the arm of his chair, and he relapsed into silence; but a few minutes later he finished the sentence he had begun:

"I wish—somebody could tell me!"

The next day he had a slight cold, but he seemed annoyed when his son suggested calling the doctor, and Amberson let him have his own way so far, in fact, that after he had got up and dressed, the following morning, he was all alone when he went away to find out what he hadn't been able to think out—all those things he had wished "somebody" would tell him.

Old Sam, shuffling in with the breakfast tray, found the Major in his accustomed easy-chair by the fireplace—and yet even the old darkey could see instantly that the Major was not there.

CHAPTER XXXI

When the great Amberson Estate went into court for settlement, "there wasn't any," George Amberson said—that is, when the settlement was concluded there was no estate. "I guessed it," Amberson went on. "As an expert on prosperity, my career is disreputable, but as a prophet of calamity I deserve a testimonial banquet." He reproached himself bitterly for not having long ago discovered that his father had never given Isabel a deed to her house. "And those pigs, Sydney and Amelia!" he added, for this was another thing he was bitter about. "They won't do anything. I'm sorry I gave them the opportunity of making a polished refusal. Amelia's letter was about half in Italian; she couldn't remember enough ways of saying no in English. One has to live quite a long while to realize there *are* people like that! The estate was badly crippled, even before they took out their 'third,' and the 'third' they took was the only good part of the rotten apple. Well, I didn't ask them for restitution on my own account, and at least it will save *you* some trouble, young George. Never waste any time writing to them; you mustn't count on them."

"I don't," George said quietly. "I don't count on anything."

"Oh, we'll not feel that things are quite desperate," Amberson laughed, but not with great cheerfulness. "We'll survive, Georgie—*you* will, especially. For my part I'm a little too old and too accustomed to fall back on somebody else for supplies to start a big fight with life: I'll be content with just surviving, and I can do it on an eighteen-hundred-dollar-a-year consulship. An ex-congressman can always be pretty sure of getting some such job, and I hear from Washington the matter's about settled. I'll live pleasantly enough with a pitcher of ice under a palm tree, and black folks to wait on me—that part of it will be like home—and I'll manage to send you fifty dollars every now and then, after I once get settled. So much for me! But you —of course you've had a poor training for making your own way, but you're only a boy after all, and the stuff of the old stock is in you. It'll come out and do something. I'll never forgive myself about that deed: it would have given you something substantial to start with. Still, you have a little tiny bit, and you'll have a little tiny salary, too; and of course your Aunt Fanny's here, and she's got something you can fall back on if you get *too* pinched, until I can begin to send you a dribble now and then."

George's "little tiny bit" was six hundred dollars which had come to him from the sale of his mother's furniture; and the "little tiny salary" was eight dollars a week which old Frank Bronson was to pay him for services as a clerk and student-at-law. Old Frank would have offered more to the Major's grandson, but since the death of that best of clients and his own experience with automobile headlights, he was not certain of being able to pay more and at the same time settle his own small bills for board and lodging. George had accepted haughtily, and thereby removed a burden from his uncle's mind.

Amberson himself, however, had not even a "tiny bit"; though he got his consular appointment; and to take him to his post he found it necessary to borrow two hundred of his nephew's six hundred dollars. "It makes me sick, George," he said. "But I'd better get there and get that salary started. Of course Eugene would do anything in the world, and the fact is he wanted to, but I felt that—ah—under the circumstances——"

"Never!" George exclaimed, growing red. "I can't imagine one of the family——" He paused, not finding it necessary to explain that "the family" shouldn't turn a man from the door and then accept favours from him. "I wish you'd take more."

Amberson declined. "One thing I'll say for you, young George; you haven't a stingy bone in your body. That's the Amberson stock in you—and I like it!"

He added something to this praise of his nephew on the day he left for Washington. He was not to return, but to set forth from the capital on the

THE MAGNIFICENT AMBERSONS

long journey to his post. George went with him to the station, and their fare-well was lengthened by the train's being several minutes late.

"I may not see you again, Georgie," Amberson said; and his voice was a little husky as he set a kind hand on the young man's shoulder. "It's quite probable that from this time on we'll only know each other by letter—until you're notified as my next of kin that there's an old valise to be forwarded to you, and perhaps some dusty curios from the consulate mantelpiece. Well, it's an odd way for us to be saying good-bye: one wouldn't have thought it, even a few years ago, but here we are, two gentlemen of elegant appearance in a state of bustitude. We can't ever tell what will happen at all, can we? Once I stood where we're standing now, to say good-bye to a pretty girl—only it was in the old station before this was built, and we called it the 'dépôt.' She'd been visiting your mother, before Isabel was married, and I was wild about her, and she admitted she didn't mind that. In fact, we decided we couldn't live without each other, and we were to be married. But she had to go abroad first with her father, and when we came to say good-bye we knew we wouldn't see each other again for almost a year. I thought I couldn't live through it—and she stood here crying. Well, I don't even know where she lives now, or if she *is* living—and I only happen to think of her some-times when I'm here at the station waiting for a train. If she ever thinks of me she probably imagines I'm still dancing in the ballroom at the Amberson Mansion, and she probably thinks of the Mansion as still beautiful—still the finest house in town. Life and money both behave like loose quicksilver in a nest of cracks. And when they're gone we can't tell where—or what the devil we did with 'em! But I believe I'll say now—while there isn't much time left for either of us to get embarrassed about it—I believe I'll say that I've always been fond of you, Georgie, but I can't say that I always liked you. Sometimes I've felt you were distinctly *not* an acquired taste. Until lately, one had to be fond of you just *naturally*—this isn't very 'tactful,' of course—for if he didn't, well, he wouldn't! We all spoiled you terribly when you were a little boy and let you grow up *en prince*—and I must say you took to it! But you've received a pretty heavy jolt, and I had enough of your disposition, myself, at your age, to understand a little of what cocksure youth has to go through inside when it finds that it *can* make terrible mistakes. Poor old fellow! You get both kinds of jolts together, spiritual and material—and you've taken them pretty quietly and—well, with my train coming into the shed, you'll forgive me for saying that there have been times when I thought you ought to be hanged—but I've always been fond of you, and now I *like* you! And just for a last word: there may be somebody else in this town who's always felt about you like that—fond of you, I mean, no matter how much it seemed you ought to be hanged. You might try—— Hello, I must run. I'll send back the money as fast as they pay me—so, good-bye and God bless you, Georgie!"

He passed through the gates, waved his hat cheerily from the other side of the iron screen, and was lost from sight in the hurrying crowd. And as he disappeared, an unexpected poignant loneliness fell upon his nephew so heavily and so suddenly that he had no energy to recoil from the shock. It seemed to him that the last fragment of his familiar world had disappeared, leaving him all alone forever.

He walked homeward slowly through what appeared to be the strange streets of a strange city; and, as a matter of fact, the city was strange to him. He had seen little of it during his years in college, and then had followed the long absence and his tragic return. Since that he had been "scarcely out-doors at all," as Fanny complained, warning him that his health would suffer, and he had been downtown only in a closed carriage. He had not realized the great change.

The streets were thunderous; a vast energy heaved under the universal coating of dinginess. George walked through the begrimed crowds of hurrying strangers and saw no face that he remembered. Great numbers of the faces were even of a kind he did not remember ever to have seen; they were partly like the old type that his boyhood knew, and partly like types he knew abroad. He saw German eyes with American wrinkles at their corners; he saw Irish eyes and Neapolitan eyes, Roman eyes, Tuscan eyes, eyes of Lombardy, of Savoy, Hungarian eyes, Balkan eyes, Scandinavian eyes—all with a queer American look in them. He saw Jews who had been German Jews, Jews who had been Russian Jews, Jews who had been Polish Jews but were no longer German or Russian or Polish Jews. All the people were soiled by the smoke-mist through which they hurried, under the heavy sky that hung close upon the new skyscrapers; and nearly all seemed harried by something impending, though here and there a woman with bundles would be laughing to a companion about some adventure of the department stores, or perhaps an escape from the charging traffic of the streets—and not infrequently a girl, or a free-and-easy young matron, found time to throw an encouraging look to George.

He took no note of these, and, leaving the crowded sidewalks, turned north into National Avenue, and presently reached the quieter but no less begrimed region of smaller shops and old-fashioned houses. Those latter had been the homes of his boyhood playmates; old friends of his grandfather had lived here;—in this alley he had fought with two boys at the same time, and whipped them; in that front yard he had been successfully teased into tem-porary insanity by a Sunday-school class of pinky little girls. On that sagging porch a laughing woman had fed him and other boys with doughnuts and gingerbread; yonder he saw the staggered relics of the iron picket fence he had made his white pony jump, on a dare, and in the shabby, stone-faced house behind the fence he had gone to children's parties, and, when he was a little older he had danced there often, and fallen in love with Mary Sharon, and kissed her, apparently by force, under the stairs in the hall. The double front doors, of meaninglessly carved walnut, once so glossily varnished, had been painted smoke gray, but the smoke grime showed repulsively, even on the smoke gray; and over the doors a smoked sign proclaimed the place to be a "Stag Hotel."

Other houses had become boarding-houses too genteel for signs, but many were franker, some offering "board by the day, week or meal," and some, more laconic, contenting themselves with the label: "Rooms." One, having torn out part of an old stone-trimmed bay window for purposes of commercial display, showed forth two suspended petticoats and a pair of oyster-coloured flannel trousers to prove the claims of its black-and-gilt sign: "French Cleaning and Dye House." Its next neighbour also sported a remodelled front and permitted no doubt that its mission in life was to attend cosily upon death: "J. M. Rolsener. Caskets. The Funeral Home." And beyond that, a plain old honest four-square gray-painted brick house was flamboyantly decorated with a great gilt scroll on the railing of the old-fashioned veranda: "Mutual Benev't Order Cavaliers and Dames of Purity." This was the old Minafer house.

George passed it without perceptibly wincing; in fact, he held his head up, and except for his gravity of countenance and the prison pallor he had acquired by too constantly remaining indoors, there was little to warn an acquaintance that he was not precisely the same George Amberson Minafer known aforetime. He was still so magnificent, indeed, that there came to his ears a waft of comment from a passing automobile. This was a fearsome red car, glittering in brass, with half-a-dozen young people in it whose motorism had reached an extreme manifestation in dress. The ladies of this party were favourably affected at sight of the pedestrian upon the sidewalk, and, as the machine was moving slowly, and close to the curb, they had time to observe him in detail, which they did with a frankness not pleasing to the object of their attentions. "One sees so many nice-looking people one doesn't know nowadays," said the youngest of the young ladies. "This old town of ours is really getting enormous. I shouldn't mind knowing who he is."

"I don't know," the youth beside her said, loudly enough to be heard at a considerable distance. "I don't know who he is, but from his looks I know who he thinks he is: he thinks he's the Grand Duke Cuthbert!" There was a burst of tittering as the car gathered speed and rolled away, with the girl continuing to look back until her scandalized companions forced her to turn by pulling her hood over her face. She made an impression upon George, so deep a one, in fact, that he unconsciously put his emotion into a muttered word:

"Riffraff!"

This was the last "walk home" he was ever to take by the route he was now following: up National Avenue to Amberson Addition and the two big old houses at the foot of Amberson Boulevard; for to-night would be the last night that he and Fanny were to spend in the house which the Major had forgotten to deed to Isabel. To-morrow they were to "move out," and George was to begin his work in Bronson's office. He had not come to this collapse without a fierce struggle—but the struggle was inward, and the rolling world was not agitated by it, and rolled calmly on. For of all the "ideals of life" which the world, in its rolling, inconsiderately flattens out to nothingness, the least likely to retain a profile is that ideal which depends upon inheriting money. George Amberson, in spite of his record of failures in business, had spoken shrewdly when he realized at last that money, like life, was "like quicksilver in a nest of cracks." And his nephew had the awakening experience of seeing the great Amberson Estate vanishing into such a nest—in a twinkling, it seemed, now that it was indeed so utterly vanished.

His uncle had suggested that he might write to college friends; perhaps they could help him to something better than the prospect offered by Bronson's office; but George flushed and shook his head, without explaining. In that small and quietly superior "crowd" of his he had too emphatically supported the ideal of being rather than doing. He could not appeal to one of its members now to help him to a job. Besides, they were not precisely the warmest-hearted crew in the world, and he had long ago dropped the last affectation of a correspondence with any of them. He was as aloof from any survival of intimacy with his boyhood friends in the city, and, in truth, had lost track of most of them. "The Friends of the Ace," once bound by oath to succour one another in peril or poverty, were long ago dispersed; one or two had died; one or two had gone to live elsewhere; the others were disappeared into the smoky bigness of the heavy city. Of the brethren, there remained within his present cognizance only his old enemy, the red-haired Kinney, now married to Janie Sharon, and Charlie Johnson, who, out of deference to his mother's memory, had passed the Amberson Mansion one day, when George stood upon the front steps, and, looking in fiercely, had looked away with continued fierceness—his only token of recognition.

. . . On this last homeward walk of his, when George reached the entrance to Amberson Addition—that is, when he came to where the entrance had formerly been—he gave a little start, and halted for a moment to stare. This was the first time he had noticed that the stone pillars, marking the entrance, had been removed. Then he realized that for a long time he had been conscious of a queerness about this corner without being aware of what made the difference. National Avenue met Amberson Boulevard here at an obtuse angle, and the removal of the pillars made the Boulevard seem a cross-street of no overpowering importance—certainly it did not seem to be a boulevard!

At the next corner Neptune's Fountain remained, and one could still determine with accuracy what its designer's intentions had been. It stood in sore need of just one last kindness; and if the thing had possessed any friends they would have done that doleful shovelling after dark.

George did not let his eyes linger upon the relic; nor did he look steadfastly at the Amberson Mansion. Massive as the old house was, it managed to look gaunt: its windows stared with the skull emptiness of all windows in empty houses that are to be lived in no more. Of course the rowdy boys of the neighbourhood had been at work: many of these haggard windows were broken; the front door stood ajar, forced open; and idiot salacity, in white chalk, was smeared everywhere upon the pillars and stonework of the verandas.

George walked by the Mansion hurriedly, and came home to his mother's house for the last time.

Emptiness was there, too, and the closing of the door resounded through bare rooms; for downstairs there was no furniture in the house except a kitchen table in the dining room, which Fanny had kept "for dinner," she said, though as she was to cook and serve that meal herself George had his doubts about her name for it. Upstairs, she had retained her own furniture, and George had been living in his mother's room, having sent everything from his own to the auction. Isabel's room was still as it had been, but the furniture would be moved with Fanny's to new quarters in the morning. Fanny had made plans for her nephew as well as herself; she had found a "three-room kitchenette apartment" in an apartment house where several old friends of hers had established themselves—elderly widows of citizens once "prominent" and other retired gentry. People used their own "kitchen-ettes" for breakfast and lunch, but there was a table-d'hôte arrangement for dinner on the ground floor; and after dinner bridge was played all eve-ning, an attraction powerful with Fanny. She had "made all the arrange-ments," she reported, and nervously appealed for approval, asking if she hadn't shown herself "pretty practical" in such matters. George acquiesced absent-mindedly, not thinking of what she said and not realizing to what it committed him.

He began to realize it now, as he wandered about the dismantled house; he was far from sure that he was willing to go and live in a "three-room apart-ment" with Fanny and eat breakfast and lunch with her (prepared by herself in the "kitchenette") and dinner at the table d'hôte in "such a pretty Colo-nial dining room" (so Fanny described it) at a little round table they would have all to themselves in the midst of a dozen little round tables which other relics of disrupted families would have all to themselves. For the first time, now that the change was imminent, George began to develop before his mind's eye pictures of what he was in for; and they appalled him. He de-cided that such a life verged upon the sheerly unbearable, and that after all there were some things left that he just couldn't stand. So he made up his mind to speak to his aunt about it at "dinner," and tell her that he preferred to ask Bronson to let him put a sofa-bed, a trunk, and a folding rubber bath-tub behind a screen in the dark rear room of the office. George felt that this would be infinitely more tolerable; and he could eat at restaurants, especially as about all he ever wanted nowadays was coffee.

But at "dinner" he decided to put off telling Fanny of his plan until later: she was so nervous, and so distressed about the failure of her efforts with sweetbreads and macaroni; and she was so eager in her talk of how comfort-able they would be "by this time to-morrow night." She fluttered on, her nervousness increasing, saying how "nice" it would be for him, when he came from work in the evenings, to be among "nice people—people who know who we *are*," and to have a pleasant game of bridge with "people who are really old friends of the family."

When they stopped probing among the scorched fragments she had set forth, George lingered downstairs, waiting for a better opportunity to introduce his own subject, but when he heard dismaying sounds from the kitchen he gave up. There was a crash, then a shower of crashes; falling tin clamoured to be heard above the shattering of porcelain; and over all rose Fanny's wail of lamentation for the treasures saved from the sale, but now lost forever to the "kitchenette." Fanny was nervous indeed; so nervous that she could not trust her hands.

For a moment George thought she might have been injured, but, before he reached the kitchen, he heard her sweeping at the fragments, and turned back. He put off speaking to Fanny until morning.

Things more insistent than his vague plans for a sofa-bed in Bronson's office had possession of his mind as he went upstairs, moving his hand slowly along the smooth walnut railing of the balustrade. Half way to the landing he stopped, turned, and stood looking down at the heavy doors masking the black emptiness that had been the library. Here he had stood on what he now knew was the worst day of his life; here he had stood when his mother passed through that doorway, hand-in-hand with her brother, to learn what her son had done.

He went on more heavily, more slowly; and, more heavily and slowly still, entered Isabel's room and shut the door. He did not come forth again, and bade Fanny good-night through the closed door when she stopped outside it later.

"I've put all the lights out, George," she said. "Everything's all right."

"Very well," he called. "Good-night."

She did not go. "I'm sure we're going to enjoy the new little home, George," she said timidly. "I'll try hard to make things nice for you, and the people really are lovely. You mustn't feel as if things are altogether gloomy, George. I know everything's going to turn out all right. You're young and strong and you have a good mind and I'm sure—" she hesitated—"I'm sure your mother's watching over you, Georgie. Good-night, dear."

"Good-night, Aunt Fanny."

His voice had a strangled sound in spite of him; but she seemed not to notice it, and he heard her go to her own room and lock herself in with bolt and key against burglars. She had said the one thing she should not have said just then: "I'm sure your mother's watching over you, Georgie." She had meant to be kind, but it destroyed his last chance for sleep that night. He would have slept little if she had not said it, but since she had said it, he did not sleep at all. For he knew that it was true—if it *could* be true—and that his mother, if she still lived in spirit, would be weeping on the other side of the wall of silence, weeping and seeking for some gate to let her through so that she could come and "watch over him."

He felt that if there were such gates they were surely barred: they were like those awful library doors downstairs, which had shut her in to begin the suffering to which he had consigned her.

The room was still Isabel's. Nothing had been changed: even the photographs of George, of the Major, and of "brother George" still stood on her dressing-table, and in a drawer of her desk was an old picture of Eugene and Lucy, taken together, which George had found, but had slowly closed away again from sight, not touching it. To-morrow everything would be gone; and he had heard there was not long to wait before the house itself would be demolished. The very space which to-night was still Isabel's room would be cut into new shapes by new walls and floors and ceilings; yet the room would always live, for it could not die out of George's memory. It would live as long as he did, and it would always be murmurous with a tragic, wistful whispering.

And if space itself can be haunted, as memory is haunted, then some time, when the space that was Isabel's room came to be made into the small bedrooms and "kitchenettes" already designed as its destiny, that space might well be haunted and the new occupants come to feel that some seemingly causeless depression hung about it—a wraith of the passion that filled it throughout the last night that George Minafer spent there.

Whatever remnants of the old high-handed arrogance were still within him, he did penance for his deepest sin that night—and it may be that to this day some impressionable, overworked woman in a "kitchenette," after turning out the light, will seem to see a young man kneeling in the darkness, shaking convulsively, and, with arms outstretched through the wall, clutching at the covers of a shadowy bed. It may seem to her that she hears the faint cry, over and over:

"Mother, forgive me! God, forgive me!"

CHAPTER XXXII

At least, it may be claimed for George that his last night in the house where he had been born was not occupied with his own disheartening future, but with sorrow for what sacrifices his pride and youth had demanded of others. And early in the morning he came downstairs and tried to help Fanny make coffee on the kitchen range.

"There was something I wanted to say to you last night, Aunt Fanny," he said, as she finally discovered that an amber fluid, more like tea than coffee, was as near ready to be taken into the human system as it would ever be. "I think I'd better do it now."

She set the coffee-pot back upon the stove with a little crash, and, looking at him in a desperate anxiety, began to twist her dainty apron between her fingers without any consciousness of what she was doing.

"Why—why——" she stammered; but she knew what he was going to say, and that was why she had been more and more nervous. "Hadn't—perhaps

—perhaps we'd better get the—the things moved to the little new home first, George. Let's——"

He interrupted quietly, though at her phrase, "the little new home," his pungent impulse was to utter one loud shout and run. "It was about this new place that I wanted to speak. I've been thinking it over, and I've decided. I want you to take all the things from mother's room and use them and keep them for me, and I'm sure the little apartment will be just what you like; and with the extra bedroom probably you could find some woman friend to come and live there, and share the expense with you. But I've decided on another arrangement for myself, and so I'm not going with you. I don't suppose you'll mind much, and I don't see why you *should* mind—particularly, that is. I'm not very lively company these days, or any days, for that matter. I can't imagine you, or any one else, being much attached to me, so——"

He stopped in amazement: no chair had been left in the kitchen, but Fanny gave a despairing glance around her, in search of one, then sank abruptly, and sat flat upon the floor.

"You're going to leave me in the lurch!" she gasped.

"What on earth——" George sprang to her. "Get up, Aunt Fanny!"

"I can't. I'm too weak. Let me alone, George!" And as he released the wrist he had seized to help her, she repeated the dismal prophecy which for days she had been matching against her hopes: "You're going to leave me—in the lurch!"

"Why no, Aunt Fanny!" he protested. "At first I'd have been something of a burden on you. I'm to get eight dollars a week; about thirty-two a month. The rent's thirty-six dollars a month, and the table-d'hôte dinner runs up to over twenty-two dollars apiece, so with my half of the rent—eighteen dollars —I'd have less than nothing left out of my salary to pay my share of the groceries for all the breakfasts and luncheons. You see you'd not only be doing all the housework and cooking, but you'd be paying more of the expenses than I would."

She stared at him with such a forlorn blankness as he had never seen. "I'd be paying——" she said feebly. "I'd be paying——"

"Certainly you would. You'd be using more of your money than——"

"My money!" Fanny's chin drooped upon her thin chest, and she laughed miserably. "I've got twenty-eight dollars. That's all."

"You mean until the interest is due again?"

"I mean that's all," Fanny said. "I mean that's all there is. There won't be any more interest because there isn't any principal."

"Why, you told——"

She shook her head. "No. I haven't told you anything."

"Then it was Uncle George. *He* told me you had enough to fall back on. That's just what he said: 'to fall back on.' He said you'd lost more than you should, in the headlight company, but he'd insisted that you should hold out enough to live on, and you'd very wisely followed his advice."

"I know," she said weakly. "I told him so. He didn't know, or else he'd forgotten, how much Wilbur's insurance amounted to, and I—oh, it seemed such a sure way to make a real fortune out of a little—and I thought I could do something for *you*, George, if you ever came to need it—and it all looked so bright I just thought I'd put it all in. I did—every cent except my last interest payment—and it's gone."

"Good Lord!" George began to pace up and down the worn planks of the bare floor. "Why on earth did you wait till now to tell such a thing as this?"

"I *couldn't* tell till I had to," she said piteously. "I couldn't till George Amberson went away. He couldn't do anything to help, anyhow, and I just didn't want him to talk to me about it—he's been at me so much about not putting more in than I could afford to lose, and said he considered he had my—my word I *wasn't* putting more than that in it. So I thought: What was the use? What was the use of going over it all with him and having him reproach me, and probably reproach himself? It wouldn't do any good—not any good on earth." She got out her lace handkerchief and began to cry. "Nothing does any good, I guess, in this old world! Oh, how tired of this old world I am! I didn't know *what* to do. I just tried to go ahead and be as practical as I could, and arrange *some* way for us to live. Oh, I knew you didn't want me, George! You always teased me and berated me whenever you had a chance from the time you were a little boy—you did *so!* Later, you've tried to be kinder to me, but you don't want me around—oh, I can see *that* much! You don't suppose I want to thrust myself on you, do you? It isn't very pleasant to be thrusting yourself on a person you know doesn't want you—but I knew you oughtn't to be left all alone in the world; it isn't good. I knew your mother'd want me to watch over you and try to have *something* like a home for you—I know she'd want me to do what I tried to do!" Fanny's tears were bitter now, and her voice, hoarse and wet, was tragically sincere. "I tried—I tried to be practical—to look after your interests —to make things as nice for you as I could—I walked my heels down looking for a place for us to live—I walked and walked over this town—I didn't ride one block on a street-car—I wouldn't use five cents no matter how tired I—— Oh!" She sobbed uncontrollably. "Oh! and now—you don't want—you want— you want to leave me in the lurch! You——"

George stopped walking. "In God's name, Aunt Fanny," he said, "quit spreading our your handkerchief and drying it and then getting it all wet again! I mean stop crying! Do! And for heaven's sake, get up. Don't sit there with your back against the boiler and——"

"It's not hot," Fanny sniffled. "It's cold; the plumbers disconnected it. I wouldn't mind if they hadn't. *I* wouldn't mind if it burned me, George."

"Oh, my *Lord!*" He went to her, and lifted her. "For God's sake, get up! Come, let's take the coffee into the other room, and see what's to be done."

He got her to her feet; she leaned upon him, already somewhat comforted, and, with his arm about her, he conducted her to the dining room and seated her in one of the two kitchen chairs which had been placed at the rough table. "There!" he said, "get over it!" Then he brought the coffee-pot, some lumps of sugar in a tin pan, and, finding that all the coffee-cups were broken, set water glasses upon the table, and poured some of the pale coffee into them. By this time Fanny's spirits had revived appreciably: she looked up with a plaintive eagerness. "I *had* bought all my fall clothes, George," she said; "and I paid every bill I owed. I don't owe a cent for clothes, George."

"That's good," he said wanly, and he had a moment of physical dizziness that decided him to sit down quickly. For an instant it seemed to him that he was not Fanny's nephew, but married to her. He passed his pale hand over his paler forehead. "Well, let's see where we stand," he said feebly. "Let's see if we can afford this place you've selected."

Fanny continued to brighten. "I'm sure it's the most practical plan we could possibly have worked out, George—and it *is* a comfort to be among nice people. I think we'll both enjoy it, because the truth is we've been keeping too much to ourselves for a long while. It isn't good for people."

"I was thinking about the money, Aunt Fanny. You see——"

"I'm sure we can manage it," she interrupted quickly. "There really isn't a cheaper place in town that we could actually live in and be——" Here she interrupted herself. "Oh! There's one *great* economy I forgot to tell you, and it's especially an economy for you, because you're always too generous about such things: they don't allow any tipping. They have signs that prohibit it."

"That's good," he said grimly. "But the rent is thirty-six dollars a month; the dinner is twenty-two and a half for each of us, and we've got to have some provision for other food. We won't need any clothes for a year, perhaps——"

"Oh, longer!" she exclaimed. "So you see——"

"I see that forty-five and thirty-six make eighty-one," he said. "At the lowest, we need a hundred dollars a month—and I'm going to make thirty-two."

"I thought of that, George," she said confidently, "and I'm sure it will be all right. You'll be earning a great deal more than that very soon."

"I don't see any prospect of it—not till I'm admitted to the bar, and that will be two years at the earliest."

Fanny's confidence was not shaken. "I know *you'll* be getting on faster than——"

"'Faster?'" George echoed gravely. "We've got to have more than that to start with."

"Well, there's the six hundred dollars from the sale. Six hundred and twelve dollars it was."

"It isn't six hundred and twelve now," said George. "It's about one hundred and sixty."

Fanny showed a momentary dismay. "Why, how——"

"I lent Uncle George two hundred; I gave fifty apiece to old Sam and those two other old darkies that worked for grandfather so long, and ten to each of the servants here——"

"And you gave me thirty-six," she said thoughtfully, "for the first month's rent, in advance."

"Did I? I'd forgotten. Well, with about a hundred and sixty in bank and our expenses a hundred a month, it doesn't seem as if this new place——"

"Still," she interrupted, "we *have* paid the first month's rent in advance, and it does seem to be the most practical——"

George rose. "See here, Aunt Fanny," he said decisively. "You stay here and look after the moving. Old Frank doesn't expect me until afternoon, this first day, but I'll go and see him now."

. . . It was early, and old Frank, just established at his big, flat-topped desk, was surprised when his prospective assistant and pupil walked in. He was pleased, as well as surprised, however, and rose, offering a cordial old hand. "The real flare!" he said. "The real flare for the law. That's right! Couldn't wait till afternoon to begin! I'm delighted that you——"

"I wanted to say——" George began, but his patron cut him off.

"Wait just a minute, my boy. I've prepared a little speech of welcome, and even though you're five hours ahead of time, I mean to deliver it. First of all, your grandfather was my old war-comrade and my best client; for years I prospered through my connection with his business, and his grandson is welcome in my office and to my best efforts in his behalf. But I want to confess, Georgie, that during your earlier youth I may have had some slight feeling of —well, prejudice, not altogether in your favour; but whatever slight feeling it was, it began to vanish on that afternoon, a good while ago, when you stood up to your Aunt Amelia Amberson as you did in the Major's library, and talked to her as a man and a gentleman should. I saw then what good stuff was in you—and I always wanted to mention it. If my prejudice hadn't altogether vanished after that, the last vestiges disappeared during these trying times that have come upon you this past year, when I have been a witness to the depth of feeling you've shown and your quiet consideration for your grandfather and for everyone else around you. I just want to add that I think you'll find an honest pleasure now in industry and frugality that wouldn't have come to you in a more frivolous career. The law is a jealous mistress and a stern mistress, but a——"

George had stood before him in great and increasing embarrassment; and he was unable to allow the address to proceed to its conclusion.

"I can't do it!" he burst out. "I can't take her for my mistress."

"What?"

"I've come to tell you, I've got to find something that's quicker. I can't——"

Old Frank got a little red. "Let's sit down," he said. "What's the trouble?" George told him.

The old gentleman listened sympathetically, only murmuring: "Well, well!" from time to time, and nodding acquiescence.

"You see she's set her mind on this apartment," George explained. "She's got some old cronies there, and I guess she's been looking forward to the games of bridge and the kind of harmless gossip that goes on in such places. Really, it's a life she'd like better than anything else—better than that she's lived at home, I really believe. It struck me she's just about got to have it, and after all she could hardly have anything less."

"This comes pretty heavily upon me, you know," said old Frank. "I got her into that headlight company, and she fooled me about her resources as much as she did your Uncle George. I was never your father's adviser, if you remember, and when the insurance was turned over to her some other lawyer arranged it—probably your father's. But it comes pretty heavily on me, and I feel a certain responsibility."

"Not at all. I'm taking the responsibility." And George smiled with one corner of his mouth. "She's not *your* aunt, you know, sir."

"Well, I'm unable to see, even if she's yours, that a young man is morally called upon to give up a career at the law to provide his aunt with a favourable opportunity to play bridge whist!"

"No," George agreed. "But I haven't begun my 'career at the law' so it can't be said I'm making any considerable sacrifice. I'll tell you how it is, sir." He flushed, and, looking out of the streaked and smoky window beside which he was sitting, spoke with difficulty. "I feel as if—as if perhaps I had one or two pretty important things in my life to make up for. Well, I can't. I can't make them up to—to whom I would. It's struck me that, as I couldn't, I might be a little decent to somebody else, perhaps—if I could manage it! I never have been particularly decent to poor old Aunt Fanny."

"Oh, I don't know: I shouldn't say that. A little youthful teasing—I doubt if she's minded so much. She felt your father's death terrifically, of course, but it seems to me she's had a fairly comfortable life—up to now—if she was disposed to take it that way."

"But 'up to now' is the important thing," George said. "Now is now—and you see I can't wait two years to be admitted to the bar and begin to practice. I've got to start in at something else that pays from the start, and that's what I've come to you about. I have an idea, you see."

"Well, I'm glad of that!" said old Frank, smiling. "I can't think of anything just at this minute that pays from the start."

"I only know of one thing, myself."

"What is it?"

George flushed again, but managed to laugh at his own embarrassment. "I suppose I'm about as ignorant of business as anybody in the world," he said. "But I've heard they pay very high wages to people in dangerous trades; I've always heard they did, and I'm sure it must be true. I mean people that handle touchy chemicals or high explosives—men in dynamite factories, or who take things of that sort about the country in wagons, and shoot oil wells. I thought I'd see if you couldn't tell me something more about it, or else introduce me to someone who could, and then I thought I'd see if I couldn't get something of the kind to do as soon as possible. My nerves are good; I'm muscular, and I've got a steady hand; it seemed to me that this was about the only line of work in the world that I'm fitted for. I wanted to get started to-day if I could."

Old Frank gave him a long stare. At first this scrutiny was sharply incredulous; then it was grave; finally it developed into a threat of overwhelming laughter; a forked vein in his forehead became more visible and his eyes seemed about to protrude.

But he controlled his impulse; and, rising, took up his hat and overcoat. "All right," he said. "If you'll promise not to get blown up, I'll go with you to see if we can find the job." Then, meaning what he said, but amazed that he did mean it, he added: "You certainly are the most practical young man I ever met!"

CHAPTER XXXIII

They found the job. It needed an apprenticeship of only six weeks, during which period George was to receive fifteen dollars a week; after that he would get twenty-eight. This settled the apartment question, and Fanny was presently established in a greater contentment than she had known for a long time. Early every morning she made something she called (and believed to be) coffee for George, and he was gallant enough not to undeceive her. She lunched alone in her "kitchenette," for George's place of employment was ten miles out of town on an interurban trolley-line, and he seldom returned before seven. Fanny found partners for bridge by two o'clock almost every afternoon, and she played until about six. Then she got George's "dinner clothes" out for him—he maintained this habit—and she changed her own dress. When he arrived he usually denied that he was tired, though he sometimes looked tired, particularly during the first few months; and he explained to her frequently—looking bored enough with her insistence—that his work was "fairly light, and fairly congenial, too." Fanny had the foggiest idea of what it was, though she noticed that it roughened his hands and stained them. "Something in those new chemical works," she explained to casual inquirers. It was not more definite in her own mind.

Respect for George undoubtedly increased within her, however, and she told him she'd always had a feeling he might "turn out to be a mechanical genius, or something." George assented with a nod as the easiest course open to him. He did not take a hand at bridge after dinner: his provisions for Fanny's happiness refused to extend that far, and at the table d'hôte he was a rather discouraging boarder. He was considered "affected" and absurdly "up-stage" by the one or two young men, and the three or four young women, who enlivened the elderly retreat; and was possibly less popular there than he had been elsewhere during his life, though he was now nothing worse than a coldly polite young man who kept to himself. After dinner he would escort his aunt from the table in some state (not wholly unaccompanied by a leerish wink or two from the wags of the place) and he would leave her at the door of the communal parlours and card rooms, with a formality in his bow of farewell which afforded an amusing contrast to Fanny's always voluble protests. (She never failed to urge loudly that he really *must* come and play, just this once, and not go hiding from everybody in his room *every* evening like this!) At least some of the other inhabitants found the contrast amusing, for sometimes, as he departed stiffly toward the elevator, leaving her still entreating in the doorway (though with one eye already on her table, to see that it was not seized) a titter would follow him which he was no doubt meant to hear. He did not care whether they laughed or not.

And once, as he passed the one or two young men of the place entertaining the three or four young women, who were elbowing and jerking on a settee in the lobby, he heard a voice inquiring quickly, as he passed:

"What makes people tired?"

"Work?"

"No."

"Well, what's the answer?"

Then, with an intentional outbreak of mirth, the answer was given by two loudly whispering voices together:

"A stuck-up boarder!"

George didn't care.

On Sunday mornings Fanny went to church and George took long walks. He explored the new city, and found it hideous, especially in the early spring, before the leaves of the shade trees were out. Then the town was fagged with the long winter and blacked with the heavier smoke that had been held close to the earth by the smoke-fog it bred. Everything was damply streaked with the soot: the walls of the houses, inside and out, the gray curtains at the windows, the windows themselves, the dirty cement and unswept asphalt underfoot, the very sky overhead. Throughout this murky season he continued his explorations, never seeing a face he knew—for, on Sunday, those whom he remembered, or who might remember him, were not apt to be found within the limits of the town, but were congenially occupied with the new outdoor life which had come to be the mode since his boyhood. He and Fanny were pretty thoroughly buried away within the bigness of the city.

One of his Sunday walks, that spring, he made into a sour pilgrimage. It was a misty morning of belated snow slush, and suited him to a perfection of miserableness, as he stood before the great dripping department store which now occupied the big plot of ground where once had stood both the Amberson Hotel and the Amberson Opera House. From there he drifted to the old "Amberson Block," but this was fallen into a back-water; business had stagnated here. The old structure had not been replaced, but a cavernous entryway for trucks had been torn in its front, and upon the cornice, where the old separate metal letters had spelt "Amberson Block," there was a long billboard sign: "Doogan Storage."

To spare himself nothing, he went out National Avenue and saw the piles of slush-covered wreckage where the Mansion and his mother's house had been, and where the Major's ill-fated five "new" houses had stood; for these were down, too, to make room for the great tenement already shaped in unending lines of foundation. But the Fountain of Neptune was gone at last—and George was glad that it was!

He turned away from the devastated site, thinking bitterly that the only Amberson mark still left upon the town was the name of the boulevard—Amberson Boulevard. But he had reckoned without the city council of the new order, and by an unpleasant coincidence, while the thought was still in his mind, his eye fell upon a metal oblong sign upon the lamp-post at the corner. There were two of these little signs upon the lamp-post, at an obtuse angle to each other, one to give passers-by the name of National Avenue, the other to acquaint them with Amberson Boulevard. But the one upon which should have been stencilled "Amberson Boulevard" exhibited the words "Tenth Street."

George stared at it hard. Then he walked quickly along the boulevard to the next corner and looked at the little sign there. "Tenth Street."

It had begun to rain, but George stood unheeding, staring at the little sign. "Damn them!" he said finally, and, turning up his coat-collar, plodded back through the soggy streets toward "home."

The utilitarian impudence of the city authorities put a thought into his mind. A week earlier he had happened to stroll into the large parlour of the apartment house, finding it empty, and on the centre-table he noticed a large, red-bound, gilt-edged book, newly printed, bearing the title: "A Civic History," and beneath the title, the rubric, "Biographies of the 500 Most Prominent Citizens and Families in the History of the City." He had glanced at it absently, merely noticing the title and sub-title, and wandered out of the room, thinking of other things and feeling no curiosity about the book. But he had thought of it several times since with a faint, vague uneasiness; and now when he entered the lobby he walked directly into the parlour where he had seen the book. The room was empty, as it always was on Sunday mornings, and the flamboyant volume was still upon the table—evidently a fixture as a sort of local Almanach de Gotha, or Burke, for the enlightenment of tenants and boarders.

He opened it, finding a few painful steel engravings of placid, chin-bearded faces, some of which he remembered dimly; but much more numerous, and also more unfamiliar to him, were the pictures of neat, aggressive men, with clipped short hair and clipped short moustaches—almost all of them strangers to him. He delayed not long with these, but turned to the index where the names of the five hundred Most Prominent Citizens and Families in the History of the City were arranged in alphabetical order, and ran his finger down the column of A's:

Abbett	Ambrose
Abbott	Ambuhl
Abrams	Anderson
Adams	Andrews
Adams	Appenbasch
Adler	Archer
Akers	Arszman
Albertsmeyer	Ashcraft
Alexander	Austin
Allen	Avey

George's eyes remained for some time fixed on the thin space between the names "Allen" and "Ambrose." Then he closed the book quietly, and went up to his own room, agreeing with the elevator boy, on the way, that it was getting to be a mighty nasty wet and windy day outside.

The elevator boy noticed nothing unusual about him and neither did Fanny, when she came in from church with her hat ruined, an hour later. And yet something had happened—a thing which, years ago, had been the eagerest hope of many, many good citizens of the town. They had thought of it, longed for it, hoping acutely that they might live to see the day when it would come to pass. And now it had happened at last: Georgie Minafer had got his come-uppance.

He had got it three times filled and running over. The city had rolled over his heart, burying it under, as it rolled over the Major's and buried it under. The city had rolled over the Ambersons and buried them under to the last vestige; and it mattered little that George guessed easily enough that most of the five hundred Most Prominent had paid something substantial "to defray the cost of steel engraving, etc."—the Five Hundred had heaved the final shovelful of soot upon that heap of obscurity wherein the Ambersons were lost forever from sight and history. "Quicksilver in a nest of cracks!"

Georgie Minafer had got his come-uppance, but the people who had so longed for it were not there to see it, and they never knew it. Those who were still living had forgotten all about it and all about him.

CHAPTER XXXIV

There was one border section of the city which George never explored in his Sunday morning excursions. This was far out to the north where lay the new Elysian Fields of the millionaires, though he once went as far in that direction as the white house which Lucy had so admired long ago—her "Beautiful House." George looked at it briefly and turned back, rumbling with an interior laugh of some grimness. The house was white no longer; nothing could be white which the town had reached, and the town reached far beyond the beautiful white house now. The owners had given up and painted it a despairing chocolate, suitable to the freight-yard life it was called upon to endure.

George did not again risk going even so far as that, in the direction of the millionaires, although their settlement began at least two miles farther out. His thought of Lucy and her father was more a sensation than a thought, and may be compared to that of a convicted cashier beset by recollections of the bank he had pillaged—there are some thoughts to which one closes the mind. George had seen Eugene only once since their calamitous encounter. They had passed on opposite sides of the street, downtown; each had been aware of the other, and each had been aware that the other was aware of him, and yet each kept his eyes straight forward, and neither had shown a perceptible alteration of countenance. It seemed to George that he felt emanating from the outwardly imperturbable person of his mother's old friend a hate that was like a hot wind.

At his mother's funeral and at the Major's he had been conscious that Eugene was there: though he had afterward no recollection of seeing him, and, while certain of his presence, was uncertain how he knew of it. Fanny had not told him, for she understood George well enough not to speak to him of Eugene or Lucy. Nowadays Fanny almost never saw either of them and seldom thought of them—so sly is the way of time with life. She was passing middle age, when old intensities and longings grow thin and flatten out, as Fanny herself was thinning and flattening out; and she was settling down contentedly to her apartment house intimacies. She was precisely suited by the table-d'hôte life, with its bridge, its variable alliances and shifting feuds, and the long whisperings of elderly ladies at corridor corners—those eager but suppressed conversations, all sibilance, of which the elevator boy declared he heard the words "*she said*" a million times and the word "*she*," five million. The apartment house suited Fanny and swallowed her.

The city was so big, now, that people disappeared into it unnoticed, and the disappearance of Fanny and her nephew was not exceptional. People no longer knew their neighbours as a matter of course; one lived for years next door to strangers—that sharpest of all the changes since the old days—and a friend would lose sight of a friend for a year, and not know it.

One May day George thought he had a glimpse of Lucy. He was not certain, but he was sufficiently disturbed, in spite of his uncertainty. A promotion in his work now frequently took him out of town for a week, or longer, and it was upon his return from one of these absences that he had the strange experience. He had walked home from the station, and as he turned the corner which brought him in sight of the apartment house entrance, though two blocks distant from it, he saw a charming little figure come out, get into a shiny landaulet automobile, and drive away. Even at that distance no one could have any doubt that the little figure was charming; and the height, the quickness and decision of motion, even the swift gesture of a white glove toward the chauffeur—all were characteristic of Lucy. George was instantly subjected to a shock of indefinable nature, yet definitely a shock: he did not know what he felt—but he knew that he felt. Heat surged over him: probably he would not have come face to face with her if the restoration of all the ancient Amberson magnificence could have been his reward. He went on slowly, his knees shaky.

But he found Fanny not at home; she had been out all afternoon; and there was no record of any caller—and he began to wonder, then to doubt if the small lady he had seen in the distance was Lucy. It might as well have been, he said to himself—since any one who looked like her could give him "a jolt like that!"

Lucy had not left a card. She never left one when she called on Fanny; though she did not give her reasons a quite definite form in her own mind. She came seldom; this was but the third time that year, and, when she did come, George was not mentioned, either by her hostess or by herself—an oddity contrived between the two ladies without either of them realizing how odd it was. For, naturally, while Fanny was with Lucy, Fanny thought of George, and what time Lucy had George's aunt before her eyes she could not well avoid the thought of him. Consequently, both looked absent-minded as they talked, and each often gave a wrong answer which the other consistently failed to notice.

At other times Lucy's thoughts of George were anything but continuous, and weeks went by when he was not consciously in her mind at all. Her life was a busy one: she had the big house "to keep up"; she had a garden to keep up, too, a large and beautiful garden; she represented her father as a director for half a dozen public charity organizations, and did private charity work of her own, being a proxy mother of several large families; and she had "danced down," as she said, groups from eight or nine classes of new graduates returned from the universities, without marrying any of them, but she still danced—and still did not marry.

Her father, observing this circumstance happily, yet with some hypocritical concern, spoke of it to her one day as they stood in her garden. "I suppose I'd want to shoot him," he said, with attempted lightness. "But I mustn't be an old pig. I'd build you a beautiful house close by—just over yonder."

"No, no! That would be like——" she began impulsively; then checked herself. George Amberson's comparison of the Georgian house to the Amberson Mansion had come into her mind, and she thought that another new house, built close by for her, would be like the house the Major built for Isabel.

"Like what?"

"Nothing." She looked serious, and when he reverted to his idea of "some day" grudgingly surrendering her up to a suitor, she invented a legend. "Did you ever hear the Indian name for that little grove of beech trees on the other side of the house?" she asked him.

"No—and you never did either!" he laughed.

"Don't be so sure! I read a great deal more than I used to—getting ready for my bookish days when I'll have to do something solid in the evenings and won't be asked to dance any more, even by the very youngest boys who think it's a sporting event to dance with the oldest of the 'older girls'. The name of the grove was 'Loma-Nashah' and it means 'They-Couldn't-Help-It'."

"Doesn't sound like it."

"Indian names don't. There was a bad Indian chief lived in the grove before the white settlers came. He was the worst Indian that ever lived, and his name was—it was 'Vendonah.' That means 'Rides-Down-Everything'."

"What?"

"His name was Vendonah, the same thing as Rides-Down-Everything."

"I see," said Eugene thoughtfully. He gave her a quick look and then fixed his eyes upon the end of the garden path. "Go on."

"Vendonah was an unspeakable case," Lucy continued. "He was so proud that he wore iron shoes and he walked over people's faces with them. He was always killing people that way, and so at last the tribe decided that it wasn't a good enough excuse for him that he was young and inexperienced —he'd have to go. They took him down to the river, and put him in a canoe, and pushed him out from shore; and then they ran along the bank and wouldn't let him land, until at last the current carried the canoe out into the middle, and then on down to the oçean, and he never got back. They didn't want him back, of course, and if he'd been able to manage it, they'd have put him in another canoe and shoved him out into the river again. But still, they didn't elect another chief in his place. Other tribes thought that was curious, and wondered about it a lot, but finally they came to the conclusion that the beech grove people were afraid a new chief might turn out to be a bad Indian, too, and wear iron shoes like Vendonah. But they were wrong, because the real reason was that the tribe had led such an exciting life under Vendonah that they couldn't settle down to anything tamer. He was awful, but he always kept things happening—terrible things, of course. They hated him, but they weren't able to discover any other warrior that they wanted to make chief in his place. I suppose it was a little like drinking a glass of too strong wine and then trying to take the taste out of your mouth with barley water. They couldn't help feeling that way."

"I see," said Eugene. "So that's why they named the place 'They-Couldn't-Help-It'!"

"It must have been."

"And so you're going to stay here in your garden," he said musingly. "You think it's better to keep on walking these sunshiny gravel paths between your flower-beds, and growing to look like a pensive garden lady in a Victorian engraving."

"I suppose I'm like the tribe that lived here, papa. I had too much unpleasant excitement. It was unpleasant—but it was excitement. I don't want any more; in fact, I don't want anything but you."

"You don't?" He looked at her keenly, and she laughed and shook her head; but he seemed perplexed, rather doubtful. "What was the name of the grove?" he asked. "The Indian name, I mean."

"Mola-Haha."

"No, it wasn't; that wasn't the name you said."

"I've forgotten."

"I see you have," he said, his look of perplexity remaining. "Perhaps you remember the chief's name better."

She shook her head again. "I don't!"

At this he laughed, but not very heartily, and walked slowly to the house, leaving her bending over a rose-bush, and a shade more pensive than the most pensive garden lady in any Victorian engraving.

. . . Next day, it happened that this same "Vendonah" or "Rides-Down-Everything" became the subject of a chance conversation between Eugene and his old friend Kinney, father of the fire-topped Fred. The two gentlemen found themselves smoking in neighbouring leather chairs beside a broad window at the club, after lunch.

Mr. Kinney had remarked that he expected to get his family established at the seashore by the Fourth of July, and, following a train of thought, he paused and chuckled. "Fourth of July reminds me," he said. "Have you heard what that Georgie Minafer is doing?"

"No, I haven't," said Eugene, and his friend failed to notice the crispness of the utterance.

"Well, sir," Kinney chuckled again, "it beats the devil! My boy Fred told me about it yesterday. He's a friend of this young Henry Akers, son of F. P. Akers of the Akers Chemical Company. It seems this young Akers asked Fred if he knew a fellow named Minafer, because he knew Fred had always lived here, and young Akers had heard some way that Minafer used to be an old family name here, and was sort of curious about it. Well, sir, you remember this young Georgie sort of disappeared, after his grandfather's death, and nobody seemed to know much what had become of him—though I did hear, once or twice, that he was still around somewhere. Well, sir, he's working for the Akers Chemical Company, out at their plant on the Thomasville Road."

He paused, seeming to reserve something to be delivered only upon inquiry, and Eugene offered him the expected question, but only after a cold glance through the nose-glasses he had lately found it necessary to adopt. "What does he do?"

Kinney laughed and slapped the arm of his chair. "He's a nitro-glycerin expert!"

He was gratified to see that Eugene was surprised, if not, indeed, a little startled.

"He's what?"

"He's an expert on nitro-glycerin. Doesn't that beat the devil! Yes, sir! Young Akers told Fred that this George Minafer had worked like a houn'-dog ever since he got started out at the works. They have a special plant for nitro-glycerin, way off from the main plant, o' course—in the woods somewhere—and George Minafer's been working there, and lately they put him in charge of it. He oversees shooting oil-wells, too, and shoots 'em himself, sometimes. They aren't allowed to carry it on the railroads, you know—have to team it. Young Akers says George rides around over the bumpy roads, sitting on as much as three hundred quarts of nitro-glycerin! My Lord! Talk about romantic tumbles! If he gets blown sky-high some day he won't have a bigger drop, when he comes down, than he's already had! Don't it beat the devil! Young Akers said he's got all the nerve there is in the world. Well, he always did have plenty of *that*—from the time he used to ride around here on his white pony and fight all the Irish boys in Can-Town, with his long curls all handy to be pulled out. Akers says he gets a fair salary, and I should think he ought to! Seems to me I've heard the average life in that sort of work is somewhere around four years, and agents don't write any insurance at all for nitro-glycerin experts. Hardly!"

"No," said Eugene. "I suppose not."

Kinney rose to go. "Well, it's a pretty funny thing—pretty odd, I mean—and I suppose it would be pass-around-the-hat for old Fanny Minafer if he blew up. Fred told me that they're living in some apartment house, and said Georgie supports her. He was going to study law, but couldn't earn enough that way to take care of Fanny, so he gave it up. Fred's wife told him all this. Says Fanny doesn't do anything but play bridge these days. Got to playing too high for awhile and lost more than she wanted to tell Georgie about, and borrowed a little from old Frank Bronson. Paid him back, though. Don't know how Fred's wife heard it. Women do hear the darndest things!"

"They do," Eugene agreed.

"I thought you'd probably heard about it—thought most likely Fred's wife might have said something to your daughter, especially as they're cousins."

"I think not."

"Well, I'm off to the store," said Mr. Kinney briskly; yet he lingered. "I suppose we'll all have to club in and keep old Fanny out of the poorhouse if he does blow up. From all I hear it's usually only a question of time. They say she hasn't got anything else to depend on."

"I suppose not."

"Well—I wondered——" Kinney hesitated. "I was wondering why you hadn't thought of finding something around your works for him. They say he's an all-fired worker and he certainly does seem to have hid some decent stuff in him under all his damfoolishness. And you used to be such a tremendous friend of the family—I thought perhaps you—of course I know he's a queer lot—I know he's——"

"Yes, I think he is," said Eugene. "No. I haven't anything to offer him."

"I suppose not," Kinney returned thoughtfully, as he went out. "I don't know that I would myself. Well, we'll probably see his name in the papers some day if he stays with that job!"

. . . However, the nitro-glycerin expert of whom they spoke did not get

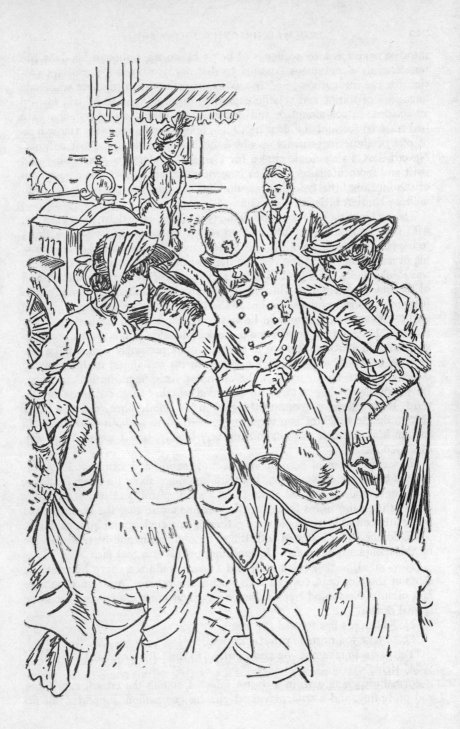

into the papers as a consequence of being blown up, although his daily life was certainly a continuous exposure to that risk. Destiny has a constant passion for the incongruous, and it was George's lot to manipulate wholesale quantities of terrific and volatile explosives in safety, and to be laid low by an accident so commonplace and inconsequent that it was a comedy. Fate had reserved for him the final insult of riding him down under the wheels of one of those juggernauts at which he had once shouted "Git a hoss!" Nevertheless, Fate's ironic choice for Georgie's undoing was not a big and swift and momentous car, such as Eugene manufactured; it was a specimen of the hustling little type that was flooding the country, the cheapest, commonest, hardiest little car ever made.

The accident took place upon a Sunday morning, on a downtown crossing, with the streets almost empty, and no reason in the world for such a thing to happen. He had gone out for his Sunday morning walk, and he was thinking of an automobile at the very moment when the little car struck him; he was thinking of a shiny landaulet and a charming figure stepping into it, and of the quick gesture of a white glove toward the chauffeur, motioning him to go on. George heard a shout but did not look up, for he could not imagine anybody's shouting at him, and he was too engrossed in the question "Was it Lucy?" He could not decide, and his lack of decision in this matter probably superinduced a lack of decision in another, more pressingly vital. At the second and louder shout he did look up; and the car was almost on him; but he could not make up his mind if the charming little figure he had seen was Lucy's and he could not make up his mind whether to go backward or forward: these questions became entangled in his mind. Then, still not being able to decide which of two ways to go, he tried to go both—and the little car ran him down. It was not moving very rapidly, but it went all the way over George.

He was conscious of gigantic violence; of roaring and jolting and concussion; of choking clouds of dust, shot with lightning, about his head; he heard snapping sounds as loud as shots from a small pistol, and was stabbed by excruciating pains in his legs. Then he became aware that the machine was being lifted off of him. People were gathering in a circle round him, gabbling.

His forehead was bedewed with the sweat of anguish, and he tried to wipe off this dampness, but failed. He could not get his arm that far.

"Nev' mind," a policeman said; and George could see above his eyes the skirts of the blue coat, covered with dust and sunshine. "Amb'lance be here in a minute. Nev' mind tryin' to move any. You want 'em to send for some special doctor?"

"No." George's lips formed the word.

"Or to take you to some private hospital?"

"Tell them to take me," he said faintly, "to the City Hospital."

"A' right."

A smallish young man in a duster fidgeted among the crowd, explaining and protesting, and a strident voiced girl, his companion, supported his argument, declaring to everyone her willingness to offer testimony in any court of law that every blessed word he said was the God's truth.

"It's the fella that hit you," the policeman said, looking down on George. "I guess he's right; you must of b'en thinkin' about somep'm' or other. It's wunnerful the damage them little machines can do—you'd never think it— but I guess they ain't much case ag'in this fella that was drivin' it."

"You bet your life they ain't no case on me!" the young man in the duster agreed, with great bitterness. He came and stood at George's feet, addressing him heatedly: "I'm sorry fer *you* all right, and I don't say I ain't. I hold nothin' against you, but it wasn't any more my fault than the statehouse! You run into me, much as I run into you, and if you get well you ain't goin' to get not one single cent out o' me! This lady here was settin' with me and we both yelled at you. Wasn't goin' a *step* over eight mile an hour! I'm perfectly willing to say I'm sorry for you though, and so's the lady with me. We're both willing to say that much, but that's all, understand!"

George's drawn eyelids twitched; his misted glance rested fleetingly upon the two protesting motorists, and the old imperious spirit within him flickered up in a single word. Lying on his back in the middle of the street, where he was regarded by an increasing public as an unpleasant curiosity, he spoke this word clearly from a mouth filled with dust, and from lips smeared with blood.

. . . It was a word which interested the policeman. When the ambulance clanged away, he turned to a fellow patrolman who had joined him. "Funny what he says to the little cuss that done the damage. That's all he *did* call him—nothin' else at all—and the cuss had broke both his legs fer him and God-knows-what-all!"

"I wasn't here then. What was it?"

" 'Riffraff!' "

CHAPTER XXXV

Eugene's feeling about George had not been altered by his talk with Kinney in the club window, though he was somewhat disturbed. He was not disturbed by Kinney's hint that Fanny Minafer might be left on the hands of her friends through her nephew's present dealings with nitro-glycerin, but he was surprised that Kinney had "led up" with intentional tact to the suggestion that a position might be made for George in the Morgan factory. Eugene did not care to have any suggestions about Georgie Minafer made to him. Kinney had represented Georgie as a new Georgie—at least in spots—a Georgie who was proving that decent stuff had been hid in him; in fact, a Georgie who was doing rather a handsome thing in taking a risky job for the sake of his aunt, poor old silly Fanny Minafer! Eugene didn't care what risks Georgie took, or how much decent stuff he had in him: nothing that Georgie would ever do in this world or the next could change Eugene Morgan's feeling toward him.

If Eugene could possibly have brought himself to offer Georgie a position in the automobile business, he knew full well the proud devil wouldn't have taken it from him; though Georgie's proud reason would not have been the one attributed to him by Eugene. George would never reach the point where he could accept anything material from Eugene and preserve the self-respect he had begun to regain.

But if Eugene had wished, he could easily have taken George out of the nitro-glycerin branch of the chemical works. Always interested in apparent impossibilities of invention, Eugene had encouraged many experiments in such gropings as those for the discovery of substitutes for gasoline and rubber; and, though his mood had withheld the information from Kinney, he had recently bought from the elder Akers a substantial quantity of stock on the condition that the chemical company should establish an experimental laboratory. He intended to buy more; Akers was anxious to please him; and a word from Eugene would have placed George almost anywhere in the chemical works. George need never have known it, for Eugene's purchases of stock were always quiet ones: the transaction remained, so far, between him and Akers, and could be kept between them.

The possibility just edged itself into Eugene's mind; that is, he let it become part of his perceptions long enough for it to prove to him that it was actually a possibility. Then he half started with disgust that he should be even idly considering such a thing over his last cigar for the night, in his library. "No!" And he threw the cigar into the empty fireplace and went to bed.

His bitterness for himself might have worn away, but never his bitterness for Isabel. He took that thought to bed with him—and it was true that nothing George could do would ever change this bitterness of Eugene. Only George's mother could have changed it.

And as Eugene fell asleep that night, thinking thus bitterly of Georgie, Georgie in the hospital was thinking of Eugene. He had come "out of ether" with no great nausea, and had fallen into a reverie, though now and then a white sailboat staggered foolishly into the small ward where he lay. After a time he discovered that this happened only when he tried to open his eyes and look about him; so he kept his eyes shut, and his thoughts were clearer. He thought of Eugene Morgan and of the Major; they seemed to be the same person for a while, but he managed to disentangle them and even to understand why he had confused them. Long ago his grandfather had been the most striking figure of success in the town: "As rich as Major Amberson!" they used to say. Now it was Eugene. "If I had Eugene Morgan's money," he would hear the workmen day-dreaming at the chemical works; or, "If Eugene Morgan had hold of this place you'd see things hum!" And the boarders at the table d'hôte spoke of "the Morgan Place" as an eighteenth-century Frenchman spoke of Versailles. Like his uncle, George had perceived that the "Morgan Place" was the new Amberson Mansion. His reverie went back to the palatial days of the Mansion, in his boyhood, when he would gallop his pony up the driveway and order the darkey stablemen about, while they whooped and obeyed, and his grandfather, observing from a window, would laugh and call out to him, "That's right, Georgie. Make those lazy rascals jump!" He remembered his gay young uncles, and how the town was eager concerning everything about them, and about himself. What a clean, pretty town it had been! And in his reverie he saw like a pageant before him the magnificence of the Ambersons—its passing, and the passing of the Ambersons themselves. They had been slowly engulfed without knowing how to prevent it, and almost without knowing what was happening to them. The family lot, in the shabby older quarter, out at the cemetery, held most of them now; and the name was swept altogether from the new city. But the new great people who had taken their places—the Morgans and Akerses and Sheridans—they would go, too. George saw that. They would pass, as the Ambersons had passed, and though some of them might do better than the Major and leave the letters that spelled a name on a hospital or a street, it would be only a word and it would not stay forever. Nothing stays or holds or keeps where there is growth, he somehow perceived vaguely but truly. Great Cæsar dead and turned to clay stopped no hole to keep the wind away; dead Cæsar was nothing but a tiresome bit of print in a book that schoolboys study for a while and then forget. The Ambersons had passed, and the new people would pass, and the new people that came after them, and then the next new ones, and the next—and the next——

He had begun to murmur, and the man on duty as night nurse for the ward came and bent over him.

"Did you want something?"

"There's nothing in this family business," George told him confidentially. "Even George Washington is only something in a book."

. . . Eugene read a report of the accident in the next morning's paper. He was on the train, having just left for New York, on business, and with less leisure would probably have overlooked the obscure item:

LEGS BROKEN

G. A. Minafer, an employe of the Akers Chemical Co., was run down by an automobile yesterday at the corner of Tennessee and Main and had both legs broken. Minafer was to blame for the accident according to patrolman F. A. Kax, who witnessed the affair. The automobile was a small one driven by Herbert Cottleman of 2173 Noble Avenue who stated that he was making less than 4 miles an hour. Minafer is said to belong to a family formerly of considerable prominence in the city. He was taken to the City Hospital where physicians stated later that he was suffering from internal injuries besides the fracture of his legs but might recover.

Eugene read the item twice, then tossed the paper upon the opposite seat of his compartment, and sat looking out of the window. His feeling toward Georgie was changed not a jot by his human pity for Georgie's human pain and injury. He thought of Georgie's tall and graceful figure, and he shivered, but his bitterness was untouched. He had never blamed Isabel for the weakness which had cost them the few years of happiness they might have had together; he had put the blame all on the son, and it stayed there.

He began to think poignantly of Isabel: he had seldom been able to "see" her more clearly than as he sat looking out of his compartment window, after reading the account of this accident. She might have been just on the other side of the glass, looking in at him—and then he thought of her as the pale figure of a woman, seen yet unseen, flying through the air, beside the train, over the fields of springtime green and through the woods that were just sprouting out their little leaves. He closed his eyes and saw her as she had been long ago. He saw the brown-eyed, brown-haired, proud, gentle, laughing girl he had known when first he came to town, a boy just out of the State College. He remembered—as he had remembered ten thousand times before—the look she gave him when her brother George introduced him to her at a picnic; it was "like hazel starlight" he had written her, in a poem, afterward. He remembered his first call at the Amberson Mansion, and what a great personage she seemed, at home in that magnificence; and yet so gay and friendly. He remembered the first time he had danced with her—and the old waltz song began to beat in his ears and in his heart. They laughed and sang it together as they danced to it:

"Oh, love for a year, a week, a day,
But alas for the love that lasts alway——"

Most plainly of all he could see her dancing; and he became articulate in the mourning whisper: "So graceful—oh, so graceful——"

All the way to New York it seemed to him that Isabel was near him, and he wrote of her to Lucy from his hotel the next night:

I saw an account of the accident to George Minafer. I'm sorry, though the paper states that it was plainly his own fault. I suppose it may have been as a result of my attention falling upon the item that I thought of his mother a great deal on the way here. It seemed to me that I had never seen her more distinctly or so constantly, but, as you know, thinking of his mother is not very apt to make me admire him! Of course, however, he has my best wishes for his recovery.

He posted the letter, and by the morning's mail received one from Lucy written a few hours after his departure from home. She enclosed the item he had read on the train.

I thought you might not see it,
I have seen Miss Fanny and she has got him put into a room by himself. Oh, poor Rides-Down-Everything! I have been thinking so constantly of his mother and it seemed to me that I have never seen her more distinctly. How lovely she was—and how she loved him!

If Lucy had not written this letter Eugene might not have done the odd thing he did that day. Nothing could have been more natural than that both he and Lucy should have thought intently of Isabel after reading the account of George's accident, but the fact that Lucy's letter had crossed his own made Eugene begin to wonder if a phenomenon of telepathy might not be in question, rather than a chance coincidence. The reference to Isabel in the two letters was almost identical: he and Lucy, it appeared, had been thinking of Isabel at the same time—both said "constantly" thinking of her—and neither had ever "seen her more distinctly." He remembered these phrases in his own letter accurately.

Reflection upon the circumstance stirred a queer spot in Eugene's brain—he had one. He was an adventurer; if he had lived in the sixteenth century he would have sailed the unknown new seas, but having been born in the latter part of the nineteenth, when geography was a fairly well-settled matter, he had become an explorer in mechanics. But the fact that he was a "hard-headed business man" as well as an adventurer did not keep him from having a queer spot in his brain, because hard-headed business men are as susceptible to such spots as adventurers are. Some of them are secretly troubled when they do not see the new moon over the lucky shoulder; some of them have strange, secret incredulities—they do not believe in geology, for instance; and some of them think they have had supernatural experiences. "Of course there was nothing in it—still it *was* queer!" they say.

Two weeks after Isabel's death, Eugene had come to New York on urgent business and found that the delayed arrival of a steamer gave him a day with nothing to do. His room at the hotel had become intolerable; outdoors was intolerable; everything was intolerable. It seemed to him that he must see Isabel once more, hear her voice once more; that he *must* find some way to her, or lose his mind. Under this pressure he had gone, with complete skepticism, to a "trance-medium" of whom he had heard wild accounts from the wife of a business acquaintance. He thought despairingly that at least such an excursion would be "trying to do *something!*" He remembered the woman's name; found it in the telephone book, and made an appointment.

The experience had been grotesque, and he came away with an encouraging message from his father, who had failed to identify himself satisfactorily, but declared that everything was "on a higher plane" in his present state of being, and that all life was "continuous and progressive." Mrs. Horner spoke of herself as a "psychic"; but otherwise she seemed oddly unpretentious and matter-of-fact; and Eugene had no doubt at all of her sincerity. He was sure that she was not an intentional fraud, and though he departed in a state of annoyance with himself, he came to the conclusion that if any credulity were played upon by Mrs. Horner's exhibitions, it was her own.

Nevertheless, his queer spot having been stimulated to action by the co-incidence of the letters, he went to Mrs. Horner's after his directors' meeting to-day. He used the telephone booth in the directors' room to make the appointment; and he laughed feebly at himself, and wondered what the group of men in that mahogany apartment would think if they knew what he was doing. Mrs. Horner had changed her address, but he found the new one, and somebody purporting to be a niece of hers talked to him and made an appointment for a "sitting" at five o'clock.

He was prompt, and the niece, a dull-faced fat girl with a magazine under her arm, admitted him to Mrs. Horner's apartment, which smelt of camphor; and showed him into a room with gray painted walls, no rug on the floor and no furniture except a table (with nothing on it) and two chairs: one a leather easy-chair and the other a stiff little brute with a wooden seat. There was one window with the shade pulled down to the sill, but the sun was bright outside, and the room had light enough.

Mrs. Horner appeared in the doorway, a wan and unenterprising looking woman in brown, with thin hair artificially waved—but not recently—and parted in the middle over a bluish forehead. Her eyes were small and seemed weak, but she recognized the visitor.

"Oh, you been here before," she said, in a thin voice, not unmusical. "I recollect you. Quite a time ago, wa'n't it?"

"Yes, quite a long time."

"I recollect because I recollect you was disappointed. Anyway, you was kind of cross." She laughed faintly.

"I'm sorry if I seemed so," Eugene said. "Do you happen to have found out my name?"

She looked surprised and a little reproachful. "Why, no. I never try to find out people's names. Why should I? I don't claim anything for the power; I only know I have it—and some ways it ain't always such a blessing, neither, I can tell you!"

Eugene did not press an investigation of her meaning, but said vaguely, "I suppose not. Shall we——"

"All right," she assented, dropping into the leather chair, with her back to the shaded window. "You better set down, too, I reckon. I hope you'll get something this time so you won't feel cross, but I dunno. I can't never tell what they'll do. Well——"

She sighed, closed her eyes, and was silent, while Eugene, seated in the stiff chair across the table from her, watched her profile, thought himself an idiot, and called himself that and other names. And as the silence continued, and the impassive woman in the easy-chair remained impassive, he began to wonder what had led him to be such a fool. It became clear to him that the similarity of his letter and Lucy's needed no explanation involving telepathy, and was not even an extraordinary coincidence. What, then, had brought him back to this absurd place and caused him to be watching this absurd woman taking a nap in a chair? In brief: What the devil did he mean by it? He had not the slightest interest in Mrs. Horner's naps —or in her teeth, which were being slightly revealed by the unconscious parting of her lips, as her breathing became heavier. If the vagaries of his own mind had brought him into such a grotesquerie as this, into what did the vagaries of other men's minds take them? Confident that he was ordinarily saner than most people, he perceived that since he was capable of doing a thing like this, other men did even more idiotic things, in secret. And he had a fleeting vision of sober-looking bankers and manufacturers and lawyers, well-dressed church-going men, sound citizens—and all as queer as the deuce inside!

How long was he going to sit here presiding over this unknown woman's slumbers? It struck him that to make the picture complete he ought to be shooing flies away from her with a palm-leaf fan.

Mrs. Horner's parted lips closed again abruptly, and became compressed; her shoulders moved a little, then jerked repeatedly; her small chest heaved; she gasped, and the compressed lips relaxed to a slight contortion, then began to move, whispering and bringing forth indistinguishable mutterings.

Suddenly she spoke in a loud, husky voice:

"Lopa is here!"

"Yes," Eugene said dryly. "That's what you said last time. I remember 'Lopa.' She's your 'control' I think you said."

"I'm Lopa," said the husky voice. "I'm Lopa herself."

"You mean I'm to suppose you're not Mrs. Horner now?"

"Never was Mrs. Horner!" the voice declared, speaking undeniably from Mrs. Horner's lips—but with such conviction that Eugene, in spite of everything, began to feel himself in the presence of a third party, who was none the less an individual, even though she might be another edition of the apparently somnambulistic Mrs. Horner. "Never was Mrs. Horner or anybody but just Lopa. Guide."

"You mean you're Mrs. Horner's guide?" he asked.

"Your guide now," said the voice with emphasis, to which was incongruously added a low laugh. "You came here once before. Lopa remembers."

"Yes—so did Mrs. Horner."

Lopa overlooked his implication, and continued quickly: "You build. Build things that go. You came here once and old gentleman on this side, he spoke to you. Same old gentleman here now. He tell Lopa he's your grandfather—no, he says 'father.' He's your father."

"What's his appearance?"

"How?"

"What does he look like?"

"Very fine! White beard, but not long beard. He says someone else wants to speak to you. See here. Lady. Not his wife, though. No. Very fine lady! Fine lady, fine lady!"

"Is it my sister?" Eugene asked.

"Sister? No. She is shaking her head. She has pretty brown hair. She is fond of you. She is someone who knows you very well but she is not your sister. She is very anxious to say something to you—very anxious. Very fond of you; very anxious to talk to you. Very glad you came here—oh, very glad!"

"What is her name?"

"Name," the voice repeated, and seemed to ruminate. "Name hard to get —always very hard for Lopa. Name. She wants to tell me her name to tell you. She wants you to understand names are hard to make. She says you must think of something that makes a sound." Here the voice seemed to put a question to an invisible presence and to receive an answer. "A little sound or a big sound? She says it might be a little sound or a big sound. She says a ring—oh, Lopa knows! She means a bell! That's it, a bell."

Eugene looked grave. "Does she mean her name is Belle?"

"Not quite. Her name is longer."

"Perhaps," he suggested, "she means that she was a belle."

"No. She says she thinks you know what she means. She says you must think of a colour. What colour?" Again Lopa addressed the unknown, but this time seemed to wait for an answer.

"Perhaps she means the colour of her eyes," said Eugene.

"No. She says her colour is light—it's a light colour and you can see through it."

"Amber?" he said, and was startled, for Mrs. Horner, with her eyes still closed, clapped her hands, and the voice cried out in delight:

"Yes! She says you know who she is from amber. Amber! Amber! That's it! She says you understand what her name is from a bell and from amber. She is laughing and waving a lace handkerchief at me because she is pleased. She says I have made you know who it is."

This was the strangest moment of Eugene's life, because, while it lasted, he believed that Isabel Amberson, who was dead, had found means to speak to him. Though within ten minutes he doubted it, he believed it then.

His elbows pressed hard upon the table, and, his head between his hands, he leaned forward, staring at the commonplace figure in the easy-chair. "What does she wish to say to me?"

"She is happy because you know her. No—she is troubled. Oh—a great trouble! Something she wants to tell you. She wants so *much* to tell you. She wants Lopa to tell you. This is a great trouble. She says—oh, yes, she wants you to be—to be kind! That's what she says. That's it. To be kind."

"Does she——"

"She wants you to be kind," said the voice. "She nods when I tell you this. Yes; it must be right. She is a very fine lady. Very pretty. She is so anxious for you to understand. She hopes and hopes you will. Someone else wants to speak to you. This is a man. He says——"

"I don't want to speak to any one else," said Eugene quickly. "I want——"

"This man who has come says that he is a friend of yours. He says——"

Eugene struck the table with his fist. "I don't want to speak to any one else, I tell you!" he cried passionately. "If she is there I——" He caught his breath sharply, checked himself, and sat in amazement. Could his mind so easily accept so stupendous a thing as true? Evidently it could!

Mrs. Horner spoke languidly in her own voice: "Did you get anything satisfactory?" she asked. "I certainly hope it wasn't like that other time when you was cross because they couldn't get anything for you."

"No, no," he said hastily. "This was different. It was very interesting."

He paid her, went to his hotel, and thence to his train for home. Never did he so seem to move through a world of dream-stuff: for he knew that he was not more credulous than other men, and if he could believe what he had believed, though he had believed it for no longer than a moment or two, what hold had he or any other human being on reality?

His credulity vanished (or so he thought) with his recollection that it was he, and not the alleged "Lopa," who had suggested the word "amber." Going over the mortifying, plain facts of his experience, he found that Mrs. Horner, or the subdivision of Mrs. Horner known as "Lopa," had told him to think of a bell and of a colour, and that being furnished with these scientific data, he had leaped to the conclusion that he spoke with Isabel Amberson!

For a moment he had believed that Isabel was *there*, believed that she was close to him, entreating him—entreating him "to be kind." But with this recollection a strange agitation came upon him. After all, *had* she not spoken to him? If his own unknown consciousness had told the "psychic's" unknown consciousness how to make the picture of the pretty brown-haired, brown-eyed lady, hadn't the picture been a true one? And hadn't the true Isabel —oh, indeed her very soul!—called to him out of his own true memory of her?

And as the train roared through the darkened evening he looked out beyond his window, and saw her as he had seen her on his journey, a few days ago—an ethereal figure flying beside the train, but now it seemed to him that she kept her face toward his window with an infinite wistfulness.

. . . "To be kind!" If it had been Isabel, was that what she would have said? If she were anywhere, and could come to him through the invisible wall, what would be the first thing she would say to him?

Ah, well enough, and perhaps bitterly enough, he knew the answer to that question! "To be kind"—to Georgie!

. . . A red-cap at the station, when he arrived, leaped for his bag, abandoning another which the Pullman porter had handed him. "Yessuh, Mist' Morgan. Yessuh. You' car waitin' front the station fer you, Mist' Morgan, suh!"

And people in the crowd about the gates turned to stare, as he passed through, whispering, "*That's Morgan.*"

Outside, the neat chauffeur stood at the door of the touring-car like a soldier in whip-cord.

"I'll not go home now, Harry," said Eugene, when he had got in. "Drive to the City Hospital."

"Yes, sir," the man returned. "Miss Lucy's there. She said she expected you'd come there before you went home."

"She did?"

"Yes, sir."

Eugene stared. "I suppose Mr. Minafer must be pretty bad," he said.

"Yes, sir. I understand he's liable to get well, though, sir." He moved his lever into high speed, and the car went through the heavy traffic like some fast, faithful beast that knew its way about, and knew its master's need of haste. Eugene did not speak again until they reached the hospital.

Fanny met him in the upper corridor, and took him to an open door.

He stopped on the threshold, startled; for, from the waxen face on the pillow, almost it seemed the eyes of Isabel herself were looking at him: never before had the resemblance between mother and son been so strong—and Eugene knew that now he had once seen it thus startlingly, he need divest himself of no bitterness "to be kind" to Georgie.

George was startled, too. He lifted a white hand in a queer gesture, half forbidding, half imploring, and then let his arm fall back upon the coverlet. "You must have thought my mother wanted you to come," he said, "so that I could ask you to—to forgive me."

But Lucy, who sat beside him, lifted ineffable eyes from him to her father, and shook her head. "No, just to take his hand—gently!"

She was radiant.

But for Eugene another radiance filled the room. He knew that he had been true at last to his true love, and that through him she had brought her boy under shelter again. Her eyes would look wistful no more.